D1566554

# PARALLEL LIVES

*A Novel*

Judith A. Ferry

Copyright © 2021 by Judith A. Ferry

Website: judithferry.com

Print ISBN: 978-1-09839-279-6
eBook ISBN: 978-1-09839-280-2

Printed in the United States of America

# ACKNOWLEDGMENTS

I wish to express my gratitude to my father, Dr. John Ferry, who read every chapter with interest and provided invaluable encouragement, and to the Beacon Hill Writers' Group, for the members' feedback delivered indefatigably over the years it took to complete *Parallel Lives*. The *Iliad* has provided inspiration for some of the characters, the themes and elements of the plot of *Parallel Lives*. Thus, I also acknowledge Professor Gregory Nagy of Harvard University, whose writings and classes focusing on the hero in ancient Greece have helped to instill in me a love for the works of Homer.

The quote at the beginning of the *Parallel Lives* is from Robert Fitzgerald's wonderfully lyrical translation of the *Iliad* (Anchor Press/Doubleday, 1974); I have substituted the more familiar "Achilles" for the more precise "Akhilleus" used by Fitzgerald. The first word of that quote, "anger," sets the stage for the conflict between Alexander Eastgard and Hector Gonzalez that drives *Parallel Lives*. Years later, when Alexander visits the site of Troy and experiences, without understanding, fleeting memories from his past life as Achilles, he recalls "the gentle girl he had loved, his prize, in grace like Aphrodite;" "grace like Aphrodite" is also from the Fitzgerald translation, and refers to Briseis.

During Julia Kaiser's brief romance with Jamie Pembroke, passages from the Bible and from the Epic of Gilgamesh echo in her mind. "Seven days and seven nights" refers to the encounter between Enkidu and the priestess of Ishtar in the Epic of Gilgamesh. I recommend the enchanting version of Gilgamesh prepared by Stephen Mitchell (Free Press, 2004) to those who wish to read the epic in its entirety.

*Anger be now your song, immortal one,*
*Achilles' anger, doomed and ruinous…*
*Iliad*, Book One

# PROLOGUE

## At Sea, July 2015

A solitary man stood immobile on the deck of the cargo ship Poseidon, leaning on the iron railing as night approached. A fair-haired man, lean, not old, but no longer young. In the west, equinox glowed in all its transitory glory, shimmering on the glaucous waters of the Mediterranean. Then slowly, the evanescent turquoise of the sky yielded to the black of night. Still the man stood at the railing, as though unaware of the passage of time.

In the infinite darkness, the sea had become pitch-black. It parted obediently for the hull of Poseidon, closing quickly and silently behind the ship as it made its way east. The sky laid out above was cloudless and crowded with constellations. Across the heavens spilled the brilliant white ribbon of the Milky Way. The man studied the sky and found three stars in a luminous triangle, Vega, Altair and Deneb, each one the brightest star in a constellation. Gleaming Vega, high in the sky, drew the man's eyes to Lyra, the lyre, forever awaiting a celestial musician. Altair shone in Aquila, the eagle, emblem of Jupiter. Deneb crowned the head of Cygnus, the swan, his body and broad wings formed by stars in the shape of a cross. Cygnus, divine lover of Leda and instigator of so much turmoil! Fearless Hercules labored directly above him, the great hero poised to slay a murderous dragon.

No matter how many times the man gazed upon the night sky, it never ceased to amaze him. Its vastness made his own problems feel small. He studied the waters below, past the stars imperfectly reflected there, as though he might see all the people he had known and loved or hated. Those he had wronged. Those he had lost. But he looked in vain.

The man was called Patrick Close. He had had another name once, and a different life. Now he was sailing to Byzantium, to marvel at its treasures. When he was ready, he would find another ship and return to New York City, the closest thing to a home that he now had. How strange that he had come to this life, this vagabond existence. So much had happened while he still had his old name, and so many had played their parts in a story, his story, over so many years, but as he recalled, it began with anger.

# PART 1

Massachusetts, 1980

# CHAPTER 1

Anger, red-hot rage roared in Alexander's head, thundered with a frantic, pounding rhythm, driving him on. Waves of fury surged through him and into his shoulders and arms, exploding into a lightning fist that smashed into Hector's jaw. Hector hit the ground with a heavy thud, and lay full length, enshrouded in dust.

Alexander stared at the prostrate form of Hector, and his mad fury receded as quickly as it had come. *What did I just do?*

A third boy, the new kid, shielded from Hector by Alexander, pulled himself to his feet and dusted off his khaki pants. "Why'd that guy hit me?" he asked.

Alexander kept his eyes trained on Hector, wary of a counterattack, but Hector remained on the ground. "That's Hector. He says that corner of the playground is his. Only he and his friends can go there."

"He can't just do that. Why does he think he can?"

"Spoiled rich kid."

"He said he was going to kill me," the new kid whispered. "So, thanks."

The 6th grade students of Brookline's Lincoln School gathered in a cautious half-circle around the three boys, amazed.

"Did you see what happened?" one of them asked.

"Alex slugged Hector, after he hit that new guy!" declared another.

"Alex, the Brain?"

"Alex must be crazy. Hector Gonzalez is the biggest kid in the class!"

"Biggest *and* meanest."

"I'm glad someone finally stood up to Hector," one boy said, and folded his arms. "Someone should've done it a long time ago."

"He tripped me once in gym when Mr. West wasn't looking. And then laughed," said another boy, who was small for his age.

"Hector is just a mean, bad person," one little girl whispered. Silently she remembered the time he called her ugly.

Giulietta Stewart, standing to one side, her round face framed by foamy red hair in two lumpy braids, and punctuated by sky blue eyes, vanishingly pale eyebrows, and a little nose replete with rusty freckles, gazed upon the scene with wonder. She had never really looked at Alex before. But now as he stood there, tall and strong, so grown-up looking, tawny hair slightly ruffled and touched with gold in the sunshine, she realized something: Alexander Eastgard was absolutely gorgeous!

Hector's partisans, Eddie and Lou, hoisted Hector to his feet as Mrs. Alma MacMillan, that day's recess monitor, widely but surreptitiously known as Big Mac, stomped over. She transected the semicircle of 6th graders and stopped short when she saw Hector's swollen lip, his pullover sweater ripped at the elbow, his jeans discolored by dirt.

"Please god, don't let him have lost a tooth- I will be in so much trouble with his nut-case mother," she muttered under her breath. "This has the makings of a real Greek tragedy. And one lasting mark on that smug face of Hector's and we're talking tragedy of epic proportions."

Eddie and Lou released Hector; he was able to stand by himself. He winced as he took a step, exposing his teeth; they appeared intact.

Mrs. MacMillan exhaled with relief. Things were looking up.

"Alright, both of you, ah, all three of you," she said, gesturing at Hector and Alex, and then at the new kid, "Get to the principal's office. Let's go."

They trudged along behind Big Mac, the way before them largely blocked by her wobbly posterior. Alex shook his head. *I never hit anyone before. I've never been to the principal's office. What happened?* The rhythmic squelch of the rubber soles of Big Mac's shoes on the worn linoleum of the school's main hall sounded a bizarre death knell, adding to Alex's anxiety.

Alex cast a sideways glance at the new kid, who looked up and gave him a tight smile. *Maybe what I did was okay*, he told himself.

Hector inclined his head towards Alex and muttered softly, "Hey, Eastgard. Hey! Better watch your back. You too, little asshole. One day you'll be sorry you crossed me."

A cold shiver ran through Alex, but he shrugged his shoulders with an indifference he did not feel. "Shut up, Hector."

Later that day the new kid let himself into his family's apartment. His mother, Pam Close, watched him enter.

"How was school, Patrick?"

"Aw, I don't know," Patrick mumbled. He understood that the question was rhetorical. "I'm going to do homework." He walked to his room and closed the door, grateful for the privacy. What a weird day. He got beat up and he got threatened. But that guy Alex seemed okay. They'd gone together to Alex's house after school. Alex had a really cool room with a giant map over his desk and posters with sailboats. And his house had a basketball net on the front of the garage. Patrick wished they hadn't moved from New Hampshire, wished he didn't have to go back to that stupid school tomorrow, but he didn't have much of a choice. He would avoid Hector and stick by Alex. He hoped it would be okay.

*

Alex lay sprawled on his bed as he thought about the day, the image of that new kid, Patrick, innocently wandering around the playground, bewildered when Hector attacked him, his own wild reaction, and then Hector lying in the dirt like he was dead. He found it hard to believe that he could become so angry that he could summon the strength to knock down someone like Hector. It was almost like he had been someone else for those few insane seconds. And then there was Hector's threat. Alex would have to be careful, but Hector would eventually find someone else to pick on. In the end, he had been lucky. Hector could have stood up and really beaten him up. Or Alex could have gotten in a lot of trouble with the principal. But Hector got in trouble at school so much that he got all the blame; Alex got off with only a warning. Today, he had done the right thing. Whatever happened later, he would not regret his actions.

Alex hauled himself off his bed and sat down at his desk. His chubby little hamster, her fur a patchwork of caramel and marshmallow white, loitered near the door of her cage. Alex noticed Angie's black eyes studying him. "I was a hero today, Angie. I was. I saved someone today. I really did."

Angie regarded him skeptically. He passed a fresh Cheerio through the bars of her cage, into her deft little paws, in hopes of eliciting a more enthusiastic response.

"Know what a hero is, Angie? It's when you save someone. You don't worry about yourself, just about the other person." He wanted to be a hero, courageous, victorious, protector of family and friends, just like Tarzan, in the book Dad gave him last month. He allowed himself the luxury of picturing himself as Tarzan, hurtling through the jungle on twisted vines, long mane of dark hair streaming behind him. Or, better yet, as champion in some ancient contest, clad in bronze, circling the field in his gleaming chariot, holding the victor's laurel wreath aloft, saluting the crowd. He glanced up at his America's Cup poster. He stepped purposefully onto the sailboat woven into the rug next to his bed, took a deep breath, closed his eyes and dreamed of being Sinbad, sailing the seven seas, braving typhoons, wrestling sharks, reveling in the wild salt-spray, the rough salute of the endless oceans. There were so many ways to be a hero!

Then he remembered his homework and set aside his dreams for later.

From his room, Alex heard the door chimes sound- his father was home from work. He heard his mother's footsteps, going to greet him, and the murmur of their voices.

"Philip, how was work?"

"Not too bad. Good to be home and out of that car."

"Your leg is bothering you again," Olivia said, observing his slight limp. "Take off your jacket and sit down."

"Thanks, Liv," Philip replied, shrugged off his tweed sport coat, uncovering a rumpled white cotton shirt. He pulled off his tie and draped it across the back of a dining room chair, unbuttoned his cuffs and folded the sleeves back from his wrists. "That's much better. Best part of the day."

"I'll get you a little something to settle your nerves," she said.

"My nerves are fine."

"There's always room for improvement." She disappeared through the swinging door into the kitchen.

Philip sat down, turned on the television, and switched the dial to the 6 o'clock news. "Christ, another murder in the Combat Zone!"

Olivia returned, the swinging door ushering her smartly into the living room. "You'd think the mayor could provide some leadership and clean all that up."

The familiar tinkle of ice against metal sounded as Olivia placed a silver tray with two cocktail glasses, a jar of queen olives and a silver-lidded cocktail shaker misty with condensation and filled with enough ice, gin and dry vermouth for two martinis, onto the coffee table.

"Alright, then. Here's that little nerve-settler I promised you." Olivia poured a generous martini, straining off the ice, and handed it to Philip. She then skewered two olives onto a toothpick, and dropped them into the drink, a little green exclamation point ending in a dot of red pimento at one side of the glass.

Philip twirled the delicate stem of the martini glass between his fingers, watching the faint ripples of the clear fluid with fascination. "Look at this. Delicious and visually appealing. This is almost too pretty to drink!"

"Drink it while it's cold, dear."

Philip leaned back in his recliner, enjoying the faint aroma of the gin and the gleam of the freshly polished silver tray. He closed his eyes, relaxing, comfortable, surrendering to the gentle limb-loosening of his cocktail. "Olivia, there is no one, bar no one, who makes this good a martini! If anything happens to me, they'll hire you as head bartender at the Ritz in a minute."

Olivia preened.

Philip winked at her and extended the foot rest of the recliner.

Alex sauntered downstairs. "Hi, Dad," he said.

"Alexander, how was school today?" Philip inquired.

"Okay I guess," Alex replied, hopeful that no news of the skirmish with Hector had reached his parents. But his Dad said no more, so Alex knew he was not in trouble.

"Alex, that was a nice little boy you brought home with you today," Olivia said.

"He's not little. He's same age as me."

"You know what I mean. Anyway, Philip, I am telling you, when I first saw him, walking in here behind Alex, he looked like a slightly younger version of our son. They could have been brothers, I thought. Now, when I took a better look, I realized that the resemblance was somewhat superficial. But there was a general similarity." She nibbled the gin-saturated olive decorating her drink.

"When's dinner?" Alex asked, although he already knew the answer.

"Soon. We're watching the news right now," Olivia said.

Translation: his parents needed time to finish their cocktails. Alex sighed; he was really hungry. What was it about drinking? His Mom and Dad changed every evening when they had their drinks. Usually they were serious, laconic, focused. But give them their cocktails and they became expansive, jovial, uninhibited, even romantic. After a second drink Mom would address the TV news anchor directly and lodge her complaints, scornfully expressing her dissatisfaction with the state of world affairs. Fifteen, maybe 20 minutes, then they'd eat. He trudged back upstairs.

Back in his room, Alex let Angie out of her cage. He held up a Cheerio and made sure she saw it, and then set it down at the opposite end of the desk. Angie tumbled out of the cage and gave Alex a quizzical look.

"If you want that, you're going to have to go get it, Angie. You need the exercise! You used to move a lot faster." Her eyes fastened on the Cheerio and off she went. She picked the Cheerio up in her little forepaws and nibbled it daintily, until nothing was left but a sparse pool of cereal dust on the desktop.

*

*I am a fortunate woman*, Anita Gonzalez reflected as she lounged on the tufted leather sofa in the great room of her home with her two younger children.

"*Mira, mamá, un A en mi examen de matemática!*" Catalina produced a crumpled paper with a large red "A" in the upper right corner. She set it down on the glass-inlaid coffee table, smoothed out the most conspicuous creases and handed the paper to her mother.

"Catalina! *Maravilloso!*" Anita hugged her daughter.

"Shhh! Big Bird's talking," Juan Carlos said, eyes fixed on the TV.

"So sorry, *mi amor.*" Anita ruffled his silky hair. Her two younger children were so sweet and good-natured. They took after their father. In business, of course, her husband could drive a hard bargain, and to be sure, he was strong as steel deep down, but his strength was subtle, almost always restrained. A logical, patient man. Hector was different though. Her older son, her wonderful Hector, was fiery, mercurial, complex, non-conformist. Sometimes those characteristics brought him trouble, as the schools were interested only in turning out studious, boring automatons oozing with respect for their mediocre teachers. Not the best environment for her Hector to flourish in but give him a few years and a little autonomy and he would show the world a thing or two. And her Hector was such a striking boy, with his black hair and shining green eyes, quite tall for his age. *He takes after my side of the family*, Anita reminded herself. *He got his green eyes from me.*

On the other hand, her Pedro was quietly brilliant, extraordinarily successful. She and her husband had come from Puerto Rico with nothing and had built a life here. She thought back on the miserable, crowded apartment her family had occupied in San Juan. *Gracias a dios*, Pedro had taken her by the hand and brought her to Boston. *It will be perfect*, he told her. *The children will have a safe neighborhood and a good education, and I will have easy access to my contacts in New York City and Miami.* Admittedly, on their arrival to the mainland, they'd had to struggle. Pedro had been forced to take certain risks, to make difficult decisions in order to establish himself. She shivered, recalling that time. *But look at us now!* She thought. *We live in a beautiful, spacious home and our three children have opportunities we never dreamed of. Catalina plays the piano beautifully; only in fourth grade and already her clever little fingers could play Beethoven! To have had a piano in our home in San Juan- impossible. And Hector was becoming quite the equestrian. What a pleasure to watch him at the horse shows, so handsome in his black helmet and tailored jacket, his lithe body one with the horse, gracefully making every jump, truly a modern-day hidalgo.*

Hector and his two friends paused on the sidewalk in front of Hector's home, a magnificent Spanish colonial-style mansion in bone-white stucco with a terra cotta tile roof.

"Okay, Eddie, Lou. When we see my Mom, just back me up. Don't try to be creative," Hector admonished his friends. "You two walk in front."

"Your house is so damn big," Eddie said.

"You been here before and you always say that. Get over it," Hector said.

The three boys sauntered up the front walk, and Lou rang the doorbell. The door was promptly opened by Anita, elegant in a vivid scarlet caftan, and wearing heavy gold earrings.

"*Eduardo! Luis! Hola. Qué tal?*" She stood aside and gestured graciously for them to enter.

"*Buenas tardes, señora,*" Eddie said, respectfully.

"*Gracias, señora,*" Lou added, a little shy with Hector's formidable mother.

The two boys stepped into the cavernous, double-height entrance hall, with its floor of glazed Mexican tile, its austere iron monastery-style chandelier, its beamed ceiling. Hector stood on the threshold and Anita got her first good look at him.

"*Dios mío, mi hijo! Qué te pasó?*" Anita gazed upon Hector with horror. Her handsome son, his jet-black hair swept back from his high forehead, the very image of a young Castilian nobleman, stood before her with a narrow thread of dried blood on his lower lip, his beautiful new sweater ripped and his jeans all dirty.

"*Mamá,*" Hector began, "There was a fight. I had to defend myself."

"Who would dare to do this thing, *mi hijo?*" Anita asked, voice shaking.

"This other kid hit me and knocked me down when I wasn't looking. The stupid principal blamed me, so I got detention."

"Hector, what happened?" little Juan Carlos asked as he strolled into the entrance hall, big brown eyes wide with concern.

"I can't talk about it anymore," Hector said, hanging his head in sorrow.

"Let him be now. A bully hit him at the school," Anita said.

"My friend Maggie has a big sister in Hector's class and she said that Hector's a bully," countered Catalina.

"Catalina, enough! We do not need this," Anita said.

They heard the sound of a door from within the house open and close. Pedro Gonzalez approached. He had a full head of thick, wavy, deep brown hair touched with smoky gray. The collar of his white polo shirt was open to reveal a gold chain with a simple crucifix. He radiated quiet strength.

"*Papá!*" shouted Catalina, bouncing around her father's feet energetically. "You're finished your work already?"

"Ah, it is my little princess, who grows more beautiful every day. And here is my little Juan Carlos, who has grown taller since this morning!" Both children beamed.

"Pedro, look, Hector brought friends home, Eduardo and Luis. But a trouble-maker injured him today. Look at our poor boy!" Anita announced. "I wonder if it is safe for him to be at that school."

Pedro turned his dark eyes to Hector. He cleared his throat, and the room went silent. "A trouble-maker. Hector, you will recall what I said last time there was a fight at school. Come with me." Pedro spoke calmly, then turned and headed back to his office. Catalina and Juan Carlos stood absolutely still. Lou studied the dirt under his fingernails; Eddie dropped his eyes.

"Pedro, he's injured," Anita whispered.

"*Sí, señor,*" Hector whispered. He shuffled out of the room, following his father.

Concha, their diminutive housekeeper, listened from the shadows of the adjacent room. Catalina tiptoed over to her and whispered, "Hector got into a fight today. He and Papá are going to talk about it."

Concha's black eyes clouded over. She grasped the rosary in her deep apron pocket and vowed to say it in full for Hector this evening while washing the dishes.

Eddie spoke. "Uh, I guess we'll get going. We'll see Hector at school tomorrow."

Lou nodded.

Eddie waited until they were out of the Gonzalez home and well down the street before he turned to Lou and said, "Do you think it's true that Señor Gonzalez is a drug dealer?"

"I don't know, and I don't want to know. Hector says he's in import-export, whatever that means," answered Lou.

"Sounds like drugs to me."

\*

That night Hector lay on his abdomen in bed, thinking about the day, too angry to sleep. *I hate him! I hate my father. I hate that stupid Alex Eastgard. It's his fault. And I hate that little whiny shit that Alex got all mad about. I hate that stupid school, and I hate the stupid principal. I hate them all.*

He started to roll over onto his back, but the soreness in his thighs stopped him. He punched his pillow in frustration. *They'll be sorry. One day they'll be sorry,* he murmured to himself.

# CHAPTER 2

Alex and Patrick raced up the stairs to Alex's bedroom. Alex flopped onto the bed while Patrick grabbed the chair from the desk and sat on it backwards.

"This is great," Alex said. "We're done with grade school."

"Yeah, I'm glad to be out of there," Patrick agreed.

"And into high school," Alex said. He had spent the last nine years of his life attending Lincoln School, and departure had been poignant, but it would be unmanly to admit that.

"And we got the whole summer off!"

"You doing anything?"

"We might go to New Hampshire for a week or something. Stay with friends from where we used to live. Mom says it's cooler than in Boston."

"We're supposed to go to the Cape. I like it there. Beaches. Sailing."

"Can you sail?"

"Not really. A little. But I love it. I want to get really good at it. In the old days they sailed everywhere. To trade, to explore, to go to war. You needed a boat."

"Yeah? I've never been sailing."

"Know what? I'd like to have my own sailboat. Sail around the world or something."

"Sail around the world? Better get a big sailboat."

"Okay. A big sailboat."

"Could be expensive."

"I could live on it. Then I wouldn't have to pay for an apartment."

"That'd be cool. What if we shared it, fifty-fifty? We could get a really nice one."

"Okay. All we'd have to do is decide where to sail." Alex turned to study the National Geographic map on the wall over his desk, a Mercator projection in heavy

13

paper. He slid off the bed and gestured toward the southern tip of South America. "There's this place called Tierra del Fuego. Means land of fire. We could go there."

"Why is it called land of fire?"

"Don't know."

"We should find out before we go."

"Or we could go the other way. We could sail across the Atlantic Ocean, past the Rock of Gibraltar, into the Mediterranean." Alex climbed onto his desk and traced their course with his index finger. "We could sail past Italy and hug the coast of Greece. And then along the coast of Turkey, Lebanon and Israel, and then Egypt. We could sail down the Nile. Wouldn't that be awesome?" Alex could almost hear the creaking of the tarred wooden planks of their boat, groaning as they struggled through the waves.

"I'm not sure if a boat that could cross the Atlantic could also sail up a river."

"Well, we have time to figure it out. When we buy the boat, we'll ask."

"What if we had girlfriends by then?"

"They could come. If they wanted."

"Don't know if girls would come with us. They need closets and bathtubs and stuff."

"We're not having a bathtub. If they want to wash off, they can take a bucket of water from the ocean and dump it on themselves. If they don't like it, they can stay behind."

Patrick nodded. "Good. Yeah, let's do it."

"Or maybe we could wait until we get to some island and meet some island girls who don't expect bathtubs. We could go to Tahiti. I bet the girls are nice there." He imagined beaching their boat on the fine sand, the sun warm on his back, the endless sky bright and clear. And pretty girls with long dark hair crowned with flowers and wearing grass skirts.

"We would have to learn to navigate so we can find Tahiti, but okay. Sure." *Alex really comes up with some crazy stuff*, Patrick thought. *I better be there to protect him from himself.*

"Want to go fishing?"

"Sure. When?"

"Now. Come on." They headed downstairs and out onto the driveway, just as Philip returned from work. He opened the car door and turned in his seat, lowering his feet to the asphalt. Before exiting the car, he paused to rub his right shin.

Alex watched without speaking.

"Darn stop and go traffic. Makes my leg hurt," Philip said.

"When I get my license, I can drive you to work. Then drive to school. Then I can come pick you up at the end of the day," Alex offered.

"We'll see. Want to shoot some hoops?" he said, jerking his head toward the basketball goal. The white cotton web of the net dangled enticingly from the metal hoop in the light breeze. He stood and walked carefully, doing his best to minimize his limp.

"We're going fishing," Alex answered.

"I'll take you both on, before or after fishing. Unless you're scared."

Alex smirked. "Okay, after fishing."

As they walked away, Patrick whispered to Alex, "Is there something wrong with your Dad's leg?"

"Yeah, he got an injury when he was in the army."

"He was in the army! Was he in a war or anything?"

"Yeah. Something exploded right in front of him and blew metal into his shin. They got it all out, but the bone still hurts him sometimes."

*

Alex lay in bed the following day, the Sunday morning after eighth grade graduation, reveling in the thought that he was now officially a high school student. A whole wonderful summer spread out before him, and he would be able to do whatever he wanted. Sunshine spilled into his room, inviting him to rise and leave the house. *Maybe I'll see if Patrick wants to go fishing in the reservoir again. Patrick's parents always make him go to church, but I could dig up some worms while he's at church and we would still have plenty of time. Or maybe Mom has some bacon she'd give me for bait.*

Alex rolled out of bed, landing on the sailboat rug next to his bed and grinned. *Or maybe I should get a job and start saving for the sailboat.* He shrugged into a fresh T shirt and pulled on a pair of jeans and turned toward Angie.

"Hey Angie, need some water?" The hamster's little black eyes followed him as he removed the water bottle. He refilled it from the bathroom, returned to the cage and slid it back into place.

"You always think I'm going to forget to bring back your water. You should know better by now," Alex said, shaking his head. He sprinkled fresh food into the little plastic dish and Angie lumbered over for breakfast. Alex walked toward the door and stopped.

"Angie! I knew something was different. No wheel. You weren't on your wheel last night," Alex scolded, and Angie returned his gaze, looking guilty. "When I get back from fishing you're getting back on that wheel and getting some exercise. Okay, see you later."

Alex smelled Olivia's coffee, its aroma rich, familiar, comforting, as he came down the stairs.

"Liv, let me get you a new coffee maker. That one must be from the Middle Ages," Philip said. He was seated at the kitchen table wearing a lightweight bathrobe, reading the newspaper.

"Philip, you know how I feel about the concept of drip coffee. For heaven's sakes. This was my mother's percolator and it makes better coffee than any of those silly new machines." Olivia extracted two slices of whole wheat toast from the toaster, expertly buttered them, cut them in half and set them on the table in front of her husband. "Alex, scrambled or poached?"

"Poached eggs are gross." Alex found the funny pages and laid them on the table.

"Scrambled then." Olivia turned to the stove.

She laid a plate with scrambled eggs and three strips of bacon, and a glass of orange juice in front of Alex. "Well?" she said, turning to Philip.

"I guess it's about time," Philip said, laying down the paper. He reached into the pocket of his bathrobe and pulled out a small envelope.

"What's that?" Alex asked.

Philip opened the envelope, pulled out three tickets and spread them onto the table. "Tickets to this afternoon's Sox game. For you, me and Patrick."

\*

"What do you think of Fenway Park, gentlemen?" Philip gestured grandly at the playing field, as they found their seats, a few rows up from the bullpen.

"These are great seats. Thanks, Dad!" Alex said.

"Thanks for inviting me, Mr. Eastgard," Patrick added.

"No problem. I think a Sunday afternoon at Fenway Park is the perfect way to celebrate 8th grade graduation."

"Dad, there's the guy with drinks. Can we get something?"

"Sure. You need something to wash down those hot dogs. What do you want?"

"How about a beer?" Alex asked hopefully. He balanced a Fenway frank with ketchup and relish on his lap. A box of hot buttered popcorn was wedged between his knees.

"Great. I'd probably get arrested and your mother would have to bail me out. Or maybe she'd leave me to rot. How about a coke, or one of those frozen lemonade things?"

"Okay. I guess the frozen lemon stuff."

"Patrick?"

"Coke?"

"Okay, here it comes," Philip said, as the vendor passed their drinks to them. "How will our boys do today, I wonder."

"They'll win, won't they Dad?" Alex said, and then took a big bite of his hot dog.

"You never know. I'd love it if they won the pennant this year. But year after year, they break my heart." Philip sighed. "Maybe this'll be the year."

"Now batting for the Red Sox, number 8, Carl Yastrzemski," the PA announced.

"Yaz is up! You know, they're saying it could be his last year," Philip said.

They watched, tense with excitement as Yastrzemski strode to the plate and glowered at the pitcher. They watched with anxiety as the pitcher threw a strike, then another. The next pitch was low; Yaz stepped back, bat on his shoulder. From the opposite side of the ball field, Alex sensed his grim determination, as he again stepped to the plate. The pitch hurtled forward; Yaz met it solidly with his bat, and the ball soared across the field.

"It's coming to us!" Alex yelled. He and Patrick and Philip raised their hands, each hoping to make a catch. The ball slammed through Philip's hands and into his forehead, just above his left eye. He grabbed it before it fell.

"You got it! Dad! You caught it!" Alex yelled.

Patrick let out a low whistle, full of admiration.

"Good catch, buddy," a man from the row behind said, clapping him on the shoulder.

"Thanks!" Philip said.

"Dad, are you okay?"

A short laceration marked the ball's point of impact. A dusky bruise, centered along Philip's left eyebrow, crept down, framing his eye with a purplish arch.

"God, that hurts!" Philip murmured. He folded a napkin and touched it to his eyebrow. When he saw the blood, he pressed firmly on the laceration, hoping to staunch the bleeding. But he turned to Alex and smiled. "It's a small price to pay for catching a ball at Fenway! Could be one of Yaz's last homers!"

"You want some ice to put on it?" Alex asked.

"No, no. We are manly men. A little bruise doesn't slow us down."

But when Alex looked away, intent again on the game, Philip covered one eye and then the other, paused, and then repeated the process. He rested his hands on his thighs and turned his attention back to the Red Sox.

*

When the game was over, they took the Green line train back to their neighborhood in Brookline.

"Alex, what are you planning for the rest of the day?" Philip asked as they approached their stop.

"I don't know. Patrick, you want to do something?"

"Sure. Is it too late to go fishing?"

"Yeah, let's go fishing." Alex turned to Philip. "Mom is going to be mad when she sees your eye."

"Probably true. You'd better take the ball. I'll try to think of some explanation that won't make her think I'm an idiot." Philip unzipped the inner pocket of his windbreaker, pulled out the ball and handed it to Alex.

Alex clutched the ball as they entered the house. "Patrick, I'm going to drop this off in my room. Then we need to get a few worms. Be right back."

Alex returned and approached Patrick. "Where are my parents?"

"Your Mom's in the living room, and your Dad went in there with her."

"Good. Come on." Alex grabbed a brown paper lunch bag from the pantry and a serving spoon from the silverware drawer and went into the backyard to the small shade garden his mother kept along the wooden fence separating their yard from their neighbors'. He crouched down by the ferns, carefully scraped aside the hemlock mulch and scooped up black soil looking for earthworms. In his experience, the best source for worms was around his mother's ferns. Indeed, within just a few minutes he had found sufficient worms for several hours of fishing. He slid the worms into the bag along with enough dirt to keep them from drying out, refilled the holes he had dug, and carefully replaced the mulch. Then the most treacherous part of this exercise: he had to get back inside and wash the spoon before his Mom found out it had been used in the garden. He wiped the excess soil from the spoon onto the grass, folded over the top of the bag of worms and returned to the kitchen. Alex successfully cleaned the spoon, dried it and returned it to the drawer without his mother learning of it. Later he would tell his Dad about this, and they would laugh together, but neither of them would dream of repeating it to Mom.

"Okay. Let's go."

*

Later that afternoon, Philip and Olivia arrived at the emergency room of the local hospital and signed in. Olivia led Philip past the sick and injured and selected a spot away from those she deemed most contagious. She and Philip sat down in chairs in the waiting room.

"Just look at these ridiculous pseudo-ergonomic plastic chairs they expect people to be able to sit in and wait patiently," Olivia snapped. "The chintzy legs are uneven," she continued, rocking the wobbly tubular aluminum frame back and forth. She picked up a magazine from an adjacent table and began absently, rapidly, nervously leafing through it. Philip remained silent.

"Philip, say something. Does it hurt?"

"No, well, yeah, it stings. Kind of throbbing too."

The receptionist came forward. "Mr. Eastgard, the doctor can see you now, if you can come with me," the receptionist announced slowly and loudly, clipboard with Philip's information at the ready.

"Thank you, dear, but we are not hard of hearing," Olivia said, testy.

"Over here on the right," the receptionist continued, with no change in tone.

"Maybe *she* is hard of hearing," Olivia muttered into Philip's ear. "It wouldn't be so bad but she sounds so nasal. Really."

Olivia and Philip entered the examining room and Olivia began to sit down in yet another plastic chair.

"Liv, you don't have to stay. I'll be okay from here," Philip said. Olivia began to protest but she recognized an unfamiliar edge in his voice and complied.

"Alright, but I'll be right out in the waiting room. If you shout, I'll hear you." She rested her hand on his shoulder and kissed his cheek. "It doesn't look too bad, Philip. Don't worry now." One more squeeze to his shoulder and she left. As Olivia waited Philip was examined, evaluated by x-ray, and returned to the exam room, where his laceration was thoroughly cleaned and sutured.

"Well, Mr. Eastgard, this x-ray shows soft tissue swelling, corresponding to your injury, but no bony damage. That is, you have no perceptible fracture of the bony orbit. I am going to give you a prescription for antibiotics, to be on the safe side." Dr. Michaelson scribbled a few words and arcane symbols onto his prescription pad and handed the slip of paper to Philip.

"Thanks, doc," Philip said. Hopefully the pharmacist could decipher this scrawl. "Um, what about my other eye?"

"What's wrong?"

"With my left eye I can see fine but my right eye, with my right eye, I don't see right. It's partly black or something, like I had a patch over part of my eye. I noticed it first after the ball hit my left eye, when I was wiping up the blood."

"Gee, let me take another look. I didn't see anything before." Dr. Michaelson peeled back upper and lower lids on Philip's right eye, and then left eye. He saw no foreign material but dropped a little saline solution into the eyes to rinse away any tiny particles that may have lodged there. "Does that help at all?"

Philip covered his right eye with one hand, and then his left eye. "No, it's the same. With my right eye it's still part dark."

"Does it hurt at all? Itch or burn?"

"No, nothing like that. Just dark."

"Let me have a look inside then." Dr. Michaelson flicked on his ophthalmo-scope and directed its little beam of light deep into Philip's left eye, then his right eye. "Well, there does seem to be something going on in the interior of your right eye. Should look nice and flat but there's a lumpy area. Left eye looks great."

"What is it? Is it bad?" Philip asked.

"I'm not sure exactly what it is, but you should definitely see a specialist. We have a list of different specialists affiliated with the hospital and you can make an appointment with one of the eye doctors." He fiddled with the head of the stetho-scope looped around his neck.

"As soon as I noticed it, I just knew it was something serious. It is, isn't it?"

"Ophthalmology is such a specialized field that it's really best to get the opinion of an expert, rather than have me speculating. So please call one of our eye doctors and get this seen to."

"Okay, I will."

"Oh, Mr. Eastgard, do you have a ride home? Maybe you shouldn't be driving after all you've been through."

"Yes, my wife is in the waiting room. She'll drive. Thanks very much, doctor." Philip sat on the edge of the examining table and watched as the doctor left the room. His sweaty hand had been clutching the prescription so tightly that the paper was visibly worn and his name, written in ballpoint pen, was smudged and barely recognizable.

*

A week and a half later, Alex and Patrick were playing basketball in the driveway of Alex's house, as the sun ducked behind the houses lining the west side of Pella Street, and the day drew to a close.

"There's my Dad," Alex said. He and Patrick stepped back out of the driveway to let Philip pull into the garage.

"Hi, Dad," Alex called into the garage.

"Hi, Mr. Eastgard," Patrick echoed.

"Hello, boys," Philip said, glancing at them but briefly.

"Hey Dad, when are you going to be able to play again?" Alex held the basketball to his chest, preparing for a throw.

"Not sure, we'll see." He turned and limped into the house.

Alex stared at the door his Dad had just passed through. "The parents have been acting even stranger than usual, ever since the Red Sox game. Wish I knew what was going on."

"Yeah, mine never tell me anything either."

"It's getting dark. Let's quit," Alex said.

"'Kay."

They sat on the front step of the house and scanned the sky for the first stars of the evening. Alex plopped the basketball on the ground and bracketed it with his feet.

"Hey, look, a firefly!" Patrick's hands shot out and trapped the tiny insect. He separated his thumbs to create a small crack and Alex peeked in.

"Cool! Fast work!" Alex said.

The front door opened.

"Oh, hi, Mrs. Eastgard," Patrick said, turning toward the open door.

"Patrick, your mother called. She'd like you home for dinner." Olivia spoke brusquely, retreated inside and closed the door.

"I thought she liked me. Not even a hello," Patrick said.

"It's not you. I told you, they're acting strange."

"Well, I better get home." Patrick opened his hands, palms up, and the firefly drifted away. Patrick mounted his bike and pedaled off.

Alex went inside and headed up to his room. Angie hadn't moved from her favorite spot in her cage since morning but her shiny little eyes followed Alex as he came into the room.

"Okay, Angie, let's get some exercise." He opened the cage door and deposited Angie onto her wheel. She took one short step and then stopped.

"Come on, girl, let's go." Alex spoke firmly, on the off-chance it might make a difference. Angie remained immobile on the wheel. Alex moved the wheel a quarter turn, but instead of taking the hint, Angie tumbled off the wheel and into her cozy wood chip bedding.

"Angie, are you okay?" Alex peered at her. He put a Cheerio at the far end of his desk, but she ignored it. He moved it closer, and she continued to ignore it. Finally, he put the Cheerio well within her reach, and her little paws skittered out and collected the treat. "I think you might be sick or something. You should get checked by the vet. I'm going down for dinner now." He put her back into her cage, where she burrowed halfheartedly into her bedding with her Cheerio.

"Mom," he began, seeing Olivia at the bottom of the stairs. He would ask her about a vet for Angie.

"Alex, come downstairs now. We have to talk." Her tone was serious. She walked into the living room, back straight, arms stiff, pace steady, and sat on the sofa. Philip sat in his recliner, an untouched martini neglected at his right hand. "Your father will be going to the hospital tomorrow to see about getting his eye fixed. He'll have to stay for a few days, then he'll be back." Her tone was matter-of-fact and did not invite inquiry.

Alex looked from his father to his mother. The hospital! A few days! From one baseball? "But then it will be okay?" he asked hopefully.

His father sat up a little and opened his mouth to speak but Olivia was too quick for him. "Yes, it will all be fine. Now let's have our dinner."

*

Three days later Olivia went to the hospital and retrieved her husband. Philip came quietly into the house and Alex ran to him.

"Dad, I'm glad you're back. Did it go okay?"

"Ah, yes. All set," Philip said. "Glad to be home. Really hate the hospital. Food's awful."

"I'd hate it too," Alex said. He wondered what had gone on there. His father seemed a gray shadow of himself, moving slowly, talking softly. And he looked a lot older. Philip retreated to his bedroom.

A few minutes later Alex hurried back downstairs carrying Angie and ran to his mother. "Look, Angie's really sick. She's been getting slower and slower, she hasn't touched her food and now she can barely breathe. Can we go to the vet in the morning?"

"Alex, Angie is just getting old. She lived a long time for a hamster. Longer than average," Olivia replied. Her tone was not especially sympathetic.

"No, please, let's at least see what the doctor thinks," Alex pleaded.

"Don't you think we have enough going on without worrying about her? She's just a rodent!"

"What do you mean, enough going on?" Alex asked. Technically Angie was not a rodent, but he let that pass.

"With your father being sick, just coming home from the hospital. Let's try to get back to normal, please." Olivia sounded strained.

"Dad is sick? I thought Dad's eye got hurt and now it's fixed!" Alex exclaimed.

"Dad had something abnormal in his eye, his other eye; he went to the hospital for that."

"Something abnormal? What do you mean!"

"Well, actually, it, well, it was a tumor. So it was taken out."

"He had an eye tumor?" Alex had never heard of that. Alex held Angie against his chest; he could feel his heart hammering at his ribs. "What does that mean? What's going to happen?"

"Everything should be alright, and now, please, let's all calm down and try to get back to normal." Olivia said, willing herself to maintain her composure.

Philip appeared suddenly in the living room. A shuffle replaced his characteristic buoyant step and he met Alex's gaze. Instead of taking his usual seat on

23

the recliner he sat on the couch. Alex sat beside his father and cradled Angie in his cupped hands. She labored to breathe, eyes closed, mouth stiffly open, little teeth on display. Philip studied her quietly.

"It was something called melanoma," Philip said.

"Daddy, what did they do to your eye?" Alex whispered.

In answer, Philip pealed back the patch over his right eye to reveal a translucent pink orb with no pupil and no iris.

"Where's your, your..." Alex's eyes slowly widened in horror as he understood. There was nothing he could say that seemed right; instead he leaned against his Dad, and Philip put his arm around Alex. They sat together like that for a long time, neither feeling the need to speak.

It was Philip who finally broke the silence. "After a while I'm supposed to go to another doctor who will give me a glass eye that looks just like my good eye. No one will know anything's wrong. Not by looking at the glass eye."

"Does it hurt?"

"Only a little. They gave me some pills to take," Philip replied. They sat together, now more comfortably, the worst of the conversation behind them.

After a while Alex spoke. "Dad, I think I should try to get Angie to drink something."

"Good idea, good idea," Philip said, his tone vague.

Alex went back upstairs and still holding Angie gently, he tapped a drop or two of water from her bottle into her mouth, with no response. He edged a Cheerio into her paws, and she seemed to take hold of it, but did not try to eat it. *That's never happened before*, Alex thought. *She just keeps breathing funny.* He set her down into the hollow in the wood shavings that marked her favorite spot in her cage and waited, but she did not move. He picked her back up, cradling her in his shirt. Time slid by, and evening darkened to night. Slowly Alex realized that Angie was breathing no longer and understood that she was gone. He stroked her mottled brown and white fur and murmured, "Poor little thing, poor little Angie."

He glanced at the clock- just after midnight. He found an old T shirt, laid Angie down on it, and folded it around her. He retrieved the flashlight from his bedside table and tiptoed down the stairs and out the back door. It was better this way, to have these last moments with Angie to himself. He dug a little hole around the ferns, but deeper than he would when searching for worms, and laid Angie in her little shroud into it.

"You were the best pet, little Angie. I'll really miss you," he said, and then filled the hole and laid a flat rock on top, to mark the spot. He smoothed mulch over the tiny grave to hide it. This spot would be his secret, his and Angie's. Tears welled in his eyes; he willed them back, but they ran down his cheeks anyway. Alex slowly walked back to the house and sat on the landing. He turned off his flashlight. The sky was black velvet sprinkled with stars, and the barest sliver of a crescent moon shone far away. He picked out the constellations he knew – the Big Dipper, the Little Dipper, Orion. He listened to the night sounds: the crickets, the rustling of the wind in the trees, the haunting melody of the neighbors' wind chimes, the occasional lonely bird call. For a long while he sat, thinking of Angie, and of his Dad, until he was very tired, and then he went in.

# CHAPTER 3

The town's reservoir was a sylvan haven, a peaceful pond surrounded by a jogging path, all enclosed by a ring of aromatic pines and broad-leafed maple and oak trees admitting filtered sunlight. For Patrick and Alex, it was the neighborhood fishing hole. They stood at the edge of the reservoir, each boy holding a lightweight fishing rod. Alex's rod bent slightly, the fishing line becoming taut suggesting a nibble; he reeled in his line hopefully but only an earthworm occupied his fishhook.

"Must've been the wind."

"I'm getting nothing either," Patrick muttered.

"I don't know but they say it's better if you get up real early to fish," Alex said.

"This is our last Monday of freedom; I wouldn't have got up early even to fish," Patrick said.

"Me either. I hope high school is okay." Alex examined the worm on his hook. It was still squirming, should still be reasonably appealing to a fish. He wondered if this worm carried any molecules from Angie. He closed his eyes for a moment, holding his emotions in check, and then leaned his rod back and with a practiced flick of his wrist made a nice cast. Sunshine sparkled on the clear water of the reservoir, shining as if in benediction on the heads of the two fair-haired boys. The water lapped gently around their lines.

"Are you going to go out for any sports or anything?" Patrick asked.

"I was thinking of track. I think I'm pretty fast. But I never timed myself," Alex said.

"Good idea. Wish I were tall enough for basketball." Patrick frowned.

"Try track."

"Yeah, maybe. Okay."

"We can time each other. You know, get an idea where we are. My Dad has a stopwatch we can use."

"Sounds good. Want to take a break? Fish must be sleeping," Patrick said.

"Yeah."

"Look what I brought." Patrick untied a plastic bag to reveal a bottle of Sam Adams beer resting in ice.

"Nice," Alex said. Then he added anxiously, "You brought an opener?"

"Of course!" Patrick pulled out the bottle and flipped off the bottle cap. "We're going to a Labor Day barbecue this afternoon. Dad is supposed to bring the drinks and the fridge is loaded with beer and stuff. They'll never miss one bottle. And anyway, beer is an important part of fishing." They admired the look of the beer with anticipation: the deep mahogany color of the bottle, the moisture clinging to it. The robust figure of Sam Adams on the label regarded them with approval.

"What's the barbecue for?" Alex asked.

"Oh, it's for my Dad's work. Bunch of nerdy accountants. So boring!" he said, handing the bottle to Alex.

The two boys sat on the spongy pine straw and passed the bottle back and forth, taking small sips of this forbidden beverage, and Alex relaxed. It was warm where they sat in the sun, and the leaves on the trees were all still bright green and abundant, but the breeze carried an occasional wisp of air cooled in nearby shade. Wordlessly it reminded them that summer was drawing to a close and autumn was about to begin.

"I found out why my parents were acting weird," Alex began.

"Really? Why?"

Alex told him about his Dad, the cancer, the glass eye.

"That sucks! I hope he's okay now," Patrick said.

"Me too," Alex said. He took a deep swig of beer and promptly belched. Both boys laughed, but the laughter died quickly.

"He'll be okay. He has to be," Patrick said. "If they took his whole eyeball out it must be all gone."

"Yeah. I hope."

They sat together quietly, finishing the beer, enjoying the mild air.

"That's it for the beer," Patrick said, with regret.

Alex took the bottle from him, leaned over, dipped it into the water of the reservoir and filled it. He stood and cast the bottle as far as he could; it landed with a splash and disappeared quickly below the surface. That bottle would be there forever, most likely. It would remain his secret, his and Patrick's, a hidden souvenir of this lovely late-summer day.

Patrick stood also. "I guess I should get back. I'm supposed to go to the barbecue," Patrick said.

The boys left the path that surrounded the reservoir and stepped through the trees and onto the sidewalk.

"Hey, there's Giuli!" Patrick said. Giulietta Stewart approached them, walking the family chihuahua.

"Hi, Giuli," Alex said.

"Oh, hi, um, how are you?" She directed the question at Patrick.

"We're good. How's your summer been?" Patrick answered.

"Um, okay. Um, I babysat a lot. And walked the dog." She gestured by wiggling the leash. "His name is Romeo." She looked at the sidewalk, blushing, trying unsuccessfully to smooth down her unruly red hair with the hand unoccupied by the leash.

"We fished a lot," Patrick said.

"Okay, see you, Giuli," Alex said, and started to walk away.

"Okay. Um. Alex," she said, finally looking at him. "I know this seems crazy, but I had this weird dream, well, that someone in your family was sick or hurt. Or something. Is everyone okay?"

Alex stared at her. "Uh, my Dad had an accident- he got hit by a baseball at Fenway Park. He had to go to the hospital, but he's okay now." He could not bring himself to mention the eye cancer again, and his Mom had told him not to talk about it anyway.

"Oh my god!" Giuli gasped, and her free hand flew to cover her mouth. "That's terrible!"

"Could that cause your dream?"

"Maybe. Sometimes I sort of get these dreams. Anyway, glad he's okay." She continued nervously wiping down her hair. "Come on, Romeo," she added in an unnaturally high-pitched coo.

"Well, see you in school in a few," Patrick said. He and Alex continued down the sidewalk.

"Giuli acts so strange sometimes," Alex observed.

"You mean that dream? Yeah, that's weird."

"No, like she's nervous or something,"

Patrick looked at him and shook his head. "Do you not know she likes you?"

"Giuli? You're kidding."

"Not kidding. It's so obvious."

Alex found it hard to believe but he let it go. "Okay, well, come shoot some hoops tomorrow if you have time. Hope you survive the barbecue."

*

Coach Joe Wainwright, a longstanding, much admired fixture at Brookline High School was a middle-aged man with a square jaw supporting a mouth set in a perpetual scowl. His graying hair was cropped short in military style. He held a brown clipboard made of compressed particle board; it carried a list of all the boys trying out for track.

"Hey, are you two brothers or what?" Coach Wainwright growled at Alex and Patrick, sitting together on the bottom bleacher after the hundred-yard dash, along with a dozen other boys trying out for track.

"No," Alex replied. I'm Alex Eastgard; he's Patrick Close."

"You look kind of alike," Coach observed; his tone was suspicious, and his left eye squinted menacingly.

"Yes sir. People say that," Patrick replied, somewhat intimidated.

"You run alike too," Coach said. His tone implied that an explanation was mandatory. The taller kid, Alex, ran like greased lightning; the other kid wasn't bad either.

"Yes sir, we've been practicing together," Alex said.

"You're not cousins or something?"

"No sir."

Coach walked off muttering and slashing at his clipboard with a pencil; Alex and Patrick exchanged a look and tried not to laugh.

"Okay, here it comes. Cross your fingers," Alex whispered.

"Okay," Patrick replied. Alex had nothing to worry about; he was the fastest one in the group. Patrick was not sure about himself though. He held his breath anxiously.

"Men, you all ran well today. I'd like to take you all, but I can only take six," Coach intoned. He flipped through the pages on his clipboard a last time and scratched the back of his head, partially dislodging his habitual blue and red

Brookline High baseball cap. "So, in alphabetical order, I want Brand, Close, Eastgard, Reynolds, Swanson and Terry. You six- practice is Monday through Friday, 3 to 4pm, right here. Rest of you, thanks for trying out. I invite you to practice and try again next year."

Patrick exhaled audibly when his name was called; he and Alex looked at each other and grinned.

"Terry, is that an earring?" Coach demanded.

"Yes sir." Michael Terry was trembling.

"You got a sister?"

"Yes sir."

"You take that damn earring off and give it to your sister and don't let me see it again," Coach Wainwright roared.

"Yes sir, no sir." Michael pulled the golden stud out of his ear lobe and tucked it into a pocket.

Alex leaned over and whispered, "Welcome to the track team, Mike!"

*

Alex skimmed over his History test one last time before starting to edge out of his chair to hand it in. Just before he stood, Hector Gonzalez sauntered by with his own test. Hector dropped the paper onto the teacher's desk with a disdainful shrug.

"Thank you, Hector," Mr. Winters said, calmly straightening the pile of tests.

Alex waited until Hector had returned to his seat before getting up to hand in his own test. An unspoken truce kept the peace between him and Hector, but Alex could sense the animosity Hector radiated whenever he was near. Alex laid his test on top of Hector's; his handwriting looked neat compared to Hector's big, loose, messy scrawl. A quick glance at Hector's test showed no answers in common with his.

"Thank you, Alex," Mr. Winters droned.

Alex returned to his desk.

*

Dusk settled, dusty mauve and gray on the outside world, as Alex lay on his bed re-reading *Tarzan*. Halfway through the first semester of his freshman year in high school he had his first report card. He was waiting for his father to get home, so he could show it to both of his parents at once. As he waited, his eyes drifted to the map of the world over his desk. He yearned to travel all over the world. What would

Zanzibar be like? Or Patagonia? He'd love to see Egypt, its temples and pyramids, the immortal Nile and its treacherous cataracts. If only he could take a year, or two, travel around Europe and then strike out eastward, through the lands of the Middle East, and on into Asia, seeing and hearing everything, tasting everything, onward and onward until he reached the eastern shores of the Pacific Ocean. He imagined cities laid out haphazardly along harbors hosting ships from a dozen countries, with merchants and sailors speaking a score of languages; vast, empty deserts with glimmering mirages always just out of reach; tribes of nomads borne by camels saddled with blankets of carmine and burnt orange; veiled women behind latticed windows in their harems; crowded bazaars selling all manner of brightly colored fruit, savory spices, intoxicating perfumes and gleaming weapons. The blood pounded in his veins with excitement. Then he heard the door chimes; his father was home. He waited a few minutes to allow his father to get settled before heading downstairs.

"Mom? Dad?" Alex saw his parents in their customary seats in the living room, about to watch the evening news, as if things were almost normal again.

"Yes, dear?" Olivia said, gaze direct, chin up, martini aloft.

"I got my first report card."

"Let's see, dear. How did you do?" Olivia held the paper before her and Philip leaned over to have a look.

"Alex, all A's! That's wonderful!" Olivia saluted him with her martini.

"Straight A's! That's great!" Philip's eyes shone. "I don't remember ever making straight A's myself. What about you, Liv?"

"I- I don't quite recall. It has been quite a while since I had a report card, dear."

"And also, here's the school newsletter. It lists kids who made Honor Roll. I made it." Alex handed over the mimeographed pages.

Olivia reviewed the list. "Honor Roll! Not too many names here. Absolutely wonderful. I see your friend Patrick made Honor Roll too."

"Yeah, Patrick got all A's except for one B in Math."

"Sweetheart, we are so proud of you." Olivia beamed.

"Yes, good work, Alex." Philip's eyes glistened.

Alex looked at his Dad. Was he about to cry? Both eyes looked kind of wet. When they took away his eye they must have left the part that makes tears.

*

Hector Gonzalez dragged his feet up the front walk of his house, his report card a leaden weight in his backpack. His parents knew that report cards would be issued today, and his father had instructed him to bring it to him as soon as Hector got home from school.

He opened the door and his mother swept into the front hall to greet him.

"Hector, *mi hijo*, how were the horses today?"

"Fine." Even a vigorous ride at the stables had not alleviated his anxiety.

"Can I have Concha make a snack for you?"

"No. Not hungry." His stomach was twisted in knots. His report card was even worse than he had feared, and his father would be angry. "Is Papá home?"

"Yes, in his study." Anita looked after Hector anxiously as he headed to see his father.

Hector knocked cautiously on the door. "*Papá?*"

"*Adelante,*" Hector heard, gruffly spoken. He entered.

Pedro sat before a large desk, papers laid out neatly before him. The late afternoon sun peeped though a small gap in the heavy crimson velvet draperies Anita had chosen for this room, admitting but little light. A tall brass floor lamp behind and slightly to the right of his father illuminated the papers on the desk. As Hector approached the desk Pedro gathered them into one neat stack, and carefully turned the stack upside down. "So?"

Hector sat down warily in a chair across from the desk. An exquisite Lladró figurine of a peasant girl on the desk aimed an enchanting smile in Hector's direction, but the boy was oblivious to her charms. The lamp shone bright in his face and he was forced to look down. May as well get this over with, he told himself. "You said to bring you my report card. Here it is."

Pedro took the paper from him and leaned forward so that his face was submerged in shadow. A heavy gold signet ring featuring a griffin with emerald eyes, a recent gift from Anita, twinkled on his right hand, the hand holding the report card, in the stark lamplight. *See, he has green eyes like mine*, Anita had told Pedro. Hector watched as the neutral expression on his father's face darkened to a severe frown, the lines on either side of his mouth deep crevices of displeasure. His eyes were unreadable, cast in menacing darkness. Hector saw him take several slow, deep, careful breaths before speaking.

"This report card is a disgrace. What do you have to say for yourself?"

"The teachers don't like me." Hector knew this question would be asked, and this was the best answer he had been able to fashion.

"That might work with your mother but not with me. Did you even go to class? Were you asleep the whole time? Did you even try?"

"I'm sorry, Papá. I will try harder next time." *Please let this be over*, Hector prayed silently.

"Do you know how hard your mother and I have worked to give you this nice home? The risks we have taken? The sacrifices we have made? To give you opportunities we never had!" Pedro's tone was hard but controlled. This topic was a common one in their household and Hector was sick of it.

"I know you work hard. You don't need to tell me again," Hector muttered.

"I want so much for you. I want you to go to college. Be a doctor. Or a lawyer. Someone important. No college will take you with grades like this."

"You didn't go to college. What do you care if I do?"

"Show some respect. I am your father."

"I know what you are." Hector threw caution to the winds and spoke his mind. "Maybe I'll go into the family business. Won't need to go to college. Won't you be proud of me?" His tone was sarcastic. He sat straight up and folded his arms on his chest.

Pedro rose and leaned forward, enraged. He struck Hector's face with a savage backhand blow. The sharp design of the signet ring opened a shallow gash in Hector's right cheek. Hector gasped, shocked. He put his hand to his face; his fingers came away marked with blood.

"Get out of my sight. And don't go whining to your mother."

Hector rose unsteadily and walked silently out the door. In a last show of recklessness, he slammed the door shut behind him. Catalina was crouched down by the side of the door. Her eyebrows shot up and her mouth made a little O when she saw Hector's face.

"What happened!" she said.

"You were spying. So, you don't need to ask."

"But…"

"I hate him," Hector whispered. "I really hate him." He strode upstairs to his room. Catalina waited for a few minutes, and then trembling, tapped softly on the door of the study.

"*Sí?*" she heard her father say. It was one syllable, but it spoke volumes of sorrow and fatigue.

"*Papá?*"

"Come in, my princess. What is it?"

"I just thought you might need a hug from your princess, that's all." She walked over to him and he embraced her, stroking her silky brown hair.

# CHAPTER 4

Alex and Patrick loitered on the worn granite steps of the high school, ready to start their junior year. Like all juniors, they were apprehensive, as everything they did this year would count when they applied to college. But they were also filled with elation. They were *juniors*, halfway through high school, on their way to college, to adulthood, to autonomy, to their future. In five minutes, the bell would ring, and the new school year would have begun.

A long line of cars queued in front of the school, advancing slowly, and one by one disgorged teenagers, some of whom emerged with alacrity, some with evident regret, and some openly somnolent. Then a wood-paneled maroon station wagon pulled up in its turn and three of the car doors opened. Two big muscular boys and a girl with curly brown hair stepped out, but did not walk forward, away from the car.

"Patrick, who are they? I don't recognize them," Alex said, nudging Patrick.

"I don't know. Look too old to be freshmen. Must be new," Patrick replied. He shivered briefly, remembering his own first day at school in this town.

The muscular boys stood, one upright with folded arms, one leaning against the car. The girl stood next to the open right rear car door; she scratched the back of her head impatiently, disrupting her curls.

"What are they waiting for?" Alex asked, squinting into the sunshine. Patrick shrugged.

Then out of that right rear door slid a pair of slender feet neatly shod in high heeled sandals; a willowy blonde girl gracefully emerged from the station wagon. The quartet, now complete, waved goodbye to the driver of their car and moved toward the front entrance of the school.

Alex stopped breathing. The blonde girl glided along the front walk and ascended the stairs. She would be passing right in front of him in a few seconds. She was so beautiful! His eyes drank in every detail and recorded them in his mind forever. Her golden hair was like silk. The perfect oval of her face rested on a long graceful neck that ended in the lace-trimmed collar of her white cotton cap-sleeved blouse.

Her dark patterned skirt swirled around her shapely legs. She was so perfect! And then suddenly she was before him and had stopped, smiling benignly in his general direction. For those priceless moments there was just her glorious smile, while her brothers and her sister were blurry images around her.

Then he heard Patrick speaking to them, "Technically they like you to stay outside until the bell rings, but once the weather turns cold nobody cares."

"Thanks. Oh, uh, I'm Charlie, and here's my brother Paul, and my sister Kelly, and this is Helen," said one of the two young men.

Helen, that was name of the angel, thought Alex.

"What year are you?" asked Patrick. He was strangely unaffected by the proximity of radiant Helen, Alex thought.

"Charlie and I are seniors, and Kelly and Helen are juniors," answered the second boy.

"Are you twins or something?" asked Patrick, noting that Charlie and Paul were almost indistinguishable; both were tall and broad-shouldered, with wavy chestnut hair, hazel eyes, healthy suntans, and friendly smiles stretching across big strong jaws beneath surprisingly abbreviated noses. Unlike Alex and Patrick, who were runners with lean frames, Charlie and Paul had bulging muscles suggesting an avid devotion to weightlifting.

"Yeah, we are, two pairs of twins. Charlie and Paul are identical, but Helen and I are not," Kelly joined in, her curls bouncing merrily around her cheeks. "Who's your friend? He's about as talkative as Helen."

"Sorry, I'm Alex," Alex replied, forcing himself to tear his eyes away from Helen. "Where are you from?"

"Small town in upstate New York," Kelly said.

"How's this school?" asked Paul.

"Oh, it's great. People love it. Teachers are pretty good and there are a lot of extracurricular activities. Sports are good. Alex and I are on the track team. He's our star, actually," Patrick offered.

"Are there other sports?" asked Charlie.

"We have football, but our team is not that good. Swim team is good. Diving is top-notch. Recently Coach introduced wrestling."

"Wrestling! No shit?" Paul blurted out. "Cool!" He grabbed Charlie and caught him in a headlock. Charlie gagged melodramatically and twisted free.

Then the bell rang.

"Coach'd love to know you're interested. Look for us at lunch, if you want," Patrick said, as he headed through the doors. He turned to Alex and spoke softly. "You see the size of those guys? The Old Man would give his right nut to have them on the wrestling team."

The two pairs of twins followed Patrick into the school. For one golden moment Helen turned her swan-like neck and met Alex's eyes.

"Helen, it was nice to meet you," Alex said. He felt he should say something more, but his mind had gone blank.

"Thank you. It was very nice to meet you too," she replied in a voice of pure honey, and Alex's heart melted. She turned her back to him and entered the school. The air around her sparkled and then she melted into the crowd of students wandering toward their homerooms.

"Hey, Alex, let's go," Patrick shouted from inside the entrance of the school, startling Alex out of his reverie.

"Patrick, did you see her? She's gorgeous!" whispered Alex, once he had caught up to Patrick.

"Who?"

"Helen! Don't you have eyeballs?"

"Yeah, they're both pretty. Kelly seemed like more fun," Patrick replied.

But Helen seemed like a princess, Alex thought, or a queen.

\*

The cafeteria at Brookline High School was a cavernous space with acoustics that indiscriminately magnified every sound. The junior and senior classes confined within for second-shift lunch created a thunderous din, interrupted by the occasional raucous howl of laughter rising above the background noise. Alex and Patrick sat at their usual table, along with several members of the track team and the ubiquitous Giuli Stewart. Giuli had taken to pasting down her foamy hair with large quantities of ultra-hold hair mousse; it encased her head in a shell of crispy red plastic.

"You do anything over the summer?" Clyde Reynolds asked between shoveled forkfuls of mashed potatoes.

"Um, yeah, I was a counselor at this boys' camp in New Hampshire. Talk about back to nature for two solid months. But I made some money," Lance Brand replied, leaning forward to be heard. "You?"

"Parents took me and my little sister to Florida for a week. It was okay," Clyde answered.

"Hey, look, there's Kelly and her sister!" Patrick half stood up from his seat and waved at them eagerly. He didn't bother calling out to them; it would have been futile.

"Helen. Kelly's sister is Helen," Alex reminded him.

"Yeah, I know."

Alex looked up and saw the girls. They each stood, holding a tray. Kelly was focused, scanning the room for empty seats. But from across the room Helen seemed uncertain, vulnerable, a little lost. Alex was seized with an urge to help her, like Tarzan protecting Jane, but Patrick had already caught Kelly's eye, and a moment later she and Helen were heading their way.

"Hi, sit down," Patrick said, gesturing at two empty chairs across the table.

"I'm glad we saw you. Charlie and Paul found the football table and abandoned us," Kelly said, scraping her chair into place and giggling. Helen sat down quietly and smiled at the group.

Alex smiled back, in such evident bliss that Giuli Stewart's heart sank. She dropped her eyes to her lunch and proceeded to grind her green peas into olive-colored paste.

Alex racked his brain for something to say to Helen, sitting across from him nibbling corn, one kernel at a time. Patrick and Clyde were chatting with Kelly, no awkwardness at all. *How do they do it?* he asked himself.

"You have Science with Peabody? I am so sorry!" Clyde groaned.

"Oh my god, I just knew I was going to fall asleep. He is so boring. I started biting my fingers to keep myself awake!" Kelly laughed, displaying a beautiful smile. "Also, not to sound whiny, but the red jello is the most interesting part of this lunch."

"Yeah, never come to school without eating a good breakfast, you want to survive," Patrick advised.

Alex leaned forward and asked, "Helen, what's your last name?" As soon as he said it he thought, that sounds so stupid.

"Fletcher. We're the Fletchers." Her tone was soft and serious, and she looked right at him with eyes of smoky blue.

"If I, if there's anything I can help you with, at school I mean, let me know. You know, homework. Anything. Any time," Alex said.

Hector Gonzalez strode up to the table, approaching from behind Helen and Kelly, Eddie and Lou in tow. He dragged an empty chair from the adjacent table and sat down, straddling it. Alex and Patrick exchanged a quick look and Alex glared at Hector, who ignored him. Helen and Kelly turned in their seats to see who was joining them.

"Hi there. I don't think we've met, and I wanted to say hello," Hector said, his voice hearty, his manner expansive. "I am Hector Gonzalez." He pronounced his name with a rich, formal Spanish accent.

"Hi, I'm Kelly, and my sister Helen."

"Hey, I'm Eddie."

"Lou." Eddie and Lou hung back a little but smiled.

Hector sat behind the girls, wearing his distressed black leather bomber jacket, long arms like powerful black wings draped over the backs of Helen and Kelly's chairs. To Alex he was a great dark bird of prey, an ugly vulture, hovering over the two girls.

"Hey, nice to meet you guys," Kelly said. Helen smiled shyly and looked down.

"And nice to meet you." He gave the girls a sly smile and a rakish wink, pushed off from his chair and swaggered off.

"Yeah, see you," Eddie said, as Lou nodded. They followed Hector out of the cafeteria.

"Wow, he's quite... dashing," Helen said, her voice finally betraying some emotion.

"No, you want to stay away from him," Alex warned. "He's bad news, always in some kind of trouble."

"Oh, don't tell Helen that. She loves the bad boys." Kelly rolled her eyes.

"He seemed very nice," Helen said, cautiously. Alex's heart sank.

*

Every year the PTO organized a Back-to-School reception for parents of students of each grade to meet their children's teachers, and tonight was the night for the junior class. Philip and Olivia filtered through the crowd with a list of Alex's classes and teachers.

"Her name tag says Henrietta Stewart, Philip. That's Alex's English Literature teacher," Olivia said, consulting the list.

"Sharp eyes, Liv. Let's go say hello."

"Mrs. Stewart? We are Olivia and Philip Eastgard, parents of Alex," Olivia said, extending her hand.

"How do you do? How do you do? So nice to meet you," Mrs. Stewart bubbled. She was a stout middle-aged lady with a pale round moon of a face resting contentedly on a double chin and decorated with tortoise-shell, cats' eyes spectacles, all crowned by a heavily hair-sprayed, bouffant hair-do in burnt sienna.

"So, uh, what will the kids be studying this year?" Philip said, trying to frame an appropriate question.

"Ah, well, we have commenced with that most profound work, *Beowulf*. Very exciting stuff, you know. I plan then to introduce some excerpts from Chaucer. The Middle English is a bit of a challenge for some of the students, even the bright ones, admittedly. But we will continue with the Transcendental poets and Shakespearian poets, including, it goes without saying, Shakespeare, but also Marlowe. Ah Marlowe! 'Who ever loved that loved not at first sight?' And of course, 'Was this the face that launched a thousand ships...' Just marvelous!"

"Well that sounds wonderful, Mrs. Stewart. You are clearly very enthusiastic about your subject," Olivia said.

"Oh my, yes! But the highlight of the course will be the study of *Romeo and Juliet*. A tragedy to end all tragedies. What an influence that particular masterpiece has played in my own life."

"How's that, Mrs. Stewart?" Philip asked.

Olivia glared at him quickly and covertly. "Why are you encouraging her?" she whispered. Philip shrugged helplessly.

Mrs. Stewart waxed lyrical, oblivious to Olivia's waning interest. "At one point in my life, I had the opportunity to play Shakespeare. I was offered the role of Juliet, a real honor! It was an off-Broadway production, but all the same, the excitement! However, it became clear that the offer was not based on talent alone. And the price for the opportunity to become Juliet – the surrender of my virtue – was just too high. So I declined, and my life took a different course. And now here I am, teaching high school. What a wonderful, romantic, impressionable group high school students are!

"And when it came time to choose a name for my lovely daughter, I named her after Shakespeare's Juliet. However! I did not utilize the prosaic Anglicized form of the name but rather the original Italian form. Yes. Giulietta. Beautiful, isn't it? And so evocative." Mrs. Stewart produced a deep, dramatic sigh.

"Well, that is quite informative. We are grateful to you for filling us in. Goodness, I see our son's math teacher. Please excuse us." Olivia pulled Philip forcefully into the midst of a dense throng of teachers and parents.

"Yes, thank you, Mrs. Stewart," Philip called over his shoulder as the crowd swallowed him.

Olivia inclined her head toward Philip and whispered, "That woman's indiscretion is really quite shocking. I hope she is more restrained with her narrative when she's in the classroom."

Philip put his arm around her shoulders and gave a squeeze. "I wouldn't worry, Liv. Kids nowadays, hard to shock them. I just hope they take her seriously enough so she can teach them something."

# CHAPTER 5

Alex sat at his desk studying AP Biology. The sudden onset of the rapid honking of a car's horn, harsh as semi-automatic rifle fire, ripped him away from the double helix. He scrambled down the stairs.

"What is going on? Who would have the bad manners to honk like that in this residential neighborhood where there couldn't possibly be any traffic!" Olivia said.

"Mom, I'll check it out and take care of it," Alex promised. He raced outside in bare feet down the sun-warmed driveway to the street, avoiding the largest of the pebbles, where Patrick and his Dad sat in their family's car; Patrick was in the driver's seat.

"Sorry! Kid shouldn't be honking like that, but he is so excited," Patrick's Dad apologized.

"So you did it? Got your license?" Alex asked.

"Yep! Here's my temporary license. Picture's not too bad." Patrick proudly handed over the little square of paper.

"What! You look like a goofball."

"I do not!"

"Just kidding. It's great."

"Well, you did it first," Patrick conceded.

Alex shrugged. "Only cause my birthday's one month before yours."

"I hope now Mom will believe I'm ready to drive. She's afraid I'll kill myself." Patrick glanced at his Dad as he spoke.

Patrick's Dad leaned toward the window to join in the conversation. "Well, she worries about you. Try to understand- you're our only child."

\*

Alex and Patrick walked together toward school one late afternoon in the middle of May of their senior year. Daylight savings time and the tilt of the globe worked together to gift their world with long evening hours of soft yellow sunlight. They routinely took advantage of this phenomenon to play a little basketball after their homework was completed but before full dark had settled on the earth. The basketball goal over the driveway of Alex's house had long been abandoned in favor of the outdoor court at school. The court was surrounded by a tall chain link fence of thousands of galvanized aluminum diamonds that was routinely left unlocked.

"I finally took a chance and asked Helen to prom, but she said she'd already said yes to Hector. Why didn't I ask earlier! I am so stupid," Alex said.

"You're so fixated on Helen! Ask someone else. You have to go. Everyone's going," Patrick said.

"I don't want to go if I can't go with Helen."

Patrick grimaced. "What about Kelly? She's so nice."

"No. She is nice, but no," Alex insisted.

"Would you mind if I asked her? We're more like friends, but she's so much fun."

"Yeah, sure, you should," Alex replied.

"What about you?"

"I don't think I'll go, but- I'll think about it." Alex shrugged.

*

Alex heard the phone ring downstairs, but he stayed at his desk. He had no interest in talking to anyone. He heard his Mom say, "Hello? Oh, just a moment, dear." He groaned.

"Alex, pick up, would you. There's a young lady on the phone," Olivia said.

As Alex leaned out into the hall he could see Olivia with a conspiratorial smile on her face, her hand covering the receiver. Alex flew down the stairs, his heart pounding. Please let it be Helen. Please let her have changed her mind. He took a deep breath and hoped his voice sounded calm.

"H'lo," he said. Olivia hovered, making him self-conscious.

"Hi, Alex, it's Giuli. Sorry to bother you."

"No problem. What's up?"

"I was wondering if by *any* chance, you would want to go to prom with me. Like as friends, I mean, but I would really understand if, you know, if you had other plans, because, well, ummm, you, uh," Giuli said anxiously, sputtering into incomprehensible.

"Oh, well, I was thinking of skipping it," Alex began. Because Hector was taking Helen. But why should Hector Gonzalez keep him away from his senior prom? "But sure, why not? Let's go together. It will be fun."

"Oh, wow, oh, that's great! Thanks, Alex!" Giulietta answered, flustered and unbelieving.

Olivia continued to stand nearby and had captured the gist of the conversation. She was tapping the hollow below her left shoulder and whispering, "Ask about what color her dress is!"

"Oh, my Mom is here. She says to ask what color your dress is." Alex paused. That didn't sound right. "I would like to get you a nice corsage that matches your dress." That sounded better, he thought.

"Oh, Alex, I- I- haven't gotten a dress yet but I'll let you know. That's really nice of you to ask," Giuli answered, astounded at her good fortune.

"Okay, well, I'll see you at school. Thanks for calling," Alex said.

Olivia beamed with pride. Her son, named class valedictorian, and so handsome that girls were calling him for dates!

*

"Mom, I need my nails done for prom," Helen Fletcher announced.

"That's nice. Nail files and 75 different colors of nail polish can be found in the medicine cabinet," Helen's Mom answered. Leda Fletcher had been a great beauty in her day, but two pregnancies, each with twins, only one year apart, had taken their toll. Her once formidable bosom was now largely deflated, and her hair remained the same color as Helen's only through the ministrations of the gifted Leticia at the Swan Salon.

"I want to go to a salon. They do a better job. I want it done professionally."

"Professionally. You're kidding. After what I paid for that dress, you want to spend more for someone to paint your nails. No."

"This is for prom. It's once in a lifetime."

"Forget it. No."

"I can't do my right hand. I can't."

"Alright then, let Kelly do it."

"Kelly's not a professional."

"Well, Kelly got into Wellesley, so she should be smart enough to help you with your nails. Not to mention your brothers, who are doing very well on their football scholarships. I haven't heard your action plan yet, miss."

Helen's so-called action plan was tenuous at best, and incompletely thought out, but it involved Hector Gonzalez, eldest son of the wealthiest family that she knew. For almost two years he had flirted with her, and now finally, he had invited her to prom.

"Helen, I can do them for you," Kelly said.

Helen puffed her lower lip out in a sullen pout and waited. After a while it became clear that a better offer would not be forthcoming. "Okay, could you?"

"Sure. But a light color with your dress."

"No, I like red." A bright red polish would call attention to her pretty hands. She contemplated her slender fingers with admiration. "*Cosmo* says to be bold with nail color."

"No. You should use clear, or maybe light pink, if you're wearing that cream-colored dress. With red you'll look like a slut."

"Oh my god."

"It will ruin the look. I know," Kelly insisted.

"Okay, I guess." To be fair, Kelly was usually right.

*

Patrick and Kelly grinned at each other as they entered the school gymnasium, which had been transformed for prom by hundreds of crepe paper streamers crisscrossing the ceiling and descending along the walls, wafting softly in the mild evening air. Too-loud music blared from the sound system set up by their hired gun of a DJ, but the dancing hadn't yet started in earnest.

"Giuli, you look so pretty!" Kelly said. "I love your dress."

Giuli wore a simple long dress in a pale turquoise; the color complemented her bright hair. "Oh, Kelly, thank you!" Giuli gushed. "When I found out I was going to prom I went on a crash diet and dropped a whole dress size. And then my Mom let me go to the hairdresser and they smoothed out my hair so I actually don't look like a freak!"

"Giuli! Why do you say things like that?" Kelly scolded.

"Oh, well, anyway, look at this beautiful corsage Alex got me!" Giuli displayed a wrist corsage with white sweetheart roses and Baby's breath.

"Beautiful, absolutely," Kelly lifted her own wrist which had an identical corsage, except that the roses were pink. "I know Alex and Patrick do everything together, and I guess that includes buying corsages." The two girls burst out laughing.

And then Helen arrived, arm in arm with Hector. Alex tried not to look at her because he knew Hector would notice, but he could not help himself. Helen wore an elegant, one-shouldered, ivory gown of some liquid fabric that clung enticingly to her slender body. Her hair was held back from her lovely face with a simple white ribbon, and her blonde hair spilled like molten gold across her bare shoulder and down her back. She was heartrendingly beautiful.

"Helen," Alex whispered. "Helen of gold and ivory, chryselephantine Helen." And then he remembered Giuli next to him and hoped she had not heard. He forced himself to look away. "Giuli, I want to tell you, this is sort of corny, but really, thank you for asking me to prom. I wasn't planning to go, and when you called, I changed my mind. We've been friends for a long time, and this is going to be a good night," Alex said, relaying the speech he had planned over the last week.

Hector slipped to his side and whispered softly close to his ear, "So, Mr. Valdadictorian, if you're so smart, why are you here with the funniest looking girl in the class?"

Alex turned, and started an angry retort, but there was Helen, the image of an immortal goddess, and on the other side, plump little Giuli with her trusting smile. Alex swallowed his anger.

"Enjoy the dance, Hector," he said calmly. He took Giuli's arm and walked away, without looking back.

*

The second Sunday in June dawned clear and bright in eastern Massachusetts. Dr. Samuel Winchell, principal of Brookline High School, stood at the podium and addressed the crowd. "It gives me great pleasure now to introduce our valedictorian, Alexander Eastgard. Alex is one of the bright lights here at our school. He is likely the fastest runner our school has ever had. During the last four years, he has led the track team to victory after victory. Many of his teachers tell me he is also a gifted scholar, not only consistently making good grades but also demonstrating an insight into difficult concepts that is remarkable for someone of his young age. Many of the students tell me he is a loyal friend, kind to all, ready to help anyone in need, especially if that need was with homework for pre-calculus or world history."

The audience laughed politely.

"He forgot to add, the most handsome student in the class," Olivia whispered to Philip, and sat up a little straighter.

Dr. Winchell continued, "And our own Alex has been awarded a full scholarship to prestigious Amherst College, based on a combination of academic merit and commitment to their track team. He intends to study history and political science, at which I am certain he will excel. I will not be surprised if in a few years we hear of him playing a role on the national stage. Without further ado, I give you, Alexander Eastgard!"

Alex stepped to the podium. His mother's assessment of her son's appearance was biased but also accurate. His mortarboard balanced with dignity over his smooth high forehead while sandy hair escaped from its sides and back. His hazel eyes shone, but his smile was poignant. He was aware that Helen was sitting behind him and slightly to his right. He would gladly give away his scholarship and all the praise Mr. Winchell had heaped on him, if he could turn to Helen for a kiss. He had been uncertain what to say but decided on keeping it short and incorporating the required words and phrases, including hope, future, challenges, lifelong friendships, striving for excellence, guidance and gratitude. And he concluded his address, "We bid you *vale*, farewell!"

The diplomas were given, Dr. Winchell delivered his closing remarks and the crowd exited the auditorium. Small and large clusters of graduates lingered outside the auditorium, reluctant to disperse and end this last time they would all be together as students at Brookline High. Giuli, her hair full and foamy again, hugged Kelly. Alex smiled and opened his arms and she hugged him too, shyly, and then turned to hug Patrick. As she touched Patrick's shoulders, her smile collapsed.

"Giuli, don't look so stricken," Kelly said. "We'll all see each other over the summer, and then we'll all be back for Christmas and we can get together and trade stories."

Tears were running down Giuli's flushed cheeks. "I don't know. Maybe not. What if this is the last time we're all together?" She glanced back at Patrick.

"Giuli, stop crying," Kelly said. She turned and spoke to the group. "I know! Let's have an end of summer party, sometime in August, before everyone takes off."

"I like it! I'll help," offered Patrick, loosening his tie. His new navy-blue suit was slightly oversized, but his mother had insisted on buying large, convinced he was in the midst of a growth spurt.

"Me too. Okay, I got to go. Parents are getting restless," Alex said. "But Patrick, later this week, let's shoot some hoops. School court, okay?"

"Yeah, sure." Patrick maneuvered himself next to Kelly. "Hey, you want to see a movie later?"

Hector and his family lingered at the other side of the parking lot, exchanging various meaningless pleasantries and fulsome congratulations with families of other graduates.

"Mamá, could I invite my friend Helen to dinner with us? She's from a good family," Hector said on impulse.

"*Claro que sí, mi hijo*. This is your day," Anita answered in an indulgent tone.

What a stroke of genius, Hector told himself. With Helen there, his father would assume the role of the Spanish gentleman, the proud and gracious father, and wouldn't give him any shit.

# CHAPTER 6

The sky was a cornflower blue, flawless, pure and innocent, stretching seamlessly from horizon to horizon. Helen Fletcher lay immobile on the bright teal and white-striped cushions of a lounge chair on the wooden deck overlooking her family's backyard. The current issue of *Cosmopolitan* lay neglected on the deck beneath her.

*Why doesn't he call,* she wondered wretchedly. *It's been three days. He should have called. If he really liked me like he said, he should have called. Even his parents liked me; I'm sure of it. He had even said, I think my Dad likes you better than he likes me. He told me about how his father refused to pay for him to go to college, and was making him get a job instead, about how upset he was about that. He trusted me with that. Could he be too busy looking for a job to call? No, that couldn't take all day. He definitely should have called.* She sighed, remembered his kisses, the harsh, sooty taste of tobacco. She was surprised that she had enjoyed the flavor of his mouth so much. It felt decadent. And his hands touching her-

*Stop thinking about it,* she told herself. *Kelly will come out here and see it on my face. Kelly will know. Stop thinking about that night, about his hands and his mouth and, and about how he hasn't called.* She laid a yellow straw sunhat, decorated with an artificial daisy, over her face to hide the tears.

*

Giuli Stewart loved her summer job at Ye Olde Corner Bookstore in Downtown Crossing, in the heart of colonial Boston. She rode the Green line each day to Park Street station and then walked a couple of blocks and there she was, at work. It was a world apart from Brookline here. There were throngs of people, Bostonians shopping, tourists drinking in their heritage, panhandlers up against store fronts hoping for some change. And she loved the bookstore with its timbered ceiling, the towering shelves crammed with books, the antique and modern maps, the posters of scenic Boston. Everyone was so nice. The tourists would ask her questions and she would answer authoritatively on topics such as how to find the beginning of the Freedom Trail, where one could find a restaurant with authentic Boston food, who had the best chowder, and was it true what they had heard about parking places in downtown Boston selling for more than a single-family home in Topeka.

"Hey, Andy," Giuli chirped to Andrea Simpson, also on duty as a cashier that day at the bookstore. Giuli hurried to the back room to stow her handbag, and then joined Andy behind the counter. Andy had milk-white skin and jet-black hair. Metal pins and buckles decorated her otherwise all-black clothing. A silver nose ring that left a little tarnish on her pale skin completed the ensemble. Andy's forbidding appearance resulted in more customers approaching Giuli with questions, but Giuli didn't mind. She knew that beneath that exterior of black leather and exposed zippers, Andy had a heart of gold. Andy also completely lacked any filter between her brain and her mouth, so one always knew just what she was thinking.

"Hey." Andy was surreptitiously touching up her black nail polish. The manager wouldn't like it, but he was upstairs and if she was quick, he'd never know.

The other thing Giuli liked about this job was the paycheck. This was her first real job, and there were things she wanted to buy. She was going to college in the fall. Her Mom was paying for tuition and room and board, but had told Giuli that anything more was her own responsibility. Giuli wanted some cute clothes, maybe from Filene's across the street. Also, she had decided to get her hair professionally straightened. It wouldn't be cheap, and her mother might kill her (she could already hear the theatrical wailing about her beautiful russet curls and the toxic chemicals that had destroyed them) but it would be worth it.

Not only was she going to college but she was going to U Mass Amherst. True, it was widely known as Zoo Mass Slamherst, but the price was within her mother's budget, and it was in the same town as Amherst College, the private college that Alex Eastgard would be attending. Maybe they would bump into one another; maybe he would see her differently without that stupid Helen distracting him. There was something so special, so different about Alex. He was so good-looking, but it was more than that. She sensed in him such an adventurous spirit, such courage. When he touched her hand at prom, she had felt it. It radiated from him, all his specialness. She wondered what his life would be, what he would accomplish. He will be amazing, she told herself.

"Quiet today, huh?" Giuli finally said, to break the silence that had settled in as Andy painted her nails and she dreamed of Alex Eastgard.

"Yeah. Tourists should be finishing their breakfasts about now; they'll be here soon. Get ready."

Giuli gripped the edge of the counter and took a deep breath.

Andy glanced at her. "You okay?"

"Uh, I feel weird."

"Go sit down in back."

"Okay." Giuli walked slowly toward the back room, pressing her hands against the bookshelves lining her path to her right and her left to steady herself. She sat down on a cardboard box loaded with books and leaned over, her head between her knees.

After a while, Andy poked her head into the back room. "Hey, you okay? You've been back here a long time."

"I- I felt dizzy."

"Are you still dizzy? Otherwise okay?"

"I guess. I'm okay now. Just, it just started with this little dot of red that kept getting bigger and bigger until everything was red. I closed my eyes for a long time and now it's gone."

"God. Are you having your period?"

"No."

"Maybe it's a migraine."

"I don't have a headache."

"Or MS. Or a brain tumor."

Giuli considered these possibilities carefully. "I don't think so. I think something bad is going to happen." She started to cry.

*

Patrick passed the basketball to Alex and then turned to pull the gate to the school court closed. Alex jogged across the court, dribbling into position in front of the goal, tall, lean, lithe and clean-limbed, in a Brookline High School T shirt and shorts. Patrick was a little shorter, but had a similar slim but muscular build.

"You look happy today," Alex said. There was no denying the ridiculous grin on Patrick's face.

"Ah- well, last night I called Kelly and asked her to go out with me this weekend. She said yes."

"Oh? Good."

"Did I tell you I took her out the night after graduation?"

"No. What did you do?"

"Movies. She kept throwing popcorn at me." Patrick sighed, blissful at the memory. "Then we got pizza."

"Yeah?"

"She's so nice. And that dynamite smile!"

"Sounds good."

"I kissed her good night," Patrick said, his voice wistful.

"Yeah?"

"She kissed me back! Can't wait for Friday. I know it's stupid but I kind of wish we weren't all going away to college. I think I'll really miss her."

"And you complain if I mention Helen! Come on, let's play some." Alex grasped the ball expertly with splayed fingers, focused, and took his shot. "Nothing but net! Beat that."

Patrick was off in his daydream. He took the ball and threw it high into the air. "How high can you throw it?"

"Kelly has turned you into a goofball." Alex also threw the ball straight up and chased it across the court as it plummeted back to earth. "Come on, make a basket now."

Patrick tossed the ball very high again, this time toward the goal.

"Look, goofball, ball's landing outside. Go get it," Alex said, and then watched him head to the gate, always so agreeable. *I'll miss Patrick when we take off for college. We've been together almost every day for the past seven years.* But Alex was also thinking how much he would enjoy the challenge of college-level work at Amherst, and the experience of learning to live alone, without his mother on top of him all the time. Sure, he would come home sometimes on the weekend. Patrick would too. UVM Burlington was only a 3-hour drive away. When Patrick would go to see Kelly, perhaps he would go along, get to spend a little time with Helen. And Helen would have to realize what a bad bet Hector was. Alex had heard he wasn't even going to college. And he looked like a big, ugly gorilla. Or a great ape, like from *Tarzan*. That brought a smile to Alex's lips.

*

Hector Gonzalez stood on the sidewalk, slowly stripped the cellophane off his newly purchased Camels, shoved a cigarette between his lips and lit it, while contemplating his reflection in the shiny plate glass store window with satisfaction. He was 6' 2", taller than his father. He had broad shoulders and a narrow waist, and had become muscular without too much effort. His biceps bulged against the bottom edges of the sleeves of his black T-shirt. *I should always wear black*, he thought. *It makes me look dangerous. And I'm bigger than my shitty old man. Let him try to beat me now.*

He inhaled eagerly, enjoying that brief rush as the nicotine hit home. That was good. And it felt good to have had her, to have had Helen the night after graduation. So sweet. He took a deep drag on his cigarette, remembering, replaying the evening in his mind. It made him feel like a man. She was always so quiet and dignified. But not then. Not alone with him. Just thinking about it made him ache for her. This was something the old man couldn't take from him. He should call her.

His walk took him past his old high school. *I'll never have to walk inside that stinking crap hole again*, he thought. *Oh, look, there are those two goody-goody assholes on the court. Who'd want to spend any more time anywhere near that place? Those two idiots! And look. The little idiot just threw the ball outside the court.*

The ball bounced and rolled, right to Hector, as if answering a fateful summons. Hector took a quick last drag on his Camel, dropped it and grabbed the ball. *Here comes the little asshole.*

Patrick ran over to Hector, now dribbling the ball slowly on the sidewalk.

"Can I have the ball?" Patrick said. He tried to stay calm, but he hated being around Hector, ever since his first day of school in this town.

"You want the ball?"

"Yeah, give me the ball."

"You threw it away. It's mine now." Hector continued dribbling, deftly turning to block the ball from Patrick.

"Come on, give me the ball."

"You're an asshole, you know?"

"Just give me the ball!" Patrick grabbed for it, and almost had it, but Hector took the ball with both hands and held it high above his head.

"Say 'I'm a fucking asshole' and I'll think about it." Hector's long arms swayed well above Patrick's reach. Patrick leapt and almost touched the ball, but Hector stepped back, laughing.

"Give me the ball!" Patrick said again, angry and frustrated.

"Say 'I'm a fucking asshole' first." Hector bounced up and down, mimicking Patrick's attempts to jump high enough to recover the ball.

"Give him the ball, Hector!" Alex yelled from inside the court. "Do it now!"

"Oh, two against one! Not very nice!" Hector said sarcastically. He feinted to the left, then to the right, each time drawing Patrick to one side or the other, like a puppet on strings. "Now what are you going to say?"

"Give him the ball, Hector!" Alex yelled again. He ran to the side of the court closest to them, glaring through the chain link fence at Hector. Hector towered over Patrick, a malevolent giant in black. Patrick looked small and vulnerable by comparison. A painful image from prom flashed into his mind, Hector with his arm around Helen's waist, pulling her slender pale figure against his towering dark form. This was bad luck. After today, with luck, they'd never see Hector again and this stupid feud would be over. "Give him the ball!"

"Give me the ball!" Patrick screamed.

"Yelling is not very nice. You should ask nicely." Hector said in a cloying falsetto, and then laughed hysterically. He had had no idea how much fun his walk for cigarettes would turn out to be.

A car whipped around the corner, a white bullet too fast for this small side street. All at once Alex took in the speeding car, the young woman driving it, the two children in the back seat, their shrieking audible through the closed windows, the woman turning toward the back seat to yell at them.

At that moment, with a malicious glint in his eye, Hector casually dropped the ball into the street.

Patrick dove for it.

"No! No!" Alex screamed, tearing at the unyielding fence before him. He watched with horror as the car collided with Patrick, throwing him in a high, terrible arc down the street. He landed with a sickening thud on the asphalt as the car skidded to a halt. Alex ran to the gate in the corner of the court and raced to his side. Patrick lay face up, eyes wide open, serene.

"Patrick? Patrick? Are you- are you- Can you hear me?" Alex knelt and squeezed his hand, but his fingers were limp and his eyes gazed back sightlessly. "Patrick? Please, can you hear me?" Alex brushed the sandy hair from his friend's forehead. He started to shake. Blood oozed from the back of Patrick's head, from his crushed skull, an expansile red circle encompassing Alex and Patrick, isolating them from the rest of the world.

Behind him he could hear the young woman, now out of her car, moaning. He was vaguely aware of police arriving, neighbors gathering, an ambulance with red lights flashing, the woman saying, "There was no one there. I turned the corner and no one was in the street. I turned around for a split-second cause my kids were fighting, but just a split-second. Then he ran into the street. He must have. I never saw him. I couldn't have stopped. Oh my god! Oh my god!"

Alex knelt silently now next to Patrick, hope all gone. People were crowding around and perhaps speaking to him, but he could not understand or answer. He studied his friend's eyes. A single reflected cloud interrupted the liquid black of his pupils. Fingers trembling, he reached forward and closed Patrick's eyes, one by one.

*

The parish priest, clad in cassock, collar and sorrow, stood attendance by the coffin at Patrick's wake. "He was too good for this world," he murmured. "Our Lord must have had some purpose for this tragedy."

"Purpose!" Olivia muttered scornfully and took a step toward the man of God. "What a stupid thing to say."

"Come on, Liv," Philip whispered and pulled her away. This was not the time for Olivia to open a theological discussion with this unsuspecting priest.

Patrick's mother sat in one of the chairs arranged in a row along the side of the reception room at the funeral home. She sat trembling on the worn velveteen upholstery, mopping her tears up with Kleenex from a flimsy cardboard box balanced on her lap, her feet bulging plumply against the uppers of her old black leather pumps. Alex sat to her right, and Kelly next to him. Patrick's Dad sat on his wife's left, clasping her hand tightly, blinking rapidly, stunned, unbelieving.

Alex sat hunched, his head to his chest. He turned his gaze to Kelly. Her head was also bowed and her curls hid her eyes. Tears coursed down her cheeks and her lips were pressed tight together. The last thing Patrick had told him was how he had kissed Kelly good night. He could imagine his gentle friend kissing Kelly's mouth and it brought a fresh wave of grief. Kelly buried her fingers in her curls and her face disappeared into her hands and her hair.

Patrick's mother cleared her throat and spoke softly. "Alex? Alex, I want you to have Patrick's wallet. There are photos of you and P-Patrick and class photos of a lot of kids." She pressed the wallet into his hands. "I – I don't even know who some of them are." She began to sob hysterically.

"I should have protected him. I'm sorry. I'm so sorry," Alex whispered hoarsely. "I could have stopped it. I could."

"No, sweetheart, you're the best friend any boy could have had."

*She's wrong*, he thought. *It didn't have to happen. I sent him out there. If I had gone instead, or if I had gone out as soon as I saw Hector he'd still be alive.*

*

Several days later Helen lay in bed, still in pajamas although it was almost noon. Day and night, ever since that terrible accident, Kelly had been screaming that Hector Gonzalez was a murderer. But she must have gone out, as it was quiet in the house, and for that Helen was grateful. Helen was just thinking about having some breakfast when the phone rang. She rolled over in her bed and picked up the phone on her bedside table. "Hello?"

"Helen?"

"Yes?"

"It's Hector."

"Oh!"

"Helen, I need to talk to you, just for a few minutes. Can you meet me at the park around the corner from your house? In a half an hour?"

"Well, I should change and get cleaned up, and,"

"No, don't. Don't dress up. Just come."

*

Hector Gonzalez lounged on a bench in the little park. He extracted a cigarette from a fresh pack and lit it. His nerves were bad, but that helped. He heard soft footsteps; before he looked up he knew they were hers. He stood up.

"Helen, thanks for coming."

"It's okay," she said, taking in his haggard face, the khaki duffel bag at his side. "Are you leaving?"

"Yeah. I'm out of here. But I wanted to tell you goodbye in person."

"Where are you going?"

"New York. I know I can make something of myself in a real city. I hate this place."

"Oh."

"But I want to be clear. The cops don't blame me. They blame that stupid bitch for reckless driving. But people are looking at me like I did something. I've got to leave." He failed to mention that he no longer had a place to stay. The old man had kicked him out of the house. His words still rang in Hector's ears. *It's never your fault. That's what you always say. And now someone's dead. Get out of this house and don't come back.*

"I'm glad you're not in trouble with the police." Helen said. It did make more sense to blame the driver of that car.

He nodded. "But here's what I want to say. The second to best night of my life was the night of prom. It was the first time I kissed you. But the best night of my life was after graduation. I'm glad we did it, Helen. It was great, just great. Other than that, my life sucks."

Helen waited a long time before speaking. "Are you coming back? Ever?"

"I don't know. No. But when I get settled, I'll let you know where I am. Maybe you'll come see me." He stood. "I have to get a bus from South Station."

Helen stood also. She touched his arm shyly. He dropped his duffel and took her face firmly in his hands and kissed her, a deep, hungry, possessive, lingering kiss that brought tears to her eyes.

"Bye now. Don't cry, okay?" He hoisted the duffel and sauntered off.

*

Philip entered Alex's room quietly and closed the door behind him. The room was stuffy and dark, and Alex lay on the bed as he had for a week, hardly moving, eating and drinking almost nothing. Philip crossed to the window, raised the blinds and opened the window, to admit fresh air and a little sunshine. He sat in Alex's desk chair for a while, watching his son. Alex remained motionless.

"Alex, I don't want you to forget Patrick. But I want you to get up. None of us knows how much time we have, and it's no good for you to be lying here in the dark like you're already dead."

No response.

"I want you to get up and come down and have some breakfast. Then we can go fishing. If you want." He paused. "Please get up, Alex. I miss you." Philip stood, walked to the door, and exited quietly. He returned to the kitchen and started to look through the newspaper.

A little while later Philip heard a creak from the top of the stairs. He held his breath, hopefully. Soft footsteps continued, coming down, coming closer. He turned slowly, and there was his son, bedraggled, noticeably thinner, but he had come. He looked somehow younger, more childlike, but also older, forced to eat from the tree of knowledge and having found the fruit most bitter. Philip stood and hugged him, and the two cried in one another's arms.

# CHAPTER 7

Alex Eastgard picked up the phone in his dorm room and dialed his home in Brookline. His Dad answered.

"Hey, Dad, just wanted to let you know about the meet with Dartmouth. Yeah. We won. Yeah. I took first in the 100-yard dash! Uh-huh. Thanks. Just wanted to let you know. Yeah, that's all. Okay, bye." Alex hung up. His hand rested on the receiver for a while as he reflected that what he had not said, but that he was sure his father had heard all the same, was that despite what had happened last June, he was functioning, living his life, able to find little bits of happiness here and there. He knew that it would comfort his Dad.

Scott Buckminster, aka Buck, Alex's roommate, listened and grimaced as he lay sprawled on his bed, reading the textbook balanced on his ribcage. *Is this guy for real*, he wondered. *He's always calling home. And just to talk.* Buck hardly ever called home. And when he did, typically it was to urgently request money to avoid bouncing a check. Buck hated talking to his parents, but this guy didn't seem to mind at all. Bizarre. He shook his head and went back to studying.

\*

Elizabeth's gaze edged up past the top of her textbook and glided down her long, denim-clad legs, past her slender white feet with their pink-lacquered toenails, to rest on the unprepossessing profile of Scott Buckminster as he sat at his desk. He did not notice; he was lost in the study of organic chemistry. For Scott Buckminster, like five generations of Buckminsters before him, was destined for the practice of medicine. Even one poor grade might bar his entry into medical school, and so he took every class, every test, every assignment very seriously.

Elizabeth lowered her eyes a little and continued her study of Buck through feathered lashes. He had gentle eyes, she thought, or were they only meek? His nose was quite attractive, nice and straight. What were the odds that that lovely nose was the gift of a skilled plastic surgeon, and not inherited? His lips were a bit fuller than she would have liked, and his chin was decidedly weak. She sighed and adjusted the pillows between her lower back and the headboard of Buck's dorm room bed. It had been a mistake to let him stay over last night. It was not awful, she conceded silently, not embarrassing, but definitely not great. She knew Buck would like to stay over again, and she just wasn't interested. Thus, her dilemma: how could she gracefully dissuade Buck from following her home tonight? Some opportunity would present itself, surely, she thought, and went back to *Introduction to the Medieval World*.

'The year 1215 was remarkable for two major events, the signing of the Magna Carta and the convocation of the Fourth Lateran Council,' she read. What was this Lateran Council that she had never heard of?

"Liz, do you remember what color the Grignard reagent turns?" Buck asked, flipping through his text.

"No. Check the index." She resumed reading. This was actually pretty interesting, she thought. Her head was down when the door opened; she finished the sentence she was reading before looking up.

Standing there was Phoebus Apollo, tall and handsome, perfectly proportioned, in sweat pants and an Amherst T shirt! The harsh fluorescent light from the hall transformed to gold and cast a shining nimbus around him as he stood in the doorway. She had noticed him before, in her Medieval History class, but had never managed to catch his name or say hello. Not knowing his name, and considering his looks, she had secretly dubbed him Apollo.

"Hi," he said to both of them, swinging his backpack down on his bed. A baritone, she thought with approval.

"Hey, Alex. This is Liz," Buck said, gesturing casually at Elizabeth.

She carefully composed her patrician features and extended her hand. "Elizabeth Hawkins," she said, reintroducing herself.

"I'm Alex Eastgard," he said, shaking her hand quickly but firmly. "Nice to meet you."

She studied his smile. It was a surface smile, she told herself, betraying nothing. Not a smile that said, I'd like to see you again, I'd like to know you better, or a tight, polite smile that said, don't waste my time; I'm in a hurry. A surface smile, noncommittal, but she sensed that a complex personality sheltered beneath it.

"I feel like I've seen you somewhere. Do you have Medieval History with Cunningham?" Elizabeth queried, trying to sound nonchalant. She was tempted to ask him where he'd left his lyre but didn't want him to think she was crazy.

"Every Monday, Wednesday and Friday at 10am."

"That's the one!"

Buck shifted in his seat. "Uh, could you guys keep it down?"

"Yeah, sorry, man." Alex grinned at Elizabeth, who smiled back.

*That is a conspiratorial smile. We are now allies*, she thought with satisfaction.

"Buck, listen, you've been at that for hours. Let's get some food." Without waiting for his reply Elizabeth stood and started filling her backpack. If he stayed here, she would have attained her goal of freeing herself of him for the evening. If he went with her, that was alright too. Perhaps he would pay for dinner. "Alex, come with us? It'll just be a quick dinner." She held her breath.

"Ah… sure. That'd be great," Alex replied.

"Okay, fine." Buck stood, stretching to the left and then to the right, while massaging his lower back. "I'm so stiff!"

"You should work out or do a run or at least take a good walk, every day if you can. That'd help," Alex offered.

"I don't have the time. I got a ton of homework, every day." Buck found Alex very irritating. He was always so calm, seemed so on top of everything. They had been roommates last year, their freshman year, and Buck had agreed to maintain that relationship in their sophomore year, because last year Alex went home most weekends, and Buck had had the room to himself. This year however, Alex had been spending most weekends on campus. But then Buck had met Liz, who had a nice little condo just off-campus. If he could hang out there, it wouldn't matter if Alex never went home.

"Try it. You concentrate so much better after a run," Alex urged, his tone sincere. Elizabeth was charmed. Buck was annoyed.

"Come on, Buck. We could all die of old age waiting on you," Elizabeth said, backpack on her left shoulder, ready to move.

They made their way to Manny's Brew House on University Drive.

"Can we eat outside? This may be one of the last days we can," Elizabeth said, spying a four-person table just off the sidewalk.

"Sure, sounds good," Alex said.

"Buck, you okay with that?" Elizabeth prompted him.

"Yeah, okay, but I would've brought a sweatshirt if I knew."

"Here, take mine. I'm not cold." Alex whipped off his hooded sweatshirt and tossed it to Buck, whereupon Buck decided that he hated him.

A waitress approached. "You're going to eat out here?"

"Apparently so," Buck replied, an ironic edge creeping into his voice.

She handed out large menus coated in heavy plastic. "I'm Lucy. I'll check back in a bit."

They studied their menus, laid them down, looked around and Lucy returned.

"Okay. Know what you want? Miss?"

Elizabeth coiled a tendril of chestnut hair around her index finger thoughtfully. "Yes. The burger, medium, no onion and a glass of house white wine."

"Okay." Lucy scribbled intently on her little white pad. "Sir?"

"Burger and fries, and a coke," Alex said.

"How do you want the burger?" Lucy asked.

"Oh, medium I guess. Doesn't matter."

"Sir?" she asked, turning to Buck, who was irritated to be here instead of studying, irritated that Alex was here, and irritated that he had accepted Alex's sweatshirt, even though it was getting cool and he was also glad to have it.

"The BLT. And a beer. Coors if you have it."

"We do. Be back shortly." Lucy hurried to turn in their order.

She returned a few minutes later with their drinks, set them down and departed.

"Alex, you don't want a beer or something?" Elizabeth asked.

"No, I've got some homework still. Booze slows me down." He popped his straw into his coke and drank.

Buck looked at his pale beer with its delicate head with regret. Maybe I shouldn't have gotten this. I have another 40, 50 pages to read tonight, he thought. Damn Alex.

Oblivious to Buck's discomfiture, Alex was looking past Elizabeth and down the sidewalk. She followed his gaze. The sidewalk was full of people, and she was unsure what he saw.

Alex scraped back his chair and stood. "Giuli? Giuli!" A redhead turned and looked their way.

"Alex!" she said, hurrying toward them, beaming, eyes bright, toting two textbooks.

"Come, sit with us. There's an extra chair. We just ordered. Do you want something?" Alex felt there was something different about her. Oh, yes, her hair: it was more vertical.

The efficient Lucy was instantly back at their table, proffering a menu.

"I'll have the Caesar salad and some water, thanks," Giuli said, after a quick look, and handed back the menu.

Alex introduced Elizabeth and Buck and told them, "Giuli and I are old friends. We were in grade school, then high school together."

"You mean, public school?" Elizabeth asked. She found the idea disturbing.

"Yes, public. Our high school had over 1,000 kids. And Alex was the smartest kid in the whole school," Giuli assured them, and the nicest and the cutest too, she thought to herself.

"It's been more than a year since we've both been here, and this is the first time we've seen each other," Alex said.

"I know, I know. Town's not that big either. I guess I'm somewhere studying most of the time," Giuli said, a little breathless, radiating happiness.

"Me too. Studying or running. That's about it." Alex reached for his coke. "School okay?"

"Yeah, I love it here. And I love coming and going when I want, no Mom checking up on me."

"I could see where your Mom could be a little intense," Alex said. "She taught Shakespeare at our high school, so we all knew her," he explained to Buck and Elizabeth.

Buck considered entertaining the group with a description of Alex's ridiculously frequent calls home, but Lucy arrived with their food.

"This is wonderful; I was starved!" Elizabeth said after sampling her burger.

"Me too," Alex said. "Great burger."

"This is so good! I never had a Caesar before college," Giuli said, wrapping a leaf of romaine onto her fork.

"Buck? Yours okay?" Elizabeth said. Who is the Giuli person Alex seems so fond of? Probably not real competition, if he had not sought her out since arriving at Amherst.

"Yeah, it's okay. Should've gotten something hot though."

A burst of wind whistled down the street, stirring leaves of gold and rust, apple-red and dusky brown, into colorful little tornadoes that promptly fragmented, scattering leaves in all directions.

"A *danse macabre* in sunset colors!" Elizabeth exclaimed. "Just beautiful!"

*Show off*, Buck thought.

Alex smiled, dunking a fry deep into his ketchup, and observed that the colors of the leaves were reflected in Giuli's bright red and Elizabeth's rich brown hair; if a blonde were also here, the colors of the autumn leaves would be well represented, right at their table. An image of golden-haired Helen flashed into his mind. But then Hector appeared at her side, contaminating the picture. Alex tried to wipe his mind clean and concentrated on his burger.

"Alex, aren't you cold?" Giuli asked. "You're just wearing a T-shirt."

Elizabeth noted that her tone was more solicitous than it needed to be and wondered about Giuli's feelings for Alex.

"No, I'm good." Actually it was a bit cold, now that the sun had set, but he couldn't ask Buck for his sweatshirt back. The image of Hector, smirking at him, popped back into his mind. *Go away!* Alex wanted to scream. A gust of wind washed over him, under and through the thin fabric of his T shirt and he shivered, craving some warmth. But then he remembered Patrick, as he often did, locked in the padded cell of his coffin forever, unable to feel or speak or see, and Alex was suddenly grateful for the cold, for the taste of his fries, for the brilliant colors of the falling leaves, for the chance meeting with Giuli. And even grateful for the friendship of poor old Buck, huddled inside Alex's gray sweatshirt looking like Old Man Winter suffering from depression. Alex choked back a laugh.

"I propose a toast to autumn!" Alex raised his coke in his right hand.

"To autumn!" Giuli echoed, eagerly.

"To autumn, if you like," Elizabeth said, tapping her wine glass to the coke glass.

"How about to mid-terms being over?" Buck asked.

"Sure, that too," Giuli said agreeably.

"Our next break isn't until Thanksgiving. I can't wait," Buck said, tone mournful.

"Well, looks like we are all about done. I have to be getting home." Elizabeth stood up, pushed her chair back into place and extracted her wallet from a zipper pouch on her backpack. "I think $20 should be about right."

"No, Elizabeth, no. Buck and I will get this," Alex assured her.

She loved the way he said her name. "Thanks."

"Let me walk you home, Liz," Buck offered. He really did not feel like hanging in the dorm room with Alex tonight, and he was annoyed that Alex had volunteered the two of them to pay.

"No, thanks, I'm so tired. I'm going straight to bed. To sleep, perchance to dream..." she said with a coy smile.

"It's no problem." Buck spoke with an undertone of desperation.

Giuli observed the scene with interest. Elizabeth seemed nice enough but she was obviously not into Buck. Giuli could relate to that!

"No, really. Not at all necessary. See you all later, I hope," Elizabeth said. She cast a last glance directly at Alex, then strode away quickly on her long lean legs, shaking out her hair behind her, and disappeared into the evening.

*

Tuesday had become Italian night in the Eastgurd household. Olivia had gone all out this evening. A red-and-white checked tablecloth covered the worn maple of their dining room table. Olivia had prepared spaghetti with red sauce and meatballs, a bowl of salad lightly tossed with olive oil and a splash of wine vinegar, and a half loaf of warm Italian bread, and had set it all on the table along with a bottle of Chianti in a straw basket. The aroma of tomato and garlic, basil and oregano filled the air.

Philip sat at the table vaguely contemplating the spaghetti and meatballs that Olivia had served him.

"Philip, why aren't you eating? I thought you loved my meatballs," Olivia said, concern in her voice.

"I'm worried about the CAT scan results. You know that."

"Philip, we both heard the same thing. There's a tiny little dot in your liver which might be nothing. Could just be large blood vessels."

"It wasn't there before. If it had been there all along, that's one thing, but this is new."

"Now the doctor said it might not have been there before because it's so small, and by chance may just have been missed. It's probably nothing."

Philip toyed silently with his spaghetti. He wanted to be persuaded not to worry, but it was hard.

"Listen, we'll go back in three months like they said, and see if there's any change. Maybe it will be gone. In the meantime, there's nothing you can do about it, so there's no use agonizing. You will make yourself sick."

"You're right, Liv. You're right." He slowly rolled one strand of spaghetti around his fork and put it into his mouth, willing himself to chew and swallow it.

They ate in silence for some minutes and then Olivia spoke.

"Philip, I think, well, when Alex comes home for Thanksgiving, please, don't say anything to him. About the scan. As I say, it's probably nothing and he's been through so much already. Why get him worried?"

Philip nodded. "I understand. You're right," he said after a long pause. He continued trying to eat, all the while contemplating just how terribly lonely he felt.

# CHAPTER 8

"Boys! This is not a scrimmage!" Leda Fletcher stood in the doorway between the kitchen and living room, hands on hips, watching in horror as her two enormous sons wrestled on the living room floor in front of the TV. Charlie slammed into the mantle around the fireplace with a resounding thump. Fortunately, there was no fire but the impact shook the vase on the mantle; Leda reached out and steadied it, just in time to keep it from crashing down on Charlie's head.

"We are the terrible twins!" Paul roared.

"No one gets past us!" this from Charlie.

"Tim, please, can you get them to settle down?" Leda directed this at her husband.

"Leda, they're just being boys. They're fine." The vase that had almost broken was from his mother-in-law. He would not have minded losing it.

"No one gets past us! That pansy-ass quarterback has it made when we're in front of him." Paul pounded his chest. Both boys dropped to their knees, facing one another and collided in a head butt.

"Tim?" Leda implored.

Tim Fletcher, also a big man, but one whose center of gravity had descended from above to below his waist in recent years, launched himself in a flying tackle into the melee. The house shook.

Leda, desperate for support, looked around. Helen was in the recliner in the corner, flipping through *Cosmopolitan*, unperturbed. Kelly sat at the dining room table, scribbling furiously in a notebook, so caught up in her work that she had completely tuned out the commotion. Helen was too passive to be of use but maybe Kelly could help.

"Kelly, could you, uh, make them stop fighting?"

"Mom, I've got to finish this to apply for that job at the Globe." Kelly looked up for a moment and studied the writhing forms on the floor. "And, no, even if I tried I could not get them to stop." She went back to scribbling.

"Well, but," Leda struggled to express her distress.

"Don't worry," Kelly added without looking up. "Half-time will be over soon and they'll be back on the couch eating chips."

Leda stood by anxiously to test this hypothesis. Sure enough, just as the announcer barked out, "Beginning of the second half, and the Lions will be receiving," the three men of her family hauled themselves off the floor and onto the couch.

"Leda, babe, can we have some more chips?" Tim asked, eyes riveted on the TV screen.

"Sure, Tim." She considered the members of her family. Her boys and her husband were so alike. The boys showed up at practice and at their games and did what the coach said and had a great time. And all the rest of the time they generally goofed off, not a care in the world. Tim was the same. He went to work, did a good job without doing extra, came home and enjoyed himself, watched TV with enthusiasm, ate his dinner with gusto and even took her out on Saturday nights, still proud and happy to have her at his side, after all these years. Kelly was in a class by herself, preparing to set the world on fire, never resting, always serious. Maybe she'll end up as a lawyer, or a politician. Secretary of State. Something big. She had changed though, Leda thought. She changed when that boy got killed summer before last. The boy's friend had shown up at their house right after it happened, all bloody, asking to see Kelly. It had been awful. She stopped smiling after that. Nowadays it had to be a very special occasion to get Kelly to smile.

And then there was Helen, her greatest source of concern. Helen would sit in that chair reading some magazine until the cows came home if she could get away with it. *I'm glad I made her get a job*, Leda thought. *At least she leaves the house on a regular basis.*

Leda kept a careful eye on the game clock. When it hit the two-minute warning, she started to bring out the food. By the time the game ended the Thanksgiving table was laden with roast turkey, onion and sage stuffing, jellied cranberry sauce, a mountain range of mashed potatoes around a valley of melted butter, gravy, carrots with parsley, cauliflower with cheese sauce and crusty rolls, warm from the oven.

"Food!" Charlie roared and bolted off the couch.

"Me first!" Paul howled, pushing past Charlie, pulling his chair out from the table with an ear-shattering screech.

"Kelly, you want to put away your work and eat?" Leda said, consciously avoiding a nagging tone. "Helen, put down the magazine. Come sit down."

"Okay," Kelly answered, but her tone was grudging. Helen sighed, laid down *Cosmo* and walked slowly to the table.

Tim and the boys began energetically loading their plates.

"Tim? Tim!" Leda began.

Tim looked up, as if awoken from a trance, serving spoon with potatoes suspended in mid-air over his plate. "Yeah, babe?"

"Don't you think we should say grace? We have a lot to be thankful for."

"Yes, okay. Yes." He laid the serving spoon down on his plate and folded his hands. "Paul, put down your fork. We're saying grace. Okay. Dear Lord, we thank you for this feast, and we thank you that we can all be together today. And also for the boys' great work on the offensive line and for Kelly being a superstar at Wellesley. Oh, and also we are thankful that Helen has a job."

"Good bread, good meat. Good God, let's eat!" Charlie added.

"Hey, you can't have both drumsticks!" Paul yelled.

"Charlie, give Paul one of the drumsticks." Leda sighed.

"Helen, do you like your job?" Charlie asked between large forkfuls of turkey.

"Not really. It's boring." Helen was a receptionist at a dentist's office. She daintily served herself plain turkey, carrots and bits of cauliflower.

"But you're making some money, right?" Charlie said.

"Yeah, some," Helen admitted. Barely minimum wage, she thought. She scraped as much of the cheese as she could off the cauliflower before eating it.

"Saving any?" Paul asked.

"Yeah, some." Not much, though, she thought. She spent most of her modest earnings on new clothes and manicures. She gazed at her left hand, lying gracefully on Leda's special holiday lace tablecloth and admired the color of her nails- springtime rose.

"What are you saving for?" Charlie asked.

"I don't know. Maybe a car."

"You take the T now?" Paul asked.

"Yeah, it's awful. So crowded and so slow. People are smelly. Or drunk. Or crazy." Maybe she should try to save for a car, she told herself. She glanced over at Kelly, who had moved her notebook to the right of her plate and continued to write. *How does she do it?* Helen wondered. *She never takes a break. Thanksgiving! I would be thankful if I could get a date with somebody good, she thought. Not like I'll ever meet anyone working for that dentist.* Her thoughts strayed to Hector Gonzalez, the only boy in whom she had ever had any sustained interest. It had been intensely painful for her when he left, but the pain had ebbed over time. Still, she thought of him often and continued to entertain the thought that one day, when he established himself in New York City he would come and whisk her away. And they would live together in the penthouse of a fancy high-rise with a uniformed doorman and with floor to ceiling windows looking out over the glittering lights of Manhattan. The kind of place where Helen Gurley Brown would live. *He can't have forgotten me, could he?* She wondered.

\*

Luis glanced at his watch. 7:00 pm. That was late enough, and dark enough. He walked slowly and quietly down the driveway of the Gonzalez home and tapped softly at the back door. Anita immediately opened the door. She must have been waiting for him, Luis thought.

"Luis, come in. *Cómo estás?*" Anita's words and gestures were as exuberant as ever, but she spoke just above a whisper.

"*Estoy bien, gracias, señora.*" Luis kept his voice down too, assuming she would appreciate it.

"Thank you so much for coming. I truly appreciate your help."

"It's no problem. I'm happy to help." Luis was always thrilled to get these calls from Anita.

"Well, if it would be possible for you to bring Hector a little care package from me, as you have so kindly done before, I would be grateful." She handed Luis a shoe box wrapped securely with cellophane several times over. "We selected a few treats for him, and here they are. I would feel better if a friend delivered them, rather than trust them to the mail."

"Sure, I can do that. No problem." Luis was well aware that beneath the treats Anita had packed was a thick wad of cash to keep Hector in style in New York City. And live in style he did! Hector's life in New York was one big party. Not much in the fridge but plenty of rum and other stuff in the cabinets. And his girlfriend Marisol was so hot! Three months ago when he had gone on one of these expeditions Marisol had invited her friend Lourdes over to party. Marisol had played salsa on the stereo, and she and Hector had danced to it while he and Lourdes looked on. Lourdes was a good-looking girl, almost as hot as Marisol. She wore this red dress so tight it looked painted on, and-

"Yes, his career in acting is developing very well." Anita's voice brought Luis back to the present. "We are very proud of him. But it will still be wonderful for him to see a friendly face from home. And here is a little something for you, to cover your travel expenses." Anita handed him an envelope. He knew that it contained enough cash to take a limo round trip to New York City and back, but Luis planned to take the dirt-cheap bus and save the rest.

"Oh, *señora*, it's really not necessary. I can..."

"No, I cannot have you spending your hard-earned money doing me a favor." She spread her fingers and laid her hand beneath her throat, a sure sign that there would be no further discussion. "Now I also want you to take some of these delicious galletas with you. *Las galletas de Concha son maravillosas!*" Luis noticed Concha in the shadows, her wizened little face transected by a broad smile, and he nodded politely at her.

"Okay, thanks for this then. And for the cookies. I will get the package safely to Hector. Don't worry." Luis turned towards the door and departed.

Catalina stood silently outside the door that led from the kitchen to the dining room. She tiptoed barefoot to her father's study and slipped in.

"Mamá did call Luis and gave him a package for Hector, just like you said," she whispered to her father, sitting at his desk. "Papá, you know everything!"

"No princess, I don't know everything, but I know your mother. She loves Hector and wants to help him. New York City is an expensive place, and he can't support himself." Pedro was aware that Anita's belief that Hector was having success with a career in acting was complete fiction. No surprise there.

"Are you still angry at him?"

"No, I'm not angry anymore." But keeping Hector at a distance was good for him, and for the family. He laid his hand gently on Cati's head, enjoying the silky feel of her smooth hair.

"Can Hector come home?"

"No, not now. Maybe one day."

"When, Papá?"

Pedro rolled his eyes. "*Princesa*, you have so many questions. Shouldn't you be helping Mamá with something?"

Catalina knew very well that Concha did all the work and that her mother did not need any help. But she could take a hint. "Okay, Papá. *Te quiero.*"

"*Te quiero también.*" He kissed her forehead and she slipped out of the room, closing the door quietly behind her.

# CHAPTER 9

"Mom, I'm home!" Alex shouted at the quiet house. No response, which was unusual for a Tuesday late-afternoon. He bounded up the stairs to his room, dumped the contents of his suitcase into the laundry hamper, and ran back downstairs and into the kitchen for a snack. A quick survey revealed the early stages of preparation of a meal. On the beige Formica counter lay one can each of tomato sauce and Italian-style tomato paste, a 16 oz. box of store-brand spaghetti and a bottle of wine in a basket. One yellow onion and two cloves of garlic lay on his mother's worn wooden cutting board. Based on the amount of food being prepared, his mother had remembered that he was coming home for spring break.

Alex was pleased with the opportunity to make himself a snack, without having to go through his Mom. He opened the refrigerator and evaluated its contents. He pulled out whole wheat bread, mayonnaise, mustard, and some thin-sliced ham that promised to harbor no more than 2% fat, prepared a sandwich, carried it to the living room and turned on the TV. It took a while to find something decent to watch; he finally settled on Jeopardy. As he picked up his sandwich, he realized he had forgotten to cut it in half. No big deal, he thought, and bit off a corner.

Just then the door opened, and Olivia walked in.

"Alex!"

"Hey, Mom. I just got home."

"We weren't expecting you so early." Her attention flicked to the end table next to the couch. "You know you're supposed to cut sandwiches in half. Otherwise they are quite awkward to eat. Dad is here too." She pronounced that last sentence a little too brightly and stepped aside so Philip could enter.

Philip gave Alex a broad smile, but his shoulders slumped and his eyes were sad.

"Dad, what's the matter? How come you're coming home together?" Alex said, standing.

"Ah, well, I, we were just, it's-," Philip stammered.

"Dear, it's a long story. We can talk about it later." Olivia turned and walked purposefully toward the kitchen.

"Dad?"

"World Religions for $300," Alex Trebek's energetic voice filled the silence. Alex shut off the TV.

"Let's sit, okay?" They sat together on the couch, Philip sitting back, and Alex perched on the edge of the couch, turned toward his Dad.

"So, what's up?" Alex prompted.

"Well, well." Philip paused and took a deep breath. "I don't know if you want to hear about all this. It's not something for you to worry about."

"Dad, please tell me. I will worry if you don't tell me."

"Well. Well. Let's see. Alright. So, remember when I had that problem with, with my eye?"

Alex thought for a moment. "Years ago, yeah. I remember."

"Well, there was always the chance that the, ah, the disease in the eye could spread." Philip folded his hands and leaned forward, resting his arms on his thighs.

"But they took your, your whole eye out, right?" The details of that frightening episode came rushing back to him. His heart started to pound.

"Yes, but still, there was always the chance. So I was seeing the doctor on a regular schedule, sometimes getting a CAT scan. The longer you go with nothing showing up, the better your chances. But then in November they found a tiny spot that hadn't been there before. Said it was probably nothing. But said come back in three months for another scan."

"November? You mean before Thanksgiving?"

"That's right, it was the middle of November. A couple of weeks ago I went for the scan and it was still there, maybe a little bit bigger. They still said, could be nothing, but better get a biopsy and see. So we got up early today and went into the hospital and got a biopsy."

"A biopsy? Of what?"

"Oh, yeah, it was of my liver." Philip gestured toward the right bottom edge of his rib cage. "They kept me at the hospital for a few hours, make sure there was no bleeding or anything. They just let us go a little while ago and we came home."

"Well, ah, when will you know something?"

"Next week. I have an appointment with the doctor to sit down and get the results."

"I'll come with you."

"Oh, Alex, no; this is your spring break. You should be relaxing."

"No. I want to go with you. I want to be there in case I can help."

"Well, alright. But if you change your mind it's okay." He gave Alex a smile.

"Dad, are you okay? You seem so, so calm." Was his father calm or rather, resigned, Alex asked himself.

"Yes, well, maybe. Thing is, it's out of my hands, nothing I can do. I just have to wait. Also, well, I'm glad I could tell you. We thought you wouldn't get home until later, and your Mother felt it was better not to worry you, so we weren't going to say anything. But then we got home and there you were, and I thought I should tell you."

Alex nodded slowly.

"Did I do the right thing, saying something?" Philip asked anxiously.

"Yes, I'm glad you told me. I'm glad. It's just a lot to think about," Alex said. He did his best to keep his voice even and strong, as his heart raced and rattled in his chest like a caged animal.

"Actually, I feel better that I told you, kind of unburdened. Not saying anything, that would have felt like lying, and that's not me, you know?"

"I do, I understand." Alex rested his hand on his Father's shoulder.

*He's turned into a man,* Philip thought. *What a son I have! I'm lucky in that, so lucky.*

Olivia waltzed into the room with the martini shaker, two etched highball glasses and a jar of olives on a tray. "Oh, Alex, I wasn't thinking," she said, glancing down at the tray. "Would you like a martini? I suppose that now you're in college you are entitled."

"No, Mom, that's okay. Thanks."

Philip sat forward. "Liv, I have discussed my, my situation with Alex, and he will be coming to the doctor with us next week," Philip said firmly.

"But Philip, we had agreed…"

"This is better. This, my, the problem affects all of us."

"Mr. Eastgard? Let me show you into the doctor's office now," a cute little receptionist chirped, opening the door that led from the waiting room to the inner sanctum of Dr. Richard Cumberland's office.

Philip stood. "My wife and my son are here with me too. Okay if they come along?"

"Of course. This way, please." She ushered them down the hall and waved them into the doctor's office, although after so many visits to Dr. Cumberland, Philip hardly needed an escort. The three Eastgards seated themselves in chairs facing the doctor's desk. Alex leaned back, feeling the fabric-covered chair pressing gently against him. He looked around the room, noticing long rows of hardbound medical texts on shelves behind the desk, crooked piles of medical journals near one edge of the desk and one broad-leaved houseplant in a white ceramic pot on top of a metal file cabinet. *That plant doesn't look too healthy*, Alex thought. *Probably doesn't like the fluorescent light.* He imagined that the leaves of the plant were reaching toward the window, straining to reach the sunlight. He could relate to that. He wished that they didn't have to be here today, that he and his Dad could be out doing something else, not sitting here waiting to get news that would be good or terrible.

Dr. Cumberland strode into the room, stethoscope tucked into the pocket of his long white lab coat. "Philip, thank you for coming," he said.

Alex had a bad feeling about that. If the results were good, he would have said, good to see you. But he didn't; he said thank you.

"Dr. Cumberland, you've met my wife Olivia. This is our son Alex," Philip said, willing himself to speak calmly.

Dr. Cumberland had a manila folder with Philip's name on the tab. He opened it and straightened the papers it contained. "So. I received the biopsy results. Unfortunately, the news is not good. The biopsy shows spread from the neoplasm that arose in your eye."

Philip nodded slowly, not speaking, looking down at his hands.

There was a pause and then Olivia spoke. "Now, Doctor. What should my husband do at this point? We would like to know what treatments are available and how good they are. Whichever is best, that is what we would like my husband to have."

"Well, Mrs. Eastgard, unfortunately, we do not currently have any therapy that is really effective for this type of tumor. You never know, perhaps something new will be developed, and I will keep checking for anything that sounds promising. But for the present there is nothing that I could in good conscience recommend."

"What should be our next step then?" Olivia insisted, dissatisfied with the idea of doing nothing.

"Well, it has been about six years since the initial diagnosis, so it is possible that the tumor has been growing very slowly and may continue to grow slowly. I would ask Philip to come back in three months for another scan to gauge the rate of growth, if any. I know this is so difficult, and I'm so sorry the news isn't better. But the disease may take years to run its course. Don't dwell on this bad thing. Enjoy life. Be grateful for each other." Dr. Cumberland closed the manila folder. *Terrible disease, and such a nice man with such a nice family,* he thought. "Please ask Jane to give you an appointment three months from now. And if anything changes or you have any questions, please call."

His parents started to stand. "Wait!" Alex burst out. "What does this mean? What's going to happen?"

"Well, every case is different. It's difficult to predict for the individual patient," Dr. Cumberland offered, his tone conciliatory, although he looked somewhat ill at ease.

There was a moment of silence, and then Philip cleared his throat and spoke. "Dr. Cumberland and I discussed this at length in the past, at my request, when what's happening now was just, ah, theoretical." He paused, swallowed and continued. "This type of tumor is very bad if it spreads. It tends to go to the liver and damage the liver, and you can get liver failure. And you can die of that. It can spread past the liver too. It could go to the lungs, and you have trouble breathing, and could even go to the brain, then you- you may not be yourself anymore. I do hope it stays out of my brain." He paused again. "I always had a feeling this day would come. Always felt I was living on borrowed time. I guess fate has caught up with me."

Dr. Cumberland listened quietly as Philip spoke. He recalled their conversation, several years ago, one of the few times he had come alone, without his wife. Philip had pressed him and pressed him for more information, for more details, for more possibilities. He had told Philip over and over, but it may never come to this. You may be cured. But Philip had asked, what if, again and again. And now here we are, just as we discussed.

Philip stood, gently touched Olivia's back, and said, "Thank you, Doctor. Come on, Liv."

Alex was stunned but he managed to stand. He turned and followed his parents out of the office.

\*

Alex lay in bed, trapped in a nightmare- his father was sick and was going to die, would suffer and die, and there was nothing he could do, nothing. He struggled to understand this senseless cruelty, this terrible twist of fate. And then he felt a soft touch on his shoulder, and a gentle shake.

"Alex, it's Daddy. Wake up, sleepyhead!"

"Daddy! You're okay! I had a bad dream! It was so scary; you got sick and…" Alex tried to sit up in bed, so happy, the terrible weight on his heart all gone. It had just been a nightmare. But then where had his father gone? He tried to sit up but struggled against sweat-soaked sheets twisted around his arms and shoulders. He peeled away the sheets and kicked off the covers. Then he was fully awake and the memory of the day before came flooding back to him. Alex took a few deep breaths and cradled his head in his hands. There was something terrible growing in his father's body, something for which there was no good treatment, and sooner or later it would cause his father's death.

Alex's gaze wandered to the clock radio on his bedside table. It was almost 6:00. Pitch black outside, but it would start to get light soon. He dreaded the thought of trying to sleep more and having his nightmare come back. He swung his legs onto the little sailboat rug next to his bed, stood, pulled off his sweaty T shirt and shivered as the air hit his torso. He dressed quickly, grabbing a clean T shirt, spongy white cotton socks, his Amherst sweatpants and a fleece jacket, and slipped downstairs. His parents were not up yet; abruptly he realized he was glad for the solitude. He pulled on the running shoes he had left by the back door, and quietly let himself out of the house.

Alex started to run. He ran down the driveway of his home, onto Pella Street, past Patrick's old apartment building and up and down the dark streets of his neighborhood, north on Fisher Avenue and west on Dean Road. He found himself running next to Brookline High School, along the side of the basketball court; realizing where he was, he ducked his head and quickened his pace. He ran faster and faster, sailing through the early morning air, like a ship at sea, borne by gusty trade winds. He soared along, imagining he was astride a powerful stallion, galloping with his companions down the banks of meandering Granicus, thundering up the other side, to access broad Sardis, across Gordian onto Issus, and then southwest onto a little dead-end street called Siwa; he turned around, retracing his path, and proceeded to Susa Street. Strength surged through his legs; he had never run like this. As he ran, palatial Victorian homes on their small lots merged into a towering walled city that he must circumnavigate, chasing a foe forever elusive.

The cold morning air filled his lungs and cleared his mind, and he was able to think. The situation was bad, he thought, as the first pale lights of dawn came peeking out over the tops of the leafless trees that lined the streets. The deck was definitely stacked against them. But there was reason to hope. If it weren't for those CAT scans, his father would not even have known he had cancer in his liver. The doctor had said that the tumor might be slow-growing. What if it took another six or seven years for the tumor that he had to double in size? It would still be very small. And there was no good treatment now, but what about six or seven or 10 years from now? Something might be discovered that could help his father.

And another thing. He wouldn't let his parents keep him in the dark about Dad's illness. He would insist on knowing what was going on. He swung around and headed for home.

# CHAPTER 10

The second Tuesday in April was gloomy and gray, raw and chilly, with sonorous bouts of rain periodically interrupting the tenacious mist. Alex donned a sweater, then a rain jacket, and started for the door. The phone rang.

"Hello?" he said.

"Alex, it's Mom," Alex heard her voice, clear and crisp, brisk and efficient.

"What's up?" It was his Dad who usually called him just to talk. Calls from his Mom were less frequent and typically had a specific purpose. He was seized with apprehension.

"Well, Dad asked me to call and... update you. We went to the doctor to discuss his scans. Alex, it isn't good news. The one spot has more than doubled in size, and now there are some new ones."

"Oh," Alex managed to say.

"Dad is sorry he didn't feel up to calling you himself."

"That's okay." That sounds so stupid, Alex thought, as soon as the words left his mouth.

"Well, we can talk more, but I should probably let you go. Will you come home this weekend?"

"Yes, of course. I will."

"If you want anything special to eat, just let me know."

"Okay, if I think of something," he said. Olivia hung up. Alex stood for a long time, dazed. The door opened, and suddenly he realized he was still holding the receiver to his ear. He hung it up quickly.

Buck walked in, damp and cranky, leaving wet footsteps as he made his way to his desk. He deposited a stack of books with a thud. "I hate organic chemistry," he intoned dolefully.

"Organic chemistry. You're pre-med!" Alex said, his eyes suddenly alight.

"Alex, what have you been smoking?"

"Can we talk later? I'm late for class."

"Sure, whatever."

*

Alex returned later that day and found Buck in his customary pose, slumped over a large textbook, with a mildly disgruntled expression on his face. Buck looked up as Alex entered; Alex actually looked flustered, Buck noted with surprise.

"Buck, I think I'm going to switch to pre-med," Alex declared with intensity, as he stripped off his dripping jacket.

"To what do we owe this epiphany?" Buck asked sarcastically. Great, just great. Knowing Alex, he would get that one spot at med school that had been destined for Buck. And Buck's Dad would probably disinherit him because of the disgrace of not getting into med school. Buck would become the family embarrassment, the one who couldn't get into med school, living out his life in poverty and obscurity.

"Buck," Alex began, dragging his desk chair over to Buck's side of the room, "My Dad has been sick lately."

"Oh. Is it serious?"

"Yeah. Seems to be."

Buck laid down his pen, and silently chastised himself. "Oh, wow, I had no idea. I'm sorry."

"Yeah, it's not too good. But I've been thinking about it, and it has been making me think about my major. What am I really going to do with that? But if go into medicine, well, I could really make a difference," Alex continued. He envisioned himself in a white lab coat, wearing protective glasses and surgical gloves, seated on a hard stool before a black counter with rows of test tubes, doing something amazing. Maybe he would find the gene that caused melanoma and figure out how to fight it.

Buck nodded slowly. "I understand, but won't you miss studying history? You seem to love it."

Alex shrugged, as the image of himself in the lab coat faded. "I do, but I can pick up a book and read any history I want, any time. I think medicine is where I should focus. I just talked to my advisor. He says if I take a Biology and a Chemistry over the summer, and then change my curriculum going forward I will still be on track to finish in four years."

"You were going junior year abroad. You were going to England. What about that?"

78

"Yeah... I will miss those Plantagenets. Not to mention the Tudors and the Stuarts, and all the rest." Alex paused and let his mind wander. He had nurtured such big plans. He was going to Oxford, or possibly Cambridge, to study in depth the history of England, the origins of the British Empire, its glories, its benefits, its tragic errors, its ultimate downfall. He had imagined the huge lessons that could be learned. He had wondered if he might one day play a role in government policy, in diplomacy. Now that all seemed unrealistic. "But only a small proportion of people who study history truly use what they learn to change the world for the better. Medicine is where I can make a real contribution."

"Well, sounds like your mind's made up. Good luck. Let me know if I can help."

"Thanks, man. That means a lot," Alex said. "I'll be going home this weekend and I'll let my parents know."

Buck's usual reaction was bliss when he heard that Alex would be away for the weekend, but not today. Buck surprised himself when he responded, "I am sure they'll be proud of you."

\*

Philip sighed and pushed away his plate of Chinese take-out. "I love this stuff, but I just can't eat it any more. The heartburn is awful!" He didn't really have heartburn. But every time he ate he imagined that the food was going to feed not him, but his cancer. For some reason this feeling was more intense with spicy, savory foods. He paused and then continued, "God takes away your little pleasures one by one so you won't mind dying so much when the time comes."

"Philip," Olivia began. She wanted to scold him for his maudlin attitude but then stopped, sighed and rested her head in her hands. Then she tried again. "Philip, I think you are so afraid of the future that you can't enjoy the present. Please, well, fine, act however you want when it's just the two of us, but when Alex comes home this weekend, please try to put on a brave face. It will be hard enough on him as it is. No need to make it worse."

"You're right, Liv," he said, smiling sadly at her. "I will, I promise."

\*

It was a beautiful warm mid-August day as Alex and Philip waited together in Dr. Cumberland's office.

"Philip, how are you feeling today?" the doctor said as he entered, extending his hand.

"I actually feel pretty good. It's just the idea of this thing growing in me, I guess."

"Well, we can work with that. Can you put your illness out of your mind and focus on something else? Is there something you want to do? Someplace you want to go? You should do it now while you are feeling well."

"I'll think about that." Philip nodded. What he really wanted was to live a long time and see Alex grown and married with children of his own. He would love to see what a child of Alex's would be like. Probably wonderful. His mind conjured up the hazy image of a fair-haired boy awkwardly but persistently trying to mount a small bicycle with training wheels. "I do have some interesting news to report. Alex is switching majors at college. He's going to study medicine. He just finished summer school. Took Biology and Organic Chemistry, got an A in both."

"Alex, that's wonderful news. The field of medicine can use a good man like you."

"I want to do something. I want to be in a position to help people like my Dad."

Dr. Cumberland leaned back in his chair, folded his hands together and relaxed. Discussing prevention was a favorite topic of his. Much easier than giving patients like Philip one piece of bad news after another. "There is something you can do that's fairly easy, but people tend to forget, or neglect. Especially young people."

Alex sat forward. "What is it?"

"This disease your father has, melanoma, arose in his eye. But ocular melanoma is very rare. Melanoma arises much more often in the skin, and it's related to sun exposure, as are several other types of skin cancers, although melanoma is the worst. Looking at you, I see you're tanned."

"Yeah, I'm on the track team. I run outside just about every day."

"Well, there you go. You keep that up and you are at risk for skin cancer."

"Really?" Alex was stunned. A cold shiver swept through him. His plan was to fight disease. It had never occurred to him that he could be on the receiving end.

"Absolutely. And it is easy to cut your risk. If you have to exercise outside, do it early or late in the day, when the sun is not so intense. And use sunscreen. And wear a hat when you can, to protect your face."

"A hat?" Alex was still recovering from the news that he could get skin cancer and wearing a hat did not sound very manly.

Dr. Cumberland nodded firmly. "I have no problem getting women to wear hats; I just tell them it will keep their skin looking younger. But men, that's a different story. But think about it. A broad-brimmed hat is best. If you really can't bring yourself to wear any other kind of hat, at least get a baseball cap. But then be sure to put sunscreen on your ears."

Philip spoke. "If Dr. Cumberland suggests this, you should do it." Alex, ill at ease with having become the subject of the conversation, remained skeptical.

Dr. Cumberland stood and came around his desk to stand before Alex and Philip. "Alex, let me have your arm for a moment. Here, on this side, nice and tanned, healthy looking skin. Until you turn your arm over to look at the more protected side. See how smooth and white the skin is? The tanned side is lined and damaged compared to the protected side."

Alex turned his arm over and back, examining his skin with horror. This line of discussion was not what he intended. He would have been much happier if the topic had been dropped after Philip announced that Alex was going into medicine.

"Alex, I don't mean to scare you. You're young. Protect your skin going forward and you will be at low risk."

Alex nodded. "Okay, I'll do it. And when I can, I'll get other people to protect their skin also."

"Good. Then this has been a most productive meeting. And of course, sun protection is most critical for those with fair skin, as they don't have much natural protection. You and your father have fair skin, so it is especially important for you to stay vigilant. Your mother has more of a Mediterranean complexion, so she has a little more leeway, but she should also make efforts to protect her skin. We all should." Dr. Cumberland spoke with authority and conviction.

"Okay, I'll remember." Alex and Philip stood and walked to the door.

# CHAPTER 11

The graduation ceremony ended, and Alex filed, elated, out of the auditorium along with his fellow Amherst graduates, scanning the crowd for his parents. But there was Buck- he wanted to say goodbye before they parted ways for good.

"Hey, Buck, good luck next year! New Orleans will be so much fun."

"I don't know. I interviewed in November and it was fine, but the heat and humidity are supposed to be awful all summer long."

"Don't worry so much. It'll be great- the music, the food, no snow...and Tulane has a great med school." Alex gave Buck's upper arm a quick, firm squeeze. "Let's stay in touch, okay?"

"Sure, sure. Good luck in New York."

Alex resumed his search for his parents. Before long he saw his mother and headed toward her. Olivia was dressed in her one good suit, a severely tailored navy-blue combination of a straight skirt and a jacket with three-quarter sleeves. Alex recognized that suit- it was older than he, and only emerged from Olivia's closet for select events. She also wore a short pearl necklace and clip-on earrings of clustered pearls, jewelry she typically reserved for weddings and funerals.

"Mom! Mom!" Alex headed toward her.

"Oh, Alex, we are so proud of you." Olivia hugged him, something she hardly ever did. It took Alex by surprise and his mortar board wobbled on his head; he reached up quickly to steady it.

"Where's Da-," Alex started to ask, when a faded little gray man with stooped shoulders stepped forward and took his hand.

"Alex, I'm so proud. So proud. Congratulations," the gray man said, and Alex realized, stunned, that it was his father, who looked to have aged half of a long lifetime since he had last seen him a few weeks ago.

Alex managed a smile but was unable to speak.

"Alex!" It was Elizabeth Hawkins, elegant in a silk sheath of muted gold, on the arm of a tall, dark-haired, meticulously groomed gentleman who held her academic robe over his other arm. Elizabeth's nails sparkled with gold-colored nail polish, chosen because it matched her dress and would scandalize her preposterously conservative mother.

"Elizabeth, congratulations. Here are my parents," Alex gestured.

Elizabeth nodded politely to Philip and Olivia. "My parents are here somewhere but let me introduce my fiancé. This is James Pembroke. He works on Wall Street. We'll be living in Manhattan after our wedding." Elizabeth was exceptionally pleased with herself for landing James. He was five years older than she, and already well established in his career in finance. The odds of him becoming obscenely rich were excellent. And he was devastatingly handsome, with that olive complexion, those mysterious dark eyes, that adorable dimple in his chin! And that business about him being descended, even remotely, from British nobility made him even more intriguing. After living here in Amherst for four years, the idea of moving to New York City was intoxicating. Life would be perfect. It had piqued her vanity not to have Alex show some interest in her, and she was happy to have the chance to show James off to him. Alex was beautiful in his golden way, but James was just as gorgeous, and with a romantic Mediterranean look. Moreover, Alex would be a penniless med student for the next four years and would then be working for slave wages during his residency. She would have been miserable living in such circumstances. James in contrast already had a nice little apartment in Greenwich Village and a respectable income.

James extracted his arm from Elizabeth's and shook Alex's hand firmly. "Nice to meet you," he said.

"Congratulations also on your engagement. Maybe I'll see you and Elizabeth around. I'm going to med school at NYU."

"I hope so. It would be fun to have our own little reunion," Elizabeth said, joy and excitement evident in her tone. She was so looking forward to having her own dinner parties and exploring the better restaurants of Manhattan.

"Alex graduated summa cum laude," Olivia interjected, a bit off-topic.

Elizabeth smiled knowingly. "Of course he did. I would expect nothing less from Alex."

"Elizabeth graduated magna. Me, I just got out of college by the skin of my teeth, but the investment houses don't care. Just have to pass Series 7, and then keep making them money," James said, his tone jovial.

"Well, I should go locate my parents. Good luck with med school!" Elizabeth plucked James's tie from his chest, twisted it around her fingers and tugged gently. She shook out her mass of chestnut hair and strode away, a slender, long-legged golden knife slicing through the crowd. James followed, smiling broadly. When she took hold of his tie like that, it was a sure sign that she would be in the mood later.

*

That summer was difficult for Alex. He had taken a job as a lab assistant at Massachusetts General Hospital, the best he could get on short notice, and in view of his imminent departure for medical school. Halfway through the summer, in the middle of July, Alex came downstairs as he always did, to have breakfast with his father, before leaving for work.

"Hi, Dad, how'd you sleep?" Alex asked as he poured maple syrup over his buttermilk toaster waffles. The deterioration in Philip's health was evident on a near-daily basis, and it was painful for Alex to watch.

"Not too bad, not too bad," Philip replied. He sipped his black coffee cautiously. He would not burden Alex with the information that he did not ever sleep through the night anymore, because of anxiety and because his swollen liver made him uncomfortable. He also failed to tell Alex that he made a point of getting out of bed in time to join him for breakfast. Alex probably thought that he stayed up and did things around the house during the day, but in fact Philip would return to bed as soon as Alex left, return to bed with his pain and his fatigue and his fear, and would only arise again in time to get dressed and greet Alex when he came home from work.

That evening, as he did every evening after work, Alex spent time with his father. These were unhurried interludes that would have been relaxing if the specter of Philip's cancer had not been hovering nearby, creeping closer and closer, impatient to take Philip away. Sometimes they talked, but often they remained quiet, or spoke only intermittently. The weather was especially fine that day; the air was dry and fresh, and shifted from warm to cool as the sun dipped below the horizon. They sat together on the patio in back of the house overlooking Olivia's shade garden of hostas and luxuriant ferns. It was silent except for the occasional car that happened along their quiet street and the rustling of leaves in the mild breeze. Olivia was in the kitchen preparing a dinner that Philip would praise but not consume. Philip spoke first.

"Alex, do something for me. It's about Mom. Your mother, as you know, she's a strong woman. A very strong woman. Independent." Philip paused, and swallowed before continuing. "But to be happy, to be satisfied with herself, she has to feel needed. So, let her, you know, cook for you or something. Ask her to mail you cookies or brownies while you're at school. Remember to tell her how delicious they were. How much your friends liked them. You have no idea what it means to her, that kind of thing." Philip realized that since it had become apparent that he would

84

not long survive this disease, Liv's focus had slowly been shifting from him to Alex. That was how she would cope, he knew, by focusing on the surviving member of the family. This would not be apparent to Alex though, and Philip hoped that Alex would take this hint.

Alex nodded silently.

"Another thing," Philip continued. "A few months ago, I started going to church. When I could see that things weren't looking too good, I started to think about, well, about my- my end, you know?"

"Dad, please..."

"Alex, I have to tell you this. Please listen. I'm sorry to mention this after so long, but I recall when there was the funeral for Patrick, the priest had some nice things to say, some comforting things, in the midst of that tragedy."

Alex thought back to that funeral. He closed his eyes, and the horror of it all swept over him, as painful as though it had happened yesterday. He had been a walking ghost, immersed in grief, blind and deaf to his surroundings, and remembered nothing of what the priest had said, but he nodded silently again.

Philip had been watching Alex's face as he spoke and sensed the effect his reference to Patrick had had. "Alex, I'm sorry. I'm so sorry."

"No, go ahead. What about the priest?"

Philip dropped his eyes and paused before speaking. "He's still there. Father Francis. I went to talk with him about my, my illness."

Alex nodded, dragging himself back from the past, willing himself to focus on his father's words.

"He was good to talk to. He really listened to me. I'd like, well, I'd like him to do my funeral Mass."

"Dad," Alex began. "You don't have to talk like this."

"No, Alex, I want this in order. Look at me; how much longer can I last?"

Alex studied his father's face, and let his eyes travel down along his body. He was near-emaciated, with wasted limbs and hollow temples. His skin had a sickly yellow cast and his remaining eye, his warm, caring eye, was all yellow, like the eyes of a wolf, or a devil, a devil who had possessed him and who was destroying his body, cell by cell. The artificial eye rested serenely beneath his eyelids, clean and unstained. Alex dropped his eyes.

"It's all over my liver. I'm getting liver failure. My liver is mostly tumor now."

Alex nodded yet again, but this time he shook and tears collected in his eyes.

Philip raised one bony hand and rested it on Alex's shoulder. "I'm so sorry to hurt you, Alex. I'm so sorry. I need, I have to say one more thing. I need for you to do something. Your mother won't listen. I've tried." As Philip's hand lay on his son's shoulder he recalled the very first time he had seen Alex, had touched Alex, the day Alex was born, the indescribable, unexpected joy of this child appearing in their lives after so many years of marriage. Olivia had been 39; he, 42. She was sitting there in that hospital bed like it was a throne, wearing the biggest smile he had ever seen, cuddling a tiny baby swaddled in a little white blanket. She had pulled back the blanket to reveal a little head with tufts of fair hair and dark eyes that gazed on him unblinking. Philip had placed his hand carefully, reverently on the little head, the same hand that now rested on his son's shoulder. But look at Alex now, grown up, strong, brilliant, but also sensitive, and in pain. Philip withdrew his hand.

"I'm sorry. Whatever you want." Alex sat up and wiped back the tears.

"After I, after the funeral, you know, I want, I don't want to be buried," Philip began.

Alex looked at him, surprised. "What do you mean?"

"What I want, is I want to be cremated. I do not want to spend all eternity in a pine box with my cancer. If I have to go, I want it gone too, burned away. To ashes. Dust to dust, you know?"

Alex covered his face with his hands and sobbed. A little squirrel with an exuberant gray tail scampered down from a tree, regarded them cautiously, and when Alex shifted in his seat, scurried away. The neighbors' wind chimes tinkled sweetly in the distance. Venus gleamed before them as equinox ebbed and darkness covered the earth.

"Alex, I'm so sorry, I'm so sorry, and so angry. It's so unfair. I want to be here and see you become a doctor and get married and have kids and I want to get to play with them." His voice shook. "I'm so sorry to dump this on you, but if I can't have what I really want, I'll settle for Father Francis saying my Mass and for cremation. I've tried 10 times to talk to your mother but she won't face reality. She thinks if she keeps making good meatloaf and gets the martinis just right that life will continue as before." Philip's face contorted with emotion; he forced his features to smooth out.

Alex absorbed this. He could certainly understand what Dad was saying about Mom. After a long while he was able to speak. "Let me call NYU. They would let me start a year later, I'm sure. I want to spend this time with you."

"No." Philip shook his head emphatically. "I don't want that. Don't put your life on hold for me. Call me if you want. Come home for the weekend if you can."

The back door opened and Olivia peaked out. "Dinner is just about ready. Want to come in and sit down?"

They sat around the kitchen table, all in the same spots they had occupied for the last twenty years. Olivia took Alex's plate and loaded it with roast potatoes and broiled chicken.

"Mom, that's enough."

"You didn't eat enough at college. It's so nice that you're home for the summer, and I plan to feed you properly. You are so thin! Philip, let's have your plate."

Alex watched silently as she put a chicken breast and potatoes on Philip's plate. She just was not going to admit to herself how bad things were with Dad until she absolutely had to. His eyes met his father's across the table. *See what I mean?* his father's eyes said.

\*

"Mom, you really didn't have to drive me to South Station. I could have left a little earlier and gotten here on the T," Alex said, leaning forward from the back seat.

"Now, Alex, it's not every day our son leaves for medical school. We can certainly drive you, at least this once," Olivia replied.

"That's right, Alex. And you have two heavy suitcases. Just makes sense," Philip added.

Traffic was heavy as they inched toward the station. One lane of the street was occupied by a utility vehicle and workmen in hard hats creating a rapidly expanding hole in the asphalt with the loudest equipment possible in order to access a water main. The noise prevented normal conversation. Olivia pulled over carefully to let Alex out once they finally reached the front entrance. Alex leapt out of the car and extracted his suitcases from the trunk, checked his jacket pocket for his wallet and his tickets, and started to wave goodbye. Then he saw his father struggling to exit the car, feet on the pavement, yellowed hands feebly gripping the car door, awkwardly, ineffectually trying to stand up. Alex returned to the car, took his father's hands and pulled him to his feet and embraced him, his arms around Philip's frail frame and then stepped back. The man he saw before him was wasted and jaundiced. His abdomen protruded, tense with fluid. His father was dying.

The roar of two jackhammers was punctuated by the honking of taxis, and Alex realized that they had pulled up in a taxi stand. The driver of the taxi just behind them yelled out of his window, "Hey grandpa, either get back in the car or go in the station. You people got to move."

"Okay! Okay!" Alex yelled back. "Dad, better get back into the car." Alex helped him into his seat.

Philip gazed at him intensely and whispered, "I love you, Alex. Good luck in New York."

"Will you people wrap it up? You're holding everyone up!" the taxi driver howled. "We only got one lane to work with here."

"I love you too, Dad," Alex replied. He stood back from the car and watched his parents drive away, following their car with his eyes as long as he could, until it disappeared into the crowded streets. Leaving for New York now felt wrong, and Alex wondered if he should just go home. But his father had said he did not want that. *I'll go home next weekend,* Alex thought. *There's still time.*

# PART 2

New York City and Beyond, 1991

# CHAPTER 12

Alex strode down the hall of his dorm toward his room, #1126, last room on the right on the eleventh floor of the medical students' dormitory, overlooking FDR Drive. It was Friday afternoon of his first week of school, and after a week packed with hours of Anatomy and classes in Biochemistry and Physiology, he was hurrying to his room to grab a small suitcase and get to the station to catch a bus to go home. Ben Goldberg and Steve Kirkpatrick, classmates with rooms across the hall, loitered outside their rooms.

"Hey, guys, shouldn't you be studying?" Alex grinned at them. There was already an easy camaraderie among many of the medical students; they knew that they would be working together, day and night, on and off, for the next four years. They would be spending more time with one another than with family or friends, and that realization drew them together.

"Yeah, well, first I have to give Steve some advice on how to dress. No decent girl will go out with him when he's dressed like a nerd."

"It's not how I dress. I'm afraid I smell like my cadaver."

"There's this invention called a shower."

"I don't know. I feel like I can't get the smell off me."

"Well, I guess you can go without a date for a semester."

"Easy for you to say."

"Did you know there's a nursing school down the street?"

Steve turned to Ben. "Nursing school? No."

"Student nurses. They look up to us. It'd be like shooting fish in a barrel."

Alex laughed. "Ben, you're going to give us all a bad name. Hey, is that my phone?" He fished in his pockets for his key and hurried to his door.

"Somebody's been trying to get you. Someone with OCD. Phone rings five times. Then stops for a count of five, then rings five times again. Like clockwork," Steve reported.

"You are so anal. I'll bet good money you end up in Psychiatry," Ben said.

"Look who's talking. You already know DSM-3; you're cut out to be a shrink. I'm going into whatever will get me laid," Steve said.

Ben pondered this critical issue. "So what kind of doctor would girls consider hot? Not sure. Surgeon, maybe?"

"Maybe. But not general surgery. Thoracic surgery? Cardiovascular surgery?"

Alex opened his door as quickly as he could, but the phone had stopped ringing. The vibration of the phone's last ring hung in the air and then dispersed, to be replaced by the incessant rumble of traffic from FDR Drive. "I missed it. I wonder who it was."

"Count to five and it will ring again," Steve advised.

Alex dropped his books onto his desk and stared at the heavy black rotary phone. A wave of anxiety swept over him, and he half hoped that whoever it was would give up and not call again. But sure enough, after a count of five, the phone rang.

"Hello?" Alex answered.

"Alex, it's Mom." Alex's grip on the phone tightened. Something must be wrong. No, he corrected himself; something must be worse. His father had died. He felt dizzy, and took hold of the back of his desk chair to steady himself.

"Alex, I wanted to catch you before you left. Dad has... has taken a turn for the worse. I- we're not at home; we're at Mass General. Baker Building 632. So don't go home. Just come to the hospital. That's where we'll be."

Dad was in a hospital room. He was still alive. "I'm leaving right now. I'll be there as soon as I can."

"From South Station, take the Red Line to Charles/MGH."

Alex rolled his eyes. "Mom, I know how to get there."

"Alright then. Be careful."

Alex pulled on a sweatshirt, slid some books and a notebook into the side pocket of his suitcase and hurried out of his room.

All the while Steve and Ben had continued their conversation. As Alex emerged from his room, Steve inquired. "Alex, if you had to pick a specialty based on likelihood of getting laid, what would it be?"

"Something that important, I'm going to have to think about it," Alex replied.

"Where you heading?" Ben asked as Alex hurried back down the hall.

"Home," Alex replied.

"Hey, have a good weekend," Ben said. "Bring some food back with you."

"Will do. See you." Alex raced down the hall and waited impatiently for the elevator, to begin his trip back to Massachusetts.

*

It was almost 9 o'clock by the time Alex reached the hospital and found his way to his father's room. Alex opened the door quietly and saw his mother, her back to him, spine ramrod straight, sitting on a chair next to his father's bed. A curtain concealed his father from his view. He stepped forward and looked past his mother to see behind the curtain. There was his father, or rather what was left of his father, sleeping. Nasal prongs delivered oxygen to his lungs while an IV in the dorsum of his hand kept him hydrated.

"Mom?" Alex whispered.

Olivia's head whipped around. "Oh, Alex, I didn't hear you come in."

Alex dragged a chair over next to his mother's and sat down. "What happened?"

"Well, two days after we dropped you at South Station, your father was so uncomfortable that we went to the hospital to get the fluid drained from around his stomach. They took away, I think they said three liters of fluid. I don't know what that is in quarts, but it seemed like a lot. That went okay and he said he felt better, said he thought he'd be able to sleep."

"He wasn't sleeping?"

"No, he laid awake most nights, as best I could tell."

"I didn't know."

"Yes, well, he's been very uncomfortable, for quite a while."

"I didn't realize." Alex felt foolish; shouldn't he have known? He studied his father's face. The skin slid down his cheeks like melting wax.

"Anyway, after the fluid was drained, he said he felt more comfortable but just didn't think he could get up and walk. So they admitted him to the hospital, and then he kept getting sleepier and sleepier and he hasn't been awake at all since yesterday."

"Mom, he's been in the hospital for days and you didn't tell me?"

"Well, I didn't want to worry you while you were trying to study, and..."

"Mom! You didn't want to worry me?"

"I kept thinking, well, I kept hoping, that he would get better enough to come home before the weekend, and then what would have been the point of calling you and upsetting you? But he just didn't."

"You should have let me know right away."

"Alex, I believe he was holding on so he could see you leave for medical school. I can't tell you how proud he was of you. That whole day after you left and the next day, he was saying, 'Alex must have arrived in New York by now; Alex must have gone through orientation by now; I wonder what classes Alex will have in the morning,' things like that. And then we went to the hospital and he hasn't been able to leave."

Alex turned away from his father and studied his mother's face. She looked like a shadow of the commanding woman he knew. "Mom, when did you last sleep? You look tired."

"Well, I've been catching cat naps here and there."

"You haven't been home?"

"Well, no. I didn't want to leave in case there was some change, and... well, no."

Alex reached over and took his father's hand; he would have touched his face, but the waxen flesh was too forbidding, too foreign. He squeezed his father's hand, softly and then firmly, hoping for some sign, but the hand lay limp and unresponsive in his own. He glanced at his mother again; she radiated fatigue.

"Mom, Dad doesn't know we're here. Let me drive us home. You need to sleep. We'll come back first thing in the morning. Come on." He laid his father's hand down respectfully on the covers and stood. He wanted to stay, would have welcomed the opportunity for a solitary vigil with this man that he loved so well, would have welcomed the opportunity for quiet, unhurried reflection, but it was his mother who needed him now.

"Alright, Alex." Olivia stood unsteadily, and they walked together to the door.

*

Giuli Stewart awoke the next morning with terrible nausea. She lay in bed, evaluating this sensation. She had not eaten anything unusual yesterday, and she wouldn't have her period for another two weeks. The more she thought about it, the more she sensed that it had something to do with Alex. But he should be in New York City, in school by now. As the nausea ebbed, she was able to get out of bed and get dressed. She had a couple of hours before she had to be at work at Ye Olde Corner

Bookstore, where she now worked full time as an assistant manager. She snapped a leash onto little Romeo, now quite elderly, and urged him to the door.

"Come on, Romeo, let's go see what's up at Alex's." It was a long walk, and between the dog's short legs and his advanced age, progress was slow. Impatient, Giuli scooped the little chihuahua up in her arms and hurried toward Pella Street. She then casually set Romeo down as they rounded the corner onto Alex's street. She then walked slowly, looking and listening. A sense of foreboding still nagged at her but as they passed the house, all looked peaceful.

"I don't know, Romeo. I guess I'm imagining things. Let's go home." She led the little dog home as quickly as she could; she didn't want to be late for work.

*

Father Francis spoke beautifully at Philip's funeral. In the few months before Philip's death, he had come to know him well, and his words reflected a deep understanding of the kind and patient man Philip had been. At the end of the service, the priest announced that later that afternoon, the Eastgard family would host a reception at their home, welcoming their friends to join them.

Alex took his mother's arm as they left the church, and waited on the sidewalk, watching the coffin being loaded into the hearse. He knew that soon his father would be reduced to ashes. He fought back the tears, not wanting to appear weak, not wanting pity.

"Goodbye, Daddy," he mouthed silently as the hearse drove away.

*

Alex sat on the couch in their living room, hoping to be left alone. The house was full of sympathetic well-wishers, some from the church, some from the neighborhood, some from Philip's work. He knew he should be greeting people but he just couldn't. His mother seemed to be doing fine on her own as the sorrowful but dignified widow, thankful for the support of the community.

Halfway through the reception Tim and Leda Fletcher arrived, and sought out Olivia.

"Mrs. Eastgard? I'm Leda Fletcher, and this is my husband Tim. I'm not sure we've ever met, but our daughters were friends with your son in high school. This is Kelly, and our other daughter, Helen, is here too, somewhere. We're all so sorry for your loss."

Tim extended his big strong hand and shook Olivia's. "Anything you need, just let us know."

"Well, thank you very much. Thank you," Olivia said graciously.

"And we weren't sure if you could use this, but anyway, I made a casserole." Leda extracted a large covered Pyrex dish from a heavy brown paper grocery bag.

"Leda is a great cook, I'm telling you, otherwise I'd be a much slimmer guy," Tim said, patting his abdomen with satisfaction.

"Thank you; that's very thoughtful." Olivia took the casserole from Leda. "I'm going to put this out on the table." She nodded to them and stepped toward the kitchen.

Alex thought back on the times he had spent with his father. He remembered the day Dad had come home with a basketball goal and fixed it to the garage. He had handed Alex the big orange basketball, and encouraged him to get it through the net, but Alex was little and couldn't throw high enough. Finally, Philip had lifted him up, high enough to reach, and Alex had lobbed the ball through the goal. His father had assured him that before he knew it, he would be tall enough to score goals without help. Alex had been so happy that day. He almost smiled, even now, enjoying that memory. Then he heard voices, dim and indistinct, but coming closer, and he tensed.

"Alex, I'm so sorry! I had no idea your Dad was sick," Kelly said, and sank down onto the couch next to him and hugged him, tears in her eyes.

"Kelly! Thanks for coming." *And thank you for not being some stranger I don't want to talk to*, Alex thought. "It is so sad, but my Dad was really suffering, and there was nothing they could do for him. It's been going on for a while."

"I heard you're in med school."

"Yes. NYU. I switched majors largely because of my father's illness. It made me realize how important medicine is."

"You know what? You'll make a great doctor."

"But look at you; you look so grown-up!"

Kelly wore a dark suit, a white cotton blouse with button-down collar and no-nonsense loafers. Her curly hair was rolled up and contained on the back of her head by a large tortoise-shell hairclip.

"Oh, well, I work for the Boston Globe. I'm learning investigative reporting. I can't look like a kid, you know, or no one will take me seriously."

Alex nodded. And then when he looked up, there was Helen. Despite this sad occasion, despite all the years that had gone by, and her simple black dress, there she was, like pale gold Aphrodite, timeless, still so beautiful. Alex stood.

"Helen, thank you for coming."

Helen shook his hand awkwardly. "I'm really sorry," she said softly in her honeyed voice.

"Helen? Helen, come here, sweetie; you didn't meet Mrs. Eastgard," Leda called from across the room.

Helen smiled sadly at Alex, ducked her head and started towards her mother.

"Mom, wait. Come say hello to Alex," Kelly called out.

Leda approached cautiously. She knew Alex as the best friend of that boy who had died, and she knew that that tragedy had forged a strange bond between him and her daughter Kelly. But as he shook her hand politely and thanked her for coming to their home, she saw before her a nice-looking, neatly dressed, serious boy who was apparently coping well with the challenges of his life.

"Mom, Alex just graduated from Amherst College, and now he's in med school at NYU," Kelly said.

"That's very impressive. I am sure you've been making your parents proud."

"Thank you," Alex responded.

"Let's go see Mrs. Eastgard, okay? I looked for you as we were saying hello but you had gone missing," Leda said to Helen.

Alex watched Helen depart, her blonde hair a bright spot in the dark throng occupying his home.

Alex sat back down next to Kelly. "What's Helen doing now?" he asked.

"Nothing much. She's working as a receptionist in a dentist's office. Still living at home. My Mom has encouraged her to take a few classes in community college or something but she's just not interested. She's leading this, this rudderless existence, just waiting for life to happen to her."

Alex nodded. "What about you? Did you move out?"

"I did!" Kelly responded. "I finally have my own apartment. It's on the bad side of Beacon Hill but I can afford it."

"Better than me. All I have is a dorm room."

"My place is tiny, really tiny."

"It can't be smaller than my one room."

"I get about one quart of hot water a day to shower. The landlord's so cheap."

"At least you have your own bathroom; I share a hall bathroom with 30 other guys."

"I have mice for roommates."

"Okay, you win." Alex and Kelly shared a strained smile.

Gradually the house emptied, and Alex and his mother were alone. Olivia stood in the kitchen, squeezing leftovers into their refrigerator, absently brushing crumbs from the table into her hand.

"Alex, now that Dad has...passed on, do you, will you still be coming home some weekends?" Her tone was uncharacteristically wistful and uncertain.

"Of course, I will. Of course."

# CHAPTER 13

"Mom, I'm going for a run!" Alex called out and let himself out the front door. He had dutifully protected his skin with sunblock as he always did when he was out during the day. He ran aimlessly up and down the familiar streets, looking neither to the left nor the right and never looking back, only straight ahead. Faster and faster he ran, anything to occupy his mind, to dispel the thoughts, banish the images that flooded his consciousness, of his father's sickness, his death, his funeral. Flashbacks to happier times struggled to claim Alex's attention too, glimpses of everyday joy: Dad teaching him to ride a bike, Dad giving him *Tarzan*, summer vacations on the Cape. But these sweet recollections only served to heighten the pain Alex felt for the loss of his father. And so he ran, running away from his thoughts, praying for fatigue profound enough to still his mind.

As he ran he realized he was passing the path to the reservoir. He slowed, then stopped, reminded of the other sorrow. It had been four years, a little over four years, since he had come to the reservoir. Was that enough time? Should he venture down this path? Were the ghosts of his childhood waiting for him in the shadows of the surrounding woods? And would they welcome him gently or rebuke him? Chastise him for failing to prevent a tragedy? He stepped cautiously onto the path leading to the reservoir, listening for accusations, but all he heard was the slight rustle of the leaves of ancient trees swaying softly in the mild breeze, the soft crumbling of fallen leaves beneath his feet, the sudden snap of a little twig.

Alex passed through the ring of trees and emerged into the sunshine. All was quiet. No admonishing whispers taunted him from the shadows. He reached the edge of the water and surveyed its sparkling surface, just as beautiful as he recalled it. He remembered the day Patrick had purloined a bottle of Sam Adams, and how they had joyfully shared it, here by the edge of the reservoir, before casting the bottle into the water. *I'll bet that bottle is still out there somewhere*, Alex thought. "We had some good times, didn't we, Patrick?" addressing this question more to himself than to his lost friend.

The reservoir was always beautiful, even on the day that Patrick died, and Alex had wandered here, trying to find someplace to be alone. He turned and saw the bench where he had sat, where he had collapsed, on that terrible day. The bench had aged, the wooden planks more worn than they had been four years ago. There had been so much blood on his clothes and his skin, Patrick's blood, and he had left its mark on that bench. Alex recalled sitting toward one end of the bench; he studied the wood for blood stains but could see nothing but graying wood with a scarred and pitted surface. Slowly he sat down, in the middle of the bench, next to the spot where he had last sat. This is where his father had found him. Philip had heard what had happened, and somehow knew to come to this place to find Alex and bring him home. He wondered now, how long had his father looked for him? Was this the first place he had come? Or the tenth? Alex had never asked. He had never thought about it before, and now he would never know.

Slowly, filled with apprehension, he lowered his hand to the very spot on the bench where he had sat spattered with the blood of his friend. He half-expected his touch to release some evil, some demon to punish him, but all he felt was the warmth of the sunshine soaked up by the wood.

"Patrick, I want to say I'm sorry. I could have stopped it. I'm so sorry," he whispered to himself. "I wonder what you'd be doing now. Job? Grad school? Would you have married Kelly?"

From far, far away, or perhaps from deep within his heart, he heard very faintly, "Not your fault."

"Patrick?" Alex's asked, unbelieving, but only the rustling of the leaves replied. He waited a long time, wondering how he could have imagined hearing Patrick's voice, but reveling nonetheless in the illusion of the unexpected gift of absolution.

Alex spoke again, in a voice no louder than breathing, "My Dad died. Just two weeks ago. The eye cancer got him after all."

"Not enough time," the faint voice responded.

Alex's head snapped up, and he scanned the surface of the reservoir, the ring of trees, and listened. The sound of the breeze, the lapping of the water, the disinterested squawk of a crow, the distant hearty bark of a dog, the faraway voices of carefree people: surely these had somehow combined and in the chaos of his mind, turned into the sound of his friend's voice. He sighed and stood to continue his run back home. His mother would have dinner on the table at 6:00, and he would disappoint her if he was late.

Olivia sat in her usual armchair, watching the evening news and sipping her martini, as Alex came through the door.

"There you are, dear. You just have time to take a shower before dinner."

"Okay, Mom," Alex replied, patiently, dutifully.

"Alex, I made up two martinis in case you'd like one. Still nice and cold." The familiar cocktail shaker glistened with its accustomed condensation on the table beside Olivia.

"I don't really like martinis. Do we have any beer?"

"Beer! I hadn't thought of that." Olivia sat up even straighter in her chair. "I can get some for next time you come. Is there a certain type?"

"Yeah, Sam Adams. Can't go wrong with Sam Adams."

"Sam Adams. I'll remember that." She nodded slowly and pursed her lips, as if to seal this critical memory inside her head.

Alex bounded up the stairs for his shower. When he returned his mother was still in her armchair, glaring at the news anchor and muttering.

"What's wrong, Mom?"

"It's a disgrace. You elect people to public office, and this is what you get in return. Corruption, Alex, corruption!"

Alex noticed that the lid was off the cocktail shaker, which had been emptied while he showered.

"Another thing, Alex. This is important. To make a good martini, keep the gin in the refrigerator. Then, when you shake it with ice, there's not much melting and your drink isn't watered down. And don't overdo it with the vermouth. Just a dash. Your father used to say, just pass the cap over the glass, no need to pour any in."

"Mom, I don't like martinis."

"That's because you're young. Wait until you're older. It takes time to learn to appreciate a good martini," she stated with conviction. "Your father loved my martinis," she added dreamily.

The news ended, indicating that it was 6:00. Olivia turned off the TV, stood and marched to the kitchen. "You go sit down, dear. I'll bring it all out."

"Looks great, Mom," Alex said as Olivia loaded the table with enough food to feed 10 hungry med students.

"Thank you, Alex. I think the beef stew came out very nicely. The meat is so tender. I usually get stew meat; it's quite economical. They sell that in chunks, you know. But choice sirloin was on sale so I splurged. You can tell the difference."

"Smells great."

"Yes, now I wasn't sure if you wanted stew over rice or over mashed potatoes, so I made both," Olivia said, proffering the two bowls.

"Oh, ah, potatoes, I guess." Alex spooned mashed potatoes onto his plate, hollowed out the center and filled that with stew. "It's delicious."

"We have French bread also. Want some? And real butter, not margarine."

"Oh, sure, thanks." Alex broke off one end of the long crusty loaf and buttered it thoughtfully.

Olivia gave herself a small serving and ate slowly, pausing to sip the last of the martini. "So how is school going?"

"Fine, I guess. It's still early in the year." *For god's sake, all I think about is Dad; getting through the day is hard for me,* Alex wanted to say, but he decided it was easier to play the game her way than to have a real conversation.

"Do you have a favorite class?" she asked eagerly. She leaned forward, eyes bright.

"It's too early to say." Alex studied the interesting geometric distribution of vegetables and meat that lay on the bed of mashed potatoes.

"Do you have friends?" This time her tone was solicitous.

"Sure. All the guys on the floor of my dorm are great. Kind of crazy, but good guys," Alex answered casually.

"Crazy? How do you mean?" Olivia was intent on getting to the bottom of any irregularities that might impinge on Alex's education.

Alex recalled Ben and Steve's conversation about girls, but knew it was unfit for his mother's ears. "I don't know. People just like to let loose. Play their music loud, you know." Alex hoped that response was sufficiently innocuous.

"Loud music? Are you able to study? You must have to go to the library. Is the library open late? When your father and I were in school there were rules about that sort of thing." Her mental image of medical school as a sacrosanct academic haven was beginning to crumble.

"It's not a problem, Mom. You worry too much." She talks about Dad like the high school sweetheart she hasn't seen for 40 years, he thought. An idealized version of a fond memory, already poignant rather than painful.

"Well. I will tell you one thing I worry about. When are you going to return that casserole dish to Mrs. Fletcher?" Olivia set down her martini glass with a distinct clank.

"I don't know. Soon, I guess."

"How about tonight? I feel quite awkward having held onto it for so long. What if she had wanted to use it?"

"Okay."

"Be sure to tell her it was delicious."

"Okay." Alex didn't recall what kind of casserole it was and was pretty sure he hadn't tried it. Hopefully he wouldn't be asked too many exploratory questions if he complimented the dish.

*

As Alex hurried outside, lovely autumn hurried along with him; sunlight dwindled with each minute that passed. The crescent moon, guardian of the darkening sky, was a scimitar of old ivory sailing above him as Alex and the spotlessly clean Pyrex casserole dish reached the Fletcher home. He stood outside the door and rang the bell. He recalled the last time he stood on this threshold and shivered. He should get back to New York. There were too many memories here; struggling with them would be the end of him.

As he waited by the door, he heard, indistinctly, female voices.

The door opened, and there was Helen. Alex had assumed that Mrs. Fletcher would answer the door, receive the casserole dish from his grateful hands, and he would depart. It never occurred to him that Helen would make herself available for mundane tasks like answering the door, and yet there she was. His heart started to pound.

"Helen! Hi, I'm, ah, my mom sent me to return this dish to your mom," Alex said.

"Oh, hi, Alex, thanks." She took the dish carefully from his hands. He allowed himself several quick seconds to take her in. Her hair was back in a heavy ponytail, and she was wearing pink and white-striped pajamas. Standing before him like this, she did not seem as tall as he had thought she was. Perhaps she usually wore high heels, he hypothesized, and glanced down. The fabric at the bottom of the pajama legs puddled around her little white feet. She must have noticed his look, as she self-consciously slid her right foot over her left so that only one bare foot showed.

"I'm sorry, were you about to go to bed? I guess it's kind of late," Alex apologized.

"Oh, no, I just took a shower, no, it's not late."

Alex looked at her face, free of make-up, child-like and innocent, and greedily inhaled her sweet, just-showered smell, knowing that this moment was about to end. "Well, thank your mom for us. Casserole was delicious. We really appreciated it."

Leda Fletcher appeared at the door. "Helen, who's- oh, Alex, come in."

"Thanks. I was just returning your casserole dish. We really appreciated it. I'm sorry it's so late. Sorry to disturb."

"No, no, come in. Helen and I were just about to watch a movie. Come on in." Leda stepped back and ushered Alex into the house. "Tim is at his poker game, and you probably know, Kelly moved into Boston. So it's pretty quiet tonight."

"Thanks."

"Sit down, sit down. Feel like watching a movie?" Leda gestured toward the sofa, as Helen curled up in the old recliner she favored.

"Sure, what movie?" Alex eased himself slowly onto the end of the sofa next to Helen in her recliner, hoping she would not slip away.

Leda gestured with a videotape. "*When Harry Met Sally*. It's really cute."

"Sounds good. Thanks."

"Our tradition is, I make a big bowl of microwave popcorn for me and Helen, and she eats three kernels, and I end up eating all the rest and getting mad at myself. If you could help out with the popcorn, I'd be grateful."

"Sure!"

"Good! I'll go pop the corn." Leda hurried out of the room.

Helen smiled at Alex and tucked in her feet.

So here he was, all alone with Helen, Alex thought, and he couldn't think of one clever thing to say.

"Kelly said you had a job. Do you like it?" he ventured.

"No, it's really boring. And I have to take the T. I'm trying to save up for a car, so I can at least stop riding the T."

"Oh, that's good. Are you almost there?"

"No. Long way to go. Doesn't pay very well." Helen looked down. "It's not a very good job."

"Could you look for something better?"

"I guess, but..."

Leda returned with an aromatic bowl of butter-soaked microwave popcorn and a thick wad of napkins. "Let's start the movie," she said cheerfully, and hit the remote. "Helen, Alex, take some," she said, handing the bowl to Alex and sitting down toward the other end of the sofa.

"Oh, Helen, baby, are your feet cold?" Leda hauled herself off the couch, retrieved a plaid throw from a cabinet and tucked it around Helen's lap, as Helen leaned to one side of Leda's torso to see the movie.

"Alex, you okay? Need anything? Can you see okay?" Leda asked.

"Yeah, fine, thanks."

"Isn't Meg Ryan the cutest little thing? I just love her," Leda exclaimed. "Here, take this popcorn. Your turn," she said, as she passed the bowl to Alex.

Alex had trouble concentrating on the movie. There was Helen, just two feet away from him, curled up in pajamas. The smell of the popcorn aggressively filled the room, but once in a while Alex could discern Helen's sweet fragrance wafting delicately through the scent of artificial butter. At one point, Helen took her hair out of its ponytail and fluffed it up. Alex watched this display out of the corner of his eye and could scarcely breathe. Could she be doing this for him, because he is here? But she seemed to be engrossed in the movie, seemed to have forgotten he was there.

"You ask me, she should be able to do better than Billy Crystal. Look how cute she is!" Leda downed some more popcorn.

Helen was silent. Alex felt compelled to respond. "But Billy Crystal is funny. She'd never have to worry about being bored."

"Maybe. She could still do better," said Leda, the die-hard Meg Ryan fan.

"Helen?" Alex whispered as he held out the popcorn bowl.

"Oh, thanks." She took the bowl, ate a few kernels and handed it back.

Time passed, and as the popcorn bowl rotated among the three of them, Alex was able to calm down and enjoy the evening, peppered as it was with Leda's commentary.

"Oh, Alex, I forgot. Something to drink? Coke? Beer?" Leda asked.

"Oh sure. I'll take a beer."

Leda hurried into the kitchen and returned with a frosty bottle of Sam Adams. "This okay?"

"Absolutely, thanks. My favorite." Alex relaxed a little more.

"Oh, look, I love this scene." Leda sighed.

"You are really into this movie, Mrs. Fletcher!" Alex said, and surreptitiously turned toward Helen and winked. She smothered a giggle.

"Yeah, it's one of my favorites. I think Meg Ryan looks something like Kelly, except that Kelly's a brunette. Helen, what do you think?"

"Aw, Mom, I don't know. I hope she can find someone cuter than Billy Crystal."

Leda nodded. This assessment passed for wisdom in the Fletcher household. "Not only cuter but less neurotic."

Alex laughed. "I think Kelly's too busy with the Globe to worry about dating."

"You're right there," Leda replied. "I think she's found her niche. And our boys, well, Charlie's got a job as an assistant coach at Boston College. Paul decided he wants to do physical therapy, so he's back in school. His dream is to work with the Patriots."

"I didn't know about Charlie and Paul. That's great."

"Mom, don't you want to see the movie?" Helen asked, her tone verging on whiny. She had extended her feet, keeping them wrapped in the throw.

"Sorry! I'll be quiet," Leda said in a stage whisper. "More popcorn, anyone? I can make more," she said, holding the empty bowl aloft.

Alex shook his head.

"No, no more," Helen added.

Leda exited to drop the bowl in the kitchen. As she set the bowl down in the sink, she paused and permitted herself a little smile. She was proud of her kids. Her big strong boys, on track to do what they loved, and Kelly who had worked so hard and landed her dream job! Her Kelly, so sincere, so ardent, so uncompromising, more of a grown-up than Tim in a lot of ways. Helen was the only one who hadn't found her calling yet. But it would happen, surely. She hoped it would happen. Having Alex show up had been a nice surprise. Nice for Helen to spend time with someone her own age. Amazing how after all he'd been through, he really seemed quite nice.

Helen turned to Alex. "It's all about Kelly, all the time, except when it's about Charlie and Paul," she whispered. *She never has anything good to say about me; I'm the family disappointment*, Helen thought, unwilling to voice this out loud.

"Oh, Helen, I'm sure that's not how she meant it. Your Mom seems so nice." Alex was surprised to hear the bitterness and resignation in her soft voice.

Leda re-entered the living room to view the closing scenes of the movie.

On the way home, Alex replayed the evening in his mind. There was much to consider. First there was Mrs. Fletcher. She seemed so *normal* compared to his own mother. He liked Leda's friendly, open, come-right-in approach, her efforts to make him feel welcome in their home. And then there was Helen, a Helen he had not known before this night, an approachable Helen, a Helen with insecurities, not the goddess on a pedestal he had always thought her to be. Her '*Hey, Alex, thanks for coming. It was great to see you*' still echoed like an enchantment in his ears. Had she sounded a little sad? He thought so. He wondered if there was something he could do for her. And he wondered if there was any chance she might possibly have any interest in him. He didn't get the sense of that; she spoke to him as an old friend, nothing more. If that is how things were to be, he could accept that. As he approached his own front door he reflected that this was the most tranquil he had felt for a long time. He paused to study the night sky; his gaze wandered over the glittering constellations as he allowed himself to wonder, to hope, that life would be easier, happier in the future.

Alex quietly entered his home. The TV was on; Olivia was watching the 10:00 news. Except for the half-hearted glow from their old TV, the room was dark.

"Mom?" Alex asked. His mother was sitting in her usual spot in front of the TV, enveloped in darkness. She sat up a little straighter in her chair, adjusted the neckline of her robe, pressed her hands to her face and then calmly folded her hands in her lap.

"Alex, there you are. It took quite a while to deliver that casserole dish."

"I stayed to watch a movie with Helen and her Mom."

"You might have called; I was worried something had happened to you."

"Oh, I'm sorry. I should have called. I'm beat; I'm going to bed." He had meant to work a little this evening, but it was getting late and his eyes were too tired to start reading now. He would get up early tomorrow and get some studying in. He started up the stairs, but then paused and turned around.

"Mom, don't you want some light?" he said, flipping on the light at the foot of the stairs. He was startled to see that his mother's eyes were red, her cheeks marked by the tracks of tears.

"Are you okay?"

"I'm fine dear," she said. "I was just concerned for you, that's all."

That's all? He thought. Poor Mom. He recalled with guilt how only a few minutes ago he had compared Helen's mother favorably with his own Mom. He hurried to her and wrapped his arms around her as she sat in her chair, and she hugged him back with an intensity that took him completely by surprise.

# CHAPTER 14

It was still early, and Ye Olde Corner Bookstore was quiet. The lone customer was an elderly woman who had purchased a poster displaying the equestrian statue of Paul Revere in front of the Old North Church. Once she had limped out, Giuli and Andy were alone in the bookstore.

"Andy, can I tell you something?" Giuli asked cautiously.

"Yes, Miss Stewart? How can I be of assistance?" Andy answered, each word sheathed in frost. Since Giuli had been promoted to assistant manager, Andy had been disgruntled, and blamed Giuli.

*Shoot*, thought Giuli. *This may not work. Not my fault I got promoted over her. If she could take out the nose ring during work hours, and trade in the leather for clothing made of fabric, she'd have this job, not me.*

"Andy, come on, I want to tell you something. I want your perspective," Giuli tried again.

"Doesn't the assistant manager report to the manager? Take it up with that bozo," Andy said. *The one who made you, not me, assistant manager*, she thought loudly.

Giuli heard her, as surely as though she had spoken aloud. "Andy, just listen. You were here when this happened before. So maybe you'll know what it means, or what I should do."

Andy grunted, grudgingly. She would not admit it, but she was a little curious to know what the impetus for Giuli's bloody verbal diarrhea was.

"Okay. Listen. Remember, when it was my first summer here," Giuli began.

"Yeah, I remember," Andy muttered. *That was before you stabbed me in the back and took the job I'd been wanting!*

"And one day I got sick and dizzy, and I went and sat down in the back. Do you remember?"

"Not sure. Wait, yeah, I remember. I thought sure you had a brain tumor."

"No, I didn't. But something terrible happened that day. One of my class-mates from high school got killed. Car hit him. It happened just a couple of hours after I started feeling sick."

Andy grunted.

"Well, a few days before that happened, at graduation, when I hugged him, saying goodbye, I had this weird scary sensation that something was going to happen. To him, I mean."

"So?" Andy's tone was sarcastic but at least she was listening.

"So back in September I started feeling sick again, but not dizzy like before, instead really nauseous. And I got better, and just figured it was some virus or food poisoning or something."

"So?" Andy's expression was non-committal. One by one she squeezed each of the six stud earrings dotting the helix of her right ear to be certain their backs were firmly engaged.

"Well, my mother was in the grocery store recently and ran into the mother of another kid in my class in high school, a good friend of mine, and turns out the father of my friend died that week." Giuli rushed the words, anxious to air them all while Andy was still listening, but she did pause momentarily to give thanks that she had not been present for the meeting of those mothers. It was bound to have been humiliating.

"What week?" Andy asked impatiently. "When the mother was out shopping?"

"No, no. He died back in September. He died exactly when I was feeling sick. But we just learned about it recently."

"Sounds like a coincidence."

"Maybe, but even more years ago I had this episode where everything went black, and I had this premonition that something was really wrong at the house of this friend, same friend whose father died."

"Yeah?"

"Turns out, I found out later, that the father had a cancer in his eye and got his eye taken out, same time as I was having this, this visual black-out. Then when he died, it was of this cancer."

"Cancer in the eye? That is so gross! But, there are only three, maybe four times this kind of thing happened?"

"Once in a while I have a feeling about something, like I know something might happen before it does, and sometimes it does happen. But not always, and not intense like the episodes I told you about. Those times I had this awful sense of impending doom. It's so scary when it's happening. What do you think? Do you believe in ESP, or second sight or whatever you call it?"

"I don't know. I don't believe in any of that ESP crap but it's hard to explain what you're telling me. Maybe it's just chance. But maybe you have a gift." Andy's nose ring vibrated gently as she spoke. She peered intently into Giuli's eyes, looking for some clue to the truth. "If it happens again, tell me."

Giuli nodded. "I will. Thanks for listening."

*

On Old Olympus's Towering Top, A Finn and A German Viewed A Hop, Alex muttered to himself. O-O-O: Olfactory, Optic, Oculomotor are first, second and third. Okay. T-T, fourth and fifth: Trochlear, Trigeminal. Sixth is A- Abducens. Seventh is F- Facial. A German. G is glossopharyngeal. What is A for? He checked the anatomy textbook. The eighth cranial nerve is vestibulocochlear. So what is A for? Stupid mnemonics, he thought. He skimmed the text. Ah, vestibulocochlear nerve is also called auditory. Okay, Viewed, V is for vagus. A for accessory, or rather spinal accessory, and Hop, H for hypoglossal. All set with cranial nerves; what's next? He flipped to the next page of the Atlas of Human Anatomy. The base of the skull. And each of the many little bumps and divots and full-thickness holes had a name he had to learn. When Alex decided to switch to pre-med, he had no idea that this was how he'd be spending his time.

Alex stood and stretched, first his hamstrings, then his quads. He bent over, clasped his ankles and held for a count of 10. He had switched majors halfway through college, and while he had met the requirements for medical school, he had had a lot less biology than many of his classmates. For them, much of this material was a review while Alex was learning it for the first time. He glanced at the clock. 9:15. He would sit and study for another 15 minutes, then he would treat himself to another cup of coffee. Three months into med school and he was already a caffeine addict!

He sat down again and studied the complex anatomy of the base of the skull. As soon as his clock radio hit 9:30, he stood, crossed his small dorm room and poured a cup of strong coffee. He pulled a carton of half and half from his tiny refrigerator and added enough to ameliorate the coffee's bitterness. As he stirred the coffee with his one and only metal spoon, he recalled studying history and how that all seemed to come to him more easily. There were a lot of names and dates to remember but each name was associated with a personality and an interesting story. He could still list every Plantagenet from Geoffrey, Count of Anjou and his son Henry II, the first

Plantagenet king, to Richard III, the last of the Plantagenets. And he knew something about each of them, almost like family. But this Anatomy class, you barely had time to learn the names of the structures much less what they do, when another load of body parts to learn gets dumped on you. Okay, back to the desk. He resolved to sit and study without stop until 10:30.

When 10:30 arrived Alex stood and stretched again. He looked out his east-facing window, past the chaos of FDR Drive, into the wide blue expanse of sky. What a beautiful day, he thought. What a way to spend a Saturday! He glanced back at his desk. His nemesis, the Anatomy textbook and its fraternal twin, the Anatomy atlas, glared back at him. *I need a real break*, he told himself. *I can study later*.

Alex grabbed a change of clothes and took a quick shower. He returned to his room, dropped his dirty clothes onto his bed, pulled on his windbreaker, grabbed his wallet and started back down the hall toward the elevators.

Sarah, one of six in his cadaver group, had grown up in Manhattan, and while painstakingly dissecting the facial nerve, she had shared information on the attractions of the city. Sarah had raved about the Metropolitan Museum of Art, and Alex had decided he would go and have a look.

He exited via the plate-glass doors on First Avenue and walked west until he hit Lexington Avenue, looked around and spotted the dark rectangle in the pavement marked with a placard on the railing proclaiming this to be the entrance to the subway. He descended, determined which way was north and made his way to the platform. He paced for a while, waiting for the train, past an unconscious drunken man sprawled face to the wall on one of the benches. Dark blue tiles set in a background of smooth white ceramic tiles covering the walls of the subway tunnel indicated that this station was at 33rd Street. Alex found a different bench and sat. It was quiet except for the distant rumble of a faraway train and the intermittent snoring of the drunk. When the train arrived, Alex stepped aboard, abandoning his temporary companion on his bench. He wondered idly if he would ever see the man on the bench again, perhaps as a patient in Bellevue, the big city hospital affiliated with his med school.

As the train sped north, Alex watched as the numbers of the street for each of the stations whizzed by, streaks of midnight blue against a white background, only legible once the train had almost come to a halt. He carefully noted each stop, to avoid overshooting his goal. There was 42nd Street, he thought, peering out the train's windows at letters settling into focus. 42nd Street, Grand Central Station. And then 59th Street, which he knew was Central Park South. When he reached 86th street, he stepped quickly off the train and headed for the exit.

As Alex emerged on the Upper East Side he was greeted with tentative sunshine and a bracing wind. He pulled the sleeves of his windbreaker down past his wrists and evaluated his surroundings. Not bad, he thought. The apartment buildings looked much more elegant, clad in creamy white stone, their doorways marked by spotless awnings, than the pedestrian red brick and mortar buildings he was used to around his med school. As he reached 5th Avenue, the imposing facade of the Metropolitan Museum of Art sprawled before him, occupying a broad swath of the eastern edge of Central Park. He passed between carts on the sidewalk selling hot dogs and pretzels and strode up the expansive staircase. If it weren't quite so cold and windy today, this would be a great place to sit and watch the world go by.

He entered the museum, reverently, and looked around. The ceiling of the spacious lobby soared above him, and a crowd of museum-goers, swept inside by the forceful wind whistling down Fifth Avenue, surged around him. He squeezed through them, intent on scoring a map and figuring out what he wanted to see.

Alex wandered toward the galleries. He found himself in a Greco-Roman sculpture hall and cast his eyes on the figures around him. There was a bust of Hadrian, the great builder, with sightless eyes regarding him sternly. And a Roman matron with a complicated hair-do who looked past him impassively. And statues from classical Greece, and from the Hellenistic period, their images trapped for all time in gleaming marble. Along the walls were cases displaying coins in silver and gold corresponding to the times of the sculptures. Alex studied the coins. Tiny little works of art, each one.

An exquisite tetradrachm displayed the handsome profile of Alexander the Great's helmeted head gazing forward into eternity. Alex edged to his right and focused on another coin. Ptolemy, what a profile he had! His chin was a bit more protuberant, his cheeks a little fleshier, and his nose distinctly less straight than Alexander's pure classical image with its perfect aquiline nose. Ptolemy's wavy hair was held back by a simple diadem. Probably more of a real likeness than that one of Alexander the Great, Alex decided. *I sense your power, oh Ptolemy,* Alex said silently to the coin. *I can hear you shouting orders, I can see you passing judgment, I can imagine you laying claim to Egypt and establishing the Ptolemaic dynasty.*

Alex stepped back to the coin showing Alexander, reverently touched his fingers to the protective glass and looked more closely. He felt the energy, the drive, the ambition of this young king as though they were his own. Was there a flicker of awareness in his silver eyes? *Speak to me! Turn to me and speak!* he commanded in a soft whisper, but the image paid no heed.

Alex let his eyes drift to the next row of coins. One showed the head of a curly-haired, clean-shaven man with three dolphins swimming in a circle around him, while another showed a four-horse chariot rendered in meticulous detail. *This is amazing! I could be here forever and never get bored.*

With regret he forced himself to look at his watch. Almost 4 pm. While he felt some guilt for taking such a long break from studying, he couldn't leave without taking a quick look at the second floor. He was greeted by a huge number of marvelous paintings. He didn't know much about paintings, he admitted to himself, and looked around, uncertain where to begin. Then he caught sight of a face he recognized: a stunning portrait of sly Richelieu, elegant in his cardinal's robes. *I should get back and study*, he told himself. *You'll see me again, Cardinal*, Alex thought, casting a lingering glance at the master diplomat, who acknowledged Alex with a condescending sneer.

Alex reached his dorm room around 5 pm, took off his jacket and prepared to study. Today was good, he thought. He had seen works of art created over a span of thousands of years, none of which had anything to do with memorizing cranial nerves. It helped to put life into perspective. *I should do this every week. Once a week, every week, I should do something non-medical.*

He extracted the map of the museum from his pocket, unfolded it and laid it down on his desk. His finger traced the rooms he had visited. There was much more to see, he realized. He turned the pamphlet over and spied a paragraph about something called the Cloisters. 'The Cloisters is a branch of the museum dedicated to medieval art and architecture,' he read from the brochure. Visions of Plantagenets swirled in his mind's eye. Located in the northernmost part of Manhattan, in Fort Tryon Park, it says, accessible by subway or bus... Maybe next weekend.

As Alex carefully folded the map, he thought how much he would have liked to call someone to talk about all he had seen and done and learned today. He would have loved to be able to call his father and tell him about it. Or Patrick. What would Patrick have said? Probably would have rolled his eyes and told him to stick to sports. Or maybe not, Alex mused. He could call his mother, but her only concern would be when he would next be visiting Brookline. The day had been glorious, but now there was a hollowness to it. He sighed and opened his anatomy textbook.

*

The group of five clustered around their diminutive cadaver, a little old lady they had affectionately named Minnie. The sixth member of the group, Jerry Grossman, spent every weekend with family on Long Island, and was frequently missing on Monday mornings; his tardiness went unremarked.

"Sarah, I took your suggestion about the Metropolitan Museum and went Saturday. It was great. Thanks for the recommendation," Alex said.

"Glad you liked it. It's a favorite of mine," Sarah responded.

"Hey, Ben, move the Isro out of the way. You're blocking the whole thoracic cavity," Steve complained.

"Nothing wrong with my hair. The ladies love my unshorn locks. They call me Samson," Ben replied, standing up and shaking his dark curls.

"Please," Cheryl groaned, as she held the heart steady for Sarah, who was clipping the coronary arteries away from the myocardium.

Sarah was back in New York City after four years at Berkeley. She had long brown hair with blond highlights that had not been refreshed since before the school year began. As the left anterior descending artery came free, Sarah paused in her dissection, shoving wire-rimmed eyeglasses up her nose with the back of her latex-gloved wrist and then resting her hands on the edge of the open rib cage.

"What do you think?" Sarah said.

"I'd say Minnie has atherosclerosis." Steve said.

Just then Jerry sauntered in, looking relaxed and well-fed after a weekend of maternal pampering. "What's going on? How was everyone's weekend?" he asked, his voice booming across the lab.

"Nice of you to show up. Some of us are working here," Sarah grumbled.

"Don't be mad, Sarah; Mom packed me more treats than I can eat, and I promise to share," Jerry said, snapping on disposable gloves.

"Guys, come on. Someone start on the circumflex," Cheryl whispered.

Alex smiled quietly. He really liked his cadaver group.

*

Alex emerged from the subway at the southern end of Fort Tryon Park and looked around. The sunshine was brighter and the wind less vindictive today than it had been last week when he visited the Metropolitan Museum of Art. A soothing landscape of rolling hills and clusters of trees greeted him. This late in the fall, the trees were bereft of their leaves, and the park's color palette consisted of shades of brown rather than lush greens. It must be beautiful here once the weather turns warm, he thought. To his left Alex could hear the rumbling of water; that must be the Hudson River. If this were merry old England, Alex told himself, any king would be glad to have such a park as part of his realm. He could hardly believe he was still in Manhattan.

Alex strode briskly along the road to the Cloisters, enjoying the tranquil surroundings. Scanning the way before him, Alex was greeted by a square tower protruding over the tree tops. He quickened his pace, and the trees parted to reveal the stony mass of the Cloisters. He hurried to the entrance. Few other visitors had made their way here today, and the place was quiet. Faintly he heard strains of period music, as he wandered about. He walked softly through rooms of finely dressed stone hung with huge tapestries, conscious of his footsteps echoing into the vaulted ceilings. He saw a chapel sternly flanked by saints against pillars and containing a magnificent altar, and sarcophaguses in number topped by reclining images of their one-time occupants in Gothic style. He walked among the sarcophaguses, studying their effigies. Here lay a noblewoman, her arms modestly crossed against her chest; there a warrior, depicted in his armor; then a nobleman, even in pitted gray stone, richly attired. He walked around the chapel and then returned to the warrior. *Who were you?* Alex wondered. In the eerie silence he could almost imagine the ghost of the dead man rising from his sarcophagus, striding noiselessly toward him and announcing that he was Edward the Black Prince, clad in the very raiment he wore when laying waste to broad swaths of France. Alex waited, but no ghosts materialized. He slowly slipped out of the chapel.

He found his way to the interior courtyard and the surrounding walkway, the cloisters, delimited by an arcade of elegant columns topped by capitals with intricate stonework. Alex was surprised to see that the capitals were not uniform. Birds with scaly wings, whimsical animals and strange faces that might have been human were woven into curling tendrils of stone decorating the capitals.

His explorations took him to the upper level, where he found an herb garden, each section meticulously labeled in English and Latin. Alex could imagine a diligent monk, clad in coarse brown robes tied with a hempen belt, carefully placing the labels. He felt he had stepped into the past, into a world apart. Approaching the parapet, he looked down and discovered a breathtaking view of the Hudson River rippling past him. He rested his forearms on the rock wall and gazed for a long time at the water, thinking of nothing at all, just enjoying the beauty of the place.

The music he had heard indistinctly earlier now seemed closer. After a while it ceased, and he heard a man's voice, formal, measured, although Alex could not discern the words. Curious, he re-entered the interior and walked toward the sound. In another stone chamber he found the source of the voice. A wedding was underway; bride and groom stood side by side before a clergyman conducting the ceremony. To either side were groomsmen in tuxedoes and bridesmaids dressed for cool weather in velvet gowns the color of red wine. Alex smiled as he watched from the shadows. What a wonderful place for a wedding. As he watched, the bride turned and a ribbon of fair hair came into view.

Helen! Alex's heart skipped a beat and he stopped breathing. That's Helen. That's her hair. Helen! He put his hand on an adjacent column to steady himself and forced himself to take several deep breaths. He watched the couple intently. The groom was not at all familiar to him, and after observing the bride for a while, he decided it was probably not Helen, just his imagination playing tricks on him. He retreated into the shadows, returned to his post in the herb garden and thought about what he had seen. And then it came to him, like a bolt of lightning. It was a message, clear and true. It was a warning: at any time, Helen might meet someone and get married and be lost to him forever.

Thoughts tumbled in disorder into and out of his mind. He recalled the night he had visited her home to return the casserole dish; he had had such a nice evening with her. It was refreshing, just like his visits to the Metropolitan Museum and the Cloisters. She had been so nice to him that night. He should have called her afterwards. It would have been easy. But he didn't. He was so preoccupied with the loss of his father, concern for his mother, the burden of schoolwork, and also, he was afraid, deep down, that she would reject him. Would she go out with him now? She was so reserved it was hard to know what she was thinking. But if she was just living with her parents, working at a job she didn't like, perhaps she would like to be asked out. Unless she was already dating someone else. It had been a couple of months since he had seen her, so it was possible.

Alex leapt to his feet, hurried to the exit, raced down the road to the subway and rushed toward the platform, taking the steps two at a time, bounding onto a southbound train just before its doors slammed shut. Alex collapsed into a seat and tried to be optimistic. But then the memory of what had happened the one other time he had asked Helen out, when he asked her to go to prom with him, flared before him. She turned him down, because Hector had just asked her. Alex broke out in a cold sweat. What if that happened again? Not Hector, he was gone, but someone else. Why hadn't he called Helen before? What was he thinking?

When the subway finally reached his stop, Alex erupted onto the street and ran all the way back to his dorm. When he reached his room, he tried to calm down, drank a cup of water from his coffee mug, and practiced what he would say, trying to keep his voice from shaking. He dialed the number, which he knew by heart.

Helen answered, "Hello?"

For a few agonizing seconds, Alex could not speak. When his voice returned, he said, "Helen?" but with a humiliating squeak in the middle of the first syllable. Angry with himself, Alex tried again. "Helen, how are you?"

"Fine. Who's this?"

"Oh, sorry, it's Alex. Sorry. Were you busy? I don't want to interrupt."

"No. No, not at all. Just hanging out."

"Oh, good." Get to the point, Alex told himself. He took a deep breath. "Helen, I'm planning to go home next weekend, and I was wondering if I could take you to dinner on Saturday."

The silence seemed to last an eternity, but when it ended, the wait proved worthwhile.

"Sure, that would be nice." Her tone was non-committal, not enthusiastic, but she had said yes. That was enough, and he was grateful.

"Okay, great. I'll come by around, around 7, if that's okay."

"Sure, that's fine." Her tone was so neutral; he wished he knew what she was thinking.

"I'm so glad you can go. I'll make a reservation somewhere nice," Alex said, relief finally loosening his tongue.

"That sounds good."

"Okay, see you next Saturday," Alex prepared to end the phone call.

"Okay, thanks," Helen said. A pause and then she added, "Alex, thank you for thinking of me. I'm really looking forward to it."

Those last few words rang so sincerely, and with such a heart-wrenching undertone of vulnerability, that Alex's heart almost stopped.

"Me too, Helen. Thank you," he managed to say.

Leda Fletcher approached from the kitchen, where she had been preparing dinner. "Who was that, sweetie?"

"Alex. You know, Alex Eastgard."

"What did he want?"

"He invited me to go for dinner next Saturday, when he's home from school."

"Oh, that's nice. Nice boy. And a medical student. Must be smart. And a hard worker."

"I guess so."

Leda sensed that this was an opportunity not to be overlooked. "Well, wear something nice. Do you want to get your hair done?"

Helen looked at Leda. "Mom, what is with you? I'm just having dinner with a guy I went to high school with. I mean I'd like to get a haircut, but this is not some big thing."

Leda turned away and crossed the fingers of both hands. Over her shoulder she said, "I know, I know, but anyway, it's always nice to look your best. I'll make you an appointment with Leticia at the Swan."

# CHAPTER 15

When he reached the reservoir, Alex paused in his run and sat down on the bench close to the edge of the water. It was December, nearly the winter solstice, and although it was only mid-afternoon, the western horizon already embraced the sun with open arms.

"So, Patrick, I've been dating Helen Fletcher for a year now. I really love her. It makes me so happy to talk with her, just to be with her. She's so beautiful, so elegant. When we're together I feel like the luckiest guy in the world. The few hours I spend with her when I come home are what I live for. I'm thinking, I'm planning to ask her to marry me." Alex recalled their first date with pure joy. She had looked so pretty and seemed so happy. They had spoken of many things. Although now that he thought about it, perhaps he had done most of the talking. But she didn't seem to mind. He remembered asking her what she enjoyed doing. She was reluctant to say at first, but finally she said she liked going to the movies, and so he had invited her to go to the movies with him, for their second date. Since then he had been coming home every other weekend, and always took Helen out on Saturday night.

He wouldn't propose until he had enough saved to get a respectable ring though. While there was enough money for his basic living expenses, buying a good ring was not in the budget. Alex had gotten a job drawing blood 2 hours a day, before classes started in the morning. It didn't pay too well, and the loss of precious sleep left him terribly fatigued, but his savings were growing.

"Are you sure?" Alex thought he heard in reply.

"No doubt about it, Helen's the one for me. I can't imagine not having her in my life. Not after this year, being able to see her." Alex thought of the kisses they'd shared, her lovely mouth against his, his fingers against her silky skin. He let his gaze rest, unfocused, on the glossy surface of the frigid water and waited.

No reply.

"There's just one thing," Alex whispered, as dappled light struggled to penetrate the trees, their branches smoky indigo against the backdrop of the setting sun. "Do you think Helen ever had, Helen was ever, was ever, with Hector?" Alex could not bring himself to pronounce the word "sex" in this context. He considered the indescribable pleasure it would give him to make love to Helen, if she would have him, but this one thing had held him back.

"Don't know," came an ephemeral reply.

"That's the only thing. If she ever did, just the thought of that, thinking of him... touching her...I think that would bother me. I don't know how to find out though. I don't think I can ask Helen. I don't think it would be right."

"You can't ask her," came the reply.

"I'll just have to live with not knowing, I guess." Alex spoke softly to the sunset. The darkening air slipped under his clothes, dissecting the layers, seeking his skin, and he realized that he was cold. As he stood to resume his run, three words echoed in his mind- *Are you sure?*

*

"Helen, think about it. You've been dating Alex for almost a year now. He's a very serious person. He's going to ask you to marry him. I just feel it. You have to think about how you're going to respond." Kelly scanned her sister's face intently, but Helen returned her intensity with indifference.

"I don't know. We'll see what happens." Helen sat forward in the recliner to reach her diet Coke, took a sip, then leaned back. "Why worry about something that might not happen?"

"Helen, come on. I think he loves you deeply. And I don't get the sense of the same depth of feeling from you." She inclined her head toward Helen, hoping for a real discussion. Kelly had cut her hair short, and a cap of saucy curls bounced around her head whenever she spoke.

"Why is this your business?" Helen continued complacently flipping the pages of last month's *Cosmo*, not bothering to meet Kelly's eyes. What if Alex did want to get married? He was always so nice to her, made her feel like someone special. No one else had ever been so good to her. And doctors could be really rich. If she and Alex were married, they would have a nice house together, maybe nicer than her parents'. And go on good vacations, and she wouldn't have to work at the stupid dentist's office.

"Because Alex is just about the best person I know, and he deserves to be with someone who's right for him. He's loyal and hard-working and smart and nice. Do you think you're right for him?" Kelly evaluated her sister with a critical eye. Sure, Helen is pretty, although if Alex could see her right now in the old T-shirt and the baggy sweatpants, he might get quite a shock. And her head is absolutely empty. Alex should be with an intellectual.

"What's that supposed to mean?" Helen asked, trying to remain calm. She turned the pages of her magazine, thinking about what marriage with Alex might be like.

"If you were to get married, would you be good to him? Would you be good *for* him? Would you deserve someone with so much integrity?" Kelly persisted.

"Don't get all Wellesley on me. Just because I didn't go to some fancy college." Kelly could be very irritating. One thing nagged at Helen though: Hector. When she was with Alex, she often mentally compared the two of them. Alex just wasn't as, as hot as Hector. Alex made her feel pretty and respected and appreciated, but Hector had made her feel sexy, sensuous. She and Alex had kissed a lot, and it was fine, but it surprised her that he had never pushed her to go to bed with him. Was he afraid she would say no? Could he possibly not believe in sex before marriage? Was he just that much of a gentleman? Her mind drifted back over the years and she remembered the feel of Hector's mouth on hers, his hands, strong and insistent on her body, that loss of control she experienced. Although she had not heard from Hector in years, she longed to know what had become of him, yearned for some explanation of why he had never contacted her, after what they had shared at the end of senior year. Maybe it just wasn't that big a deal to him, although that possibility was painful to consider. If only she could talk to him, understand what had happened, put it behind her. She sighed.

Leda came in from the kitchen, accompanied by the aroma of tarragon-cream sauce. "What's up?"

"I just think that Helen should understand the implications of dating Alex. I think he's going to propose," Kelly said.

"That would be wonderful. I really like Alex," Leda said, beaming. What a relief it would be if Helen would make a real start on her life.

"That's not the point," Kelly said, frustrated. "The point is, Alex is an intelligent person with a complex personality. Could Helen be his equal in a marriage? If not, it would become apparent over time. I don't want her to disappoint him."

"You don't want me to disappoint him? What about me not getting disappointed? Don't my feelings matter? You know what I think? I think you're jealous! You're jealous because you don't have a boyfriend and I do." Helen threw *Cosmo* to the floor.

*I had a boyfriend*, Kelly fumed silently, *and your prom date killed him*. An image of Alex at their door, all covered in blood, Patrick's blood, flashed before her.

"Come on, Kelly, let her have a little fun. I'm glad he's taking her out," Leda said.

"Neither one of you gets it." Kelly would not mention Patrick's name; they would just say it was so long ago and that she should move on. She hated their complacency, hated not being taken seriously, and despised Helen's lackadaisical approach to life. She pushed herself up from the couch and stood in a formal pose before them, hands on hips, eyes on fire, glaring at Helen. "Look at me. Listen to me. You're wrong for him. I predict that you will marry Alex and that you will make him miserable. I predict you will ruin his life. If I'm right, and if you do, I swear, I'll, I'll, be tempted to strangle you, so don't screw up!"

Helen stared at Kelly and felt the blood drain from her face. Kelly could be scary when she got worked up.

"Kelly, come on, calm down, get off your high horse and be nice," Leda said in a soothing tone.

Kelly cast a last furious glance at Helen. "Don't forget what I said," she shouted, and stomped out of the room.

\*

Alex opened the door, breathing heavily, and leaned against the wall as he pulled off his running shoes.

Olivia approached, her fingers lovingly encircling a cocktail glass that did not contain a martini. Instead of water-clear, the beverage was tawny brown. A maraschino cherry danced within.

"Mom, what's that?"

"Ah, this. It's a Manhattan."

"Oh, sure. You're switching from martinis?"

"I started drinking them in your honor. When you're not home, and I have one of these, I think of you, at school in Manhattan."

"Can I try it?"

"Of course." She handed the glass over a little reluctantly.

Alex took a sip. "Wow! Don't spill that on the car. It'd eat right through the paint!"

"Alex, really. As if I would be in a situation where I would pour my cocktail onto our car!"

"I'm only kidding." He handed back her drink.

"Can I make you one?"

"No, that's okay."

"The other thing wonderful about them is that on a cold day like this, they warm you right up." She took a sip and gave a satisfied sigh. "That's delicious. Alex, will you be having dinner at home at last? I am roasting a lovely chicken, and I have new potatoes to go with it."

"Oh, no, not tonight. I'm seeing Helen."

"For goodness sakes. I barely see you!"

"Mom, I'm sorry, but I go to school out of state; I can't be here all the time." Alex knew that was not what she meant, but he tried deflecting the argument away from the main issue.

"I know where your school is. I understand the constraints. But when you're here in Brookline, you show up midday Saturday, barely say hello, drop your bag of laundry and go running. And then you'll be gone for hours!"

"You offered to do my laundry."

"Yes, so you could focus on your studies. Instead you go off to spend time with that girl, what's her name." Olivia crossed her arms, the hand holding the Manhattan thrust slightly forward.

"Helen. Mom, you know her." Alex wondered how long this conversation was going to last, and how he might curtail it.

"And then you go to your room, fall asleep, wake up at dawn to study, and then you slip down the stairs and you head back to New York. People ask me how you are. I hardly know what to reply." Olivia put her cocktail to her lips.

"I only get to see Helen for a few hours once every couple of weeks. She's important to me." As soon as the words left his mouth, Alex realized they would backfire.

"What about me? Am I not important to you?" Olivia demanded.

"Come on. Don't say stuff like that."

"And this, this Helen is important to you? How important? She seems like a silly little," she saw Alex's face darken, and stopped herself from saying 'twit.' "A silly little thing. Not well spoken. In fact, she hardly speaks at all."

"She's shy. And yes, she does tend to be quiet. But that one time I brought her here to meet you, you made her nervous. You don't realize it, but you can be intimidating."

"Intimidating! That's ridiculous. I was overly polite."

Alex sighed. No way to win this one. "Let's do this. Can we have the roast chicken tomorrow for lunch? A nice lunch, just you and me," Alex offered in his most appealing tone, hoping this would placate her.

"Well, alright," Olivia said, her tone softening. "You know, let me see if we have some Chianti to have with lunch. That will help you relax on the bus back to New York."

"Okay. I have to go shower. Sorry, but I've got to go." He hurried up the stairs.

"Fine, fine, I'm used to it." She took a sip of her Manhattan.

# CHAPTER 16

Giuli Stewart lay in bed. The pain in the left side of her head was horrendous, as though a vicious madman had slammed a dagger through her skull and into her brain and was slowly, mercilessly twisting the blade back and forth. The pain radiated from the top of her head, down its side and into the bones on the left side of her face. Any sound or light escalated the pain from excruciating to unbearable, and she breathed as softly as possible, minimizing movement, to avoid worsening the pain.

The door whipped open. "Giulietta! What are you doing? You should be up and dressed." Her mother Henrietta was a blur of red and blue standing in the doorway in front of the brightly lit hall. Giuli weakly dragged a teddy bear to her face and pulled it over her eyes to block the light.

"I can't go," Giuli replied, her voice barely audible.

"This is your friend's wedding. It will surely be seen as rude!"

"My head hurts so much. I think I'm having a migraine," Giuli whispered.

"Giulietta, I can hardly hear you. Can you speak up?" Henrietta craned forward while keeping her hand on the doorknob.

"Mom, please, I'm sick. I can't go. Please go and apologize to Alex for me." Giuli raised her voice a little and was rewarded with a violent twist of the imaginary knife.

"What? You're friends with the boy? You're not a friend of the bride?"

"Tell Helen sorry too," Giuli muttered.

"I remember Alexander. I had him in my English literature class. A promising young man, scholarly in a most endearing manner. I could discern that his love for literature was sincere," Henrietta reminisced. "I have no recollection of this Helen Fletcher. I wonder if she took my class. What is she like?"

Giuli moaned softly in response, but she answered the question silently: *Helen is beautiful and skinny and has gorgeous blond, non-frizzy hair.*

"I'll wager that if you got up and showered you'd be right as rain in a jiffy. Come along then, Giulietta!" Henrietta chirped, her voice absurdly bright.

*Oh my god, why do I have to have Mary Poppins for a mother at this moment?* Giuli wondered. "Can't. Go without me."

"Could you try, dear?" delivered in more of a croon. "After all, they invited you. I'm just your guest."

Giuli wordlessly clutched her teddy bear tighter.

"Very well then, have it your way! I suppose I'll be off." Henrietta sighed theatrically and finally departed, shutting the door hard enough to send a fresh wave of agony through Giuli's throbbing head. Giuli lay as quietly as she could, listening to the front door open and then close, the car's engine revving in the driveway, and finally the car driving away. She forced herself to relax, to focus on her breathing, and slowly, very slowly, the pain began to ebb.

*

Helen Fletcher stood in the back of the church, clinging to her father's robust arm, preparing to walk down the aisle. Her wedding dress was lovely, white satin with a fitted bodice, sweetheart neckline and full skirt with a layer of delicate lace overlying it all. But as she stood there in the warmth of the August afternoon, the heavy long-sleeved dress was making her flushed and sweaty. She wished she had picked a different dress, a sleeveless dress that left her shoulders bare, which would be cooler.

The pastor asked the congregation to rise in honor of the bride. They all looked at her, twisting and peering this way and that. Helen trembled nervously. The wedding march began. Helen had wanted that traditional march they always played at weddings. The choral director at the church had helped her pin it down. He had explained to her that it was from some opera called Lohengrin. Helen didn't know anything about opera, but she had listened to the music and confirmed it was the correct piece, and now here they were. The music she had chosen rose from the old pipe organ and filled the church. No turning back now. Her father, resplendent in an enormous black tuxedo, started to walk. Her slender arm was entwined with his big, meaty one, and she had no choice but to follow along. One step in front of the other.

There was Alex up front, looking cute in his tux with a huge smile on his face, and she felt somewhat reassured. Just across from Alex stood Kelly, her maid of honor, her face frozen in a mask. What if Kelly was right? What if she wasn't smart enough for Alex? Did she really love him? Yes, she did, she told herself. She did. What if it was true, what Kelly had said about ruining his life? Kelly could be so mean. Helen couldn't see how she could hurt Alex. She was making him happy, and he would be good to her, and she in turn would be happy. She made an effort to smile and look the part of the radiant bride, but inside she was very anxious.

Then an awful image popped into her head. From that old movie, *The Graduate*, when the guy comes into the church and takes the bride away with him, away from her groom. What if Hector were to show up right now and try to take her away? Would she go with him? Her breath came more quickly and she paused, lightheaded. No, she would not. She certainly would not. She would say, *who do you think you are, showing up here after seven years, and just expecting me to run off with you? No thank you.* At least, that's what she thought she would say, certainly what she should say. Without meaning to, she slowly, cautiously turned her head to look over her shoulder, toward the door of the church, but was unable to see past her father's big frame. Their eyes met and he smiled at her fondly. As she inched up the aisle, she thought, this is not so unusual, to have cold feet. Lots of people get nervous before they get married. *I'm fine*, she told herself. *I'm normal. It will all be fine.*

*

Henrietta Stewart waltzed through the front door and into the living room, where she found Giuli in her bathrobe curled up on the couch sipping chamomile tea. Romeo, their chihuahua, and the light-blocking teddy bear placidly shared Giuli's lap.

"Ah, I see you have recovered from your little episode." Henrietta seated herself across from Giuli, radiating satisfaction. "You missed a lovely ceremony and a most enjoyable reception."

"Mmmm. Sorry I missed it. What was it like?" Giuli asked sleepily.

"Well, the bride was beautiful, in such an exquisite gown, although in my estimation she was rather bony. And she had that long stringy hair that you girls seem to admire so much. And she seemed very stiff and artificial. Perhaps she was nervous. Some people don't like the spotlight, I suppose."

"Mm-hmm." *If only Alex had been interested in me, but he never looked at anyone but Helen*, Giuli reflected. *I'm just not pretty enough for someone like Alex. I hope they'll be happy. Or do I?*

"Giulietta, why don't you stop subjecting your hair to those dreadful chemicals and let it go back to normal? Your curls were poetically beautiful." Henrietta tilted her head, furrowed her brow and pursed her lips, waiting anxiously for a response.

"Mom, if you bring that up again, I'm moving out," Giuli said in a voice drained of emotion.

"Very well! No need to be so testy," Henrietta said, looking away from Giuli.

"What else? About the wedding?" *Come on, Mom, don't pout. You're too old for that.*

"Oh, yes. The best man was a friend of the Alex's from college. His name was Buck. That must be some sort of nickname, as he most definitely was not an adult male deer."

Giuli looked down. *It should have been Patrick*, she thought. "Did he give a toast?"

"Oh, yes, what a rousing toast young Buck delivered. Very entertaining. Do you know he began by stating that initially he hated Alex, for being so perfect!" Giuli winced at the notion as her mother continued. "But then he said that he realized that Alex was a, 'a sincerely nice guy,' he said, with the same sorts of problems we all have, and then he finished by saying that anyway, Alex had to be perfect to win this most beautiful bride."

"Oh, that's sweet," she said, although her words lacked enthusiasm.

"And the maid of honor was the sister of the bride," Henrietta reported, her tone definitive.

"Kelly. Helen's sister is named Kelly. She's really nice."

"She may be exceptionally congenial but she became thoroughly intoxicated at the reception. At one point she was crying. I believe the expression is 'sloppy drunk.' Quite embarrassing."

*If I had been there, I would have cried with her.* "But other than that, nothing bad happened?" Giuli asked cautiously.

"What an odd query. No, nothing untoward occurred," Henrietta said with a little shake of her head.

"Mom, you look very nice." Giuli offered, relieved that her headache had no special significance.

"Why, thank you very much! It's not every day I go to such an affair, and I bought this dress and had my hair done especially for the occasion. I chose this dress in royal blue as it sets off my red hair so nicely." She patted her carrot-colored bouffant hair. "Do you think I overdid it? I would hate to be accused of trying to upstage the mothers of the bride and the groom."

Giuli groaned silently. *Poor woman doesn't get out much.* "Mom, I'm sure your outfit was appropriate."

"Well, the party is over. I shall change out of my fancy dress and into my mundane clothing and resume daily life!" Henrietta pranced out of the living room. Giuli followed her with her eyes, wondering wistfully if she would ever see Alex again.

"Here, let me do your back," Alex offered. He took the bottle of Coppertone from Helen, squirted suntan lotion into his hand and spread it carefully over her beautiful shoulders and back, and up the back of her long, slender neck, still in awe that this amazing woman had become his wife. He studied the bottle skeptically. "Do you think this is strong enough? I don't want you to burn."

"It's fine. Do under the straps too, okay?" Helen murmured lazily as she lay on a colorful beach towel on a picturesque sandy stretch presided over by the east-facing lighthouse in Chatham, Massachusetts.

Alex obediently spread lotion under the straps of her bikini top and down to the edge of her bikini bottom, along the sides of her torso, allowing his fingers to linger briefly at the edges of her breasts. Helen lay perfectly still as though hypnotized by the sun and the sound of the surf. He found it incredibly erotic.

"Thank you," Helen whispered into her towel as she lay below him.

"What do you think about being on the elbow of Cape Cod?" Alex asked, trying to think about something other than Helen's body.

"It's so nice. I really like it," Helen said, dreamily.

"Is it okay for our honeymoon? Is it fancy enough? It's not a disappointment?" Alex asked.

"No, I really like it here. It's so comfortable and all around it's so pretty." Helen congratulated herself silently. She had done the right thing. Alex was really wonderful. And the look of surprise on that smug dentist's face, when she gave notice, that would make her smile for a long time.

"That's the whole Atlantic Ocean spread out in front of us. Think of all the ships that have come this way. And the shipwrecks! Do you know that shipwrecks were very common off the coast of Cape Cod? That's why they built the lighthouses."

"Mm-hmm," Helen responded drowsily, nestling deeper into the sand.

Alex gazed down at Helen, her flawless body, her golden hair. Always so poised. She maintained her composure all the time, strangely, he thought, even during sex. He made love to her with all of his heart and his soul, but it seemed to him that she remained somehow outside the experience. She would sigh a little and say she liked it, but she seemed emotionally uninvolved. Maybe she was just shy. Over time perhaps she would learn to let herself go more.

Alex watched as the sky over the Atlantic began to darken, and the sun started to set behind them. The sea breeze blew more urgently, taking the warmth of the day with it. "We should go, sweetheart. I don't want you to get cold."

"Okay." Helen sat up slowly and yawned. "I think I fell asleep. It's so nice and relaxing. I could stay here forever, just like this."

"That's good, sweetheart. I'm so glad you're happy. Give me your bag; I can carry it. Don't forget your hat."

They walked together back to the little cottage Alex had rented for the week.

\*

That night they sat together on the back porch of their cottage, the white painted railing delimiting the little deck from the inky blackness of the backyard. A bottle of white wine stood in a pot filled with ice cubes, an improvised wine bucket, on the planks of their outdoor table. Alex filled Helen's glass and then his own.

"Helen, I want to tell you something. I want to confess. I never told you this when we were dating because I thought you might think I was crazy and dump me."

"Oh, Alex, what do you want to tell me?" She smiled and took a sip of wine.

"I want to tell you, I want you to know, that I loved you from the first moment I saw you, at the beginning of junior year. You and Kelly and your brothers came up the stairs to where I was standing, and I swear, I had never seen anyone as beautiful as you. I was just smitten."

"Oh, Alex, I'm glad you think such nice things about me." She smiled her gentle smile and butterflies raced around Alex's stomach.

"You know, for so long I was afraid to call you. I thought you might not go out with me. But here we are. I'm so happy, sweetheart."

"Alex, you're so sweet, really."

"Do you really like your ring? The jeweler said it was the same style as Prince Charles gave to Diana, with a sapphire and diamonds, I mean the stones are smaller, of course, I'm no Prince Charles, but still it's the same style. Because you're my princess." Alex looked at her anxiously. He had no experience purchasing jewelry and he hoped and prayed that he had chosen well.

"Silly, I've told you a hundred times that I love it. I couldn't ask for a better ring." She looked down and admired her left hand with its perfect manicure and beautiful engagement ring, now joined by a simple wedding band.

Alex gazed upon Helen as she sat serenely, pale in the glow of the porch light against the dark of the night.

"She doth teach the torches to burn bright," he murmured.

"It seems she hangs upon the cheek of night,

As a rich jewel in an Ethiope's ear;

Beauty too rich for use, for earth too dear."

"That's so pretty. Where is it from?"

"It's Shakespeare. From *Romeo and Juliet*. You don't know that part? It suits you perfectly, as though old Will wrote it just for you."

"You're so romantic!"

"You bring it out in me, my wonderful Helen," he said.

"You're very sweet."

"Wait a moment." Alex went inside and turned off the porch light. He took Helen's hand and led her carefully down the steps and into the pitch-black backyard.

"Helen, look up. Look at all the stars! There's a lot less light here than at home. You can see so much more of the night sky." Alex had his head tipped back, scanning the sky for constellations he recognized. "Oh, wow! Did you see it? A shooting star!"

"No, I missed it. But it's so pretty. It's amazing." She squeezed his hand and his heart contracted with bliss.

"And look there! In the bushes. Fireflies! I don't remember when I last saw fireflies." He felt like a little boy again, when the small gifts of nature had all seemed new and miraculous, before he had lost so much. Here with Helen though, he felt reborn, renewed. She gave him hope for the possibility of happiness from life. He could not ask for more.

"Oh, yes, I see them now," she said, peering into the backyard. They stood like that for a while until Helen spoke. "Alex, um, I think it's getting a little buggy. Can we go in?"

"Of course." He led her back to the porch. "Be careful on these steps in the dark."

# CHAPTER 17

Sunshine poured through the windows and danced in Helen's golden hair as she and Alex sat side by side in the train heading south to New York City. She pulled her sunglasses out of her handbag and put them on. *How thrilling*, she thought, *to be moving to Manhattan!*

"Look at you; you look like a movie star!" Alex said.

"Oh, Alex, you're so silly!" Helen replied, but he could tell she was pleased.

"Helen, I hope it will be okay, the married couple's suite in the dorm." He knew that it was definitely a few steps down from a single-family home in Brookline. "It's just not possible to get an apartment in the area. Even if we could find one, the rent would eat all of our cash wedding gifts in a few months."

"Don't worry, Alex," she answered. "Like you said before, let's make that money last. It will be fine."

"I was able to score a window air conditioner, and also a small TV from people graduating. Practically giving them away," he said proudly.

"Window A/C?" Helen had assumed that everything in the glittering metropolis of Manhattan had central air.

"Yeah. Seems silly to build a dorm without air conditioning but I guess they figure people are in class or the library or in the hospitals most of the time, and it wasn't necessary. Also, it's not a new building." He studied the slender fingers of her graceful hands as they rested in her lap. "But the window unit works great. Really powerful. The TV is only black and white though."

"Black and white? I didn't know they even made those anymore." She removed her sunglasses and looked at him.

"They probably don't. This TV is sort of a relic, I guess. It must have been passed down from one set of med students to the next for years. Decades. Only cost me 50 bucks though. And it works fine. We'll leave it behind for the next generation when I graduate and get a real TV when we get our own place."

"It will be fine," Helen responded calmly. She wasn't sure how she felt about this black and white TV thing though. Maybe she could hint around to her parents for money for a color TV for Christmas or something. Although Christmas was a long way away.

"I'm so excited to show you around New York City! There's so much to see and do. The place is full of characters. Even the concrete has personality. And we have only this one year before I finish and get my residency, but no telling where that will be, so we should enjoy New York while we can." Alex had grown to love the city during the three years he had spent there, and the idea of introducing Helen to it, acting as her personal tour guide, appealed to him immensely. "There are two more days until I start my surgery rotation. So tomorrow, let's do some sightseeing."

"I'd like that!" Helen had never been to New York City and was looking forward to seeing Times Square and going to plays and ballets and eating in fancy restaurants and going shopping.

"Tomorrow let's get up and go to Central Park. I'll show you about riding the subway. It's easy," Alex said. "And Central Park is beautiful. And huge!"

"The subway? Is it safe?" Helen had heard stories about violence, theft and severe crowding on the subway.

"Sure, it's safe. It's not luxurious, but it gets you where you need to go."

"I thought people in New York took cabs." She envisioned herself on Fifth Avenue toting several shiny shopping bags from upscale boutiques, hailing a yellow cab with her free hand, settling into the security of its leather interior, and listening to the cab driver's amusing anecdotes while being driven back to their place in safety and comfort.

"Yes, that's true, some people do, and we can once in a while, but cabs are expensive. And they get stuck in traffic if it's rush hour, so you can just sit there thinking it would have been faster to walk while the meter ticks away. Also, the taxi drivers, a lot of them are maniacs. Maybe the job makes them crazy. Better to walk or take the subway."

"I think I'd be scared to go on the subway by myself," she said, anxiously. Her vision of daily life in New York City was fading fast.

"Don't worry, sweetheart. It's easy. You'll see. And I don't want you to do anything that scares you, okay?" He reached across her lap and squeezed her hand.

"Okay." She gave him a little smile.

They sat back in their cushioned seats, silent for a while. Helen glanced down at her sandaled feet and was annoyed to see that her expensive pedicure wasn't holding up very well. *Calm down*, she told herself. *It will be easy to touch up as soon as we reach New York and unpack.* The rhythmic motion of the train was soothing, and Helen relaxed. *It will all work out.*

*

Alex and Helen squeezed into the elevator of his dorm with their suitcases. "We're on the 14th floor," he said. "The view is great! You'll see."

"Okay. Sounds pretty high," she replied.

"This way, to the right," Alex said as they emerged from the elevator. "Here, let me take your suitcase."

Helen followed, noting that the hall was plain and unadorned, with an institutional feel. No fancy light fixtures. No wainscoting. The floor was mottled gray-blue linoleum.

"Here we go," Alex said, opening the door with his key.

Helen studied the interior as Alex hauled her suitcase and his own smaller one into the room. The linoleum flooring flowed unimpeded from the hall across the floor of their suite which consisted of a single room with an attached private bathroom. The furniture included a full-size bed, a plain desk and desk chair and one additional worn chair stuck in a corner. No table. Open shelves stretched above the desk and the diminutive kitchen area. The promised black and white TV perched at one corner of the desk. It was tiny, Helen noted. She peeked into the bathroom. It had a small stall shower, no tub. Too bad, she thought. She so enjoyed soaking in the bathtub.

"I know it probably doesn't look like much, but except for the married students' floor, all the floors just have hall bathrooms. This is a big step up for me!" Alex said cheerfully. "And with the dishes and all that we got as gifts, for me this will feel like luxury. See here," he said, gesturing to a toaster oven, a scratched red hot-pot, a plate, a bowl and a coffee mug, the latter holding a fork, a knife and a spoon, all neatly lined up on the counter. "Up until now, all I had was this stuff to cook with. And we have a real stove." He nodded at a miniature stove with two coiled electric burners.

Helen nodded slowly as he spoke.

"I know it's small, but is it okay? We'll have a much nicer place when I get out of school and have an income." Alex studied her face.

Helen continued to assess the room. It was very small. And she hated the linoleum and the primitive kitchen. Then it occurred to her that she didn't know how to cook anyway and hoped to get a lot of take-out, so the kitchen didn't really matter. And in comparison with that awful dive that Kelly called a studio apartment

133

in Beacon Hill, this place was smaller, but it was in a better state of repair. "It's fine," Helen said. "It's just for this one year."

Moreover, her mother would not be hovering, nagging her about everything. And as long as she didn't say anything about the shortcomings of this place, no one would ever know she wasn't living somewhere wonderful. She walked over to the window and looked out. "The view is great!"

Helen opened her suitcase and started to unpack her clothes. She hadn't brought much, thinking it would be easy to go back and forth to Brookline and get different things to wear as the seasons changed. She carefully peeled the bubble wrap off the 4 place settings of their everyday china and their flatware and arranged them on a shelf over the stove. She went to the bathroom and hung up the few towels she had brought from home, these items comprising the bare minimum of their wedding gifts set aside to accompany them to New York.

"Oh, sweetie, look at that. It looks so much better, like a real home now. Thank you!" Alex said. "Say, it's getting late. Do you want to try to make our first dinner here?"

"Ah, sure," Helen said. She hoped Alex would take the lead on the dinner prep.

"There's a grocery store a block away. We can go there and get something to cook. That's the great thing about New York; you can get just about anything you need within a three-block radius from where you live," Alex explained.

"Okay. Where'd I leave my purse?" As she considered the prospect of preparing a meal, Helen's mind wandered back to the dinner they had had the night before with Alex's mother. Olivia had pulled Helen aside and handed her a small plastic box. Helen had raised the lid, revealing multiple index cards separated into groups by tabs neatly labeled 'Fish,' 'Poultry,' 'Meat,' 'Vegetables,' 'Beverages' and 'Desserts.' Olivia had spoken quietly, so Alex would not hear, and had explained to her that these were Alex's favorite recipes. Those marked with a red star were his special favorites. Her words, *Now, dear, he does love beef stew, but be sure to cook the stew until the meat is completely tender or he won't eat it. He won't complain; he'll just push the meat to the side and eat the vegetables,* still echoed in her ears. *And if you ever have any questions about these recipes or anything else, you just call. It takes experience and a lot of work to be a good homemaker,* she had said. Helen had not thought much about work, experience or homemaking before getting married. She planned to take it a day at a time and see what happened. She was relieved that a couple hundred miles separated her from Alex's mother.

# CHAPTER 18

Alex turned off the shower, stepped out and opened the door of the bathroom to let out the steam. Helen sat perched near the corner of the desk, talking on the phone, looking lovely in a clingy blouse and a skirt imprinted with little flowers. She rocked her slender bare feet back and forth as she spoke.

"Yeah, it's really great. It's a high-rise. Well, maybe not a high-rise, more of a mid-rise. We're on the 14th floor. You should see the view! That's right. That's right. No, we're not in Brookline anymore, Mom, that's for sure. Oh, listen, I should go. We're going to the theater tonight, and I should finish getting ready. Broadway. Yes! *Cats*! Yes, I am lucky."

Hearing this, Alex shouted, "I'm lucky too!"

\*

"Oh, Alex, this is so exciting!" Helen clung to his arm as they squeezed through the crowd in Times Square. "It's bright as daylight! And all these people! People all dressed up and people who look like bums."

"Bums? They're homeless. I met quite a few during my Psych rotation. Listen, hold onto your purse. Someone will snatch it and disappear into the crowd and you'll never see it again. Now, we want to go in that direction, see? That's our theater. The Winter Garden Theatre."

"Okay, yes, I see it."

"Hang onto me; I'm going to mount an offensive." Alex turned sideways and glanced back at Helen. "Don't look so worried. Just pretend we're Romans fighting hostile Gauls for Julius Caesar."

Helen's eyes popped wide open. Alex said the strangest things.

"Don't worry. Julius Caesar always won. Well, until his own people turned on him. But that was later. Come on."

Alex took Helen's arm and sliced through the crowd, apologizing when meeting resistance, drawing Helen after him. He finally paused when they reached an open pocket near the front of the theater. "Okay we did it. You still in one piece?"

"Yes! Of course. I'm fine. Is it always so crowded?"

"Well, it's Saturday night, and the weather's nice, so this is about as crowded as it gets. Except for New Year's Eve."

"New Year's Eve! Can we come here then?"

"Sure, anything you want. I hope the seats are okay. You know I got them at a discount through the med school activities office."

"I'm sure they'll be great. I can't believe I'm going to a real Broadway play!"

*

Hector Gonzalez took a deep drag on his cigarette. Why the hell did fucking Chewie want to meet in fucking Times Square? Hector hated it here. He shifted his weight from one foot to the other, turning away from the garish lights. Chewie said, in a crowd like this you were invisible. Maybe he was right. He hoped Chewie would be reasonable about giving him a little more leeway on payment. He should be getting more money from home soon, probably tomorrow; even a moron like Chewie could understand that. Hector took another drag, finishing off the cigarette. He dropped it to the pavement and ground it out with his foot. Truth was, though, the money he got, it was enough for the rent and for food, but not enough for a New York lifestyle. And nowhere near enough when he was stuck treating Eddie and Lou, just because they delivered the cash from his mom. And fucking Marisol. She never paid for anything. He told Lou, next time he came, it was his turn to buy the coke. Lou could stay at his place, screw Marisol's friends, whatever. But he buys his own stash, and enough to share. Hector drew his pack of cigarettes out of his pocket and extracted one. Only three left. This was his last pack and he'd have no cash until Lou or Eddie came. His hands shook as he lit the cigarette. He held it firmly in his lips and focused on breathing as deeply as he could, drawing the smoke throughout his lungs, maximizing the nicotine rush. That was good. He could make it to tomorrow. He could.

His eyes scanned the crowd for Chewie. Where the fuck was he? Wait, that girl there, the blonde. Fuck! That's Helen from high school. What's she doing here? Where'd she go? Was that really Helen? His eyes scanned the crowd but there was no longer any sign of her.

As he enjoyed his cigarette, his mind wandered back to high school. He thought of the time he had invited Helen to the equestrian competition their senior

136

year. He had seen her watching him, ringside, excited and nervous, eyes wide, lips parted, so pretty. He had loved the horses, loved the feel of the powerful muscles of his chestnut mare under his thighs. That day, knowing she was watching, he showed off for her. He admitted it. He was daring, fearless, took every jump at a gallop, cleared them all. Took first place. Flush with his achievement he had taken an unauthorized victory lap, tipping his black velvet cap at Helen as he rode past her. Did she light up! He could always light her up. A lot of things to like about Helen, he recalled. Her small, careful movements and her soft voice, so different from the sweeping gestures and melodramatic behavior of his mother. He pulled thoughtfully on his cigarette. That was a long time ago. That girl he saw, maybe it wasn't Helen anyway, just someone who looked like her.

Fuck! There was Chewie, glaring at him.

"Hector, how's it going?" Chewie was a stocky, stone-faced Mesoamerican with no sense of humor and a limited imagination, and yet with a healthy respect for capitalism.

"Good. Good." Hector knew he should offer him a cigarette but with only three left…

"You got my money, my friend?"

"I'm a little short right now, but I'm getting money tomorrow, Chewie. It's on the way. I'll pay you."

"Tomorrow."

"Yes, tomorrow."

"You're always late, Hector. Not a good customer. I like customers who pay. On time."

"I know, I know. But the rent went up and Marisol needed some stuff and I don't know. I can pay you tomorrow."

"So you come here tomorrow, same time."

"No, it might be late. Come to my place if you want. When it comes, you get what you're owed." Marisol could always put him in a good mood, Hector recalled.

Chewie was silent for a while, flat face expressionless. Finally, he spoke. "Tomorrow, your place."

"Yes, good. Good. We'll see you then."

Chewie turned to leave.

"Ah, Chewie, do you think you could give me just a little to see me through to tomorrow? Marisol, you know, I don't want to disappoint her."

Chewie's eyes narrowed. Hector Gonzalez was one whiny bastard. "You know what, Hector? For Marisol. Sure. Just a little bit more, but tomorrow we settle up or we're done." Chewie smoothly drew his wallet from the inner pocket of his jacket and flipped it open. As he ostentatiously studied the contents of his wallet he quickly slid a small plastic packet from the underside of his wallet and passed it to Hector.

Hector slipped the packet into his own pocket. Just touching it made his heart race with anticipation. Maybe he would stop somewhere quiet and try it on his own before going home. Yeah, good idea, then Marisol's bitching wouldn't get on his nerves so much. He lovingly caressed the little packet between his thumb and index finger. Marisol. As he thought about his tiny pinch of coke, and about Marisol, all the things she did that annoyed him faded into the background. He remembered instead her luscious body, her big, soft breasts with their blackberry nipples, the indescribable feeling of getting inside her. He hurried back to his apartment.

# CHAPTER 19

Helen Eastgard rolled over in bed, away from the sunshine that streamed through the window, onto her face and through the delicate skin of her eyelids. She lay like that for a while, enjoying the warmth of the sun on her shoulders. *This feels decadent*, she thought, smiling to herself. *No stupid job. No Mom nagging me to get up and go get a new job. Just Alex kissing me goodbye and tiptoeing out. Wonderful!* She stretched luxuriantly in the silky new sheets that caressed her and dozed again.

When she finally reawakened, she realized she was hungry and would have to get up and find something to eat. Slowly she eased herself into a sitting position, pushing the covers away, swung her rosy little feet onto the floor and made her way to the kitchen counter. She smiled. Even though Alex left at some god-awful pre-dawn hour to do something called "round on his patients," he always washed out the coffee pot before he left so it would be clean for her to use. He was sweet.

As the coffee brewed, Helen opened the refrigerator. Nothing too appealing: part of a head of lettuce, a couple of potatoes and half a bottle of cheap wine. Helen sighed and poured a cup of coffee. If she were at home, Mom would make her scrambled eggs. She went back to bed, and drank her coffee sitting against the headboard. No, she realized. That was wrong. That wasn't home anymore. *This* was home. Her eyes wandered over the ugly linoleum. But when we get a real home of our own, there would be no linoleum. And they'd have a bigger bed. A queen. No, king-sized. Why not? And a nice big house with big rooms, big enough for a king-sized bed, and a dining room big enough for a nice long table, a nice shiny dark table of cherry wood, or even mahogany, big enough to have a lot of people over for dinner. She paused. Before that she might have to learn to cook, but there was plenty of time for all that. Right now she had to get breakfast.

She decided she would starve to death if she took a shower before getting something to eat, so she pulled on jeans and a T-shirt, combed her hair and popped it into a ponytail, and took the elevator downstairs. She hoped no one would see her without make-up, but all was quiet as she made her way to the exit onto First Avenue. She would go to a nearby deli she knew on Second Avenue. A five-minute walk.

"Good morning," she said, approaching the counter at Arthur's Delicatessen. The attendant was a great big guy who made her nervous.

"You know what you want?" he barked from behind the counter without looking up.

"Um, what kinds of muffins do you have today?" Helen asked, timidly.

"Lady, look in the case. I think we got blueberry, chocolate chip, choco-late-chocolate chip, corn, apple. You like any of those?"

"Um, okay. I'll take one apple muffin. Oh, and one chocolate chip muffin also. For my husband." She enjoyed being able to say she had a husband. She wondered if this man was Arthur, but she had no intention of inquiring.

"Lady, I don't care who you buy muffins for. You want anything else?"

"No, thank you." Helen watched with fascination as his enormous hands engulfed each muffin and shoveled them into a white paper bag.

"That's it? You sure?" Whatever she decided, he made it sound like an error in judgment.

"Yes, thank you," she said, taking her little bag and fleeing back to the med school dorm. Back in their room, she turned on the little TV, found a talk show, laid her muffin out on one of their new dishes and nibbled it while watching TV. She set her empty dish on the counter and picked up this month's *Cosmopolitan*, flipping through it while people on TV yapped away. Kelly had gotten her a subscription to *Cosmo* as a wedding gift. Kelly had meant it as a joke, Helen knew, a gag gift, but Helen was glad to have it. There was nothing wrong with *Cosmo*. A lot of the stuff in it was quite sophisticated.

Helen glanced at the clock. 2:00! No wonder she was hungry again! She ate Alex's muffin for lunch, took a shower, got dressed and tried to think what she should do about dinner. By the time Alex got back it would be late, too late to go out to eat, too late to shop for something to cook. She made fresh coffee while reviewing her options. She could go to the grocery and buy something to cook. That would require a lot of effort. She could go back to the deli and get something else. Bagels with cream cheese? That would be easy but not a very good dinner, and she would have to talk to that man again. What about that Chinese place on the corner? She could get take-out. Perfect!

\*

It was dark outside. Alex should be home soon. Helen lined up the little containers of Chinese food on the counter: ginger beef, Szechuan chicken and white rice, along with two fortune cookies. That Chinese food had cost more than she had expected. She had wanted to get a pedicure but maybe she should do it herself and save a few dollars. She turned on the TV again, saturated a cotton ball with nail polish remover and started to remove the old polish. Once she was satisfied with that, she filled a pot with warm water, sat on the edge of the bed and soaked her feet. *Far cry from the Swan Salon*, she thought, as she wiggled her toes in the aluminum basin. She waited 15 minutes, withdrew her feet and vigorously pushed back her cuticles. That done, she had only to select a nail color.

The phone rang. She hurried to the desk and answered.

"Hi, Helen. It's me."

"Hi, how's it going?"

"Well, good, except I have to scrub in on an emergency surgery. I'm going to be home late."

"Oh, that's too bad. I got Chinese."

"Something spicy, I hope. Well, save some for me. I'll be home as soon as I can."

"When will you be home?"

"Ah, by the time we get started it'll be another half hour, and then, well, it'll be more than two hours, closer to three."

"Three more hours! It's already after seven."

"I'm sorry, sweetheart. The Surgery rotation can be just brutal. But it's temporary, don't worry."

"Okay, come as soon as you can." Helen hung up the phone. This was only the second week of Alex's Surgery rotation. She barely saw him. Six and a half weeks to go. Hopefully the next rotation wouldn't be so intense.

She sighed and went back to her short row of bottles of nail polish. Tudor Rose would do just fine.

Helen was back in her pajamas and ready for bed when Alex finally returned.

"There you are! It's after 11!"

"Oh, well at first we couldn't find an anesthesiologist, so we couldn't start, and then the surgery turned out to be more complicated than we thought. The fellow had a belly full of adhesions. Every step took longer than usual."

"Will he be okay?"

Alex paused. Their patient's chance of long-term survival was very poor. He had presented to the emergency room with acute onset of peritonitis, due to a perforation of his colon. As they resected the damaged segment of intestine they found that the underlying problem was a cancer that had eaten through the wall of the bowel. The attending surgeon had gestured to Alex and told him to palpate the mass, and then some smaller lumps in the adjacent mesentery, spread of the cancer to lymph nodes, he had said. The mass and the lymph nodes were hard and irregularly shaped, distorting and replacing the normal tissue. Is this what the cancer in his father's liver had been like, Alex wondered. He had not met the patient before surgery. When he turned to look at him, he half expected to see his father's features. But the patient was an older man with an unfamiliar face.

"Alex?" Helen asked.

"Well, he pulled through as well as can be expected. He's stable now." Alex didn't want Helen thinking about cancer and perforated bowel. He didn't want to bring that unhappiness into their new little home. "So, where's that food I've been dreaming about?"

*

Morning again. Helen Eastgard rolled over in bed and stretched, pointing her toes and swishing her legs back and forth in the lovely new sheets.

She sat up and slipped her feet into her fluffy slippers and shuffled to the bathroom. Hungry again, she thought, as she brushed her teeth. She wiggled into her clothes and steeled herself for a confrontation with her nemesis at the deli.

She opened the door to the deli, unsmiling, and walked in without removing her sunglasses. Without speaking she crouched, scanned the muffins in the glass case and stood.

"Two pumpkin spice and two chocolate chip muffins," Helen said, keeping her voice flat.

The burly man grunted, and Helen sensed a hint of approval in that primal monosyllable. She paid and left with her muffins without speaking again. Elated, she hurried back to the dorm room.

Helen turned on the TV and changed channels until she came to The Young and Restless. She selected one of the pumpkin spice muffins and ate it slowly. This was good, she thought. She never was able to watch the soaps because of her stupid job, but now she could. That muffin was delicious; since she had bought four, she wouldn't feel guilty about eating another. Chocolate chip this time. She turned the dial on the TV until she came to Oprah. Interesting. Then, The Price Is Right. Fun show, but she found she was pretty bad at guessing prices. Too bad the TV was black and white; the shows would be so much better in color.

Helen stood and strolled over to the bathroom to take a shower. Afterwards she got back into bed and reread part of *Cosmo*. She wished it came out more often than once a month. This was her third time through the September issue. As she leafed through *Cosmo*, she realized she should think about dinner. Since yesterday, when she remembered the breakfasts her mother prepared, she had been craving scrambled eggs. She was pretty sure all that was needed was eggs. She would go to the grocery store on First Avenue and get a dozen eggs.

*

Helen leaned back against the headboard of the bed as she watched the evening news. Eggs were a bargain! Dinner would be much cheaper tonight than last night. The phone rang.

"Helen, hi, it's me."

"Hi, how's it going?"

"Not too bad, but just as I was getting ready to leave, Barry comes up and tells me one of my patients ripped out his IV. So I have to go replace it."

"Oh, okay. Will that take long?"

"Shouldn't take too long."

"Why did he pull out his IV?"

"Who knows? He's in withdrawal, probably doesn't know what's going on."

"Okay, come home soon."

"Will do. Did you get anything for dinner?"

"I got eggs. Do you know how to make scrambled eggs?"

"Oh, sure. Want me to do it?"

"Yeah, could you? I'm not too sure, you know, my mom did all the cooking."

"No problem," Alex said, laughing. "I'm going to start that IV; see you soon."

*

"Alex, there you are! It's after 9!" Helen said, swinging her feet off the bed and standing. "Have you been doing that IV this whole time?"

Alex sat down heavily on the bed and flipped off his shoes. "No, after that, the guy we stayed late operating on last night coded, and we tried to bring him back."

"Did he make it?" Helen asked, looking down at him.

Alex looked down. "No. We couldn't get a heartbeat. We really tried. His wife was there. She was hysterical. We tried to calm her down, but it was hard."

Helen stood silently, then turned to the fridge, pulled out the wine and poured a big glass for Alex, and a smaller one for herself. She sat down next to him.

"Thanks, sweetie," he said, tasting the wine, and taking her hand in his.

Then he set aside the wine glasses and kissed her, caressing her smooth, flawless limbs, so different from the tissues replaced by the terrible cancer that had killed their patient. He made love to her with desperation, with intensity, replacing the sorrow of the day with her sweetness, her beauty. An exorcism. Afterwards he fell into a deep sleep. Helen lay quietly in his arms for a while, but then realized they had never had dinner and she was very hungry. She didn't want to wake Alex, so instead of trying to cook something she had the second pumpkin spice muffin and the rest of her wine. Then she too slept.

*

Helen awakened to the rat-a-tat-tat of rain spattering against the window pane. She lay curled up in the covers, enjoying the warm dry coziness, glad she didn't have to be outside today. *I wonder what time it is*, she thought, rolling over in bed, and lifting her head to have a look at the clock radio. After 10! She rolled back over onto her back and closed her eyes to contemplate how she could have slept so late. Of course! It was all wet and gloomy outside today. It was the sunshine that usually awakened her.

The staccato chatter of raindrops on glass, echoed by the hollow plop of rain on the top of the window A/C followed Helen as she pried herself out of bed and stumbled over to the counter. Her head felt as cloudy today as the gray sky; she really needed her coffee. When a small cup's worth was ready, Helen pulled out the pot quickly and poured the contents into her cup as 2 or 3 drops of coffee hit the heating element and sizzled menacingly. She replaced the pot and returned to bed, to drink her coffee.

She also realized that she was very hungry. Three muffins yesterday- that's all she had had to eat. Alex was long gone and wouldn't be back until late; she couldn't wait for him to do something about the food situation. She could *try* to cook something. How hard could it be to make scrambled eggs? She poured herself a second cup of coffee and dialed her home in Brookline.

"Mom? Hi, it's Helen."

"Helen, how are you? How's Alex?"

"We're fine. But can you tell me how to make scrambled eggs?"

"Helen! You really don't know how to make scrambled eggs?" Leda's sigh was loud and prolonged.

"How should I know? You did all the cooking."

"You think you might have noticed at some point."

"You never wanted us in the kitchen!"

"Now Helen, that's just not true. When you were little, yes, I didn't want you burning yourselves. But not later. And Kelly knows how to cook." Leda knew that because she had been to Kelly's apartment and noticed piles of unwashed dishes in and around the sink.

"Can we please not turn this into another discussion about how Kelly is the better daughter?"

"That is not what I said, I just said, well never mind. I'm sorry if it came out wrong. I can certainly explain how to make scrambled eggs," Leda said, anxious to change the subject. "It's easy."

"Okay. I have eggs. What do I do?"

"Get a pan and melt a little butter in it over low to medium heat."

"I need butter?"

"Yes, or the eggs will stick."

Helen started making notes on the back of an envelope. "Then what?"

"Okay, put one or two eggs into a bowl and add a splash or two of milk, and stir it up with a fork."

"I need milk too?"

"Yes, you do. Or cream if you want it to be richer. Then sprinkle in salt and pepper. You do have salt and pepper, I hope."

"Yes, of course we do." They always set aside extra packets of salt, pepper and condiments that came with take-out to use later.

"So just pour the eggs into the butter, let them cook for a little, then stir them a little so they cook evenly. Should only take a few minutes for the eggs to firm up."

"Okay, I'll try it. Thanks, Mom."

"Okay, good luck, sweetheart. Call if you have problems. I hope you and Alex come visit soon."

Helen gazed out the window. Rain was pouring down in sheets. *Maybe I'll go to the grocery store later*, she thought, but then her stomach growled fiercely, vetoing that plan. She put on her raincoat and made her way to First Avenue. She pulled her hood tightly around her face, wishing they had an umbrella, and waited shivering in the downpour for the light to change. A taxi whizzed through a huge puddle, spraying her and leaving her pants drenched from knee to ankle.

"You jerk," she muttered, wondering why going to the grocery store had to be so hard.

Finally, the light changed, and she was able to cross the street. She found milk and butter as quickly as she could, paid and hurried back to the dorm to get into dry clothes.

*

It was 9:30 when Alex finally returned to their room that night.

"Hi, sweetie. Sorry to be so late again. What'd you do today?"

"Well, I made scrambled eggs. I did a pretty good job, I think." Which was eventually true, although she had burned the first batch and had to start over.

"That's my clever sweetheart! I wish I could have been here to help."

*

Helen Eastgard was fast asleep Monday morning until she was awakened by the sharp ring of their telephone. It took her a few moments to realize what the sound was; then she got up and stumbled across the room to answer the phone.

"Hello?" she said, stifling a yawn.

"Helen? It's Olivia. I hope you are well. Is Alex there?" Her mother-in-law's crisp syllables vibrated uncomfortably in Helen's ear.

"Oh, no, he's gone already." Helen glanced at the clock on the desk. 7:15. Yes, Alex was long gone.

"I see. It's quite early. Is he ordinarily at work by now?"

"Yes, ma'am. He goes quite early."

"No need to call me ma'am. You may call me Olivia. Or Mom if you prefer."

"Okay, I'll try to remember. Um, thanks."

"Alex hasn't called in weeks. I hardly know if he's dead or alive. Will you tell him to call?"

"Yes, but, you know, he works really long hours."

"Well, at any rate do tell him to call. Now, are you using those recipes I gave you?"

146

Helen was still half asleep. What recipes? What had she forgotten? Panic set in.

"You must recall- the nice file box I gave you. Surely that must come in handy."

"Oh, yes, of course. Thank you again."

The call over, Helen eased herself back into bed, pulling the covers over her head to block the sunlight. As she drifted back to sleep, she wondered if it might be possible for Alex to unplug the phone before he left for work in the morning.

Two hours later Helen reawakened. She got up, made coffee and thought about breakfast. She hadn't had a muffin since Thursday. She had made scrambled eggs on Friday, and over the weekend, they'd had bagels and cream cheese for breakfast. Yes, it was time for a muffin.

Fifteen minutes later she returned to their room toting a bag with two lemon poppy seed muffins, clutching the October *Cosmopolitan* to her chest. Good thing she'd remembered to check their mailbox. She leafed through *Cosmo* while nibbling one of the muffins. A quiz! She loved *Cosmo*'s quizzes. She read, question number one.

A. Always, no matter what.

B. Almost always but if there were a natural disaster it might slip his mind.

C. He usually remembers but it's good to give him subtle hints starting two weeks ahead.

D. He remembers less than half of the time.

E. He never remembers.

Helen paused, chewing gently on her lower lip. She hadn't had her birthday since they'd been married but Alex certainly remembered it when they were dating. He was very reliable. She circled A.

She continued to question 2. How often is he on time?

A. He's always on time, no matter what, even if a car hits him and he has to get to you in a wheelchair.

Helen chuckled. Sometimes Cosmo came up with these scenarios that were hard to believe.

B. He's always on time, unless circumstances beyond his control, like really bad traffic, make him late.

C. He's on time for about half of your dates.

D. He's on time for less than half of your dates.

E. He's basically never on time.

Helen paused. This was tricky. Alex was always on time when they were dating, but on a daily basis, he usually got home late. A normal time to leave work was 5pm. Even with bad traffic her Dad was always home by 6pm. Alex just had to walk home so he should be back by 5:30 at the latest, but since he had been on his Surgery rotation was never back by then. She hated to choose E; it seemed harsh. D seemed fair, even generous. Yes, she would go with D.

She continued until she had finished the quiz. Each A response equaled 5 points, with 4 points for each B, and so on down to 1 point for each E. Helen calculated her score. 70 out of 100. She checked the rating. For a score in the range of 60-75, it said, "This relationship needs work. Talk to your guy and make him see the light, or he'll be seeing you walk out the door."

Helen set down the magazine, troubled. Here they were, just married, and with a score of only 70%! Did *Cosmo* take into account special circumstances, like medical school? It did say to talk to your guy. There never seemed to be time to talk with these crazy hours Alex worked. But she could try.

*

Alex returned to their room around 9:00 and collapsed onto the bed, shutting his eyes.

"What a day!"

"What happened?" Helen asked.

"Another emergency surgery. Guy had his surgery yesterday but then today his pressure starts falling and we took him back in for a look. Suture line was done badly and he'd started bleeding. The chief resident had done that suture line and the attending was ripped, really tore into him afterwards. Anyway, the patient is stable. But another half hour and he wouldn't have made it."

"Oh, wow." What would *Cosmo* say concerning this situation?

"I am starving! Did you have a chance to get anything for dinner?"

"Oh, no, sorry. I, it slipped my mind."

"That's okay. Let's, let's go to that diner across the street. Portions are huge." Alex said, but lay on the bed unmoving.

"Okay."

"Okay. Good. Now I have to get up." He pushed his torso into a sitting position, leaned forward and forced himself to open his eyes and stand up. "Let's go."

"Okay. Um, do I have time to put on make-up?"

"Oh, sweetie, you look beautiful. You don't need make-up. And if we don't go now I'm going to be asleep in 30 seconds."

"Oh, well, okay. I just need my shoes."

They sat across from one another on cranberry-colored vinyl benches in a booth at the diner.

"I'm having the meat loaf dinner. What about you?" Alex snapped his menu closed and set it down.

"I guess the pasta primavera."

"Sounds good. Where's our waitress?" Alex said, peering past the cranberry piping that marked the edge of their booth.

"Alex, I was just wondering..."

"Oh, miss, can you take our order? We are starved."

"No problem. What'll you have?" She took the order on her little pad and sauntered away with it.

"Alex, I was wondering, well, I know it's the Surgery rotation and all, but, well..."

"What, sweetie?"

"Well you're hardly around, really. Can you not come back a little earlier?"

"I wish I could, but I just can't. I'm so sorry. I'll make it up to you when I finish. I'm so sorry."

"Well, it's just that, well, it's kind of lonely."

"Oh, sweetie, I'm so sorry. Haven't you met anyone here? No one to talk to during the day?"

"No, not really." There was the man at Arthur's, but she didn't even know his name and he liked her better when she didn't talk.

"But, you know, you don't have to stay cooped up in the dorm all the time. You should go out and see the city. Go to a museum. Or just walk around. New York is such an amazing place."

"Oh, I, I don't think I would feel right. I'd rather wait and go with you."

"Would you want to volunteer at the hospital? I'm sure they'd be happy to have you."

That would be awful, Helen thought, panicked. She forced herself to sound calm and said, "I don't think I'm cut out to work in a hospital. You know, the way you describe it, it seems a little crazy."

Alex nodded. "Oh, thank god, here's our food." He loaded his fork with meatloaf and mashed potatoes and sighed as the food hit his taste buds. "Delicious! How's yours?"

"Um, good."

"But, sweetie, I don't want you to be unhappy. Oh, and I just remembered, this weekend coming up is my weekend on call. I'll go in Saturday morning and won't be back until Sunday evening. So it will get even worse before it gets better. I really feel terrible."

"Oh, well, I know you can't really..."

"How about this? Do you want to go stay with your parents for a few days? Relax, let your Mom cook for you?"

This was not what she wanted. She wanted him to commit to being home at a reasonable hour. "Um, maybe. I'll think about it."

*

Helen Eastgard was fast asleep Tuesday morning until she was awakened by the sharp ring of the telephone. She realized with horror what the sound was. She had forgotten to tell Alex that his mother had called and now she was calling back. She hurried to answer the phone.

"Hello?" she said.

"Helen? It's Olivia. Is Alex there?"

"Oh, no, he's gone already." Helen scanned the room to confirm this, and then glanced at the clock on the desk. 6:45. She closed her eyes and rested her head on one hand to help her endure the rest of the conversation.

"Helen, you sound sleepy. Were you asleep?"

"Well, yes, I was," she replied, and waited for Olivia's apology.

"I certainly hope that doesn't mean you're sleeping through Alex's departure. You should get up with him and make him breakfast while he gets ready."

"Oh, yes. I'll remember. I'll tell him you called," Helen managed to say, feeling utterly defeated.

As Alex crossed the threshold that evening, Helen spoke. "Your Mom called this morning, and I told her I'd tell you. Also, I'm really sorry, but she called yesterday too, and I forgot to tell you."

"That's okay."

"One other thing. I think I will go to Brookline for a few days, if you're going to be working this whole weekend."

Alex nodded. "You should. I don't want my sweetheart sitting here all lonely." He sat down on the bed and pulled off his shoes and his tie.

"Will you call your Mom?"

"Yeah, of course."

"Okay, but please call her back tonight because she's going to keep calling, earlier every day, trying to catch you before you go to the hospital."

"She's been waking you up?" Alex knew his mother very well.

"Yeah."

"Okay, I'll call her."

"Tonight?"

"No," Alex said, grinning. "Tomorrow when I wake up."

Helen burst out laughing.

*

Alex returned to their room the following night and sat down to eat part of the pizza he had just bought. Helen had left that afternoon, to stay with her parents for a week. It was empty here without her, without his Helen of ivory and gold. But she'd be back.

# CHAPTER 20

Helen relaxed in her favored recliner in her family's living room back in Brookline, flipping through *House Beautiful* while watching TV. This was so much more comfortable than anything in that little dorm room she shared with Alex.

Leda bustled into the room, picked Helen's empty cereal bowl up from the end table and rested her empty hand on her hip.

"Helen! You're still in your pajamas!"

Helen glanced down at her clothing. "So?"

"Do you lounge around your apartment in New York all day without getting dressed and doing something?"

"Of course not. I get up early every day," Helen said, her voice testy. "I'm exhausted half the time. So what if I take it easy while I'm here and catch up on my rest?"

Leda exhaled audibly. "Fine. Listen, I'm going to the grocery store. Why don't you throw on some clothes and come with?"

Helen looked past her at the TV. "Um. Okay. When?"

"Well, now." Leda shifted her weight from one foot to the other.

"But Young and Restless is on. Can we go after?"

"Helen, I hope you're not spending your time watching TV in New York instead of doing something productive."

"Um, no, I'm very busy."

Realizing no meaningful conversation could take place until Helen's soap was over, Leda grimaced and stormed off toward the kitchen. She paused and turned toward Helen. "Should be over at half past. Ten minutes from now. Can you get dressed after that so we can go?"

"Sure," Helen said absently, eyes glued to the screen.

"Well, that was nice, having you for company for grocery shopping, honey," Leda said, as they drove back home from Stop and Shop.

"Thanks, Mom," Helen muttered, hoping Mom was not going to get sentimental.

"Just like old times. You and Kelly used to love going shopping with me. You'd ride in the cart like a princess in her carriage, while Kelly would run around investigating everything." Leda's eyes shone, and her lips curved gently into a whimsical smile. Her girls had been so adorable.

Helen was silent.

"And now Kelly's with the Globe, still investigating! And you're married and living in New York!" Leda observed brightly. "I hope Alex treats you like a princess."

Helen rolled her eyes before responding. "He does, when he's around. He works so much though. He's not around until late. At least on this rotation."

"You told me. Well, it's all temporary."

"Yeah, I know."

"So... any grandchildren on the way?" Leda asked hopefully.

"Mom," Helen groaned. "Please."

"I'm just asking. I can dream, can't I?"

Helen nibbled her lower lip and gazed out the window. Truth was, since Alex had been on Surgery, they didn't have sex that much. He usually showed up, ate dinner with her and fell into bed.

"Oh look, that must be a funeral. At St. Mary's," Leda said. "I wonder who died."

Helen turned to look, disinterested. As they drove past, she noted the tall, dark-haired woman in a black dress; a man, her husband surely, wearing a black suit, attentively at her side; along with a young woman and a tall skinny boy, both in dark clothing. They looked so sad. Who were they? They were sort of familiar. Then her breath caught in her throat as she realized- that was Hector's family, his mother and father, and his little sister and brother, grown up! But Hector had not been there. She had had only a glimpse, but she was sure. He was not there. Was it, could it have been, Hector's funeral? Her heart pounded, and she felt lightheaded. She turned her head to look again but the black-clad family was barely visible in the distance. Her breaths came quick and shallow.

"Helen. Helen! Did you hear me?" Leda asked.

"What?"

"Weren't you listening?"

"What?" Helen answered, hoping her mental turmoil was not apparent.

"I just said, do you want beef stroganoff or roast chicken for dinner? I can do either. Dad likes both. Your pick."

"Um, the chicken, I guess." Maybe Hector was there but was still inside the church. Or maybe he had gone to get the car for the rest of the family.

"I'll make rosemary potatoes to go with that. How does that sound?"

*How can I find out who died,* Helen wondered, her head spinning.

"Helen?"

"Oh, sure, sounds good."

They pulled into the driveway and got out of the car. Leda went to the trunk while Helen headed for the house.

"Helen, want to give me a hand with these groceries?" Leda called out.

Helen returned to the car and lifted two bags from the trunk.

"Just leave them in the kitchen; I can put everything away," Leda said, pushing the straps of her handbag up onto her shoulder, and gathering the remaining bags from the trunk.

Wordlessly Helen entered the house and deposited the groceries on the kitchen counter. How could she find out who died? How could it be Hector? He was young. Too young to have some disease. But anyone could die in an accident. Maybe it was just a friend, not a family member. But by the way the Gonzalez family was acting, it must have been someone they all loved. It could have been Hector. Wait! Helen recalled that Hector hated his father. If Hector had died, perhaps Hector's father would not have seemed so sad. So maybe it was someone else. The thought lifted her spirits. But she still had to find out whose funeral it was, to be sure.

She walked back into the living room and sat down in the recliner, musing on how best to solve the problem. Leda had taken a subscription to the Boston Globe when they gave Kelly a job. Today's Globe lay on the coffee table, smelling of newspaper chemicals, reminding everyone how Kelly had a job and she did not. However, the newspaper might say who had died in the Boston area. She flipped through the paper, eventually found the obituaries and started to skim down the columns.

"Helen! What are you doing? This is the first time I've seen you reading the paper," Leda said. She was pleased. Maybe living in New York with Alex, Helen was picking up an interest in current events.

"What? Oh, I'm just having a look." *Mom, go away! Could you be any more nosy?* She kept her head down, looking at the names of that day's dead people. No one named Gonzalez. But this was today's paper. Maybe she should check other days as well. She folded the paper and left it at one end of the coffee table and started to flip through the magazine rack that held earlier issues of the Globe.

"Helen, are you looking for something in particular?" Leda asked.

"No, just looking." *Mom, don't hover!* Helen shoved the old papers back into the magazine rack, returned to her recliner and turned on the TV with the remote. She waited, and eventually her Mom returned to the kitchen. Helen snatched two of the older papers and slipped upstairs to her bedroom to review them in peace. No, still no clue to the identity of the dead person. She crept downstairs and took the last two Globes, but they were equally non-revealing. She returned all the newspapers without her Mom noticing. Although that gave her some satisfaction, she was no wiser than before.

What to do? She could, maybe she could go over to Hector's house and just say she wanted to say she was sorry. She knew that the proper thing to say was 'express my condolences.' She whispered the words, to get the rhythm and the tone right. *I saw you at St. Mary's and I just wanted to express my condolences.* She could do that. It would not be hard. She was just a neighbor expressing concern. Expressing condolences. Yes. Helen went upstairs to take a shower and change into clean clothes.

"Mom, I'm going to borrow the car for a bit, okay?" Helen said casually.

"Borrow the car? Where are you going?"

"I don't know. Just around."

"Well I don't want you joy-riding randomly around Brookline. Gas is not cheap, you know."

"I just wanted to have a look at the neighborhood, see how it's changed."

"Changed? A month and a half ago, you lived here. How much could it have changed?"

"Never mind," she said, resigned.

"If you want to look at the neighborhood, go take a walk. You've been in that chair all day."

"Have not. I went to the grocery store, for one," she said defensively. She returned to the recliner to think. Hector's house was at least a mile away. It would be a long walk, but she could do it.

"Mom, I think I will go for a walk after all. See you later," Helen called and headed for the door.

"Have a good walk then, honey," Leda called.

Helen Eastgard walked resolutely down the front walk of their home and onto the sidewalk. She turned left and headed towards Hector's neighborhood. She would just say, *I would like to express my condolences.* There was nothing wrong with that. She could do that.

She recalled the last time she had been to Hector's house, the things they had done. How upset she had been when he hadn't called her. She flushed at the memory. And then there was that accident, that terrible accident, and he was gone. She had waited for so long, hoping to hear from him. She was such an idiot, she told herself. She was lucky to have Alex even if all he did was work.

Nevertheless, the memory of Hector's muscular body, his emerald green eyes, narrowed, studying her, shimmered like a mirage before her. *Stop!* She told herself. She shouldn't be thinking about him like that. Should she go back? No, she had to know. She strode onward, determined.

Helen finally turned onto Warren Street, Hector's street, Hector's old street. It seemed a long way from the corner as she went, walking, walking, past one little ranch house after another on either side of the street, and then a smallish Colonial on her right, and then suddenly she was standing before Hector's family's home, a grand house with columns and balconies and a professionally maintained lawn. She paused on the sidewalk, hesitant to step onto the front walk. A kid on a bike whizzed past, looking back at her curiously. Well, she didn't want to make a spectacle of herself; she couldn't just stand there. She fluffed her hair nervously and walked to the door of the Gonzalez house. She rang the doorbell and waited. Helen heard people talking inside. Then the door swung open.

"Hello?" A pretty young woman with eyes and hair of soft brown greeted her.

"Are you, are you, Catalina?" Helen asked.

"Yes, and, sorry, who- oh I remember! You're Hector's friend! From high school! Helen!"

"Yes, I am, yes. You're so grown up!"

"Oh, thanks. Do you want to come in?"

"I came, um, I came to offer my condolences," Helen said, stepping across the threshold.

"For, ah, what?" Catalina said.

Helen had a moment of panic. Had she mistaken some other family for the Gonzalez family leaving the funeral? But no, Catalina was one of those she saw. "I thought I saw, I'm sorry if I made a mistake, but I thought I saw your family at a funeral yesterday, and I thought I would, I should say how sorry I was."

"Oh, yes, it didn't occur to me that anyone noticed us. Thank you for coming to see us."

And then Helen asked the question that had haunted her since yesterday. "Could I ask, um, do you mind if I ask, who died?" *Tell me, was it, Hector? I didn't see him with you, and I saw all the rest of your family.*

"It was our housekeeper Conchita. She was quite old and a few days ago she said she was tired, and she went to bed. In the morning when she didn't get up we went and checked on her and found she had passed away in her sleep."

"Oh, I'm glad to hear that, I mean, I'm not glad to hear about Conchita, but I'm glad because you see, I really thought it might have been Hector, and he's so young, it would have been so sad, and..." Helen's words spilled out in an anxious rush.

"Hector? Oh, no, he's-," Cati began but stopped abruptly as she heard footsteps behind her.

"*Quién está aquí, princesa?*" Helen heard a man say from within the house. Must be Hector's father.

"*Una amiga de, de Hector, de la escuela. Se llama Helen. La te acuerdas?*"

"Helen. *Ah, sí. Claro que sí.* Of course, I remember lovely Helen. We were honored to have you join us for dinner that evening after our older son's graduation." He stepped forward, smiled warmly, took both of her hands in his and squeezed tightly, pressing the setting of her engagement ring so hard against her middle finger that it hurt. But Helen smiled, relieved at the kind reception, and surprised that they remembered her so well.

"I- I saw your family in front of St. Mary's yesterday, and I just wanted to stop by and offer my condolences," Helen repeated.

"How kind of you. Won't you come in?" Pedro stepped aside and gestured toward the interior of their home.

"Oh, yes, thank you." Helen stepped into the home, recalling the last time she was here, with Hector, intoxicated by his proximity, thrilled to be invited into his home. That was seven years ago, she thought. Seven years. A lot had changed since then.

"Please, have a seat," Pedro said graciously, inclining his head toward the sofa. "Anita will be so sorry she missed you. She's having her hair done."

157

"Helen, can I get you something to drink? A little something to eat?" Catalina said.

"Um, I'm not hungry, thank you."

"Nothing? Some coffee or tea?" Catalina persisted.

"Oh, well, perhaps coffee," she replied, adding quickly, "If someone else is having some."

"Absolutely. We drink coffee all day long. I'll get you a cup," Catalina said and headed for the kitchen.

"I suppose Cati told you about losing our Conchita," Pedro said. "She has been with us for decades, and with my wife's family before that."

Catalina returned with three cups of coffee, cream and sugar on a tray and set it in front of Helen. Cati watched anxiously as Helen sipped her coffee.

"Is it okay?" Catalina asked.

"Yeah, delicious," Helen replied.

"You see, my princess here has been helping out a lot since Conchita left us. We hardly know how to use the coffeepot!"

"I learned to make coffee in college. You need it to survive. But I just learned from roommates, not from anyone who really knew anything. So, I try, and I'm glad you like it!" Catalina looked pleased.

"And what are you doing now, young lady? I do not believe I have seen you since high school graduation." Pedro sprinkled a spoonful of sugar carefully into his coffee and stirred.

"Well, I was working for a while. Trying to save some money, you know," Helen began.

Pedro nodded, the expression on his face sober and approving.

"And then just this August, I got married, and we're living in New York City," Helen said. *Please don't ask me where I went to college, she pleaded silently.*

"You got married! Who to?" Catalina asked.

"Oh. Um, I'm not sure if you would know him. Alex Eastgard. We met in high school and now he's a medical student at NYU. This is his last year."

"No, I don't know him. What's he like?" Cati asked.

"Oh, he's so sweet and he's so cute. He's really handsome," Helen replied but then wondered if it was rude to praise Alex when she had dated Cati's big brother. Was it like saying Hector wasn't handsome? She flushed and lifted her cup to her lips.

Pedro sat back, careful to keep his smile in place. Alex Eastgard, she had said. He couldn't quite place the name, but he had a vague recollection of something negative, some problem, most likely related to some trouble with Hector. He often wondered whether Hector was doing anything useful with his life. Based on the amount of money he ran through, he certainly had not managed to get a decent job.

"Congratulations, then, young lady. I hope you will be very happy." He stood and said, "I hope you will excuse me. I have some work that won't wait."

"Okay, Papá," Cati said.

"Oh, of course. Thank you," Helen said shyly, hoping she was not overstaying her welcome.

Cati watched her father leave the room. "You know, Hector's in New York City. He's trying to break into acting, but it's really hard."

"Oh? I- I'm sorry to hear he's having trouble. I hope he can make it," Helen said, stumbling over her words.

"I didn't want to mention it while my Dad was here cause he and Hector had kind of a falling out, and Dad gets all tense if anyone mentions Hector's name."

"Oh, I didn't know," Helen said, even though she did.

"You should give him a call. I bet he'd be really happy to hear from you," Cati said and headed for the kitchen, returning a few moments later with a note pad and pen. "Here's his number," she said, writing carefully and handing the small square of paper to Helen.

The paper burned red hot in Helen's fingers; she set it down on the coffee table. "Thanks. Um, I guess I should get going. The coffee was very good." Helen stood.

"Okay, well, thank you for coming. It was very thoughtful for you to go out of your way and come see us," Catalina said.

"Oh, it was my pleasure," Helen said and then wondered if that was the right thing to say, seeing that she had come here because someone had died. She walked toward the door.

"Helen, wait, you forgot Hector's number." Catalina handed it to her again.

"Oh, thank you," Helen said, slipping the paper quickly into the side pocket of her blazer, and she headed back towards her house.

As she walked, she thought of the paper in her pocket, the number jotted on it, a link with a life she had left behind. She let her hand touch the outside of the pocket, feeling the slightly different texture imparted by the crisp little piece of paper within. Finally she slid her hand into her pocket, and gently rubbed the paper between her thumb and index finger, reminding herself of Hector, his beautiful face, his commanding voice, his disdainful saunter. All that time she had spent wondering why he hadn't contacted her, wondering what he was doing! All she had had to do was to go to his house and ask after him and they would have given her his number. She pulled her hand abruptly out of her pocket and quickened her pace toward home. She entered the house.

"How was your walk, honey?" Leda asked, pleased that Helen had finally gotten out of that chair and done something besides watch TV.

"Fine," Helen answered.

"Where did you go?"

"I just walked around." Helen went up the stairs to her room and took off the blue blazer. She slipped her hand into its pocket, withdrew the scrap of paper, crumpled it and started to toss it into the little white wastebasket next to her bed. But she couldn't do it, couldn't open her hand and drop the paper into the trash. It felt too much like a betrayal of someone who had once been important to her, too much like saying Hector was trash. Helen smoothed out the paper and slid it back into the pocket of her jacket. She took off the jacket and returned it to her closet, where it would stay when she returned to New York City.

# CHAPTER 21

Alex Eastgard entered a patient room on the pediatric floor, pulled a curtain to separate the two beds in the room, and sat down in a chair next to 10-year-old Essam's bed. The boy looked uncomfortable and scared. His eyes followed Alex as he sat down.

"Essam, Mrs. Noori. Essam has appendicitis. The surgical team has discussed his case and reviewed all his tests. Essam needs an operation to take out the appendix."

Mother and son fixed their dark eyes on him. "Are you sure, doctor? He has always been so healthy. He always gets better on his own," the mother said.

"Yes, we are sure. And we should do the operation soon. Otherwise the appendix could burst and he could get worse." Alex spoke calmly but firmly.

Mrs. Noori started to cry.

"Ma'am, it will be okay. Essam will be under anesthesia, he'll be asleep for the operation, and then when he wakes up he'll be sore but we have medicine to help him feel better."

She shook her head. "I know about that part. It's, well, we don't have money for an operation. My husband lost his job, and he can only find odd jobs. It is barely enough to buy food."

"Ma'am, they should have explained. This is a city hospital. If you need medical care, you get it. You don't have to pay."

She extracted a kleenex from her sleeve and dried her eyes. "Truly? Truly? This is wonderful. Thank you! Thank you! *Allahu akbar!*"

"Essam, I'm going to need to draw a little sample of your blood so we can check it before you go into surgery. Okay with you?" Alex asked.

Essam gave a little nod. Alex extracted a syringe with a needle and a small tourniquet with velcro closure. The boy's eyes went wide; his brown eyes floated in a broad halo of white.

"Okay, first we kill the germs with this alcohol." Alex swabbed the boy's antecubital fossa. "Now, we let the alcohol evaporate. Otherwise it stings. Now you just keep your arm steady and I'll be done very quickly." Alex watched Essam's face out of the corner of his eye as he collected blood for a CBC and an SMA6. The kid was scared as hell, but he didn't flinch.

"Okay, I'm going to have your blood checked and then later today we will take you to have that surgery. You just hang in there. It'll be okay," Alex assured them. "Cameron! Were you listening in?" Alex said to the kid who had slipped from the other bed in the room and was now peering past the edge of the curtain. Cameron was an undersized child with congenital heart disease whose only hope for survival to adulthood was a transplant he was unlikely to get.

"Yeah, well, is Essam going to be okay?" Cameron asked timidly.

"Yes, he's going to be fine. You need help getting back into bed?" Alex slipped the tubes of blood into his white coat to free up his hands.

Cameron, still clinging to the curtain, shook his head.

Essam leaned forward a little. The movement made his tummy hurt worse but he needed to say something. "Um, Mister Doctor, will you be there, for the surgery? While I'm asleep?"

"I sure will. And thank you for calling me doctor but I'm still a student for a few more months. The chief resident will do the surgery. He is very experienced, so don't worry. Try to relax now. I need you to be patient for just a little longer. Cam, you be good." Alex nodded at them and left to deliver the tubes of blood.

*

Alex headed downstairs to grapple with the Coffee Dragon whose lair was on the first floor of the hospital. Essam's surgery had gone smoothly, and he was in Recovery. Alex now wanted a cup of coffee and he wanted it hot. When he was within sight of the coffee stand, he slowed his pace and studied the situation. No one was at the counter at the moment. The Coffee Dragon used the interlude to fill several styrofoam cups with coffee and snap on plastic lids. She added these cups to one of several tall columns of full coffee cups. She was clad in one of those shiny satin tunics she typically wore, bright green today, with her hair up in a striped gold and red turban. Her nails were ridiculously long and painted bright red. But it was not her clothing, nor her claw-like nails, that were responsible for Alex's unspoken designation of Coffee Dragon. It was her personality. An unsuspecting woman approached and asked for coffee. Alex noted that the Dragon selected a cup from one of the columns, but not the one she had most recently added cups to. The customer paid and went away, not yet aware that she was about to drink lukewarm coffee. The Dragon filled another cup and reached to add it to a column as Alex arrived at the counter.

"Can I have a cup of coffee?" Alex asked, using a stern tone. He watched as the Dragon set down the most recently poured cup and reached for one from the opposite side of her workspace.

"Not that one. Pour me a fresh one." Alex knew he would never get her to pour him a cup of coffee, but it was a good way to start the negotiations.

"They all fresh," she said in a harsh rasp, and crossed her emerald sleeves across her chest, waiting for his next move.

"No, they're not. They're mostly cold." Someone else was approaching for coffee. That was good, because the Dragon would try to settle with him before her next customer arrived.

"No, they not. They all hot." Reflections of the hospital's fluorescent lights glittered in the gold of her headdress.

"They are not. You've got coffee you poured this morning." That was a conservative estimate. For all he knew, some might be from last week. "I want a fresh cup that's hot."

"I ain't pouring no new coffee when I already poured all these others." Her voice was a sullen husky hiss.

"Okay, I'll settle for the cup you just set down," Alex said. If she were ever to smile, would he see fangs?

She reached for a cup from the top of one of the precarious towers.

"Not that one. The one you just put down. No. To the right. No. One more over. Fine." Alex pulled a dollar from his pocket and set it down on the counter. "Why don't you just wait until people come up and then pour the coffee?"

"You know what? You do your job, I'll do mine. I been at this 20 years. I don't need no kid telling me how to do my job." Metaphorical smoke erupted from her nostrils.

"Okay. See you tomorrow," Alex said. She glared at him as he turned away. Sarah was in the ER this month. Maybe he'd drop in for a moment and see what was going on.

He crossed the lobby and pushed open one of the swinging double doors that led to the ER, stepped aside and lifted the edge of the lid of his coffee. Hot!

What a victory! He didn't always win. Sometimes he was in too much of a hurry to spar with the Coffee Dragon, and he ended up accepting cold coffee. But not today!

From the interior of the ER came an anguished roar, then multiple voices, medical voices, struggling to stay calm. A woman's voice, words coming faster and faster, taking on a tone of hysteria. That was Sarah! Alex hurried forward. The crack of heavy plastic on linoleum. The roar again. Alex came to the end of a tiled wall and looked past it, taking in the chaotic scene. A young man lay shirtless in restraints in his heavy hospital bed, straining against the belts holding him down, thrashing from side to side, with Sarah standing helplessly to one side, clutching her stethoscope. A big turquoise hospital tray and the components of a hospital lunch lay scattered on the floor. A blob of chocolate pudding clung to the leg of Sarah's blue scrub pants.

"Mr. Lopes? Mr. Lopes. You need to, could you," Sarah sputtered helplessly, as with a tremendous effort the young man threw himself to the right, wrenching the left side of the bed off the floor. The bed teetered on two legs and fell over, landing on top of Mr. Lopes, who continued to roar, oblivious to any injury he may have sustained. An IV pole crashed to the ground, along with a bag of normal saline. Sarah let out a high-pitched yelp. She shielded her face with her clipboard and hopped backwards as pudding slid down her pant leg.

"Sarah! Jesus Christ! What's going on?" Alex said, running to her side. "That bed almost landed on you."

Sarah had squatted down and was peering through the hand rails of the bed. "Mr. Lopes? Are you okay? You can't do that, okay? We're going to flip you over, but please don't do that again, okay?"

Mr. Lopes answered with a blood-curdling howl.

"Do you want to try to turn the bed right side up?" Alex asked a muscle-bound orderly. Mr. Lopes thrust his hands through the hand rails, grasping wildly, but the leather bands on his wrists kept him from reaching too far. Sarah scooted back a little in an attempt to ensure her safety.

"Oh, Alex, hi, what a mess. This guy is high as a kite on god knows what. Maybe PCP. I can't believe he flipped the bed! Oh, man, half of my hair came loose." Sarah took out her hair clip, shook out her long hair, twisted it, rolled it back up and enclosed it in the hair clip. "Maybe he is better off down there," she said, peering uncertainly at the patient, his thrashing making the mattress flop around.

"Could be angel dust. Is there an attending?" Alex asked.

"I went to the desk before, asked someone to come. Everyone's busy," the orderly intoned.

"Butch, you stay so calm. Have you ever seen a bed flip?" Sarah asked the orderly, adjusting her wire-rimmed glasses.

"I seen everything, but no, I never seen that. Not 'til today."

"I think we should flip the bed over. He could suffocate under the mattress," Alex said.

"Okay," Sarah said. "Butch, you okay with that?"

"Not really, but I'll be in deep shit if this gomer kicks the bucket on my shift." Butch snapped on a pair of disposable rubber gloves and bent over to take hold of the bed's guard rails on one side. Alex and Sarah stepped up on either side of Butch. "Watch out where you put your hands. He'll grab for anything."

"Okay, on three. One-two-three," Sarah said. Together they managed to push the bed onto its side and then back upright. Mr. Lopes howled, unfazed by his recent experience.

"I think he's tiring out," Butch opined.

"Yeah, maybe his roar has lost its edge. You think he won't flip again?" Sarah asked.

"Doubt it." Butch pulled off his gloves and flipped them into the trash.

Alex cautiously approached the troublesome Mr. Lopes. His bare torso glistened with sweat. The tangle of sheets was drenched with sweat, and judging by the smell, with urine as well.

"What are you doing for him?" Alex asked.

"Tox screen is cooking. Took three people to hold him down while I drew the blood, which was not easy. His veins are shot. Took like an hour to get that IV going." Sarah picked up the IV pole and checked the IV. Miraculously the needle was still neatly taped in place, and normal saline still flowed rhythmically, drop by drop, into Mr. Lopes's scarred veins.

"If he'd messed up this IV, no way I was redoing it," Sarah said.

"Kind of makes you miss gross anatomy. Little old Minnie never gave us problems," Alex reminisced.

"Tell me about it. I'm doing the 24-hour ER shift. It sucks! All I can think about is getting out of here and taking a shower and getting some sleep." Sarah plucked an errant tendril of hair from her forehead and tucked it behind her ear.

"I'm on Peds Surg for two weeks. I really like the kids. But there are some kids that you can't do much for. Really sad."

"Yeah, it's sad," Sarah agreed, but her voice was flat.

A nurse strolled in. "Dr. Rosenberg said if this patient's stable there's another admit he wants you to do."

Sarah turned around to inspect Mr. Lopes. He lay quiet on his soggy mattress. "Mr. Lopes, I have to go for now. Feel free to call if I can do anything for you," Sarah said.

Mr. Lopes howled and thrashed in response but his efforts were half-hearted.

"Do I detect a note of sarcasm?" Alex asked.

Sarah grimaced.

"Okay, I'm going to check on my little guy who had his appendix out. He should be back in his room by now." Alex reached for his coffee which was cold now, his struggle with the Coffee Dragon all for naught.

"Okay, thanks for coming by." She turned to the nurse. "As soon as the tox screen comes can you let me know?"

"Sure, if it comes to me." The nurse waddled off.

"Just great," Sarah muttered to Alex. "My job is to track down lab results on top of everything else."

"How much longer do you have?" Alex asked.

Sarah glanced at her watch. "Seven hours and 22 minutes."

"You'll make it. I have confidence in you," Alex said and grinned. He turned to leave.

"Oh, hey, Alex, we're having a little birthday party for Cheryl, Thursday, 9 pm, eighth floor of the dorm. We're just meeting in the hall. Can you make it?"

"Sure. You don't mind if I bring Helen, do you? She'll be back by then."

"Absolutely. I'd love to meet the famous Helen. See you," Sarah said and hurried toward the intake area.

*

Alex entered the hospital room quietly. Essam was asleep. Even in the dim light, he could tell that he was resting comfortably, his color good, his respirations slow and even. Alex's eyes drifted to the foot of the bed, where a little boy was kneeling. Alex stopped breathing. It was Patrick; it was Patrick looking like he did on the day they first met, a vulnerable little fair-haired kid. Patrick turned toward him, his face serious. And then the spell was broken, and it was Cameron, not Patrick, Cameron keeping watch over Essam. Alex shook his head. Crazy hospital lighting. Or maybe lack of sleep.

166

"I thought I'd sit here for a while in case Essam needed anything," Cameron whispered. "His parents were here but they left a little while ago. His brothers were making noise and the nurses got mad and told them to go home cause he was going to be out until morning."

Alex nodded.

"How come you were looking at me funny?" Cameron asked.

"Was I?" Alex asked, pulling up a chair and sitting down.

"Yeah, you looked surprised or something."

"You know what? Just for a moment you reminded me of a friend of mine. You look something like he did when he was a kid."

"I do?" Cameron sounded flattered. "Does he live around here? Does he work in this hospital?"

"No, not around here. He- he's in Massachusetts. That's where I'm from."

Cameron nodded slowly as he absorbed this information.

"Okay, buddy, I'm heading home." *I should really get some sleep*, Alex told himself. "You go get in your own bed."

"Okay." Cameron took a last look at Essam, slid out of his bed and climbed into his own. He adjusted the curtain so he could see Essam.

"Good night, Cam," Alex said, going toward the door.

"Good night, Dr. Eastgard," he answered.

Alex exited the hospital and began the short walk back to the dorm in the cool autumn night. His gaze wandered up and he examined the sky. A distant wind drew a translucent veil of high, thin clouds across the face of the full moon. What was Helen doing, he wondered. Was she seeing this same brilliant moon? Was she thinking of him?

\*

That night Alex had the nightmare. He wound his fingers around the metal of the chain link fence and pulled as hard as he could, shook the fence with all of his strength, and yet it stayed intact, as he watched the horror of Patrick's death replayed before his eyes. He awakened, shaking and covered with sweat. He would be glad when Helen was back; she kept the nightmares away.

# CHAPTER 22

Helen Eastgard relaxed in the recliner, absorbing every detail of that day's episode of Young and Restless while nibbling her breakfast, one Cheerio at a time. The phone rang. Helen frowned, reluctant to answer and be distracted from her show. The phone rang a second time. Maybe Mom would get it. No, she was in the shower; Helen could faintly hear the low whistle of water running in the bathroom upstairs. The phone rang a third time. Helen tried to ignore it. It rang a fourth and fifth time, and then a sixth. Helen sighed. Must be one of those annoying people who doesn't know to hang up after five rings, she concluded, and grudgingly reached to answer the phone.

"Hello?" Helen said, eyes still focused on the TV.

"Leda. It's Olivia. I'm glad you finally answered," Alex's mother's distinctive voice erupted from the receiver.

"Oh, no, it's Helen, not Leda," Helen said. "She's in the shower at the moment. I'll tell her you called."

"Helen! That explains it. I've been calling Alex's room, but no one answers." Olivia sounded irritated.

"Well, Alex was probably working and I'm spending a few days in Brookline." *How can I get off this phone call*, Helen asked herself.

"In Brookline? Shouldn't you be in New York with Alex?" This Helen that Alex had incomprehensibly selected to marry was absolutely hopeless. Olivia would never have left Philip to fend for himself.

"Um, well, I'm just here for a few days, and, um...," Helen began, stung by Olivia's harsh reproach, wondering what response could possibly be acceptable. And then suddenly it came to her. "I hate to leave Alex alone, of course, but I missed my Mom so much. I just had to come back for a few days."

"Well, that is understandable. Your mother is a fine woman," Olivia said, wondering whether Alex ever felt the same way about her. He had spent very little time at home since Philip died, and since marrying this silly little blonde, he barely found time to have a telephone conversation with her. "When do you return to New York?"

"Tomorrow afternoon," Helen answered. Would Olivia please get off the phone and out of her hair so she could get back to her program?

"Tomorrow afternoon. Fine. Will you have your mother call me? We must discuss coordinating for Thanksgiving dinner."

"Thanksgiving? That's over a month away."

"That's correct. Just over a month left. No time to waste. Have your mother call me. Don't forget, please," Olivia said, recalling the apparently unheeded requests she had made recently, asking Helen to tell Alex she had called.

"Um, sure. Of course," Helen replied. Could she get back to her show now? She shouldn't have to be Olivia's secretary.

*

The following day Helen was comfortably ensconced in her recliner, enjoying the last episode of Young and Restless she would see before returning to New York. The doorbell rang, interrupting her train of thought. *I'm not getting it*, she told herself. Maybe Mom will get it. Maybe it's someone looking for a donation and they'll go away.

The doorbell rang again, twice in quick succession.

"Helen, can you get that? I'm not dressed," Leda called down the stairs.

"I'm in pajamas," Helen called back.

"But you're right there. Just go see who it is," Leda said.

"Okay," Helen muttered, reluctantly sitting up and rising from her seat, keeping her eyes on the TV screen, as she shuffled to the door in her slippers. The doorbell rang again, a prolonged chime set in motion by the finger of an impatient visitor. Helen opened the door.

"Helen! You're still in pajamas?" Olivia stood on the front step, her visage serious, her tone critical.

"Um, well, I've been getting ready to pack, so..." Helen stammered.

"Aren't you going to ask me in?" Olivia said.

"Oh, um, sure," she stepped aside to make way for Olivia, while surreptitiously trying to catch a little more of Young and Restless.

"Now, I have assembled some things for you to take back to New York. There are certain foods that Alex likes, and I've prepared several of them for you to take with you." She set down a large shopping bag with a heavy thud. "Most of these should be kept refrigerated until just before you leave. I have included several cold packs to keep things cold, and those should go into the freezer until you pack these things back up. I double-bagged everything in these two good sturdy shopping bags from Filene's. They should hold just fine."

"Um, thank you."

Leda descended the staircase. "Olivia, what a nice surprise."

"How are you? I'm just dropping off some food I prepared for Helen to take back to New York." She inclined her head toward the shopping bags.

"How thoughtful! Helen is still learning to cook, so I know they'll appreciate it."

Helen wondered if it might be alright if she were to quietly watch the last of Young and Restless. She started to sit down in her recliner but realized that Olivia was blocking the view from that seat. Helen stepped over to the far end of the couch and started to sit.

Olivia fixed her laser vision on Helen. "Helen, as I mentioned, several items in this package should really be refrigerated and the cold packs should be stored in the freezer until just before you leave."

"Um, okay." Helen stood and took the shopping bags and headed for the kitchen. Weighs a ton, she thought, with a last mournful glance at the TV.

*

Alex and Helen stepped out of the elevator and into the hall that ran down the center of the eighth floor of the dormitory.

"Hey, Alex!" Cheryl called. She and Sarah and Ben and a few others were seated in the hall in chairs dragged from adjacent dorm rooms.

"Cheryl, hi, happy birthday," Alex said, bending down to kiss her cheek. "This is my wife, Helen."

"It's so nice to meet you, Helen. Alex talks about you all the time," Cheryl said.

"Oh, thanks, and happy birthday," Helen replied, speaking softly.

"So this is the famous Helen, the face that launched a thousand ships," Sarah quipped, but not unkindly.

Alex dropped to one knee in front of Helen, "Sweet Helen, make me immortal with a kiss, and none but thou shalt be my paramour!"

Helen ducked her head. "Oh, Alex, really, you're too much!" She studied Cheryl and Sarah from under feathered lashes. Both of them were so dowdy! *If these are the kind of girls he's used to, no wonder Alex thinks I'm so great.*

Alex leapt to his feet. Helen was a little embarrassed but he knew she enjoyed the praise.

"Alex, you're awful." Sarah rolled her eyes.

That Sarah could be attractive if she half-tried, Helen thought. But there she was, with her baggy clothes and long stringy hair that badly needed a shampoo.

"As I recall, you started it," Alex said, smiling. "We brought a few things to contribute to the party. Here's a bottle of red wine, not great but decent, and a dozen brownies."

"Brownies?" Ben's eyes lit up. "Baked with pot?"

"No, sorry. At least not that I know. Mom made them along with a bunch of other stuff and gave it all to poor, unsuspecting Helen to haul from Massachusetts to New York. There's another dozen brownies back in our room. As well as meatloaf, fried chicken, mashed potatoes and, what else?" Alex looked at Helen.

"There was a box of cinnamon-apple flavored instant oatmeal. I learned it was your favorite breakfast and you had it every morning growing up," Helen said.

"Really?" Alex laughed. "I don't even remember what I used to eat." As he opened the wine, Cheryl grabbed a stack of white plastic cups, and held each in turn for Alex to fill, then handed them around. As Cheryl gave Sarah a cup, Helen noted that Cheryl had clearly never had a decent manicure. And Sarah! It looked like Sarah must bite her nails. Helen could hardly believe how some women could let themselves go.

"Maybe we should move the party to Alex's room then," Ben suggested. "I wouldn't mind some fried chicken to go with the wine."

"Hey, here comes Steve!" Cheryl said.

"If Jerry Grossman shows up, we'll have a reunion of our entire cadaver group," Ben said, raising his glass to toast his observation.

"I invited Jerry; he might come," Cheryl said, taking a sip of the wine. "Alex, this wine is okay."

"I'll give you 3:1 odds that if Jerry shows up, it's with a bimbo in tow," Sarah said.

"Sarah, better drink your wine; I think that ER shift made you disillusioned with all mankind. Jerry's not a bad guy," Alex said.

"You like everybody. There's something wrong with that," Sarah complained. She set down her wine and cleaned her wire-rimmed glasses with the bottom of her T-shirt. "You'd probably even like that Lopes guy if he were your patient."

"What Lopes guy?" Cheryl asked.

"This patient I had in the ER. He was screaming and howling and he flipped his bed over," Sarah answered.

Cheryl's eyes widened. "He flipped the bed over? I didn't think that was possible."

"He was so high. He had no idea what he was doing," Alex said.

"Listen to you, making excuses for him!" Sarah said with scorn.

"You think that's bad. I had a patient, came in with fever and a murmur. Of course, we needed to get blood cultures and an IV going until we could rule out endocarditis. But he had no veins whatsoever. Nothing." Steve gestured with his cup of wine. "So, the chief resident said we needed to start a central line. Which we did. I mean the chief resident stood there and told us exactly what to do, but it was not easy and took a long time. We get our cultures and start antibiotics, and the guy defervesces and is feeling better. Then on rounds this morning, he's gone. Went AWOL with his central line."

"Wait, what was wrong with him that he didn't have veins?" Helen asked.

"Has Alex really not told you about this?" Sarah asked, incredulous.

"I try to spare her," Alex replied.

"Understood," Steve said, nodding. "A lot of our patients are IV drug users, mostly heroin, and if they keep shooting up, after a while the veins just scar down. You can't draw blood or start an IV or anything. And they can even have trouble finding a vein to shoot into. But this guy left with his central line, which is like gold for him. He can shoot up all he wants into the line we started, no problem."

"But even a central line can't be left in indefinitely, so he'll probably be back after it gets infected, and the whole cycle will begin again," Alex said. "It's really discouraging. A lot of the time I feel I'm more of a technician whose job it is to draw blood than a student who's supposed to be learning."

"Okay, enough of that. This is Cheryl's birthday. We've got cake and wine and brownies. Let's talk about something more pleasant," Sarah said, and drained her glass. "Alex, can you fill this up?"

"Okay, something more pleasant. Helen, tell us about yourself. How did you and this joker meet?" Ben asked. He gave his dark curls a good shake as he spoke.

"Oh, um, Alex and I met in high school, and after graduation we went our separate ways. Then a couple of years ago we reconnected and then got married, and now here we are," Helen said with a smile.

"What were you doing before you moved here?" Sarah asked.

"Um, I was working in a dentist's office, trying to make some money, nothing exciting." Helen took a small sip of her wine.

"Do you like New York? Some people find it intimidating. People either love it or hate it. No in-between. I've lived here my whole life, except for college, and I can't imagine living anywhere else," Sarah said.

"Oh, well, I know what you mean about it being intimidating. But Alex has been so great, showing me around and all. There's so much to see," Helen said.

"Yeah, I mean, I spent four years at Berkeley, and it was a great school, but California is not New York. I'm glad to be back."

"Wow, I can imagine," Helen said agreeably.

"Where did you go?" Sarah asked.

"Huh?" Helen blinked.

"Where did you go to college? I mean, is NYC a real culture shock for you?" Sarah continued.

"Oh, I didn't, um, actually go. To college." Helen felt herself flush.

"You didn't go to college?" Sarah glanced at Alex and then turned back to Helen.

"Well, no, actually. I was never sure what I wanted to study so I never applied, and time just went by, and then I had my job which kept me busy." Helen was sure her face was beet-red, from the roots of her hair to the tips of her ears.

"Hm. Makes sense, I guess," Sarah said, shrugging.

Helen felt everyone's eyes on her. She fought back the tears that threatened to spill onto her cheeks. "I think I'll have a brownie after all," Helen said, turning away, slowly unwrapping a brownie from its plastic wrap, hoping that when she turned back around, someone else would be the topic of conversation. Dimly she was aware of Ben and Steve trading opinions about this year's Yankees, and she was able to relax a little. The rest of the evening she sat in silence, reluctant to take part in the conversation, afraid of saying something that would be considered stupid. She recalled how nice Hector's father and sister had been to her. They didn't quiz her about college.

"Well, we should be getting home. Rounds are early on Surgery," Alex said. He stood, taking Helen's hand. "Night all. I hope you had a good birthday, Cheryl."

Helen remained silent on the way back to their suite, but once the door closed behind them, she sank onto the desk chair and started sobbing.

"Helen, what's the matter?" Alex knelt before her and hugged her. "What's wrong? Tell me!"

Helen continued to cry.

"Sweetie, come on. I've never seen you like this! What's wrong?" Alex had heard that women could be moody, but he assumed Helen was an exception. She was always so poised, so composed. He felt helpless. He hurried over to the sink and filled a glass. "Come on, now, drink this and tell me what's wrong."

Finally, she spoke, sobs interrupting her words. "I was so humiliated!"

"Why? For god's sakes, Helen, what could you be humiliated about?

"The way they all looked at me when I said I didn't go to college. It was awful." She raised her head and looked at him with red, puffy eyes.

"Sweetheart, I don't think they cared. Not everyone goes to college."

"Yes, they did. They thought I was stupid." She had spent so much time that day, getting dressed and doing her hair and make-up, and no one cared. They just cared about where someone went to college. Kelly would fit right in here.

"Now, sweetie, that's just not true. No one thought that. Maybe you're right not to go to college if you don't have a specific interest. There's no point to spend all that money and time if you don't know what you want."

"They don't think that. They think I'm not good enough for you." She let her head drop into her hands and sobbed some more.

"Well, that's ridiculous. I'm the luckiest guy in the world. Listen, if you want, why don't you look into going to college? You could go part time; it wouldn't be hard, and maybe you'd find it enriching. And it would give you something to do while I'm working."

This was not where Helen had hoped this conversation would go. She already had plenty to do, with all the cooking and everything. She had no interest in going back to school. She just wanted Alex to know how upset she was. She wished that he would understand how awful those people were, to make her feel bad like this. But he wouldn't. That was one thing that snooty Sarah with the stringy hair was right about- Alex liked everyone. It wasn't just these people, either. There was Alex's awful mother who wouldn't leave her alone. And now with these people tonight, it was the first time since she'd come to New York that she wondered if this was really the right place for her. Had she really chosen well? If only there were someone she could talk to, but there wasn't. It was horrible not having someone she could confide in.

"Um, that's an idea, I guess, but for now I don't think I have much time for something like that. Maybe in the future." Helen sniffed and wiped her eyes.

"Okay, then, but don't cry, bright angel. You'll always have me on your side," Alex said, and kissed her smooth forehead.

# CHAPTER 23

"Kelly, you too, let's go!" Mike Sullivan barked at her without so much as a sideways glance in her direction. She grabbed her pad of paper and a pen, stood so fast that she stumbled, caught herself, and then followed him as quickly as possible into his office.

Mike, a section editor at the Globe, was her boss. He was a big, tough man, rough-hewn from granite of gray and rusty red. A powerful Cro-Magnon jaw supported his square face. When the jaw moved, it emitted terse phrases in a Boston accent a mile wide. Kelly worshipped him.

Mike pulled his chair back from his desk with an awful screech and sat down with a thud. Kelly timidly slipped into a straight back wooden chair as she noted that the two other reporters present were North End resident Tony Salvatore and former police officer Johnny Callahan. Just as Johnny started to shut the door, the new guy, Aggie, appeared from somewhere, caught the door in his hand and slipped into Mike's office. Aggie scanned the office, noted the absence of empty chairs, and stepped to the back of the room to lean against the wall. Kelly was the youngest present, and the only woman. She sat up straighter and tried to look calm and serious.

"We're going to do a series on drug-related crime in Boston and the surrounding area. I want it to be a real exposé, with fresh stuff, not the usual rehash. Ideas?" Mike roared.

"How about young kids getting involved because of older kids in the neighborhood, or even parents, who used? We saw it all the time," Johnny offered with a sad shake of his head. He reached into a pocket and surreptitiously unwrapped a piece of nicotine gum.

"I want fresh, not a rerun of the same old soap operas," Mike said.

"But you could go to a prison, pick a couple of young guys to interview, let them say how they ended up locked up. Interview their relatives, their friends. People'd eat it up," Johnny persisted. He resumed chewing his gum.

Mike growled softly. "Tony?"

Tony pushed a broad swath of dark hair off his forehead. "How about what's being done around the schools to keep dealers away?"

"Jesus," Mike grumbled. "People will be falling asleep on their morning paper. Aggie, tell me about drugs in Texas."

"Well, I don't know. I mostly shoot tequila," Aggie said in a pleasant drawl.

"I don't mean you personally! I meant, aw, forget it. Kelly, you got anything to contribute or what?"

Kelly took a deep breath. This just might be the opportunity she had been waiting for. "Well, I don't know if it's what you'd want, but there was one fellow in my class in high school, whose parents were originally from Puerto Rico. Everyone knew his dad was a drug dealer," Kelly said cautiously. Mike leaned back in his swivel chair, eying her through narrowed lids. Kelly continued, fighting back her intimidation. "Big time, not one of those guys on the street corner. I honestly can't say how we knew; it was just accepted and not discussed."

"What do you mean? Why did you all think that?" Mike asked suspiciously.

"The family had, well, they have an enormous house, bigger than any other house in their neighborhood. And every underemployed Puerto Rican in the greater Boston area would hang around their house, mowing the lawn, raking leaves, trimming the shrubs, driving the younger kids around, running errands. Whenever the parents showed up at school, the mother always wore a lot of jewelry, often set with gemstones. I recall in particular a heavy gold necklace with emeralds that she wore to graduation."

"Emeralds? Colombian connection, I wonder." Mike interrupted. "Go on."

"That doesn't necessarily make him a drug dealer," Tony said. "Any jewelry store will sell you emeralds. My mother has a ring with emeralds. And some people are rich and have big houses, come by them honestly."

"Kelly, what did the guy, the father, supposedly do for work?" Mike asked, ignoring Tony, and leaning forward to plant his elbows on his desk. Mike loosened his tie and rolled up the cuffs of his sleeves. Mike started each day with his tie in place and shirt cuffs buttoned. As the day progressed, the knot of the tie descended and the cuffs ascended. One could almost tell time by checking the position of Mike's cuffs. They typically hit his biceps around 5 pm, indicating quitting time.

Kelly's glance flicked from Tony's neo-pompadour to Mike's salt and pepper military-style buzz-cut. "I asked the son that once. He said his father was in import-export. I said where, does he have a store in Boston? He said his dad's connections were all over but mainly in Miami, New York City and Puerto Rico. But there was no store or anything. His dad just moved stuff that needed to be moved," Kelly replied.

"Sounds like drugs to me," Aggie responded agreeably.

"Did he say what he imported and exported?" Mike persisted.

"Yeah, I did ask. He was vague, said he didn't know, all kinds of stuff," Kelly said.

"Did the kid, your friend, do drugs? Was he a source for the other kids?"

"He wasn't my friend," Kelly said, too quickly. She forced herself to slow down. "But no, he didn't even smoke pot. We knew the kids who used drugs. He was not one of them."

"No drugs, huh? Straight arrow?"

"No, not at all. In trouble at school all the time. Made bad grades, although he did graduate on time. Always had a lot of money to throw around. He did do a lot of drinking. Smoked a lot too. But cigarettes only."

"Interesting. As though drugs were strictly forbidden, to avoid any link, any suspicion. Anything else?"

"No, sir. That's it. Nothing definite." For long seconds, the only sound in the room was Johnny chewing his gum. Kelly was uncertain whether she should feel proud for piquing Mike's interest or foolish for throwing out accusations she was unable to prove.

Finally, Mike spoke. "I'd like to know more about this family. Kelly, see what else you can dig up. Aggie, you go with her, make sure she doesn't get into trouble. Johnny, I guess if you want to make a draft of your tearjerker crap, go ahead and let me see if there's any potential. Okay, all of you get out of here. Go earn your paychecks!"

As they exited Mike's office, Kelly thought she heard Tony mutter *sotto voce*, 'that girl' and then something she couldn't make out.

Kelly flushed, and turned to the new guy. "Is Aggie your real name? Is it short for something?"

"He's from Texas. That makes him an Aggie," Mike shouted from inside his office.

"Actually sir, I went to Baylor, not Texas A&M. I'm not actually an Aggie." He called back toward Mike's office.

"If I say your name is Aggie, that's what it is. I want no insubordination in my section."

"Well, yes sir, but," Aggie started.

"What's your real name?" Kelly interrupted.

"Marvin."

"Marvin. You know what? Aggie suits you just fine."

*

Kelly and Aggie sat in lumpy upholstered chairs in the parlor of the Pleasant Street Retirement Community, sipping tea from unmatched cups, across an aged Queen Anne-style coffee table from their hostess, retirement community resident Ruth Berkowitz. Kelly sniffed, and caught the scent of harsh commercial disinfectant.

Ruth peered at them uncertainly through hefty trifocals. "Yes, we did own the home at 170 Warren Street. I and my Yitzhak. We decided we should sell when he found out about the cancer. He wanted we should make aliya, but the cancer spread too fast. So, we stayed in Brookline. My Yitzhak was taken from me 22 years ago this August."

"I'm so sorry. We don't want to impose but we had a few questions about the family who purchased the home from you," Kelly said.

"You say you got my name from Town Hall?" Ruth queried.

"Yes, ma'am. Real estate transactions are public record. According to those records, you sold your home to Pedro Gonzalez and his wife," Kelly said, leafing rapidly through papers she had brought in a manila folder.

"You mean they gave you my name? They do that?" She raised her eyebrows and her forehead crinkled like Venetian blinds above the top rim of her eyeglasses.

Aggie broke in. "Yes, ma'am, they did give us your name and we found your number in the phone book. We hope you don't mind us dropping in like this, and we apologize for any inconvenience."

*Look at him,* Kelly thought. *He's good. I need to slow down.*

"So, ma'am, you did sell your home to the Gonzalez family?" Aggie continued.

"Not just me. Yitzhak too. He was still clinging to life at the time of the sale. I think he was holding on to see me settled here before passing on." She sighed heavily.

"We wondered if you could give us any information about the couple," Kelly waited hopefully.

"What terrible people! I wish we had sold to someone else, but they came forward with cash. A lot of cash. Enough to cover all the medical bills. Still, if I'd known what kind of people they were," she lowered her head and moved it side to side slowly.

Kelly and Aggie exchanged a quick look.

"All cash, you say? That's very unusual," Aggie prompted. "How did this couple have so much cash? Did they say?"

"No, I don't know. I should have known better. People like that."

"Why do you say they're bad people? What did they do, Mrs. Berkowitz?" Aggie said, sincerity oozing from every syllable. An errant spring just below the fabric of Kelly's chair nudged her thigh uncomfortably. She shifted to avoid it.

"All those years! All those memories!" Ruth dropped her head into her open hands.

"Please tell us what happened. Why were they bad?" Aggie continued patiently.

"Yitzhak and I, we raised three wonderful children in that house. A beautiful ranch house with a nice yard and a little vegetable garden. I grew all my own tomatoes." She sighed, and a little smile crept onto her face as she reminisced. "My girls had to share a room, sure, but my boy had his own room. It was a wonderful home. But then sometime after Yitzhak passed, one of my friends, Rivka Kellerman, came by. She said, 'Ruth, have you been by your old house?' I said, 'No, why?' Rivka said, 'Ruth, I don't mean to cause you pain, but your home is gone. The lot is all bare. I think they're building from scratch.' It broke my heart! All the memories those rooms held, taken away by some bulldozer like it was some shack, some hovel, not a nice family home."

"Mrs. Berkowitz, are you in touch with anyone from your old neighborhood?" Aggie inquired.

"Oh, sure. My friend Rivka I mentioned. We talk all the time. She has a house on the same street. She lost her husband too, but she was smart. The house was too big for her all by herself. But her daughter and her family moved in. Her son-in-law's a doll. It's wonderful for her. To have family around all the time."

"Do you think Rivka would mind talking with us?" Aggie said. "About the neighborhood, and how it has changed. You know."

"Sure, Rivka loves to talk. Let me write down her number for you."

*

Aggie held the door of the retirement home and ever so lightly touched Kelly's back with his free hand. "Please, go ahead."

There was something about that split-second touch, Kelly realized, and she flushed as she passed through the door. They walked together to the car.

He turned the key in the ignition. "Let's find a phone and see if we can chat with Rivka."

*

Aggie and Kelly stood at the door of a small but well-maintained colonial-style home. Aggie rang the doorbell.

A woman with short-cropped dark hair and piercing black eyes opened the door but remained behind a closed screen door.

"Hello. Is this the residence of Mrs. Rivka Kellerman?" Aggie asked, tone formal.

"Yes. What is it?" she answered, her voice radiating distrust.

"Yes, well, I'm Marvin Harris, and this is my colleague Kelly Fletcher. We're the ones who called earlier. From the Boston Globe."

"Hello," Kelly said, smiling pleasantly. The woman's gaze flicked to Kelly's bare knees and she frowned. Was there something wrong? Kelly was proud of her stylish new suit in lightweight burgundy wool, with its short pencil skirt and fitted jacket.

"Oh. Alright. Come in then. I'm her daughter."

She offered no name. Kelly decided that Black Eyes would be a good designation.

Rivka's daughter held the screen door open as Aggie entered. As he stepped across the threshold Kelly noticed that he respectfully touched a little oblong box attached to the doorframe, and that Black Eyes took that in with what Kelly imagined was approval. Black Eyes led them into the dining room and gestured at an elderly woman seated at the table. "Ma, here are those people who called. Marvin Harris and his assistant."

"Kelly Fletcher. I'm Mr. Harris's co-worker."

"Come in! Sit down! I would be polite and get up, but at my age, that's a lot of effort so I make my own rules." Rivka Kellerman smiled broadly. Kelly noted that given her girth, she was probably right.

"Well, thank you so much for seeing us on short notice, Mrs. Kellerman," Aggie said. "What a beautiful home you have."

Kelly glanced at Aggie. Was he on the level? All dark and somber, in shades of dingy brown. And overseen by that nasty Black Eyes.

"Ah, thank you, thank you. We are very comfortable here," Rivka replied, nodding, pleased.

"Your friend Ruth Berkowitz says that you've lived in this neighborhood a long time," Aggie began.

"Yes, oh yes. Forty-two years now."

"Wow. You must have seen a lot of changes," Aggie continued.

"Oh, yes. My daughter who you met grew up in this house. My son too. Jeremiah. Jerry. He married a nice girl from Brooklyn and they live there. They have four children. Four! Three boys and a girl. And another on the way. He's a dentist. Very successful," she said, nodding again and beaming with pride.

What, does Black Eyes not have a name? Maybe saying it is bad luck, Kelly speculated.

"And Zipporah has the two. Miri is here somewhere. Benjy's," she paused and glanced at a black-framed clock on the wall. "Benjy's davening mincha with his father just now."

Black Eyes does have a name. Zipporah. And what is Benjy doing? Aggie seems to get it. Kelly composed her features, trying not to look confused.

"There's my little Miri. Come here, come here." Rivka gestured at a skinny female standing in the threshold of an adjacent room. "Don't be shy, Miri. Come."

Miri approached. She wore a simple white blouse, an oversized sweater, a faded skirt of mid-calf length, white socks and tennis shoes. From a distance her clothes make her look middle-aged, Kelly thought, but up close, she's just a kid. High school probably.

"Hello," Miri said, barely audible.

"Miri, sit down with us," Rivka gushed.

Miri cautiously pulled out a chair and seated herself next to her grandmother.

"Forty-two years! That's quite unusual nowadays," Aggie said.

"Yes, the world's changing too quickly, I say," Rivka intoned.

"Yes, that's for sure," Aggie said, nodding. "Now your friend Ruth said that one change that distressed you both was that her home was demolished by the couple that bought it."

182

"That, yes, that was awful. A tragedy. A real loss. I still feel for Ruthie. To lose her husband and then that. Terrible!"

Aggie shook his head in sympathy. "Do you know why they would do that? It seems so wasteful."

"Have you seen what they built? A monstrosity!" Rivka's voice trembled with emotion.

"Yes, I have. Why would anyone need such a huge house?" Aggie let his voice rise a little.

"I'll tell you why. Just to show off their money. And another thing, when they built that big house, everyone's taxes went up. Everyone on the block," Rivka said, leaning forward for emphasis.

"Ma, you don't know that. No one at Town Hall would ever say," Zipporah called from the kitchen.

"Zippy, I know what I'm talking about. Just because no one would admit it doesn't make it a lie," Rivka said, directing her voice toward the kitchen. "Another thing," she said, turning back to Aggie and Kelly. "Do you know about square foot ratios?"

Aggie and Kelly exchanged glances. "No, ma'am," Aggie answered.

"That's because you're young. You'll learn. But in Brookline, you're not allowed to build a house bigger than a certain number of square feet depending on the size of your lot. That's the ratio. You've seen that house and the yard. It can't be within the square foot ratio."

"Yes ma'am?" Aggie prompted.

Rivka leaned forward again and shook her index finger at them. "They paid someone off. To get the building permit."

Zippy's voice echoed from the kitchen. "Ma, no one could ever prove that. Will you let it go?"

Rivka lowered her voice to a hoarse whisper. "I know Brookline politics. My husband was on the Town Council. Someone was paid off."

"That's amazing! They really caused you a lot of grief then too, not just Mrs. Berkowitz," Aggie replied. "Is there anything else unusual about the family?"

Rivka paused before speaking. "Well, they're Spanish. And the man doesn't go to work. A man should get dressed in the morning and go to his office and work at his business. But this man, he never goes anywhere on a regular schedule. How can he afford that house if he doesn't go to work?"

Kelly glanced at Miri, and realized Miri was studying her. Miri dropped her eyes.

"And another thing. All those Spanish people coming and going, all the time."

Zipporah appeared in the doorway that led to the kitchen.

"Ma, you know those are the yard people and the cleaning people. If they're rich and they can pay, let them." She turned toward her daughter. "Miri, if you're just sitting there, you can come in the kitchen instead. I could use some help with dinner. Because I don't have that kind of money." Miri complied, silently.

Rivka looked at Aggie and Kelly. "My daughter is too trusting." Kelly smothered a laugh. "I think they're up to no good," Rivka continued.

"Ma, what do you always tell me about *loshon hora*?" Zipporah called out.

"Is there anything specific that makes you say that? Anyone in particular who seems suspicious?" Aggie asked. "Other than the man not going to work outside the home."

"I just know."

"But is it a feeling or something definite you saw or heard?"

Rivka paused again before answering. "It's not *just* a feeling. I know. I just know."

The clock chimed 6:00. Zipporah entered the dining room with a stack of dishes and laid them on the dining room table with a loud clunk. She turned and re-entered the kitchen.

"Well my goodness, it's later than I thought. We should really be on our way. We don't want to take any more of your time, and it looks like you're getting ready for dinner," Aggie said, standing.

"It was a pleasure to speak with you and your assistant," Rivka said with a smile. Kelly bit her lower lip.

"The pleasure was all ours. And actually, Miss Fletcher is my colleague, not my assistant. She's the smart one. They send her along to keep me in line." He winked at Rivka.

Rivka chuckled. "What a world! Well, come again, any time." She planted one hand on the table and the other on the back of her chair and attempted to stand.

"Mrs. Kellerman, please, no need to get up. We can let ourselves out." Aggie and Kelly smiled at her and left the house.

"Well that was interesting," Kelly began, once they were back in the car. "I mean, I know there are a lot of Orthodox Jews in Brookline, but I had never been to any of their houses. Never knew any of the kids. I think they all go to private schools."

"Probably. They would go to religious schools instead of public school if the family could afford it," Aggie responded.

"But you seemed to be familiar with all this. I was clueless. What was that little box on the door frame?"

"Oh, that! That was a mezuzah. There's a little prayer rolled up inside it. You see one of those on the doorframe and you know devout Jews live there."

"How do you know this? I had no idea."

"My grandparents were Orthodox. I made my bar mitzvah and everything."

"Are you still religious?"

"Nah, that's all ancient history. Now I'm just a happy-go-lucky reporter." Aggie winked at her.

"I tell you what. Mrs. Kellerman was a sweetie. Classic grandma. But old Zippy did not like me. She liked you okay, cause you touched her little box on the way in."

"Do not repeat that to Mike Sullivan when we're back at the office. It might be misunderstood."

Kelly laughed and then said, "Why didn't she like me? Did I imagine it?"

"Well, she's happy to have a handsome young Jewish guy in her home, but a pretty shiksa... Don't take it personally."

"I'm not going to comment on your hypotheticals," Kelly said, but she smiled. "We did get some interesting information though."

"Yeah, the building permit business is intriguing but it's so long ago now, hard to know if it would help us."

"What do we do next?" Kelly asked.

"Let's get back to the office and review everything and make a plan." Aggie put the car into reverse and looked over his shoulder to make sure the driveway was clear.

"Aggie, wait." Kelly touched his arm. There was Miri slipping out from the back of the house and hurrying toward the car. She went to the passenger side and Kelly quickly put down her window.

Miri looked at them intently for a moment as though gathering her nerve.

"Maybe you should know. About the people coming and going. Five days before the end of the month, every month, one of those men Grandma mentioned, they come. Always after dark. Sometimes just after dark, sometimes later. They stay inside for a little while, and then they leave with something. A tote bag or a shoebox, something like that. Never anything big. But always carrying something."

"You've seen them?" Kelly asked.

"Yes. I can see their house from my bedroom. I'm usually doing homework that time of day."

"Thanks. This is so helpful," Kelly said. "Thanks so much for coming out and letting us know that."

"It's okay. Also," she said shyly, "I love your outfit."

Kelly grinned. "Thanks! I got it at Filene's Basement. It was a real bargain."

# CHAPTER 24

The sky was an uncompromising gray that day, a gray that erased the bright colors of autumn and threatened an early winter, a gray that shot bolts of frosty air at the unwary few who found themselves carelessly outside without a warm coat. Alex stood close to Helen, blocking her from the worst of the wind as she pulled out her house key and opened the door of her family's home. Leda hurried to meet her and Alex as they stepped inside.

"Alex, honey, we are so glad you were able to get a few days off and spend Thanksgiving with us. Helen's been telling us how hard you work," Leda said. "Helen, take Alex's coat. How was your trip?"

"Crazy! First, we had to get up around dawn and had so much trouble getting a taxi to get downtown to catch our bus, and then the bus was packed! Everyone had loads of luggage and no one would stick it under the bus," Alex said, shrugging off his coat.

"You took the Chinatown bus again?" Leda asked.

"Yeah, the price was right! But the traffic was terrible. I thought we would be stuck in Connecticut until Monday," Alex said.

"I was afraid we were going to miss Thanksgiving dinner," Helen moaned.

"Listen to her. She's exhausted!" Alex said, giving her shoulder a squeeze. "She's not used to getting up so early, poor thing."

"No, you made it in plenty of time. Dad's setting up the living room with 12 different kinds of junk food to sustain those who want to watch the game. He and I are the only ones here," Leda said. "Why don't you put your suitcases upstairs and come down and have a little something to eat and drink, and just relax while we wait for the others to arrive?"

Alex collapsed onto the overstuffed sofa with an expression of bliss on his face, pulling Helen after him. "This is awesome! We are actually sitting! I have no beeper! And I'm here with my wonderful Helen!"

"Oh, Alex, really, my Mom is going to think you're crazy," Helen shook her head.

"What about your Dad? Don't you care what I think?" Tim said cheerfully. Proffering a large, heavily laden bowl he continued, "Alex, Doritos?"

Leda stuck her head out from the kitchen. "Alex, Bloody Mary or mimosa?"

"Bloody Mary would be great, thanks." He leaned back into the enveloping sofa and shut his eyes, enjoying this decadent comfort.

"Helen? Mimosa?" Leda asked.

"Yeah, a mimosa." Helen smiled. It was nice to be home for Thanksgiving, nice that her parents liked Alex. Thinking back, she had been silly to get all upset about what Alex's stupid friends might think about her not going to college and all. Everything would be fine.

Leda emerged from the kitchen and handed Alex and Helen their drinks.

Alex took a sip. "This is delicious, so spicy! Here I was thinking things couldn't get any better, but they just did."

"The secret is- red *and* green Tabasco sauce," Leda called over her shoulder as she hurried back into the kitchen.

The doorbell rang. Tim hoisted himself to his feet. "The gentleman of the house will now greet the next guest." He headed for the door with his lumbering gait.

"Olivia, you come on in! Great to see you!" Tim ushered her in. "Alex and Helen are here already."

"Happy Thanksgiving, Tim. Let me give this to Leda- it's the pies." Olivia's penetrating voice filled the first floor of the house. Helen felt herself tense.

"Hi, Mom! Happy Thanksgiving!" Alex said, hurrying to greet his mother. He hugged her and kissed her cheek.

"Alex! I'm pleased to see you looking so well. I was afraid something might be wrong, considering how infrequently I hear from you," Olivia responded, shoulders back, chin up. She wore a long-sleeved A-line dress the color of the day's gloomy sky.

"Come on, med school is crazy. Let me get through it and I promise to reform and call you more," he said, but his tone was unrepentant.

"Well, time will tell, I suppose," she replied with a sniff.

"Mom, come sit down," Alex said, resuming his spot at the end of the sofa.

"Olivia, can I offer you a Bloody Mary or a mimosa?" Leda called from the kitchen.

Olivia crossed the living room and went to join Leda in the kitchen. "If it wouldn't be too much bother, would you mind if I had a Manhattan? Bloody Mary and mimosa are made with those acidic juices and they don't sit quite right with my stomach."

"No problem at all. Tim makes a mean Manhattan. Tim? Can you make Olivia a Manhattan?" Leda called across the room. She turned back to Olivia and said confidentially, "I have to try to get some work out of him now, before the game starts. After that, there's no hope."

"I am on it, Leda baby. One Manhattan coming right up," Tim said enthusiastically. He stepped over to the glossy maple wood credenza at one side of the living room and set about assembling his materials. He extracted whiskey and sweet vermouth from the cabinet and flipped a bar glass right side up. "Olivia, you want that straight up or on the rocks?" He reached for the ice bucket, conveniently lodged next to the Doritos.

"Straight up, please, on a cold day like this. And I don't need a cherry. It makes the drink overly sweet." Olivia followed Tim's maneuvering with her eyes as she sat down in Helen's beloved recliner, next to Alex's end of the sofa.

"Alex, tell me what's new in New York. What are you studying?" Olivia began.

Alex turned to Olivia, but the doorbell rang again. "Who is that?" he asked.

"That'll be Kelly, and she's bringing a date!" Leda called out.

"Kelly has a boyfriend?" Helen's interest was piqued. She conjured up the image of the kind of guy Kelly would attract. Pasty pale and stoop-shouldered, wearing glasses with heavy black plastic frames. A nerd, like her.

"No, I shouldn't have said 'date.' She's bringing a friend from work. I haven't met him," Leda answered, hurrying to the door.

Kelly strode from the front hall into the living room. "This is Aggie," she said, nodding at the young man at her side.

"Hello. Oh, Mrs. Fletcher, we brought some wine," Aggie said, handing a bottle to Leda.

Alex stood and hugged Kelly warmly and shook Aggie's hand. Helen remained seated. She greeted Aggie with a smile. His looks were not what she expected. This Aggie fellow was about as tall as Alex, with an athletic build, cute face and thick, wavy dark hair. And no glasses. Much more attractive than she had predicted, although he could use a haircut. So why was she disappointed?

"Helen, how do you like New York City?" Kelly asked. Her voice had an unfamiliar disinterested quality to it, Aggie noted. The Kelly he knew radiated intensity. Was something wrong between the two sisters?

"It's wonderful. We have a nice place with a fantastic view," Helen responded. Is this the first time they've spoken since Helen moved to New York, Aggie wondered. They got married a while ago. Long time for sisters to go without speaking.

"And we've been able to see a lot of the city together," Alex said.

"Alex has been an amazing tour guide," Helen said, turning to him with a smile. "We've seen so many beautiful and interesting things."

"What have you liked best?" Kelly asked, stirring her Bloody Mary with her celery cautiously to avoid spilling.

Helen sat up. "Oh, let me think. Maybe, that wonderful home with the gorgeous dining room. Alex, where was that?" Kelly fought the impulse to roll her eyes.

"Dining room? Oh, yes, of course. At the Frick Collection." He turned toward Kelly and Aggie. "Frick was a filthy rich entrepreneur and associate of Vanderbilt who had a mansion on Fifth Avenue, across from Central Park. He left the mansion to the city to be used as a museum. His art collection is fantastic."

"So, analogous to Isabella Stewart Gardner?" Kelly asked.

Alex nodded. "Yes, although Frick's taste was, I'd say, less eclectic, less fanciful, than Isabella's."

"And it has the most magnificent dining room, with a huge, long table and fancy chairs. Just imagine the kind of dinner parties he must have held!" Helen's eyes shone.

"What I like about the dining room is the paintings. Above the fireplace is a portrait of Henry VIII by Holbein, a real masterpiece. On either side of old Henry are good portraits of Thomas Cromwell and Thomas More. Frick had some sense of humor lining those three up on the wall." Alex drained the last of his Bloody Mary. "And on that note, I think the time has come for a refill." Alex stood and walked into the kitchen.

"Alex," Olivia began, as Alex returned from the kitchen with a fresh cocktail.

The doorbell rang again. "My turn to get it," Alex said.

Charlie and Paul stormed into the living room, their heavy footsteps making the floor vibrate.

"Hey, everybody! Helen, Alex. Happy T-day, Mrs. E!" Charlie said, clapping a big hand on Olivia's gray-clad shoulder.

"Why, thank you, ah, thank you-" Olivia said, unable to distinguish Charlie and Paul, and reluctant to take a guess and embarrass herself.

"Whoa, Kelly, did you bring a date?" Paul asked, gawking at Aggie.

"Hi there, I'm Aggie. I work at the Globe with Kelly." Aggie said, extending his hand. Paul grabbed it and pumped it enthusiastically.

"Everyone! Quiet! The game is on!" Tim commanded. He picked up the Doritos and handed them to Kelly. "Pass these around, honey," he said without taking his eyes off the TV.

"Alex, how are things at school? Still making straight A's?" Olivia asked, speaking softly, leaning toward Alex.

"Things are good," Alex began. "We-"

"Look at that sucker run!" Charlie yelled.

"Touchdown! Touchdown!" Tim and Paul howled together. Alex leapt to his feet and cheered.

Olivia frowned. She looked past Alex and caught Helen's eye. "Dear, how are things going with the cooking? Are you picking up the knack?"

"What's that? Sorry, they're all yelling," Helen said. Olivia made her nervous. She wished she would leave her alone.

Olivia drained the last of her Manhattan. "I believe I'll go help Leda," she said. No one acknowledged her comment, she noted with displeasure, and Tim did not offer her another Manhattan, even though she was standing with extended arm ostentatiously holding an empty glass. She cast a withering glare at the oblivious football-watching crowd. She started for the kitchen, paused, and then walked behind the sofa over to the credenza, where all the ingredients for preparing a drink were still laid out. From the corner of her eye she saw Charlie (or Paul) leap off his improvised seat on the coffee table and onto the recliner Olivia had vacated. She shook her head silently as she prepared a fresh Manhattan. Thus fortified she made her way to the kitchen, head held high.

"Olivia," Leda said, reaching around to the back of her waist to untie her apron, "I believe that blasted game is almost over. Let's start putting out the food." She hoisted the platter with the oversized golden-brown turkey firmly in both hands and pushed the kitchen door open with her back.

"The table is lovely, a real work of art, Leda," Olivia said, taking a sip of her third Manhattan. "Everything smells wonderful too."

"Thanks! Let's hope the ravening hordes appreciate it." Leda set down the turkey and headed back to the kitchen for the stuffing.

"Good bread, good meat. Good God, let's eat!" Tim, Charlie and Paul chanted in unison.

"At least they'll pause a moment to say grace," Leda whispered to Olivia. Olivia nodded, her hands neatly folded in her lap, as she waited for food to be passed.

"Leda, baby, this looks fantastic!" Tim stood and started carving thick slices of turkey breast. He distributed them, starting with Olivia, who acknowledged his gesture with a gracious nod, and continuing with the other guests before serving his family.

"Dad, come on, the drumsticks!" Paul prompted, fork and knife in hand, ready to go.

"Cool your jets and eat some stuffing," Tim replied.

Leda smiled apologetically and scanned the table. "Usually our boys take the drumsticks. Does anyone mind?"

Alex replied, "No, of course not."

Aggie shrugged. "I prefer white meat."

"I couldn't say. I've never tasted a drumstick," Kelly looked at Aggie and gave him a smile that said, *this is my family*.

"Turkey's perfect, babe! Dee-licious!" Tim said, as he devoured his slab of meat. "Boys?"

"Yeah, it's all great, Mom," Paul said.

"Yeah, really good," Charlie echoed. He held his drumstick in his left hand, using it to push mashed potatoes onto his fork.

"Kelly, it's almost dark!" Aggie whispered. Their eyes locked.

"We have to go! Sorry to run off." Kelly leapt out of her chair and ran for her coat.

"What, are you vampires or something?" Paul chuckled. Pretty clever, he thought, turning to Charlie for confirmation. Charlie pounded the table and laughed while Paul sat back, looking pleased.

"Thank you, thank you all. It was great meeting you," Aggie said as he slid his arms into his overcoat.

"Why, Kelly, where are you going? We haven't had dessert yet." Leda set her silverware down on her plate and looked perplexed.

"Mom, sorry. It can't be helped. It's for work. If we finish up early, we'll be back," Kelly called over her shoulder. The front door opened and slammed shut, and they were gone.

Olivia frowned. She had labored over the pies, even making the crusts from scratch. She had calculated for the total of nine who would be at dinner, that three pies- pumpkin, apple and chocolate cream- would provide a generous amount of dessert for each person. Now if that number dropped to seven, three pies would be a ridiculously large amount of dessert. Had she known, she would have skipped the chocolate cream pie. All that time she had spent melting chocolate in the double boiler, and stirring the filling waiting for it to thicken, wasted.

"Hey Paul, you think they reserved one of those rooms you get by the hour?" Charlie asked, with a nudge to his twin's elbow.

"Charlie! Shame on you! That's your sister you're talking about!" Leda said.

He shrugged. "Well she's supposed to be an investigative reporter. If I was a reporter trying to figure out why they ran out of here like their hair was on fire, that's all I can think of."

*

Aggie turned off the car's headlights as he turned slowly onto Warren Street. He parked two car-lengths from the Gonzalez's driveway and studied the shadowed monolith of the Gonzalez home. A soft amber glow from the downstairs windows spoke of order and serenity within.

"Aggie, look," Kelly said, pointing towards the ranch house where Rivka Kellerman and the disagreeable Zippy resided. "Isn't that Miri in the window?"

Aggie turned and saw the slender dark silhouette partly blurred by sheer curtains. "I think you're right."

"No action from the Gonzalez's," Kelly commented.

"Don't be so impatient! We just got here." Aggie extracted the night vision goggles borrowed from Mike Sullivan. Mike, in addition to other colorful aspects of his background, was a lieutenant in the army reserves. He had indicated that night vision goggles were an essential component of their annual bivouac, held in the forests of western Massachusetts. "These are great!" Aggie whispered as he settled the goggles in front of his eyes.

Kelly's gaze flicked from the driveway of the Gonzalez house to Miri's window. Miri was immobile and the driveway remained empty.

"Do you think it could be the wrong night? Maybe it's tomorrow," Kelly said.

"Well, Miri said five days before the end of the month. We figured if 30 days hath November, the night of the 25th would be the right night," Aggie replied, scanning the street with his goggles in place.

"I don't know. It's getting late. Could we have missed it?" Kelly said, peering anxiously into the darkness.

"You want to go knock on Zippy's door and ask to talk to Miri? Clarify about which night?" Aggie grinned.

"Oh, yeah, that'd fly like a lead balloon."

"Calm down. We're on a stake-out. You have to be patient."

"Yeah, we are. We're on a stake-out! Kind of cool, huh?"

"That's the spirit. Here, try the night vision goggles." He handed them to Kelly.

"Wow! These are amazing!"

"Military grade! Only the best!" He cautiously lifted his right hand to Kelly's shoulder, then rested his fingers gently on the bare skin of Kelly's neck.

Kelly's head whipped around and she glared at him through the goggles. "Aggie, come on. We're on a stake-out."

"No harm intended. Can I take you to dinner Saturday?"

"Fine. Just let's concentrate on this for now," Kelly snapped, as she studied the street.

A car drove past them and parked on the street in front of the Gonzalez's house. A young man in a heavy sweatshirt got out, shut the door and locked it. He walked along the sidewalk toward them, turned onto the driveway and sauntered toward the back of the house. Kelly's hands were shaking as she adjusted the goggles.

"He looks familiar. I think that's, that's Luis Vargas, from our high school class."

"He would know Hector?" Aggie asked, as he tried to memorize all that he could about the young man who had just walked past them.

"Oh, yes! Luis was one of Hector's best friends. If it's Luis coming here, there must be some link with Hector," she said, trying to contain her excitement.

Aggie nodded. "Okay. It's 8:22. Let's see how long he stays in there."

The minutes crept by slowly. "What do you think they're doing?" Kelly whispered.

"I don't know. Being polite. Having coffee or something. Don't be so impatient."

"Look, here he comes!"

"8:45. He was in there for 23 minutes." Aggie pulled a small note pad from his jacket pocket and noted the times.

Luis walked quickly back to his car, rubbing his arms vigorously to warm them. A small shopping bag swung from his left wrist.

"He's got something! He is carrying something!" Kelly exclaimed. "It's a bag, looks like a paper bag, a small shopping bag."

Luis reached his car, opened the door, carefully folded over the top of the shopping bag, and thrust it under the front passenger seat. And then he was gone.

Kelly and Aggie looked at one another. "Oh my god! I think this is for real!" Kelly said.

"Next month is December. 31 days. The pick-up will be on December 26th. Day after Christmas," Aggie calculated. "We have to go to Mike. Next time we should get police to stop the guy and see what's in the bag."

"Can we do that?"

"Mike will know. Let's go." Aggie started the car and they drove away.

*

Olivia drained the last of her Irish coffee. "Well, it's getting late. I think I'll be on my way," she said, rising unsteadily from the Thanksgiving table.

Alex watched with concern. "Mom, let me drive you home."

"Alex, it's not necessary. And how would you get back here?"

"I don't like you driving- ah, by yourself this late at night. A lot of accidents happen over Thanksgiving. And after all this food, I'm thinking a run would feel great. Let me change clothes and I'll drive you, then run back. It's not far."

"Well, in that case, I suppose it would be nice." Olivia carefully lowered herself back into her chair.

Alex reappeared minutes later in running clothes. He walked to his mother, firmly took her arm and led her to the door. He was glad he had offered to drive her. Her gait was distinctly unsteady as she leaned against him. How much had she had to drink? The Manhattans. Wine with dinner, then Irish coffee. Should he say something? Maybe not. She would be offended and defensive. Perhaps rightfully so. Tonight was unusual. Surely she didn't always drink this much.

"Mom, do your seatbelt," Alex said as he started the car.

"Alex, I don't need you to remind me to fasten my seatbelt. Really." Olivia sounded testy.

How to mollify her? "Mom, the pies were delicious. You must have spent all of yesterday baking."

"That's true, I did. Except for the chocolate cream pie. The filling is made in a double boiler on the stove." Her tone was a little softer.

"Did you make the crust yourself, rolling the dough out like you did when I was a kid?" That would put her in a good mood.

"That is correct. I did. I really believe that a crust prepared from fresh ingredients in one's home is far superior to those pie crusts you buy frozen from the grocery store."

"Well, all your work was well worth it, Mom," Alex said. "Everyone enjoyed the pies."

"Except that Kelly and her boyfriend fled before dessert was served, offering no substantive explanation. It was rude, if you ask me," Olivia said, her voice darkening.

"It must have been something important. Kelly is a very serious person. She wouldn't run off like that unless it was necessary." So much for trying to placate his mother. Alex sighed.

"Did you enjoy the dinner, Alex?" Olivia asked.

Alex paused. He feared that this simple question was more than rhetorical. "It was great. Sure, I enjoyed it very much."

"I ask because Leda served a sausage stuffing. She asked me what we typically had for Thanksgiving, and what in particular you and I liked, and I told her we always had a bread stuffing. You love my bread stuffing. I gave her my recipe! But she made a meat stuffing instead. I hope you weren't disappointed."

"No, of course I wasn't disappointed. I do love your stuffing though. Maybe you can make it another time for me and Helen."

"I would be happy to cook for you, and also for Helen. But you have to come over. That doesn't happen very often."

"Okay, Mom. We'll figure out a time."

"And you know, you could have stayed at our home rather than with Leda."

"Okay, thanks, we'll do that sometime." Helen would love that, he thought ruefully. He pulled into the driveway and walked with Olivia to the door. "Here are your keys, Mom. Can I help you, ah, up the stairs or anything?"

"Alex, really. I'm not that old. I can certainly ascend the stairs by myself." Olivia took the keys and opened the door.

"Okay then. I guess I'll run back now. Good night, Mom." He waited until she had entered the house and closed and securely locked the door, and then he began his run back toward Helen's house. The wind had died down, so that the weather seemed much milder than it had earlier. He took the long way back, making a broad loop that led him past the reservoir. It had been a long time since he had passed this way. He slowed and detoured down the path to the reservoir. It was deserted, as was fitting for this late hour on a holiday near the end of autumn. It was also very dark; there were no streetlights nearby, and persistent clouds still blocked the light of the moon and stars. Alex found his way to one of the benches and sat down, his gaze passing from the glistening black of the water of the reservoir to the matte black of the surrounding trees. The absence of light and sound, the absence of sensory input, was somehow comforting to Alex. It cleared his mind and felt peaceful.

He sat for a while, enjoying the tranquility. Then he whispered into the blackness, "Patrick? I had Thanksgiving dinner today with Helen and her family. My Mom came also. It was so nice." Even though Alex knew no one was really listening, he would not mention Kelly's friend Aggie. It didn't seem right.

A gust of wind stirred some leaves at Alex's feet and carried a faint reply, "Thanksgiving, so nice."

"I wish you had been there, and my Dad," Alex continued. *My Dad, for me, but even more for my Mom. I wish he had been there.*

"Me too," the wind responded. And then all was silent again. He sat for a little longer, and then fleet-footed Alexander rose and ran back to his Helen.

# CHAPTER 25

"This was a spectacular weekend. Probably the best Thanksgiving I ever had! All I did was eat, drink and sleep. I feel so rested. I think I'm in much better shape to face the world," Alex said, as he finished packing and zipped close his suitcase.

"Yes, it was very relaxing. My parents just love you," Helen said.

"And *I* love you." He paused. "Listen, we should get going. Your Dad thinks we should allow at least half an hour to drive to South Station. I'm taking my suitcase down. Can I take yours?" Alex asked.

"Sure, thanks," Helen answered, quickly tossing the last few things she had laid out on the bed into her suitcase and closing it. "I'm all done packing."

Alex wrapped his fingers around the handles of his suitcase and Helen's, lifted them and bounded down the stairs.

Helen turned and reached for her coat, hanging from the doorknob, and then realized she was wearing only a tee shirt with her jeans. She should have put on a sweater so she wouldn't have to wear her coat in the bus all the way back to New York City. In her hurry to finish packing, she had thrown her favorite baby blue sweater, the one that always made Alex say it made her eyes look even bluer, blue as the vaulted heavens, he would say, into her suitcase.

"Alex?" she shouted, but the front door banged shut just as she yelled for him. She went to the window. There was Alex dropping their luggage into the trunk of the car. She didn't want to ask him to bring her suitcase back in. She would find something else. Anything would do. She walked across the room and after a brief search in her closet extracted a lightweight navy-blue jacket, put it on, and put her coat on over that. She scanned the room quickly with her eyes to be certain nothing had been left behind.

About half an hour after the bus pulled out of Boston's South Station, Helen had finally warmed up enough to slip off her overcoat.

"I don't remember that jacket; it looks nice on you," Alex said.

"Oh, it was in my closet," Helen said, glancing down. In her hurry she hadn't taken a good look at it before. Her heart sank. Her fingers cautiously swept along the outside of the right-sided pocket and confirmed the presence of a crisp little square of paper within, a paper with a phone number she had meant to leave in Brookline.

"You okay?" Alex asked, watching her face.

"Yes. Yes, of course," she said quickly. She cleared her throat. "So now that Surgery is over, how will your schedule be?"

"Well, I have my Internal Medicine sub-internship starting tomorrow. We start a little later in the morning than on Surgery but it's still every third night on call, and the other days will be pretty long." It sounded like a confession.

"Oh, Alex, really? I thought Surgery was the only bad one!" Helen groaned.

"I'm sorry, Helen. For Medicine, I have to be in by 8, not by 6:30. That's a huge improvement. And then after Medicine, they do get much easier," Alex said, his tone conciliatory.

"But I just sit there alone all day!" she moaned.

"You don't have to. You should go out and do things," Alex said.

"I don't want to go out all by myself!" She crossed her arms below her breasts and pouted.

"I'll do my best to be the most efficient sub-intern ever, and get home at a decent hour, every day, I promise."

Helen looked out the window, away from Alex. The sun in her golden hair traced a glimmering halo around her head as the scenery floated by.

\*

Sunshine poured across FDR Drive and in through the window, onto the perfect oval of Helen's face. She rolled over in bed and forced open her eyes. The clock radio said it was 9:05 am. It looked like Alex was long gone. Would it be possible to get blinds so the sun didn't wake her up so early? She pulled the covers over her head but it was no good; she could not get back to sleep. She pushed back the covers and rolled into a sitting position, rubbed her eyes and stood, clumsy with sleep. She shuffled over to the counter and made coffee, sliced open an English muffin, toasted it, spread it with margarine, and settled down to find a TV show to watch. Before long, the Young and Restless came on. Helen watched it attentively, flipping through *House Beautiful* during the commercials. Once that show was over, she changed channels until she found The Price Is Right. Then that was over.

Hours until Alex was likely to show up, and she had nothing to do. She began to pace around the room, a short winding path past the door to the hall, past the bathroom, along the kitchen counter, past the TV, past the bed. As she passed the closet, through the door she had forgotten to close, she saw the jacket, or at least the right sleeve of the navy-blue jacket she had worn yesterday, peeking out seductively from the mass of other tightly packed clothing hanging to the right and left of it. She slowed, and then stopped in front of the closet, extending one hand to clasp the sleeve of the jacket.

In that moment the clock radio flipped its digital display to 4:00, and the phone rang. That'll be Alex, she thought. She was still annoyed with him about his long hours. Medical school is so stupid. You work so hard and you get paid nothing. She let the phone ring four times, and on the fifth ring she answered in a sleepy voice, "H'lo?"

"Oh, sweetheart, did I wake you?" Alex said, apologetically.

"No. No, not really," Helen said, sinking onto the bed.

"The Medicine rotation isn't bad, or at least today it wasn't too bad. By the way, did you cook anything for dinner yet?" Alex asked.

"No." Why would he assume she had nothing to do but sit around cooking?

"Good, then don't. I just wanted to make sure. I'll get take-out for tonight, okay? And I won't be late."

Helen turned back to the closet, firmly grabbed the sleeve of her jacket and folded it deep in among the other clothing so she couldn't see it.

At 6:30, Alex whipped open the door, presenting Helen with Chinese take-out, a bottle of red wine and a bouquet of white carnations laid against a background of ferns. "I took the liberty of picking the Chinese food, Szechuan chicken and beef and peppers, one spicy and one mild. I hope that's okay." Alex had wanted to get Helen roses, but they just weren't in the budget. Fortunately, she seemed to like the carnations. Already she was busy putting them into a vase they had received as a wedding gift.

"Sure, it smells delicious. And thanks for the flowers. That's so sweet. They're beautiful!" If he could get home by this time on a regular basis, the Medicine rotation wouldn't be too bad, she thought.

"Hey, know who's in my medicine team? Cheryl Anderson. You met her at her birthday party. Remember her?" Alex reached for the wine, unscrewed the cap and poured a glass for each of them. "This is that same wine I got for that night; everyone seemed to like it."

Helen groaned. "Don't remind me of that night. Those people were awful. Especially those two girls."

"Not Cheryl. She's truly a gentle soul." Alex deposited rice onto Helen's plate and covered it with beef and peppers. "Here you go. Is that enough?"

"The other one was worse. What was her name? Sarah," Helen said, taking the plate without looking at it.

"Sarah. Well, she can be overly self-confident sometimes, I guess. Sorry, sweetheart, I shouldn't have said anything." Helen was so sensitive. Sarah could be pretty self-righteous, and some people found her hard to take, Alex knew, but no need to mention that. Alex got on fine with her. He scooped up Szechuan chicken with his chopsticks. "How's your dinner?"

"Good." Helen struggled with her chopsticks, but after a while frustration led her to switch to a fork. How did Alex learn to use those silly things? She watched with fascination as his chopsticks swooped, twirled, crossed and uncrossed. Maybe he's had a lot of Chinese over the years and just picked it up. Maybe his family would go out for Chinese food when he was a kid. Maybe he ate a lot of Chinese in New York before they got married. Maybe it's just one more item on the very long list of things he does well. She shrugged and continued to eat with her fork.

*

On Tuesday Helen had Cheerios for breakfast. She ate slowly, as always, one Cheerio at a time, while listening to Oprah. When she finished she glanced at the clock. Now she had basically nothing to do until lunch. Except for watching Young and Restless. She watched that intently for half an hour but all too soon, the show was over. She sighed. She toasted an English muffin, spread it with peanut butter and sat down to watch a Beverly Hillbillies rerun. The English muffin finished, Helen climbed back into bed and watched more TV. This was very boring, she thought. She glanced at the clock. 4:15. Alex had called yesterday at 4:00. Would he be checking in today as well?

At 5:15 the phone rang. Helen emerged from her pillows and answered.

"Hi, sweetheart, it's me. Looks like I'll be a little later tonight than yesterday, but not too late."

"Oh. Okay. Well, come home as soon as you can," Helen said, and re-entered their bed, her expression glum. She lay there another 15 minutes, and then threw off the bedclothes and stood. She marched to the closet, pulled out her jacket and slipped the little square of paper out of its pocket. She gazed at it for a long time, that 10-digit number beginning with 212. Abruptly she shoved the paper back into the pocket and the jacket back into the closet.

*

Alex Eastgard hurried along the hall of the 14th floor of the city hospital. He had successfully drawn blood on all of his patients needing testing this evening and was on his way to deliver the tubes to the appropriate labs. As he passed room 1404, he heard a man's voice, angry, whiny, shout, "Stupid bitch! Leave me alone."

Then a woman's voice, soft, placating, and the loud response.

"I don't give a rat's ass what you think I need, lady. You're not sticking me again."

Alex paused in his headlong march to the elevators and entered the room.

"Hey Cheryl, what's going on?" Alex motioned her to come out of the room.

"I've tried and tried. I can't find a decent vein. The guy's so mean. But I need to get the blood drawn. He's just been started on Coumadin, and he needs to be monitored. Plus his LFTs were a mess on admission. We need to see how they are today." Cheryl's voice trembled. She wiped the beginning of a tear from her left eye.

"Give me your tubes," Alex said. "And wait here."

Alex entered room 1404 and closed the door.

"What, are you that stupid cow's replacement? Why can't you people leave me alone? I gave blood yesterday!"

"The young lady you are referring to does not deserve to be called any of the names you've been throwing at her. She's trying to help you, you know."

"Great, now I got Mr. Goodie Two-Shoes here."

"May I take a look at your arms, please?" Alex asked, but did not wait for an answer. He took the man's right arm, searching for veins from biceps to wrist. He turned the arm over and examined the man's hand. No veins to draw from. Alex dropped the right arm and picked up the left; it was worse.

"Okay, here's what we're going to do. You really need this blood work done. You've got no veins that I can see. I'm leaving these three tubes. Here's a needle; I'm attaching it to this syringe. Here's my tourniquet. You draw the blood yourself," Alex said, carefully laying the materials down on the bedside table, leaving the needle in its plastic cap.

The man's eyes glittered in the halogen spotlight over his bed when he saw the fresh shiny needle, and his breath quickened.

"I'm going to need the needle back; you cannot keep it." The patient's face collapsed with disappointment. Alex continued, "Here also are alcohol wipes. Wipe your skin off thoroughly before you draw the blood. You can keep the extra alcohol wipes."

The man observed Alex with an inscrutable expression.

"I'll be back in 10 minutes. If those tubes are full, we're done." Alex waited for an acknowledgment, but there was none. He stepped into the hall, closed the door and looked at his watch.

"What'd you do?" Cheryl asked.

"I told him he could draw his own blood," Alex said. "I gave him 10 minutes."

"What?" Cheryl asked.

"He knows where his veins are. Maybe his feet. Maybe his ankles. I don't know and I don't care. He'll fill those tubes. But nobody goes in or out until he's done and I get the needle back from him." Alex leaned against the doorframe and crossed his arms across his chest.

"You look like a bouncer!"

"Missed my calling, I guess," Alex said, glad to see her smiling.

After a while, Cheryl said, "It's been about 10 minutes."

Alex re-entered the room and found the tubes of blood neatly lined up on the bedside table and the patient with a smug expression on his face.

"The needle and syringe too; let's go," Alex said, making his voice deep and brusque.

The man sighed and reached under his pillow and set the used needle and syringe next to the tubes of blood.

"Thank you very much, sir," Alex said, collecting his equipment.

"We done for tonight?" the patient demanded.

"Yes sir, we are. You have a pleasant evening," Alex said and exited. He handed the tubes to Cheryl. "This takes care of today's blood work. We'll worry about tomorrow when it gets here."

"Okay, Alex, thanks a million. Really," Cheryl said. "Want to get coffee?"

"No, thanks, I'm going to drop off these tubes and get home. Helen's waiting. I think she gets lonely, you know?"

"That's too bad. Tell her I said hi," Cheryl said, and headed down the hall.

\*

Wednesday. Cheerios. Again.

Oprah. Young and Restless. The Price Is Right.

The Chinese food was all gone; she wondered what they would do for dinner. As she was re-reading *House Beautiful*, the phone rang.

"Hi, sweetheart, how are you?" Alex asked.

"Fine. How's it going?" Helen replied, as she studied photos of a gut renovation of an estate in the Hamptons.

"Not too bad. No real disasters so far today."

"That's good. Um, what do you want to do about dinner?"

"Helen, I'm so sorry. Remember I'm on-call every third. I won't be home tonight."

"Oh, I forgot." He should have reminded her. "Well, good luck. I hope you get some sleep."

"Ha. Fat chance! I should go. See you tomorrow, at least." Alex hung up.

Helen looked out the window. It would be dark soon. She put on her coat and hurried to the grocery store to find something to eat. She returned with two TV dinners and a new bottle of nail polish, a bright red called Brazen. If they couldn't afford for her to get a manicure once in a while, she should at least be able to get some new nail polish. Helen ate one of the TV dinners while watching a M.A.S.H. rerun.

After she had finished eating, and during a commercial, she wandered around the room, ending up in the bathroom. Her face in the mirror returned her solemn gaze. If she was so beautiful like Alex said, what was she doing all alone here at night? Looks don't last forever. When she was old, would she look back on this time and think that she had spent what should have been the best time of her life sitting in a dorm room in a city where she didn't have any friends watching TV all by herself? The horizontal line of her lovely mouth drooped, her rosy lips trembled and tears collected at the corners of her eyes of celestial blue.

*This is ridiculous*, she told herself. She marched to the closet, found her navy-blue jacket and pulled Hector's number out of the pocket. *He's an old friend from high school. I'm a respectable married woman. I just want someone to talk to, so I won't be so lonely.* As she examined her conscience, she realized she was not so much lonely as bored. Either way, she was just not happy.

She stepped to the desk and sat down. Why shouldn't she call Hector, after all? The reasons flooded her mind- Hector had played a role in the death of Alex's best friend, and even before that there had been bad blood between them. Alex would not be happy if he knew she was thinking about calling him. Even more, a little voice in her head told her, she was still hung up on Hector. What if they met and she was still attracted to him? No, it couldn't be, she told herself. She was married now. She wouldn't let herself feel that way. Also, after all these years, maybe he wasn't good-looking anymore. Maybe he had gotten fat or gone bald or prematurely gray. She would call. She needed to hear a friendly voice.

Fingers shaking, Helen dialed the number on the paper. The phone rang three times, then four. *I'll hang up after the fifth ring*, she thought. At the beginning of the fifth ring, someone answered.

"Hello?" Hector's voice. Helen would have known it anywhere. Her throat closed and she was suddenly unable to speak. "Hello?" she heard again, impatient this time. She couldn't get any words out. She hung up.

She went to bed that night after watching the Tonight Show, but she was unable to sleep. The need to call Hector, the challenge of successfully making the call and being able to speak normally loomed mercilessly before her.

She awoke Thursday morning, badly rested, but resolved to call Hector and prove she could do it. There was nothing wrong with calling him, she told herself over and over. There was no need to feel awkward. She had felt awkward on her way to the Gonzalez's house, but once she got there, Catalina and Hector's father had been so kind. It would be the same with Hector. She dialed the number, her fingers a little less shaky than the night before.

"Hello?" he answered.

Her voice cracked as she managed to get out one word, "Hector?"

"Who's calling?" He sounded suspicious.

"I'm not sure if you remember me, but this is Helen. Helen Fletcher. Well actually, now, um..." Helen found herself unable to continue.

The pause that followed lasted what felt like an eternity. Then she heard, "Helen! Of course! Of course, I remember you. How could you think I wouldn't?" And suddenly his voice sounded bright, happy.

"Oh, I- I don't know. It's been years and all, you know." Helen realized that she should have planned what she was going to say, but she hadn't thought past placing the call.

"What are you doing now?" He actually sounded interested.

"I'm living in New York City," she said.

"Did you come here for work? Found a job here or something?"

"No, I don't have a job at the moment, actually," she confessed.

Hector laughed. "Welcome to my world! It's hard as hell to find a decent job in this city. Tough place to do well."

"Yes, it is. You're right," Helen said. Maybe the best strategy would be just to agree with him. She was too light-headed to develop original thoughts.

"Let's have a drink and catch up. What do you say?" Hector offered. How refreshing to have a woman say he was right. Marisol was constantly telling him he was wrong.

"Oh, that would be so nice. Um, when?"

"What about tomorrow?"

"Um," Helen quickly calculated that if Alex was on call overnight on Wednesday, he was not on Thursday or Friday, but he would be again on Saturday. Saturday would be best. Otherwise she could go for more than 24 hours without communicating with another human being. "Saturday would be better. For me. If it's okay for you." She waited, heart pounding.

"Ah, sure. Saturday. Is afternoon okay?" Hector asked. Marisol would gut him if he made other plans for Saturday night.

Helen's heart sank. He's not available Saturday night. That means he has a girlfriend he's taking out Saturday night. *I shouldn't care!* Helen told herself. *I'm married! If he has a girlfriend, good for him.* "Sure, that's fine."

"Great! Could you meet me at, let's say 3 o'clock at, what about the Waldorf? They have a lounge just off the lobby."

"The Waldorf?" Helen had heard of it.

"Yes, the Waldorf-Astoria," Hector said. "It's huge hotel. Been around forever. It's on Park Avenue, between 49th and 50th Street. Just take a cab."

"Okay," Helen said, giggling a little. "3 o'clock at the Waldorf, this Saturday."

"Good. Can't wait to see you," Hector said.

That was easy, Helen thought. She had a friend of her own right here in New York, and she was going to get out of this dreary dorm room for a few hours this Saturday. What would she wear? Something nice enough for the Waldorf, but not dressed up like for a date. How about- And then she realized with horror that she had not mentioned she was married. No telling what impression or expectation Hector had about Saturday. Well, she would tell him right up front when they met, so there was no misunderstanding.

Helen wandered through the day in a haze. When Alex burst into the room at 6:00 with a hearty take-out dinner of roast chicken and mashed potatoes, from the First Avenue diner across from the hospital, Helen looked up in surprise. "You're home so early!"

"You mean at a normal hour! Yes, that is early for me. I have dinner and a bottle of wine, white this time."

"I meant, I didn't even realize it was evening," Helen said.

Alex glanced out the window. "It's dark outside, sweetheart. Of course, it's evening."

"I guess, I guess, I've just been so busy, I don't know where the time went."

"That's great. I don't want you feeling like you're wasting your time. What did you do?" Alex asked as he laid out their take-out.

"Oh, um, I don't know. I just cleaned up and stuff like that."

"Did you have a chance to get out and do anything?"

"No, not today. But I'll try to get out."

"Good! Brave girl." Alex turned to the TV. "Hey, look, Jeopardy's starting. I used to watch with my parents. Let's watch it, okay? Come sit with me."

"Sure," Helen said, sitting down next to him on the foot of the bed. She never really watched Jeopardy although Kelly and her Mom liked it.

"I'll take British nobility for $200," one contestant said.

"And the answer is, 'This son of Edward III built a magnificent residence in London known as the Savoy Palace,'" Alex Trebek's voice rang out.

"Oh, easy one. John of Gaunt. Did I ever tell you he was my favorite Plantagenet?" Alex asked.

"No, I don't think so." Sometimes she had no idea what Alex was talking about. He and Alex Trebek were clearly on the same wavelength though, as Alex proceeded to get every answer in that category correct.

"Helen," he said after final jeopardy was over and Rachel had triumphed over Paul and Susan, "I want to thank you for being so patient and so wonderful. I have call again Saturday night, but the next day, since it's Sunday, I don't have to work a full day. I should be home by noon. So you pick something you want to do. Whatever you want. Okay?"

"Oh, that's nice. I'll think about it." Helen nibbled at her chicken. Sunday! She couldn't think about Sunday until after Saturday. Two more days. It would be hard to wait.

# CHAPTER 26

Hector Gonzalez strolled up Park Avenue, a cigarette dangling from his lips. He paused as he approached the entrance to the Waldorf, inhaling deeply as the cigarette burned down to its filter; he dropped it to the sidewalk and ground it beneath the heel of his cordovan leather boot. He glanced at his watch; with regret, he saw that there was not enough time for another smoke. He entered the Waldorf, found his way to the bar and selected a table toward the back, but with a view of the entrance.

What the fuck was he doing here? he asked himself. Probably wasting his time. What did he remember about Helen Fletcher? She was pretty, he recalled. She had pretty blonde hair. Beautiful hair, that's right. Golden blonde. Kind of skinny, wasn't she? He wondered what she looked like now. Had she gotten fat? Old? Women can lose their looks fast. She sounded sweet on the phone. Innocent. Nervous. He lifted his glass and sucked Jack Daniels past ice cubes. What the fuck could she want, calling him after all this time? He glanced again at his watch. She was five minutes late. If she showed up, she showed up. If she didn't, no loss. He'd just finish his drink and go.

Helen Eastgard entered the Waldorf-Astoria and gazed in wonder at the magnificent lobby. Like a ballroom in a palace, she thought. She hesitated, anxious about proceeding, and instead stood, studying the decor, waiting for her heart to stop racing.

A uniformed attendant approached her. "Miss, could I be of assistance?"

Helen flushed. Did it look like she was lost? "Oh, um, yes, thank you. I was told there is a lounge off the lobby. I am supposed to meet a friend there."

"Yes, of course. Just along this side of the lobby and off to your right. Please enjoy your visit to the Waldorf-Astoria," he said, punctuated with a courteous half-bow.

Helen watched him walk away. She slipped off her bulky overcoat. When she walked into that bar, she wanted Hector to know that she hadn't gotten fat. Not that it should matter, because she was married, but still, she wanted him to know she hadn't let herself go. She took a deep breath and walked toward the lounge. Helen paused as she entered, scanning the room for Hector. Her eyes traveled down the long gleaming hardwood bar, silently checking each swivel barstool for someone familiar. He saw her first and stood. She looked good, he thought. Still had that hot little body. Her hair was still that golden blonde that he remembered.

Then she saw him: a lone figure standing before her, a dark silhouette in the light from the Tiffany lamp behind him. Hector. She was sure. Helen smiled, and walked slowly toward him.

"Helen! You look beautiful. Come, sit." Hector gestured at the chair opposite him and sat down.

Helen slid into the chair. Hector hadn't changed much, she thought. He looked a little older, but more mature, not old. Not a kid anymore. He was still tall and muscular, with shining black hair swept back from his face, and those green-green eyes, just as she remembered. Seeing him, it was like stepping back in time.

"Well, thank you for calling, Helen. It was wonderful to hear from you. So, tell me what you are doing in New York City," Hector said, the sound of his voice a rich melody in her ears.

Helen felt his emerald eyes upon her, studying her. "Well, ah, not too much, actually. Um, I should say, um, I should tell you, I got married and I'm here because my husband's in school here."

"Married! You didn't wait for me." A statement, not a question. Actually, he had hardly thought about her since he had left home, but as she was safely married, it seemed like the right thing to say.

Her face collapsed.

"Oh, no, please, I'm sorry. I wasn't serious. I shouldn't have said that." He leaned back, bowing his head.

Helen was silent. He hadn't called or written or anything. She hadn't known how to contact him. He had known how to contact her. Had she really hurt him? She felt terrible.

"Who did you marry? Anyone I would know?" Hector asked. He steeled himself for some polite chitchat.

"Alex Eastgard," Helen said. "He's in medical school here."

Alex Fucking Eastgard! Hector was stuck in New York, cut off from his family because of that fucker and his idiot friend. "Medical school, huh? He was always a good student, I seem to recall." Hector's hand slid up and down his cocktail glass. He could really use a cigarette. "Well, what about you? What are you doing while he's in school?"

"Well, that's just the thing. Not much. I'm on my own a lot. Alex is studying or working in the hospital all the time. Like today, he went in early, and has to work overnight and he won't get home until tomorrow morning, at the earliest. He's on call like that every third night."

"My poor beautiful Helen! You must be lonely!" He shook his head softly.

*He understands me!* Helen thought. *He seems to care.* She told him about the funeral, and about going to his house. "When Catalina gave me your number, I thought, why don't I call? Then when you suggested meeting, I thought it would be nice to get out of that awful dorm and not feel so lonely for a while."

"Helen, I am so touched. You were really worried I might have died? I don't know anyone else who gives a damn." Strictly speaking, that was untrue. He owed Chewie a bundle. When last month's money came through, he gave a good chunk of it to Chewie, right off the top, but he was still in the red. Chewie wanted him alive until he was able to pay off his debt.

And then Helen told him everything, about the mean man at Arthur's deli, about their tiny dorm room with the linoleum floor, about Alex's awful, snobby friends who made fun of her for not going to college, and worst of all, Alex's terrible mother who wouldn't leave her alone.

"But in all this, I hope that Alex, himself, is good to you," Hector struggled to pronounce 'Alex' in an even tone, without betraying his enmity.

"Oh, Alex is so good, and works so hard, and he is very good to me when he's around. He brings me flowers and all. I know he's working hard like this so we can have a better life in the future."

"But for now, it's difficult. I understand. I'm glad that he is good to you, at least when he is able," Hector said. *She is still one damn good-looking piece of ass*, he thought. *Totally wasted on fucking Eastgard.*

"Yes, he is. He does his best. But-," Helen began.

"But what?" Hector said, the predator in him sensing vulnerability. He leaned forward.

"Well, I know it's mean and unfair to say, but Alex is, almost, too good. He's good at everything! He's at the top of his class in everything! He knows everything. He can use chopsticks better than Chinese people. Everyone likes him. My own sister thinks I'm not good enough for him. Even my parents think I'm a loser compared to him; I'm not kidding."

"Oh, Helen, poor sweet Helen," Hector began. "What can I do to help?"

"You're helping me so much by just listening. I- I'm really sorry. Here I am going on about my problems. Tell me what you've been up to."

"Me? There's not much to tell. I had hopes of breaking into acting. I occasionally get some small part, nothing that would even make the playbill, and I've had an odd job here and there." This was misleading. The only work he had ever had in the theater was putting a few actors in touch with Chewie; Hector had gotten small commissions for those referrals. "But it's hard. It's a hard city. The people are hard."

Helen nodded her agreement. The man at Arthur's was a perfect example. New Yorkers were hard, just like Hector said.

"Listen, I should get going, but it's really been so nice speaking with you. Would you like to get together again?" Hector said. He had promised to take Marisol someplace upscale for dinner. The better the dinner, the better the sex would be when they got home.

"That would be nice, sure," Helen said.

"How about Tuesday afternoon?" Hector suggested.

"That would be perfect. Alex will be at the hospital all night, so he-, so I don't have to worry about having dinner ready at a certain time."

"Yes, and I hate the idea of you being alone all that day and part of the rest," Hector said, his tone sympathetic. "Let's go get you a taxi."

They walked together to the front entrance of the hotel. Hector considered what thought he might leave her with before parting. "There was such a nice bond between us when we were in high school. I wonder what would have happened if, well, if I hadn't had to leave Brookline."

"Yes, I wonder," Helen murmured.

"There's a yellow cab for you," Hector said. He pulled out a thick wad of cash in a gold money clip, peeled off a twenty, and gave it to the cab driver, saying, "Take the young lady wherever she wishes to go." Hector stepped away from the taxi, extracted a cigarette from the pack in his pocket, lit it and smoked thoughtfully as the taxi pulled away. *I wonder what she's like in bed now.* He turned around and headed for his apartment.

He had only had that one time with Helen, he recalled. He cast his mind back through the years to the night after graduation. His family had had dinner at Il Cibo, his mother's favorite Italian restaurant. He had invited Helen to come along at the last minute. After dinner they had all gone back to the house and hung out. His parents seemed to like Helen, especially his Dad. They asked her so many questions, and she answered so sweetly, stammering sometimes, like she wasn't used to the attention. He had sat there quietly, listening and not listening, thinking what she would look like with her clothes off, what she would feel like, how she would act. He had imagined slipping his hand under her dress, up her thigh, and imagined the feel of her soft skin against his hand. How would she react? he had wondered. He decided that most likely she would try the shy act at first and play hard to get, but then cave in pretty quick. He had waited patiently for the conversation to die down.

"Well, should I drive Helen home? It's getting late," Hector had said.

"Yes, dear, that's a good idea. Always a gentleman," Anita had crooned. "Helen, it was such a pleasure to meet you. I hope we see you again soon."

Hector stood and escorted Helen politely to the door, but instead of going to the car, he had walked her around to the dimly lit backyard with its swimming pool.

"We have a nice pool. You should come over and swim sometime," he had said.

"I would like that. You just have to invite me," Helen had answered enthusiastically.

"I bet you look good in a bikini," he had said.

"Oh..." She had looked down, shyly.

Then he had held her tight, kissed her, run his hands along her body, meeting no resistance. Encouraged, he had walked her over to a lounge chair and laid her down. She got nervous then. He had to talk her into staying put. There she lay, so pretty and soft, and he had wanted to get into her so bad it hurt, and then didn't she say- yeah, she did, she said, "Hector, I love you; tell me you love me!" So he told her. It made her so happy. She had let him do everything he wanted. Twice. Then he helped her get dressed, walked her to the car and drove her home. A gentleman, just like his mother had said. He had been her first; he could tell. He grinned as he remembered.

God, that had been great! Now she was married to that asshole. The surviving asshole, he thought. Abruptly the swagger drained out of him. That had been a bad day, the day the little asshole died. Even though it wasn't his fault. His life changed that day. Kicked out of his house forever, never able to see his family. Now he was in New York City; every day was a party and he could screw Marisol whenever he wanted. Once in a while, someone else. Once, Lourdes. Marisol didn't know about that. She was okay, but not like Marisol. But all that had gotten old. He was still basically in exile. Hector lit a fresh cigarette; there was time for one more before he reached his apartment.

*

212

Alex burst into their dorm room at 10:00 Sunday morning. He had gotten out of the hospital earlier than he expected, the weather was cool but not bitter, and brilliant sunshine lit up Manhattan from Fort Tryon Park to the Battery. He couldn't wait to have this beautiful day together with Helen. He wondered what she would want to do.

"Helen?" He saw her curled up in the covers of their bed, so lovely with her fair hair spread across the pillow.

"Mmmm... I'm awake. Sort of."

"It's such a beautiful day. Do you want to get up and go somewhere? Did you decide what you'd like to do?"

"I'm still resting," she said lazily.

"I'll come rest with you," he said, and lay next to her, sliding his hands under her hair and across her shoulders, and down her slender torso.

"No, I'm too tired," she said, pulling the covers tighter around herself.

"Why are you so tired?"

"Up late watching old movies..."

He contented himself with combing her hair with his fingers. He knew she was not happy about his hours. And she had gotten so upset at Cheryl's party. It would explain why she had not been interested in sex the last couple of weeks. And then over Thanksgiving, she said she felt weird about it, as they were in the room next to her parents' bedroom. He sighed.

*

Helen awoke and rolled over in bed, shielding her eyes from the sun. *It's Tuesday!* She threw back the covers, leapt out of bed and hummed to herself while making coffee. She spent the next hour choosing an outfit for her date with Hector. No, she told herself, it was not a date. She was just meeting an old friend from high school. She had been very up-front with him about being married. They were only getting together to talk. She gave herself a manicure, using her new nail polish, Brazen. She felt good about herself, confident. She had someone to talk to, someone who thought she was interesting and who cared about what she had to say. She studied her nails. That was one bold shade of red! Crimson, really, or scarlet. She didn't usually wear such a bright shade. But today, she felt like it. Half an hour before she was to meet Hector, Helen departed the dorm room, and took the elevator down to the ground floor to find a taxi. *This is easy*, she thought, settling herself against the

213

muted blue vinyl rear seat of the taxi. And to think just a week ago she had been scared to go out by herself. How foolish she had been!

She exited the cab, and gracefully removed her sunglasses and shook out her hair as she entered the Waldorf. She walked straight to the bar, without hesitation, and there she found Hector, seated at the same table. He stood and helped her take off her coat.

"Thanks," she said.

"What will you have?" he asked. "I'm having JD on the rocks."

Helen gave a pretty little giggle. "I think I should stick to white wine."

"Very good. Let's get a bottle." Hector beckoned to the waiter and instructed him to bring a well-chilled bottle of Pouilly-Fuissé.

Hector emptied his glass of Jack Daniels as the waiter deftly opened the bottle of wine, poured a little into a glass, and offered it to Hector to taste.

"The lady will taste the wine and see if it suits her," Hector said, deferentially.

"Oh, I've never done this before!" Helen said. She timidly reached for the glass.

"Helen, inhale the wine's aroma. Swirl it around in the glass and see if you like the look of it. Then taste," Hector advised.

The waiter stood at attention. Helen watched the wine spin around the glass, sparkling in the light of the Tiffany lamps. She held the glass to her nose and breathed in, and then she tasted it. "It's wonderful!"

The waiter nodded his approval. "The Pouilly-Fuissé Louis Jadot is our most popular French white," he said as he filled Helen's glass and then Hector's. He plunged the bottle into a silver ice bucket, draped a towel over it and quietly withdrew.

"That was so much fun! Just like in the movies!" Helen said. "How did you learn so much about wine?"

Hector knew almost nothing about wine. However, he recalled that his mother occasionally served Pouilly-Fuissé on holidays and figured that was a safe choice. "You flatter me. I don't know much at all."

Helen's gaze fell on the cork lying on the table. When she and Alex had wine, it usually had a screw cap. It was thrilling to be drinking fine wine from a bottle that came with a cork, in this beautiful, fashionable hotel. The Waldorf-Astoria! A year ago she was living in Brookline, working in that dentist's office. Who would have thought back then that one day she'd be sipping French wine in the Waldorf?

"Here, let me give you a little more wine," Hector said, reaching for the bottle. She held her glass for him, arranging her fingers gracefully around the stem of the goblet. "Let's see your hands," he said. She obediently held them out for inspection.

Helen was glad she had used that new polish. It had caught his attention. She liked the idea of being bold once in a while. Hector slipped his hands over hers. "Beautiful hands, you have beautiful hands."

"Thank you," she murmured. This felt more like a date than she had anticipated after all. *What a silly thought*, a voice in her head countered. *You're just meeting an old friend from school to talk and catch up. An old friend, a trusted friend.* Helen thought about that. It seemed logical enough. *It's the wine. I'm imagining things.*

Hector refilled her glass. She drank it, a little too quickly. "Oh, um, this wine- it's gone straight to my head!" She reached for her water glass.

"Well, the wine's gone. Perhaps we should take a walk, clear our heads?" Hector suggested. He signaled for the waiter, paid their check, helped Helen on with her coat, and taking her arm, walked with her out of the hotel. He headed west with her, and as they walked, moved his arm to around her waist.

"Are you warm enough?" he asked solicitously. He stopped and adjusted the collar of her coat, allowing his fingers to brush across the bare skin of her throat. Then he put his arm back around her waist and drew her on.

"I live nearby. Shall we go to my place and have some coffee?" Hector asked. "I'd like to get you out of this cold."

"Oh, I really shouldn't. I should get back," she replied. Perhaps it would be better to return to the hotel, get a taxi there.

"Please do come. Just come and get warmed up and then we can get you a taxi. They come right past my building all the time." Hector delivered a reassuring smile.

"Well, alright." Hector had been so kind. She didn't want to offend him.

"Good. I'm glad." He steered her along the sidewalk and into the front entrance of his apartment building.

They entered the small lobby, walking across a floor of Carrara marble. Uniformly framed architectural prints decorated walls the color of parchment. *What an elegant lobby!* Helen thought.

"The elevator is over here," Hector said. The elevator was a gleaming box of steel with a mirrored ceiling that whisked them silently to Hector's apartment on the 20th floor. Helen looked up; there was her reflection, the face of a stranger who drank French wine in fancy places, a little pale face framed by her dark coat, with

Hector standing tall and strong beside her. They exited the elevator and walked down a quiet hall lit by unobtrusive recessed lighting. Thick, springy, dark teal carpet led them to apartment 20E. He unlocked his door and ushered her in.

"Hector, it's beautiful!" Helen exclaimed, as she absorbed the chic modern apartment with large south-facing plate-glass windows. Years ago, when she thought of Hector in New York City, she had imagined him in just such a place. What did that mean? All those long years ago, was she seeing the future? Or was it just a coincidence? Or a good guess? And yet, now that she was finally here with Hector, it didn't feel the way she thought it would. It felt- more complicated.

"Thank you. I'm glad you like it," Hector said. "Please sit down. I'll make coffee." He looked quickly around the apartment to see that nothing was out of place. He had personally instructed the cleaning lady to put every piece of Marisol's crap away where he didn't have to look at it. Looks like she had done a good job.

Helen sank down onto the sofa and gazed out the window. She recognized the Empire State building and, far in the distance, the twin towers of the World Trade Center. *What an amazing view*, she thought. *Definitely beats our view of FDR Drive.*

"Here's the coffee," Hector said, setting down a mug for each of them. His face turned serious. "Helen, I'm concerned about you. You're such a sweet person, so uncomplaining, so accepting. But because of that you've landed in this difficult situation."

Helen nodded in agreement. Hector was so understanding.

Hector watched the slight rise and fall of Helen's breasts beneath the thin fabric of her dress as her breath came and went.

"Speaking as a friend," he said as he took her hand, "Speaking as a friend, I want you to know that I'll do whatever I can to help you."

"Oh, Hector, that is so nice of you." She gazed at him with trusting sky-blue eyes.

"You're so beautiful! To leave a woman with your beauty all alone is really a crime. What a waste!" Hector assumed an aggrieved expression. He leaned forward and kissed her.

"Oh, no, I can't, I'm sorry, I can't," Helen whispered.

"Helen, listen. I'm making no demands on you. I know one day, not long from now, you'll have your own life apart from me, but if we two lonely people can find a few hours of happiness now and then, at this difficult stage in our lives, how could it be wrong? It would be our secret. No one would know. We've already been together. Remember? Do you remember that night? I think about it a lot. It was magic, Helen. I don't think it was fair that we only had that one night. That I lost you right after I found you, after I found out what a treasure you were."

"Oh no, Hector, I just can't," Helen said, shaking her head sadly.

"I know what it is. It's the kid. The one who died. You blame me. Do you blame me?" Hector put on his most mournful expression.

She lifted her head and looked at Hector. "You mean- Patrick?"

"Yes, him. If you blame me, and I hope you don't, I can understand why you wouldn't..."

And then Helen's heart melted. "No, Hector, of course not. It was an accident." She put her hand against his cheek.

"You're just so beautiful, so beautiful. I won't hurt you, Helen, I swear," he murmured into her ear. She trembled as he undressed her, as he covered her body with his. "Don't be afraid, Helen. This will be our secret. I'll never hurt you."

Helen whimpered and quivered beneath him. Getting her off was lot more work than with Marisol, but when she finally came, she screamed and gasped for breath, and he was pleased. A little extra effort was worth it. Look at her, he told himself. He studied her as she lay beside him, eyes closed, recovering. Perfect white skin, unmarred by tattoos, her hair silky gold and smooth as doll's hair.

"Hey, I think you needed that," Hector told her, his expression smug.

Her breathing slowly returned to normal. *What have I done?* she asked herself.

He admired the curve of her back, her firm little buttocks, and moved his fingers lazily down the length of her torso, back and forth, until he wanted her again and entered her. She lay unresisting, still limp, moaning softly as he took her, but whether from desire or despair, he did not know, nor did he care.

Later, he helped her to dress. She was silent, lost in her thoughts.

"Helen, what we did, it wasn't wrong. I know it has to remain between you and me, but it wasn't wrong. Never think that. Okay?"

"Okay," she whispered, barely audible.

"I want to see you again. Can we meet again at the Waldorf in three days?"

She nodded.

"Good," he said. "I'll walk you down and get you a cab." If she turned all weepy, he could call this off any time. But he didn't think she would.

This worked out well, Hector thought, congratulating himself. Timing was perfect. It'll be an hour before Marisol gets off work, plenty of time to straighten up.

Helen hadn't changed much since high school. He had just had to find the right thing to say and she caved. And it had been great. Not only was she good-looking, but she was Alex Fucking Eastgard's wife. It gave him a lot of pleasure to fuck Alex over. Too bad he wouldn't know. Funny, he thought, as he lit a cigarette with a self-satisfied grin: Helen never once mentioned being married today.

# CHAPTER 27

Alex and Helen stood together waiting for the elevator to take them down to the dormitory lobby. Helen studied her new leather boots, gleaming against the ugly old scuffed linoleum floor. The boots were a gift from Hector. Last week, after they had made love, they had fallen asleep in one another's arms. Hector had woken her, with an excited tone in his voice. *Let's get dressed. If we hurry, we can get to Lord and Taylor's before they close. I can't let you leave for Christmas without getting you a gift,* he had said. They'd taken a lovely walk to Fifth Avenue, arm in arm, weaving among other pedestrians on the over-crowded sidewalks, laughing, twice stopping to exchange kisses, his mouth hot against hers in the brisk December air. When they reached the department store, he told her to pick something out. Whatever she wanted, he had said.

"Helen," Alex said softly, "I want you to know how much I appreciate your being willing to stay at my house for Christmas. It means so much to my Mom."

"It's no big deal," she replied calmly. She looked up from her boots and gave him a dazzling smile. Hector had paid cash, counting twenties off a roll of bills that made the salesgirl's eyes pop.

"It is a big deal. It really is. I know she drives you nuts. She drives me nuts too but I'm at the hospital so much she can't get to me."

Helen continued to smile and remained silent, but her mind was singing. This was a small thing she could do for Alex, staying with his mother for three days over Christmas, such a small thing, compared to the magic of her relationship with Hector. At first, she had been uncertain, plagued by guilt, but Hector had been so supportive, so insistent that their time together was a gift, nothing to be ashamed of or feel guilty about, and that they must make the most of it, as it might not last much longer. Once Alex's schedule lightened up, Hector told her, he knew he wouldn't be able to see her as often. He respected her commitment to Alex. Even though, he pointed out, Alex was neglecting her shamelessly. Helen had grown to love her afternoons with Hector. She looked forward to their meetings with such enthusiasm that it wiped away the silly little problems of daily life that used to trouble her so much. And then after they parted she would replay their hours together in her mind, remembering what he had said, what he had done with her, how he had made her feel. How he sometimes liked to dance to salsa with her, before. He said his mother liked that music, would play it all the time when he was a kid. It reminded her of being young in Puerto Rico, Hector said. In her mind Helen could hear the lively, sensuous music above the hum of traffic from the streets below. If Olivia got on her nerves she would just smile and think about last Thursday.

The elevator arrived. Alex picked up their suitcases and they stepped in.

*

"Well, come in," Olivia said, holding the front door open. "Alex only has a twin bed in his room, so I made up the fold-out couch in the living room for the two of you to sleep on."

"Mom, it looks absolutely festive in here!" Alex said, setting down the suitcases. A small Christmas tree decorated with a string of white lights and gold and red ornaments stood across the living room from the couch, and a red velvet ribbon ran up the banister of the stairs leading to the second floor. "Look at this, Helen. It's all the Christmas paraphernalia we've had since I was a little kid. The angel chimes, the fancy gold candles...even that little statue of Frosty the Snowman,

"That's so cute, Alex," Helen said.

"Mom, this is great. Thanks for doing all this," Alex said.

"It's nothing, no problem at all. I'm just glad you enjoy the decorations." Olivia's tone was restrained, but she was pleased that Alex noticed and appreciated her work.

*

"As it is Christmas Eve, I prepared a special dinner. We have a nice tender roast beef, baked potatoes with your choice of sour cream, bacon bits and chives, and green beans with slivered almonds," Olivia said proudly. "I bought a bottle of Chianti to go with it."

"It looks wonderful, Mom," Alex said. He sat down between Olivia and Helen and poured the wine.

"It certainly does," murmured Helen, arranging a napkin in her lap. She ate slowly, enjoying the home-cooked meal. Her manicure still looked good, she thought, even though she had done it herself several days ago. Over the past month she had changed her nail color several times, sometimes using a girlish light pink and sometimes even a classic clear. But for her last meeting with Hector before Christmas, she had again used brilliant red Brazen. She wanted him to remember her that way. Bold. Sensuous. That's how he made her feel. Helen smiled to herself.

"What a beautiful smile you have tonight, sweetheart. Now that I think about it, you've seemed so happy these last few weeks. What's your secret? Is it the Christmas season? Are you finally getting used to New York?" Alex asked her.

Olivia frowned. Helen had such a stupid smirk on her face. How could Alex find that attractive? And that flashy nail polish Helen insisted on painting her nails with showed a lack of maturity. And of modesty.

Helen smiled a little more broadly. "New York just doesn't make me as nervous now." She lifted a fork with a nibble's worth of mashed potatoes to her mouth. Her time with Hector was not only good for her and Hector; in a strange way it was good for Alex too. He knew her moods. When she was happy, as she was now, it made him happy. He didn't have to waste time worrying about her; it decreased his stress.

"The wine is great, Mom. We're used to the kind with a screw cap, so this is a real treat," Alex said, tasting his Chianti. "Can I give you a refill?"

Helen smiled at that. She was no longer used to screw cap wine, but she would keep that to herself. Her mind wandered. What would the future hold? Alex might get a residency far away, and she would have to go with him, and possibly never see Hector again. If that were to happen, she imagined a tearful scene at their last meeting, with promises of endless devotion and undying affection, like in some movie. Or Alex might end up somewhere close to New York City, and perhaps there would be a chance for the occasional discreet meeting with Hector. But the uncertainty about the future made the present all the more intense and exciting.

When they had finished dinner, Alex asked, "Want to see what's on TV?"

"Sure," Helen replied, and started to follow him into the living room.

"Helen, could I have some help with the dishes?" Olivia asked. She couldn't believe Helen was going to walk away without even offering to help.

Helen groaned inwardly. They had just gotten in from New York, and she had been so nice about staying here rather than with her own family where she would have been a lot more comfortable. And already she was being put to work. Her nails were going to chip for sure doing dishes. But she couldn't really say no.

*

Daylight crept in through the living room windows, interrupting Alex's sleep. What an unheard-of luxury, he thought, to be still in bed while it was turning light outside, with his sweet, lovely Helen beside him.

"Merry Christmas, sweetheart!" Alex whispered, hugging her, as they lay together on the thin mattress of the fold-out couch. He ached to make love to her but knew she would not be comfortable with that here in the open living room, only a short staircase away from his mother's bedroom.

"Merry Christmas," Helen murmured. She wondered what Hector was doing for Christmas.

*

Hector Gonzalez rolled over in bed and looked at the clock. Almost noon. He got up, made coffee and returned to bed. Marisol lay, still fast asleep beside him, her wild black hair strewn over the pillows. He had made a mistake last Thursday, the last time Helen came over before Christmas. After he made it with Helen, they had both fallen asleep. He had awoken just in time to get up and get Helen out of the apartment before Marisol got home. It had been close, too close. One look at Helen and Marisol would hack off his balls. And then laugh about it and leave him to bleed to death. He thought about Helen, sweet Helen with her pretty face and beautiful hair, and then his thoughts strayed to Marisol, lying so close by. He got up quietly, went into the kitchen, did a quick line of coke and returned to the bedroom. Thus fortified, he lay down again beside Marisol.

"Stop it, I'm sleeping," Marisol muttered.

"Not any more. I need it," Hector said, filling his hands with her splendid body, her abundant breasts.

She continued to complain, but Hector ignored her, and had his fill of her before leaving her to sleep.

*

Helen ascended the staircase and entered the bathroom to take a shower. She and Alex and Olivia would be going over to her family's house for Christmas dinner. As Helen undressed, she remembered Hector undressing her earlier this week, and all the other times. It made her feel tingly all over. She opened the cabinet to find a towel. There she also found inexpensive shampoo and conditioner and a big opaque white plastic pack of two dozen super-absorbent maxi pads. Apparently, this was Olivia's idea of hospitality. Gross, Helen thought. She always used Tampax. She pulled out a fresh towel and started to close the door of the cabinet. Then a cold shiver ran through her. When had she last had her period? Before Thanksgiving? Calm down and think! She told herself. Yes, it was just before Thanksgiving. She didn't have it over Thanksgiving, or she would have remembered. If she'd had it any

222

time in December, she would have remembered, because she would have had to tell Hector, and she never had. She had been so worried about everything else that she forgot to worry about- that. Maybe she was just late, she thought desperately. No. She was never late. This was really terrible. She studied her abdomen. Was it possible that it was already bulging? Her whole body trembled as she showered and dressed. She didn't know what to do, but Hector would. He would help her.

\*

"Hector, I need some money," Marisol demanded, hands on hips.

"What the fuck for?" *Fuck you, Marisol, we all need some money*, Hector thought, sitting on the couch, looking out the window.

"I'll tell you what the fuck for. We need some food. Everyone needs food, in case you didn't know. I'm hungry and the refrigerator's got nothing worth eating. And I need to pick up my prescription."

As she spoke, a chunky gold crucifix bounced merrily on the convex trampoline of her breasts. Hector briefly contemplated taking her to bed, but he was too preoccupied. Tonight, Luis would be arriving with this month's money. Just in time. Hector owed Chewie a lot. More than what he'd be getting tonight, but Chewie would let him pay it down. He had to stop using so much coke. And he would tell Marisol she could fucking pay for her own. Well, he could try, cautiously casting a glance in her direction. He looked back out the window and onto the street as though watching would make Luis arrive sooner.

\*

Aggie and Kelly resumed their post on Warren Street around sunset on December 26. They noted a blunt-nosed sedan of uncertain color in the fading light parked across the street. Hard to be sure, but it looked like two men were sitting in the front seat. Almost certainly undercover police.

"Hey, Kelly, Christmas with your family was really nice. Thanks for inviting me," Aggie said.

"I'm glad you could come," she replied. "And thank you again for the necklace." She put her fingers to her throat and touched the delicate gold chain.

"My pleasure! I'm glad you like it."

\*

Pedro Gonzalez arose from the dinner table and went to his library. He knew that this was the day of the month when one of Hector's friends would arrive to pick up money from Anita and bring it to Hector in New York City, and he wanted to be absent for that transfer. Pedro gave Anita a generous amount of money for household expenses, and while he knew that a good portion of that was siphoned off and delivered to Hector, he preferred to act as though he was unaware.

Pedro sighed. He picked up his little Lladró figurine. She greeted him with her winsome ceramic smile. A thing of beauty, the little Lladró peasant girl. His life was a good one, he thought, gently setting down the figurine. Not perfect, but good. He lived in this beautiful home and he had a wonderful wife who was absolutely dedicated to him. Of his three children, two were real treasures. And then there was Hector, the biggest disappointment of his life. Hector, so beloved by his mother, such a handsome boy, but a complete loss. So spoiled! Not even able to support himself after all those years in New York City. This foolishness about breaking into acting was such a charade. He should tell Anita she should cut back on what she sends Hector. Make him get a job. But the other two made up for Hector. Catalina was such a good girl, so smart and hard-working and respectful. College graduate, the first in their family. He was glad she still lived at home. He would miss her deeply when she eventually moved away. Juan Carlos was a good boy too.

Through the closed door of his library he heard, faintly, a door open and shut, Anita's effusive greeting, and a response, the words indistinct. He waited patiently, while reviewing his accounts. His ledgers were neat and orderly, with notations meticulously entered. There were no names, just code numbers. The names he kept in his head. After a while, the door opened and closed again, and Pedro knew that whoever had come had departed. He would finish up the last bit of work he had to do and rejoin his family.

\*

Luis Vargas stepped off the landing at the back door of the Gonzalez home and set down the Bloomingdale's shopping bag. He reached into the bag and slipped the small packet of cocaine he had bought into the shoe box inside, on top of the packet of money. Hector had told him not to show up in New York to party unless he brought his own blow. Luis had never even bought coke before; it had been a hassle to figure out where to buy some and it was expensive. Hector was a real bastard, Luis reflected. Hector was lucky that he or Eddie took the time to bring him his cash. He'd be broke without it. Luis walked up the driveway toward the street, unlocked his car, stowed the shopping bag under the front passenger seat and took off.

Kelly and Aggie watched as Luis drove away and the car from across the street made a U-turn and took off after him.

Come on, Aggie," Kelly shouted, pounding the dashboard. "Let's go!"

The sedan following Luis traveled sedately, allowing the distance from the rendezvous to grow. About a mile from the Gonzalez home, the driver turned to his colleague. "I say he's swerving across the center line."

"I agree. Sure. Could be intoxicated," came the reply.

"Put out the siren then, Gene," the driver whispered.

Gene Bryant opened his window, placed a siren on the roof of the car and turned it on. The driver, Dan Abrams, brought their car up immediately behind Luis. Flashing lights passed through Luis's rear windshield, filled the car and spilled onto the street as the harsh siren pierced the quiet of the neighborhood.

*What'd I do?* Luis wondered frantically. Shaking, he pulled his car over to the curb. A dumpy-looking guy in a khaki zipper jacket and a Red Sox cap approached his window.

"I am Detective Abrams," the man said, flipping open his badge quickly and then replacing it in his jacket. "License and registration, please."

Luis fumbled in the glove compartment, found the registration, and passed it to the detective along with his license. What kind of phony cop was this?

"Mr. Luis Vargas? Do you know why we stopped you?" the goofy-looking cop asked.

"No. Why?" Luis asked, trying to sound tough, but he had a bad feeling about this.

"You were swerving, once or twice over the center line. Are you intoxicated, sir?"

"What? No! I haven't been drinking. I never swerved or anything." Luis knew his driving had been just fine.

"Step out of the car please, Mr. Vargas," Abrams commanded. "Are you transporting any alcohol in this vehicle?"

"No, of course not!"

"This is Detective Bryant. He will have a look in your car to confirm what you're saying." Abrams inclined his head toward his partner, a black guy, younger than Abrams, wearing a bomber jacket and plaid scarf over a white T shirt.

"I didn't do anything. Can I please go?" The shopping bag was sticking out from under the passenger seat. If they looked in the car the first thing they'd find was the money. And the coke.

"Sir, please exit your vehicle and stand aside while Detective Bryant checks your car."

"Let me take a breathalyzer. I'm totally sober. I swear."

Bryant and Abrams exchanged a quick look. The guy was close to panic. Car must contain something interesting. "Please just wait while Detective Bryant checks your car. This is for everyone's safety."

Luis stood with heart pounding, waiting for the inevitable.

Bryant emerged from the car, gripping the shopping bag, his hands in disposable rubber gloves. "You got a late Christmas present there?"

"No, it's not a present." Luis hoped against hope they'd beat it and leave him alone.

Bryant carefully reached into the shopping bag and lifted the lid of the shoebox. He whistled softly. "You win the lottery, man?" Bryant asked.

"No, no. It's not for me. It's for a friend."

"Uh-huh. That cocaine tucked in there with the cash?" Bryant continued.

"I, no, it's not like that. Someone told me to get it and bring it. It wasn't my idea, I..." Luis stammered. Sweat trickled down his face.

"Better Mirandize him," Abrams muttered.

"Mr. Vargas, it is my duty to inform you that you have the right to remain silent. Anything you say can and will be used against you in a court of law. You have the right to an attorney. If you cannot afford an attorney, one will be appointed for you by the court. Do you understand these rights?" Bryant intoned.

Luis stood, stunned, unspeaking.

"You need me to repeat that in Spanish? In español?" Bryant asked.

"No. I speak English," Luis managed to spit out.

"He was speaking English, Gene," Abrams muttered.

Bryant shrugged. "Let's go then." Bryant cuffed him while Abrams stood guard. They walked him over to their car, deposited him in the caged back seat and drove away.

*

"Fuck!" whispered Hector under his breath, as rosy-fingered dawn appeared outside his window. He had been up all night waiting for Luis. Now it was daylight and he still wasn't here. He tried calling Luis's cell, but there was no answer. Cell phones sucked. Worthless pieces of crap. Could be service was bad some places between Boston and New York City. Or Luis was out of battery or maybe he lost his phone. But Luis had never been late before. Hector sensed impending doom.

Anita and Cati sat at the kitchen table later that morning drinking coffee. Anita was flipping through the day's newspaper while Cati was deep into *War and Peace*, a half-finished bowl of Cheerios before her. Juan Carlos, a gangly boy with uncombed brown hair, clad in rumpled T-shirt and gym shorts, stumbled into the kitchen, dragged a chair out from the table and slumped into it. He folded his arms on the table and dropped his head onto them.

Anita rose, went to the refrigerator and poured some orange juice. "Here you go, Juan Carlos. This will wake you up." She set the juice down. "And here's a bowl for your Cheerios, whenever you're ready." She moved the box of Cheerios to within JC's reach. Cati turned to the next page of her book.

"How is your book, my angel? It's very thick!" Anita sat down and straightened her newspaper.

"Good," Cati said, not looking up. "But I'm glad we don't live back then."

Juan Carlos remained seated, face down. The doorbell rang.

"I'll go get it," Cati volunteered.

"Papá is right there," Anita pointed out. Pedro had gotten up early and was working in his library, which was to the left off the front hall of the home, with a view of the front yard.

"Yes, but he's busy. I can go so he won't be disturbed," Cati replied.

The doorbell rang again, three times in rapid succession.

"My goodness!" Anita exclaimed.

"I'm coming, I'm coming!" Cati muttered and stood, but before she took a step, the heavy brass doorknocker sounded four times, a pause and then another four.

Anita caught her wrist. "Catalina, don't go. Look out a window and see who it is first." Their lives had been so quiet since moving to Brookline. Before that, before Pedro consolidated his business, he'd had rivals who had given him trouble. Those times had not been easy, but Anita had thought they were long gone. What if one of those old enemies had quietly built a coalition to oppose Pedro? What would they do? Surely they would not hurt her family. Not their children, dear God, let them not hurt her family, she prayed silently.

"Okay, Mamá." Cati started toward the front of the house.

The doorknocker banged again.

Pedro dashed into the kitchen, his usual calm demeanor replaced by the agitated face of a stranger.

"Anita, take this. Hide it." He had something wrapped in a hand towel, something small, rubbing it vigorously with the towel. He handed it to Anita. Anita took it, realized what it was and looked at him, terrified.

"Anita, *mi amor*, no matter what, always remember that I love you. Leave it in the towel. Don't touch it. Now hide it. You all stay here. I will answer the door." He tried to compose himself and then headed to the door.

"Pedro. Do you know who it is? Who's at the door?" Anita asked.

"It's the police." Pedro headed to the front of the house to face them.

Juan Carlos lifted his head as Anita looked around frantically. Her eyes locked on the box of Cheerios. She whipped the wax-paper bag of cereal out of the box, deposited the towel-wrapped item into the box, and then replaced the bag.

"Don't touch this box. Don't say anything about it. Nothing." Anita warned.

"I wanted some Cheerios," Juan Carlos said, a little whiny.

"You just wait. Don't say anything to anyone." Anita glared at him.

"I don't..." he began.

"Just do it, JC. It's important. Mamá and Papá will explain it all to us later," Cati said, her voice a harsh stage whisper. But inside she felt very afraid. She stood, clutching her robe around her, uncertain whether she should join her father. Before she could decide, three police officers strode into the room, hustling Pedro along with them.

"Mr. Gonzalez, please be seated here with your family. Is there anyone else in the home?" asked one of the officers.

"No, there's no one else," Pedro said. He turned to his family. "They're here looking for drugs. I told them there are absolutely no drugs in our home, but they insist. They say they have a search warrant," Pedro said with as much dignity as he could muster.

"Sir, we showed you the duly executed search warrant and just to clarify, we are here to examine this premises not only for the presence of illegal drugs but also for evidence of drug trafficking and distribution," another officer said. Indistinct conversation punctuated by small and large sounds, pounding, ripping, banging, came from the front of the house. The police were examining the house room by room, starting with Pedro's library.

Anita sat at the table, head buried in her hands, her body jerking with each violent blow to her home. Pedro sat statue-like, expressionless, at the table. Cati had a hundred questions but knew she could not ask them now. She had the sense that life as she had known it, was over. JC looked at Cati, bewildered. She reached over and rubbed his back but could not meet his eyes. Two hours passed, and then the police were done. The box of Cheerios stood on the table, undisturbed.

"Mr. Gonzalez, we'd like you to come down to the station with us to answer some questions," one of the officers said.

"Do I have a choice?" Pedro asked.

"No, sir, you do not. Your daughter there can get your coat and you can come with us. The rest of you please remain seated," the officer said. Catalina hurried to comply, gathering her father's wool overcoat, cashmere scarf and leather gloves and returning to the kitchen. And then Pedro and the police were gone.

Then the phone rang. Cati looked at her mother uncertainly.

"Don't answer it, my love. I can't talk to anyone now. Don't answer it." Probably some reporter or a nosy neighbor, Anita thought. When the ringing had stopped, Anita stood and unplugged the phone. She took the box of Cheerios and put it into the pantry. "No one touches this box. Just leave it there. We will worry about it later."

Catalina wandered through the house. It was in shambles. She found herself in her father's library, horrified to see desk drawers pulled out and emptied onto the desk in big messy piles, the cushion of the desk chair slashed open, the wall board on either side of the fireplace pried away from the wall to reveal broad pink strips of insulation. There on the desk, knocked over and partly obscured amidst writing tablets, envelopes, stacks of family photos, old-fashioned fountain pens and mechanical pencils dumped from the drawers, was her father's favorite little Lladró. Catalina gently picked her up and set her right side up in a small empty spot on the desk. Her dainty little foot had been broken off at the ankle. Catalina sank into the ripped desk chair and wept.

# CHAPTER 28

Alex and Helen boarded a bus with a vicious-looking Chinese dragon painted on its exterior. They sat together in silence. Alex sensed that she didn't want to talk, so he pulled out the most recent issue of the New England Journal of Medicine, read the key articles and studied that week's Case Records of the Massachusetts General Hospital. He thought about the case presented, the abnormalities on physical examination, the results of laboratory assays and the EKG and echocardiogram. So what was the diagnosis? Sounds like systemic amyloidosis, he told himself. He turned the page and allowed himself a smile. A diagnosis of amyloidosis had been established on the basis of a kidney biopsy. He was correct!

He turned to laconic Helen, but she was gazing out the window at the scenery. "Helen?" he asked. She slowly turned and met his eyes.

"Bright angel, there are clouds in your eyes of ethereal blue. What is it?"

"I haven't been able to sleep on that lumpy mattress," she said. "I'm just tired." Helen reflected that with this fib she was laying the groundwork to avoid ever having to stay with Olivia again, although she hoped the whole problem would soon be moot.

She had turned the possibilities over and over in her mind. The best was to talk to Hector and offer to leave Alex and stay with him. What would Hector say? He never talked about the future, except to say that it was uncertain. But she had never mentioned willingness on her part to leave Alex for him. Hector would probably be overjoyed. She could imagine herself living happily in his glamorous apartment. They would have a beautiful child together, and everything would be fine. But how could she tell Alex? It would be so hard, but the sooner the better. As soon as she had spoken with Hector. Maybe Hector would come with her, help explain it to Alex. Explain how it had started innocently, because she had been so lonely. They never meant to hurt him.

She suppressed the tears that threatened to spill onto her cheeks. When she was with Hector, she was better, confident, a real woman. Now she felt like the old

Helen again, the stupid Helen who couldn't do anything on her own, who couldn't even take care of herself.

*

Helen was glad that she and Hector had set up a time for their next rendezvous before leaving for Christmas. She and Alex returned to New York on the 27th, and she and Hector were to meet as usual at the Waldorf the following day. She chose her clothing carefully, an outfit more serious, less sexy than usual. She removed her bright red nail polish (it was chipped anyway) and replaced it with clear. She arrived at the Waldorf, quietly entered the bar and sat at their usual table. She was disappointed to see that Hector had not yet arrived; he almost always reached the bar before she did. She had waited so long to see him, and now she would have to wait longer.

"Nice to see you again, Miss. May I get you something from the bar?" their usual courteous waiter asked. "Shall I bring a bottle of Pouilly-Fuissé?"

"Um, no, could I have a cup of coffee? For now anyway, please." She had heard that alcohol could be bad when you were pregnant and decided to play it safe. She stirred cream into her coffee and tried to wait calmly. But it was no good; she was panicked. She watched the entrance to the bar as though by keeping watch, she could speed Hector's arrival. But Hector was now half an hour late. This had never happened before. What could have happened to him? He could be sick, or injured, and unable to come. Maybe he needed help. She would find a phone booth and call him.

She finished her coffee. The waiter approached.

"May I get you anything else, Miss?" he asked. Helen imagined she heard pity in his voice.

"No thank you. Just the check." Good thing she didn't order wine; she had barely enough money with her to pay for coffee.

Helen found a phone booth outside, on Park Avenue, and dialed Hector's number. She listened to ring after ring, with no response. She wondered if she should go home. That was tempting, in a way, to postpone this awkward meeting with Hector. But she couldn't. She had to see him. She had to speak with him and figure out a plan. She walked the few blocks to Hector's apartment building. A middle-aged man in a gray overcoat stepped into the vestibule at the same time as Helen. He unlocked the door and held it for her.

"Thank you," she murmured. She took the elevator to Hector's floor and walked down the hall to his apartment. She paused, knuckles in the air, wondering if she should knock, or if she should just leave and call Hector the next day. No, she had to knock. She rapped softly at the door.

*

Hector Gonzalez paced around his apartment, paced like a caged animal. His head throbbed. He stopped to light another cigarette and continued his circuit around the living room, inhaling and exhaling deeply and rapidly. What could have happened to Luis? Luis wouldn't have disappeared with the money, would he? No, never. He had always been right on time before. Could he have gotten mugged or something? Maybe. Shit happened. He kept calling home, hoping to speak with his mother, to confirm that the money had been sent, and no one answered. When did that ever happen? Someone was always there.

The phone rang. *Fuck! I'm not getting it,* Hector thought. *Probably Chewie. Wants to be paid. I'm not answering it.* The phone kept ringing. How many times was the fucking phone going to ring? He took five long strides over to the phone, tentatively planning to smash it, but it stopped ringing and he put it down. He resumed his agitated pacing. After a while someone knocked softly on his door. Who the fuck could that be? Not Chewie. He would pound on the door. Hector quietly went to the door and peered through the peephole. Fuck! It was Helen. Was he supposed to meet her today?

Hector opened the door. "Helen," he said, as he stepped aside to let her in. Things just kept getting worse. Marisol had gone out but could be back any time.

"Hector, weren't we supposed to meet?" she asked, trying to keep the tremor from her voice.

"Wow, I'm so sorry. There's a family emergency and I can't reach anyone," he said.

"I- I'm sorry for that. I'm sorry but I have to talk to you," Helen said.

"How about we meet in a few days, after this gets straightened out?" He gave her a reassuring smile.

"This is kind of an emergency too. I mean, um, Hector, I'm pregnant." There. She had said it.

This can't be happening, Hector thought. It can't be real. It's a nightmare. "Are you sure? It could be a false alarm," he managed to say calmly.

"It's certain. I did one of those tests from the drugstore." Even now she could see the blue dot shining brightly before her, like one of her eyes, unblinking, confronting her.

"Helen, how can you be sure it's mine anyway? You are married, after all."

"Alex and I haven't...been together since before Thanksgiving. I think. It's been one thing or another. It can't be his."

Hector felt a twinge of pity for Alex. *Poor bastard*, he thought. "You're married to a medical student. Aren't you on the pill or something?"

Helen was startled by the annoyance in his voice. "Well, no, we thought we'd just see what would happen, and when nothing did, I thought maybe I was one of those women who didn't get pregnant that easily." She spoke in a voice saturated with despair.

What kind of stupid dingbat was she? Even fucking Marisol knew to be on the pill. Helen was a nice little break from Marisol, Hector thought, but he couldn't help her with this shit.

"If you want me to, I would leave Alex. We could be together," she said, looking at him wistfully. The expression on Hector's face was not what she had been hoping for.

"Helen, it's not possible. It's just not," Hector replied. "Can't you just get an abortion?"

"An abortion, oh! I don't know if I could. And anyway, I don't have any money." *This was his baby. Could he really want that?*

"You could go to the city hospital. It would be free," he suggested.

Perfect. She'd probably run into Alex and his nasty friends. "I can't. Alex works there. If it, if that was the only way, would you come with me somewhere else? Could you pay for me?"

Another fucking parasite wanting money from him! "That's part of the problem with the family emergency. My parents have been helping me and the situation has changed. I may not be getting that help for a while." He tried to sound patient and concerned. What did he have to do to move her out of here before Marisol returned?

She tried again. "Hector, just say the word and I'll leave Alex. I will. I'll help you with your family emergency. I can help you make ends meet. I could get a job. Anything."

Seconds ticked by, agony for Helen as she waited for Hector to speak. Finally, he said, "I just don't..."

The door opened and in walked Marisol. She immediately absorbed the scene: the skinny blonde girl wiping red eyes with a kleenex, and Hector standing there looking guilty as hell.

"Who the fuck is she?" Marisol demanded of Hector.

"A friend. She came to me for help." Hector feigned virtue unconvincingly.

"Yeah, I bet. I can guess what kind of help," Marisol replied sarcastically.

"*Ella es como una hermana para mi,*" Hector said, with all possible dignity.

"Like a sister! Fuck you, Hector. I'm not stupid!" Marisol screamed.

Hector stood, and there was Marisol's face, contorted with rage, her voice, ugly with jealousy. He struck her in the face, a savage blow that sent her staggering backwards.

Helen's eyes widened in horror.

Marisol ran at Hector, nails poised to claw him. Hector deftly grabbed both of her hands.

"Helen, you'd better go," Hector said. Helen grabbed her purse and wordlessly fled, slamming the door behind her.

Hector pushed both of Marisol's hands behind her waist and caught both wrists firmly in his left hand. He unbuttoned her shirt with his right hand.

"Hector, you fucking bastard, stop it!" She struggled against him, trying to kick him, but Hector moved quickly, having practiced this routine previously, and few of her kicks did much damage.

"I'm saving it for you, baby. How can you think something else? You really think I'd go for that skinny kid? Come on, don't be mad." He buried his hand in her breasts. "If I let go, will you be nice? You will? Okay, that's better."

Helen flew from the apartment building and onto the sidewalk. By this time, it was almost sunset, and the air was turning uncomfortably cold. She checked her wallet. Not enough for a cab after paying for coffee at the Waldorf. She could take the subway partway home, but it would still be a lot of walking. She should get started. She walked as fast as she could in her high heels, wondering what to do. The horrible scene at Hector's place wouldn't leave her mind. What had happened? Hector was a completely different person than the one she thought she knew. And he didn't want her. After all the nice things he had said, ultimately, he didn't want her. Tears streamed down her cheeks. This being New York City, nobody on the crowded sidewalks gave her a second look.

If only there was someone she could talk to. Someone like Kelly. She would know what to do. Kelly knew all kinds of things. Not that it did her any good because Kelly would kill her if she found out about this. What else might work? Sometimes women had miscarriages. If that happened, she'd be okay, off the hook. But that wasn't something you could count on. What about an abortion? She had no idea where to go. She had no money to pay for one, and anyway maybe she'd need someone to go with her and bring her home. But she, Helen, had no one. Not even Hector, the father of this child. If only she and Alex had been together sometime in December, but they hadn't, not even once. And who was that awful woman? That awful witch, with her wild dark hair and hefty build? Was she his, his regular girl-friend? Was she the reason he never took her out in the evening? Why he had never asked her to stay overnight? That terrible woman! And Hector! He had hit her! She wouldn't have believed it if she hadn't seen it with her own eyes.

She stumbled along, heading east, back towards the dorm, her bare face and hands, her pretty legs almost bare in sheer pantyhose, so cold, while her toes sliding forward in the narrow high-heeled shoes screamed for relief. What had she been thinking? Why had she gone with Hector? Alex had been so good and so kind. She didn't have it so bad. Why had she gone and spoiled it? She was stupid. Kelly was right- she wasn't good enough for Alex. But what about now? She had to do something.

\*

The next evening, Alex walked home slowly, dragging his feet. As he left the hospital, one of the pediatrics residents had seen him, called out to him. His little patient Cam had been readmitted a few days ago, in heart failure, complicated by pneumonia. They tried everything they knew, but Cam's little body did not respond, and he had died.

When Alex opened the door, dejected, Helen stood ready to greet him in the loose-fitting, snow-white, lace-trimmed nightgown she had worn on their wedding night, her hands clasped together in front of her waist. Her shining beauty, as though offered in compensation for the loss of Cam, revived him.

"You look like an angel!" Alex said.

Helen managed a smile. "I made dinner."

"Later," Alex said, dropping his coat on the foot of the bed.

Afterwards, they lay quietly together. He ran his fingers through her won-drous hair and gently touched her face. But when his fingers brushed her cheek, he found tears.

"Helen, I've hurt you. I'm so sorry. You have to tell me. I'm so sorry."

"No. No, you didn't. It's okay," she said, but against her will, she started to sob, and her whole body shook.

"What's wrong? Did I do something?" Alex lifted himself on one elbow and studied her face.

"I- um, it's nothing. I'm just emotional, I guess. Maybe hormones or something. I'm fine." *Shut up, Helen*, she told herself. *Shut up and stop crying. Everything will be okay.*

# CHAPTER 29

Sunshine poured in through the dormitory window and onto the wan oval of Helen's face. She lay unmoving, willing the nausea to subside. It was only several weeks since she and Alex had had sex, too soon for morning sickness. Too soon, that is, if she wanted Alex to believe he was the father of the baby she was carrying. She absolutely could not let Alex know about her morning sickness for at least a couple more weeks. She grasped a small wastebasket awkwardly and drew it toward her, waiting for the nausea to peak. She thrust her head out over the wastebasket, and her stomach delivered a few dry heaves. She whimpered helplessly. *Maybe I deserve it*, she thought. *Maybe I'm being punished. For those few days, no, not even days, those few hours of happiness. Maybe I deserve it, but I'm sorry, I'm so sorry. When will it end? Please let it end.*

*

"They say March comes in like a lion, but today feels more like a lamb. Why don't we take a walk?" Alex said.

"I just feel so awful. And fat." Helen's eyes surveyed the lump below her belly button. "Sweetheart, it's a baby. You're not fat," Alex said. "You're…"

"If you say I'm beautiful one more time, I'm going to scream."

Alex sighed. What was he supposed to say? The change in contour of Helen's body was already obvious, but he certainly would not point out that the small bulge she had now in her lower abdomen was just the beginning.

"And I'm so hungry but everything tastes funny. Everything makes me sick to my stomach."

He put six saltine crackers on a plate, spread them with peanut butter and set the plate in front of her. The nurses on the OB floor had shared this dietary tip with him. "Here, sweetheart. You can eat this. It won't taste funny."

Helen nibbled at the crackers cautiously. Alex was right- this didn't taste weird.

"Do you feel up to a walk?" Alex asked, taking the empty plate from her.

"I don't know." She sat pouting on the one desk chair.

"Come on. You have to get out. You can't stay cooped up in here forever."

"Alright. Let me get my stuff," Helen said. She found a coat and put it on. The khaki all-weather coat was worn, but it would provide the right amount of warmth for the day. She pulled on her boots, her gift from Hector, with a grimace. She hadn't bothered to clean them or polish them since Christmas, and much of their luster was gone. She wanted to throw them away, but Alex would ask where they went, and anyway, they were her only warm boots.

Alex and Helen exited the medical center and turned right onto First Avenue, heading north.

"Look there, Helen," Alex said as they approached 34th St. "The Empire State Building! Let's go left here." They crossed 1st Avenue and headed down 34th Street.

The Empire State Building soared above its neighbors. Helen took a deep breath and kept walking. The last time she had seen the Empire State Building had been from Hector's apartment. She shuffled like a prisoner in its direction, ahead of her and slightly to the left, a reminder of her infidelity.

"Alex, 34th St is so crowded, with all these stores and all. Can we walk on a different street?"

"You don't want to look in the stores? Look at all these shoe stores! I thought a new pair of shoes would cheer you up."

"No thanks."

"You sure? Even if there was a sale? You found those boots you're wearing on 34th St., right? You said they were a steal."

Helen shook her head. "Not in the mood."

"That's okay, sweetheart." Alex turned right onto 2nd Avenue, and then left at 35th St. Helen looked around. She could no longer see the Empire State Building and felt a little better. They continued to walk west until they reached Fifth Avenue, and then turned north.

"Look, there's the New York Public Library. The lions out front are really wonderful."

"Oh, um, yes. They look very...fierce, I guess."

"Majestic, I'd say, but fierce too, I suppose. Let's walk around behind the library to Bryant Park. We can sit down and you can get a little rest."

"Okay."

"This is a beautiful park. I mean, it will be much prettier when the weather warms up and the gardens are in bloom. But it's still a nice space now. Here's a bench; let's sit down," Alex said. "Guy's selling pretzels over there; you want anything?"

Helen shook her head. Alex took her hand and squeezed it. The warmth of the sun reached them in grudging intermittent dollops, alternating with cool bursts of early spring air. Helen wished she had put a sweater on under her coat.

"Hey, I think- see that woman over there? She reminds me of someone I went to college with," Alex said, leaning forward on the bench.

"The one with the stroller?" Helen asked.

"Yes. Now that I think about it, her fiancé worked on Wall Street; they were planning to get married and live in New York."

"So it could be her," Helen said.

"Let's go see if it's her; do you mind?" Alex asked.

"Sure."

Alex drew Helen to her feet, and they walked over to the neighboring bench.

"Elizabeth?" Alex asked.

The woman looked up. Helen saw an attractive young woman with chestnut-brown hair in a lightweight fitted wool coat the color of aged cognac, with black velvet piping along the edges of the collar's lapels.

She looks so elegant, Helen thought miserably, noting with envy the rose-gold necklace and earrings gleaming against her VSOP coat.

"Yes?" She said and then her eyes opened wide. "Alex!"

"Yes! I thought it was you. This is my wife, Helen. Helen, this is Elizabeth Hawkins; we were in the same class at Amherst."

"Nice to meet you," Elizabeth said, extending her hand. "Now it's Elizabeth Pembroke."

"Oh, yes, that's right. I'd forgotten your fiancé's name."

"James Pembroke. We got married that summer after graduation and we've been here in New York since." Her smile radiated self-satisfaction.

"And you have a baby!" Alex said, peering into the stroller.

"Yes, this is little Jamie." Elizabeth adjusted the blanket carefully around the baby's shoulders and smiled indulgently. "He's quite the handful, but he's asleep now, so I can enjoy sitting for a few minutes."

"He's a good-looking little fellow," Alex said.

"Congratulations," Helen murmured.

"We're expecting a baby ourselves. In early fall," Alex said.

"That's wonderful! And what are you doing now? You were planning to go to med school, I think," Elizabeth said.

"Yes. I'm at NYU, graduating in less than three months."

"You mean to tell me we have both been inhabiting this island since graduation, and this is the first time we've run into one another?" Elizabeth inclined her head as she spoke.

"Unless you were at Bellevue Hospital, it's not likely you would have seen Alex. That's where he spends his time," Helen said. Elizabeth noted with interest the edge in Helen's voice.

"In June we're moving to Boston. I just found out that I got my residency there. Which is great because the residency program is top-notch and Helen and I are both from that area, so we'll be close to family."

"Which branch of medicine are you going into?" Elizabeth asked.

"Pathology," Alex replied.

"Alex, really? Isn't that cutting up dead people?" Elizabeth crinkled her nose.

"No, mostly not. It's mostly reviewing biopsies under the microscope and identifying cancer." *And I'll never have to draw blood again!*

Elizabeth eyed him with skepticism. "That's not how it was on *Quincy*."

"Quincy was a forensic pathologist. I'll be doing surgical pathology. You get to see the disease process right in front of you, and understand it better, distinguish benign from malignant."

"Sounds positively Manichean!" Elizabeth said, shaking her head.

Alex threw back his head and laughed. "I never thought of it that way. I'll keep it in mind."

"You have a nice laugh. I always liked your laugh, Alex. Helen, you're lucky. Such an appealing feature is uncommon among the men of today," Elizabeth said.

"I have a feeling you keep poor old James on his toes 24/7!" Alex answered.

"Quite right! As it should be," Elizabeth confirmed with a nod. James needed a lot of direction. However, he was quite capable in the workplace. If his numbers were good again this quarter, he'd get a raise, and they should be able to afford a nice two-bedroom co-op.

Helen smiled agreeably. "Your coat is so pretty."

"Oh! Thank you. James got it for me during our honeymoon. In Paris."

Helen looked down. She regretted her last remark.

"I bet that was wonderful. We had a really nice honeymoon, closer to home though. In Chatham. I think it's the nicest town on Cape Cod. I'd love to have a second home there one day, but the real estate is out of our reach for now," Alex said.

Elizabeth nodded. "Maybe sometime we'll look into that."

"Alex, should we get back to our walk?" Helen whispered.

"Oh, sure, sweetheart. Elizabeth, it was such a nice surprise seeing you. Good luck with young Jamie!" Alex took Helen's arm.

"And you, good luck with your baby, and good luck next year with residency," Elizabeth said, her tone gracious. She and James had talked about the possibility of a place with three bedrooms, but they were hard to come by, and anyway, a third bedroom would mean her mother would stay with them when she came to visit. Two bedrooms were plenty. Let her mother stay in a hotel.

They turned away. Helen murmured, "She was flirting with you. I couldn't believe it."

"Helen, she wasn't. She's a respectable married lady, just like you." Alex gave her arm a squeeze.

Helen shuddered. "She just acted, I don't know, pushy."

"Oh, no, no. Elizabeth is not like that. But she has a certain presence, like she's, she's..."

"Queen of the world or something?" Helen muttered bitterly. The one good thing about this meeting was seeing how good Elizabeth looked after having a baby. It gave Helen hope that her own body would recover from this assault.

"Helen, no. She has a certain patrician quality about her, I admit, but she's very nice." Alex studied her with concern.

"Yeah, you like everyone. I remember." Helen ducked her head, hiding her face behind a curtain of blonde hair.

Elizabeth watched them stroll away. The way they looked, the way they dressed, they seemed so, so underfunded. She had made the right decision, marrying James.

"Kelly, I have something to show you." Leda carried a large, flat rectangular package into the living room and proceeded to strip off its brown paper wrapping. Kelly watched with curiosity.

"Here we go," she said, letting the last of the brown paper fall to the floor and holding the rectangle aloft. "I had the front page of the Globe with your big story mounted on foam board and framed. What do you think?"

A simple black frame surrounded the newspaper. "Drug Lord Arrested-Fortune Seized" the headline proclaimed. The story, hers and Aggie's, followed below.

"That is so maternal. I'm having a flashback to the days when my stuff would go on the refrigerator."

"Come on, you love it. And Dad and I are so proud of you!"

Kelly accepted the gift and studied it. "That's actually really nice."

"It will look great in your apartment."

"Thanks. Really. It's very thoughtful."

"And, I thought, while I was at it, why not have one made for Aggie too? So here's a second one, identical to yours. Just leave it in the wrapping paper until you can give it to him."

"Will do. Say, you don't mind if I borrow the car, do you?" Kelly asked. "I need to run an errand."

"No problem. Will you stay to dinner?"

"Sure, I'll stay for dinner. Want me to pick anything up while I'm out?" Kelly selected a large bottle from the cabinet, filled it with water, screwed on the cap and slid it into her tote bag.

"No, we've got everything we need. Try to be back by 6, 6:30, okay?"

Kelly's first stop was Harvard Street in Coolidge Corner. After the usual struggle to find parking in this retail area of Brookline she entered a florist shop, selected a nice bouquet of pink roses along with a greenish vase and stashed them in the car. Next, she drove to West Roxbury and pulled into the drive of a cemetery. Although it was now almost eight years since she had last been here, she remembered exactly where to go. She walked in a zigzag along the lonely bluestone pathways laid into spongy new grass until she reached her destination. She knelt down by Patrick's grave and carefully, respectfully arranged the flowers in the vase, and poured water into the vase from the bottle she had brought. She set the flowers before the headstone.

*So, Patrick,* she thought, *I did my best to avenge you. We brought down Hector, or, at least, we brought his family down. His father's in jail and will hopefully stay there for a long time. Hector never got a job. He was living off his family, off his father's drug money. But that's all over. I think he'll self-destruct without that income. Look, I got you pink roses, just like you got me for prom. Rest in peace, my sweet friend.*

*

Hector slumped into the couch and lit a cigarette. He gazed at the vacant wall, reflecting how much he would miss the TV, but he needed some smokes, and needed to pay down what Chewie said he owed. He had gotten decent money for that TV, not what he had paid originally, but still good money. Money'd last longer now that he was off cocaine. Chewie had cut him off. *You got champagne taste on a beer budget, my friend,* Chewie had said. *Switch to H. A little more trouble to use, but cheaper and you still get a nice high.* Chewie had been right. Hector glanced at the little drawer in the end table; that's where he kept his stuff. Knowing it was there within easy reach comforted him.

Hector drew on his cigarette, making every breath count, pulling the nicotine deep into his lungs, waiting for Marisol. Once the money dried up, she had flounced out of here pretty quick. *I'm going to live with my mother,* she had said, over her shoulder as she hauled her ass out the door. Now she wanted to talk. What the fuck could she want?

Marisol opened the door and stomped into the living room. "Where's the TV?"

"You can't knock? You don't live here. You left. You shouldn't have kept a key." Hector slumped deeper into the sofa. He wanted to enjoy it while he could. It might be the next to go. He contemplated Marisol. Her tits were enormous, even bigger than he remembered. She had really packed on the weight since she moved out. Eating too much of her mother's greasy food. If she's here asking to move back in, he would say no. He didn't want to live with a porker.

"I don't want to be here. My mother told me I had to." Marisol collapsed into a chair and stared at Hector.

"Your mother told you to come here? She's so sick of your sorry ass she sent you here to give me shit?"

Marisol glared at him.

"If you think you can move back in, you're wrong. I've had enough of your crap." Damn! Could he even find her snatch now through all the blubber?

"That's not why I'm here." Marisol kept her tone even. "Even though you're a fucking bastard, my mother told me it was your right to know. I'm pregnant."

"Congratulations."

"It's yours."

Hector lit a cigarette and blew smoke in her direction. That was it. She was here for money. Not from him, not today. "You're a lying bitch."

"I'm not lying."

"You were on the pill. How could you get pregnant?"

"I kept asking you for money for my prescription. You wouldn't give it to me, and you wouldn't stay off me. That's how I got pregnant, you asshole."

"So. You're getting an abortion or what?"

"No. In my family we respect life. I won't do that." She put her fingers to the crucifix she wore around her neck.

"Good for you. What're you going to name it?" he asked sarcastically.

"I don't know. Do you care?"

"Of course, I care." Hector's tone was flat. "How about Pedro, after my fucking father?" *My father who's in jail, hope he rots there.*

"What if it's a girl?" Marisol's voice had a caustic edge.

"How about, how about, Elena?" Hector sucked on his cigarette and closed his eyes. He hoped she would leave. Maybe if he ignored her.

Minutes ticked by. Finally, Marisol pulled herself to her feet. "Okay, so I told you. I'm leaving."

"Uh-huh. Bye." Hector kept his eyes closed. He held his cigarette close to his mouth, ready for the next puff.

Marisol slammed the door on the way out.

# CHAPTER 30

"Helen, he is really beautiful," Alex said. "And so tiny!" He rested his hand on the head of the blotchy-faced newborn swaddled tightly in a little blue blanket. A crop of dark hair stuck straight up from his reddish scalp. Helen, shining among women, Helen, his philosopher's stone, his own beloved, had worked this magic. "I have a little son! I can't wait to play with him."

Helen sighed. "I think you'll have to wait a while before you can play with him."

"No, look, didn't you see? He just smiled at me!" The baby opened his eyes cautiously to reveal slits of misty green iris.

"Helen, Alex, congratulations!" Leda said, beaming as she entered the hospital room, carrying a large bouquet and setting it down on the window sill.

Kelly sailed past her. "Helen, you look awful. Was it bad?"

"Thanks a lot," Helen said. "What a night! I am so glad it's over!"

"Kelly! Let's see how you look when it's your turn," Leda said.

"Note to self- make sure Aggie doesn't want a big family!" Kelly mouthed, *sotto voce.*

"It's so wonderful that you're back in Brookline, so we can all be with you." A tear appeared at the corner of Leda's eye.

"And this is the best hospital in Boston for OB. They took such good care of Helen last night," Alex added. "Having my residency here is working out really well."

"So. Let's have a look at the little fellow. How big is he?" Kelly continued. She leaned over the baby, cradled in Alex's arms.

"8 lb, 14 oz, 21 inches," Helen recited. "Apgars, 9 and 10."

"Ouch! A big one. No wonder you look like crap," Kelly said.

Alex glanced at Helen, who was starting to tear up while trying to maintain a smile. He studied her face. Her usual flawless ivory complexion was streaked with shadows of violet, a testament to her extreme fatigue. "Kelly, no. Helen looks beautiful. Have you ever seen such an intriguing smile? A Mona Lisa smile. And I have a little something for the very beautiful mother of my son."

Alex returned the baby to Helen, snapped open his briefcase, extracted a Tiffany's bag and handed it to Helen. He was delighted to see her eyes light up when she recognized the gift bag's signature pale turquoise color.

"Alex! Something from Tiffany's! This is so extravagant!"

"I hope you like it," Alex said. He held his breath, hoping he had chosen well. "Here, let me hold the baby while you open it."

Helen carefully passed the baby to Alex. She pulled a glossy jewelry box from the bag and quickly untied the white satin ribbon holding it closed. She lifted the lid to reveal a lovely necklace of graduated white pearls with a tiny gold clasp.

"Alex, I love it! I just love it!" Helen gently ran her fingers over the gleaming pearls. "I've never had anything so pretty. And I've never had anything from Tiffany's."

"The lady who helped me said it was a classic, and that no woman should be without such a necklace. I am so happy that you like it," Alex said, relieved. He missed the quick glance of satisfaction that Helen shot at Kelly.

"Wow, Helen, you got one of the good guys. That's for sure!" Kelly said.

Helen put on the pearls. Alex gazed at them shimmering against the glowing skin of Helen's throat. They reached the inferior edge of her manubrium, which was a very good length, Alex thought. Not too short, and not too long.

"What are you going to name him?" Kelly asked.

"We're thinking Mark. Mark Eastgard. It has a nice ring, don't you think?" Alex said. He studied the baby. "His eyes are such an interesting shade of greenish blue. Halfway between my hazel and your blue eyes. His hair, his hair is rather dark."

Helen started to shake. A full confession trembled on the tip of her tongue. *I was so lonely. I'm sorry. I'm so, so sorry.*

"My mother will be pleased," Alex continued. "The baby, I mean Mark, must have gotten that from her."

"You can't go by that," countered Leda, seasoned veteran of years of child-rearing. "Some babies born with dark hair turn blond after a few months. When Helen was born, her hair was so pale that wet it was almost transparent. And she stayed blond. But my boys both started with brown hair, and then it grew in blond, almost as light as Helen's. Eye color can change too."

Helen suppressed an urge to sob with relief. She concentrated on controlling her breathing.

"Helen? Helen?" Alex was asking.

"What? Sorry, I'm so out of it." She forced herself to meet his eyes.

"I was just asking if you wanted anything. Coffee?"

"Coffee would be wonderful. Starbucks, if there's one nearby."

"Absolutely. Tall with cream?"

"Um, can you get me a grande? With cream and one Sweet and Low."

"I'm on it." He handed the baby to Helen and left the room.

Helen contemplated her son. *Little Mark,* she thought, *is it possible that I am going to get away with this, slut that I am?*

Leda leaned over the baby. "Hello there! Hello, young man. I'm your grandma. Yes, I am. I'm your grandma!"

Kelly rolled her eyes.

"You know," Leda said, "I thought being a grandmother would make me feel old, but I don't. I just feel elated." She leaned over Mark and cooed.

"And I guess that makes me an aunt," Kelly said, although less effusively. *When the goo-goo noises start, it's time to hit the road.* "He's really sweet, Helen. Listen, I have to go. I still have work on my desk to get done today."

"Okay, thanks, Kelly," Helen said, watching her leave. She wished Kelly liked her more, like when they were kids. She turned to her son. *You really are beautiful, and I know I messed up, but I will be good mommy, I promise. If I'm really good and really careful, things might just be okay.*

*

Hector Gonzalez lay on the floor of the living room of his apartment, his head on a pillow pulled off the bed, his mind wandering somewhere in the vicinity of reality. Someone was banging on the door. Who could it be? He vaguely recalled some papers shoved under the door, something about eviction, something about rent not being paid. Was it those people banging? Let them bang. He couldn't move. He didn't have any money to pay them. Someone else could pay. That girl Helen maybe. She told him she would help him. She would get a job and help. He would tell them to call Helen. But they were still banging on the door. Didn't they know to call Helen? Then he heard the door open, someone walking toward him. He had his needle and all wrapped in a T shirt; he slid that to his side so they wouldn't take it. He would keep his eyes closed. If they thought he was asleep, they would go away.

"Hector!" Marisol stood over him, glaring down.

"I'm asleep. Go away," he said, barely audible.

"Where's the couch?" she asked.

"Helen can pay," he muttered. "Ask her for money."

"Someone named Helen bought the couch?" she demanded and waited for him to answer.

Hector breathed slowly in and out, enjoying the air briefly unadulterated by noisy words.

"Hector! Wake up! Where's the couch?" Marisol punctuated her query with a firm kick to his left buttock.

She wouldn't leave. "Couch? No, Chewie took it. High quality leather. He always liked it."

Marisol stomped away and it was quiet again. He gratefully drifted back into sleep. But the blessed silence remained for only a few minutes.

"Hector. Wake up. I got to talk to you. Wake up."

He lay quietly, willing her to depart.

"Hector? Hector!" She stood over him and poured a glass of ice water onto his face.

"Holy crap! What the fuck!" he said, coughing and sitting up.

"I need you to wake up. Here's coffee. I just made it."

Hector tried to focus. Marisol had not come alone. There was a stroller with a sleeping baby. Oh, fuck! She had said she was pregnant.

"Are you awake now? Are you listening? Okay, here's the baby. Your baby. I named her Elena, like you said. I've done my part and I'm done. Chewie says I can move in with him, but I can't bring this kid." *No more living in that damn convent my mother calls home.*

Hector contemplated her, bleary-eyed, but managed to swallow some coffee.

"Okay, are you listening? I brought diapers and bottles and an extra blanket they gave me at the hospital."

"Wait. You can't leave that kid here."

"Yes, I can. Your turn to do something. Get your ass in gear and you figure out what to do with her." She paused. "I want to tell you something. In all seriousness.

I told you in my family we respected life. Whole time I was pregnant, I never used. That baby is healthy." *You can thank Mamá for that. Not even booze allowed in the goddamn house.*

As the caffeine from the coffee kicked in, the enormity of this new problem began to dawn on Hector.

"Marisol, no! I can't take care of a baby."

Marisol folded her arms beneath her copious breasts. "If I were you, I'd get your mother to take her. Your family is rich."

*Was rich*, Hector thought.

Marisol turned and walked to the door. The baby started to whimper.

"Marisol, please, baby, let's talk about this. Don't leave. Sit down, let's talk."

"I'm through with you, Hector. If she cries, change her diaper and give her a bottle. Oh, and her birth certificate is in the side pocket of the diaper bag," she said, hand on the doorknob.

"Diaper bag?" Hector whispered. He tried to stand, to stop her, but couldn't get to his feet in time.

"Good luck!" she said sweetly. The door slammed shut.

*

Hector opened the door and Eddie and Luis entered the apartment.

"Okay, Hector, we're here. What's the emergency?" Eddie asked.

"Why'd you need both of us? You never asked us to come together before," Luis asked. He had been dreading this meeting with Hector. When he had been caught with all that money and the coke last December, it led to Hector's dad being arrested. He had half-expected a hit-man to greet them, but only Hector was here, and he didn't even look mad, just wasted.

"Where's the TV?" Eddie asked, stepping over an empty pizza box. "What'd you do with the couch?"

"Long story." Hector let out a deep sigh. "Sit down." He gestured at several bed pillows on the floor.

Luis lowered himself onto a pillow, knocking over the half-finished can of Pabst Blue Ribbon that stood in place of the couch. "Damn, I'm sorry. Let me get a towel."

"Fuck it," Hector said. "Just sit. They're kicking me out anyway. Either of you can spare a smoke?"

"Sure, here you go," Eddie said, proffering a pack of Marlboros.

Luis lifted a bottle from a brown paper bag. "I brought Don Julio along. Enough of him and it will feel like a party."

Hector nodded. "Thanks, we'll need it."

"Come on Hector, cut the shit and say what's going on and what you want from us." Eddie replaced his cigarettes in his shirt pocket.

Hector's hands shook as he lit the cigarette. He drew deeply on it before speaking. Luis and Eddie exchanged a glance.

"That fucking whore Marisol. She showed up today." He looked down, studying the grain of the shiny hardwood floor, tracing it with his free hand. He had never really noticed it before.

"What'd she want and what's that got to do with us?" Eddie prompted.

"She, she brought over this fucking baby. Dumped it on me so she can move in with Chewie. Fucking Marisol would run off after anyone who'll get her her next fix."

Luis quickly uncapped the tequila, took a swig and handed it to Hector.

Eddie eyed Hector skeptically. "I don't see no baby. You've lost it, man."

As if on cue, a little whimper sounded from the bedroom.

"There she is. That whore's baby." Hector put the bottle to his lips and chugged tequila.

"So, ah, why are we here exactly?" Luis asked, nervously.

Hector wiped his mouth with the back of his hand and gestured with the bottle. "I want you to take the baby, take it to my mom."

"Ah, Hector, if Marisol has been sleeping around, why should your mom take it?"

Hector finished his cigarette and took another swallow of tequila before answering.

"Marisol's not really a whore," he muttered. "Tell my mom it's mine. Ask her to take care of it. Birth certificate's in the, the, what do you call it, diaper bag."

Luis looked at Eddie. It was not what they wanted to hear, but no baby left alone with Hector would survive for long. "I guess we can do that." He stood, took a deep breath, put his shoulders back and headed for the bedroom. He returned pushing a stroller containing a tiny infant.

The baby looked up with eyes of emerald green and started to cry. "Damn, it looks just like you, Hector," Eddie said.

"Marisol says it's a girl. Elena. Pretty name, huh? Means Helen." His voice was flat, as the baby's cries escalated to a quivering howl.

"I think you're supposed to give it milk if it cries," Luis offered.

"Yeah, I think Marisol left some. Can you check the fridge?"

"What about you? What are you going to do?" Luis asked, looking around the empty room.

"I don't know. I guess stay until they carry me out. Then find somewhere else."

"Well, why don't you come with us? Move back into your old house? Your dad's, ah, gone. I bet your mom'd love to have you back," Luis said

Hector swallowed more tequila and paused before answering. "Can't. I've got contacts here I can't leave. I- I owe Chewie. Got to pay that back." He turned his gaze to the plate-glass window and let it linger on the magnificent skyline. He gave them a sardonic smile. "Leave all this? No. I love New York."

# PART 3

Louisiana, 2001

# CHAPTER 31

Gail Julia Kaiser was nervous. Things were changing too quickly. For one thing, she was about to start kindergarten, and she wasn't sure she was ready. For another, just two weeks ago Mommy had gone to the hospital and had come home with not just one baby but two. Julia was the big sister to twins. Both of them were boys and their names were Aloysius and Beauregard. Babies were supposed to be cute, but these two were funny-looking. She wondered if her parents knew how ugly they were. She felt bad for her Mommy. All that work and not much to show for it. Plus these babies were so annoying, always crying or needing something. Worst of all, Mommy never had any time for her any more. *I don't think she likes me, now that she's got those dumb babies.*

That night she climbed into bed and looked around the room. She was glad to see the pale stripes of moonlight that crossed the room. She knew that moonbeams were a barrier to the monsters that lived in the closet. Dark nights meant the monsters could come out and get her, so on those nights she would keep very still and quiet so they wouldn't know she was there. But tonight the moonbeams were brighter than ever, so she was safe. She tiptoed to the window and gazed on the big solemn face of the moon and thought how pretty it was. She returned to bed and started to climb back in, but then she had an idea. She took her pillow and wedged it deep under the covers at the foot of the bed and burrowed in after it. *Maybe if I sleep upside down, I'll wake up different. Special. Maybe life will change and Mommy will like me again.* She lay like that for a while, decided it was too stuffy, put her pillow back into its original position and finally went to sleep.

# CHAPTER 32

Julia's father Guy Kaiser was a non-confrontational, soft-spoken man who was reasonably responsible but not particularly ambitious. He craved peace and quiet and enjoyed a good football game. The closest he ever came to passion was a restrained display of elation when the LSU Tigers scored, or a quiet despondence when their opponents were victorious.

That afternoon Julia sat silently by his feet, skinny legs crossed to support her Math notebook as she worked through her assignment.

"This is the Sugar Bowl, Julia. LSU vs. Notre Dame. This is big!" Guy sat tense in his easy chair, leaning forward. Would he see one of his boys playing in Tiger Stadium one day? They were strong and energetic. What he wouldn't give to see a jersey with "Kaiser" on the back!

"Well, here we are at just 90 seconds until half-time. The Fighting Irish have really dominated the first half, Bill. Will LSU be able to respond in the second half?" the announcer queried. Guy grimaced. As an LSU alum, he took the implied criticism as a personal affront.

"Well, Tom, the Tigers have some fine young men on their team this year, some really talented young men. I think they can still give Notre Dame a run for their money," countered Bill in a hearty baritone.

"Well, Bill, LSU has their work cut out for them," Tom bantered. "There's the snap. Notre Dame's quarterback is looking for a receiver. Look at the movement on this field! He's getting some pressure, but he has time, and look at that pass."

"Interception! Interception! LSU number 76 intercepted on the 50-yard line!" Bill broke in enthusiastically. "Look at him run! What a sprinter! 30-yard line! The crowd is going wild! 20-yard line! He's going all the way! All the way! Touchdown! Touchdown LSU!"

Guy clenched his fist and hoarsely whispered, "Yes!" He took a long swallow of his Abita beer. This was nerve-racking. "See that, Julia? That's what it's all about."

Julia looked up from her Venn diagrams, puzzled.

"Who is that #76, Bill? What do we know about him?" asked Tom.

"Fine young man, fine athlete. Name is Landry, hometown is Lafayette, deep in the heart of Cajun country, Tom. He's a junior now at LSU," Bill replied, his voice smoothly confident.

"Well that was quite a play! The Tigers have the extra point. They are back in the game, Bill, and now we'll be heading into half time," intoned Tom.

"Okay, if I know what's good for me, I better go change those light bulbs like Mommy said." Guy rose from his chair. "We have about 20 minutes before the second half starts."

It was quiet in the house. A good time to call Grandma, her father's mother. She slid the receiver under her dark hair and dialed the number.

"Grandma! It's me, Julia."

"Hello, sweetheart. What are you doing today?"

"Watching the Sugar Bowl with Daddy. But it's half time."

"Oh, I bet he likes that."

"He does. No one else watches with him."

"How is your Mom?"

"She's fine. She's grocery-shopping."

"That's good. Your mother is such a good cook. I'm sure she'll make you a wonderful dinner."

"Yes, I know."

"Do you help her around the house?"

"Yes." *But not that much*, thought Julia. "I'm going to set the table in a little while."

"That sounds perfect. What a treasure you are!"

"Okay, I should go do that. I love you." Julia knew she would be in trouble with her mother if this long-distance call got too expensive.

"I love you too. Thank you for calling, my angel."

Just as the second half of the game was underway, Julia's mother Aura Lee returned from the grocery store, with Alo and Beau roaring into the house in her wake. They were identical twins, big for 6-year-olds, with vocal capacity to match their size.

"I'm an airplane!" Aloysius said, arms held straight out, running figure eights in the TV room. Guy leaned from side to side, trying to catch all the action on the TV screen.

"I'm a fighter jet! I'll shoot you down!" said Beau. He ripped off his Batman sweatshirt and threw it against the wall. "Ratatatat! Ratatatat! Pow! Direct hit! You're supposed to crash now, Alo!"

"Oh! Okay! Boom! I exploded!" yelled Alo.

Guy leaned forward for the remote and activated the closed caption function. He grinned, embarrassed, at Julia and said, "That's better."

"Where's Julia? Alo and Beau want to go to the playground. She can help out and take them," Aura Lee said, brusquely.

"She was right here just a moment ago," said Guy. "Bound to be here somewhere."

"Julia! Julia!" Aura Lee yelled. No response. "Where is she?"

Guy concentrated on the TV, hoping that things would settle down soon without his intervention.

"Guy, can you take them? They need to burn off some of their energy or they'll drive me nuts. I need a break," Aura Lee said, depositing a gallon of milk and a bag of fresh shrimp into the refrigerator.

"I can take them out, throw the ball around some, after the game." He raised his voice slightly. "Beau. Alo. Y'all want to go throw the ball around later?"

"Got ya! You're dead, Beau!" Alo yelled.

Beau fell to the ground, jerked his legs spasmodically and groaned.

"They want to go now. I want them to go now too before they destroy the house."

"Honey, come on, it's the Sugar Bowl. It's once a year," Guy said, eyes fixed on the TV, a pleading tone creeping into his voice.

"Fine, I'll take them after I put away the groceries. For a little while." She quickly laid rice, dried red beans and a can of plum tomatoes onto a shelf in the pantry, pivoted and shoved a small jar of bay leaves into her spice cabinet. "I will speak to Julia when I get back. She could help out more." Aura Lee flounced out of the room. "Aloysius, Beauregard, if you still want to go to the park, let's go." The door slammed behind them and the house was quiet again, except for the football game.

"Whew, dodged that bullet," Guy muttered.

Julia slid out from behind the couch, and silently resumed her spot near her Dad's feet. Being small had its advantages, she thought.

"Julia, where were you? Mommy wanted you to take the boys to the playground."

"I know. I didn't want to go." She plucked a dust bunny from her pants.

"Why not? The playground is nice," Guy asked.

"I wanted to watch the game with you," Julia said. That was true, more or less, but more important, she really did not want to go to the playground. It meant pushing the twins on the swings without a break. And if they got dirty, she would be the one to get yelled at. No, thanks.

"Are you going to tell on me?" asked Julia.

"Tell what?" He tousled her hair. "Look now, LSU has the ball. Let's see how they do."

Announcers Bill and Tom resumed their mildly jocular interchange.

Suddenly the door opened.

"Stay where you are," commanded Aura Lee. "Do not take one step farther into this house. I'll get some towels."

Aura Lee stormed into the TV room, followed close behind by the twins.

"They went into the sandbox. At their age! With all those little children, those little toddlers, and there were Alo and Beau, biggest kids ever to get into the sandbox. And Alo threw sand into Beau's hair. And then Beau threw sand at him. And then they started wrestling and kicked up sand and the little kids got scared and started to cry. And this rude woman came and complained to me that her whiny little brat was crying. Said my boys got sand in his eyes. And what a mess. Sand everywhere! All through their clothes! And their shoes! I'm going to get some towels. Don't let them move from the back hall." Aura Lee turned and realized that the twins were right behind her. A path of sand marked their transit from back door to TV room. Alo scratched his head, releasing more sand from his brown hair.

"I told you to wait by the door while I got some towels. *Don't move!*" Aura Lee repeated.

*Dodged that bullet,* Julia thought.

"Why don't you take them outside and hose them off?" Guy suggested.

"Guy, it's January!"

"Oh, I forgot," he mumbled and sank back into his chair.

"And you!" glaring at Julia, "Where were you when I called you before? Why can't you help out more around here?"

"I set the table for dinner at halftime," Julia said innocently, hoping the topic of where she had been would be dropped.

"Oh, fine, so that makes it all okay because you did one little thing!" Aura Lee stomped away.

Julia felt mildly guilty. "I'll go sweep up the sand, Daddy," she said.

"That would be nice, Julia baby. Mommy would appreciate it," Guy said, eyes never leaving the TV.

"After the game."

"Sure, baby. After the game."

# CHAPTER 33

Julia Kaiser assembled three boxes of cereal into a barricade blocking her from the rest of the family. She just couldn't deal with the twins today. She skimmed the pages of the Sunday *Times Picayune* as she stirred butter into her grits. An ad for the Versailles Hotel in New Orleans promised to provide the quintessence of luxury to the upscale traveler. Alo made an awful face at Beau, opening his mouth as wide as he could and sticking out his tongue as far as possible.

"Now Beau, stop it. Your face is going to freeze like that," Aura Lee scolded.

"That's not Beau; it's Alo," Julia said, peering out through a crack in her cereal box triptych.

Aura Lee did not respond.

"Mom," Julia said, looking up. "What does 'quintessence' mean?"

"Do I look like a dictionary?"

"Mom, come on, just tell me what it means."

"Can't you see I'm busy?"

"Is it something bad?"

"Well, why don't you look it up and figure that out for yourself? You got that nice dictionary for your birthday."

Julia sighed. She finished her breakfast, slipped out of the kitchen and returned to her bedroom. Could it be that Mom doesn't know that word? She pulled the well-thumbed red hardbound Webster's New Collegiate dictionary from her shelf.

Quintessence, Julia read. The first definition was 'the fifth and highest essence in ancient and medieval philosophy that permeates all nature and is the substance composing the heavenly bodies.' That seemed to be a more complicated idea than would fit with what she had read. The second definition was 'the essence of a thing in its purest and most concentrated form.' That was more like it. Quintessence. Quintessence. A lovely word!

That night, while Mom was busy doing dishes and Dad was watching the news and the terrible twins were in bed, Julia tiptoed outside and walked to the end of the driveway, along the sidewalk, away from the house. Darkness engulfed her. It was nice outside, now that it was cool and there were no mosquitoes. She gazed up into the pure black of the sky and recognized the Big Dipper. She cupped her hands around the sides of her eyes to block out more of the surrounding light. That brought out a lot more stars. *This is so cool*, she thought. *I'd love to learn about stars and galaxies sometime.*

As she marveled at the spectacular display above her, she had an idea, and then words and phrases to describe it tumbled into her head. She rushed inside, back to her room, but quietly, to avoid alerting her parents to her movements. She pulled out a notebook, opened to a blank page and wrote:

Magical Sky

The ever-endless universe garbs in a velvet blue

That ancient, ageless, changeless cloak waxed old when Time was new.

The only light within this cloak is that known as the Sun,

And still that orb's the coldest shade of so few great things done

Comparing with the quintessence of joy and wisdom true

That shines without that velvet cloak, that cloak of velvet blue.

And sometimes when the threads wear thin, they prove I have not lied:

What we call stars are tiny holes that hint of light outside.

Julia leaned back and exhaled. She had written a poem! Tomorrow she would call Grandma and read it to her and see what she thought.

# CHAPTER 34

Stars twinkled distantly in the cold pre-dawn sky as Aura Lee bustled out the door.

"Hurry up! Hurry up! We have to get to Grammagrampa's! It's Thanksgiving!" Aura Lee urged. Each member of the family complied grudgingly, dragging heavy feet.

"What's the matter? Let's go!" Aura Lee continued. "Guy, be careful with those pies."

"It's 6:00 am! It's still dark! Why do we have to leave so early?" Julia demanded.

"The traffic on the interstate will be awful if we don't get going! You know how tense your father gets."

Guy looked up in surprise but offered no contradiction. He opened the trunk and laid boxed pies neatly in a row, hoping they would survive this road trip intact.

Guy and Aura Lee buckled themselves into the front seats. Julia opened a back door and sat down next to the window, while her brothers climbed in from the opposite side, Beau first, followed by Aloysius. Alo was a mess, as usual, hair not combed, no socks, shoes untied, and with his T shirt actually on backwards. But at least he had made a token effort. Beau, in contrast, was still in pajamas, and had limped out to the car toting a pillow and the green velour throw from the couch in the TV room. Wordlessly he laid the pillow on Julia's lap, curled up on the seat next to her, pulled the throw up to his chin and closed his eyes. Julia looked down, irritated, and started to push Beau and his pillow away from her, but then stopped. *What's the difference*, she thought. She rested her hand on his head and stroked his hair lightly. It was softer than she expected. Alo was slumped on top of Beau, completely unconscious. She looked out the window. Too dark to read. Beau was smart to bring a pillow. There's nothing to do but sleep, Julia thought ruefully, and reluctantly closed her eyes.

Julia awoke in discomfort. Her head was wedged against the window and the weight of Beau on her lap had made her leg go to sleep. She rubbed the side of her head and shifted the pillow a little, to give herself some relief while avoiding awakening Beau. But now there was daylight, enough to read by, so she pulled out her paperback copy of *The Count of Monte Cristo* and began to read.

Her parents spoke softly in the front seat.

"Guy, it's so cute! They are all fast asleep!"

"I'm not asleep. I'm reading," Julia countered.

"Well, most of you are asleep," Aura Lee replied in a stage whisper. "The boys look so innocent!"

"An illusion at best. Don't let your guard down, is my advice," Julia muttered.

The car continued its inexorable passage along the interstate, seeking that very special exit that would lead the family to Aura Lee Pelletier Kaiser's childhood home. Julia didn't mind the trip so long as it was reasonably quiet and she had her book.

"Guy, we should be there in half an hour, wouldn't you say?" Aura Lee eventually said.

"Sounds about right," Guy replied.

Aura Lee peered into the back seat. "I wonder if we should wake the boys up. I want them to be bright and chipper when we arrive."

"Really, who says 'chipper'?" Julia rolled her eyes.

"Dear, it's just an expression," Aura Lee said. It was early in the day, so her tone was still soothing.

Beau started to stir, cautiously opening one eye. When he realized Aloysius was half-lying on him and sharing the throw, Beau squirmed to dislodge his brother. Alo remained unconscious. Suddenly Alo rolled over and sat up.

"Oh, gross! Beau farted! Right in my face!"

"Keep your face away from my butt then!"

"It stinks!" Alo shouted.

"Whoever smelt it dealt it!" Beau asserted.

Alo and Beau started kicking each other. Julia withdrew as far as she could to her side of the car and continued to read. Edmond Dantès despaired in the terrible Chateau d'If as Alo managed to give Beau a wedgy.

"Owww!" howled Beau. Julia gripped the pillow and held it vertical, making a barrier between her and the boys, and assumed a pained expression.

"Look, everyone! We're here!" Aura Lee exclaimed. "Now be sure to give Grammagrampa a big hug and thank them for inviting us. And when we eat tell Gramma that everything's delicious, even if it's not your favorite."

Alo and Beau dutifully rolled out of the car and went to hug their grandparents. Julia slid out of the car as well and waited patiently for her turn to greet them. She recalled a saying that when people are married for a long time, they begin to look like one another. This was true of her grandparents. They stood next to one another, both shaped like footballs standing on end. Both had short-cropped white hair and near-identical wire-rimmed reading glasses. Gramma wore an apron, and Grampa wore suspenders to hold up the pants belted ineffectually beneath his generous abdomen, but otherwise, even their clothing- long-sleeved plaid shirts and khaki slacks- was similar. Aura Lee, standing next to her mother, was well on the way to football shape herself, Julia reflected with a mixture of fascination and horror.

"Aura Lee, look at her! Don't you feed her?" Gramma scolded, her gaze fastened on Julia.

"Mom, I do what I can, but she does all this exercise and jogging. Nothing sticks to her bones!"

"Girls nowadays have image problems, you know. If they can't be model-skinny they think they're obese," Gramma opined. "Julia, you should eat more. If you want a boyfriend one day you can't be so skinny."

Julia considered the possibility of having entered a parallel universe, where normal logic did not apply. There was Beau in pajamas, not to mention Aloysius dressed like a schizophrenic, but just because she was petite, she was the object of derision.

Gramma ushered the group into the house. "Y'all watch out for that front step. Don't trip."

"Aura Lee made pecan pie- my favorite!" Grampa said, reaching into the trunk of the car.

"Okay, everyone, you're here nice and early, so we have plenty of time to relax before dinner.

Turkey's in the oven. It will be about two hours until it's done," Gramma said, beaming.

Grampa took over from Gramma. "So, what shall we do for two hours?" He winked at Gramma.

"A nice walk in the neighborhood?" suggested Gramma.

"We could look over old family photos. We have lots of albums," suggested Grampa.

"Come on, say it!" pleaded Beau.

"I know. I could help you with your homework. Did you bring it along?" asked Grampa.

"You know what we want! Come on, Grampa!" Alo shouted.

"I'd like to know why we left before dawn just to get here two hours early," Julia muttered.

"What's that, honey?" asked Gramma.

"Oh, I said I can already smell the turkey," Julia replied.

"Don't change the subject! We want our tradition!" Beau yelled.

"Oh, I know, the big football game!" Grampa said.

"It's three hours until kickoff," Guy said, checking his watch.

"No, no, you know what we want!" Alo was jumping up and down.

"Papa, you'd better do what they want before one of the boys busts a gut!" Gramma said.

"Okay, okay," Grampa said. "We don't want any bust guts." He reached behind a houseplant in a brightly painted ceramic pot and pulled out a videotape recording of *Talladega Nights*.

"Hooray! At last! Let's go!" Beau and Alo yelled. They trailed after Grampa as he made his way to the spare bedroom, where an old 19-inch box TV was hooked up to a VCR.

Alo and Beau leapt onto the bed and sprawled across the blue and red striped, vintage J. C. Penney's bedspread and rolled around, pummeling each other as Grampa turned on the TV and inserted the videotape.

Julia remained in the living room with her mother and grandmother.

"Sweetie, don't you want to watch the movie with your brothers?" Gramma's voice was annoyingly cloying.

"No, I've already seen it five times, each of the last five Thanksgivings. I think I'll pass this year," Julia said. "I'm going to read my book."

"You always have your nose in some book. Thanksgiving is for being with family," Aura Lee said.

"Fine." Julia went into the bedroom where *Talladega Nights* was in full swing. She inserted the earbobs of her iPod, turned up the music, curled up in a chair in the corner and proceeded to read *The Count of Monte Cristo*. Edmond Dantès admittedly had it rough, but he did not know what real suffering was.

Soon however the movie became so loud and her brothers became so noisy that even with ears plugged she couldn't read. She returned to the living room where her Mom and Gramma were sipping spicy Bloody Mary's, another Pelletier family tradition, observed religiously at all major holidays. Grampa and Guy were drinking beers.

"Did you read this month's *Ladies' Home Journal*?" Gramma asked her daughter, gesturing to the open magazine in her lap. She took a bite out of the celery in her drink with a loud snap.

"I did. 'Can this marriage be saved' was so interesting. My heart really went out to Christine."

"That's my favorite section too! I can't believe the lives some people live," Gramma answered, shaking her head. She moistened her finger and used it to flip the page.

"Dad, what do you think LSU's chances are this year?" Guy inquired of his father-in-law.

"Well, I don't know. Those boys have a lot of potential, but the coach! I think he holds them back," Grampa replied.

"I agree with you!" Guy replied.

"You know, I never told you, but when Aura Lee told us she was dating you, we asked what you were studying. And she told us Engineering, and I said, Baby, he must be one smart fellow if he's in Engineering. You just hang on to that one," Grampa said, nodding and saluting Guy with his beer.

"Dad, don't you make his head swell up, now," Aura Lee said.

"It's true. We feel lucky to have you as a son-in-law. And those two boys! All that energy! They like football?"

Guy laughed. "They like TV. I do try to get them outside, throw the ball around."

"I'd be real proud to see them playing for LSU, you know, if it were to work out," Grampa said.

"Me too! That'd be great," Guy answered.

"Dear, thanks so much for that subscription. I think it's the best Christmas present I've ever had," Gramma said to Aura Lee, waving *Ladies' Home Journal* aloft.

"I'm so glad you like it. Did you see the recipe for black-bottom pie? I think it was on page 32."

"Wow! It must be good if you remember the page number," Gramma said. "I could try it, but you know your father's cholesterol. I'll have to check the ingredients. Might not sit well with his digestion."

*It's not as loud here but the conversation is almost as inane as in that awful movie,* Julia decided. She found an inconspicuous corner and opened her book and continued reading. Another half hour of *Talladega Nights*, then dinner, then the game. Another four and a half hours of misery and then they could leave. She hoped her book would last that long. She would read slowly.

# CHAPTER 35

Julia walked into the house, pulling the door shut behind her, and groaned. "36 more days to go at the Misconception this year. It can't end soon enough." Julia referred to her high school, Academy of the Immaculate Conception.

"That's not a very respectful way to speak about your high school," Aura Lee said. She sat at one end of their old brown faux leather sofa, a cup of coffee at her side, reading a paperback from the grocery store.

"It's about as much respect as they deserve." She frowned at the romance novel her mother was reading. The cover featured a woman with impressive décolletage and disorderly blond hair swooning in the arms of a devastatingly handsome young sailor in dress whites.

"Mom, why don't you read something decent? Let me get you a good book, something more worthwhile," Julia said.

"A big, fancy literature critic and you're only 15!" replied her mother, eyes scanning page 28.

"Not exactly," she answered calmly. Then suddenly inspired, she added, "In my last incarnation I lived to be old, and I read everything worth reading."

"I can't believe the things that come out of that mouth of yours," her mother said, shaking her head, without looking up from the novel.

"At least it's a step up from the cookbooks you usually read."

"For your information, cooking is an art. I don't hear you complaining at dinner time."

Julia proceeded to the stairs and stomped loudly up to her room to study.

*

Sunday morning at 8:05 Julia burst into the house, and the door slammed behind her. She had just finished her daily run. Attempting exercise outside in early September any later in the day would be suicidal. She was breathing fast and deep. Her face was flushed and a light sheen of sweat covered her slender body. *Two more years. This is the beginning of junior year, then there's senior year, and then I'm out of here!* Julia strode into the family room wearing skimpy running shorts and a crop top.

Her parents sat next to one another on the brown sofa, wearing his and hers blue and pink terrycloth bathrobes, sipping coffee from matching coffee mugs and sharing the Sunday paper. Her Dad bent over the weekly crossword puzzle while her Mom reviewed TV shows for the coming week from the Arts and Entertainment section. Julia took in the scene and thought, oh my god, they are absolutely plastic. It is Ken and Barbie turned middle-aged. It is the Stepford parents, no two ways about it.

"Guy, what about redfish for dinner tonight? I can't remember when we last had redfish," Aura Lee said.

"Great. I love your redfish."

"Or, if they don't have nice redfish today, I could get catfish. Farm-raised kind they have at Robichaux's is always delicious."

"Can you do your fried catfish?"

"Sure. That's what you want?" Aura Lee looked up, saw Julia and frowned. "Gail Julia Kaiser! Look at the way you're dressed. Your midriff is showing and that top does not even cover your bra. And your bottom is hanging out of those shorts! What are people to think?"

"First of all, my bottom does not hang. If and when it does, I promise to wear old lady shorts to cover it. Second, no one in this black hole of a neighborhood is awake yet to see me, and third, you are so concerned about how I look but believe me, even if there were people around and awake, they would barely realize I'm a female much less notice my outfit. Truth is, I could do my run naked and no one would look. Boys don't like me. Doesn't matter what I wear."

Aura Lee looked to her husband for support, but he had wisely decided to stay out of the conversation. He sheltered behind the hastily erected firewall of the newspaper's sports section.

Aloysius and Beau stomped down the stairs, in alphabetical order, Julia noted.

"Boys, what about the way your sister is dressed? Shouldn't she wear something more modest outside the house?" Aura Lee appealed to her sons.

Alo piped up, "What'd she say, she was going to run naked? For once she's right. No one'd look at her. She's a nerd. They're sexless."

Julia glared at him. "There's a reason Aloysius rhymes with malicious." She swept out of the family room and up the stairs to her bedroom, laid out a towel and started on her daily 100 crunches. With her head close to the floor she could hear talking; the tone was light and happy, but the words were indistinct. Then suddenly a peal of laughter. That was her mother. Probably laughing about her. She felt tears starting, hot in her eyes. She wiped them away angrily, and focused on her crunches, moving furiously, and reciting loudly the conjugation of irregular French verbs, anything to drown out the sound from below. With her exercises all done, Julia felt better. She showered and went downstairs to have breakfast.

Her brothers were having breakfast, shoveling a milk-soaked, tan-colored, semi-solid substance into their mouths. "Can you chew with your mouths closed?" Julia demanded. "I don't want to see that nauseating emulsion."

Alo responded with a sly grin, opening his mouth even wider and chewing with exaggerated slowness.

Julia averted her eyes in disgust.

"Mom, more monkey vomit," Alo said.

"I didn't hear the magic word, mister!" Aura Lee responded.

"Do you have to call it that?" Julia interjected. "It's disgusting."

"Mom! I'm still hungry!" Beau said.

"Not until I hear the magic word!" Aura Lee repeated.

"Mother dearest, could I please have some more of that delectable monkey vomit?" Alo said, a big smirk on his face.

"Now, that's more like it," said Aura Lee. She pulled 8 graham crackers out of their wax paper packet, carefully broke each one into 4 squares, and deposited them into Alo's cereal bowl, and then poured milk over the fragmented graham crackers. Alo stirred and mashed the graham crackers until a thick tawny brown stew formed.

"Grade A monkey vomit if I've ever seen it," Alo declared.

"Mom, thanks for getting the cinnamon graham crackers. They're really good," Beau added.

"You little suck up!" Julia glared at Beau.

"They have chocolate graham crackers now. Can we try them? It'd be chocolate monkey vomit," Beau asked. "And I'm still hungry. Can I have more? I mean can I please have more?"

"Well, finally! I was beginning to think I had only one polite child," Aura Lee said. She prepared a second bowl of the graham cracker breakfast for Beau.

"Can't you call it something besides monkey vomit? It's so gross!" Julia begged.

"What's in a name? A rose by any other name…" Guy began, and then thought better of it, and reverted to silence.

270

Julia opened the cavernous avocado green refrigerator, found an English muffin, carefully cut it in half, toasted it and spread it with exactly one level tablespoon of crunchy peanut butter. In the meantime, Aloysius and Beauregard relocated to the adjacent TV room.

"Mom, make them clear these bowls of disgusting slime if they're done. I can't sit here and eat with this anywhere near me," Julia said.

"If it bothers you, dear, you could move their bowls. Clearing dishes isn't really a job for boys," Aura Lee said. She turned to refill her coffee cup.

"This family is impossible!" Julia grumbled. She surreptitiously studied her mother's build, her buttocks spreading complacently in the generous folds of her bathrobe. She wondered if she was destined for a similar future, despite her now-slender body. No. She would never let that happen.

Then her gaze fell on the couch, where Aloysius sat playing a video game and Beau flipped through the comic strips.

"Look at the two of you! You're burning daylight! What will you accomplish today?" Julia demanded. "You have to have a strategy, or you will end up as complete failures and dribble into obscurity!"

"Someone could mow the lawn," Guy suggested cautiously, his voice muffled behind the newspaper. "It's been two weeks."

"Well, I'm going to prep some more for the SATs." Julia clutched the plate with the English muffin and stormed back upstairs, closed the door of her room behind her and settled down at her desk. The surface of her desk was all divided into three parts: in the middle was the hefty, bright yellow SAT prep book, opened to page 273; on the left was the pile of homework yet to be done; and on the right was a tray equipped with fresh index cards, mechanical pencils, blue and black ballpoint pens and two lightly used Pink Pearl erasers.

Julia drummed her fingers on the SAT prep book. "Okay," she whispered, addressing the book. "This is it- you're my ticket out of here."

# CHAPTER 36

Monday morning, just before leaving her room to catch the school bus, Julia began her weekly ritual. She vigorously shook a can of Raid Ant and Roach Killer and sprayed along the baseboards of the walls of her room, delineating a pomerium across which any prudent cockroach would be reluctant to venture. She wished her mother would break down and get an exterminator, but she was too cheap. Julia headed downstairs and toward the front door.

"Mom, can't we please get an exterminator? I hate roaches."

"We hardly have any roaches," Aura Lee said, seated at the table, drinking coffee.

"Hardly any roaches! Are you kidding?"

"No one else seems to mind. Anyway, the boys enjoy chasing them."

Julia groaned and left the house. Less than two years, and she was out of here.

Julia stood with Alo and Beau on the sidewalk in front of their house, waiting for their school buses. She checked her phone. It was only 7:30 but it was already 82 degrees. The early morning air, supersaturated with humidity, promptly deposited a layer of water on her skin, cool as it was from the AC inside. The condensate accumulated and began to trickle down her legs. What I wouldn't give for a little shade, Julia thought. But her parents didn't want trees in the front yard, for fear that a hurricane would uproot them and drop them on the house. She could feel her face reddening. She slipped her phone into the front pocket of her book bag and pulled out a notebook to fan herself.

"I got to go to the bathroom," Alo whined.

"You should've gone before. If you go in now you'll probably miss your bus," Julia said.

"I can't wait!"

"You are way too old for this."

"If the bus comes, tell him I'll be right out," Alo said.

"No way. You just want to wait in the AC, while Beau and I are stuck out here," Julia countered.

Beau stealthily crept up behind Alo and grabbed at his midsection.

"Ow, don't tickle me!" Alo dropped his backpack and his lunch bag and chased Beau across the front lawn. Beau, weighed down by his own backpack, was quickly caught and knocked to the ground by Alo.

"Oh my god, you two will look like vagabonds by the time you get to school. Stop it!" Julia ordered.

"What's a vagabond?" asked Alo, looking up. The distraction allowed Beau to escape, although not without grass stains on his khaki uniform pants.

"Look, there's your bus!" Julia exclaimed.

How do you know it's ours? Could be yours," Alo said. Julia didn't see any stains on his clothing, but his shirt was mostly untucked.

"How do I know? It says, right on the side, 'St. Anselm's School for the Criminally Insane and Mentally Deficient!' Get your sorry asses into it."

Both boys stared at her blankly, and then climbed aboard the bright yellow bus, joining a crowd of boys who looked no better groomed than they. Julia saw them bouncing in their seats and could hear the yells even through the closed windows. One of the particularly energetic bouncers disappeared suddenly from the window. Probably irritating the hell out of the kid he was next to and got thrown under the seat, Julia thought. The rubber-edged folding doors of the bus slammed shut. Julia looked down and saw Alo's brown bag lunch lying on the lawn.

She scooped up the bag and banged on the door. "Hey, open up, please! My brother forgot his lunch!" The driver, sporting a grimy baseball cap worn backwards, ignored her. She banged more forcefully until he finally looked up and opened the door partway.

"You break that door, you pay for it. That's municipal property," the burly driver said, taking a swig of his Barq's root beer. His short sleeves revealed several colorful tattoos.

"Sorry! My little brother forgot his lunch. Alo!" she shouted as she thrust her arm into the narrow opening in the doors, proffering the brown bag. As Alo scuttled forward to retrieve his lunch Julia had two thoughts: first, she prayed that the unpleasant driver would give her time to withdraw her arm before the bus took off, and second, she felt surprised that the driver had known and used in an appropriate manner a word as long as municipal. Four syllables. Not bad.

Mercifully she was able to retrieve her arm, hand still attached, before the scowling bus driver re-slammed the door and took off. But her bus had still not arrived. The combination of the heat, the humidity, absence of shade and the confrontation with the driver of the St. Anselm bus had made her hotter than before. She stood on the sidewalk, in heat radiating up from the concrete. She felt a few drops of sweat trickle down her back, between her shoulder blades. She saw a cloud in the distance; she willed it to come this way, to give her a little shade, but the cloud was impervious to her prayers. She felt sweat collecting under the waistband of her hideous navy blue pleated uniform skirt. There was no escape. She stopped fanning herself with her notebook and opened it up, holding it above her head to provide some protection from the sun. It helped a little, but after a while her arms were tired and she went back to fanning herself. Finally, her bus arrived. She glanced at her phone again. 7:50.

"What's going on? The bus is like 15 minutes late," asked Julia. "My homeroom teacher doesn't accept the bus being late as an excuse for me to be late."

"Engine overheated about 20 minutes into the route and we had to stop. And air conditioning is out. Come on in, we don't need to be any later than we already are," the female counterpart of her brothers' bus driver commanded. She was a middle-aged obese woman named Marla; she wore an unflattering tank top that revealed an imposing mammary apparatus and flabby arms replete with freckles. Her face was flushed and sweaty, and the strands of hair that had strayed from her dun-colored ponytail were stuck to her forehead.

Julia held onto the back of the first row of seats and peered into the bus. There was an empty seat next to her friend Dahlia.

"Hi, Dally, how are you?" asked Julia as she sat done on the vinyl bench seat. She leaned back but contact with the back of the seat made her white cotton-polyester uniform blouse stick to her sweaty back. She sat with knees apart and lifted her legs as far as she could by pointing her toes, to separate her sweaty thighs from each other and from the vinyl.

"Hi. I was okay until I got on this stupid bus. It must be a hundred degrees in here and it smells bad. You'd think by high school people would've heard of deodorant," Dally twisted her ash brown hair into a ponytail and held it away from her neck.

"Did you try to open the window? Might help a little," Julia suggested.

"Let me see." Dahlia tugged at the window, then stood up and tried again, without success. "It's jammed shut, sorry."

"Let me try," Julia said; she also stood and tried pushing, pulling and wiggling the window but there was hardly any movement. "Oh well, we tried."

"Give me a shot at it," said a boy in the seat behind them. He leaned across the back of their seat and grasped the edges of the window. It moved a little, but not enough to let air in. He thumped the sides of the window, hard, with the heels of his hands and tried again. This time he was able to shove the upper pane all the way down, giving the girls some fresh air at last. Dahlia watched his muscular arms at work with appreciation.

"Thanks soooo much," cooed Dahlia.

"Yeah, thanks!" Julia echoed.

"No problem! I think it's rusty or something," the boy said. He was good-looking, with sun-bleached hair, lively blue eyes and an athletic build.

"That was nice," Julia admitted.

"Do you know who that is?" whispered Dahlia.

"Um, not really. He's not in our grade, I'm pretty sure," Julia said.

"That is Bobby Bergeron! He's a senior! He was named starting quarterback just last week. He is so cute! And nice too!" she whispered. "Do you think he can hear us?" she added, glancing back to be sure Bobby had already sat down.

"Well, it's September, so here we go again!" Julia teased. Dear sweet Dahlia fell in love with someone pretty much every year since fifth grade. Typically, this happened before the end of September, so she was right on schedule.

"Shhh! He'll hear you!" Dahlia slid down in her seat, out of the line of Bobby's sight, and started to comb her hair.

"Dally, he's a jock," Julia whispered. "Probably dates some cheerleader."

A few minutes later and they had arrived at the Academy of the Immaculate Conception. The bus pulled into the big semicircular drive and students spilled out.

Dahlia slowed her pace.

"Dally, come on, we'll be late for homeroom. Sister Maleficent already hates me and would love to mark me late!" Julia urged.

"Just a moment, okay?" Dahlia whispered. "There he is!"

"Hey, thanks for the help with the window!" Dahlia turned and said to Bobby Bergeron with a dazzling smile.

"Ah, anytime you need a window opened, just give me a call," he said, smiling back. "Hey, what's your name?"

"I'm Dahlia. I go by Dally though." Julia recognized the catch in her voice and knew she was nervous.

"I'm Bobby."

"It's nice to meet you!"

"Same here. Okay, see you," Bobby answered and jogged off.

"Oh, Julia, he is so gorgeous and so nice. I am in a cold sweat. I could barely get the words out when he asked me my name. I could feel my throat closing up on me. Oh my god, he's so cute," moaned Dahlia.

"Fine, but now let's get to class. At least he wasn't one of the smelly ones on the bus," Julia observed.

"You are so unromantic. One day some guy will sweep you off your feet and you'll see," said Dahlia.

# CHAPTER 37

Every last fried shrimp had been gobbled down, Aura Lee noted. No surprise. They were beautiful shrimp. "Alright, let's bring our dishes into the kitchen so we can do Julia's birthday." She brought out a cake and candles, and a half gallon of Neapolitan ice cream.

Sitting around the table, her family sang happy birthday to Julia and she successfully blew out the candles. *Now I'm sweet 16,* Julia thought. *Maybe things will be different.*

Her birthday present was wrapped in paper with footballs and baseballs, left over from the twins' birthday. This could be a bad sign. She pulled back the paper to reveal a box from Macy's. Please let it be something nice, please, please, please! Julia thought. She removed the top of the box, unfolded the crisp white tissue paper, and saw an assortment of Buster Brown kids' clothes, size 14, including a light blue cotton turtleneck sweater, a navy blue and green plaid jumper and matching opaque navy-blue tights. But there was more underneath, and she set aside the first bolus of clothing to find 6 pairs of white cotton underwear, also size 14, full-sized baggy briefs, providing coverage from waist to thighs. She swallowed her disappointment as quietly as she could.

Beau shyly handed her something smaller and weightier. "I made it at school," he said.

Julia carefully unwrapped Beau's gift. It was a white coffee mug with her name in upper case pink letters.

"I painted it myself. Mr. Bradford put it in the kiln and fired it."

"Beau, it's really, really nice." Julia realized that he had had to plan ahead to produce this gift, as his art class met only twice a week, and the painting, glazing and firing were all done on different days. Maybe there's hope for him.

"That's beautiful, Beau! Very professional," Aura Lee said.

"Uh, why'd you use pink?" Guy asked nervously. Bad enough they never wanted to play a little football, but now Beau was painting with pink!

"Dad, girls like pink," Beau muttered.

"Thanks everyone for the presents. I really love the mug Beau made me. Mom, umm, these clothes are nice and all, but you know I'm small for my age, and they're not going to fit. Maybe could you return them, and I could pick something out on my own?"

"Julia, this is a very good brand, and you're bound to grow into them," Aura Lee countered.

"Mom, honest, I don't ever think I'll be this big," Julia replied, unfolding the jumper and holding it in front of her, showing that it dwarfed her tiny frame.

"Just wait till you hit your growth spurt. Then they'll fit. You could set them aside for senior year or even college, you know, if you go to college. I think they'll be perfect!" Aura Lee said brightly.

Julia stood silent. Did her Mom actually think she might not go to college?

Seeing the downcast look on her daughter's face, Aura Lee sighed. "Fine, we can return those nice clothes if you insist. There's one more thing I think you're old enough to have now. It's from Granny Kaiser," Aura Lee said, offering her a small unwrapped cardboard box.

"Grandma has been dead for more than a year now, Mom."

"Yes, well, she wanted you to have this. We weren't sure it was appropriate for a child to have, as it is quite valuable, but it was her wish, and now you're 16," Aura Lee continued.

"She was very fond of you," Guy said.

Julia opened the cardboard box, which contained a turquoise velvet jewelry box. On top of the velvet box was a note card with "Gail Julia" written on the envelope. Julia turned the card over to open it, then stopped.

"This card has been opened. It looks like it was sealed, but someone else opened this card!" Julia said.

"Just open the box," Aura Lee advised. Typical Julia. Neither of the boys would have cared about the card, and certainly would not have noticed if it had been opened previously. Aura Lee told herself that she had done nothing wrong when she opened the note card to read it; she had just wanted to make sure her mother-in-law hadn't been getting in one last dig directed against her in this note. Still, if this came up again, a thin layer of Elmer's carefully applied along the line of the original adhesive would avoid this embarrassing situation.

"Fine," Julia said. "I will read the card later on my own, so I don't waste the valuable time of those already familiar with its contents." Aura Lee squirmed but did not speak.

Julia opened the jewelry box to reveal her grandmother's exquisite heirloom necklace. A large oval opal was rimmed by small rubies and seed pearls, laid in an ornate gold setting and suspended on a simple but heavy gold chain.

"This is so beautiful. I will really treasure this." Julia fled to her room, set the jewelry box down on her dresser and whipped the card out of the envelope.

"My dearest little Julia," it began, "I want you to have this necklace. It is old fashioned, but you admired it once years ago, so I hope it is still something you like. I think it is well suited to you and will look lovely on you. Think of me when you wear this. If St. Peter lets me, I will be watching out for you. Much love from your Grandma."

*

Julia pulled out the books she would need for her afternoon classes and shut her locker.

"Julia! Julia!" Dahlia rushed up to her. "You won't believe it!"

"Slow down, what is it?" Julia replied.

"I made the cheerleading team! I'm one of the Fabulous Five! Me! Can you believe it?"

"That's great, Dally! I had no idea you were trying out."

"I didn't say anything cause I figured I wouldn't get picked. But I did! They just told us at lunch break. I can't believe it!"

"I guess it should be fun, and, well, should look good on your resumé. Colleges like to see participation in school activities."

"Oh, Julia, all you think about is college! What about the here and now? This is going to be so amazing!" Dahlia said, dizzy with excitement.

"Well, congratulations! I'm happy for you!" Julia said, but she knew where this sudden interest in cheerleading came from: Bobby Bergeron. As a cheerleader Dahlia would be in his sights almost constantly. Oh, Dahlia! She had so much potential, but she was so boy-crazy.

*

Julia sat cross-legged on her bed, algebra homework on her lap.

Her phone rang. "Dally, hey, what's up?" Julia said.

"Julia! I can almost do a split! I think I'll be ready for the first game."

"That's great. You'll have to show me. I couldn't do splits, for sure," Julia was glad Dally was happy. She wondered what it would take for her to be happy like that.

*

It was the first football game of the season. The announcer, Lennie Thibodeau, called out over the loudspeaker, "And there you have the starting line-up of Immaculate Conception's Fighting Gators! And now, everyone's favorite part of football season: the Fabulous Five! This year's gorgeous cheerleaders are Sarah, Candy, Dally, Missy and Wendy! Let's hear a big Gator roar for our athletes and cheerleaders!" The fans howled their support and the cheerleaders shook their pompoms vigorously.

One of the students, clad in a truly ridiculous, mottled brown outfit that was intended to make him resemble an alligator, served as the school mascot. He scrambled around the sidelines, mainly at the feet of the cheerleaders, shaking his long tapering tail. *Probably trying to look up their skirts,* Julia concluded, as she looked down the field.

The Gators had the ball, and Bobby Bergeron threw a pass caught by a teammate, for a first down. The fans went wild with emotion, cheering loudly, and the stadium shook.

Julia stood at the railing at the bottom of the bleachers. *So much energy! Where does it go?* Julia wondered. *Is it stored somewhere? Does it affect the balance of the universe? Was that what they called an aura? If this energy somehow survives, perhaps that is our immortality, the sum of all our emotions, all our energy, positive and negative…*

"Hey, hey, are you deaf?" a boy called out from behind her.

"Are you talking to me?" Julia asked timidly, snapped abruptly back to real life.

"Yeah, move, you're blocking my view!"

"Look how skinny she is, how can she be blocking your view?" another boy snickered.

"Okay, okay. Hey, stick figure, stay if you want, just turn sideways, you won't be in the way." The first boy called out.

"Stick figure! That's a good one" the second boy laughed.

Julia tiptoed away from the railing and found a seat far away from the scene of her humiliation. She tried to concentrate on the game, but it was no use. She could see that Dally was doing really well as a cheerleader. *Look at that. She just did a full split! Good for her,* Julia thought. *She fits in and she's happy. I wish I fit in…but not here. This isn't the place for me.*

*

Alan Prudhomme, Buster Lagarde and Sammy Brewster loitered in the second-floor hall of the school building before first period.

"You going to Homecoming?" Alan asked the others.

"Game yeah, not the stupid dance," Buster replied.

"I might go. To the dance. Maybe. I'd have to find a date though," Sammy said, meaning he'd have to find a girl shorter than he was.

"I can't go. My parents volunteered to be chaperones," Buster grumbled.

"Hey Sammy, what about her? Bet she doesn't have a date," Alan gestured toward Julia, who was across the hall, spinning the dial of the combination lock on her locker.

"Her! Aw, you're kidding. She's a total nerd. She'd want to talk about history or something," Sammy laughed.

"God, look at her. She is flat! No boobs!" Buster snickered.

Julia slammed her locker shut, collected her material and strode past the boys, eyes narrowed. "Do you think I can't hear you? You're all morons." She strode onward as the three boys guffawed, unfazed by her criticism.

"She does have nice legs, give her that," Alan opined as she walked away.

# CHAPTER 38

"Dally, you got highlights!" Julia said, as Dahlia ascended the stairs of the Kaiser home.

"Yeah, you know, my hair is naturally the color of Bambi. I just needed a change. I want to look my best for the team and the fans," Dally said. She ran her fingers through her newly streaked hair.

*And for Bobby Bergeron.* "It looks good," Julia said. They sat down in Julia's room.

Aura Lee tapped on the door and walked in. "What are you girls up to?" she asked.

Dahlia smiled. "We're wondering who our dates will be for Homecoming, Miss Aura Lee."

"I'm wondering if I'll have a date for Homecoming. Actually, I'm not. I know I won't have one," Julia said sadly.

"Well if you would just eat something so you weren't so skinny and be nice someone might ask you," Aura Lee said.

"Mom, give it a rest," Julia said and drummed her fingers on her Biology textbook.

"What about you, Dahlia, anyone special?" Aura Lee asked.

"Well, I don't know," Dally blushed.

"In my day, if we wanted to tell who liked us, we'd get an apple and twist the stem while saying the alphabet, until the stem broke off. And whatever letter you were on, that was his initial."

"Unimpeachably scientific. Thanks, Mom."

*

Dahlia came home to find her mother on the couch watching a DVD. She dabbed her eyes with a tissue as she sniffed sadly. Dahlia glanced at the screen. *From Here to Eternity.* For the 75th time.

"Mom, do we have any apples? I have a craving for a good apple," Dahlia finally asked.

"Check the fruit bowl, honey. We should have some apples," Dahlia's mother answered. She blew her nose.

Dahlia lifted the shiny Red Delicious from the bowl and studied it. "My fate is in your little hands," she whispered, excited, and started to twist the stem while reciting the alphabet. She gave a good tug at B, but the stem was not prepared to detach so close to the beginning. She kept turning the stem, but sadly now, as B had come and gone.

"M, N, O, P, Q, R," she whispered and abruptly the stem was between the fingers of her right hand while the apple rested in her left.

"R! Do I even know anyone whose name starts with R? Randy Meyers? No, no way. Rick Rodrigue? No. Russell Miller? No. Rob, Robert... Oh my god, Bobby's real name is Robert! Bobby loves me! Please let it be true!" Dahlia blissfully bit into the apple and threw herself giggling onto her bed. She finished the apple and tossed the core into her wastebasket. As she wiped her fingers on the front of her jeans, her cell phone rang. She glanced at the caller, but it was not one of her contacts and she couldn't place the number.

"Hello?" Dally said.

"Hi, Dally, this is Bobby, from the team. Bobby Bergeron. Hi," a boy's voice sounded from her phone.

"Bobby?" Dally's throat contracted and she could not squeeze out any other words.

"Hey, am I catching you at a bad time?"

"No, no, I was just, um, finishing an apple, sorry," Dally managed to say. "You just surprised me. I didn't know who was calling."

"Wendy gave me your number; I hope it's okay," Bobby said. Then it dawned on Dally that Bobby was nervous too.

"No, no problem at all. What's up?"

"I was wondering, if you didn't already have plans, could I take you to Homecoming?"

"I, I would love to go with you."

"That's great! I think it'll be a great night. The school broke down and agreed to pay for a live band."

"Well, thank you so much for asking me. I haven't been to the Homecoming dance before," Dally said, and instantly cursed herself. She didn't want Bobby to think she was previously too pathetic to get a date to Homecoming.

"Really? Well, we'll have to make up for that this year. We'll have an extra-great night."

"That sounds wonderful! I'm so excited. I'll have to get a dress… oh sorry, dresses probably wouldn't interest you."

"Whatever you wear you will be pretty, I'm sure."

"Bobby Bergeron! I am glad you are not here to see how you made me blush!"

"You're teasing! Okay, I am so glad you can go. I better get back to Chem homework cause at the moment I have a C- in that class."

"Okay! Thanks, Bobby. I'm really looking forward to it." As Bobby hung up, Dally held the phone against her heart. I think that really happened, she told herself. She ran to the door of her room and leaned out into the hall.

"Mamaaaa!" Dally howled. "I need a dress for Homecoming!"

Dahlia ran back into her room and sat on her bed and concentrated on remembering to breathe. She grabbed her phone.

"Julia! *Julia!*" Dahlia cried into the phone.

"What? What's wrong?"

"Nothing! But your mom is some kind of psychic!"

"Psychic! You must mean psycho. What's going on?"

Dahlia told her.

"That's great, Dally. He seems really nice."

"Julia! Do you know how exciting this is? Julia, don't you know what this means to me?"

"Dally, of course, but,"

"No, you don't. You are hopeless. Where should I go for a dress?"

*

"Julia, thanks for coming over. I am so nervous!" Dally was vigorously fanning herself with a *Seventeen* magazine.

"Dally, you look amazing!" Julia was astonished. Dahlia wore a beautiful ice-blue strapless gown with a fitted bodice and a full skirt of satin overlaid with a layer of airy tulle. The shimmering fabric sparkled with silver highlights. Dahlia's hair was arrayed in a complicated up-do, leaving her smooth fair throat and shoulders bare. She looked lovely and innocent and vulnerable and so hopeful.

Dahlia's mother tapped at the door and entered. "Baby, don't you look just like Grace Kelly!"

"Who?" Julia and Dally asked simultaneously.

"Never mind. Baby, you look unbelievable! You look so grown up!"

"Mama, don't cry, please!" Dally begged. "I'm nervous enough. Now, really, do I look alright?" Dally turned slowly. Julia reached forward and straightened a fold of her skirt.

"Bobby is a lucky guy. You'll be the prettiest girl there," Julia said.

"It's like a dream. I still can't believe he called *me*," Dally marveled.

"Dally, look at yourself. You're beautiful, and you're the nicest person I know. You deserve a good guy."

Dally chewed on her lower lip as she studied herself in the mirror. Julia stood next to her and glanced at her own reflection. She was small and skinny, almost boyish, in her build. But she had silky dark brown hair and a pretty face, with delicate features and violet eyes. Her eyes were her best feature, she thought, the only thing about her that was special. She wished someone would notice. She wished that someday a handsome boy who was not an idiot would look at her and stop in his tracks, arrested by the intoxicating violet of her eyes. No, intoxicated by the arresting violet of her eyes...

"I hear a car," Dally said. "He's here! Oh my god. Okay, shoes, purse, phone…"

"Here's your pretty little lace shawl, Baby," Dally's mother said. "Put that around your shoulders."

Dahlia descended the stairs in her heels with great care. Bobby and her father stood near the bottom of the stairs, waiting. Bobby looked outrageously handsome in his shiny black tux, still aglow from the afternoon's victory over Lafitte High School. She watched for a reaction from Bobby, apprehensively, but when he saw her, a big smile lit his face. He hurried to the bottom step and offered Dahlia his arm. Dahlia at last relaxed. Everything will be fine, she thought.

"You look gorgeous! Wow!" Bobby exclaimed. "Wow! I am so glad I cleaned the car! I didn't know I was taking a princess to Homecoming!"

"Oh, Bobby!" Dahlia beamed. She turned to her parents. "Okay, I guess we'll be on our way."

"Alright, Baby, have fun," her mother said.

"You drive carefully now, Bobby," Dally's father said, unsuccessfully trying to look stern. And they were gone.

Julia was peeking out the window of the living room; all the lights were off, so she had no concerns about getting caught spying. "He opened the door for her and helped her into the car," she reported.

"I'm glad he has nice manners. Dally seemed very happy that he asked her. I hope they have a good time. Oh, to be young like that again and carefree..." Dally's mother sighed.

*

The dance had been wonderful. Reluctant for the night to end, Bobby and Dahlia had come to the park overlooking the bayou, climbed out of the car and sat together on a picnic table. And now beneath a midnight sky embroidered with stars, with Spanish moss drifting softly in the slight breeze, her gown gossamer in the moonlight, now at last alone with Bobby, Dally was suddenly nervous again.

"You look so beautiful. I mean, you always looked so cute in your cheerleader outfit, but tonight you're really beautiful," Bobby said softly, touching her cheek.

"Thank you. It's so sweet of you."

"No, it's true. I'm just saying what anyone could see." Bobby brushed his fingers along her lips. "You know what else? In that cheerleader outfit, you're Dally. Tonight, you're Dahlia. Dahlia is nicer; that's what I'm going to call you."

"Bobby, I didn't know you were such a romantic!" Dahlia shyly ducked her head.

"I mean it, look at you! This dress, and your little hands, so soft and light," he held her small hands in his. "And your hair and your eyes, all so pretty. You're like a butterfly, that's what you're like." Bobby lifted her chin and looked into her eyes. "Why do you look down? Are you shy with me?"

Dally's brown eyes widened. "No, I mean, maybe a little."

"Little butterfly girl, are you going to fly away? Don't fly away from me," Bobby whispered into her ear.

"I won't. I won't fly away," Dahlia whispered back. *In all the wide world there is nowhere I'd rather be than right here with Bobby Bergeron.*

Bobby slipped his hands to the back of her neck, his fingers in her hair, gently pulled Dahlia toward him, and kissed her lightly. He felt her trembling and heard her catch her breath.

"Don't be shy with me, little Dahlia, little butterfly," he said, and kissed her again.

"No one ever talked like that to me before. No one makes me feel the way you do, Bobby."

"I'm glad, little Dahlia. Come here," and he kissed her again, like nothing she had ever known, in the light of the faraway moon.

# CHAPTER 39

Julia stood on the sidewalk in front of her home, awaiting the school bus as usual. Then she heard it, the distinctive rumble of an un-mufflered car, approaching. The rumble grew louder, evolving into a sustained roar as the vintage orange Camaro turned onto her street and pulled up in front of her.

"Come on, Julia, get in. We'll give you a ride!" Dahlia said. She smiled blissfully from the front passenger seat, while leaning as close as possible to the driver, Bobby Bergeron.

"No, that's okay. Three's a crowd." As Julia watched, Bobby rubbed Dahlia's knee possessively.

"Not with us. Come on," Dahlia urged, then turned to Bobby and giggled. "You know my knees are ticklish!"

"Look, there's the bus. I'll see you in homeroom."

Bobby silently saluted Julia with his aviator sunglasses, accompanied by what could only be described as a shit-eating grin, wrapped his right arm around Dahlia's shoulders and drove away, his left hand controlling the steering wheel.

Julia watched the car disappear noisily into the distance, spewing grayish fumes from its tailpipe. Bobby had saved for a long time to buy that Camaro, and he was so proud of it, despite the noise pollution and lack of emissions control. He drove it to school every day, except when it was in the shop, and Dahlia was always with him, riding shotgun. Julia missed getting to talk to Dally on the bus. They couldn't have a real conversation in Bobby's car because of the noise and because Dahlia was constantly pasted up against Bobby, usually giggling and whispering in his ear. It was rather nauseating, Julia reflected, but they both seemed very happy with one another.

*

*Merry Christmas*, Julia told herself, as she slipped out of the car and headed for the house. The family had just returned from the annual Christmas mega-dinner at her grandparents' home, and Julia ached to get to her room and close the door and enjoy some peace and quiet. Her cell rang as she closed her door behind her.

"Hi, Dally, what's up?" Julia asked.

"Well, Merry Christmas!"

"Oh, yeah, Merry Christmas. We just got back from my grandparents'. My Mom's parents. Trapped in that house for hours. I thought they were going to hold me down and force-feed me sweet potatoes baked with marshmallows."

"We stayed home and Mama cooked. Bobby came and joined us for dinner. My parents really like him."

"That's great. Sounds like a more civilized experience than mine."

"And he is so sweet! He gave me a beautiful sterling silver heart necklace. Real jewelry store jewelry, not the cheap kind."

"Well, he must really like you."

"Yeah..." Dally's voice went all dreamy.

"What are you going to do next year, when he's at LSU and you're still here?"

"We'll stay together, I know it. LSU's not that far. He'll be home on the weekends."

"There's a lot going on at college on the weekends. Maybe he won't always come home. Plus he'll have to stay in Baton Rouge for games, or travel to the away games, on weekends."

"Well, maybe I'll go to wherever he is. It'll work out."

*Like your parents will let you just drive to LSU and spend the weekend with some boy.* Julia waited.

"You know what else? I wrote down 'Bobby' next to 'Dally'- the consonants and vowels are in the exact same spots in both our names! That has to mean something."

"Dally, um," Julia began.

"Oh, got to go; Bobby's calling."

The call ended abruptly. Julia watched the shiny face of the cell phone fade to black.

*

*April is the cruelest month,* Julia read. Not really, though. Weather is not too awful right now. And there are no hurricanes in April. The cruelest month is July, when the heat and humidity hit their peak. August is a close second. The heat was unbelievable. And the humidity- it was more than just weather. It was a hot animal, a heavy beast with furry arms, seizing her, choking her, every time she set foot outside the house. She would definitely go to college as far north as possible. She rearranged the pillows and returned to her assignment.

The doorbell rang. Kind of late for anyone to come by. Julia listened but did not stir from her bed.

Aura Lee answered the door. "Dahlia! Come on in. You okay?"

"Yes ma'am."

"You don't look too good."

"I'm okay. Could I speak to Julia?"

Julia jumped out of bed and ran to the top of the stairs. "Come on up." Julia watched her ascend. Her eyes were red, and each slow step hinted at some deep sorrow.

Dally climbed onto Julia's bed, hugged her knees to her chest and looked around with bloodshot eyes. Julia closed the door.

"Dally, what's wrong?"

"Well. Ah, Bobby and I broke up. Well, really, Bobby broke up with me."

"Why?" Julia asked.

"I don't know. He got mad at me."

"Why?"

"I don't know, I just don't know!"

"Dally, did something happen? I mean out of the clear blue he broke up with you?"

Dahlia lifted her head and looked up at Julia. "I'm pregnant." She whispered it, as though that would make it less real. She started sobbing, big gulping sobs, with tears pouring down her cheeks. "I really love him. I thought he'd stand by me. I can't believe it."

"You're pregnant? Are you sure?"

"I wish I wasn't. But I am."

"What, what are you going to do?"

"I- I don't know."

"I mean, are you going to keep it? Or,"

"I don't know. I don't know." Dally sat on the bed with tears streaming down her cheeks. "He thinks I got pregnant to keep him from going to LSU next year and playing football. Like I would do something like that. I did think he'd help me or something, at least, or at least be nice about it. But he wasn't. He got so mad." She started to sob.

"Listen, Dally, every bozo with a Y chromosome in every high school in the state of Louisiana dreams of playing football for LSU. He is just like all the rest of them." Julia said.

"I thought he was different. I don't want to take that away from him! I just thought he'd stand by me." Dahlia shook her head slowly. "I loved him so much. I don't feel whole anymore. It's like he broke off a big chunk of my heart and threw it away."

*

As the rest of the class straggled into the classroom, Julia quickly took her seat and opened her textbook to 'The Love Song of J. Alfred Prufrock.' *This is so much more straightforward than 'The Waste Land,' thank god*, she thought.

Lindsey Perkins sat down across from her and whispered something to Wendy that included the words, 'Bobby Bergeron.' Wendy gave a restrained squeal, leaned forward and squeezed Lindsey's shoulder. Lindsey smiled smugly.

"What did you say?" Julia whispered.

Lindsey and Wendy exchanged a look. "I was just saying Bobby Bergeron invited me to go to senior prom," Lindsey said.

"He's Dally's boyfriend."

Lindsey shrugged. "He told me they broke up."

"It'd be nice if Dally's so-called friends wouldn't rush to go out with him and give him and Dally a chance to work out their issues."

"To me, it didn't seem like," Lindsey began.

Ms. Bryn Wilcox rapped her knuckles loudly on her wooden desk. "Let's begin. Today we discuss 'The Love Song of J. Alfred Prufrock.' Despite its sexist, patriarchal overtones, it does have powerful and compelling imagery. Can I have an example of imagery from this poem?" Ms. Wilcox paused. "Did anyone read the poem?"

"Julia, I want you to know," Lindsey whispered.

"Don't speak to me," Julia muttered. She turned away and directed her gaze towards Ms. Wilcox. Lindsey sank into her desk chair and studied her fingernails.

Julia's phone rang. She tossed her Chemistry textbook onto her bed and answered it.

"Julia?"

"Hey Dally, how are you holding up?"

"I- I'm okay. I wanted to call, cause it's hard to talk at school without everyone hearing you. Anyway, I made a decision. I'm going to keep the baby. No matter what. If Bobby never talks to me again or whatever. I want this baby. I will love it and take care of it."

"Are you sure?"

"Yeah. Yeah, I am."

"What about school?"

"I'm going to finish up this year, and not say anything to anyone. But once it's summer, I'll go to Sister Rita and all of them and explain and tell them I want to keep going to school and graduate."

"I think that's good, I guess. You don't think they'll rag on you?"

"Well, it's a Catholic school. They're supposed to act like Jesus, I would think. I don't believe pregnant girls bothered Him."

"Dally, did you, um, talk to your parents?"

Dally paused before answering. "I did. I finally made myself. After I decided to keep the baby. Mama, she cried and everything, and Dad, he ran to the closet and got his rifle and said he was going to teach Bobby a lesson, and then Mama said, no, they'll put you in jail; let's just call his parents. They may not even know. They went to Bobby's last night and they talked, and nobody got shot, but Bobby's still going to LSU and far as I know he still wants, he wants nothing to do with me." Her voice lowered to a sad whisper as she spoke the last few words.

"Are your parents doing anything to you?"

"They're not kicking me out or anything. Mama keeps moaning and groaning about where they went wrong. Stuff like that. I feel bad about making her all upset. But I think it will be okay, eventually."

"That's good. It's really good, Dally. It sounds like you're doing the right things."

"Thanks. Okay, I'm going to go. I know you're studying."

"It can wait."

"No, I'm okay. See you tomorrow."

# CHAPTER 40

*Senior year. One more year to go. I can do this,* Julia thought.

The class just after lunch was World Literature with Bryn Wilcox, and in preparation for a section on poetry, Ms. Wilcox had assigned each student to write a poem. "This will help you to understand the agony and the ecstasy of the poet," she had intoned dogmatically. This was the day when the students would read their poems to the class.

Lindsey Perkins went first; it was a weak effort at best, Julia thought; it was in free verse and soundly condemned global warming, so Ms. Wilcox loved it. *Suck-up,* Julia concluded. *In fairness,* she told herself, *I hate her intensely ever since she went to Prom with Bobby last year. That broke Dally's heart.* Julia would despise whatever she wrote.

Ms. Wilcox nodded. "Good. This is good. We all learned from this. Alright, let's sample a different genre. Julia, you have written a piece called, 'Half a Heart'. Please come up and read it to the class."

"This poem is dedicated to my friend Dahlia who can't be with us today," Julia said in a matter-of-fact tone, but she heard murmuring among her classmates. Then silence as she began to read.

"Half a Heart

I gave the love you begged of me

And then you asked to set you free

From the chains we forged and placed

Around our hearts that interlaced

Thus proving that you weren't true.

Sadly though I still loved you.

Merciless you broke the chains

And caused my soul the worst of pain

For though you loved me then no more,

Half my heart was part of yours:

Half a heart I'd never see

And half a heart inside of me.

I died when finally we did part;

I couldn't live with half a heart.

All those who love, if they love true,

May they beware, as I of you!

Alas, behold my secret then:

An unseen fault as in a gem

Might cause the gem to fall apart,

Or destroy it, like a heart.

You were my love, my life, my jewel

And knowing this you were so cruel

To me. You broke my love apart

And left me dead with half a heart."

Jason Cramer burst out, "Wait! You mean Dally is dead?"

"No, I meant death in the metaphorical sense," Julia explained, restraining herself from adding, 'you idiot.'

Ms. Wilcox cleared her throat, "Now that is an old-fashioned sort of poem. Furthermore, the author is apparently quite self-absorbed."

Julia flushed crimson.

Ms. Wilcox folded her arms on her desk and continued, "In my view and that of many others, poetry should be a mode of guiding society, through the vision of the thoughtful, sensitive poet. I would prefer to hear something more socially relevant. Lindsey's poem beautifully illustrated the interplay and interdependence of humankind and nature."

Julia muttered, "Thank you" and started to return to her seat, and then turned again toward Ms. Wilcox.

"Pardon me, but how is what happened to Dahlia not socially relevant? We all liked her. She was nice to everyone. She wouldn't hurt a fly. She loved one person too much and wasn't willing to do what some girls would to cover up an accident, so now she's kicked out of school," Julia said, her throat tight, so it was hard to get the words out. She sat down quickly in her desk and tears filled her eyes.

"I think that's enough melodrama," Ms. Wilcox said, her tone somewhere between sarcastic and disgusted. She exhaled loudly. "Who's next? Jason?"

Lyssa leaned over from her right and whispered, "You know she hates all that romantic stuff; couldn't you of picked a different topic?"

Lindsey leaned over from the left and whispered, "I thought your poem was really good; I love Dally too."

"Really?" Julia hissed, eyes narrowed. "You have a funny way of showing it."

"I had no idea about Dally being, you know, pregnant. I thought they just had broke up."

"Yeah, right."

"I never, ever meant to make things any worse for Dally. If I could do something to fix it, I would, I swear."

"Yeah? Well, either do something or shut up about it."

Lindsey leaned back in her desk chair and thought about that.

*

The following Tuesday in World Literature class Julia struggled to concentrate. Ms. Wilcox had the peculiar gift of being able to ruin even the most beautiful and moving works of literature with that awful nasal monotone of hers. On the bright side, this would be the last class she would ever have with Ms. Wilcox. Second semester World Lit would be with Sister Mary Amelia, who was at least a nice person.

"For tomorrow, read section 6 of our text, including 'Ode on a Grecian Urn'," she intoned. "You will recognize the sexist themes, but it is illustrative of the style popular in the 19th century. Also I have your poems to hand back. Some of you are promising young poets."

"I got an A!" squealed Lindsey.

Julia looked at her poem. "A D! She gave me a D!"

Lindsey's eyes went wide and she shook her head, "That's just not fair!"

Then the bell rang, and the students shuffled out of the classroom.

"You know what? This is my first D ever. This is a milestone. I'm going to post it on Facebook," Julia told them. "I guess we can't all be A students like Lindsey."

Lindsey responded. "This is my first A."

"What did other people get?" Julia asked.

"I got a B."

"I got an A-."

"I got a C," Jason said.

"What was yours about? I forget," Julia asked.

"It was about hoping the Saints get into the Superbowl. Here," Jason passed her his poem. It was four lines long and at a quick glance she saw two words misspelled.

"Jason, you know what? This is very sincere." Julia handed his paper back.

*

A week later, Julia stepped out of the bus and strode along the sidewalk toward the front drive of her high school, lugging a heavy tote bag, lumpy with books and notebooks. *Christ on a crutch, what's going on?* Julia stared at the Fox News van parked on the street near the front of the school. Students crowded around a professional news camera mounted on a tall metal stand on the sidewalk in front of the school. Julia approached cautiously. Hopefully this did not mean there had been a shooting or something. The absence of police or a black-clad SWAT team presumably made that less likely. She reached the edge of the crowd and squeezed toward the center, trying to see what was happening.

An elegant blonde woman in a closely fitted, scoop-necked beige sheath in raw silk spoke into a microphone, "I'm here with Lindsey Perkins at the Academy of the Immaculate Conception, a Catholic high school in southern Louisiana. Lindsey, you and I have discussed the shocking story that unfolded recently at your school, but can you tell our audience, in your own words, what happened?"

Lindsey faced the attractive reporter and her fellow students and nodded seriously. She looked unusually well-groomed today.

"We had this assignment to write a poem in one of our classes, and I wrote one about trees because our teacher really likes all those green issues. Honestly it was kind of a lame poem, but I got an A, so I mean I'm not complaining."

"Tell us, Lindsey, what is your concern?" the reporter asked.

"Well, my concern is fairness. Someone else in our class wrote a really romantic sad poem, and it was pretty, and she got a D," Lindsey asserted.

"The audience knows there's more to this story. Go ahead, Lindsey," the reporter encouraged her.

"Well, last year one of the cheerleaders got pregnant, and she didn't want to have an abortion and she also wanted to keep going to school but they wouldn't let her," Lindsey stated, trying to keep her voice even.

"Lindsey, who is they?" the reporter pressed her.

"The school. They didn't want her. They said it would be too distracting," Lindsey replied.

"What has that got to do with the poetry assignment?" the reporter continued.

"The girl who got a D said her poem was about our friend who got pregnant. Well, she didn't use the word pregnant in class, but everyone knew what she meant," Lindsey explained.

"Lindsey, one more question: was the teacher who gave the student a D involved in the decision to bar the cheerleader from school, despite her courageous and life-affirming choice to carry her pregnancy to term?" the reporter demanded.

Lindsey took a deep breath and paused for dramatic effect. "Yes," she answered. "That teacher is one of the vice principals. She would have had a say in that. Look, here is Julia Kaiser, who wrote the poem about Dahlia, I mean, about our friend," Lindsey burst out on seeing Julia. Thirty pairs of eyes swiveled to Julia.

"Julia, I'm here from Fox News to let our viewers know about the amazing drama that is unfolding here in your town. What do you have to add to what Lindsey has already told us?" the reporter queried, focusing intently on Julia while thrusting the microphone close to Julia's mouth.

"Um, I am surprised to see Fox News here at our school today. I- I guess- I would like to thank you and your audience for your interest in this situation and thank you for your support. I guess that's it," Julia said, nervous at suddenly being in the spotlight.

"Are you planning to dispute the D you received for your poem? Some think it's very unfair," the reporter said, tensely waiting for Julia's response.

"No, evaluating poetry is subjective. Ms. Wilcox is entitled to her opinion. I am sorry that she didn't like it more though," Julia replied. "I never made a D before."

"If you had it to do again, would you submit a poem more likely to get a better grade?"

"Absolutely not. Sometimes you have to speak up and be willing to live with the consequences. If we worry about what grade someone will give us every time we have something important to say, the world would be an even bigger mess than it already is."

"Well said, Julia." The reporter turned to the camera and addressed her viewers. "We want to let our viewers know that we tried to contact the remarkable young woman, a former cheerleader, who is the silent mover behind this drama, but she and her family have asked for privacy in this emotional time. This is Heather Adams, reporting live from the Academy of the Immaculate Conception high school in Iberia Parish, in Louisiana for Fox News."

The Fox News crew retreated to their van, and most of the students drifted away. Julia and Lindsey were left alone on the sidewalk, watching the crew load their equipment.

Without turning to look at Lindsey, Julia spoke softly. "Thanks for doing that. It will make a big difference to Dally."

Lindsey nodded her acknowledgement. They walked together to homeroom.

# CHAPTER 41

Aura Lee carefully folded down the corner of the page with the recipe for Better than Sex Cake. "Why do you need to apply to Harvard? No one from our town has ever gone there."

"Well, of course not. Harvard doesn't accept people who can't read!" Julia retorted.

"Julia, why can't you try to fit in?" Aura Lee asked, a frustrated tone in her voice.

"I don't want to fit in; I want to stand out." Julia crossed her arms and glared at her mother.

"You'll need a stepladder then," observed Aloysius.

"Neanderthal spawn!" Julia groaned.

\*

The Committee for Undergraduate Admissions consisted of four men and one woman, all professionally attired in Harris tweed or lightweight wool in muted tones, seated around an oval mahogany table in a small conference room overlooking Harvard Yard. Stacks of application packets, each in a manila folder, lay on the table, and in this session, the committee members would decide which applicants in the current batch would be accepted to Harvard University, and which would be, with polite regret, declined admission. About halfway through the session they reached Julia's application.

"Next, Gail Julia Kaiser. Comments?" the committee chair queried.

"She's from Louisiana. We get very few applicants from that state. I've never even heard of her town. It must be tiny," the gentleman to his left observed.

"She's a National Merit Scholar," the sole woman on the committee observed.

"National Merit Scholars are a dime a dozen. What else does she offer?" the gentleman to the chair's right queried.

"Not a great deal," the gentleman to the left observed. "Although her grades are outstanding."

"While her grades are excellent, and her SAT scores are impressive, she has nothing to speak of by way of extracurricular activities," the gentleman to the chair's right intoned.

"I've heard that in some of those small towns down South there isn't much in the way of extracurricular activities except for football. Or, for girls, cheerleading. Maybe she hasn't had the opportunity," suggested the lady of the committee.

*Catherine was such a bleeding heart when it came to the female applicants*, the gentleman to the right thought. "Surely even in Louisiana there is opportunity for community service! I see nothing in that vein reflected in this application."

"So, in her favor, origin from a state that would enhance the diversity of our student body and excellent grades and test scores but lacking outside activities that would demonstrate a commitment to school or community. Perhaps she is nothing more than a bookworm," the chair summarized. "I believe we can do better, but let's take a vote."

The gentleman across the table from the chair had been silent up until that point but now he asked, "One moment, may I show this?" He extracted an iPad from the leather satchel by the side of his chair and turned it on. "When I reviewed this application, I kept thinking that I had heard that name, Julia Kaiser, somewhere. I did a Google search. And I found an entry on something called the YouTube." This was partly true, but he was not going to admit to his fellow committee members that he watched Fox News, and that was the source of his recollection.

"William, you are so progressive! An iPad," Catherine cooed.

"Well, actually, it belongs to Douglas, my son. And I have to return it right away after this meeting or he will be sorely vexed, let me tell you!" Douglas had shown him exactly what to do, which icons to tap and so forth. He hoped it would work. He held his breath as he hit play, and there was the video clip from the Fox News interview at Conception High School. The committee members leaned forward and watched with interest.

"She's tiny," Catherine said. "The other students look absolutely burly compared to her."

"She stood up for her friend who had gotten pregnant and was then expelled from high school. The straight A student accepted a D on her assignment nonchalantly, because it was more important to make a statement than to get a good grade," William said.

"She apparently has a fabulous sense of right and wrong," the gentleman to the chair's left said.

"Yes, she remained poised even with that aggressive reporter sticking a microphone into her face," William said.

"Alistair," intoned the chair, addressing the man to his right, "what say you now?"

Alistair sniffed, and his round wire-framed spectacles wobbled on the bridge of his nose. "Well, in view of this new information, in conjunction with our stated goal of promoting geographic diversity, I suppose we could give due consideration to this candidate."

"I like her. Let's give her a chance," Catherine said.

*

Julia saw the letter with Harvard University in the return address. She snatched it from among the bills and junk mail and ran up to her room. She held it to her chest and then started to open it, but her fingers were shaking too violently. She set it carefully down on her desk and forced herself to take a few deep breaths. She stared at the letter for a long time, until her hands stopped shaking. *I will open this now, for better or worse.* She slid her finger under the back flap and worked the envelope open.

"Julia! Juliaaaaa!" Julia heard her mother bellow, shaking her out of her reverie. "You were supposed to set the table!"

Julia went scrambling down the stairs and ran into the TV room.

"I'm in! I'm in! Harvard accepted me! I can't believe it! I can't believe it!" Julia exclaimed. "I'm going to Harvard! I am so out of here!"

"Well, that's nice. I don't know why you would think they wouldn't accept you. You have good grades and all," Aura Lee calmly replied. "Now can you please set the table?"

"Yes! I can set the table! No problem! Not only am I going out of state for college, but I am going to Harvard University!"

# PART 4

Massachusetts, 1999

# CHAPTER 42

"Daddy! Daddy!" Mark toddled to the door on sturdy little legs as Alex let himself into their apartment. Helen wore a T-shirt and jeans; her fair hair was rolled up in a plastic hair clip.

"Fair Guinevere! Your loyal Arthur has returned from his day of battling dragons and vanquishing wrongdoers. How does my lady?" Alex set down his briefcase and executed a courtly bow.

"I'm fine. How was the hospital today?"

"Crazy as always. Good to be home."

"Up! Up! Up!" Mark gripped the khaki fabric of Alex's pant leg and pulled vigorously. Alex grinned, grabbed Mark around the waist, flipped him in a full somersault, and popped him onto his shoulders.

Alex held Mark's feet firmly and said, "Hey buddy, want to go for a run before dinner?"

"Yaaaa!" Mark pushed against Alex's head and tried to jump down.

"Hey, big guy, hang on. You're supposed to wait for me to put you down." Alex spun him in a reverse somersault and deposited him on the floor. "Okay, go get ready."

Mark scampered away and returned a few minutes later wearing Winnie the Pooh sunglasses and clutching a plastic dinosaur. "All ready!"

"Look at him, Helen! Can you believe he's already two and a half?"

"I know! He's growing like crazy."

"Want some water to take with you, buddy?" Alex asked as he tied the laces of his running shoes.

"No wa-wa! Aaaapoool!" Mark said, pounding on the refrigerator.

"Apple juice. Okay." Alex filled a cup with juice. "Let's go. Helen, we'll be back in half an hour, 45 minutes."

"Okay. Try to tire him out, please," Helen called after them.

"There's your race car. Hop in, buddy."

Mark clambered into the bright red jogging stroller and took a swig of juice as Alex buckled him in. Alex pushed the stroller to the sidewalk and started to run, pushing Mark ahead of him.

"Hey, Mark, want to go see Grandma?"

"Yeah!"

Alex quickened his pace. He turned onto Fisher Avenue and then onto Pella Street. He pivoted at the end of the driveway of his old home and parked the stroller just outside the garage.

"Daddy! Daddy! Me! Me! Me! Up! Up! Up!" Mark yelled, straining at his seat belt.

"Okay! Okay. Here you go." Alex lifted Mark from the stroller and held him up in front of Olivia's door. He pushed on the doorbell, once, twice, again and again, laughing.

Olivia opened the door. "Why, I couldn't imagine who it could be at the door. I thought maybe the mailman. But it's my little grandson. Come on in, sweetheart. Alex, come in."

Mark ran inside and threw himself against the refrigerator. "Aaapoool!" He called, waving his cup.

"Alex, the child is thirsty. Probably hungry too. Doesn't Helen know how to take care of him?" Olivia opened the refrigerator and pulled out a bottle of apple juice. Mark jumped up and down as she filled his cup.

Alex smiled. No verbal response was required.

"I have the news on. Come sit down." Olivia walked toward her chair. "Oh, wait. You're all sweaty." She left the living room and returned with a bath towel, folded neatly. She laid this on the couch. "You can sit here."

Mark struggled to climb up and sit next to Alex, but the couch was too high. Finally, he backed up and ran toward it, catapulting himself at the last moment halfway onto the couch. Alex put out his hand to keep Mark from rolling off.

"I'm having a martini. Want one?" Olivia gestured at the silver canister. "There's enough here for you."

"No thanks. I'm driving." He watched with fascination as Mark labored to get onto the couch, fingers gripping the upholstery, feet kicking wildly.

Mark finally realized the futility of his attempted ascent. He slid down and started to climb onto Olivia's chair. "Here you go, sweetheart." She pulled him onto her lap.

"See dino. See?" he said, waving the plastic dinosaur in front of her face.

"I do see. How scary! Will he bite me?"

Mark shook his head. He held the dinosaur against his chest and petted it.

Olivia sipped her cocktail. "He's so sweet!"

"I think he takes after you, Mom."

"Oh, Alex, I don't know. Well, maybe."

"We should get going. Helen is making dinner."

"Good luck. I'll pray for you." Olivia waved her hand dismissively.

"Come on, Mark. Time to go see Mommy. Let's get the race car."

"Woo! Woo!" Mark yelled, waving his dinosaur as Alex strapped him in. They started for home.

"Hey, Mark, how does the dinosaur go?"

"Grrrrrr!"

"How does the doggie go?"

"Ruff! Ruff! Ruff!"

"How does the kitty cat go?"

"Mee-owww!"

"How does Tarzan go?"

"O-o-o-ah-ah-ah!" Mark pounded his chest.

"How does Mark go?"

"Aaaapoool!" He waved his cup.

"How does Daddy go?"

"Lov-oooo!"

*

Giuli Stewart snapped a leash onto Tybalt's collar. "Let's go, big boy," she whispered. "But be quiet. We don't want to wake Grandma!" Her Mom knew her boss had wanted her to be into work an hour early today to discuss something important. God forbid her mother get up and take a turn walking Tybalt any time before noon. No, she just relaxed and enjoyed her nice teacher's pension from her easy chair in front of the TV.

The feisty little West Highland terrier needed no encouragement. He bounded out the door and onto the pavement, eager for his morning walk. Giuli and Tybalt's early morning stroll through the neighborhood was marked by Tybalt's lunging for a pair of terrified chipmunks and an attack on a squirrel, ending with the squirrel escaping to the upper reaches of an enormous old copper oak at the corner of Pella Street.

"Now, Tybalt, you know your big brother Romeo was not nearly this aggressive!" Giuli missed her little chihuahua, who had eventually died of advanced old age, at least in dog years. Tybalt was little Romeo's replacement. Giuli stopped short. She knew she was on Alex's street. She often walked this way, but she hardly ever saw him. But today, she was out earlier than usual, and there was Alex, leaving for work. She stepped behind the broad trunk of the oak tree, embarrassed for him to see her without make-up, with her hair a mess, and before she had taken a shower. And yet she couldn't resist watching from a distance. Alex stood on the doorstep, handsome as always, and looked back into his house. Helen emerged, and he took her in his arms and embraced her. *Wouldn't that be wonderful, to have him hug me like that?* she mused. As she watched, Alex kissed Helen, on the mouth, then on her forehead. He strode to the car, waved goodbye and drove away. Giuli collapsed against the tree and sighed. *He really loves her!*

*

Giuli and Andy sat side by side in their boss's small office on the second floor of Ye Olde Corner Bookstore. He paced back and forth before speaking.

"You two have been great. You've worked here for years, and, I hope you don't think I'm weird, but honestly, I feel like you're my own daughters." He removed his glasses and wiped his face with his handkerchief.

"Joey, that's really sweet," Giuli said.

"I have a feeling a 'but' is coming. Out with it, for god's sake," Andy grumbled. She slumped in her chair.

He replaced his glasses and continued to pace, then stopped, leaned back against his desk and looked them in the eyes. "Okay. Here it is. Straight. We're closing. We're losing money. It's not sustainable. I'm so sorry to have to say it, but come the end of the year, I won't have a job for you."

Giuli sat speechless. This bookstore was almost her whole life.

"I'll be goddamned," Andy muttered. She grasped the edges of her black leather vest and ground her knuckles together.

"People just don't buy books anymore. At least, not from bookstores." He sighed heavily. "You have some time, a few months, to figure out what you'll do next. If I can help, you know, please ask."

Giuli rose unsteadily to her feet. Joey stood and extended his hand. Giuli shook it. He reached out to Andy, but she crossed her arms and scowled at him. They shuffled silently from the office.

"The guy who can't make a profit from a store on the Freedom Trail wants us to ask him for career advice? Fuck that!" Andy said.

"Aw Andy, it was hard for him. To tell us, I mean. I feel terrible for us but I feel bad for him too. Do you have any idea what you'll do?" Giuli asked.

"None." She snorted loudly past her silver nose ring. "I got no savings. I got to have some job."

"I have some saved, but it won't last if I'm out of work. We have to think of something."

"I got nothing."

"I do feel bad for Joey." She paused. "You're going to think I'm nuts, but when we shook hands, I got this feeling that he hasn't told his wife about us closing yet and that when he does, it won't go well."

"Wait. This might be really crazy but let me run it by you. You know how you have these, like, premonitions about certain people? Maybe you could use that. Learn to control it, focus it. Be a fortune teller or something." Andy looked at Giuli expectantly.

"What? Like in Salem?" Giuli laughed. "I can't do that."

"Listen. I never told you this. But remember that time you said you were afraid I would get into an accident on the way home?"

"Yeah?"

"Well, I didn't tell you what happened, because I was afraid you'd be annoying about it."

"What happened?"

"I took the T to the train station where I leave my car, like always, but you had kind of freaked me out. So I went and got a cup of coffee, killed a few minutes, before driving home. Then when I got on the road, there had been this huge crash. I thought, god, that could have been me if I'd left a few minutes earlier. Then I told myself it was just a coincidence and kind of forgot about it. But maybe there's something about you where you can tell things."

"I don't know. I can't imagine doing that, making a living telling fortunes."

"It was just an idea." Andy sulked.

*

Alex and Helen and Mark walked past the New England Aquarium and toward a sleek black and white, multideck ship, the Calypso, anchored in Boston Harbor.

"Mark, how do you like being on this big boat for your fifth birthday?" Alex asked as they crossed the gangway. He held Mark's hand tightly as he studied the dark water below.

Mark nodded enthusiastically. "Good," he said.

"This is a harbor cruise. We won't go too far today. But one day, wouldn't it be fun to sail the seven seas? Just take off and sail and sail?"

"Would there be TV?"

"Sure. We'll have a special boat with TV."

"Okay." A pause. "Daddy, did you have a boat when you were little?"

"No, I didn't. I had a rug with a sailboat, but that was a pretend boat."

Alex stood at the railing with his family as the late afternoon sun played on the glittering water and gently warmed his skin. It was late August, still summer, but the ferocity of July's heat had waned in preparation for autumn. Alex inhaled the pungent aroma of the sea water and the sharp smell of boat fuel, as water lapped hungrily around the pilings of the dock and the hull of Calypso, and the seagulls soared and wheeled above. Their ship proceeded from its mooring with a raucous chug-chug. As it turned, they found themselves facing west.

"Look at the sunset! Magnificent!" Alex said. Golden light spilled across the city of Boston and onto the water around them.

"It's like butter! Butter on popcorn!" Mark shouted, throwing his arms wide.

"Butter on popcorn! I like that! Young man, you have the makings of a poet," Alex said, gazing down at Mark.

As their ship continued its turn, a rogue wave slammed into it and sprayed the edge of the deck. Helen squealed as the water splashed her, and Mark laughed. Alex smiled, silently reveling in the caress of the wild salt spray across his cheek, in the light of the setting sun, in the company of the best family he could ever have hoped for.

On the ride home, Mark dozed in his car seat. Alex spoke softly as they headed back to Brookline. "Helen, I want to talk to you about something. About New York."

*He knows! He knows!* Her mind screamed in utter panic. "Yes?" she said out loud, her voice a little shaky.

"I'm not sure if you remember, or, well, maybe I never mentioned him, but there was a professor, Dr. Rheingold, kind of a hot-shot researcher type from NYU. His focus is on melanoma."

Helen nodded attentively. *Maybe this isn't about Hector. Please, please let it be so.*

"Anyway, he called me today. He's gotten an NIH grant, a big one, and he's looking to expand his staff."

*Where was this going,* Helen wondered.

"I'd always respected, well, even revered him for his work. Everyone did. He called and asked if I'd come work in his lab. I told him I'd be thrilled to work with him, especially on melanoma, but I needed to talk to my wife first."

Helen could just imagine herself running into Hector on the streets of New York, Mark in tow. That was a meeting she did not want to happen. That was all behind her. She would never agree to this move, but she needed a reason. "What about the job you have here? They need you at the hospital. And what about our nice home we were finally able to buy? We'd just leave it?"

"Oh, the house! We could sell it. We'd make a profit for sure in this market. And my job- I would give enough notice for them to find a replacement."

"What about schools? Mark is signed up to start kindergarten in a few weeks."

"We'd probably have to send him to private school. Which would be expensive. One thing is that as a research position, it wouldn't pay as well as the job I have now."

Helen started to cry. Visions of the ugly linoleum from the med school's dorm loomed large in her imagination. "New York is so expensive. We'd be poor and miserable. We're happy here. You have a good job and we have our nice home. Why should we give this up?"

"What if I could contribute to finding treatment or even a cure for melanoma? So people like my Dad wouldn't have to suffer."

She turned to him with tear-stained cheeks. "Well, um, what about your Mom? It would break her heart if you left."

Alex sighed. He had thought that moving away from his mother would appeal to Helen. This looked like a no-go.

*

Alex sat in a lounge chair on the little deck in the back of their home, enveloped in black silence. Helen had been right. Buying this house was smart, a good investment. Miraculously, the real estate market had dipped simultaneously with their decision to buy a home in Brookline. Prices had crept mercilessly upwards ever since; they would not have been able to buy this house if they had waited.

The scraping sound of the sliding door opening announced an interloper. Mark's footsteps, cautious in the dark, approached.

"Daddy, what are you doing?"

"I'm stargazing!"

"What's that?" Mark asked.

"It's fun. Look up and see if there's anything you recognize. Do you see anything you know?" Alex hoisted Mark into his lap.

Mark paused thoughtfully before replying. "The moon!" he said, triumphant.

"That's right! Is it a full moon or a crescent moon tonight?"

"I say full, Daddy!"

"You are right! Did you know that the moon changes the tides of the oceans here on earth?"

"Daddy, you are making it up."

"No, I'm not, it's true!"

"Na-ah!" insisted Mark in his high childish trill.

"Do you know what happens to little boys who doubt their daddies?" Alex asked him.

"No!" but Mark started to laugh uncontrollably with anticipation.

"I'll tell you what happens to them," said Alex. "They get tickled!" And Alex proceeded to tickle Mark as the little boy shrieked with delight.

The sliding door screeched again. "Alex, please stop. That child will never go to bed," Helen said, sounding faintly irritated. "He has school in the morning."

"Don't worry; I'll see that he gets to sleep soon," Alex assured her. She retreated into the house.

"Okay, we'd better settle down for Mommy. Now, did you know that the stars make shapes, kind of like big pictures in the sky?

Mark shook his head.

"Well they do. Look up there. See those three stars straight in a row? Yes? Those are Orion's belt. The stars above and below make up the rest of his body."

Mark looked skeptical.

"You have to use your imagination. Orion was a mighty hunter."

"When Daddy?"

"Long, long ago." Alex gazed at the night sky and silently picked out Betelgeuse, marking Orion's shoulder, and Rigel, below.

"Were you alive then?"

Alex threw back his head and laughed. "I haven't been alive *that* long. Orion was in the sky long before I was born." Would humans ever be able to travel so far, to visit those distant stars? Not in this lifetime. *If I had been born in the future, the distant future, and they were putting together a crew for an interstellar space mission, I would volunteer. No matter how dangerous. I would go.* He held Mark tight and imagined it.

"How did he turn into stars? How did he get so high?" Mark's voice was sweet and trusting.

"Those stars are not really a person. In the old days people used to think that groups of stars made things they could recognize. Those groups are called 'constellations.' Someone a very long time ago thought some of the stars looked like this famous Orion, and so the name just stuck."

"Daddy, you know everything."

\*

Alex slid the heavy silver coin out of its plastic envelope and onto the leather panel set into his desk. He drew his magnifying glass from the drawer to his right and studied the coin. The face of the coin featured the profile of Alexander the Great in the guise of Heracles, wearing the skin of the Nemean lion as a cloak, with the head of the mighty lion serving as a hood. *What an amazing work of art! The detail is unbelievable,* Alex thought as he peered through the magnifying glass. *Where has this coin been for the past 2300 years, who was the artisan who made it, and who has touched it since?* He leaned back in his chair. Wouldn't it be wonderful to go on an archeological dig and look for pottery and coins and the foundations of ancient buildings? Maybe there would be an opportunity someday to volunteer for a dig, somewhere near a nice resort for Helen and Mark. He would set out each day on a worn and rusty local bus that would struggle down dusty, unpaved roads to the archeological site, where he would find other similarly dedicated volunteers under the supervision of professional archeologists, with the requisite gray-haired, bespectacled professor, careless of his appearance but obsessed with his field, furiously puffing away at his pipe, overseeing the entire operation.

Mark tiptoed into the room. "Daddy, did you get a new coin for your collection?"

"Yes, I did. It shows Alexander the Great. Come see."

"He had the same name as you?"

"Yes, he did. What do you think?"

"It's nice, but I like the gold one better."

"The gold stater? That one's also nice."

"Is it pure gold, Daddy?"

"Oh, yes. It would have to be," Alex said.

Helen paused in the doorway, listening.

"How do you know?"

"In those days, the king could put you to death for adulterating pure gold. So people making the coins would be unlikely to take the risk."

"Wait, Daddy, what's adult- ah, does it mean a grown-up?"

"No, it means to mix the gold with some other metal, so it's worth less."

"And they could kill you for that, even if it was an accident?"

"Adulterating gold is never an accident. And in those days that could definitely get you killed."

"How could they even tell, unless they saw you do it?"

"Mark, that is a very good question. I'll tell you how one man figured it out. Long ago, in ancient times, there was a brilliant scientist named Archimedes, and he lived in the powerful city of Syracuse. Now the king of Syracuse gave a goldsmith some pure gold to make into a crown. But then after the crown got made, the king suspected that his crown was made of adulterated gold, not pure gold."

"Can you tell again, adulter, um...?"

"Adulterated means impure. Like if you mix a cheap metal into the gold so it costs less to make something, but you tell the person buying it that it's pure gold. If you do that, you're cheating. You're dishonest."

"Okay." Mark considered this. "Then what happened?"

"The king called Archimedes and said, 'Help me figure out if my crown is pure gold, or whether I got cheated.' So Archimedes thought and thought and then one day while he was soaking in the baths in the great bathhouse of Syracuse,"

"Wait, Daddy, why didn't he take a bath at home?"

"That's how it was in the ancient world. Lots of people didn't have their own bathtubs. People would go to the public bathhouses to bathe. You could go and take a bath in a huge bathtub with your friends."

"That's funny!"

"No, it was a good idea. Anyway, Archimedes, he figured it out. About how to tell if the crown was unadulterated or not. He leapt out of the bathtub and ran naked through the streets yelling, 'Eureka' which means...Look, here's Mommy, my woman of pure gold!"

Helen stood in the doorway. A cold shiver passed through her. Unadulterated. Adulterated. Adulterate. Adultery. Years had gone by, and much of that time she was able to put that whole episode with Hector behind her. Then today the letter came, the letter that she hid and would read later. Did Alex know about it? Had he found it? Was he toying with her, talking about being adulterated? There he was, looking at her with his easy smile. No, Alex did not know. It was just a coincidence, the letter and these words, innocently chosen and without malice.

"Okay, Mark, let's get washed up for dinner," Helen said.

"Mommy, please! I want to know if the guy's head gets chopped off."

"Mark!"

"Listen, buddy, if Mommy says to go get washed up, you'd better get going."

Helen returned to the kitchen and poured 2% milk into a Red Sox souvenir cup for Mark and set it at his place.

"I don't like milk. I'm not drinking it."

"But sweetie, it's good for you. Come on, like a good boy."

"I'm six years old. I'm not a baby. Milk is for babies." He folded his arms across his chest and scowled.

"Mark, if you don't finish your milk, there's no riding your bike after dinner," Helen said as she stirred the mashed potatoes. She used instant potatoes; it was a lot less work than making mashed potatoes from scratch. Alex never complained; maybe he couldn't tell the difference.

"That's not fair! Milk is for babies. If I can ride a bike, I'm too old for milk."

Alex approached. "Listen, Mark. I have an important secret to tell you," he whispered. "When I was your age I hated milk too. But then my Dad told me a way to make milk taste good. The secret is to drink it while it's super-cold. You put your cup into the freezer, and let it get almost frozen. Then you drink it right away before it has a chance to warm up. Want to try it?"

Mark nodded. Alex took the Red Sox cup and wedged it carefully in the freezer between the frozen corn and the frozen broccoli, and said, "Now we wait ten minutes. Can you tell me when ten minutes are past?"

Alex began to flip through the day's mail, left on the kitchen counter. A bill from the electric company; he set that aside to be paid. A bill from the gas company; he laid that on top of the first bill. Multiple catalogs, from local and distant stores. As he picked up the Land's End catalog featuring women's clothing a letter that had been wedged inside it dropped onto the counter. The letter was addressed to Helen in big, loose, messy script.

"Helen, what's this, addressed to you?" Alex asked. The handwriting seemed vaguely familiar; he struggled to recall the context. Something about it disturbed him, but he could not explain why.

"What? What's addressed to me?" Helen said, but when she saw the letter Alex extended to her, she snatched it from him.

"Helen, what's the matter? What is that?"

"That? It's nothing. I left the water running. Sorry!" she said and dashed out, tucking the letter into the pocket of her jeans.

"Helen?"

"Daddy, it's been ten minutes!"

"Oh, okay!" Alex responded. Helen was known to overreact on occasion; better not to bother her. "So now we are going to do the experiment: does milk really taste better super-cold?" Alex extracted the cup from the freezer. "Now try it, big guy," he said to his little son.

Mark took a small sip. "Hey, it's not too bad! Thanks, Daddy!"

"Mark if you keep drinking milk that fast you'll be taller than me before you know it!" Alex assured him.

"Really?" Mark gazed up at Alex in wonder. Such a thing was unfathomable.

"And another thing I've learned," Alex told Mark. "I have learned that my favorite cereal is Cocoa Krispies. Know why?"

Mark shook his head, earnestly waiting to hear the reason.

"Because it turns the milk chocolate. Ice cold milk over Cocoa Krispies for breakfast. It just doesn't get any better than that!"

"Daddy, does Cocoa Krispies also make me tall like you?"

"Only if you have them with milk." He ruffled Mark's hair fondly. "Milk is very important because it has good things in it to help you grow. Most important is the protein. You absolutely need protein to build up your muscles."

"Really?"

"Yes. And do you know that in your body you have 640 muscles? And each one has a name. Hey, for fun do you want to learn the name of one muscle every day? Then if you want to become a doctor when you grow up you'll be ahead if you already know all the muscles."

"Okay."

Shall we start with the biceps? It's this muscle." Alex flexed his arm. "You try it."

"Biceps!" Mark said and flexed his arm.

"Technically, you have two biceps. One in each arm, so now you know the names of two muscles. Left biceps and right biceps!"

As they finished dinner, Alex said, "Mark, you want to take a short bike ride? Over to Grandma's? She'll be surprised to see how well you can ride."

Mark nodded. He loved his bike.

"Okay, good. I'll run with you while you bike. Helen, what was that letter you got?"

"Oh, nothing. Someone wanting a donation. I threw it out." Her throat constricted as she spoke, but she managed to pronounce the words. The letter had been from Hector. Nothing from him for over six years, no contact since that awful day in his apartment when that awful woman had shown up. He had written to apologize, he said, to apologize for any pain he had caused her. He hoped that she did not mind that he had gotten her new address from their high school's alumni office. He regretted how long it had taken him to contact her, but as he had not been in a position to help her, he had not known if she would want to hear from him. Finally, he could bear it no more; he had to know how she was doing, and if she was angry with him. It was a good letter, she thought. Very touching. Except that he never asked about the baby. Their baby. And he finished the letter with an appeal for money. Now that Alex was a doctor, surely she could spare a little money to help an old friend who was in need, he had said. She had nibbled at her dinner, in turmoil over how to respond.

A little while later Mark, sporting a shiny new silver bike helmet, flanked by Alex in running gear, set off. Mark was a little unsteady on his new bike but stayed upright. As they approached the corner, a car turned onto their street, heading toward them, in the opposite lane.

"Mark, get over! Get toward the sidewalk!" Alex shouted, running to put himself between the car and Mark.

The car continued on past them at a leisurely pace.

"What's a matter, Daddy?" Mark asked. He had stopped his bike and was looking at Alex.

The pounding of Alex's heart slowed back toward normal. "I was afraid the car would hit you. I was very scared."

"It didn't come by me. I'm okay."

"Well, to be safe, let's have you ride on the sidewalk, until you're a bit more grown-up, okay?" Mark was right; the car was driving slowly and had stayed in its lane. There had been no real danger.

Alex and Mark made their way to Pella Street. Mark carefully parked his bike and then hurried to ring the doorbell, but since he was a big boy, he only rang it three times.

Olivia came to the door and looked down at him. "Who are you?"

"Grandma, it's me, Mark! I rode over on my bike!"

She peered at him. "No, my grandson Mark is a little boy. You're a big boy. You shouldn't tease me like that."

"Grandma, it is me! I promise."

"And my grandson Mark can't ride a bike. You're a big boy who can ride a bike."

"Daddy taught me! Look, it's me." He unstrapped his new bike helmet so she could see him better.

She bent over to study him more closely. "Why, you may be right after all. I hardly recognized you, you grew so much."

Mark turned and looked at Alex with wonder. "Did the milk make me taller?"

Alex shrugged. "Apparently so."

As soon as Alex and Mark left the house, Helen found some paper and an envelope. She had considered throwing Hector's letter away and not responding, but what if he wrote again? Or called? What if Alex were to answer the phone, or open a second letter coming from Hector? She had to answer and put an end to this. She wrote quickly, thanking Hector for his letter but asking him not to write to her again, as Alex would not like it. She was enclosing a little money, she wrote, because she wanted to help him, but she would not be able to do this again. She then paused, intending to write, *Our son is named Mark. He is a wonderful boy*, but stopped. He didn't even ask about the baby! Perhaps he thought she had gotten an abortion and didn't want to say anything about it. She shut her eyes for a moment, and Mark's happy face shone before her. The idea of undoing that smile, that little life, was an awful one now. At any rate, either he didn't know or didn't care about this child of theirs, and she would not be the one to enlighten him. Let it be her secret. She went through her wallet and the top drawer of their desk, collecting five $20 bills. She folded the money inside two sheets of paper, so it could not be seen through the envelope. She sealed the envelope and affixed a stamp. She shoved the letter deep into her purse; she would mail it the next day.

What to do with Hector's letter? Alex could be back any moment. She should destroy the letter, not just throw it into the trash. She opened the drawer to the right of the stove and extracted a box of matches. She held Hector's letter over the sink, struck a match and lit a corner of the letter. She dropped the letter into the sink and with satisfaction watched it burn. As the last of the letter turned to ash, she began to relax. Everything would be okay. Suddenly a shrill alarm sounded. *What was that?* She wondered, panicked. *Oh, no, the smoke alarm.* She raced to the sink, turned on the water and rinsed the ash down the drain, and then hurried to the window and opened it. The alarm stopped as fresh air filled the room. Helen sank into a corner of the kitchen and started to sob. Would she ever be safe? She wondered miserably. Would this ever be gone, really gone, and behind her? She had made a mistake, yes, but it wasn't so bad, the way it had worked out. Mark was such a good boy, well, most of the time, and Alex loved him dearly. Did it really make a difference, the thing that happened, years and years ago?

Through the open window she heard Mark and Alex chatting as they returned home. She pulled herself to her feet, quickly wet a dishtowel with cold water and wiped her eyes. Everything would be okay.

That night Alex had the nightmare- the terrible day when Patrick died played mercilessly in his mind's eye. He felt his fingers wrapped around the chain link fence, the tough metal unyielding, separating him from Patrick. And then the car, speeding; Hector's evil face, laughing; and Patrick, lunging into the street for the ball. He woke abruptly, panting and sweaty, to find the room dark and quiet, with Helen sleeping peacefully beside him. *I'm sorry, Patrick. I'm so sorry. I should never have sent you out. I wish I could do it over. I'd give anything, anything.*

# CHAPTER 43

Sunshine poured into the kitchen of the Gonzalez home on Warren Street. Elena scampered into the room and ran to her grandmother.

"There's my little treasure. Good morning, little Elena," Anita said, hugging her.

"Good morning, mi Abuelita!"

"*Tienes hambre? Quieres el desayuno?*" Anita asked.

"Yes, I'm hungry but I don't know what I want." Elena went to the pantry and scanned the shelves for something good. Not oatmeal. Boring. "Abuelita, are there any donuts?"

"No, my treasure. I'm sorry. They are not so healthy, you know."

"Okay," she whispered. What other choices were there? Bran cereal. Only Tía Cati ate that. It was disgusting. What was this box at the far left of the shelf? Cheerios. They were boring too but not as boring as oatmeal. She was pretty hungry by now and Cheerios would have to do. She pulled the box off the shelf and it fell from her hand and hit the floor with a loud thud.

"What was that, Elenita?" Anita asked.

"The Cheerios. They're so heavy! Why are they so heavy?" Elena bent down to pick up the box. She opened the top and started to unfold the bag inside.

Anita leapt out of her chair and hurried to Elena. "Don't touch that, my treasure. Let's put that away." She closed the Cheerios and slid the box onto a higher shelf, out of Elena's reach. She should have taken care of this before now. But what could she have done? She would like to dispose of the- item, but she didn't know how, or where. And she was sure that the government kept a watch on their home. She was so afraid that if she took it away to get rid of it, someone would stop her and catch her with it, and arrest her. They might even tie it in with that earlier phase in their lives, before they came to Massachusetts, and make Pedro stay even longer in jail. And then she might never see Pedro again comfortable and happy in his own home. And what if poor little Elena would be left with no one? Better to leave it where it had been these past years, hurting no one.

"What is it?" Elena asked, merrily dancing around Anita.

"It's something from a long time ago. It's not a toy. Just please don't touch it," Anita said, resuming her seat at the kitchen table, and trying to regain her calm.

"But why, Abuelita?" Elena tipped her face up at Anita and assumed her most innocent and sincere expression.

"I'll explain one day when you're older. But for now, let's find you something else for breakfast, alright my angel?" She gave Elena a reassuring smile.

*

Alex loped into the TV room of their home, where he knew he would find Mark.

"Hey, Mark, guess what I found today?" Alex asked. *He is so cute in those Red Sox pajamas!*

"What, Daddy?" Mark said, turning away from the TV.

"Instead of going to the closest T stop to come home, I walked along the river, on the Esplanade, and I was planning to cut over to the T stop at Arlington Street. But then on the Esplanade, what did I see but a place where you can take sailing lessons and then sail on your own! It's called Community Boating. Anyone can join."

"Wow, can we go sailing?"

"As soon as they let me, I'll take you and Mommy out. And when you get a little older you can take lessons and learn to sail on your own."

"Can you and me get our own boats and race?"

"Sure. Why not?" Alex smiled. Mark was even more enthusiastic than he had expected. Sailing would be a wonderful thing for them to do together.

"That'll be so fun!"

Alex sat down on the couch. "What are you watching, big guy?"

"Disney channel." Mark watched until a commercial came on, then turned toward Alex. "Did you watch Disney channel when you were my age?"

"No. There was a Disney show once a week, but it wasn't the same as now. I didn't watch much TV. I used to read a lot."

"Why? Grandma made you?"

"No, because I liked it. TV wasn't as good as it is now, I'll admit."

"What'd you read?"

"Oh, different things. When I was a little older than you, I used to read *Tarzan*."

"I didn't know there were Tarzan books. I liked the movie. Remember when we went?"

"Of course, I remember. But those are great books. I loved reading them."

"Why?"

"Because Tarzan was so brave, a real hero."

"Aren't you a hero, Daddy?"

"Oh, no, I'm not a hero, not a real hero."

"What's a real hero?"

"A real hero is someone who does more than he's supposed to do and does it very well. Who will risk everything, even his life, to achieve his goals. A hero is more courageous than anyone."

"Then why aren't you a hero? You're brave."

Alex leaned over and smoothed Mark's hair. "Well, I do what I am supposed to do and I do it as well as I can. But I don't take big risks or do anything extraordinary, beyond what I'm supposed to do. Here's an example. Let's say a fire-breathing dragon came to our neighborhood and started burning down people's houses. Most people would do the sensible thing: get in their cars and drive away. A hero would go out and fight the dragon and kill it." *A hero would have gotten to Patrick and kept him from running into the street. A hero would not have sent Patrick out to confront Hector on his own.*

"Can I be a real hero? I would fight the dragon." Mark asked, his tone hopeful.

"Sure, you can. But you could get killed fighting the dragon. You'd be a hero, but you'd be a dead hero. So you have to think carefully whether you would want to take that risk." The commercials ended, and Alex could see Mark's eyes drifting back toward the TV. "Okay, big guy. I'm going to change."

# CHAPTER 44

Helen Eastgard stood in front of the full-length mirror in the bedroom of the rented cottage in Chatham. She couldn't wear a bikini anymore, but she looked okay, reasonably okay, in this tank suit. She sighed and turned away from her reflection. She opened a beach bag emblazoned with "Cape Cod" in navy blue, and selected towels to take to the beach. The Cape was nice, but perhaps next year they'd finally be able to go to Hawaii. As she folded a Lion King towel for Mark to use, the peaceful atmosphere of the quiet town was shattered by a blood-curdling shriek. It sounded like Mark! She pushed the window up and leaned out anxiously to see what had happened. There were Alex and Mark, on the deck at the back of the house. Mark gave another shriek, but this one was only half-hearted, and ended in a prolonged fit of giggling.

"What are you two doing? I almost had a heart attack!" she shouted.

"Daddy's making me sun-scream!" Mark said. "It's cold on me."

Alex stood with a canister of spray-on sunscreen, looking sheepish. "I don't want him to burn. Or get skin cancer later in life." His friend Geoff Drucker in Dermatology had noticed a rough spot on the helix of Alex's ear two weeks before, as they sat together in a multidisciplinary conference. Geoff had insisted it be excised. It was an actinic keratosis, not exactly malignant, but a sign of sun damage. Geoff had scolded him for not protecting his ears better. His Dad's oncologist had also warned him about the sun, years ago, he recalled. Alex had thought he was careful, but apparently not careful enough. A baseball cap wouldn't do it, Geoff had said. He needed a hat with a brim. Alex had obediently gotten one of those nice khaki hats that looked appropriate for a safari. He would wear that today to the beach.

"Do you have to make him scream?"

"I think he's overreacting. It's not that cold. I hope you put on sunscreen. I can help if you need me too."

Helen groaned and shut the window. Alex and his sunscreen!

"Hold still, Mark. One more spray!" Alex commanded.

A little later, they arrived at Lighthouse Beach, presided over by the sturdy lighthouse that gave the beach its name. Helen headed eastward across the sand shod in rattan sandals, toting the beach bag, while Alex followed close behind with the cooler. He turned his gaze upward to the sky of clear blue. A mild breeze ruffled his hair.

"It is hot!" Helen exclaimed.

"But it's not too hot, because hot means summer vacation and we love vacation. Right, Mark?"

"Right, Daddy!"

"Let's get Mommy settled under this umbrella and we can go cool off in the water. Wait for me now." Alex pulled the ice chest right next to Helen. "Want something?"

"Iced tea. The diet kind."

"Here you are- diet lemon iced tea." Alex handed her a can and gazed out at the ocean. "I was thinking. What if we do something different next year for vacation? I get four weeks a year. I'd love to use that time to go somewhere exotic, work with Doctors Without Borders. Maybe they have a site where there was someplace nice nearby for you and Mark to stay. We could go somewhere in Africa and save some time at the end to go on safari. What do you think?"

"Well, I don't know, um," Helen began. She had no interest in going anywhere to be eaten by bugs and catch a disease. "Do you think that group of doctors has a station in Hawaii? I really want to go there."

"Hawaii? I doubt it. We can look into it." Alex sighed.

"Oh, god, there he goes. Go get him!" Helen said, as Mark raced toward the water.

"Hey, Mark, slow down!" Alex ran after him.

Mark reached the surf and jumped in, howling with delight. Alex caught up with him, standing near him in the water while Mark jumped and bobbed in the water. After a while, Alex spoke. "Hey, Mark, what about a little break? The water's kind of cold."

"Na-ah, it's fine!" He dived down again, this time emerging with a portion of a seashell. Seeing that it was incomplete, he planted his feet in the sand and hurled it away. The next wave knocked him over, and he came up coughing and laughing.

"Look- your lips are blue! Let's take a break." Alex threw an arm around Mark's waist and lifted him from the water, and then strode back to Helen reclining beneath the umbrella. "This child has not noticed that the waters of the North Atlantic Ocean are frosty as hell. We both should warm up." Alex deposited Mark on a towel next to Helen.

"Na-ah, Daddy. It's warm."

"And there might be sharks. This is the summer home of the great white shark."

"I don't see any sharks."

"You don't see them until it's too late."

"There's no signs. There would be a shark sign if they were around."

"Listen to that. You are just too smart for your own good!"

"Let's go back, please!"

"Mark, it's so cold!"

Helen sat up and set her magazine down on her lap. "I noticed someone with a wetsuit on earlier. Maybe you should get one, and you could stay with him without freezing."

"Look! Look!" Mark yelled, pointing at the sand. "Seagull footprints!"

"That's a great idea. Someone around here should have a wetsuit for sale," Alex said.

"Yaaay! Daddy's going to play with me!" Mark danced in the sand, running circles around their station on the beach.

"Remember the first time we were here, on our honeymoon?" Alex asked.

"Yes, it was very nice." She lowered her magazine and looked off toward the ocean.

"The weather was beautiful that week, just like now."

"Daddy! Daddy! Tomorrow can we go to Thunder Beach?"

"What's Thunder Beach?" Helen asked.

"Oh, he means Coastguard Beach, cause the water's so rough," Alex explained. "I know. What about Oyster Pond? That's got a nice little beach and the water's warmer."

"No!" Mark yelled. "That's for babies who can't swim! Thunder Beach! Thunder Beach!"

Helen shook her head. "Better get that wetsuit." She turned back to her magazine.

# CHAPTER 45

"My little treasure, when you are finished with your dessert, bring your dish to the sink, alright?" Anita asked. "I'm going to take a bath."

"Okay, Abuelita," Elena said. She dipped her spoon into the chocolate ice cream thoughtfully and watched her grandmother leave the kitchen. She listened as Abuelita went upstairs, step by step, to the second floor. She heard her turn on her music, music from her old home in Puerto Rico. Salsa, she called it. Then the sound of her bathroom door closing, and after a pause, the sound of running water. Ever since that day when her grandmother was so mysterious about the heavy box of Cheerios, Elena had wondered how she could find out what was in the box. This house was so boring. Could there be something interesting in that box?

Now that her grandmother was in the bath, Elena leapt into action. She was still too short to reach the shelf with the Cheerios, even on tiptoe, but she was able to drag a chair over to the pantry and stand on that and reach the box. She put her left hand on the doorframe of the pantry and with her right hand gripped the box. She lifted it tentatively, to be sure it wasn't too heavy for her, and then slid the box from the shelf. She climbed down from the chair, opened the box, and then opened the bag inside and shook it. Nothing but old Cheerios. The heavy thing was under the bag. She withdrew the bag and set it carefully on the floor. There was something, wrapped in a kitchen towel. She slid that out of the box and laid it reverently on the floor. She unfolded the towel to reveal a small gun, a pistol, in shiny silver metal. Elena started to shake. This is not what she was expecting. Frightened, she quickly folded the towel back over the gun and slipped the gun back into the cereal box, praying all the while that the gun would not fire. She replaced the box on the shelf and moved the chair back to the table.

\*

A mound of mail lay on the table, waiting to be sorted. Mark started to flip through it with his free hand.

"Look at this! Worst handwriting I ever saw!" Mark said with a laugh. "Mom, it's for you."

Helen's heart skipped a beat. "Let me see." She pulled the letter a little too hastily from Mark's hand.

Alex looked up and followed the letter as it passed from Mark's hand to Helen's, and then into the pocket of Helen's jeans, catching a glimpse of an envelope addressed in a loose, messy scrawl. He had a vague recollection of a similar letter for Helen many years back, and how she had become flustered when she saw it.

"Who is it from?" Alex asked.

Helen retreated into the kitchen, let the door swing shut and started to run water into the sink.

"There wasn't any name, just a return address in New York," Mark replied.

Helen felt a shiver of panic as water splattered loudly in the sink. Should she open this now? Should she stash it somewhere? What if Alex found it? She had burned the other letter she had gotten from Hector but there was no time for that now. Fingers trembling, she ripped open the envelope and pulled out the letter. Her eyes scanned it quickly, to get the gist of the contents. Some of the writing was so bad that she had to guess at the words. In essence, Hector was desperate. He had no one else to turn to, and she was so kind, could she send him some money? He'd had a run of bad luck. Anything she could spare would help him get back on his feet. She ripped the letter and the envelope and shoved the pieces deep into the trash. She took a deep breath, loaded meatloaf and roast potatoes onto a platter and returned to the dining room. "It's your mother's recipe, so you should like it," she announced with forced cheerfulness. She served them, and then sat and helped herself.

"This came out great. I'll tell my Mom. She'll be so happy," Alex said. Helen made no reference to the letter, and Alex decided not to ask.

Helen smiled. Olivia wouldn't be impressed with her cooking even if she suddenly turned into Julia Child. "My guys must have been hungry- that meatloaf is almost gone!"

Alex tapped Mark's foot with his own under the table. "Yeah, it's really good, Mom. Dad, can we go to the new Lord of the Rings movie this weekend?"

"I don't know. The orcs are supposed to be scary. Will you get scared?"

"Dad! I'm not a little kid anymore. No stupid pretend orcs are going to scare me."

"Okay. We'll figure out a good time."

Later, Alex and Helen had cleared the table and loaded the dishes into the dishwasher, while Mark marched off to do homework. Alex took great pleasure in sharing the daily routine, these small chores, with Helen. It spoke of comfort and stability. He returned to the table, laptop in hand. He sat and swirled the last of the wine in his glass as the encryption software hummed and clicked and finally prompted him to enter his username and password. He complied. He sipped his wine as the laptop hummed some more. Then he had the option to view his e-mail provided he enter another username and password.

"Wifi is so slow!"

Helen slid into a chair across from him. "I know. But what can you do?" She set a mug of decaf down on the table and started to flip through this month's issue of *House Beautiful*. Alex had not said anything about the letter.

"Finally!" Alex said as the contents of his Inbox became visible and then groaned. "87 new e-mails." He had cleared his Inbox in the morning before sign-out. If he read all of his e-mails and dealt with them during the day, he would never be home in time for dinner with Helen and Mark. He would have preferred to relax now, but he couldn't put off his e-mails anymore. Thankfully most could be deleted without response.

The elevators would be out of order for the rest of the day in the Fairbanks building. Magnum Laboratories urged him to purchase their laboratory equipment. Expedia announced 50% off hotels when purchasing a round trip airline ticket to selected cities. Selena in Nigeria wanted to transfer six million dollars to him; could he forward $10,000 to her to facilitate the transfer? Thomas and Sadie Caldwell had donated two million dollars to be used for research in pediatric oncology. The Radiology Department had obtained a new MRI machine to decrease patient wait time. Nine e-mails had to do with a case he was peripherally involved in; he had been copied on the initial e-mail and on all 8 replies. Alex deleted them all. Internal Medicine Associates welcomed two new outstanding attending physicians, Dr. Sharon Knowles and Dr. Scott Buckminster, to their faculty, to help with increased patient volume. They would be starting on the 15th of the month. Alex reread the last line. Buck! Buck was coming to work at his hospital.

"Helen! You won't believe it. Remember Buck?"

"Yeah, sure. Why?" Helen forced herself to speak casually as she turned to an article on a tasteful refurbishing of a vintage carriage house.

"He's joining the Medicine Department at the hospital here. Supposed to start in three weeks. After our wedding, I'd completely lost touch with him. I didn't know what he was up to. I'll check in with him and let him know we're here. Maybe he'll need some help finding his way around." Alex looked up. Excitement shone in his eyes.

"That would be nice." Helen looked up and smiled. Alex was now engrossed with thoughts of reuniting with his friend; the letter, Hector's letter, had likely been forgotten. She relaxed. "You know what? I think I'll go take a nice bath. I feel grungy."

"You're never grungy!" Alex said.

Helen shook her head and walked to their bathroom, glad for the privacy. She wished Hector had not written again. She had already told him once not to contact her, and he had not respected that. Last time she had replied, sending him a little money. This time there would be no response, no money. Hopefully he would never write again.

Alex sat for a while, finishing off his e-mails. After a long time, Alex rose and entered the kitchen. His eyes absently scanned the counters, coming to rest on a short stack of catalogs. He flipped through them; nothing but catalogs. He rested his forearms on the cool granite of the counter as the hum of the water into Helen's bath echoed above him. As he stood there, his gaze continued along the edge of the kitchen and stopped at the trash can. As though hypnotized, he walked over to it, eyes fixed on the shiny aluminum cylinder. He opened the trash can and looked in. There, mixed with cucumber peels, fragmented eggshells, onion skins, packaging from ground meat, strips of plastic wrap and crumpled paper towels, were tiny scraps of paper, perhaps from a letter, shredded far beyond legibility. He shook the trash bag gently, looking for some more solid clue to the nature of the mail Helen had received. There was the envelope, torn in two and only a little stained on one corner by something oily, perhaps from the meatloaf. The handwriting was atrocious, but there was something familiar about it.

*What am I doing?* He asked himself. *I'm a grown man who trusts his wife absolutely and I'm going through trash to see who sent her a letter.*

He took the trash bag, knotted it firmly and carried it to the trash barrel outside. But he took the two halves of the envelope and slid them face down into the middle drawer of the desk in his study, underneath some other papers.

\*

Alex and Helen sat together at a table for four at Toscano's on Charles Street in Beacon Hill.

"I wonder what's holding them up?" Helen asked.

"Denise was supposed to meet Buck at work and they were going to walk over. Maybe she's having trouble getting into town." Alex glanced at his watch. They were already 15 minutes late.

"Mmm. Could be." She was glad she had gotten a French manicure this week; it had a sophisticated look.

"They'll be here. In the meantime, I have you to myself." He reached over and squeezed Helen's hand.

She looked up at him. He really was so good.

"I love this place. It's so cute and cozy," she said. She had chosen a wrap dress in heathered gray for this evening's dinner; it was simple yet elegant, not too formal for a Thursday night dinner. And with control-top pantyhose underneath, it made her look a little more slender and toned than she actually was.

"I agree. The embossed tiles on the walls, the patterned woodwork and the lighting fixtures create such a nice atmosphere. Really makes you feel like you're in Tuscany."

"Mmm," Helen replied.

"We should go there sometime. Tuscany, I mean. What if we rented a cottage or something in the countryside, but close enough to Florence so that we could go there during the day and take in the sights?"

"We could. Also, we keep saying we're going to go to Hawaii," Helen said, taking a small sip of her Chianti.

"But just think of it: Florence is the cradle of the Renaissance. It's a beautiful city, so they say. The countryside is supposed to be gorgeous. Many an artist has made a pilgrimage to Florence to study her art and to try to capture the ephemeral Tuscan light. And what a great experience it would be for Mark," Alex said. "And you- you would be the 21st century's Simonetta Vespucci." In his mind's eye he saw Helen, just as she had looked at prom, but then her beautiful ivory dress dissolved and she stood in place of the goddess in the center of Botticelli's Birth of Venus, tendrils of fair hair caught in the gentle wind- the breath of Zephyr, her slender feet balanced on a seashell, attended by Pomona who waited anxiously on the shore, eager to offer a robe to cover the goddess's flawless body.

"I, ah, don't recall who," Helen began.

"Look, that must be them." Alex interrupted. He stood as the maître d' conducted a couple in the direction of their table.

A broad smile crossed Buck's face. He touched his wife's shoulder and gestured in Alex's direction.

"Buck! Are you a sight for sore eyes or what! It's great to see you," Alex said, shaking Buck's hand energetically.

"It's great to see you too. Let me introduce my wife Denise. Denise, this is Alex, my roommate from Amherst, and his wife Helen."

"Nice to meet you." Denise inclined her head graciously. She wore a short boiled wool jacket in fuchsia over a dress of Impressionist-inspired floral print. Her hair-do indicated a recent trip to the beauty salon.

"So sorry to be late. We're not used to this kind of traffic. I had taken the train in this morning, and Denise drove into Boston to meet me, on- which way did you come?"

"93, it's called. Awful. Just ludicrous. I am lucky to be alive," Denise said, speaking with a distinct drawl.

"Sounds like a bottle of wine is in order, then," Alex suggested.

"Great idea. Hey Alex, you look great. You must not have gained a pound since college," Buck said. He pulled out a chair for Denise, and then sat down.

"He runs for exercise. I think that's his secret," Helen said. She would have liked it if Buck had said something similar to her.

"You don't look half bad yourself, Buck," Alex said.

"Aw, you're just being polite. I've put on 25 pounds since you last saw me," Buck said.

Denise cleared her throat. "30."

"Maybe. Maybe closer to 30," Buck admitted.

"Buck, I'm going to tell you, I thought I'd never see you again. After our wedding, we just never heard from you. I wasn't sure where you'd gone."

"Oh, I'm not the best at staying in touch," Buck said. He looked away, embarrassed.

"Well, at least you finally surfaced." Alex turned to Denise. "Denise, where are you from? How did you and Buck meet?"

"I'm from New Orleans," she said. "My father was hospitalized at one point at Tulane for some heart issues, and Buck was one of the residents on the team taking care of him."

"That's right," Buck said. "Even after that rotation was over for me, I kept going back to check on Denise's Dad, hoping to run into Denise. I finally worked up the courage to ask her out."

"That's such a nice story," Helen said.

"Yes, she's quite a catch, my Southern belle. Her family lives in one of those beautiful old mansions in the Garden District. Denise was a debutante; she made her debut at the annual ball for the Krewe of Endymion during Mardi Gras."

"Mardi Gras! How exciting!" Helen said. She laid her hands gracefully on either side of her dinner plate, to show off her manicure. She glanced at Denise's hands. The color of her nails was a near-perfect match of the vivid color of her jacket; however, Helen noted with satisfaction, she had short, stubby fingers. Even the best manicure couldn't fix that.

"Oh, well, the balls are nice, but the city gets so crowded with all the tourists, and you can't get around like you want. I'm always glad when Mardi Gras is over," Denise said.

"You won't have to worry about Mardi Gras crowds if you're living up here. Say, did you find a place?" Alex asked.

"Maybe. There's a house in Swampscott that's nice. Single family. Decent yard," Buck said.

"That place needs a lot of work. With Buck's hours, he's not going to be able to manage all that, so we'll have to pay a contractor, and we'll have to put a fortune into it before it's livable. We saw one house that was quite lovely but it's in someplace called Peabody, and I just don't think it's right for us. I wish we had looked into the real estate prices here before Buck accepted the offer they made him." Denise made a mournful face.

"Keep looking. Don't settle for the first thing the realtor shows you. You'll find your new home," Alex said.

*

Alex sat at the swivel chair by the desk in his library, spun away from his desk, and planted his hands on the antique globe that stood beside him. He gave the globe a push and watched it whirl before him. He smiled as it slowed, and he could read the names, all in Latin, inscribed over its parchment-colored surface. He especially liked the sea monster coiled in the middle of the Atlantic Ocean. *Was I born in the wrong time?* He wondered. *Could I have been one of the great explorers who found and mapped the New World? To have sailed with Columbus or Amerigo Vespucci! Or with Magellan, who circumnavigated the earth, proving it was possible. What courage the man had. What a feat!*

"Alex, dinner's ready," Helen called from the kitchen. Alex gave his globe a final spin, and then headed to have dinner with his family.

Alex, Helen and Mark sat down to dinner.

"I have some news," Mark said casually.

"Oh, what sweetheart?" Helen asked. Alex looked up with interest.

"I made the track team!"

"That's great, Mark. I didn't know you were trying out," Alex said.

"Well, I was afraid I wouldn't make it, so I didn't say anything till I was sure."

"You're too modest. You're a natural athlete," Alex said.

"Yeah, well, actually the coach said, didn't I want to go out for the football team. He thought my build was better for football."

"What'd you tell him?" Alex asked.

Mark muttered into his plate, "I said, well, my Dad was a track star and I wanted to do track too."

"Oh, Mark, thank you. What a nice thing to say." Alex said.

Later Helen and Alex sat together in Adirondack chairs on the patio in back of the house, finishing their wine. The muted greens and blues of the flagstones faded to non-descript gray as evening turned to night.

"Beautiful weather, isn't?" Alex said. "I love sitting out here. It's so peaceful."

"Yes, it's lovely," Helen whispered in reply.

*This is so wonderful. Let it stay just like this for a long time,* Alex told himself. Growing up he had yearned for a life of adventure. Sometimes, he still did. Ironically, he and Helen had settled down to a life not so different from that of his parents. His father. He missed his father. If only he could have met Mark. Alex would have loved to have other children, but none had come. But Mark was such a great kid. One great kid. That was enough. This life, this peaceful life with Mark and Helen, this was enough. He was content.

# CHAPTER 46

"Okay, Mark, now you're in high school. If anything happens to me, you're the man of the family," Alex said.

"Aw, Dad, is this going to be one of those serious discussions?"

"Sort of." Alex pushed his chair away from his desk and stepped over to the cabinet where he kept a small safe. "The combination to the lock of this safe is 8-23-14."

"Is 8-23 for my birthday?"

"Right. And you're in the high school class of 2014, so 14." Alex extracted the album containing his coin collection and gestured toward the interior of the safe. "Look in there. There's money for emergencies. So if anything ever happens where you or Mom needs cash and I'm not here, you can get money from the safe. Okay?"

Mark peered inside the safe. Two thick stacks of bills bound by rubber bands lay against the back of the safe. "Okay."

Alex opened his coin collection. "These coins of mine are also quite valuable. They could be sold in an emergency." He turned the heavy pages. "You know what I'd like to have? I'd really like to have coins with all five of the main successors of Alexander the Great."

Mark pondered before replying. Asked for more detail, his Dad could go on for quite a while, and would probably tell him much more than he wanted or needed to know. But Mark was curious, so he responded cautiously, "What do you mean, successors? Didn't he have a son who took over when he died?"

"He did, he had a son, born after he died, but the son was murdered."

"Wow. Why? Was he a bad ruler?"

"No, no." Alex shook his head vigorously. "He was killed while still young. He never got to rule. Alexander's generals had fought long and hard for him, and when Alexander died, the generals figured it was their turn. They didn't want to turn everything over to some kid to benefit from."

"Wow, sucks!"

"Yeah, true. The boy was the child of his wife, a beautiful Bactrian princess named Roxana. They were both killed- Roxana and the son, who was also called Alexander- some years later, in great secrecy. The generals weren't taking any chances."

"And this kid didn't do anything wrong?"

"Only to carry the blood of the great Alexander in his veins. Alexander had only one full sister; she was named Cleopatra. She was murdered too. The generals wanted no rivals."

"Cleopatra, like from Egypt?"

"Same name but different lady. The Egyptian Cleopatra was almost 300 years later. She came to a bad end too. She committed suicide rather than march in chains in Octavian's triumph. I have two coins with the Egyptian Cleopatra on them." Alex flipped the chronologically ordered pages. "See?"

"Kind of ugly." Mark was hazy on who exactly Octavian was. His Dad would gladly tell him all about it, but Mark had had his history lesson for the day and decided not to ask.

"Julius Caesar didn't think so. I believe the coins don't do her justice." The scene played out in Alex's mind: a beautiful supple carpet unrolled, and out tumbled a flushed teenager, desperate, uncertain, bold, proud, beautiful, the young Cleopatra, direct descendant of Alexander's general Ptolemy. What was the expression on Julius Caesar's face when he saw her? Shock? Surprise? Amusement? Was he instantly smitten? *What I wouldn't give to have been there*, Alex thought. *Mark is right about the coins- she does look rather severe.*

"Uh, maybe. I'll remember what you said about the safe," Mark said.

"Are we sailing tomorrow?"

"Yeah, definitely."

"Okay, see you at 5:30?"

"Yeah."

"Dinner's ready," Helen called from the kitchen.

"Let's go, big guy," Alex said and walked out of the library. He carried with him a copy of this month's *Archaeology*.

They sat together at the dining room table.

"This is delicious, Helen."

"Thanks," Helen said. Most of it was prepared food from Whole Foods that she had warmed up. Part of her felt that she could be making more of an effort in the kitchen, but if the people at Whole Foods do such a good job, why shouldn't she take advantage of it?

"Look at this article in *Archaeology*," Alex said, waving his magazine. "They've found a trunk with a treasure in coins, mostly from the time of Alexander the Great, in the ruins of the house of someone named Apollodorus. In Halicarnassus. There were some scrolls that have information about him, and some other things as well. He was a physician who served in the household of Antigonus, one of Alexander's generals. The scrolls haven't been fully translated yet. But they say here that the treasure will be on display at the archeological museum in Istanbul starting in May. What if we go there this summer for vacation?"

"Just to see some coins?" Helen said. Alex came up with some strange ideas.

"Well, no. We could fly into Istanbul, and there's so much to see there, and then we could visit some other places in the western part of Turkey. Think about it: Hagia Sophia, the Blue Mosque, Pergamon, Ephesus... It would be wonderful!"

Mark made a mental note to investigate the drinking age in Turkey.

"Oh, Alex, I'm sure it would but we finally found that beautiful resort on Maui that we all enjoyed. I was so hoping we could go back there again. Couldn't we?"

Mark remained silent. Never mind about the drinking age in Turkey.

*

"Mamá! Enough! I am one woman with a job that doesn't pay all that well. I cannot continue to pay for the taxes and upkeep on this huge house *and* for Elena's private school," Catalina said. *It would also help if you didn't need botox every six weeks,* she wanted to add, but held back. "Why don't you sell this house and move to a nice little apartment? You'd get plenty for the house and there'd be so much less maintenance to worry about."

"I can't move. You know that. I want to be right here when your father comes back. He bought me this house." Anita's voice dropped to a whisper. "Bad enough that he is wrongly imprisoned on some trumped-up charges. What a slap in the face if I turned around and sold his home!"

Cati decided not to address the issue of wrongful imprisonment. "Papá would not care. He's a practical man. You could talk to him about it, you know."

"Why don't you and Ricky move in here, and get rid of your apartment? There's plenty of room." Anita gestured at the broad expanse of the kitchen and the spacious family room beyond it.

*Because you drive Ricky nuts and it will end with our divorce!* "No, it's better for me and Ricky to have our own place. We like our apartment."

"Each to her own. But I am not moving from the house your father gave me! It is our home."

Catalina waved the tax bill. "I can't pay this, Mamá. Not with everything else."

Elena had been hovering silently near the door. "Abuelita, Tía Cati is right. It's too much for her. If it will help, I can go to public school in the fall."

Anita paled. "Oh, no, Elenita! I want you in a good Catholic school."

"Your children survived public school. I turned out okay. So did JC. Why can't Elena go?" *And why the hell can't Hector get off his butt and earn a few dollars to help out?*

"Let me, please. I want to help." Elena looked at Anita with gleaming emerald eyes. She hated the bossy old nuns who ran her all-girls' school. Brookline High School couldn't be half as bad as St. Anastasia's.

*

Elena was pleased. Abuelita had consented to her leaving that dreadful St. Anastasia's School. She would be attending Brookline High School in the fall. BHS was a huge high school with lots of clubs and sports and activities and lots of boys. She would actually look forward to going to school. And now, Tía Cati had gone home and Abuelita had gone to take a nap. She was alone.

She tiptoed to the kitchen and began her special ritual. She pulled the over-heavy Cheerios box from the shelf, pulled out the waxed paper bag, extracted the underlying heavy object and laid it on the floor. She carefully unfolded the towel to reveal the silvery pistol. She brushed the cold steel with the tips of her fingers. She smiled when she recalled the first time she had done this. She was just a kid then. She had needed a chair to reach the box, and she had been afraid to touch the gun. She had just opened the towel and folded it right back up. But now she was familiar with it, her secret friend. She had figured out how to check for bullets, and she knew it was loaded. She picked it up slowly and held it, like they held guns on TV. She tossed her mass of wavy black hair behind her shoulders and posed like that, with the gun.

She wondered whose gun it was. Probably her grandfather's, the one she had never met. Abuelita insisted that he was in the witness protection program, and couldn't come home for a few more years, but Elena knew that he was in prison. She had read about it on-line. She really wanted to meet him; he sounded cool. Or maybe, could the gun belong to her mysterious father? Abuelita said he was the most handsome boy she had ever known, but he couldn't come home because of his career in acting in New York City. It took all of his time and concentration, she had said. Her evil mother Marisol had abandoned Hector and Elena when they had needed her most, and Hector had given Elena into the care of his own mother, because he trusted her to raise Elena right. Elena had talked to her father on the phone a few times, but he always sounded sleepy or sick or something. Some actor. No wonder he didn't get hired. One day she would meet him in person, Abuelita had promised. Elena used to look forward to that so much, but after so many years of waiting, if he ever showed up, she would tell him to fuck himself because he was such a shitty father.

Elena heard a small sound from upstairs. Abuelita! She might be on her way down. Elena quickly folded the gun into its towel, replaced it in its box and quietly closed the pantry door.

# CHAPTER 47

Alex hovered near the entrance to the hospital cafeteria and peered down the hall. At last, there was Buck, hurrying towards him.

"Hey, let's eat. I'm starved. I'm going for a burger." An empty cafeteria tray hung vertical from Alex's right hand.

"Denise has been nagging me about my weight. I guess I'll hit the salad bar," Buck said, and sighed.

"Okay. Whoever gets food first, head towards that corner and grab a table." Alex gestured to his left, using the tray.

A little while later they sat together at a table topped with beige Formica.

"Congratulations on finding a house. It sounds great," Alex said.

"Yeah, it's a nice little house, three bedrooms so Sandra and Leo can each have their own room. Near Newton Center, which Denise says she finds charming. It cost more than we were hoping to spend but turns out there's an opportunity now for covering extra ER shifts. I think I'll do that, bring in some extra money so Denise can get all the furniture she wants."

Alex shook his head. "I'm glad that phase is behind us. We were able to buy in Brookline, a bargain for that town, but a real fixer-upper. It's finally done and furnished, but I wouldn't want to do it again. Helen's happy with it; that's what's important."

"Yeah, what is it with women and houses? Does it really matter that much? I'd be okay renting an apartment, but Denise won't hear of it."

"I agree. Back when Mark was little, I asked Helen, look, what if we just took off for a year, took a plane to Greece, got a boat and sailed from one Greek island to another? I had just finished my residency and Mark wasn't in school yet. We wouldn't have another chance to do this for years. We had saved money for a down payment on a house. I said let's use that and have an incredibly special year. But she was scared, probably thought I was crazy. I said we could make that money back easily. I was an able-bodied man with an M.D. and a good residency on my CV. We wouldn't have anything to worry about. Then she started to cry, saying she really wanted us to have our own house. Stuff like that. Just about broke my heart. So I shelved that plan, took a staff position here and here I've been ever since. Maybe one day. Maybe after Mark finishes school."

*

Mark Eastgard and his friends Gary and Ringo slouched on a bench near the main entrance to Brookline High School.

"Should we go in?" Ringo asked.

"No. No way. We have five minutes more of summer vacation and I'm not giving up a millisecond," Mark said.

"Want a cigarette?" Gary proffered a pack of Marlboros to Ringo.

"Sure." Ringo took one and lit it from Gary's cigarette.

"Mark?" Gary asked.

"Nah. I want to do track again this year. Smoking slows me down."

"Fine, Mr. Health-conscious. I don't want to corrupt you."

A vintage Mercedes pulled up to the front of the school, the right front door opened, and a teenage girl with a mass of wavy dark hair stepped out. As soon as the car drove away, the girl slipped off her zippered sweatshirt to reveal her magnificent breasts, bulging against a hot pink tank top.

All three boys followed her movements with interest.

Ringo whistled softly. "Damn, I never saw tits like that before."

"Me either. Not on anyone in high school. They're huge," Mark said.

"That is one set of bodacious tatas." Gary ground out his cigarette against the seat of the bench and leaned forward. "Nice junk in her trunk too."

"I'm going to say hello," Mark said.

"No, you won't. You don't have the balls," Ringo said.

"She's new. I'm just trying to be nice. Polite. That's all." Mark stood.

"Someone like that, she has a boyfriend already. Probably some guy in college," Gary said, and leaned back. He wondered if there was time for another cigarette.

"Why shouldn't I talk to her? I can be very charming," Mark said and grinned.

"10 to 1 she tells you to fuck off," Gary said.

"I'm going over," Mark said.

339

"Bullshit," Gary muttered.

"I'll enjoy seeing you crash and burn. Go ahead." Ringo rested his elbows on his thighs.

"Here I go, asshole. Just watch me." Mark sauntered over while his friends stared.

"She's not going to talk to him," Gary opined.

"Look at him. Trying to be cool." Ringo snickered.

"Girls do think he's hot. Sometimes, anyway."

"He looks so gay! Pretty face, you know."

"Girls go for that."

"Yeah, true."

"Damn. She's smiling at him. Damn. Look at her, shoving her tits in his face. He's got all the luck." Gary groaned.

"God, they're huge. Each one is bigger than Mark's head. I'd love to get my hands on them."

"Too late now. Look at her, giggling and throwing her hair around. She loves the attention."

"I know. I mean, we *gave* her to him. That could be one of us over there."

"The world is just not fair."

*

"Well, Buck, I just realized it's been six months since you started here. Let's toast." Alex lifted his Coke and tapped it against Buck's Diet Coke. "How do you like it so far?" He and Buck sat in molded plastic chairs at the cafeteria table they always occupied on Tuesdays at 1pm.

"It's okay, not bad. Pace is faster than where I was before, but it's okay."

"Are you still doing those extra shifts?"

"Yeah, well, Denise decided we needed some renovations after all, so I'm still doing that. You know, the salaries are not bad but everything up here costs so much more than what we're used to."

"I'm just asking cause you look kind of, I don't know, tired," Alex said.

"I am! I drink too much coffee. I'm so caffeinated I have a tremor." Buck extended his hand to demonstrate. "Good thing I'm not in surgery!"

Alex laughed. "I can relate. A lot of days I feel like I'm running on Starbucks and borrowed time."

"So even Pathology is busy? Where I was before they never worked past 5. In fact, Path was usually dark, with phones sent to voicemail by 4."

"It's really busy here. Lots and lots of biopsies to review, then struggle with the computer to sign them out. Plus, we have so many meetings! Yesterday I had 3 hours of meetings and didn't leave until 8 at night. No meetings and I could have left at 5. Plus, the atmosphere has changed over time. There used to be a slower pace, a sense of history and tradition, time to pause and think. Now, things are different. More corporate. But health care has changed so much, and I guess the hospital has to do what's necessary to survive. But the bureaucracy!"

Buck nodded thoughtfully. "Yeah, you think it's going to get easier, but it doesn't."

"Exactly," Alex responded. "Here I am, over 40, and every morning I'm up at 5:30 and hit the ground running and barrel through the day just to keep up. I mean, I don't mind, I work with great people, and I think I do a good job getting patients their diagnoses. But mostly I think I'm willing to work this hard for my family, to make their lives better."

"Preaching to the choir."

"I think about it sometimes- when was the last time I had a significant amount of free time? That was in high school. Then Amherst was pretty tough, and in med school, it was a challenge to find the time to eat and sleep. Now, it's better than that but still quite stressful."

"I know, I know. I wonder how much longer I can keep up this pace. When this round of renovations is paid for, I'm dropping the extra shifts before I drop."

"You get to spend time with the kids?" Alex asked.

"Some. On the weekend. When I'm not on call. I get home late on weekdays."

"It's hard, I know. I bring work home and do it after dinner, so I can have a chance to spend time with Helen and Mark. And in summer at least twice a week I leave in time to go sailing with Mark after work. No matter what. I'll stay late the next night to catch up."

"That's good. I should just focus and move faster. I need to get home earlier."

They paused in their conversation to take a few bites of their lunch.

"Say, Alex. Do you ever regret changing your major from history? You really loved it."

"I don't know. I don't think about it. I still read a lot of history, so it's not as though I've given it up."

*

Alex looked up from his microscope. *How do I feel?* He asked himself. *Tired,* he answered. He stood and walked to the secretarial area and poured himself a cup of murky coffee from the last pot of the day. It was scalding hot, and thick and bitter after several hours of sustained heat. Alex returned to his office. He was lucky to have such a big window. He used to have a wonderful view of Beacon Hill, but sadly, so many new towers had sprung up at the hospital that they now comprised his view. He couldn't see the sky at all. He could see the reflection of the sky in the mirror-shiny Manchester Oncology Building across a small courtyard from his office. He gazed at the clouds drifting across the glossy surface of the new building and sighed.

This month's edition of *Science* lay on his desk. Professor Rheingold's lab had published a paper describing dramatic response of a subset of patients with advanced melanoma using targeted therapy. *I wish I'd been part of that,* Alex thought, profoundly regretful. *But Helen would have been unhappy, and anyway, the important thing is that it got done.*

As evening approached, the reflection of the setting sun bounced off the Manchester Building and blazed into his office. He wondered if he could get shades or something. He could ask but would probably be told it was a capital expense and would have to wait for the next budget cycle.

# CHAPTER 48

Anita and Elena emerged from the Starbucks on Harvard Street. Anita had finished her cafe latte inside, but Elena still had half of her frappuccino. Elena stopped suddenly.

"Abuelita, see that boy across the street? The tall one, in front of the taco place. See him? Isn't he cute?"

"Very. When I was your age, we'd call someone like that *un papacito.* '*Mira qué papacito,*' we would say."

"He's in my grade at Brookline High School. He's really nice. His name is Mark. I like BHS so much better than St. Anastasia's." Elena waited until Mark had turned in her direction, then she waved. He smiled and waved back. Knowing his eyes were on her, Elena gently took the plastic straw of her drink in her fingers, opened her mouth and lowered it to the straw. She pursed her lips around the straw, closed her eyes as if in bliss, and drew frappuccino slowly into her mouth. She raised her head, opened her eyes, smacked her lips and gave a deep, contented sigh. Mark watched transfixed.

"You certainly are enjoying that drink!" Anita said.

"Yes, it's delicious." Elena turned her back on Mark, threw him one last quick smile over her shoulder, took her grandmother's arm and swaggered down Harvard Street.

*

Alex sat at their regular table in the far corner of the cafeteria. No sign of Buck yet, but he often got held up in clinic. Alex took a bite of his sausage pizza and let his eyes scan the room. *There he is!* Alex waved, and then popped open his Coke.

Buck dropped into the chair across from Alex. His white styrofoam tray held a cup of soup with a plastic lid and a cellophane package of two saltine crackers.

"Are you trying to make me feel guilty? You could have gotten some real food. Take some of my pizza," Alex said.

"No, I have to watch my weight," Buck whispered. He hung his head.

"Hey, Buck, what's the matter?" Buck looked awful; was he starting to tear up?

"It's okay. It's nothing."

"Hey, buddy, come on. What's on your mind?"

Buck listlessly stirred the watery minestrone but would not meet Alex's eyes.

"Everything okay at work? At home? I mean, you don't have termites in that nice new house or anything?"

Buck shook his head. "Nothing like that."

"Then what's wrong? Can I help?" Alex set down his pizza.

Buck stopped stirring his soup and folded his hands together. "It's Denise. She's not happy. Partly, she's away from her family in New Orleans. She doesn't know anyone here." He laughed sadly. "No, that's wrong. She doesn't know many people here."

"But she liked Newton, liked the neighborhood. It just takes time to get to know people. Helen could take her around, introduce her to her friends."

Buck kept his head down. "We had a big fight last night. She said I didn't make time for her and the kids. I worked all the time, she said."

"But you were doing the extra ER shifts so she could fix up the house! Just stop doing that and spend the time with her instead."

"Alex, it might be too late for that."

"What do you mean?"

"I think, I believe, she is, ah, cheating on me."

"Oh, Buck, no. It can't be. Are you sure?"

Buck nodded. "They meet during the day while the kids are at school."

"Have you talked to her about this? Did she admit it?"

"No, not exactly, but, see, she'd been raving about this chiropractor she found, how wonderful he was. So last night I said, since when do you need to go to the chiropractor 3 days a week? That's when she started in about not making time for her, and I just know, I just know she's been, you know…" He shrugged miserably.

"That doesn't really sound definite. Why don't you take her someplace nice, romantic, for dinner and discuss all this?"

"It's definite. I looked on her phone. You should see the texts." Buck picked up his spoon and resumed absently stirring his soup.

"You looked on her phone?" Suddenly Alex recalled his fishing through the trash to see who had written to Helen. He looked away for a moment.

"Okay, I'm not proud of it but I had to know. Now I know." He propped one elbow on the table and rested his forehead against his hand.

"Buck, I'm so sorry. If I can do anything, let me know. If you want to stay with us, you're welcome, any time."

*

That night, after dinner, Alex waited until Mark left the table. Then he turned to Helen. "I had lunch with Buck today. He told me Denise is seeing another man. Buck is just broken. He bent over backwards for her, and this is how she treats him."

A cold shiver swept through Helen. She forced herself to speak calmly. "That's terrible. Buck is so nice."

"I know. He's a great guy."

"You know, I didn't really like her. That time we had dinner. There was something, I don't know, snooty about her." Helen spoke softly, murmuring into her coffee cup.

"Whatever she is, she did the worst thing a woman can do to a man."

Helen was silent. From far away she imagined the sound of harsh laughter, directed at her.

*

Alex watched as Buck approached their regular cafeteria table. He looked even worse than he had last time they had met. His hair was badly combed and his tie was askew. Buck pulled out a chair and sat.

"Alex, I-, I talked to a lawyer today. It's bad. Not the money part, I mean, although," he laughed nervously, "I'll be basically ruined financially. But she's saying I'm neglectful. Can you believe it?"

"That's so unfair! You were working extra to make her happy and provide a better home."

"I know! I know! But she's trying to keep me from the kids. She says she wants full custody."

"Wait a minute. If she has the kids all the time, how is she going to spend time with the chiropractor? It just doesn't make sense. I think she's trying to manipulate you. Or maybe it's not her. Maybe her lawyer. Sometimes they make things worse."

345

"She says I'm unfit. Unfit!" Beads of sweat dotted Buck's forehead.

"Why? In what way? You work too much?"

"What she says, well. With all this going on I've been stressed out of my mind. Can't sleep. So I've been taking a few pills to get through it. She found them and says I have a problem. Like half of Boston isn't on Prozac. She said, wouldn't the Board of Registration in Medicine like to know about the prescriptions I'm writing for myself. Stood there, hands on hips, and snapped that out at me. I mean, I could lose my license."

Poor Buck, Alex thought. "That sounds really extreme. I'd be happy to speak up for you, speak to your character. Write a letter. Anything."

"Yeah, that wouldn't hurt."

"And the Board won't revoke your license without proof. Writing yourself scripts for a few pills for a few weeks won't do it. But what a thing to threaten!"

Buck sat silent for some moments before speaking. "There's something else. When we first got together for dinner, remember you said I had been out of touch?" Buck asked, then abruptly he stopped.

"What is it?" Alex prompted.

Buck gave a heavy sigh. "I had had to take a year off. I couldn't cope. I was diagnosed with depression. I took that year off and got my act together, and I was fine. I met Denise not long after that. She knows about the whole thing. So the other night she kept saying I had to disclose that, I had to disclose that, had I disclosed that, when I applied for my Mass license. If I didn't, I would lose my license, she said. And I certainly wasn't fit to care for the kids."

Alex reached over and put his hand on Buck's shoulder. "You got through it once; you can do it again."

He glanced around and then leaned close to Alex. "Oh, no. I'm not done. It keeps getting better. This wasn't good, but I need to tell someone." He paused and looked around again. "As she was harassing me, I just got so down. I'd had a drink. Then maybe one or two more."

"Were you, ah, okay?"

Another pause. "Not really. No, I was not okay. She was really baiting me, and I started yelling at her. I- I even threw an empty wine bottle at her. I mean, I missed. But it was terrible. I- I was terrible. Kids were home. Sandra started crying. Leo came out, Leo came out and put his arm around Sandra, as though to protect her. I was so ashamed! And worst of all, that witch taped it on her phone. She taunted me about that. 'Wait'll the court sees this of you yelling like a crazy person and waving a bottle!' She said." Tears collected on his eyelashes. "I'm going to lose everything!"

"Jesus, Buck, I'm so sorry."

# CHAPTER 49

Alex checked his cell phone: 5:08 pm. He dropped the phone into a side pocket on his gym bag and hoisted the bag onto his shoulder. As he reached for the knob of the door of his office, his cell spewed forth its customary jangle, indicating an incoming call. He pulled it out and answered it, while pulling his door shut behind him.

"Buck, what's up?"

"Listen, do you have time for a cup of coffee? I need a break. I need to see a friendly face." It was a plea.

"I'm just on my way to the Esplanade to go sailing with Mark. Why don't you come?" Alex purposely made his tone upbeat. He felt for Buck, but he needed to get out of the hospital, into the fresh air, out onto the water.

"I- I don't know. I wouldn't be good company."

"Come on! Weather's beautiful, and it won't be warm enough to sail for much longer this year."

"I- no, I wouldn't want to intrude."

"You wouldn't be intruding. You'd enhance our experience. Mark loves to show off!" Alex spoke enthusiastically but he was ambivalent. He wanted to help Buck if he could, but Buck would likely cast a dark shadow on their boating, and it wouldn't be the carefree activity with Mark he treasured so much.

"No, I'm not in the mood."

Alex hid his relief. "Okay, fine, but will you come for dinner after? We usually go to King and I."

There was a long pause as Alex hurried down the main corridor of the hospital. Had the call dropped? But finally, Buck answered. "Sure. Thai sounds good. Call when you're back on dry land."

Alex strode across the footbridge to the Esplanade. There was Mark, approaching from the opposite direction. He was a good-looking boy. With dark hair, like Alex's mom. Funny how that skipped a generation. When had he gotten so tall?

And then they were in their sleek little sailboat, racing into the glittering water, sailing upriver to the BU boathouse, and then back downriver, all the while zigzagging back and forth across the river.

"Can we avoid the other innocent sailboats, please?" Alex asked. "That last one was close."

"Ah, you worry too much. I was nowhere near them." Mark waved jovially at the sailboat he had nearly sideswiped. The two girls on board laughed and waved back.

"Yeah. Just close enough to check out those girls. I used to be young, you know."

Mark laughed and headed back to the dock.

Alex watched with approval. *My wonderful son. Smart. Strong. Capable. Handsome too, no doubt about it. This is tame compared to the sailing I used to imagine for myself, but it's with Mark, and that's good. It's enough.* They climbed onto the dock and secured their sailboat.

"Buck's not answering," Alex said and frowned. He hit call again and waited. No answer. "Do you mind if we swing past his office?"

"Yeah, sure."

"I'm looking forward to you meeting him. We were roommates in college, then he was the best man at our wedding." Alex pocketed his phone.

"Oh, cool," Mark said automatically. His Dad and this other guy would be reminiscing about Amherst all through dinner. Thank god for iPhones! He pulled out his phone, hit the Facebook icon and grinned. Elena had posted some new photos. Looked like that vacation she had taken in Mexico over the summer. There she was, her gorgeous body in a skimpy red bikini, sipping a frozen umbrella drink, flanked by several guys. Mark frowned. Then he realized they were dressed as waiters, not fellow-vacationers, and felt better. She looked right at him with bright green eyes half-covered by lids heavy with thick black lashes.

"What are you smiling about?" Alex asked.

"Oh, just checking Facebook. Some people have posted new pics."

"This way. His office faces Cambridge Street. Look, there's an ambulance. And a police car. I hope nothing happened."

Alex flashed his hospital ID and they entered the building. As he headed toward Buck's office, a pair of grim-faced EMTs passed them, heading outside. Alex felt his heart start pounding. He walked faster. He glanced at Mark, blissfully unaware of any problem, texting on his iPhone as they walked. A large policeman blocked the door to the suite where Buck had his office.

"Officer, could I ask what's going on here?" Alex asked, trying to see past the policeman.

"There's been an incident. You should be on your way unless you have business here."

"Well, actually, I do. I was meeting a friend for dinner. His office is through there. I called but he didn't answer his phone."

"Friend's name is what?"

"Dr. Scott Buckminster."

The officer half-turned and called out over his shoulder, "What's the decedent's ID?"

From within, someone responded, "Buckminster."

"Decedent?" Alex whispered.

"Go on through. They may want to take a statement from you," the big officer said, stepping aside.

"Dad, I'll wait out here," Mark said, and found a chair.

Alex walked softly into Buck's office. Before him on the ground was a body, under a white sheet. Another policeman stood guard, while a detective and personnel from the office of the medical examiner stood nearby, speaking in hushed tones. The variegated blue-toned institutional carpet all around was stained rusty red with blood.

Alex knelt down by the body. "Can you tell me what happened? He was my friend. We were supposed to have dinner tonight."

"He was a friend? How long you know him?" the detective asked.

"Many years. We were roommates in college and he was best man at our wedding."

"When did you last see him, or speak to him?"

"A couple hours ago we talked on the phone. I was going sailing with my son. He wouldn't go sailing with us but agreed to come to dinner after."

"He called your cell?"

"Yes. Yes, he did."

"Mind if I take a look at your phone?"

"Sure." Alex pulled out his phone, entered the password and brought up his recent calls. "There's his call. From Buck."

The detective noted the time of the call. He tapped 'Buck office' on Alex's phone. After a short delay the phone on Buck's desk began to ring. The detective nodded and ended the call. "We have his wallet with his license, but can you also confirm his identity?"

"Yes, of course."

The detective pulled the sheet back, exposing Buck's bloodless face, staring up at him wide-eyed.

"Yes," Alex said, voice catching. "That's Buck, Scott Buckminster." His right hand trembled as he reached over and closed Buck's eyes.

The detective stood and spoke. "Cleaning lady was emptying trash. Door to this office was locked but she saw the fresh blood oozing out from under the door and called her supervisor."

"What, ah, how did he...?"

"Looks like the poor devil slit his wrists. Would he have had any reason to do himself harm?"

"He, ah, was in the beginning of a bad divorce." He lapsed into silence, and finally added, "His wife had broken his heart."

The detective nodded sadly. "I see. Well, leave us your contact information. We may have some additional questions."

Alex complied and left, stunned.

When he returned to the lobby, Mark looked at him anxiously. "It was your friend?" Mark asked.

Alex nodded.

"Did he, I mean, what,"

"It was pretty bad. Let's go home." Alex paused. *When Buck asked me to have coffee, why didn't I go? Mark wouldn't have minded. This might not have happened. It didn't have to happen. But now it's too late.*

They headed for the garage.

That night Alex lay awake, the day's tragedy playing over and over in his mind. Buck must have done it right after they talked. It would have taken a while to lose so much blood, and they had found him less than two hours after their phone call. Maybe Buck had held the blade in his hand while they were on the phone. Alex imagined him pressing a razor, or a scalpel blade, against his skin while they spoke, and slicing deep into the soft tissue of his wrist as soon as the connection was broken. While they had sliced through the water, Buck had sliced through his veins. He imagined Buck slumped over, completely alone as his life slipped away from him, alone and miserable. When Alex finally slept, he dreamt of Buck. There was his pale face, drained of blood, eyes bulging out at him, and then the face blurred and it was Patrick, staring at him with big sad eyes. He awoke with a start, gasping for air and sweating. He turned toward Helen. She lay peacefully on her side of the bed, her flawless profile just visible in the in the faint glow from the streetlights that filtered in through the sheer curtains of their bedroom. She slept quietly, lost in her dreams, covers pulled primly up to her shoulders. *Look at her, so peaceful, so innocent, not weighed down by my cares and my- my guilt. She really keeps me going, she and Mark do.*

# CHAPTER 50

Helen stood in front of the mirror, tying the frothy bow at the neck of her crêpe de chine blouse and frowned. Where did this double chin come from? She had to do something about her weight. She wasn't fat. Not at all, not really overweight. She was a size 10, at least with the better brands that were not so stingy with fabric. More often a 12. That was only average. Not bad, compared to how some women let themselves go. Although there had been that awful episode at Lord and Taylor's when the salesgirl, trying to be helpful, handed her a size 14 dress to try on. Helen had told the girl she didn't want that dress after all and had fled. But she used to be size 4! Now size 4 was a distant memory. She sighed.

Then there was Alex- he still looked great, she reflected, not an extra pound on him. All that running he did outdoors had aged his skin a little, and he had a touch of gray at his temples, but otherwise he had barely changed since they married. She glanced at the clock. She had to hurry and finish getting ready to go to the restaurant. Today was for Mark, a celebration for him, with the whole family. She descended the stairs. There was Alex, the perfect gentleman, holding her coat for her. Mark stood nearby, looking so grown up and handsome in his new Brooks Brothers suit, texting away as usual.

"You'll need your gloves, sweetie; it's gotten so cold," Alex reminded her. And then they were off.

Alex had decided to splurge; he had reserved a private room at Toscano's for this family dinner. Helen's parents arrived first, then Olivia and then Kelly and Aggie and their children. Alex noted with surprise that in addition to her special occasion pearl jewelry, his mother was wearing a new dress, with ecru lace trim at the cuffs.

"You look nice, Mom."

Olivia gave a tight little smile and nodded a thank you.

"Mark, look at you, in a suit! You're just perfect!" Leda shook her head in wonder, as Mark hovered on the threshold, flanked by his parents.

*You're just perfect.* Helen's mind wandered back over the years. *You're just perfect,* Hector had said. She lay naked on his bed, waiting for him, his music playing softly in the background. *I can't decide which perfect part of you to enjoy first. Or next.* She started to sit, to extend her arms to him. *No,* he had said. *I forbid you to move. Lie down.* She lay back, trembling. He knelt at her feet and gripped her ankles. A glistening drop of semen crowned the peaked column of his penis, dusky in the dimly lit bedroom. And then the irresistible dance of his hands along her limbs, her face, her body. His fingers, along her lips, and in her fair hair. His breath came harsh and fast, keeping time with the rhythm of his salsa. Then he had touched her, to see if she was ready for him. And then- was that the beginning of Mark?

What would he think of her now? He might not even recognize her. She was no longer the perfect girl he knew. Nobody gave her a second look on the street anymore. And he- Hector- he had been so beautiful. His physique, his thick black hair. What did he look like now?

Kelly snapped her fingers in Helen's face. "Where are you? Come back to us!"

Kelly's children Orrin and Ellen exchanged a glance. *Mom is so embarrassing,* it said.

Helen flushed and looked down. "What? Oh, sorry, I was daydreaming."

"About what?" Kelly asked, with a hint of sarcasm in her voice.

"About when Mark was- very young. He was always a wonderful boy," Helen said. And indeed, he had been. She and Alex had raised him together, and he had stayed wonderful. She watched as Mark leaned over to speak to Alex. Alex smiled and clapped Mark on the back. Perhaps it had worked out for the best, after all. Despite wanting more children, none had come. Having Mark was a thousand times better than being childless, even if he had not started off the right way. Her affair with Hector was wrong, but she had been stupid, lonely and bored, and away from home for the first time. The result was Mark, who was perhaps meant to be. She gazed across the table at Alex. He was so good and caring and responsible, the opposite of Hector. Whatever Hector had been to her, that was an illusion. Alex was real. She had grown to love Alex, not with the madness she had felt for Hector, but with a better, longer lasting, comfortable kind of love. She was lucky. She didn't deserve all the good things she had ended up with, and she was very grateful. Alex had not been so lucky, at least not lately. He had reconnected with Buck after so many years, and now Buck was gone. It had been several months, but Alex had still had not recovered from Buck's death. Today he was quiet, but he was smiling a little. Perhaps he was starting to get over it.

"That's right! Mark is a wonderful kid. Let's toast!" Tim raised his glass. "To Mark! Congratulations on getting into BU."

"That's right! Congratulations! Boston University is one lucky school." Leda echoed.

"Thanks! I'm glad they took me and I'm glad the decision where to go is behind me," Mark said.

"I'm glad you'll still be close by. Feels safer," Helen said.

"What are you going to major in?" Leda asked.

"Pre-med. Like Dad."

"Only do pre-med if that's what you love. Don't do it for me," Alex said.

"It is what I love. You worry too much," Mark said.

"Y'all hear that? Study hard and you can get into BU pre-med like your cousin, and from there you can, I don't know, save the world or something," Aggie said.

"It could use some saving!" Kelly proclaimed.

Orrin and Ellen exchanged another glance. This one said, *Mom, give it a rest!*

"Olivia, is your drink okay?" Leda asked. Olivia was usually on her second Manhattan by now, but her first one sat in front of her, barely touched, and she had been unusually quiet. "We can have the waiter freshen that one for you."

"Oh, ah, no, I have a bit of indigestion today," Olivia replied. She paused, opened her mouth to speak, then stopped, pursed her lips and shuddered.

"Mom, are you okay?" Alex asked. He rose from his chair and started toward Olivia.

Suddenly she lurched forward and vomited blood. Three waves of spasms seized her, dashing her against the table, each time with a violent torrent of bright red blood. Olivia frantically tried to contain it with her napkin, but it covered the table, spilled into her lap and splattered onto the floor.

"Mark, call 911!" Alex shouted and ran to Olivia's chair. There was so much blood! Could she have an ulcer? A bleeding disorder? Leukemia? But the vomiting stopped, as suddenly as it had started. Mark's fingers shook as he tapped out 911 on his phone and handed it to Alex. Kelly stood, anxious to help, but uncertain what to do. Helen watched, silent, horrified.

Little Ellen leaped from her chair to cling to Aggie, covering her eyes with her hands and sobbing. "Daddy? Is it okay now? Can I look?"

Olivia sat, head bowed, sobbing. "I'm so sorry! What a mess I've made. I'm so sorry."

Leda dipped her napkin into her water glass and came to her side. She gently wiped her face. "Don't apologize. You got sick, that's all."

"But what a mess! I've spoiled Mark's dinner. I'm so sorry." Olivia covered her face with bloody hands. Blood dribbled from her hands to the lace cuffs of her dress, and she sobbed.

"Don't worry about that. Let's worry about you," Leda said, her tone soft and comforting.

"An ambulance is on the way. I'm going to go with Mom," Alex said.

Mark leaned close to Olivia. "I love you, Grandma. It will be alright."

Tears streamed down Olivia's cheeks in response, and a little more blood dribbled from her mouth. Wordlessly she shook her head.

*

Four days had passed since the evening of the family dinner. For four days Olivia had lain in a hospital bed, waiting for the results of blood work, upper endoscopy, radiographic studies and finally, a liver biopsy. Alex was now back in his office after visiting his mother and discussing the results of all the studies with her mother's doctors. He rubbed his tired eyes. *Poor Mom! Alcoholic cirrhosis, with esophageal varices, the cause of her bleeding episode. There would have been some hope, but a hepatocellular carcinoma had silently arisen in the cirrhotic liver. Inoperable. She didn't have long. Dad is gone. Mom will be gone soon. I knew she drank too much. Why didn't I sit down with her, make her stop?*

As he rubbed, the skin moved across the bones of his face. Just as he lowered his hand he thought, *Sometime, maybe not so long from now, the skin will be gone and the bone will be all that's left of me.* His fingers returned to his cheek and traced the edge of the bone slowly, thoughtfully. Then the world will belong to Mark. It will be Mark's world. Or Helen's. He and Helen were the same age, but he couldn't imagine outliving Helen. Helen, still so beautiful. Alex felt like Anchises, espoused to Aphrodite. He grew old and weighed down by life, while his immortal goddess remained untouched by time. He sighed as he gazed upon a stack of resident evaluations, overdue as usual. *Forget it; I'm leaving.* He stood and made his way home.

# CHAPTER 51

Alex and Helen and Mark sat together at the dinner table.

"Mom has decided to stay at home. She doesn't want to go into the hospital if they can't offer her meaningful treatment," Alex said.

"She'll be there alone?" Helen asked.

"No, I have a visiting nurse coming every day for a few hours, and I'll go see her every day after work."

"Will a few hours a day be enough?" Helen asked.

"Mom said she didn't want a stranger hanging around and disrupting her routine. Her routine! She's only willing to have the nurse come and check on her, see if she needs something, and then leave."

Helen nodded. They sat in silence until Mark spoke.

"Mom, sorry to bother you about this, but can I have a check to pay for prom?"

Helen paused before answering and sighed. "Sure. Let me get the checkbook while I'm thinking of it. You have a date?"

"Yeah."

"Is she a nice girl?" Helen asked.

"Yeah." Seriously, what did Mom expect him to say?

"You know how you can tell a real lady? You look at her hands. A real lady takes good care of her hands," Helen said. She glanced at her own manicured fingers with satisfaction.

Alex raised his head and looked at Helen. "I say you look into her eyes. Windows into the soul. It's an old saying, but it's true."

Mark knew that getting a check for prom would require some polite listening to parental philosophy. He sat quietly waiting for it to finish.

"What's her name?" Helen asked.

"Elena."

"Elena. That's Spanish for Helen. Sounds promising," Alex said.

"You've never mentioned her before," Helen said. Helen told herself this was just a coincidence, but she had the inescapable sense of a net tightening around her. She cleared her throat and asked, "What's her last name?"

"Gonzalez," Mark answered.

"Gonzalez! Who are her parents?" Helen asked, hysteria creeping into her voice.

"Um, not sure," Mark answered. "Her grandmother raised her. Her mom abandoned the family and ran off and her dad lives in New York. He's too busy, and I mean he didn't know how to take care of a kid so anyway she got sent up here to be with her grandmother."

"What's the grandmother's name?" Helen asked desperately.

Mark shrugged. "I don't know. Mrs. Gonzalez. They live on Warren Street."

Helen began, "Mark, um,"

"Mark, they're not a nice family. You should stay away from them," Alex said, an unusual harshness in his voice.

Mark looked at Alex. "She's really nice. You'd like her." What was going on? He had long grown accustomed to an enviable only-child status, where everything he did met with approval.

"Dad is right. Stay away from her and her family. Please!" Helen wished that she understood. Did Hector have another child? Maybe with that witch he apparently lived with? Had Hector actually named that baby after her?

"I- I already asked her. I can't un-ask her. Why are you being like this? I'm worried about Grandma too, but," Mark said.

"This has nothing to do with Grandma. I don't like that family. They're bad people. If you already asked her, okay, take her to prom and then after please stay away from her and her family," Alex said.

"Promise us, Mark!" Helen said.

"But why?"

"For one thing, her grandfather is in jail," Helen said.

"Not just jail. He's in federal prison serving a long sentence for drug trafficking," Alex said.

"You can't hold against her something her grandfather did. Do you think I'm doing drugs or I will if I go out with Elena? Because I don't do drugs and neither does she."

"Mark, I need you to listen. That whole family is bad. Nothing but trouble," Alex said.

"This makes no sense." Mark pushed back his chair and stood up. "I'm going to do homework."

Alex watched him ascend the stairs. Mark knew, everyone knew, that Alex's best friend from high school had died in an auto accident but he had probably never heard about Hector's role in it. So Alex's reaction, and Helen's, seemed illogical to Mark. Part of Alex wished he could tell Mark the full story and make him understand. But another part of Alex could not bear to recount the details. And what if Mark responded that it was so long ago, before Elena was even born, why should it matter? It would break Alex's heart.

*

Olivia sat in her customary chair in front of the TV, aware that the news was on, but not really listening. She was tired, but if she tried she would be able to stand and get around alright. What should she do with her remaining good days? She dragged herself to her feet, shuffled to the pantry, pulled out a trash bag and headed for her bedroom. She would start with her undergarments. She critically examined each bra, each pair of underwear, each slip. Any that was not in pristine condition was dropped into the trash bag. *When I'm gone, I don't want people going through my things and finding worn underwear*, she told herself. She collected all the bottles of all the alcohol that she had in the house, emptied them all in the sink and put the bottles out for recycle. *They say that my cocktails are what have made me sick; it seems ridiculous. Right or wrong, they won't find any evidence of it here in my home.* Cocktails now made her nauseated anyway. She was terrified of vomiting and starting to bleed again. Better to throw it all away. Day after day, she went room by room, slowly, painstakingly vacuuming, sweeping, dusting. At times the pain and the fatigue were almost more than she could bear, and she would lean against the wall to steady herself before continuing. And eventually the house was rendered immaculate. *People will be amazed at how clean this place is*, she told herself. *If I can do this, maybe I have some time yet.* But she sank onto the couch, completely drained of energy, abdomen swollen with fluid, the pressure of the cancer against her back a throbbing, incessant ache that became worse every day. She looked out onto the backyard, sitting as still as possible to diminish the pain, and watched as afternoon slowly evolved to evening, and light became dark.

Olivia was sitting on the couch wearing a loose house dress and sandals over flesh-tone nylon peds when Alex arrived. He noticed her abdomen, distended by fluid, as he sat down across from her.

"Don't ask me how I am. I feel awful." She spoke haltingly. The fluid pressed up against her diaphragm, Alex knew, and it was hard for her to fully inflate her lungs.

"Okay." Alex paused. "Can I get you anything?"

Olivia sat silent for a long while before responding. "I think I'd like to go to the hospital now. I'd like them to drain this fluid."

"Mom, I'll do whatever you want, but you understand- the fluid will come back after a while."

"I fully realize that. But anything would be an improvement. Perhaps, perhaps also there is something stronger they can give me for pain." No emotion showed on her face, but Alex knew it was hard for her to ask for help.

"I'll take care of it, Mom. Whatever you need," Alex said.

*

Olivia sat in her hospital bed, back ramrod straight, as usual. "Alex, I know this thing will end my life one day. It's frightening, having no control." She squeezed his hand.

Alex sat next to her, his head bowed, amazed that she clasped his hand so tightly, she who had always been so aloof, so controlled.

Olivia continued, "I wonder how many more times I will say, 'thank you for my tray, because I just love hospital jello; thank you for this tea.' How many more times will I change my clothes or do my hair? I wonder if I will ever walk around the block again. I suppose I won't ever buy shoes again. Isn't that strange to think? I wonder how many more times I will awaken?"

"I hope you will awaken many more times, Mom," Alex mumbled and forced himself to smile. He studied his mother's visage. The edges of her platysma had separated and now they stood as rigid cords tethering her chin to her torso.

"You know, I look at that tube of Colgate in there," she gestured toward the bathroom, "and I wonder whether I or that tube of toothpaste will run out first." She paused and then, "the way I feel today, I think the toothpaste will last longer. And I'm afraid to go to sleep, because I know I may not wake up in the morning."

For some minutes there was silence and then she said, "Alexander, you are the best son any mother could have. I love you so much."

Alex trembled. His previously omnipotent mother rarely expressed emotion. "I love you too, Mom." Tears streamed down his cheeks.

Alex returned the following night to his mother's hospital room. Olivia appeared alert, but weak and apprehensive. They exchanged a few sentences, but when the nurse arrived, she seemed eager to receive that evening's morphine, which allowed her to ease into sleep. The next two nights, she was more drowsy but seemed comfortable, and she murmured a few short replies to Alex's simple queries. But the following night when Alex arrived, without opening her eyes, she muttered a few words that he could not understand. He sat in a chair next to her bed, waiting for her to speak. He took her hand, but she did not seem to know. As the minutes passed into hours she entered a deep sleep, and he could not awaken her. Her breathing turned strange, labored, irregular, punctuated by harsh snoring. Her mouth was open, baring her teeth. It was terrible, heartrending. But as he sat there an old memory floated up from deep within his mind. Alex remembered his poor little hamster Angie, and her struggles to breathe as she lay dying in his hands and thought with despair that his mother and little Angie would leave the world looking the same. A little later her breathing stopped. He wept then, for her and for Angie, and for himself, for the loss of the last link to his childhood. He kissed her on the cheek and left to call the nurse.

\*

Alex sat silently at the table, a tuna fish sandwich untouched before him, while Helen tidied the kitchen. Mark descended the stairs, two at a time, no challenge for his long legs.

"Mark, I made tuna fish. You want some?" Helen asked as she dropped the cutting board into the dishwasher.

"Sure." He pulled back his chair and sat at the table.

"That's my kid- always hungry. I'll make you a sandwich." Helen opened a cabinet to get a fresh plate.

"Take mine- I'm not hungry," Alex said. He pushed his plate toward Mark.

"Thanks." Mark pulled the plate toward himself and picked up the sandwich. He glanced at Alex, still as a statue, immobilized by sorrow. Better to leave him alone for now, he thought.

"I'm going to, ah, do some reading," Alex finally said. He stood and walked slowly to his study and opened the beautifully illustrated edition of Vasari's *Lives of the Artists* he had started to read before his mother died, without looking down at the pages. His gaze drifted unfocused on the afternoon sunshine. He sat without moving for an uncertain period of time.

A soft tap at the door. "Alex?" Helen said. *Her voice was so sweet.* "I'm going to Stop and Shop. Can I pick something up for you?"

"No," he answered, barely audible. "Thanks."

Alex listened, unmoving, as the car pulled out of the driveway.

# CHAPTER 52

Mark and Elena sat side by side at a little table in the Starbucks in Coolidge Corner. Mark nursed a grande coffee of the day while Elena sipped a venti passionfruit iced tea sweetened with honey.

"So, we didn't talk, after prom. Did you like it?" Elena asked.

"Yeah. Yeah, it was great," Mark replied.

"What'd you like about it?"

"I liked the way you looked." He paused. "You were so hot. That dress- wow!"

"Thank you! I'm going to admit, I wasn't sure if you had fun, cause you know, you didn't call or anything. More than a week!"

"Hey, I'm sorry. Things have been crazy at home."

"Yeah? How?" Elena asked. *Here it comes. That excuse already sounds pretty thin, and it will probably be downhill from there.*

"Well, the day after prom, my grandma got moved into the hospital. She had cancer and they were going to do some stuff to make her, you know, more comfortable. It was too much, uh, advanced, they said, to try to cure her. Then she was at the hospital for a couple of days and then she just kind of went into this coma and didn't come out, and then she passed away. We had the funeral two days ago. My Dad's all depressed and my Mom and I are just laying low around the house, trying not to bother him."

"Oh, I didn't know she was sick. I'm so sorry!" Elena said. So Mark actually had an acceptable excuse for not calling.

"Yeah, she was a good grandma. I used to ride my bike over and visit her. I was her only grandchild." Mark took another sip of his coffee. "When I saw you today at school, I was so happy to see you. After this depressing week, there you were, with your smile and all. Anyway, I'm glad you had time to meet after school."

"Mark, if I can do anything, anything, just let me know."

"Just seeing your beautiful face is such a big help." He took Elena's hand. She was so sensitive and kind, Mark reflected. His parents were just being unreasonable, misjudging her as they did. "So, you're still planning on taking a gap year?"

"Yeah. I need to figure out what I really want." Elena didn't really like studying, and there was no money set aside for her to go to college, so it would mean taking loans to do something she wouldn't enjoy. Screw that.

"I want you to do what you want. That comes first. But if you're taking a gap year, I sure am glad I'll be going to BU next year. It'll make it so much easier to see you. If you want."

"Of course! I'd love that." She folded her hands in her lap, and with her upper arms squeezed her breasts so they bulged from her low-cut blouse.

# CHAPTER 53

Helen and Alex and Mark returned to their home, following Mark's graduation. Alex retreated to his study and quietly closed the door, to pass the time with the ghosts of his past.

"Sweetheart, I'm sorry we didn't plan any celebration, but with Dad so sad and all..." Helen said.

"Don't worry, Mom, I'll take a rain check." His academic robe was draped over his left arm, while he held his mortar board and his diploma in his right. He gazed out the window into the backyard. Now that he had graduated, he suddenly had nothing specific to do.

Helen went to their bedroom, to change into casual clothes. Now that Mark was finished at BHS, she hoped that their link to the Gonzalez family had been severed for good. That episode today had been uncomfortable. She and Alex were standing together with Mark after the ceremony, preparing to leave, when Mark had said, *Look, there's Elena, and her grandmother. Please come with me to say hello.* Helen had glanced at Alex; he was lost in his own thoughts and had not heard. Helen looked in the direction Mark indicated. Sure enough, there was Anita Gonzalez, older but still with jet black hair and that heavy gold jewelry. A teenage girl, Elena, stood next to her, wearing her graduation robe and shiny red stilettos. From that distance, Helen could not tell anything else about her appearance, except that she was fairly tall. *Not now. Please. Look, let's get Dad home,* she had said. Mark was disappointed, but he had obliged. Hopefully Elena was going to college far, far away.

\*

The following day Mark met Elena at Starbucks. He slid into the chair next to hers and gave her a warm smile. Elena leaned over and softly brushed Mark's cheek, as they sat together at a small table. "Thanks for the frappuccino," she said. "It's yummy. But it makes me so cold!"

As she shivered, her nipples poked into the thin fabric of her tank top. Mark watched, mesmerized by her perfect breasts. *What would they look like without that top over them,* he wondered. *What would they feel like?* Elena rubbed her bare arms vigorously to warm them, apparently oblivious to his attention.

"Ah," Mark said, feeling he should say something and stop staring. "What did you think of graduation?"

"Oh, it was okay. My grandmother and my aunt and her husband and my uncle came. Then we went for a nice lunch at Elephant Walk. It was good."

"Did, um, did your father get to see you graduate?"

"My father! That asshole! Oops, sorry, but he makes me so mad. The absentee father. What a jerk. No, he did not make an appearance." Elena crossed her arms and frowned.

"I'm sorry. I shouldn't have asked."

"Don't worry about it. I've gotten used to it. But can you imagine- he has a child, and he's never even seen me, not since he gave me away to my grandmother to raise. He makes no effort. None. You'd think he could get on a bus or a train and come see me in person. Out of curiosity, if nothing else. But no. And after he ditched me with his mother, he doesn't even help her with expenses. She has to scrape together the money for everything."

"But why would he do that?"

"Oh, my grandmother is always talking about the stress of his acting career, but let me tell you, there is no evidence that he has any such career. It's just a lie. You know what I think? I think he's a drug addict or something."

"Really? Why?"

"Really! Once, oh, years ago, my aunt Cati and her husband went to New York to try to find him. I think they found him, but he wouldn't leave, wouldn't come home. I heard them whispering about it, telling my grandmother what had happened, and I heard Cati say something about addiction."

"Oh, wow, I'm so sorry."

"He's the worse person I know. He should get the worst father of the century award. I mean it."

Mark put his arm around her shoulders and pulled her to him. "That's terrible. I guess I made out okay with the parents. My Mom is just sort of nice and kind, and my Dad is amazing. He's the smartest person I've ever met. He taught me most of what I know, I mean, how to ride a bike, how to swim, how to sail, always helping me with homework, giving me ideas."

"He sounds nice." Elena sounded wistful.

"He talks to me a lot, about, about everything. Don't get me wrong: he's a total nerd, totally off on cloud 9 half the time about some historical trivia. But he was never too busy, you know? Never yelled at me."

"Who would yell at you? You're too good."

"Are you trying to butter me up or something?" He ran his fingers down her ribs and she giggled.

"I'm ticklish! Don't!" Elena squealed, but Mark thought she enjoyed it. He moved his arm back to her shoulders. Mark couldn't understand what his parents' problem was with Elena. Was it that she was the first girl he'd ever talked about? Couldn't be. Last year he went out with Susan Patterson a few times and they had had nothing to say. And so what if Elena's grandfather really was some kind of criminal? That all happened before she was born. She had never even met her grandfather either, much less her mother, who sounded like a real winner. She had had it really hard, and she was still so nice. What would his parents do, what could they possibly say, if he continued to see her? What if he invited her over and there she was when they came home; his parents were both polite people. They wouldn't say anything to hurt her feelings. He felt sure of that. He glanced at his phone. 3pm. Neither of them would be home for a while anyway. This was his mother's day to get her hair done, and his Dad would still be at work for hours.

"Elena, want to go to my house and hang out for a while?" Mark asked.

"Sure, sounds good." She snuggled against him.

*

Alex sighed as he slid into his car. He would be so happy to get home today. His job was stressful enough under optimal circumstances, but with the deaths of Buck and his mother still so recent, it was hard to concentrate. And then at today's staff meeting, he and his colleagues were informed of additional budget cuts that would basically lead to them working more for less. As he turned the key in the ignition, he pondered whether he should make a serious life change. They had plenty of money set aside for Mark to go to college. The mortgage was paid off. What if he were to go half time? Have more time for sailing, or travel, or maybe go back to school and get a degree in history. Perhaps at least he should take a look at his schedule, move things around and block a couple of weeks off-service to get his head together.

*

Mark took Elena's hand as they walked up the front walk to his house.

"I don't think my Mom's home." He rang the doorbell.

"You ring the doorbell before you go into your own house?" Elena laughed.

"Um, it's sort of a sore subject." No one had answered, so he let go of Elena's hand, knelt down and turned over a rock next to the walk. He flipped open the little compartment at the bottom and extracted a key. "I was always forgetting my key, or losing my key, so my Dad got one of these fake rocks and hid a key inside. Now I don't even bother carrying one." He opened the door, returned the key to its compartment and turned the rock over. "It's only plastic but unless you look close, it looks real."

Elena nodded. "Good idea."

"Come on in," Mark said, gesturing for her to enter.

"Nice," Elena said, looking around. Mark's home wasn't as big or fancy as hers, but it looked like it was in better condition, very clean, with no water stains on the ceiling or peeling paint. When Mark flipped the light switches, all the fixtures had working bulbs.

"Let's go into the TV room, see what's on."

"Wait. Listen to this instead. Salsa. Isn't it sexy? Do you want to dance?" She set down her iPhone and music filled the room. She stepped to face him, and he put his arms around her.

"Elena, there's something about you. You're different from everyone else. It's like you're under my skin, all the time." Mark whispered.

"In a good way, I hope," she said and smiled coyly.

"Of course, in a good way. Like we're on the same wavelength."

"I think we're soulmates," she replied. She moved his hand from her shoulder and placed it on her breast.

Mark's hand reveled in the feel of her big, soft, pillowy breast. He had imagined this so many times and now it was real and it felt wonderful. They continued to stand, swaying gently to the sound of the music, neither speaking.

"What are we doing?" Elena whispered.

"Whatever you want. What do you want?" Mark asked.

"I want, I want you. I do," Elena said.

Mark kissed her, while his hand stroked and squeezed her breast.

"Oh, god," Elena moaned.

Mark kissed her neck, inhaling the scent of her skin. *She tastes so good*, he thought.

"Mark, wait, I need to tell you something."

"What?" he murmured.

"I haven't done this before. Not really. Have you?" She had never done it where it really counted. There had been Manuel, their gardener. Abuela had had to let him go because she couldn't afford to pay him anymore. Elena had felt bad for him. He was about five years older than she, so he knew how to do it. The last time he had come to mow, she had approached him. She wanted him to know that they appreciated him and didn't want him to stop coming, it just had to do with money. And then there had been those few days on vacation in Acapulco with Jorge the gorgeous bartender. But never with a real boyfriend.

"Of course," Mark scoffed. Susan Patterson was nothing special but at least he had learned a few things. "Do you want to go upstairs? To my room?" He was going to have her big beautiful tits all to himself. He couldn't wait to get her shirt off and touch them, kiss them. Run his hands all over her body, see how she would react- she was so hot!

"Yes, let's go," Elena said, breathlessly. She picked up her phone. Mark walked her to the stairs and they started up the staircase. They paused partway up the stairs and kissed passionately.

Helen walked into the house. She paused in front of the mirror in the entrance hall; they had done a good job on her hair at the salon today. But the lines at the corners of her eyes and around her mouth were getting more obvious every time she looked. She sighed. Then she stopped- what was that music? That was, could that be, the same music Hector used to play? Was this some bad joke? No, it must be Mark, must be some coincidence. She cautiously looked for the source of the music; the sound was coming from upstairs.

"Mark?" Helen called as she approached the stairs. There was Mark, looking startled, and a girl, a girl with wild dark hair and huge breasts. Elena. It must be. She was the image of that awful woman from Hector's apartment, the same, but younger. That woman's daughter. With Hector's emerald eyes, and a sullen pout on her face, instead of the wild rage of her mother.

"What, what are you doing?" Helen asked, panic creeping into her voice.

"We, ah, I was going to show Elena my room. I guess," Mark said, embarrassed. "Oh, um, Mom, this is my friend Elena."

"Hello, Elena. I need to speak with Mark, so if you could excuse us, please," Helen said.

Elena tossed her black curls and wordlessly headed for the door.

Mark watched her go. "I'll text you," he called after her, utterly devastated.

Helen waited until she had gone. "Mark, what's the matter with you? Dad and I both asked you to stay away from her. And you brought her here?"

Humiliated, disappointed, he turned to her, "I have no idea what you have against her. She didn't do anything wrong. She's never even met her grandfather. She's really so nice, and she's had it pretty hard. I wish you'd calm down and let it go."

"I will not calm down. We asked you this one thing and you ignored us."

"I feel like you're not giving me a reason. What is the problem? She's a nice girl."

"She's not!"

"How do you know? You don't know her."

"If one member of the family is bad, usually the whole family is bad. Be friends with someone else."

"That's ridiculous. That's not a reason."

"It is. Dad agrees."

"What is it really? Do you not like Hispanics? Is that it?"

"No, of course not. I have nothing against Hispanics." *If only I had*, Helen thought.

"This doesn't make sense. I want to be friends with her. It means a lot to me."

"No, Mark, please! Please stay away from her!"

"Mom, come on. You're being completely illogical. And no matter what, she's my friend. If she's not welcome here, well, she says I'm welcome at her house. I'll see her there. Or just out somewhere."

"No, Mark, no, please!" Helen was now sobbing. She walked away from the stairs and into the TV room and sank onto the couch. She covered her face with her hands and rocked back and forth.

Mark followed her into the TV room. "Come on, Mom. You're never like this. What is it?"

"Promise you'll stay away from her!"

"No! You've given me no reason!"

Helen shook her head sadly. "Please, Mark."

"Look. When Dad gets home, we can talk about it. I bet Dad will get it, and if he does, I bet you'll be okay with it."

*Oh, god, what if Mark is able to change Alex's mind? It couldn't be any worse.* "I don't care if you're friends with her, but she can't be your girlfriend."

"What is that supposed to mean? What is going on?" *A platonic relationship with Elena? Impossible!*

Helen raised her head and looked him straight in the eye. "Please, have you, have you, been, um, with her?"

"I don't have to answer that! Why is that such a big deal?"

"Please tell me. Please say you haven't," she said desperately.

His mother looked terribly miserable, so Mark answered quietly, "No."

Helen gave a sigh of relief. That was something. "Mark, you can't date her. You just can't."

"Why not?"

Helen raised her tear-stained face and sighed. "I'm so sorry."

"Sorry for what?"

"If I tell you, you have to promise you won't tell anyone else."

"Tell them what?" Mark's voice rose with impatience.

"Something you have to keep secret. You can't tell anyone. Not your friends. Not even Elena."

"Dad?"

"No!" Helen exclaimed, then lowered her voice. "No. Not Dad."

"Okay. What is it?"

"Do you promise? Do you swear? It has to stay a secret between you and me."

"Fine, I promise!" Mark said, exhaling loudly.

"You can't, because, because, she's your sister," Helen whispered.

"My sister!" Mark shouted. "What are you talking about?"

"Half-sister," Helen sobbed.

"What does that mean? Who are my parents? Am I adopted?"

"You're not adopted. You're my son." Helen covered her face in her hands.

"You can't, I mean, is Dad, is he not, my dad?" Mark asked.

"I'm sorry, I'm so sorry," Helen whispered.

"Wait, what, who, who is..." Mark stammered.

"You and Elena have the same father," Helen sobbed.

"That guy, Hector?" Mark stared at her.

Helen nodded; she cautiously looked up to see Mark's reaction.

"Does Dad know?"

Helen shook her head and started to cry.

"It's Hector Gonzalez?" he asked. According to Elena, the worst father in the world.

She nodded miserably.

"Helen! No!" It was Alex, standing at the threshold of the room. "What are you saying? What did you do?"

She stared at Alex horrified, without speaking. All these years, the thing she had most feared had finally happened.

Alex strode into the room and stood over her. "Helen, what did you say?" His voice was different, hard, angry.

Whimpering, Helen tried to defend herself. "You left me there all alone in your dorm room. I didn't know anyone. I was so lonely! I was so bored!"

Alex strode across the room, grabbed her wrists and pulled her to her feet. "You were bored! So you committed adultery with the person who killed Patrick! It had to be Hector? He took my best friend from me, and now, now..." *The loose messy handwriting on that envelope- it was Hector's!* He saw in his mind's eye, that messy scrawl, vibrating faintly and then condensing onto Helen's face. He saw Helen's name, her address, their address, inscribed on her fair skin, the words moving across her forehead. He hit her, slapped her cheek hard, leaving the angry red imprint of his hand; the words went spinning away, receding into the distance. He let go of her wrists and Helen sank back onto the couch.

He looked down at her. The magic of his love, the spell that had kept her forever young and fair in his mind's eye, the spell was broken. The goddess, the angel, that he had always seen was gone; instead he saw a husky, middle-aged woman, with the years weighing heavily on what had been the perfect oval of her face.

"Those letters! They were from Hector!" Alex yelled.

"He- he wrote to me, begged me for some money, and I, I," Helen stammered.

"He took you from me! He took you from me and then he wanted money? You were sending him money?" Alex stared at her.

Mark jumped between them. "Don't, don't hurt her."

Alex turned to Mark. There he recognized for the first time Hector's strong face, tempered by Helen's delicate features. "Oh, no," he whispered. He backed out of the room, ran to his study, retrieved the torn envelope from his desk, and ran from the house, slamming the door behind him.

Mark sat down next to Helen. They sat in silence as Alex started the car and drove away.

*

Alex parked at the hospital, left his cell phone in the glove compartment, took the T to South Station, paid cash for his bus ticket and waited in line to board. He looked around; he recognized no one. On the ride south to New York City, heart pounding, furious, gripping the envelope so hard his fingers hurt, Alex looked straight ahead, set on vengeance. He would rip Hector Gonzalez apart with his bare hands. He would end his life, just as Tarzan vanquished Kerchak, Beowulf felled Grendel, Achilles killed Hector, David slew Goliath. He would drag his bloody body by the ankles through the streets of New York. He should have killed him long ago. Should have hit him hard enough to kill him that day defending Patrick. When the bus finally stopped in New York City, he steeled himself to step calmly off, and then strode off into the dark streets to find the return address on the envelope. It corresponded to a seedy bar named Paris, which bore absolutely no resemblance to the City of Light.

"What'll you have?" the barrel-shaped bartender grunted.

"Is Hector Gonzalez here?" Alex asked.

"He owe you money?" the bartender asked, leaning across the bar.

"No," Alex responded, surprised.

"Fine. I'm first in line to get paid back, just so we're clear. Not that I expect it," the bartender muttered. "He's around back." He gestured with a jerk of his head.

Alex walked cautiously around to the back of the building, which was separated from its neighbor by a small alley. The dim light of a low-wattage bulb over the back door of the bar reluctantly illuminated the far end of the alley. A few moths danced a circle around the light, casting odd little shadows. The odor of garbage rose from a row of mottled aluminum trash cans lining the back wall of the bar, silent witnesses to whatever was to come. As Alex's eyes adjusted to the poor light a dark figure emerged from the gloom, a crumpled scarecrow of a man squatting on the threshold of the bar's back door. The gaunt figure slowly lifted his head and turned toward Alex- it was Hector Gonzalez.

Swift as a lion, Alex leapt at him, grabbed his arm. Hector looked dazed. His skinny arm flopped loosely in a sleeve now too big for him. His whole body seemed flaccid. Alex dropped his arm and stepped back.

"Do you remember me?" Alex snarled.

"No, dude. You got the wrong guy," Hector responded after a long delay.

"You should remember me. Look at me," Alex demanded.

Hector slowly lifted his head and squinted at Alex. "Sorry, man. Say, you got a smoke?"

"I'm here about Helen." Anger seethed in Alex's voice.

"Who, man?"

"Helen! Don't you know? Helen! Helen Fletcher!"

Hector shook his head. "Dunno, man. You got a smoke for a brother?"

"Helen! You- you-," Alex struggled to find the words. "You were with her. More than once. Almost 20 years ago. Helen!"

"I dunno. Don't fuck with me."

"Helen Fletcher. The most beautiful girl in school." Alex's voice caught in his throat at that. Why did he call her Helen Fletcher? She was Helen Eastgard, but he couldn't say it.

"Ahhh, maybe. Oh, yeah, blonde girl. Nice girl." Hector spoke slowly.

"And you got her pregnant, didn't you?" Alex demanded.

"I dunno. Bitches fucking lie," Hector mumbled. His head dropped between his knees.

"You had a son with her! Do you remember?" Alex grabbed Hector's hair and yanked his head up.

"No, man, I dunno. Where? You got a smoke?" Hector whined. He twisted to free himself from Alex's grasp.

Alex grabbed Hector's bony left wrist, pushed back the sleeve and held his arm out under the light. Hector did not resist. Needle tracks, Alex observed, and dropped his wrist, disgusted. He stood, looking down at Hector. *I could kill him,* he thought. *I could kill him with my bare hands, but he's gone. He's dead already. So this is how he ends up, Hector with the grand house and the horses.* He stood for a while contemplating the wreck that Hector Gonzalez had become, and finally turned and started to walk away.

"Hey, man, hey," Hector said softly.

Alex paused and turned.

"Hey, I never wanted that kid to die. Just picking on him a little. Never thought he'd go for that ball. Never," Hector whispered.

Alex listened, silent.

"I got to live with that, you know? I can still hear that thud." Hector's voice shook.

"Patrick, my friend Patrick!" Alex groaned.

"Who?" Hector shook his head, the lucid moment past. "I dunno, man. Hey, you got a smoke?" he pleaded. He leaned back against the brick wall and closed his eyes.

Alex turned and started to run, run away from Hector, run away from those memories, from that terrible day. But the scene played out before him: there was Patrick lying dead on the ground, in a pool of blood. Someone had called an ambulance, and Alex managed to give them Patrick's name and address. A crowd had gathered; someone among them said, look, he's all bloody, take him to the hospital too, then the ambulance driver saying, looks like the other kid's blood. If he's not injured he can't come in the ambulance. Alex had stood there, his clothing drenched in Patrick's blood, as the crowd dispersed. One or two people asked him if he needed help, if he wanted them to call someone for him. No, I live nearby, he had answered mechanically. Then in a daze he had walked to tell Kelly. Her mother had come to the door; he remembered the look of horror on her face when she saw him standing there. But she had called Kelly and stood close by as he told Kelly what had happened. Then he asked if he might call Patrick's home; he had to do it. It was his responsibility. He told Patrick's mother about the terrible accident. He should have gone in person, out of respect, but seeing Patrick's blood on full display would have made the horror even worse. He recalled then Mrs. Close, crying, sobbing, murmuring Patrick's name, over and over. *My son, my boy, oh Patrick*, she had said, in anguish. Then somehow Alex found his way to the reservoir and sat on the bench, looking out over the water. He still couldn't recall how he got there, but he did remember thinking about that empty bottle of Sam Adams, probably still sitting at the bottom of the pond. And there he had sat, for hours, most like, until his father had found him and brought him home.

And now Alex headed cross town, until he hit Broadway, and turned south. He walked for minutes, or hours, the streets finally nearly quiet, past variable façades in shades of gray in the dim light, simple flat building fronts with tall rectangular windows, handsome buildings fronted with paired arches resting on Corinthian columns, another with Doric columns, another with bricks that might be red when daylight returned. Façades of pitted brownstone. Plate-glass windows protected by heavy retractable metal grates. A few newer buildings of glass and metal, buildings of concrete. He continued south. Suddenly on his right, the Freedom Tower glittered impossibly tall and silver in the moonlight. Past that, the unexpected appearance of an exquisite Gothic Revival church marking the foot of Wall Street. Trinity Church. Next, the huge iconic bull, lowering his head to charge. Alex continued south until he reached the darkened Staten Island Ferry station. He turned to one side and found himself in Battery Park, and collapsed onto a bench, exhausted but unable to sleep. He watched the stars above him, hypnotized. He lay there for a long time, unable to move and uncertain where to go if he should arise. Finally, he looked at his watch. 3:45 am. He forced himself to sit. It was still the middle of the night. Where should he go? He couldn't stay here forever. He could retrace his steps and return to the bus station and be back in Boston by late morning. And then decide. He arose unsteadily and started the lengthy return walk up Broadway. The way uptown was slower; his feet hurt and the muscles of his legs were stiff with fatigue. As he limped north, he noted a glow on his right. He turned and watched spellbound as the sun rose and cast golden light along the eastern edge of Manhattan Island.

Alex stopped at a diner, already open for breakfast, and approached the counter. "Can I get a large coffee to go?" he asked.

A trim brunette with curly hair and a crisp white apron handed him coffee in a disposable cup marked with a Greek key design. "Hey, mister," she said briskly, "Not my business, but you look awful. Take a look around. It's a beautiful day in the greatest city on earth. Try to smile."

Alex met her eyes. "Thanks." The events of the past 12 hours seemed unreal. He, the good father, the good husband, had been living a lie for nearly 20 years. Enraged, he had come here to kill Hector, but there wasn't enough left of him to kill. He couldn't return to his old life; that was gone, forever. He would return to Brookline and keep working and stay in his mother's house until he figured out what to do.

"That's better. You have a good day."

*The greatest city on earth*, she had said. He looked around at the modest surroundings, and farther off, at the majestic skyline. New York City. A city of extremes, a city both passionate and indifferent, magnificent and unlovely, a polyglot city of wealth and privation, of fame and blessed anonymity.

# CHAPTER 54

Alex exited the bus at South Station and made his way to his car. He pulled his cell phone from the glove compartment and checked the time. His secretary would be at her desk. He called her number.

"Phoebe?" he said.

"Yes, Dr. Eastgard?" she replied.

"I'm going to be in late today. Something came up regarding my mother's house that I need to deal with. I'll be in as soon as I can."

"No problem. I'll let people know."

"Thanks. I'll see you by this afternoon at the latest." Good. That was taken care of. He didn't want anyone from work calling his house asking where he was.

Phoebe hung up and turned to Meredith, at the desk next to hers. "Dr. Eastgard is so nice. He's so sad about his mother passing. You can hear it in his voice."

Alex drove the car to his mother's house, entered, and slowly ascended the stairs. He headed for his bedroom, physically exhausted, but too emotionally distraught to sleep. He sat at his old desk and opened the drawers one by one, uncovering in each the relics of his childhood. There, face side down in the top drawer, lay a picture. Alex extracted it and turned it over. It was his high school track team, with Coach Wainwright standing to one side. He and Patrick used to call Coach the Old Man. He couldn't have been older than Alex was now. He wondered if anyone called him the Old Man behind his back. He used to have this photo proudly on his desk, but when Patrick died, he put it away- it had hurt too much to look at it. He studied the photo- two rows of boys smiling for the camera. He and Patrick stood next to one another. People used to say they looked like brothers, or maybe cousins, Alex recalled. He examined the photo. On casual inspection, there was a resemblance. Next to them were John, Kevin and Mike, and then, who was that, next to Mike? He couldn't remember. He took one last look at his own image, and Patrick's, before returning the photo to the desk drawer.

He opened the second drawer and the baseball from the Red Sox game and all the memories it carried rolled toward him. Way in the back of the drawer he found Patrick's wallet. He had not touched it since the day of Patrick's funeral, when Mrs. Close had given it to him. He opened it and slowly turned the clear folders it contained. Most held formal black and white senior photos of his friends. Photos from before Patrick's life ended and his own life was ruined. Most of the track team. Giuli, with her curly hair. Patrick's own picture: Alex ran his index finger slowly over the photo. Facing Patrick's photo was Kelly's, like Patrick said, with that dynamite smile. Then he saw his own photo, an impossibly young and innocent Alex Eastgard. And finally Helen. Helen forever fair in this tiny rectangle. The memory of her from the very first time he had seen her, as she and Kelly and her brothers had approached the school, materialized within his mind. He had never seen anyone so beautiful. He had so badly misjudged her. He was an idiot. But still, with all that had happened he could not blame himself for falling in love with such perfect beauty. A final clear window contained Patrick's driver's license. Alex gazed at it. It showed Patrick's full name, his address, his date of birth, his height and eye color. And his license number. Alex recalled that back in those days the world was a more trusting place, or at least more naive, and the license number was the person's social security number. Patrick's social security number. He hadn't gotten much use out of it. Alex closed the wallet and returned it to the drawer.

By this time, Alex was so tired that he struggled to find the strength to rise from the desk chair, but he finally stood, collapsed onto his old bed and fell into a fitful sleep.

\*

For the next several weeks, Alex stayed at his mother's house and went to work as usual. Knowing Helen's usual schedule very well, and guessing at Mark's schedule, he chose a time to return to his house to pick up some belongings when he thought they were both likely to be out of the house. It seemed absurd- sneaking into his own home, but he couldn't face Helen or Mark. Not now. Maybe not ever.

One day, after a long day at work, Alex drove to his mother's home, parked, and then headed for the reservoir on foot. He walked silently along the path to the water, grateful to find himself alone in this hallowed place. He slowly approached the old bench he used to occupy, he and Patrick, and sat on the worn, gray, wooden planks. He sat quietly for a long time, gazing at the dark water, as sunset came and went, and darkness crowded in around him. *What do I have?* Alex asked himself. *What do I have to lose? I've worked so hard to be a good doctor and husband and father and son, and I have nothing. No parents, no children. A wife who cheated on me in the worst possible way. Everyone who loved me is gone. I've chosen so badly. What a fool I've been.*

Alex finally spoke into the black waters of the reservoir. "Patrick, it's been a long time since I've been here." Alex paused. "I came because I want to ask you something. I need to ask whether you would think, if I were to do something, that it was wrong." Alex explained, and heard a reply, drifting across the water in the breeze: *It's not right, but I would understand.*

# CHAPTER 55

Alex had been studying the forecast. All week it had been unnaturally hot and steamy, and he knew that a storm was brewing that would clear the air. As he went through the day, he kept himself going with the promise of a sail on the river after his work was done. As he strode toward the Esplanade, the heat was miserable. It was so hot that the asphalt below his feet yielded to his weight. He could feel it shifting slightly with each step he took. He ducked into the shade of some trees on his way, but once he was forced back into the sun, the earth exhaled her heavy, feverish breath all around him. It would be cooler in the water, he told himself. Today was the perfect day for his sail. He approached the dock and asked to take out a sailboat.

"Hey, doc, looks like it's about to pour," the attendant said. "Take a look at that sky."

"I just want to take a quick spin across the water. Need to decompress- what a day I've had!" Alex said.

"Yeah, but, looks like we're in for a monsoon." He looked anxiously at the steel gray of the overcast sky.

"First raindrop, and I'll head back in," Alex said.

"Well, you know what you're doing, but be back soon, okay?"

"Will do. Thanks," Alex said. He zipped his wallet and cell phone into his backpack and stowed it in the little boat. He pushed off from the dock, and his spirits soared as the smoldering wind swept him into the middle of the river. Alex guided his boat down the river as the sky darkened. He looked back. He was out of sight of the docks, but it would still be easy to return if he wanted to. His little boat surged bravely onward, farther and farther away, his familiar landmarks now out of sight. He closed his eyes and imagined he was sailing in the South Pacific, approaching the enticing shores of the Fiji Islands, or circumnavigating a little Greek island capped with a village in blue and white stucco, or exploring the craggy coast of Norway, seeking the fjord that would lead to the sturdy stone cottage that was his home.

The air gathered around him, thick and heavy, beneath an implacable sky of lead; clouds of dense purple and mauve emerged from the dusky background like hard, angry gods from long ago, lusting for sacrifice. A waxing gibbous moon appeared briefly in the east and grudgingly cast reflected light as through a smokescreen, only to be quickly engulfed by the hungry clouds.

Suddenly, a jagged bolt of lightning, a glorious incandescent streak, transected the dark sky, and thunder erupted all around him. And then the rain began, and he didn't mind that, because it was part of being a man of the sea. Then the heavens opened, and there was nothing, except the deluge that surrounded him. A torrential baptism that embraced him, absolved him, purified him as though he was one newly born. And that, Alex loved, because the pounding rain on his skin reminded him that he was still alive.

*

Helen and Mark sat in silence at the dinner table. Wordlessly Helen passed Mark the beef and peapod stir-fry she had purchased earlier; Mark shook his head and she set the dish down. She was relieved that her credit card still worked. She had wondered if Alex would cancel all their credit cards, or send her a scathing letter, or file for divorce, but so far neither she nor Mark had heard anything directly or indirectly from Alex. It had been three weeks since that awful night when Alex had stormed out. Since then, nothing. A week ago, she had called Alex at work, knowing his secretary would answer. She had said she was calling from Dr. Jones' office; could he speak with Dr. Eastgard? The secretary had replied, *of course, he's right here; please hold and I'll connect you.* Helen then hung up. So Alex was still going to work as usual. Perhaps he was staying at his mother's house. She would just have to wait. She raised her eyes to look at Mark, her amazing son. What an awful person she was to bring him to this.

"Mark, I'm so sorry," she whispered. She should have left Alex. When she found out Hector didn't want her, she should have gone home to her mother and confessed. Kelly would have rained abuse on her, would have said, *I told you so!* Alex would have been hurt, but not nearly as much as she had hurt him by keeping her secret. It would have been awful for a while, but all the commotion would have died down, and Mark would still have had a good life. And wouldn't have had this horror unloaded on him. Why hadn't she done that? Why? She was a coward. She was weak. She thought she would get away with it. What she had done- it seemed like the easiest thing at the time.

"Mom, you don't have to keep saying that." Mark pondered his existential conundrum. His secure status as beloved only child was gone, abruptly erased by

381

an incredibly unlucky sequence of events. Instead he learned he was the result of adultery, the biological son of a man he had never met, but a man who by several accounts was neglectful, irresponsible, selfish, a miserable failure, and possibly overtly evil. Yet without his mother's infidelity with this man, he would never have been born. Part of him wanted to scream and scream and scream at his mother, but she sat there so low, so devastated, that he could only pity her. She had been open with him about what had happened, the longstanding enmity between Alex and Hector, the death of Patrick just after they had all graduated from high school, the role of Hector in that tragedy. After holding so much in for so many years, his mother had seemed relieved to unburden herself of all this. It was cathartic for her, he knew. *I'm so sorry to dump all this on you*, she had said. *No, I want to know; I need to understand*, he had answered.

"Look at you! You are wonderful! You are the only good thing I ever did," Helen cried, tears in her eyes.

"Don't say that, Mommy," Mark said, slipping into childhood parlance. "You do so many good things."

They gazed sadly at each other, the silence broken only by the steady thrum of the heavy rain against the roof and windows. Abruptly the doorbell rang, shattering the quiet of the moment. Helen stood and hurried to the door. When she opened it, a middle-aged policeman wearing a mournful expression was standing before her.

"I'm Officer Connelly, Brookline Police Department. Is this the residence of Alexander Eastgard?" he asked.

"Ah- yes, it is." Helen's heart hammered in her chest. Was she going to be arrested? Had she committed an actual crime?

"You're his wife?"

"Yes, I am Helen Eastgard," she said, as firmly as she could manage.

"Has he come home from work yet today?"

"No, not yet," she answered cautiously.

"When did you last speak to him?"

"I, ah, haven't spoken with him today during the work day. But he often doesn't call from work, as he can get very busy."

"Okay," the policeman said. "Let me make note of that."

Helen watched as he pulled a small notebook from his pocket, flipped through it and scribbled a few lines on a fresh page. "Could I ask, why, I mean, is there a problem?" She held her breath.

"Well, Boston Police got a call from Community Boating, which they're following up. Then Boston called us. Since you are Brookline residents, policy is for us to be involved too. Mrs. Eastgard, it's too soon to be sure, but there may have been a sailing accident. He does much sailing?"

"Oh, yes, he's very experienced."

"Well, apparently he took out a sailboat, promised to be back quick, and then didn't get back to the dock. At least, not yet. Got stuck in this thunderstorm."

"He went out in this storm?" Helen started to cry.

"Now, ma'am, there's nothing definite. We're conducting a search along the river, and we will probably get the Coast Guard involved, just to be thorough. We'll keep you informed."

"Thank you, officer," Helen said.

He nodded to her and returned to his cruiser.

*

A day passed, and Alex had still not appeared. Kelly decided she should check in on Helen; she was suspicious that some stupidity on her sister's part had precipitated this catastrophe. She rang the doorbell.

Leda answered the door. She had been keeping a vigil with Helen since early that morning. "Kelly! It's nice of you to come. Helen and Mark are inside."

Kelly walked into the living room. There was Helen, sitting on the couch, hands clasped, head bowed, face all red and puffy. Mark paced back and forth, unspeaking.

"Thanks for coming, Kelly," Helen sobbed. "Um, there's coffee if you want. In the kitchen."

Kelly helped herself to coffee and then sat down in a chair next to Helen. "Helen, do you know what happened? Why would Alex go out in a boat in that storm?"

"No, I don't know. I have no idea." Helen glanced up at Mark, but he continued his pacing, with no apparent intention to contribute to the conversation.

Kelly took a sip of coffee and made a face. Helen still couldn't make coffee. "Well, do you think it was just an accident? Poor judgment?"

"I don't know. I don't know!" Helen choked on her tears and moaned.

"I mean, his Mom just died. Maybe he was depressed. I just wonder if, you know, he might have gone out into the storm on purpose," Kelly said. "You didn't have a fight or anything, did you?"

"No!" Helen squealed into her kleenex.

Mark finally paused in his pacing and spoke. "And you know his friend from college committed suicide not long before Grandma got sick. Dad was really down about that."

"That's right. I'd forgotten. Why did he commit suicide?" Kelly asked.

Helen's voice cracked as she answered. "His wife was cheating on him. She wanted a divorce."

"Sweetheart, don't take this wrong, but this isn't the Globe. Don't ask your sister so many questions right now," Leda said softly.

Helen shook her head slowly back and forth. "We were such a nice family. Such a nice family. Why? Why?"

Kelly gazed upon her grief-stricken sister. Perhaps she had been wrong about Helen. Perhaps she really did love Alex.

Mark's phone pinged. He glanced down and saw a text from Elena. *Can we meet?* She asked.

He texted back. *Sure. Starbucks at 5?* Since their last meeting, he had struggled to devise an approach to take with her, but since the sailing accident, he had completely forgotten about her. After their last meeting any follow-up was bound to seem illogical to her. He couldn't see her anymore, not in the same way, but he owed her some kind of closure.

"Mom, you mind if I go to Starbucks?"

Helen shook her head.

"You go on, Mark. We'll call right away if we hear anything," Leda said. "We'll take care of your Mom."

*

Mark looked at Elena. She had said they were soulmates. Now he knew there was a bond, a very special bond, between them. He studied her face. There was a certain resemblance between him and her. Her hair was darker than his, almost black, but his Mom was blonde. Elena's mother probably had dark hair. They were both tall. Hector must be tall. That's how he got to be taller than his Dad. His Dad. What was he supposed to call him now? He spoke the words he had put together and practiced on his way over. "Elena, you are the most wonderful girl, but I can't see you now. Things are rough at home, with my Dad missing. My Mom is hysterical. I'm the only one she has, and I just have to be there for her."

"I understand. But why don't you let me be there for you?" Elena asked.

"You are so sweet, thank you, but this is something my Mom and I have to deal with together." His cell rang. "Grandma? They did? But not, I mean nothing else? Okay, I'll be back in a little while."

Mark turned to Elena. "That was my grandmother. My mom's mother. They found the boat my Dad was sailing in. It had made its way out into the harbor and then got beached on Deer Island. His backpack and his phone and wallet were on the boat in a storage hatch. But they didn't find him."

"Well, that's progress, at least. I hope they find him and he's alright after all," Elena said. If only Dr. Eastgard turned up alive, she and Mark could resume their relationship where they left off. Elena was disappointed that Mark couldn't see her under these circumstances, but he had said he couldn't see her *now*. He would get past this; give him some time, she told herself. They were meant to be together; she knew it.

"I got to go." Mark stood and hugged her tight, for a long time, all the desire that consumed him before replaced with intense affection. His sister. His sister! He wished he could tell her what he'd found out, but he couldn't. If they still knew each other after they were both old and gray, after their parents were gone, maybe he would tell her then.

*

Giuli Stewart opened the door to her apartment after a long day at work, to find her mother riveted to the TV. Giuli sighed. "You may wonder why I'm later than usual," she said, seeking some sign of recognition from her mother. "Just as we were about to close, several people came, asking for readings, and I hated to turn them away." Pause. "Mom?"

"What's that? Oh, here it comes again. I've been watching for updates." Henrietta Stewart kept her eyes on the TV.

"Updates on what?" Giuli asked impatiently.

"There has apparently been a tragedy, involving one of your old classmates. It seems that lovely young man, Alexander Eastgard, has drowned in a sailing accident."

"Alex drowned?" Giuli whispered. She steeled herself for a crushing headache.

"That's what they say. Remember how you couldn't go to his wedding because you were having one of your little headache episodes? It was a lovely wedding, but to have the marriage end this way, what a tragic turn of events!"

Giuli bit her tongue, to forestall the retort she longed to give her mother for belittling her migraines. Her mother was right, though, that a headache had prevented her from attending Alex and Helen's wedding. From all she knew, their marriage had been happy, and now that Alex had, had died, she had no symptoms. Perhaps the timing of her headaches was just a coincidence, and the idea that they were associated with Alex was a silly fancy of hers. Or perhaps she didn't sense Alex's passing because she had seen him so little in the many years that had gone by, and whatever link they had was broken.

"I saved some tuna casserole for you," Henrietta said.

"I'm not hungry." Giuli turned toward her bedroom. Alex, gone. Alexander Eastgard, the cutest and nicest and smartest guy in school, her long-ago prom date, drowned in a sailing accident. Tears collected in her eyes as she closed the door behind her.

*

Lonely Mickey's was a hole-in-the-wall bar in the East Village. True to its name, it was almost completely empty that night, except for the eponymous proprietor of the establishment and a laconic middle-aged patron seated in the shadows two stools from the far end of the bar. Mickey, an older man with a receding hairline and a striped dish towel across his left shoulder, gestured at the wall-mounted TV.

"It's crazy, this story about the guy drowned sailing. They say he's a Harvard professor. He don't look like no professor I ever seen. He don't look like he's in his forties. He looks like some kid." Mickey directed his gaze at his customer. *Lucky bastard still has a full head of hair, although it is starting to go gray around the temples.* "Although, could be they're showing his photo from when he started working wherever he was working. Never got a new one taken," Mickey continued.

The customer glanced up at the TV. He shrugged and took a sip of his Manhattan.

"And another thing- who would be stupid enough to go out sailing in some god-awful storm? He'd have to be a retarded idiot. You don't see no one from New York going out in a storm. People in Boston are idiots. And those Red Sox! Don't get me started." Mickey pulled the dish towel off his shoulder and started to buff the wooden surface of the bar.

The customer finally spoke. "Those people who get to be professors- some of them have no common sense."

Mickey nodded. "You're right, buddy. That kind, they don't live in the real world, like me, like you."

The customer nodded his agreement, drained his glass, left cash on the bar, and exited without waiting for change.

# PART 5

Massachusetts, 2014

# CHAPTER 56

Julia Kaiser emerged from Terminal B at Logan airport, dragging an old, soft-sided suitcase with a grape juice stain, courtesy of Beau, on the front. She paused to catch her breath. Only a few hours ago, she had boarded a plane in Lafayette, Louisiana, where the heat and humidity had been brutal. After changing planes in Atlanta, she had arrived in Boston. The air in Boston was warm but not hot, and only a little humid. She looked up and saw a whipped cream sky full of fluffy white clouds. *Surely this is an omen! Everything will be wonderful*, she told herself. *Harvard, here I come.*

*

Julia flopped down on the bed in her room. The fabric of her comforter cover, still crisp and new, greeted her with a quick aromatic puff of whatever manufacturing by-products remained in the cloth after its purchase. *What a crazy place this is*, she thought. *All these amazing old buildings! It looks so historic, like a movie set!* Their dining hall looked like a big old castle from a thousand years ago. Or maybe like the great hall in Harry Potter. But her favorite place was the Widener Library. It was awesome and beautiful, like a big temple to learning, and it was associated with a tragic story. The wealthy Widener family had a son coming home on the Titanic, and he drowned. The library was built in his memory.

It had taken her three trips to the library before she finally found the courage to mount the steps and enter, shyly tap her ID, and find a place to study. The first two times she had been too intimidated, wondering if she might somehow not warrant admission to this monument to the written word. Finally inside, she ascended the broad staircase, and marveled as she found herself before the room that represented a shrine to the young man who had drowned, a reproduction of his own library, it must be, magnificently appointed. At the threshold of the room was a Gutenberg Bible. Julia leaned over to examine it and sighed- it was open to the story of Jonah. It was so sad- Harry Widener had died young, before having much of a chance to experience life. But thousands and thousands of people knew his story; his memory would live forever. If he had just taken another ship, he would have made it safely home, and lived a good long life, but no one would know about him. Strange sort of trade-off.

She tiptoed away from young Widener's room, and encountered reading rooms, too luxuriously decorated for her to feel comfortable studying in. Off to the left she found the floors with the treasure trove of books that gave this library its heart. She loved wandering around the closely packed stacks that must contain all the knowledge in the whole world. Surely somewhere on these crowded shelves must rest the secrets of alchemy- how wonderful to learn to change base metal into gold! Indeed, if she studied all these books she might well discover the secret of life itself. She had crept from one Carrara marble-paved floor to the next, each step marked with a resounding echo. On the top floor she found books in Hebrew and Yiddish; that floor had the most intense musty, old-book smell. She would go there and breathe deep, and imagine she was drinking in the knowledge of the centuries. The floor below had books all about France and French- history, literature, books in French, while the one below that had a similar selection, but about Germany. Then just below was her favorite floor- it had books about many different religions, archeology, Egyptology, the Greco-Roman world. She had a favorite desk on that floor, too. She would walk straight across the floor to the far wall, turn right and find the desk overlooking one of the main gates into Harvard Yard, with a view across the street to Angel's. Angel's Heavenly Bakery. Once a week, on Sunday, she would go and select a delectable treat from Angel's. Day after day, while Angel baked and the world bustled outside the window, Julia would come to this spot and study, safe and secure in this little corner of what was quickly becoming her new home.

# CHAPTER 57

Julia paused on her way across Harvard Yard to perch on a stone bench facing the grand colonnade of the Widener Library. The cold of the stone penetrated the thin fabric of her skirt on the chilly, early-October night. She shivered, drawing her cardigan tighter across her chest. *It's cold here,* she thought, *so different from home. And I'm really here, I really escaped, I'm really at Harvard!* In the moonlight that filtered through the network of autumn branches, her face broke into a broad smile. She stood and smoothed her skirt down and headed back to her dorm.

Back inside, Julia rubbed her arms vigorously to warm them. It hadn't occurred to her she'd need a warmer sweater tonight- it was only October. Glancing down the hall she saw Campbell McDade, a big-boned, athletic girl who had announced, when they first met, that she excelled at something called crew. Now Campbell loitered near the door of her own room wearing Madras plaid shorts, with a short necklace of pearls visible beneath the collar of her Wedgewood blue polo shirt, chatting with another girl whose hair was dyed blue.

"Aren't you cold in those shorts?" Julia called out.

"No, I'm fine. You're not cold, are you?" Campbell countered.

"Well, it is kind of chilly outside," Julia said. Campbell's teeth were supernaturally straight; seeing them made Julia regret not having worn her own retainer more regularly.

"Hey, I'm Betsy. Don't think we've met," the blue-haired girl interjected. Betsy had

thin, fine, stick-straight hair a remarkable shade of turquoise through which her ears protruded.

Julia found herself staring. "Sorry, but what a pretty color your hair is!"

"Oh, thanks! You know what it is, is that I have a Dionysian disposition but Apollonian hair. The color makes my hair more in synch with the rest of me." Betsy fluffed her hair, temporarily covering her ears.

"Great idea!" Where did these people get their material, Julia wondered as she retreated to her room. Before she climbed into bed that night, she unlatched a window and opened it a crack. A flood of the cool dry air of a New England evening in autumn filled the room. Julia closed her eyes and breathed deep. "It tastes sweet," she murmured to herself as she curled up in bed.

*

Julia headed for her room, book bag over her left shoulder, clasping a bag from Angel's.

"Hi, how's it going?" Campbell strode along the hall, toting a hefty backpack.

"Oh, hey! Good."

"What've you got there?" Campbell asked, eyeing the crisp white bag.

"Mocha brownie from Angel's. Want some? No way I can eat the whole thing."

"Sure."

Julia opened her door, set the enormous brownie down on her desk and cut it into quarters. "Help yourself."

Campbell took a piece. "This is awesome!" Campbell scanned Julia's room. "Who's that? Brothers?" she asked, eyes fixed on framed pictures of Alo and Beau.

"Yeah, the Neanderthals. Aloysius and Beauregard. My Mom sent me their school pictures because she said she was sure I'd be missing them. Right," Julia said, rolling her eyes.

"Mmm. I've got just one brother. Two years older. Very un-Neanderthal. In good and bad ways."

"Sounds more interesting than my brothers."

"He's interesting, all right. Definitely want to stay on his good side." Campbell directed her attention to Julia's closet, the door of which stood open. "Will they be sending you your winter clothes soon?"

"Winter clothes? I mean, I've got a coat and some boots."

"This coat?" Campbell asked, pulling the sleeve of a lightweight satin-lined wool coat out for inspection.

Julia nodded.

"Where are your boots?"

Julia pulled out a pair of black vinyl rainboots.

"Those are galoshes. They're not lined. Do you have any other shoes for winter?"

Julia pulled out a pair of ballet flats. "These are closed-toe."

Campbell shook her head in disbelief, then turned to leaf through the clothing in the closet. "Julia, listen. These clothes will get you through November, but you need warmer clothes to survive. You know what they say: Winter is coming."

"Oh, wow. I thought if I wore the coat over a heavy sweater I'd be okay. I really need other stuff?"

"You really do. A down jacket, and real snow boots for a start. If you have to be outside in a good-going blizzard, having ski pants is nice also."

"A blizzard," Julia whispered. Of course they had snow up here. She should have thought of that. "Where should I," she began.

"Hold on, I have an idea." Campbell checked the calendar on her phone. "Monday is Columbus Day. We have a three-day weekend. My family will be at our home in Marblehead; why don't you come along? I have a ton of stuff in good condition that I've outgrown. You'd be welcome to have whatever you wanted."

"Oh, I wouldn't want to get in the way of your time with your family."

"Not at all. Please come. My family's a hoot. Hard to describe unless you meet them."

"Well, okay, thanks! Sounds great." Julia smiled.

*

Campbell had donned khaki pants, a blush pink polo shirt and a flannel-lined windbreaker for their trip home to Marblehead that weekend. "Can you wait here with our stuff while I get the car?"

"Sure," Julia had answered. She hoped her blue jeans and high school sweat-shirt over a tee shirt were within the dress code in the McDade household. As Julia contemplated this, Campbell pulled up in an ancient Volvo. "This old clunker was my Mater's car."

"Big and comfortable- this is great!" Julia said and climbed in. And then they headed north, through little towns with unfamiliar architecture and landscape bursting with trees ablaze with the colors of autumn.

"Wow! This is beautiful. At home we have mainly pine trees, and their needles don't change color, except they turn brown when they die."

"If you think this is different, wait'll you see the snow!" Campbell replied as she guided the car onward. "Here we go; that's our house, up ahead."

Julia gaped at the enormous Victorian home that rose before her, ensconced on a rocky outcropping, complete with gabled roof and towers and turrets and a wraparound porch with an ornate balustrade, dusky purple in the lingering late-afternoon light. As soon as Campbell parked and pulled the key from the ignition, Julia could hear in the distance the crash of waves against land. "Is that the ocean?" she asked, but not loud enough to be heard.

Campbell jumped from the car and yelled, "I'm home!" At the sound of her voice what looked to be the hound of the Baskervilles bounded forth from the home that could easily have been Wuthering Heights. A young man who looked like a masculine version of Campbell strolled behind the dog at a leisurely pace.

"Hello there, Cambrian," the young man said. He exuded self-confidence.

Campbell ignored him. "Satan! How's my baby? I missed you sooo much!" Campbell dropped to her knees to greet the dog and it licked her enthusiastically, forepaws on her shoulders. Campbell threw her arms around the dog. "Oh, you missed me too! Good boy! Good boy!"

"Dog! You beat me home this time!" Campbell addressed this not to Satan, but to her brother, in a belated acknowledgement. "Julia, this is my brother Russell."

"Dog?" Julia asked, looking from Campbell to Russell.

"Of course. I could call him Rusty, but that's so conventional. Russell also brings to mind Russell terrier, so I could call him Terrier, but that takes longer to say than Russell. So I just call him Dog. Short and sweet. Easy to spell. Sign of affection."

"Campbell! You're looking well. And this must be Julia." Mrs. McDade stood in the front doorway, in the shadow of the broad porch. She was a middle-aged, slender woman with brilliant blue eyes and a nice tan, her light brown hair swept up into a neat French knot. She was wearing a navy-blue sheath with a little white collar decorated with anchors. She was shod in what Julia had recently learned to recognize as L.L. Bean docksiders. Julia reflected that Mrs. McDade's outfit could accurately be described as jaunty, an adjective she had heretofore never had occasion to apply.

"Mater! Yes, this little scrap of the Deep South is Julia. Wait until you hear her talk! She says 'y'all' sometimes!" Campbell remained crouched and Satan continued to slobber on her.

"Hello, yes, I'm Julia, and I don't think I have an accent."

"Well, Campbell does tend to exaggerate but we are quite fond of her nevertheless. I'm Maggie McDade," she said, extending her hand, which Julia shook politely.

"You might want to let your father know you're home, if you can tear yourself away from Satan," Mrs. McDade continued. To Julia, she said, "I will be mortified if our pastor ever finds out we have a pet named Satan. I think that's why Campbell insisted on that name."

"Yes, Mater. Come on, Satan! Good boy! Good boy! Doesn't your mama love you! Yes, she does! Yes, she does!" Campbell stood and addressed Julia, "Come on, let's find Pater."

"He's in the library, dear." This from Mrs. McDade.

Campbell set off down a circuitous hall hung with innumerable family photos, with Satan and then Julia trailing behind. Julia glanced cautiously at Satan; he was bigger and stronger than she but seemed quite tame.

"Pater!" Campbell stood on the threshold of a large room. "It's your second-born child reporting for inspection."

"Campbell, let's have a look at you. How are your studies going?"

"Very well, Pater," she replied.

"Maintaining that GPA, are you?"

"It's early in the semester but I'm on track for straight A's."

"Good. Staying out of serious trouble as well?"

"Absolutely. Squeaky clean, as usual," Campbell assured him.

"That is all good news. Entirely satisfactory indeed. Tuition dollars well spent," Mr. McDade replied.

"Let me introduce you to my friend, Julia Kaiser." Campbell said, grabbing Julia's arm and thrusting her forward. Julia's gaze travelled up and around the library. She felt she had stepped back in time and entered the inner sanctum of a colonial governor from the Victorian age. Surely the British viceroy of India would have found this chamber much to his satisfaction. The ceiling soared to at least 14 feet. Built-in bookcases of dark mahogany with ornate crown molding and packed with books of all sizes and shapes lined most of the walls. There was even a sliding ladder to access books on the higher shelves. A bank of tall windows of mullioned glass admitted wrinkled sunshine, the last of the day, to the room. The pale marble fireplace, complete with a pair of solemn caryatids, harbored a few glowing embers from a dying fire. Blackened logs rested on andirons fronted by heavy brass structures resembling bishops from a game of chess. Over the fireplace was a wonderful oil painting of a clipper ship barreling through a choppy sea, with a setting sun shedding rosy light onto the water's surface in the background. An Oriental carpet of crimson and ivory with sapphire accents lay before the fireplace. An enormous grandfather clock stoically marked the seconds as they passed. Dominating the room was Mr. McDade's oversized, ornately carved desk inlaid with burl wood.

"Nice to meet you, young lady. I'm Martin McDade. Campbell was telling us about the challenges you face adapting your wardrobe to the Massachusetts weather," Mr. McDade leaned back in his chair. He had a full head of tawny hair swept back from a serious face, and a sinewy build, a tautness to his muscles, an alertness about him reminiscent of a lean old lion about to pounce. His hazel eyes viewed Julia through wire-rimmed glasses.

"Yes sir, she's helping me a lot, thank you," Julia replied.

"Please call me Marty. Well, must get back to the salt mines," he said, gesturing at the single-spaced contract spread out on his desk. "I'll see you girls at dinner," he said, smiling urbanely. And yet Julia had the distinct impression that she was in the presence of the preppy version of Lord Tywin.

The girls and the dog withdrew. Julia whispered to Campbell, "Wow, I have never been in a room like that before! It looks like it's right off the History Channel." She recalled the cracked brown vinyl couch in her family's living room and decided that Campbell would not be visiting her home.

"Yes, well, Pater is old school, you know. There's nothing in that room, Pater excluded, that is less than a hundred years old. And his law firm is the best in Boston. His job is what he refers to as quite remunerative, so he is able to get the kind of trinkets he likes."

"Something to think about, I guess," Julia said. By the way, why do you call your parents Mater and Pater? It's pretty unusual. Although compared to Dog…"

"Oh, well, they made me take Latin in school, not my first choice. 'Knowledge of Latin is indispensable to the study of the Law,' Pater often says. My teacher was so old that classical Latin may well have been his native tongue. He used to fall asleep in class, which was great because then the other kids and I could catch a nap too. The only time I use Latin since prep school is greeting my parents. They don't seem to mind. Here's my room."

Campbell's bedroom was endlessly cozy, with its two twin beds with simple white headboards, blue and white striped bedspreads and matching curtains, a hand-hooked oval rug and numerous stuffed animals. It smelled faintly of Satan. Satan curled up on the rug and Campbell sat next to him and scratched his head.

Julia walked to one of the dormer windows. "This room is so pretty. And you have a view of the ocean! This house is so cool!"

"Home sweet home, all right. Now. Let's go see about the primary purpose of this visit. Finding you rational winter clothing," Campbell said and slid off her bed.

"Thanks. I really appreciate it," Julia answered.

"No problem. It's my good deed for the day. I am taking pity on you and allowing you to benefit from my longstanding experience with winters in New England," Campbell said, but her tone was kind. "Let's head down to the basement."

The basement of the house rivaled the Roman catacombs in its extent and complexity of layout. Campbell confidently led Julia down a narrow hall, turned to the right, took another right turn, stopped, rested her hands on her hips and said with satisfaction, "Here we are."

Julia looked up and saw innumerable identical clear plastic bins on shelves built into the wall.

"These are clothes I've outgrown or don't want anymore, arranged in chronological order, like archeological strata," Campbell explained. "The top shelf has clothes from senior year in high school, and some things from junior year. Shelf below that contains most of my stuff from freshman and sophomore year. Below that, from grade school." She selected a bin corresponding to the first year of high school, unfolded a sweater and held it up to Julia. "Nope. Too big. I'm going to look in 8th grade."

As Campbell rummaged, Julia asked, "Who does all this organization? And why do you keep so many clothes you've outgrown?"

"Mater does this. She is OCD, to some extent. But the clothes really do get use. All good quality, so they last. My old baby clothes all went to my younger cousin when she was born. Some of these clothes weren't even originally mine- they were passed down from older cousins. Both Mater and Pater believe that waste is absolutely abhorrent."

Julia nodded. "Does your Mom save just your things, or your brother's too?"

"The Dog's things are on shelves across the hall. Come to think of it, he may have some snow boots that would fit you. He grew so fast that he has some things he outgrew before he even wore them. We'll check over there next. Here we go- the jacket I was looking for. Try that on."

After half an hour, Campbell had laden Julia down with enough warm clothing to survive several winters. As they prepared to depart the basement, Campbell's cell phone rang. "Be right there." She hung up and turned to Julia. "Dinner is served."

Julia's favorite class was Bible and Beyond: Literary Masterpieces of the Ancient Middle East. The teacher was Dr. Jonathan Templeton, the Randall J. Montgomery Professor of Ancient Languages, a tall and gangly, gray-haired septuagenarian, long of limb and torso, with a bit of a stoop and mild blue eyes with a tendency to water. He watched with satisfaction as Julia Kaiser took her seat and eagerly laid out her notebook, ready to get started. Then two other students passed through, one muttering to the other, "Why do we have to learn about this Gilgamesh thing? When will we ever use this?"

Professor Templeton turned away with a sigh. Pity that he had not earned his doctorate in adolescent psychology; it might have proved useful. He coughed softly and then loudly to indicate that class was beginning. He wrote on the blackboard, in all caps, 'Bible' and 'Gilgamesh,' then turned to the class. "Can one compare the Bible and the Epic of Gilgamesh?"

Dead silence.

"Anyone?" A few students leafed through notebooks, as though searching for a response. Others looked down or away.

Julia glanced around. No one was going to speak. "Of course. Gilgamesh is much shorter," she offered.

Professor Templeton's eyebrows rose. "That's it? I expected a more analytical response from you, Miss Kaiser." He smiled benignly. He knew more information would be forthcoming. He was fond of this little Julia's provocative assertions.

"Well, Gilgamesh and the Bible deal with a similar time period, or, at least, the beginning of the Bible, both are set in the Middle East, they share similar literary devices, and in a nutshell, both start off with the creation of man from clay, followed by a lot of sex and violence and end with a search for immortality," Julia said.

"A reasonable summary. Now, let us discuss the significance of the Flood in the Bible and Gilgamesh..."

Julia sighed and smiled. She loved this class. She had heard that most summers Professor Templeton lead teaching expeditions to the Middle East for interested students; she planned to apply.

# CHAPTER 58

Helen gazed fondly on Mark. He sat at the kitchen table, immersed in his studies, spiral notebook in front of him, open laptop slightly to the right, and hefty hardbound inorganic chemistry textbook to his left. As a student at nearby Boston University, he could easily have commuted to class from his home in Brookline, but in order to have a more traditional college experience, he had decided to live on campus in a dorm room. Still, he came home for dinner on occasion, for which Helen was grateful. It had become very lonely at home since Mark started college.

"Mark?" Helen asked.

"Yeah?" he said, not looking up.

"I know finals start tomorrow, but want to take a break and have some dinner?"

"What? Oh sure." He pushed his chair back, stood and stretched.

"Sit here, sweetie," Helen gestured to the empty chair next to the spot occupied by his school materials. She set a dinner plate with a large rectangle of Marie Callender's meat and cheese lasagna in front of him.

"Lasagna! That's great."

"Glad it makes you happy." No need to mention it was straight from the freezer case. All she'd had to do was turn on the oven. "How's the studying going?"

"Okay," Mark said, pausing briefly to reply between forkfuls of lasagna.

"You'll be ready for your finals?"

"Hope so. First time, you know."

"You'll do great."

Mark shrugged in response.

"Mark?"

"Mm?"

"Um, well. You know how, well, we don't have a lot of cash, I mean we're fine, but we don't have a lot of cash for like, extras. Once Grandma's house gets through that probate thing we can sell it and we'll be fine. But that's taking so long."

"Mom, I know all that."

"Well, I just feel kind of bad because Christmas is coming, and it's our first Christmas without, um, Dad, and we don't have a lot of cash for too many presents and all." Unspoken between them was an agreement to still call Alex Dad.

"Don't worry. Doesn't matter."

"I shouldn't even have brought it up while you're studying for finals. Sorry."

"Really, doesn't matter."

They finished their meal in silence. Mark returned to his original seat and resumed his studies while Helen cleared the table. Mark groaned. Avogadro's number was 6.022, not 6.22, x 1023. He had to remember that. Along with about a million other things. He felt bad for his Mom, having to worry about money. Suddenly he sat straight up. Money in an emergency! How had he forgotten? He hurried to Alex's study, knelt down by the safe and opened the combination lock. He looked inside. There was the coin collection, as always. Where was the cash? He turned on the flashlight on his phone and scanned the interior of the safe. No money. He pulled out the binder holding the coin collection, and swept his hand across the shelves. Nothing. He flipped through the pages holding the coins, thinking cash might be stuck between them. Nothing. He started to replace the coin collection, and then paused. The binder seemed thinner than it once was. Mark flipped through the pages. American coins. A few foreign coins, badly worn. None of those fancy Greek coins. No gold coins. Only silver. Or copper. He pushed the coin collection back into the safe and secured the lock. Bizarre. On the other hand, it had been years since Dad had shown him the cash in the safe. Maybe it had gotten spent. He returned to the table, to study some more. Better to get through finals and forget about the contents of the safe for now.

Just as Mark stood and turned to walk from the room, Elena drove by, on her way home from the Chestnut Hill Mall. She slowed as she passed the Eastgard home and caught sight of Mark through the window. *Nice that he still spends time at home with his mom*, she thought. *And he's so cute!*

# CHAPTER 59

"So, how does it feel to be back for Christmas? Did you miss home?" Aura Lee probed.

Julia, clad in tee shirt and jeans, with flip-flops on her feet, sat at the kitchen table, bent over a copy of the annotated New Jerusalem Bible. "Actually, it's kind of nice. It's 30 degrees warmer here than in Mass," she replied. "I couldn't dress like this a week ago." She looked back down at her book.

"You've had your nose in that Bible since you got home. Why do you spend so much time reading it?"

Without looking up, Julia responded, "I enjoy the fantasy genre."

Aura Lee's mouth dropped open. "This is what comes of sending your child to one of those liberal Yankee colleges," she muttered.

Julia carefully inserted her bookmark and closed her Bible. "Okay, well, I'm going to see Dally."

\*

"Dally, hi!" Julia said, as Dahlia opened the door, carrying her baby.

"Ohhhh, Julia! You're really here! Come in! Oh my god, but you look the same!"

"You thought I'd look different?"

"Well, I don't know. I was afraid you'd be all different from being with all those smart people."

"No such luck. I'm still puny little Julia. What about you?"

"I'll tell you one thing, I swear, my butt has got so big since I had this baby!" Dahlia moaned.

"Miss Dahlia Lasalle! I do not want to hear you swear," her mother called out from within the house.

"Yes, ma'am, sorry!" Dally yelled, but she grinned at Julia and shrugged.

"I got you and Bubba little Christmas gifts." Julia handed her a small bag with two presents.

"Can I open them now?"

"Sure, I don't care. Few days early. Anyway, I want to see whether you like them."

"Okay, I'll open Bubba's first. Oh, that is so cute! A Harvard T shirt! Let's see how it fits." As soon as Dahlia pulled the shirt over his head, Bubba grabbed the hem and proceeded to chew on it. "He likes it!"

"He is so cute! Okay, now open yours," Julia urged.

"It's beautiful!" She slipped the silver bracelet onto her wrist and admired it.

"I thought it would look nice on you. I'm really glad if you like it."

"I've got something for you too." Dahlia rummaged through the gifts beneath the Christmas tree, finally extracting a small box. She handed this to Julia.

Julia unwrapped the box. "This is awesome! Business cards!" There before her was a box of 100 shiny business cards with her name, address in Cambridge, cell phone and 'Harvard University Class of 2018.' In the corners of the cards were listed: 'Scholar,' 'Poet,' 'Super brave' and 'Best of friends.'

"Dally, you're giving me way too much credit," Julia said.

"That is not true. You are all of those things."

The doorbell rang.

"Who's that, I wonder," Julia said.

"Oh, that'll be Bobby." Dally ducked her head and blushed. She walked over to the door and opened it. Bobby planted a kiss on her mouth and swaggered into the living room, as Julia looked on in shock.

Bubba crawled rapidly to Bobby and clasped his right ankle. Bobby picked Bubba up and flopped down on the couch near Julia.

"Hey, Julia, how's it going?" Bobby asked.

"Ah, fine, but, I didn't know you were…" Julia stammered, looking from Bobby to Dahlia.

"Oh, well, we recently decided we'd get back together," Dally said, shyly.

"You know what they say. Why should I have hamburger at LSU when I can come home and have steak?" Bobby said, grinning.

"Shhh. Bobby Bergeron, I don't want Mama to hear you talking like that," Dally said.

"Wow! Well, I'm really happy for you," Julia said. "But, Bobby, you be good to Dally this time. She deserves it."

"Yes, ma'am! I know," Bobby said. He had the decency to look contrite.

*

Julia returned home and sauntered through the TV room. Her father was watching LSU play Alabama.

"I don't believe it!" he exclaimed.

"What's the matter, Dad?" Julia asked.

"Their best receiver was wide open. He's caught everything that came in his direction today. What was the QB thinking? Threw instead to some kid with butterfingers." He shook his head sadly.

"Oh, that's too bad," Julia said.

"I miss the Honey Badger. Team hasn't been the same without him.

# CHAPTER 60

The winter solstice ushered in a New England January that brought short days with attenuated sunshine, long, dark nights, and a light snowstorm that left the leafless branches of trees in Harvard Yard embroidered with lacy hoarfrost. It had grown dark while Julia was studying. As the wind howled she could feel a frosty draft accompanied by a faint rattling of the window in its frame. The cold penetrated her bare fingers and permeated the rest of her body. She shivered and looked out through the window to see slender branches locked in glassy cylinders of ice. *Looks like a black skeleton lurking outside, trying to get in.* She shook her head. *Okay, enough. Done for tonight,* she told herself, and climbed into bed. She pulled the blankets up to her chin, and then to be sure of keeping the cold air out she tucked the upper edge of the covers down over her shoulders. She started off in the shape of a little ball, limbs tightly clasped in fetal position, to minimize contact with the icy sheets and slowly, slowly uncurled as her body warmed the bed.

\*

Campbell strode down the hall, backpack over one shoulder, pulling a wheeled suitcase behind her. She knocked at Julia's door. "Class will be canceled tomorrow and maybe the next day. I'm going to Marblehead. Want to come?"

"Canceled? Why?"

"The storm. A major Nor'easter is bearing down on us. Don't you check the weather?"

"A Nor'easter! Um, no, that's okay. I have so much work, I think I'll just stay here and slave away. Thanks though," Julia answered. She peered out into the hall.

Betsy with the turquoise hair struggled past them lugging a load of groceries in two colorful reusable tote bags.

"What is all that?" Julia asked.

"Supplies for the storm," she explained, setting down her bags. "Don't want to run out of Kombucha. Stores will probably shut down."

"Oh, I get it. It's like a hurricane. Do I need to tape the windows?" Julia asked.

Campbell looked at Betsy and sighed. "No, you do not need to tape the windows. But if there's anything you need, you should go get it now before the stores close."

"Trader Joe's is closing at 6 tonight. Should give all their guys time to get home before the storm gets bad," Betsy said. She hauled the bags back onto her shoulders and limped to her room.

Julia returned to her desk and tapped the keypad to bring her laptop back to life. As she worked on her paper, she reflected that the floor was unusually quiet. No foot traffic in the hall. No doors slamming. Nobody laughing, or talking, or knocking on doors. Maybe a lot of people fled for cover, like Campbell. Would this storm really be that bad? She retreated to her desk and settled down to read.

The skeletal branches tapped gently, at first gently, on her window, disturbing the silence of the night. Little by little the snow began, as a dusting on the paved walks and benches. Then the wind became audible, at first as soft whistles, but over time as high-pitched howls that drove the snow against Julia's window. The ice-covered branches rattled violently, lashed against the window panes, demanding shelter from the storm. Snow spattered against the glass, and piled against the window frame, narrowing Julia's view of the outside world. Even with the unobstructed glass shrinking, she could see the snow piling up against trees and buildings, swallowing the legs of benches.

She glanced at her phone. Almost midnight. On impulse she jumped out of her chair, pulled on a down jacket that used to be Campbell's, laced up Russell's outgrown brown and tan snow boots, and left the shelter of her building to see the storm firsthand. The wind was ferocious; it almost knocked her over. Snow pelted her face and slipped under her hood and into her hair. She stepped carefully into the fresh snow, extending her arms for balance; snow threatened to overtop her tall boots. She stood in Harvard Yard, seeing with wonder a world blanketed in white. She tipped her face up and gasped as sharp, heavy snowflakes struck her bare skin. The sky was white, all white. It was bright as day!

She struggled back to the door of her building. When she turned around, she could see that the deep hollow columns left by her footsteps were already filling with driving snow. At the entrance she stamped her feet and shook her coat to remove the adherent snow, and then returned to her room through a deserted stairwell and hall. She turned off the lights and crept into bed, the screeching of the wind a harsh New England lullaby in her Southern ears.

When Julia awoke, she reluctantly discarded the cozy chrysalis of bed sheets and blankets that had warmed her during the night. Outside, the wind had died down, and the snowfall had slowed but not stopped. The changes wrought by the night's storm were foreign to her, and amazing. The view from her window revealed a world almost unrecognizable, all covered in such a thick coat of snow that the locations of paths and benches existed in memory only. Snow drifts piled high against the walls of buildings, swallowing much of their first floors. The branches wont to rattle against her window were so weighed down with snow that they were rendered immobile. Julia put on her robe and pulled on heavy socks, made coffee and then sat at her desk to contemplate the metamorphosis of her world.

Campbell returned two days later.

"Hi, how was Marblehead?" Julia asked.

"Miserable. The roads didn't get plowed until today and our snow removal man couldn't reach us. Mater made me shovel the whole driveway. My arms are so sore!"

"Didn't Russell help?"

"The Dog? No, he stayed here. I was told this was a good lesson for me; there wouldn't always be someone else to do the heavy lifting. Some lesson!"

*

Julia looked up from her textbook and let her gaze wander through the windows of the library and across the street. The lights were going out one by one at Angel's. Julia stood and stretched left and then right, and then bent down and touched her fingertips to the ground. What she really needed was a run, but it was too cold now that the sun had set. Julia paced up and down; she was too restless to sit and concentrate. She scanned the shelves as she walked. What was this? A History of the Seleucid Empire. Never heard of it. She pulled the book off the shelf and flipped through the pages until she got the gist of it. Seleucus was one of the generals of Alexander the Great. After Alexander died, Seleucus ended up with the biggest chunk of his fragmented empire. She continued to flip the pages, wondering if there was anything about women in this book. Then she came upon the story of Stratonike. Stratonike was the daughter of Demetrius, called Taker of Cities, the son of another of Alexander's generals. And then somebody decided it would be a good idea for Stratonike to marry Seleucus. Julia radiated outrage. This poor girl was sent off to marry some guy in the same generation as her grandfather. Her father Demetrius must have been a first-class jerk. But then, Seleucus's heir, his son from an earlier marriage, met Stratonike and fell in love with her, his stepmother. He was so distressed about his feelings that he became physically ill and took to his bed. Eventually Seleucus found out what was going on, and graciously turned Stratonike over to his son. After which, one hopes, they lived happily ever after. She looked up from the book reluctantly and returned it to its shelf.

Julia packed up and headed back to her room. She read some more, and then stood and jogged in place to warm herself. The bitter cold had dried her skin, and her cheeks were peeling. She nibbled at the flaky edges of her chapped lips until she tasted blood. She would have to get moisturizer and chapstick in the morning between classes. She prepared a big mug of chamomile tea, wrapping her hands around the mug, enjoying the comforting heat, and returned to her books.

After a while, there was a crisp tap at her door. "Julia?"

Campbell stood at the door. "My parents are having a party next Sunday afternoon for a few old friends and some of Pater's clients. The main event will be that wretched play-off game, so the available activities will be watching the game, eating and drinking. Want to go?"

"Sure, thanks," Julia said.

"Would it be too much hassle taking the train home? I don't have a Monday class and I won't be driving back until Monday night," Campbell said.

"That's no problem," Julia replied.

"The trains run pretty late. I can give you a ride to the train station."

"It'll be fine. Should be fun. Your parents are so nice."

"Nice. I won't disabuse you. Okay, glad you can make it." Campbell retreated and shut the door.

*

Julia stood before her closet and nibbled her lower lip. What should she wear? A dress would be a force. Too much. But pants? Should be fine for a football party. She finally settled on black skinny jeans and a cream-colored, scoop-necked blouse with ruched sleeves, something fancy to contrast with the casual jeans. She pulled on a pair of black pumps with 4-inch heels to complete the outfit and surveyed herself in the mirror. She looked slim and fit, her runner's gastrocs straining at her tight jeans. *Not too bad*, she thought. *And with these heels, I'm almost average height. Still shorter than Campbell though. I'll have to be careful not to slip in the snow.*

Just before leaving her room she went to the drawer with her socks, pulled it out from the cabinet, and from the hiding space thus exposed, she extracted the box with Grandma's necklace. *Look, Grandma. I'm wearing your beautiful necklace to a nice party. I wish you could come with me...* She fastened the necklace, slipped on her coat and went down the hall to find Campbell.

The porch and driveway of the McDade home had been meticulously shoveled, and snow had slid off most of its steep roof to terminate in icicles decorating the perimeter of the home. It looked like an enchanted manor from a fairy tale.

Campbell walked with Julia to the front door. "Welcome back to the Winter Palace," Campbell said.

*Campbell's kidding but it's true,* Julia thought. Julia and Campbell entered the McDade home, and Julia set to stamping her feet and scuffing the soles of her shoes on the rug in the entrance hall. She would be humiliated if she dragged melting snow into this beautiful home. She looked past the entrance hall toward the formal living room.

"Who are all these people?" Julia asked.

"Oh, clients, people from Pater's firm, some investment people. Mostly from Boston, a few from New York."

Julia nodded.

"Mater, where's Satan?" Campbell asked, as her mother approached.

"I left him in your room with the door closed. This isn't his sort of event."

"Maybe not," Campbell answered.

"Julia, what a beautiful necklace! Is that an antique?" Maggie McDade asked.

"Oh, yes, it is, thank you. It was my grandmother's. She left it to me."

"Your grandmother? Were you close to her?" Maggie asked.

Julia nodded. "Oh, yes. We used to talk on the phone a lot, and I would write her letters. She was such a nice lady."

"How wonderful! Well, why don't you have something to eat? The food is laid out in the dining room, and there should be someone circulating with drinks."

"Thank you," Julia said. She and Campbell headed toward the food.

"Julia, I need to say hello to someone. I'll be right back." Campbell walked across the room.

Martin McDade joined his wife near the front hall.

"Campbell's friend Julia was just telling me about how close she was with her grandmother. She's very sweet," Maggie said.

"Yes, I agree; she has a nice way about her," Martin replied.

Julia stood alone in the living room, feeling a little uncomfortable. Campbell and Russell were chatting with a few of what must be their old friends. She wandered away from the living room, down the quiet hall, glancing at the family photos hanging on either side. Campbell and Russell as kids on the beach or at a barbecue. The whole family standing together in the snow, in ski gear, ready to mount a ski lift. Older photos- must be grandparents, or even great-grandparents.

She found herself before Mr. McDade's library. The door stood wide open- would it be okay to walk in for a moment? She took a deep breath, tiptoed in and paused before the grand fireplace with its sculpted mantle of milky white marble. She reached out and reverently brushed the cool marble face of the caryatid on the right of the mantle. Then she stepped back, to study the painting over the fireplace. It fairly gleamed with color. The rich rose and gold of the sunset cast bright highlights where sunshine danced on the choppy waves and in the billowing sails of the clipper ship, as it cut through a dark sea rendered in subtle shades of turquoise and gray.

Julia let her imagination wander, let it conjure an image of herself in a life perhaps 200 years ago. She saw herself standing on Long Wharf in Boston Harbor, wind whipping her long skirts around her ankles, waiting for this very ship to appear on the horizon and progress through the fine mist to dock. She knew she should be at home, helping with housework, but she had resolved to remain by the harbor until sunset, hoping that today the ship would return. She imagined that the capable captain was her own father, who would hurry down the gangplank to greet her, and enfold her in his arms. After that she would wait anxiously for the appearance of the first mate, her own true love, young and handsome with laughing eyes. He would pick her up, hands around her slender waist, and spin her around, delighted to see her, so happy that she had been waiting there on the wharf for them. His name would be something manly. Starbuck, perhaps. Or Quatermain. No. Armstrong. William Armstrong. She would call him Will. She would whisper in his ear, *Will, I'm so glad you're home! So glad-*

"I see you like that painting."

Startled abruptly out of her reverie, Julia looked around quickly. There was Mr. McDade. He approached, hands folded behind his back.

"I'm sorry if I shouldn't be in here. The door was open, and I couldn't stop myself from taking a closer look," Julia managed to stammer. She felt her face grow red and she looked down at her feet.

"Not at all. I'm glad you like it."

"It's beautiful. Good enough to be in a museum," Julia answered.

"True. This painting and this house were both completed in 1872. I like to think the painting gives an idea of what was going on outside the walls of this house when it was new."

"I- that is, when you walked in, I had been thinking about that, about what it would have been like, living back in the time when this ship was sailing," Julia said, but immediately felt foolish. It was very unlikely that Campbell's father cared one bit about what may or may not have been on her mind.

He nodded. "If you like this artist's work, you can see more by him at the Boston Museum of Fine Arts. Fitz Henry Lane. His ability to capture the light in the sky and on the water is quite amazing."

"I haven't been there. Yet, I mean."

"The MFA has a fine collection of American artists, and a respectable assortment of Impressionist works. I find their earlier European paintings to be less impressive. You can do better elsewhere if you are drawn to works from the Renaissance and Baroque periods."

"I will certainly check it out. Thank you." *Whatever all that means,* Julia thought.

"Sit in my chair, Julia. It's the best place to view the painting from. From the angle you have now, there's some glare from the chandelier."

"Oh, I, thank you." Julia eased herself into the cordovan leather swivel chair and turned to the painting.

"There, you see? Much better, right?"

"Yes, thank you. I see what you mean," Julia said.

"Good. Well, I should go; I shouldn't leave Maggie to greet all the guests by herself. But, please do stay and enjoy the painting as long as you wish." And with that, he was gone.

Julia gazed upon the painting for a long while and then spun the chair 90 degrees so she was looking out through mullioned glass onto the snow-covered front lawn. *These people are so nice to me. Not sure why. Kind of cool to see how rich people live though.* She leaned back into the deep cove of the back of the chair.

While she sat there enjoying the feel of the leather, she heard footsteps and voices and froze; two people had entered the library. They couldn't see her; her back was to the door and she was completely concealed by the large chair.

"You're being ridiculous. I am not the problem here." A woman's voice, low and serious.

"You've spent money faster than I could make it. Faster than anyone could make it! And now you wonder why there's not more left." A man's voice, soft, defensive.

"Not more left! There's none left, but plenty of bills. The problem here is that you've had these... missteps. Mistakes do not lead to income, dear. Not in your field." The woman's voice was sarcastic.

"If you hadn't spent so much over the years! I got you that nice house in Chatham. And I said, sure, redo it if you want. With the cost of the renovations we could have bought a palace somewhere. And then, and then! You said you didn't like it, and you hired a different designer who did even more expensive renovations."

"I didn't like it because it was cookie-cutter. Pottery Barn! I couldn't have had people like Marty and Maggie over, the way it first came out."

"Keep your voice down, for god's sake. That's what you worried about! What Marty and Maggie would think!" The man's voice shrank to a harsh whisper. "I think Marty knows more than he's saying about my... reassignment."

"That isn't the point. This doesn't have to do with Marty or anyone else. The point is that you blew it."

"Give it a rest, Liz."

"Don't call me Liz!"

"Fine. Elizabeth! I need a drink," the man said. The footsteps receded. Julia breathed a huge sigh of relief. She waited what seemed like a safe interval and then quietly slipped out of the library and back to the living room, where viewing the play-off game was in full swing. Russell was waving a bottle of beer, while talking to two other young men. Julia gasped. One of them was the likeness of her imaginary Will Armstrong: exceptionally handsome, with dark hair and a devilish glint in his dark eyes. Something Russell said must have been funny; he threw back his head and laughed, revealing a beautiful smile. If she had been more self-confident, she would have walked over to the group and introduced herself. But she didn't have the nerve. She took a seat on a sepia-toned tufted leather ottoman near the TV and focused on the game.

Martin McDade was standing behind the sofa. When an attractive mid-dle-aged couple approached him, Martin turned and greeted them. "There you are. James, good to see you. Elizabeth, as always, what a pleasure! Maggie said you'd arrived, but I hadn't seen you."

"Marty, thank you for having us to your home, this enclave of civilization in a barbaric world," Elizabeth said. Her trim, toned torso was enfolded in a cashmere cardigan the color of old gold. She studied Martin's eyes but couldn't see into them. He smiled in welcome, but it was a polite smile, a host's smile, not an ally's smile, not a sympathetic smile.

"Elizabeth, you give me too much credit. The source of any civilization in this household is Maggie. Are you still drinking vodka martinis? Grey Goose?"

"You have a good memory, Marty. Yes, thank you, with a twist," Elizabeth said, shaking back her thick chestnut hair, and adjusting the dark brown Gucci bag on her shoulder.

"James?"

"Oh, scotch. Whatever you have. On the rocks," James answered.

"Your preference was for a single malt, if I recall. We have Laphroiag and Lagavulin. Also, I've discovered this wonderful A'bunadh, which is less peaty but with an amazing intensity."

"I'll try that A'bunadh. Thanks, Marty," James said.

Martin stepped over to the bar and instructed the caterer's bartender as to their drinks.

"Has Jamie arrived yet?" Elizabeth asked. "He drove separately."

"Yes, he did, he's right over there with Russell." Martin said. He looked over his shoulder, toward the entrance hall. "My next bolus of guests has arrived; I should go."

Julia glanced again over to the cluster of young men around Russell. I bet that cute one is their son, she thought. Jamie, his mother had said. Tall, like both of them, with dark hair like his father. As she watched, a college-age girl approached the knot of young men. She was pretty, with hair like a dark silky curtain falling over her shoulders and down her back, lightened at the ends by an ombré treatment. She laid one hand on the arm of the cute one. Julia felt a stir of jealousy. Wait a minute-they look a lot alike; she's his sister. Must be. Although she knew it was absurd, Julia felt a wave of relief. *I wish I could walk over and be in that group.* And meet Jamie. Flesh and blood Jamie, not an intangible William Armstrong. But she lacked the nerve.

She turned around and focused on the game, perched on the edge of the ottoman. She followed the action carefully. The team she had chosen to root for had the ball. Julia leaned forward. A first down, and then another. Her team was in the red zone. They had momentum. They were going to score on this set of downs; she knew it. Maybe on this next play. And then the snap, and the quarterback took two steps back, and then another, scanned the field and threw. His wide receiver reached for the ball, juggled it in his hands but let it slip away from him and hit the field.

"88 was wide open in the end zone; what was the QB thinking?" Julia burst out.

The men all turned and looked at her.

"I've turned into my father," whispered Julia. She shrank down as small as possible onto the ottoman.

"Nothing wrong with that," declared Martin McDade and looked pointedly at Campbell. One of the portly clients nodded vigorously in agreement.

The game continued. Julia, wanting to be less conspicuous, slipped off the ottoman and got a glass of wine from the bar. She sipped wine and slowly nibbled hors d'oeuvres until the game was over.

On the other side of the room, Elizabeth approached her son. "Jamie, sweetheart, we'll be heading out now. You drive carefully, alright?" Her tone was indulgent.

"Don't worry, Mom. I'm always careful," Jamie replied.

"What about Caroline?" Elizabeth continued.

"She drove here in the Audi; she's all set."

"Good. Love you." She kissed her son's cheek and turned to her husband.

"James, let's be on our way. Really, we could die of old age waiting for you to make all your goodbyes." Elizabeth stood with her Gucci bag on her shoulder and a lustrous beaver coat over her arm, ready to move.

"Could be we won't be back here for a long time. What's the rush?" James allowed his eyes to wander around the room and smiled sadly.

Elizabeth made a dismissive gesture. "I'm ready to go. There's only so much small talk I can tolerate."

Elizabeth headed for the door; James padded along behind her.

Julia glanced at her watch. She was also thinking it was time to be on her way. She would find Campbell and ask for a ride to the train station. She set down her wine glass and turned around. Standing there was Jamie.

"Hey there. I wanted to say hello to the rabid football fan before heading out."

Julia turned around slowly. Her heart stopped. There smiling at her was Jamie. He was even more handsome up close than from across the room. The reflection of the chandelier sparkled silver in his dark eyes.

"Oh. I'm so embarrassed! I can't believe I did that," Julia said, ducking her head.

"I thought it was great. I'm Jamie. Jamie Pembroke," he said.

He was beautiful; his voice was beautiful... Julia struggled to respond and finally managed to give her name.

"It looked like you were really into that game. You actually like football?" said Jamie.

"I've watched a lot of football with my Dad. He's a huge LSU fan. My two brothers, Dad was always trying to get them interested in football, but they prefer computer games. I felt bad for him, you know? So I would at least sit with him when a game was on," Julia said.

"Louisiana girl? I thought I heard that in your voice. What do the parents think of their daughter living among Yankees?"

"Would you believe it, when I got into Harvard my Dad just said their football team wasn't very good," Julia said.

"Ouch! Sounds like child abuse to me!" Jamie laughed his wonderful laugh.

A blast of Arctic air swept into the room as someone exited via the front door.

"Looks like people are heading out. Did you drive?" Jamie asked. He zipped up his bomber jacket and looped a plaid scarf around his neck.

"Ah, no. I- I don't have a car. Campbell gave me a ride up, but I'm taking the train back."

"I can give you a ride. You'll freeze on the platform waiting for the train."

"I wouldn't want you to go out of your way," Julia said. This gorgeous guy was actually willing to spend an hour in a car with her.

"Not at all. I'm also at Harvard," Jamie said.

"Oh, well, okay, sure, that would be great," Julia said. "Let me get my coat." She hurried to grab her coat, praying all the while that Jamie would not have come to his senses and vanished in the meantime. But he was still there, pulling on leather gloves as she returned.

"All set?" he asked.

"Yep, all set," Julia said. They walked to the door and onto the driveway, and then over to Jamie's little sports car. He held the door for her and she dropped into the bucket seat. She texted Campbell, 'got a ride. c u tues' and slipped her phone into her handbag.

Jamie gripped the roof of the car and swung into the driver's seat.

"So what are you studying?" Julia asked.

"What am I studying? Oh, a lot of things!"

"I meant your major. You know."

"I see. You ask serious questions. Okay, I'm a music major. I love music."

"That's wonderful. What do you like best about it?"

"I love the whole evolution of music over the centuries, the ordered clarity of the music of the Classical period, the wild intemperance of the Romantic period, succeeded by atonal music, later jazz, reggae, big band. I love it all!"

"What will you do when you get out?"

"Get out? You make it sound like prison," Jamie said.

"No! I love being at Harvard." Julia felt like an idiot. Everything she said came out sounding stupid.

"Sorry for teasing you." He paused before continuing, and then his tone was more thoughtful. "I'm not sure what I'll do. I've come to realize that good job prospects are scarce with my degree. Although what I'm studying has enriched my life so much, that I don't regret a minute of it. Possible that eventually I'll go to business school and do investment banking like my father."

"Investment banking! That sounds stressful," Julia said.

"Mmm, true. Or could pursue a military career. Family tradition," Jamie continued. "I like the idea of capturing cities."

"Really? Who in your family was in the military?"

"My great-grandfather. I wouldn't be here if he hadn't gone off to war."

"How so?"

"My great-grandfather, his name was Lawrence Pembroke. From London. He was an officer in Montgomery's army, and was there in the thick of taking Italy from the Axis. After Sicily was liberated, for a while he was stationed in Palermo. And there in Palermo he met an Italian girl whose family had had a rough time in the war. Her father and two brothers had been killed, so it was only her and her mother, trying to get by. She was skin and bones but still very beautiful when they met. Francesca, her name was. She couldn't speak English. Old Lawrence's Italian was limited to 'macaroni,' so I have no idea how they communicated. But he would take her out and feed her, and she was grateful.

"Then, on one momentous occasion when he had leave, they went to Capri together for a weekend, which was quite a scandal at that time. She told him, in her poor English, that in Capri there are two moons, one in the sky above and one below, in the bay. It was true, my great-grandfather would say. That night there was a full moon, and there in the Bay of Naples was its mirror image. Somehow that struck a chord with my great-grandfather, and he started thinking of her as a spiritual woman with depth of feeling, not just a cute but helpless little waif. Make a long story short, he fell in love with her. They were married, and he brought her with him when he was discharged from the army. Most unlikely part of the whole thing is that he had gotten friendly with several officers in Patton's army, and they all ended up going to the States and going into business together. In Boston. In my family we call that 'the magic of the two moons of Capri'."

"That's so romantic! What a wonderful story!"

"Yeah, it's kind of cool," Jamie agreed, as he sped confidently south, the Atlantic Ocean on his left.

"Did you know him? Your great-grandfather?"

"Yes, sort of. He died when I was a little kid. Now my great-grandmother, she died before I was born. I never knew her," he said, eyes focused on the road as he navigated the narrow streets of downtown Cambridge. He pulled into a parking garage near Harvard Square. "The Pembrokes were one of the great noble families of England. Unfortunately, we take our descent from one of the younger sons who did not inherit the estate."

"Have you been back there? To Palermo, or Capri? Or London?" Julia asked.

"Oh, yes, we've gone back. To all of those places. My parents love to travel. Palermo's crazy. You should see how people drive! And Capri is a fantastic resort island, really beautiful. And London! Definitely one of the best cities in the world."

"That sounds wonderful. I've never been anywhere, well, except for Massachusetts. I'm from Nowheres-ville, Louisiana."

"You'll have a chance to travel. Give it time. Nice necklace, by the way."

"Thanks. My grandmother's."

"Ah. Family jewelry. What does your father do in Louisiana?"

"He works at an oil refinery."

"The petrochemical industry? Good field. Does he own the refinery?"

"No, no. He's an engineer, pretty senior, but he's not the owner."

"Too bad," he murmured. "Listen, come with me for a while. I'd like to talk some more." He unbuckled her seatbelt, got out of the car, sauntered around to the passenger side and opened her door. "Allow me, lovely lady," he said, extending his hand to help her out of the car. She put her hand into his and he lifted her up. He wrapped his arm around her waist and guided her toward his house. In silence they ascended the stairs.

*Lovely lady?* Julia couldn't believe her ears. "I hope I'll get to travel," she stammered. "I plan to go to Turkey this summer, on a sort of archeological expedition. We will be reading the *Iliad* before the walls of Troy. I think it will be amazing!"

"My family usually spends most of the summer on Cape Cod. We have a place in Chatham. It's a cute little town. Not too exciting though. You have to make a major effort to find decent night life."

"That sounds so nice though. What's it like?"

"It's across from the beach. Here, sit down." He motioned at a chair. "I'll get us some wine."

He returned with two glasses of wine and set them down on a small table, then pulled a second chair over, next to hers. "Here, I have some pictures on my phone."

Julia saw a stately two-story house clad in weathered shingle, with white shutters and trim. The windows of a third story protruded from the steep incline of the roof. Hydrangeas bursting with brilliant blue flowers lined the immaculately maintained lawn. White roses on trellises and tufts of lavender stood against the front of the house. "And see this porch? It's on the back of the house. You can see the beach from it. It's great. Hearing the surf."

"It looks wonderful. I can almost smell it- the ocean and the flowers..." Suddenly she remembered the conversation in the McDade library. Was this the house Jamie's mother had renovated twice? Then Jamie leaned over and kissed her, and she forgot about renovations. Flustered, she looked down. He lifted her chin and kissed her again, harder, more deeply, and Julia's head began to spin. *Let him kiss me with the kisses of his mouth, for his love is better than wine, his mouth is most sweet,* echoed in her mind.

Then he stood and stepped behind her and put his hands on her shoulders. "Are you tense? I hope I'm not making you nervous."

Julia managed to shake her head; no words were forthcoming.

"Your muscles are so tight; let me get out those knots. Do you like the wine?" Jamie massaged her shoulders with strong hands. His fingers slipped lower, gently, rhythmically caressed her ribcage and the muscles along her back.

"Oh, yes, it's delicious," Julia said.

Jamie leaned down and whispered in her ear, "Now let me sing you a song without words."

Then she was in his bed, with her hands on the taut muscles of his chest. Jamie's skin was smooth and olive, with a wonderful suntan, perhaps the legacy of his Italian great-grandmother. *Thou art brown but comely...* She closed her eyes and surrendered to him. Lying with her, he seemed to her both more and less than human, a hero, a god, an angel come to earth to look on this daughter of man, an incubus to possess her, a sphinx to devour her. She melted into him and dissolved in ecstasy. It could have been seven minutes, or it could have been seven days and seven nights, and she was then aware of herself as a being separate from him. But she knew that she would never be the same again.

"Jesus!" Jamie whispered, rolling off her. "You were so wet! God, was that great!"

Julia lay next to him, enjoying the warmth of his body. What a luxury, to lie in a bed already warm and cozy, despite the bitter cold outside. She drifted off to sleep, and in her dreams she saw herself in a white organdy dress, the delicate fabric enfolding her slender frame in a flattering way. She saw Jamie ambling across the broad emerald expanse of the lawn of the Pembroke's summer home on Cape Cod. He would look at her, entranced by the arresting violet of her eyes, the raven wing of her silky dark hair caressing her cheek. He would produce a freshly cut, perfect white rose from behind his back, and lay it tenderly in her delicate hands. Later they would sit together on the porch in brightly painted Adirondack chairs, looking out over the dunes into the surf spilling over the sand.

She slept well and awoke wonderfully rested at 8 o'clock the next morning. She glanced at her phone. She had an hour to get to class. Jamie was still sound asleep. She studied his face in the morning light; how handsome he was! She felt like Psyche indulging in the forbidden pleasure of gazing upon sleeping Cupid. But she knew she must go, if she wanted to be on time to class. She turned away, dressed in silence, crept to the door and let herself out. She pulled the door shut behind her and started down the hall. She stopped short. He didn't have her number. He knew her name, at least her first name, but they had not exchanged phone numbers. She didn't want to knock and wake him. Suddenly she had the solution. She opened her handbag and unzipped the side pocket. There was her packet of personalized business cards! She pulled out a card and jotted on the back, 'Here's my number-I'm so glad we met!' She slipped the card under Jamie's door, and hurried home, to shower and change clothes.

Back in her own room, she looked at herself dreamily in the mirror. "I can't be that bad," she mused. For the first time in her life, she felt like part of the world that *lived*, not part of the world that just watched. She looked deep into her eyes and studied the lavender folds of her irises. "I am the rose of Sharon and the lily of the valley," she whispered. "I am."

Then she noticed a little dried blood on her chest, just above the neckline of her ivory blouse. When she and Jamie had been together, the heavy gold of her grandmother's necklace, with its complex setting had scratched her, and she had not noticed until now. She removed the necklace and carefully put it away in its hiding place.

Julia wandered through the day in a pleasant fog, reliving the events of the night before, remembering what Jamie had said, or done, what he was wearing, how he drove his car, how he had kissed her. It had been magical. She wrote his name down on a piece of paper and wrote her own name below it. Both names started with J, both had five letters, and the vowels and consonants were in exactly the same positions in both names. They were meant to be. It was fate. She had found her place in the world at long last. She and this wonderful guy had found each other, and together they would be happy. Suspended in this transcendental state, she forgot to eat lunch, and had little interest in dinner. She crossed Harvard Yard in the icy cold, heading for her room, giggling quietly as she recalled some detail of the night before. But as she laid out her books to start studying, she realized something: it had been 12 hours since she and Jamie Pembroke had parted, 12 hours since she had slipped that card under his door, and he had not called. No phone call, no quick text message. Her mood took a nosedive. What could that mean? Surely he would contact her. They'd had such a great connection!

Julia studied as well as she could for the next three hours, but it was hard to concentrate. When she finally closed her books and climbed into her cold and lonely bed, she lay awake in the dark, trying not to cry, trying not to panic. *I am the rose of Sharon*, she reminded herself, but now it sounded hollow and preposterous.

As soon as she awoke the next morning, she checked her phone for any messages she might have missed in the night. Nothing. She arose, dressed, and dragged herself from class to class, checking frequently for missed calls and text messages. Nothing from Jamie. She continued on like that for several days before coming to terms with the fact that if Jamie had not contacted her by now, he probably never would. Alone in her room, Julia found tears spontaneously dribbling down her cheeks. When at class, it took all her concentration to keep herself from breaking down and sobbing. Then she recalled how her necklace had scratched her skin. Was this some kind of sign? If only Grandma was here! She needed a hug in the worst way. This thought precipitated a fresh round of tears.

Words began to swirl around in her head. Sadly, she pulled a pad of paper from her desk, and wrote:

"Adrift

Adrift, alone, with insubstantial dreams,

Sweet children of a moment lost in time,

How bright and sparkling that brief memory seems

Elusive, wavering vision, were you mine?

Enchanting, that exquisite adagio

Chased silver of those chiaroscuro eyes.

Upon my heart a gold intaglio,

Upon my soul indelibly incised,

My enigmatic wanderer with winged words.

I linger in forgotten lands in ruins,

The haunted silence whispering a dirge

Concerti lost in harsh discordant tunes.

The winds of time may bring you back to me

But what was real, and what imagining?"

When she had done, she looked at the paper, folded it and stuck it into a drawer in her desk. She read a little more and then went to sleep.

\*

Campbell waved at Julia as she returned from her last class of the day. "So, how did you like the big football party?" she asked.

"It was fine. Thanks again for inviting me." Julia's tone was flat.

Campbell eyed her suspiciously. Something was up. Or maybe she was just tired. "By the way, you somehow managed to make quite a favorable impression on Pater. He mostly tolerates people, thinks they're mostly idiots, but he actually seems to like you."

"Oh, thanks. Thanks for telling me that."

"Did you, ah, what did you do, other than that little comment about turning into your father that might have caught his attention?" Campbell asked.

"Oh, we talked a little about that painting he has in his library. He knew I thought it was beautiful. I guess he approved of that."

"Mmm, yes. Pater is fond of his Fitz Henry Lane. He wanted to know whether you shouldn't be studying law rather than anthropology. Actually, he calls it 'the Law.' Says someone with your intelligence would be better off studying something more substantive than anthropology. Really, I wish he'd say something about my intelligence." Campbell sighed and withdrew.

Julia smiled sadly to herself. At least Mr. McDade thought well of her.

A week passed, and then another, and Julia found herself able to function again, sometimes going for a whole hour without thinking of Jamie. Still, it felt like he had taken a big chunk out of her heart and stepped on it and thrown it away.

\*

Campbell tapped at Julia's door. "I'm going to Zorba's to get some take-out. Want to come?"

"Sure. Not really hungry but I'll take a walk," Julia answered.

It was early March, and the temperature still dipped below freezing once the sun went down, so they both bundled up before heading out. Zorba's was a popular Greek restaurant with an active take-out business and a nice lounge area with a decent bar. Its Cretan bartender only allowed Greek music on the sound system, and pretended not to understand English, unless appropriately compensated. The lounge area was packed that night with a mixture of people waiting for tables, waiting for take-out, and waiting for Cretan Idomeneus to condescend to serve their drinks.

Campbell squeezed through the crowd. "There you are," she said to Julia. "It's hard to find a short person in here. So. There's a half hour wait for my food. Don't feel you have to stay here if you have things to do."

"I'll wait. It's nice and warm in here," Julia replied.

As they stood together, Campbell caught sight of someone she recognized and gave a casual wave.

"Who are you waving to?" Julia asked.

"Oh, this fellow I know. Actually, he was at the party. Not sure if you met him. Jamie Pembroke. I'll introduce you."

Julia stood horrified, paralyzed. She contemplated flight, but people were so densely packed that it would have been impossible to do quickly. Instead she watched as Jamie swaggered toward them, smiling, confident, glass of red wine held aloft, until he caught sight of Julia. His smile flickered briefly, and the renewed smile seemed forced.

"Campbell, hey, how are you?" he said.

"Not bad although pretty hungry. Taking so long to get food tonight. Oh, did you meet Julia? At that party we had?" Campbell gestured to Julia.

"We did meet," he said to Campbell. "Hello again, Julie. And how is the little down-home country girl this evening?"

"Julia. My name is Julia," she said with all the dignity she could muster. Then she realized that Jamie was not alone. He had in tow a tall shapely blonde girl wearing cream-colored velour leggings as tight on her legs as skin on a cucumber.

"This is Amber," Jamie said.

"Nice to meet you! We just got back from Aspen. We ski. My family, I mean. I can't believe how good Jamie is on the slopes!" Amber said, shrugging her shoulders and shaking her head.

"Her family has a great ski house. Amber was kind enough to invite me for a long weekend. We had a great time," Jamie said.

"Ah. That's why you missed Dr. Manning's class last Friday," Campbell said. "I was wondering."

Jamie gave a sheepish grin but did not speak.

"Oh my god but it was so cold! I was soooo lucky to have Jamie to keep me warm. What a good boyfriend!" She tossed her abundant hair in a magnificent rendition of the entitlement flip. "I tell you what- he's even better at après ski than at skiing, if that's possible!" She linked arms with Jamie and pressed the side of her body against his. Jamie's hand rested possessively on her hip, his thumb thrust under the bottom edge of her sweater, a fat worm burrowing beneath baby blue mohair.

Amber held her cell phone aloft, pouted, leaned close to Jamie and clicked. "Look at our selfie! No, it's a weefie! Or an ussie? You look so cute, sweetie," she giggled as she admired her look in the digital image.

"Trying to butter me up?" Jamie asked.

"Can you hold my drink? I'm going to the bathroom," Amber said.

"Sure. I'll come with you," Jamie said.

Amber walked forward, but a tight cluster of Japanese tourists stepped in behind her, and Jamie was cut off. As he tried to squeeze forward, following Amber, Julia put her hand on his wine glass. He stopped and faced her.

"That caricature of a woman is your girlfriend? Seriously?" Julia whispered hoarsely.

"Hey, wait. We had a great night, but you didn't think...that we..., no. Sorry if you misunderstood," Jamie said.

His tone was condescending.

Julia withdrew her hand. He turned and forced his way through the crowd. *I hate him!* She thought.

Campbell watched the exchange with interest. And concern. "What did you say to Jamie? I can't hear a word in here unless you scream."

"Oh, nothing much," Julia responded.

By this time Campbell's order was finally complete, and they left Zorba's. Outside, a cold, heavy mist had settled on Cambridge; it congealed into tiny particles that pelted Julia's face as she and Campbell hurried into the dark night.

"Sure you don't want some of this?" Campbell asked as they returned to their floor.

"No. Thanks." Julia let her hair fall across the side of her face as she opened her door. She was tearing up again and she didn't want Campbell to see. How could she have been so stupid? She was actually taken with a guy who wanted to be with a ditz like Amber.

"Julia?" Campbell had stepped forward and could see Julia's tears.

Julia looked up. She knew she was busted.

Campbell set down the bag of take-out and parked her hands on her hips. "I want answers and I want them now."

Reluctantly, embarrassed, Julia told her what happened, the offer of a ride, then one thing leading to another, and then he just didn't call, her voice cracking as she related that part of the story.

Campbell gave a heavy sigh. "Can you please check with me before you decide to get together with someone? I mean, if it's someone you meet in my house who I'm bound to be able to fill you in about. Jamie Pembroke is a royal prick of a pseudo-Brit and if you were a little more in touch with reality you would have known that. Not to mention that he's also a ruthless narcissist, as is his Disney princess du jour."

"I just, I don't know, he seemed so nice!"

"Really, you don't have the sense that God gave a left-handed monkey wrench," Campbell said.

"I guess not," Julia said.

"He put the moves on me once," Campbell confided.

"What did you do?" Julia asked.

"I hit him." Campbell cradled her right fist in her left palm. She allowed herself a small smile, remembering.

"I feel so stupid!" Julia groaned.

"Don't blame yourself. He's a master-manipulator. If I'd seen you together, I would have warned you about him. And don't feel bad about Bambi, or Amber or whatever her name was. Jamie's not after her so much as her father. He's on the board of Citigroup. Very wealthy guy. What Jamie really wants is to make a good impression on him. Jamie's going to need some real money very soon."

"What do you mean?"

"Well, Jamie's dad is in finance, and he's had an incredibly successful run, until recently. Pater's firm serves as counsel for James, Senior's firm. And just between you and me, Pater uncovered some corner-cutting on the part of Jamie's Dad. Pater dug some more and found more irregularities. Nothing as spectacular as the Bernie Madoff scandal, but enough to interest the SEC, were they to notice it."

"Is he being fired?"

"No, the firm is not firing him. They are giving him the option to stay on, but he has been demoted and his clients are being reassigned. They probably hope he resigns."

"I thought those kinds of people got that, you know, golden parachute."

"Not in his case, no, apparently."

"So the family's income will be going down?"

"Going way down. No way they can keep up their current lifestyle."

"I see." Now the conversation she'd overheard in the library in January made sense. She also suddenly realized: Jamie's compliment on her necklace and questions about her own father's line of work were not just polite chit-chat. He had wanted to know if she was from a wealthy background. If she had been, it might have been her instead of Amber at Zorba's tonight. And she would not have understood why. A wave of disgust swept over her. *That's it. No trusting any guys. I don't need them. I'm just going to study.*

\*

Dahlia called the next night. "Bubba's asleep so I can talk. I looked on my phone. Only 40° up where you are. I feel so bad for you, with all that cold!"

"It's really not so bad, now that I've got the right clothes. And you know, the best part about being cold is how nice it is getting warm again. Curling up under a blanket, wearing thick fuzzy socks and a good flannel robe, big mug of herb tea..." *How can I explain how much I love it? The magnificent progression of the seasons: the beauty of the multicolored autumn leaves, the awesome power of a blizzard, the miracle of the world's green rebirth in springtime, the long summer days, with weather so much milder than the crippling heat of the Louisiana summer...*

"I guess. You meet any guys yet? Anyone special?"

"No, no one. I just study." She was wary of all guys after the heart-rending episode with Jamie Pembroke.

"Just wait, one day you'll meet someone."

*Been there, done that, not interested,* Julia thought.

\*

Across the Charles River in Brookline, Mark Eastgard sauntered into his family home, dropped his backpack on the table and entered the TV room, where Helen, clad in a gray fleece sweatshirt and stretch pants intently followed the exercises being demonstrated in a yoga DVD. Mark plopped down on the couch and opened a can of coke. "Mom, what are you doing?"

Helen was breathless, despite the modest demands of the yoga instructor. She wiped a strand of hair from her face and paused the DVD. "I'm trying to get back into shape. Look at me! I used to be so thin!"

"You look fine," Mark said.

"No, I don't. I- I've put on 40 pounds, since um, Dad and I got married. I'm not going to ignore it anymore. I'm going to exercise and eat healthy. After this routine is done, I'm going to walk around the block. Briskly."

"Okay, Mom. Go for it. Oh, I wanted to see if you'd mind- a few of us want to go to Florida on spring break."

"You've worked so hard. You should go. But, um, is it expensive?"

"No. Greg, he's in my Bio class, he found a deal where we can stay in Tampa for four nights for cheap. I can cover it with the money I earned last summer."

"Well, why not? Go ahead."

"Great. I'll tell Greg to sign me up."

# CHAPTER 61

Midterm exams behind him, Mark went home to pack for his trip to Florida. He checked the weather on his phone. "Mom, look at this. It's going to be cold during spring break, only in the 60's."

"I guess you'll have to stay out of the water."

"We were counting on windsurfing! We'll freeze if we try that."

"Say, ah, Dad had that wetsuit. He got it so he could go into the water with you when we went to the beach. When you were little. Want to try it on?"

"Wouldn't hurt."

"Check his closet. He always kept it on a hanger on the far left."

"Okay." Mark rose and went to check Alex's closet. No wetsuit on the left side of the closet, although there was an empty hanger. He leafed through all the suits and jackets hanging neatly in the closet. No wetsuit. He returned to Helen. "No wetsuit. Any place else I should look?"

"No, that's where he always kept it. I'll look around, but I don't know where else it might be. Wonder if he threw it away or something. It was pretty old."

"Too bad. I'll survive."

Elena Gonzalez stood in the shadows across the street from the Eastgard home. She had checked on-line and knew that BU was scheduled to begin spring break tomorrow. She wondered if Mark would be staying in town, or if he were going to take a vacation. If he was hanging around, it would be a good time to contact him and check in. During break, Mark wouldn't be stressed out. He'd be able to relax and think about her, about their relationship. She decided to text him the following day.

\*

By early afternoon Mark and his friends Greg and Rich had entered the modest hotel room they had reserved in Tampa, Florida.

"What's the wifi password?" Mark asked.

"Just the room number," Greg answered.

"Hmmm," Mark muttered.

"What is it?" Rich asked.

"This girl, she keeps texting me." Mark answered.

"So? What's wrong with her?" Greg asked.

"Nothing. She's great. But she's not for me."

"Just tell her," Rich advised.

"I try. I mean, I don't want to hurt her feelings, so I keep saying I'm busy, I'm stressed out with school, but she keeps texting. Wants to know if we can get together."

"Sure you're not gay?" Greg asked.

"No, I am not gay!" Mark groaned.

"She a dog?" Rich asked.

"No, she's good looking. Very hot. But just not for me."

"Give her my number. I'll do her. She'll forget you," Rich said.

"If I can think of a way to suggest that, I will." Mark turned off his phone. "Let's go to the beach."

Mark, Greg and Rich walked several blocks to reach the beach, a broad expanse of pale sand, heavily populated by college students, beneath an azure sky, and overlooking the Gulf of Mexico.

"Here's good. Good spot to check out the talent," Greg said.

"Yeah. Look at the one in the black bikini," Rich said.

"Not bad. The one over there has bigger tits," Greg said.

Mark laid out his towel and studied the girls on the beach. Lots of cute girls. Objectively. But since the near-miss with Elena, boobs didn't do it for him. Girls would flirt with him, all the time, but then he'd remember that episode with Elena, and all the desire would drain out of him, especially if they had big tits. Just as well, he told himself philosophically. He had so much studying to do. He put his arms behind his head and watched, amused, as Rich and Greg laid their plans to befriend some females. The more he thought about it though, the more troubled he became. What if this was permanent? Greg had suggested he was gay. It couldn't be true, could it? You couldn't just turn gay all of a sudden. Or could you? How could you tell? He was not interested in guys. Definitely not. A little voice inside his head said, *Prove it to yourself! Test yourself!* Mark closed his eyes and forced himself to imagine being alone with Greg, naked. Ughhhh! No way. He repeated the mental exercise with Rich instead. Even worse! Whatever had happened to him, he was definitely not gay.

# CHAPTER 62

It was 8:05 am. Julia tiptoed into her old home, easing the door closed behind her, not wanting to wake anyone who was still asleep. She had just finished her daily run. Attempting exercise outside in June any later in the day would be suicidal. She was breathing fast and deep. Her face was flushed and a light sheen of sweat covered her slender body. She heard her mother talking. *Must be on the phone*, Julia thought.

"No, Lydia," Aura Lee was saying, "I won't be able to go. My daughter is home from Harvard University where she is studying anthropology and making straight A's, and I want to spend some time with her before she has to leave. But thanks for thinking to invite me. I do appreciate it. What? No, she won't be here for the whole summer. No. She's going on some archeological tour of Turkey. I know. Yes, I know. I agree, but her professor says it's perfectly safe. Yes, I'll tell her to be careful. You too. Bye."

Julia turned away from her mother to hide her grin. She headed for the kitchen for something to drink.

"I'm probably wasting my breath, but do you have to take this crazy trip to the Middle East?"

"It's an educational program, led by my favorite teacher."

"You may say that now, but you'll probably end up getting thrown in some harem and we'll never see you again!"

"Nobody's going to bother putting her in their harem. Who'd want her?" Alo opined. He was settled at one end of the couch with his iPad.

"This discussion does not involve you," Julia said without turning to face her brother.

"Or you could get kidnapped by terrorists and end up getting killed or something," Aura Lee continued.

"It will be fine. I promise!" Julia said. Only a few days to go! She could hardly wait.

# CHAPTER 63

Professor Templeton and his dedicated band of students, two women and four men, gathered in the lobby of a small hotel in the town of Hisarlik, in modern Turkey, believed to be the site of the ancient city of Troy.

"You are mostly welcome," declared the hotel's proprietor with a broad grin, displaying an impossibly large number of teeth including one in front, capped with silver. He distributed heavy brass keys, nodding as each key changed hands. Julia accepted a key for herself and Betsy, her roommate for this trip. Betsy had tired of her turquoise hair; in preparation for this trip she had changed her hair color to pale silver with fuchsia highlights. Edward and Conner shared a room; Sam and Lee shared another.

In their mini-bus along their route they had started reading the *Iliad*, by turns standing near the front of the bus, one hand holding the book open, and the other hand clutching an adjacent seat, to avoid falling as they careened along bumpy roads.

Julia stood to take her turn, Book 2 of the *Iliad*.

"It is critical to establish the mood of our pilgrimage by reading of the catalogue of the ships as we travel," Professor Templeton said. "Carry on, Julia."

And so she did. The lurching of the bus became the rhythm of the waves, and the modern world slipped away, to be replaced by the world of ancient Troy. Conner read next, and then Betsy, and before nightfall, they had reached Hisarlik.

That evening the group gathered on a patio in back of the hotel. As sunset approached, it burned a stripe of vivid coral above the blue-black horizon and slowly faded, engulfed by the gathering darkness.

"As each of you reads, think of yourself as a bard, a rhapsode, travelling from one little town to another, in the Dark Ages of the Greek world, bringing the story of its glorious past to people with monotonous lives scratching out a subsistence existence in the rocky soil," Professor Templeton said. "Those people, they sit before you, exhausted from their daily labor, sore in body, but excited in mind, anticipating the golden words and phrases you will lay before them this very night."

Put in that context, it seemed absolutely magical, Julia thought.

"We begin now with Book 13, and will read through Book 14, but we will save Books 15 and 16 to read tomorrow, on the plain of Troy."

Beneath a sky blazing with stars, they read the *Iliad*, each taking a turn, using flashlight or iPhone to light the pages.

Early the next morning they gathered before the ruins of Troy and read of the death of Patroklos, beloved friend of Achilles, slain by the Trojan prince Hector, with an assist from Apollo.

"Where you stand now, this may be the very spot!" Professor Templeton declared. "Julia, are you crying?"

"No, sir," she replied, wiping away a tear.

"I still don't know that this isn't all just a story," Sam commented.

Julia poked him in the ribs and whispered, "You know that upsets him. Shut up about it."

The professor's face fell. "Samuel, the lines you read in the *Iliad* are as factual as what you read in the newspaper."

Sam nodded respectfully, but then turned and whispered to Julia, "the National Enquirer?"

"Shhh!"

And then they entered the archeological site with a local guide, and evaluated the remains of the walls, and learned that many different cities, designated chronologically by Roman numerals, had arisen on this site. As the hours passed, midday arrived, and the sky, pale and distant when they started out, was now a merciless cobalt, heavy and brutally hot.

"So, young warriors, what do you say to a lunch break?" Professor Templeton suggested. This was greeted with unanimous approval. The professor unfolded a white cotton handkerchief, removed his floppy white hat, settled the handkerchief on his head and replaced the hat, and then gestured toward the little street nearby. "We will find something to our liking along that way."

"Wait, where is Betsy?" Julia asked.

"Lee's missing also," Sam said.

"Likely climbing among the stones and pretending to be Achilles. Everyone wants to be Achilles!" Professor Templeton said, shaking his head. "Let's head back and locate them. Most likely near the Skaian gate..."

"While you do that, I can grab a table at that café," Julia said. She hurried over to the restaurant, propitiously named Andromache's Feast, and scanned it for a free table. There was one with room for their group, in row of tables along the sidewalk. The free table was near the edge of an awning, but still exposed to the hot rays of the sun. She looked around. This was as good as it was going to get. She sat down, dropped her backpack on the chair next to her, set her paperback copy of the *Iliad* onto the table and smoothed out a diagram detailing the plan of Troy, or rather, the many Troys. The famous Troy is Troy VII, she reminded herself. The diagram was pretty clear but translating that to the stones tumbled about the site itself was bewildering. At a table in the shade of the awning, a man sat by himself. He was tall, with graying sandy hair, and a lean, athletic build that set him apart from most other men of his age. A khaki-colored brimmed hat and a half-drunk cup of apple tea rested on his table. He was also reading the *Iliad*, and Julia noted with surprise that it was exactly the same edition as hers.

He looked up and noticed her. She was tiny, with silky dark hair, wearing a man's loose work shirt over a tank top, jean shorts with frayed cuffs, low boots and thick cotton socks.

He smiled. "American?" he asked.

Julia nodded. "Yes. Here with a group from school. I couldn't help but notice- we've got the same *Iliad*."

"So we do," he said. "What school are you in? Is this a high school trip?"

Julia sighed. Yes, she was short and skinny, but she wished people wouldn't always think she was younger than she was. "No, I'm in college. Harvard."

"Harvard! Very nice. What places are you visiting on your trip?"

"We've come along the western edge of Turkey, focusing on archeological sites. We visited Hierapolis, Ephesus, Pergamon, and now we're here at Troy. We'll stay here for three nights and then we have several days in Istanbul."

"That sounds fantastic!"

"It really has been. I've never been outside the US before, and to get to come here- it's unbelievable, all the things we've seen!"

"What have you liked best?"

"Oh, let's see. I think, at Ephesus, there's an absolutely beautiful building- the Celsus Library. Wait, I have a picture." She pulled out her phone and showed him. "And then at Pergamon, the Hellenistic city walls were insane. Perfectly cut stones, huge stones, still sitting right there, for more than 2000 years."

The man listened as she spoke. Here was this kid, spouting off about Ephesus and Pergamon and Hellenistic city walls, reading her *Iliad*. He knew many adults who knew nothing about any of these things.

"They told us that some of the really good stuff from Pergamon had been taken and put on display in a museum in Berlin. I wish they'd left it; I'd love to have seen it."

"I think that means you'll have to plan a trip to Berlin."

Julia looked at him. "That's a great idea! I'll have to save up some money, but why not?" She picked up her *Iliad*, holding it open and used it to fan herself. "I have heard that Alexander the Great always used to sleep with a copy of the *Iliad* under his pillow."

"I've heard that too," the man said, nodding. "So what are you doing here?"

"Visiting Troy. Our professor has us reading the *Iliad* out loud, on the bus coming here, last night at the hotel, this morning just outside the site. We're up to the death of Patroklos. Did you go there yet?"

"Yes, I spent the morning in Troy."

"What'd you think? I'm pretty confused, with this Troy I and Troy II and Troy VII and all the rocks that look the same."

"What did I think?" the man repeated. As he had walked along the paths neatly laid out by archeologists, now clean and tranquil, he had imagined it all, just for a moment: the warriors with armor of gleaming bronze strapped over muscles of iron; the roar of the soldiers; the faces, their rage, their determination, their fear when they knew death was upon them. The cheers from the ramparts as their hero marched forth; the blood, blood everywhere, spattered hot against the skin, the heavy smell of it, the taste of it. The blinding pain in the heel. The beautiful face of the gentle girl he had loved, his prize, in grace like Aphrodite...

"I mean, did you like it?" the girl asked, interrupting his memories.

"Yes. It was really something. Really something," he said. "Say, do you want to move over, out of the sun? You can have my table. I'm about to leave."

"You're sure? I'm supposed to be holding a table for my group. A couple of people got lost."

Her skin was fair and the tip of her nose was red. Brilliant sunshine glowed rose through the translucent helix of her ear. "Sure, no problem. I hope you don't mind if I mention it, but looks like you're getting some sunburn."

"I'm not surprised. We've been walking around in this blazing heat day after day." Julia picked up her backpack and moved out of the sun and over to the man's table.

"Don't you have sunscreen?" Now that she was close, he saw that the girl had eyes of deep-dark blue, almost indigo.

"No," Julia said.

The man zipped open a small green canvas tote and pulled out a tube of sunscreen. "Here. Take this and please use it. You have fair skin and you have to protect it."

Julia accepted the sunscreen.

"It's zinc oxide. It provides excellent sun protection."

"Okay. Thank you," she said but she wondered: why is it that people she barely knew went around telling her what she needed to wear and how to survive extremes of weather? "What about you? Where did you go on this trip?"

"I've been in Istanbul the whole time, except for this side trip to see Troy. You'll love Istanbul. There's so much to see: Hagia Sophia, the Blue Mosque, Topkapi Sarai, the Archeological Museum, oh, and this huge ancient underground cistern with fish in it. And the covered bazaar." The exhibit of the treasure of Apollodorus at the Archeological Museum had truly exceeded his expectations. He had never seen so many mint-quality coins from the early Hellenistic period.

"It all sounds so awesome! I can't believe I'm really here."

"It took me a lot longer to get here, but I'm glad I came," the man said. "Initially I had just planned to go to Istanbul, but then I saw how close I was to Troy and decided to make a detour. I couldn't leave Turkey without seeing the site of Troy." He recalled the moment the thought popped into his mind, and how he couldn't shake it. He had had to come to this spot. See it for himself.

"Where are you from?" Julia asked.

He paused. "New York. New York City."

"Oh, wow, another place I've never seen and want to visit!"

"Greatest city in the world, a lot of people say."

"If I were to be able to visit New York, could I call you and ask your advice about what to see and like that?"

He paused again, a long time, without speaking.

"I mean, I don't know anyone from New York," Julia said. "I don't mean,"

"Of course. Thing is, I travel a lot outside the US, so you won't be able to call me if I'm on a trip."

"Texting will still work, if you have wifi," Julia pointed out. "If you're away, you're away."

He took a small paper napkin from the table and jotted down his cell phone number. "Let me know if you come to New York."

"At last, my group is coming," Julia said, peering past him out into the sunny street.

"I'll be on my way then. Table's all yours."

"Wait! What's your name?" Julia said as he stood and started to turn away.

"Patrick," he said. "And you?"

"Julia," she said. She opened her phone and recorded his name and cell number.

"Julia. I'll remember," said the man who called himself Patrick.

"You will?"

"Not likely I'd forget the lady with the wine-dark eyes," he said.

Her face lit up. "Thank you!"

He started again to walk away and then turned around. "Listen. If I give you this hat, will you wear it? I'm returning to the U.S. as soon as I get back to Istanbul; I won't need it. You should really take care of your skin."

"Alright, if you're sure you don't need it," she said. He handed over his brimmed hat. She glanced inside the crown of the hat; there was a little white patch of worn fabric on which was written, 'If found, please call' and then a phone number. If she ever lost his number, she could just look in the hat. She put it on and tightened the cord under her chin.

"Looks great. Wear it."

"Okay. I will. I'll take good care of it," Julia said. The man called Patrick walked out of the restaurant, smiling pleasantly at Professor Templeton as they passed one another.

Professor Templeton approached, eased himself into a chair at the rickety metal table, and removed his hat and the rumpled handkerchief.

"Who was that old guy you were talking to?" Edward asked.

"From my vantage point, he looked as though he had just emerged from the fountain of youth, although I suppose everything is relative," Professor Templeton declared.

"He kind of looked like Indiana Jones," Betsy said.

"He said he was from New York and said I needed to use sunscreen and wear a hat. He even gave me his own hat. He said he didn't need it; he's about to head home. And he gave me sunscreen. Anybody want some?" Julia adjusted the cords that met under her chin and proffered the tube of SPF 70 zinc oxide sunscreen.

"Yeah, sure." Betsy accepted the sunscreen and smeared some on her face and hands.

"Rub it in, doofus. You look like a clown," Conner said.

"Now Conner, some might construe that as an ungentlemanly comment," Dr. Templeton said.

A waiter appeared, distributed menus, returned, took their lunch orders and disappeared.

"While we're waiting, I was wondering if I could read you all something," Julia said.

"Aren't we waiting until later to read more *Iliad*?" Sam asked.

"This isn't *Iliad*. I have written a poem in honor of Professor Templeton," Julia announced.

"A poem?" Conner asked, concern in his voice.

"Don't worry; it's short. It is entitled 'Professor Templeton's class.' Can I go ahead?"

Betsy and Edward nodded. Professor Templeton sat straight up, ready to listen.

Julia began,

"We hear these ancient words from realms of gold,

These tales of Bronze Age heroes, god-like men.

Majestic epics a wondrous blind poet told

Of endless blood in vengeance for a friend,

And struggles without equal to reach home.

Those fragile lyrics, shimmering with light

From tender-hearted Sappho left alone,

To work her magic in the fragrant night.

The catalogue of gods from Hesiod,

The hopeful prayers of maids and youths now gone,

The noble sorrow of famed Pindar's odes

That long ago were set to ancient song.

And from the crumbling parchments that survive,

It is our teacher brings their words to life."

The little group gave her a round of applause, and Julia smiled with delight. She turned to Professor Templeton for his reaction and was surprised to see him dabbing tears from his eyes with his handkerchief.

"In all my many years of teaching literature, no one has ever written a poem for me. And that was absolutely splendid, my dear. I am most flattered and very moved by your kindness and creativity." Professor Templeton cleared his throat, a bit embarrassed by his emotions. "I expect that before you graduate from Harvard College I may receive something from you in dactylic hexameter, and preferably in classical Greek."

Julia blushed. "I'll see what I can do," she replied.

# CHAPTER 64

Elena walked into the house and closed the door behind her. Abuela had asked her to be home by 7, but she had stopped by the Chestnut Hill Mall on the way home and had lost track of time. Now it was after 8. She wouldn't be in trouble; she had Abuela wrapped around her little finger.

"Elena, can you come in here, please?"

That was Aunt Cati, and she sounded annoyed. Maybe that's why Abuela had told her so firmly to be home by 7- her aunt had come over. So she was late. Fuck it. Shit happens. She sighed and headed for the kitchen. Better apologize and get it over with. Elena stepped into the kitchen to find Cati and her husband Ricky seated side by side. Cati's arms were crossed. The look on her face spelled irritation. Abuela sat beside them, looking nervous.

"Elena, your grandmother asked you to be home by 7. You're more than an hour late," Cati said.

"Oh, sorry, I stopped by the mall on the way home and got distracted." Elena started to walk from the room.

"Do you mind sitting down?" Cati's words were polite, but the tone was severe. "We've been sitting here waiting to see you for over an hour. We tried calling your cell, but there was no answer."

*Duh, I could see who was calling and didn't pick up.* "Sorry, I ran out of battery. I think I need a new phone. This one doesn't hold a charge."

"I'm glad you brought that up, your spending and needing this and that expensive thing," Cati said. She pulled out the last three months of statements for Elena's credit card. "Do you look at these?"

"No," Elena mumbled.

"Well, let me tell you, you need to spend less. We came tonight after work to discuss it with you. Your grandmother said she has tried to talk to you about spending less, but that you don't seem to understand, or to care."

"Isn't that between me and Abuelita?"

"No, it is not only between the two of you. Because we, Ricky and I, have been paying this bill each month to help out. But it is ridiculously high and is higher every month. Our kids don't spend like this." She turned around to Ricky for support. He nodded his agreement.

Elena shrugged and studied her feet. "Sorry," she muttered.

"We are going to pay this bill one last time. But that credit card has been cancelled, as of this evening."

Elena gasped. So that was why her card didn't work when she'd tried to buy leggings at lululemon!

"If you want to buy something, you're going to have to get a job and pay with what you earn," Cati continued.

A job! Who the fuck does she think she is, telling me what to do? "I can't. I'm taking a gap year to try to figure out what I want to do with my life."

"You can think about that while you're working."

"I don't know how to do anything."

"Yes, you do. For example, you could work at Starbucks. You're there a lot, according to your credit card statements, and you probably already know most of the drinks."

"Give me back my card; I can spend less."

"Nope. Too late," Cati said tersely.

Anita cleared her throat. "I think it's for the best, Elenita. It will be good for you to have a job. You can get out of the house and meet some nice people. And earn some spending money."

Elena eyed the members of her family. Aunt Cati is a bitch, a fucking bitch. And Uncle Ricky is a total pussy. He lets her do all the talking. Ughhh, she's yapping again. Could she and her pussy-ass husband shut up and go home? Her eyes strayed to the pantry. She really hated her aunt. If that gun was in her hands instead of in the cereal box, she'd be tempted to use it.

"Okay, I'll apply for a job in the morning." She stormed out of the kitchen without waiting to learn whether anyone had anything else to say, ran up the stairs to her room and slammed the door.

# CHAPTER 65

Campbell reached into her handbag and pulled out an envelope. "This is from my parents. Now that you're back for your sophomore year, they thought you'd enjoy it."

Julia opened the card. "A membership card for the Museum of Fine Arts. That's awesome!"

*

Campbell stuck her head into Julia's room on the morning of the last Saturday in October. "Julia, listen, let's go to Salem later today. It's really good fun this time of year. It's all decorated for Halloween, everyone's dressed up, there are haunted houses. What do you say?"

"Oh, sure, great idea. I haven't ever been to Salem," Julia replied.

"Great, let's go around 4 or 5:00. I have a paper I need to knock off, shouldn't take me past mid-afternoon to get it done." Campbell disappeared abruptly.

*

It was just after sunset as Campbell and Julia left Campbell's old Volvo in the parking lot by the train station and walked along Washington Street toward Salem's town center.

"Here, now, Julia, the thing to do is get into the spirit of Halloween. We should dress the part." Campbell led Julia to a kiosk selling inexpensive witches' hats and selected two. After admiring their new look in a blurry mirror at the kiosk they proceeded down the street.

"There's a Witch Museum!" Julia laughed.

"There are several! What would Salem be without its Witch Museums?"

"Campbell, look at the moon. It's huge!" Julia said. An unusually large moon glowed orange just above the horizon to the east.

"That's a harvest moon. Don't you have them down South?"

"Not that I ever noticed." Had she ever looked?

Julia was amazed by the array of witches, warlocks, ghouls and miscellaneous monsters prowling the streets of Salem. There was someone in a skeleton costume that lit up- the bones flashed ghostly green! They turned onto Essex Street. Several little shops had signs offering fortune-telling.

"You can actually get a Tarot reading here? That's so cool!" Julia said.

"You can get your fortune told. Of course, it's all made up, but it's fun," Campbell said.

"Sure, I'd like that!"

"Let's see. What about that one?" Campbell pointed at one of the shops.

"Ah, sure," Julia said, but something made her turn around. Her eyes scanned the street. "Wait. That one, there."

"It's your choice. Let's go," Campbell said.

The shop had a sign over the door: 'Sibyl's Fortunes: Palmistry, Tarot, Séances.' As they walked inside they were greeted with the heavy aroma of sandalwood and the delicate tinkling of door chimes. Unlit sun-catchers dangled before windows that could use a clean. Several shelves were occupied by scented candles of different colors, intended to treat different maladies: melancholy, upset stomach, heartbreak and others. Other shelves contained Tarot cards, incense, little statues of witches, and books on fortune-telling and on the history of Salem.

Campbell and Julia approached a stern, broad-shouldered woman clad in a white cotton T shirt, black leather vest and dark pants. Multiple silver stud earrings decorated the helix of her ear, and large onyx earrings dangled from her earlobes. A silver nose ring completed her ensemble.

"My friend is interested in having her fortune told," Campbell told her.

The Gothic maid gave a curt nod of acknowledgement. "You have come to the right place. Sibyl is the foremost fortune-teller in all of Salem."

"Sibyl. Where is she?" Julia asked.

"Just over there." The woman gestured.

Julia turned. Sibyl sat in a wood-paneled booth behind a little round table draped with dark blue brocade, partially shadowed by a heavy purple velvet curtain with matching fringe, held back by a short length of gold rope. She was a plump, middle-aged woman with fair skin, penciled-in eyebrows and red hair inadequately contained by a gleaming turban shot through with frayed metallic threads. Even Julia's unpracticed eye recognized that shade of red as unnaturally bright. The dim lighting and the dark drapery gave Sibyl's pale skin an eerie pall. She was in a trance, her head tipped slightly back, her eyes closed, her hands resting limply on a deck of Tarot cards. A broad opaque swath of powder-blue eye shadow covered her eyelids.

"Is she okay?" Julia asked.

"She is in communion with the other world, but she will return to assist you," the woman said.

A Siamese cat appeared, meowing loudly, and rubbed itself against Julia's leg.

"Hi, there, kitty." Julia bent down and scratched the cat's head. "He's so pretty. What's his name?"

"That is Mercutio, Sibyl's familiar," the woman in black intoned.

"A familiar!" Julia said.

"You may be seated," the woman told Julia. She gestured at a chair across from the Sibyl.

Julia slid into the chair and regarded the fortune-teller before her with apprehension.

"Very well. Sibyl will chant, and as she extends her arms, you should"

Campbell broke in. "Cross her palm with silver?"

The woman glared at Campbell. "No. she should place her hands in Sibyl's. And then Sibyl will read her future."

"Can I watch?" Campbell asked.

"No." The woman released the golden rope and the curtain dropped shut. Julia was alone in the booth with Sibyl.

Eyes still closed, Sibyl began to chant, softly at first.

"*Nam Sibyllum quidem Cumis*"

A foreign language, Julia thought. What is she saying? And yet, she felt she had heard those words before, somewhere…

"*Ego ipse oculis meis vidi in ampulla pendere,*" Sibyl continued, a little bit louder. Her plump white hands and forearms lay flaccid on the table, her palms open, ready to receive Julia's hands.

"Have you put your hands into Sibyl's?" the woman hissed from outside the curtain.

Julia took a deep breath and cautiously extended her own hands, as Sibyl continued to chant.

"*Et cum illi pueri dicerent, 'Sibulla, ti qeleis?' respondebat illa…*"

Julia placed her hands into Sibyl's. Sibyl's hands instantly locked around Julia's and her eyes snapped open to reveal pale eyes that matched her eye shadow. She peered at Julia, studying her carefully. *Her hands are shaking,* Julia realized. There was a long pause before Sibyl spoke.

"Thank you for coming to see me today," Sibyl said.

"You're welcome," Julia said. Was that what one should say?

"Fate brought you here today, my dear. I think we have some things in common, starting with our names," Sibyl studied Julia's face intently. Her hands were still shaking but not as badly.

"Our names? My name is nothing like Sibyl," Julia said. *This is so fake.*

"Oh, Sibyl is not my real name. My real name is Juliet. Well, actually Giulietta with a G. That's the authentic Italian spelling, you see."

Julia stared at her. Had Campbell called her by name since they entered the store? She didn't think so.

"Think of me as Giulietta the sibyl, not as Sibyl," Giulietta said. "Is your name anything like mine after all? Not Juliet, but perhaps Julie? No, you don't like that. Julia, I think."

"My name is Julia," she answered hoarsely, now a little disturbed by the turn of events and wishing for Campbell's presence.

"You've come to have your fortune told."

Julia nodded.

"Let me see your hands," she said, turning Julia's hands over, and peered at the creases transecting her palms. She shook her head. "You are a new soul. That much is clear. And thus you're not cautious."

"I'm not cautious?"

Giulietta nodded. "I advise you to be much more careful. You could be harmed and might cause harm to others."

Julia listened in silence.

"Possibly serious injury. You have it in you to become someone who people will follow. You must be very careful where you lead them. It is a great responsibility."

Julia stared at her.

"You are brave," Sibyl continued, "You're intelligent, but not wise. Wisdom will come to you over time if you foster it. But it won't come naturally; you've had too few past lives."

"Wait- can you actually tell how many, ah, past lives I've had?" Julia asked, sitting forward.

Giulietta paused to concentrate. "I can sense two, but both are quite indistinct. Have you ever had dreams that you were someone else?"

"No, nothing I recall," Julia answered.

"Sometimes, if a person was very strong in some way in a past life, that life may still be remembered after rebirth. The memory may be very vague or seem like a dream. Most lives are unremarkable and go unremembered."

"I see," Julia said.

Giulietta continued. "You've been unlucky in love."

Julia flushed.

"But that will change." She paused, for a long time. "I think we may also have a mutual friend, someone dear to me, someone who helped you perhaps…" Giulietta mused, trying to sort out her impressions. "They say he died more than a year ago. He was such a wonder, I often feel I can still sense his spirit on this earth. I don't believe he has crossed over. Not yet." She sighed.

"They *say* he died?"

"Yes. They never found his body. So I'm not convinced." Giuli knew the moment she touched Julia's hands that Alex was still alive. Alex was alive and had known this girl. This girl had seen him, spoken to him, perhaps touched him, and not so long ago; she could feel it. "I believe that he had many past lives. An old soul. An old soul with a destiny greater than the life he has lived so far."

"An old soul! Did he have many past lives then?"

"Oh yes. And they were remarkable! Heroes out of legend. Great warriors, great explorers. I know. I have seen them."

*This can't be for real,* Julia thought. "If he had an old soul, was he wise?"

"Having many past lives does not always make you wise. It depends upon the lives you lived, and what you learned during them. He was absolutely splendid. Was he wise? I don't know."

"I haven't been living in this area for long. Less than a year and a half. I can't think who we might both have known." Julia said. "What was his name?"

"Alexander. He went by Alex."

"I don't think I know any Alexanders," Julia said. "Wait. There's an Alexander in my Comparative Religions class."

"This would be someone my age, not your age."

Julia thought about that. Any of her teachers? Any of her parents' friends or any of Campbell's parents' friends she'd met at their home? "No, I can't think of anyone named Alex."

Giuli's face collapsed. "You're certain?" she asked anxiously.

"I'll think about it," Julia promised.

"Will you, if you remember anything, would you, could you call me?" Giuli handed her a card.

"Sure." Julia took the card.

"Farewell, child." Giulietta closed her eyes again and resumed her contemplations.

Julia pushed aside the curtain and slipped outside. Campbell was waiting on the sidewalk, enjoying the sights.

"How did it go?" Campbell asked.

"Totally creepy. I'm a new soul lacking wisdom and it makes me dangerous."

"I'll consider myself warned. Across the street, want to go to that haunted house? People have been coming out with all kinds of looks on their faces."

"Yes, let's!" Anything but fortune-telling.

# CHAPTER 66

One Sunday morning in February Julia and Betsy met in Julia's room to study. Julia lounged on her bed, propped up among pillows while Betsy sat at Julia's desk. The brilliant blue sky and the bright sunshine were deceptively inviting; outside it was only 14°. Julia finished her coffee and set her mug down on one corner of the desk, the only hard horizontal surface within reach.

"It is so cold!" Julia said.

"I know. Sometimes you feel like it will never end," Betsy replied.

"I went to the MFA yesterday afternoon and almost froze to death," Julia said.

"You are always over there."

"I am- I love it!" Julia looked up from her work and let her gaze wander unfocused across the room. "Exactly seven months ago, we were in Turkey. It was literally a solid 70 degrees hotter than it is now."

"Another month and it will start to warm up." Betsy sighed heavily. "Do you like my hair this color?"

"Yeah, the purple is nice with your complexion."

"I was thinking- what if I did rainbow hair for Pride Month?"

Julia nodded. Thank god her parents weren't here- there'd be even more moaning about the Northern liberals. "I think it's a great idea. But ambitious. Wouldn't it be difficult to do?"

"Yeah, probably. I could practice it, see how it comes out." Betsy pushed her textbooks to the side of the desk to make way for her laptop, and the mug on the corner crashed to the ground. "Oh, no, what was that?"

"My coffee mug. At least it was empty."

"I'm so sorry! I'll get you a new one."

"Don't worry about it, not a big deal at all," Julia said. She slid off the bed and scooped up the pieces and dropped them into the trash.

*

Mark Eastgard entered the Harvard Coop in Harvard Square, scanned its expansive sales floor and headed for the ladies' clothing section. His goal was to buy work-out clothes for his mother. He held up a medium-sized sweatshirt and compared it to a large. The large looked like it would be a better fit, but receiving a large might prove demoralizing for her. He decided to get a medium sweatshirt and matching pants and ask for a gift receipt. Maybe if medium was too small Mom would work harder to lose weight so they would fit. He threw the clothing he had selected over his arm and turned, colliding with a dark-haired kid who had come charging down the aisle. Mark reached out and grabbed her arm to keep her from falling.

"Sorry!" he said.

She looked up at him. "It's okay," she said, shaking off his hand.

Mark looked at her. She was a skinny little thing with silky dark hair, a pretty face with delicate features and eyes that were an unusually dark shade of blue. He'd been wrong- she was no kid. Her face said college student.

"I'm really sorry. I don't usually plow into people."

"No big deal." She was holding a large ceramic mug emblazoned with Harvard's crest.

"I'm glad I didn't break your mug. Do you go here, or is it a souvenir?"

"I go here. Someone accidentally broke my only mug this morning, and I can't go too long without coffee. So." She lifted the mug.

"I go to BU. I'm Mark."

"Julia." She smiled briefly and then headed for check-out.

Mark followed her. There was something about her. As the saleslady wrapped the mug, Mark spoke. "Julia. Since you're a coffee addict, and I am too, could I get you some coffee? I mean, would you have coffee with me?"

The saleslady listened with interest, waiting for Julia's reply.

"I don't know. I should really get back..." *Look at this guy. Tall, dark-haired, gorgeous. At least as good-looking as the execrable Jamie Pembroke. Can't be for real.*

"I realize I'm just a BU student, invading your turf, no less. But I would really like it."

She eyed him warily.

He gave her his most engaging smile.

447

She shrugged. "Okay, I guess."

The saleslady ducked her head to hide her own smile.

Julia and Mark walked together to Au Bon Pain. He had a dark roast coffee; she had a small cappuccino.

"What did you buy?" she asked, as they sat together at a small table.

"Valentine's Day gift," he said.

"Oh?" Her eyebrows rose.

"For my Mom. She's been trying to lose weight. She joined a gym but she doesn't have many work-out clothes."

"You didn't get her something from BU?"

"She has those, a full set. She needs some variety."

"It's an unusual Valentine's Day gift."

"I wanted to get her something. If I don't, she might not get anything."

"Sorry," she said. His parents must be divorced. "Are you from this area?"

They exchanged information about their past, their present and their plans for the future. Eventually Julia's phone pinged, interrupting their conversation. She glanced at her phone.

"I should go," she said, pulling on her coat.

"Can I call you?" Mark asked.

"Why?" Julia asked. This guy could do much better, if he was after a good-looking girl. No more delusions about guys who were out of her league; she had learned her lesson.

"I just thought, well, it's just that I've never seen such pretty eyes." And she was the most un-Elena-like girl he had ever met.

*Could he mean it,* Julia wondered. He did seem nice. She told him her number.

Mark entered it into his phone and sent her a short text. "Now you have my number too."

They walked together from the coffee shop. He headed for the bus back to Brookline, and she, for Harvard Yard. Julia pulled her phone from her bag to see what he'd texted. It said, "Dinner next Sunday?" That was Valentine's Day. She smiled. She actually had a legitimate date for Valentine's Day. She would have to thank Betsy for breaking her mug.

# CHAPTER 67

Julia and Mark sat across from one another at a little table in Sol Azteca, near the window overlooking Beacon Street. Sleet and freezing rain had consolidated into snowflakes when the sun set and the temperature dropped.

"I hope Mexican is okay," he said.

"It's great. This place is so cute."

"Their margaritas are awesome. I have a pretty good fake ID I use when I go out with the guys, but I thought it might make a bad impression if it got confiscated while you were here to witness it."

"Can I see it?" Julia asked. "I wish I had a fake ID."

"Here." He handed it over.

"Ha! This is great. Says you're from Muncie, Indiana."

"Yeah, everything is true except that, and the year of my birth. Only one year to go and I'll be legal."

"Me too. Say, what's good here?"

Mark scanned the menu. "Everything's pretty good, the enchiladas, the fajitas... I'm going to get the chiles rellenos."

"What about these enchiladas de mole verde?" She spoke haltingly.

"They're really good, but..."

"But what?"

"You never studied Spanish, did you?"

"No, four years of French. No Spanish. There's a lot of French influence where I'm from. Why?"

"That's what it is- you're pronouncing it like it's French! Have you had Mexican before?"

"Hardly ever, actually." Her one and only trip to Taco Bell did not count. "Am I saying these things wrong?"

"I'm sorry to tease you. I took Spanish in high school. My Dad said he used Spanish a lot when he was in med school in New York City. Since I'm pre-med, I went with Spanish."

"Makes sense. But if this were a French restaurant..." Julia smiled. She'd done really well in French. She looked outside. A C-line train forged through the snowstorm, spraying snowflakes that glittered in its headlights. "This is a nice area. I haven't been here before."

"No?"

"I've mainly hung around Cambridge. In September someone gave me as a gift a membership for the Museum of Fine Arts. So I've gone there a lot, but still there are so many places in Boston I've never seen."

"Well, what about the North End? It has so many awesome Italian restaurants, one after the other."

"I haven't been there, no."

"We have to go! What about Boston Common and the Public Garden and Newbury Street and Boylston Street? Boston Garden? The Esplanade?"

"No. This is so embarrassing."

"Fenway Park?"

Julia laughed and shook her head.

"Have you been anywhere besides Cambridge and the MFA?"

"I've been to Marblehead a few times. A friend's family lives there. They've been so nice to me. They're the ones who gave me the MFA membership."

"I admit, I've never been to Marblehead. One point for you."

"I've also been to Salem, during Halloween this past fall."

"I've never been to Salem either. You're making me look bad. What did you do there?"

"Oh, looked around at all the people and the crazy costumes. It was a total mob scene. Also, I had my fortune told."

"What did they say?"

"Well, the fortune-teller said I was a young soul and not cautious and not wise." *She also said my lack of caution could hurt people, but no need to mention that. She said I would be lucky in love, but I'll keep that to myself as well.*

Mark laughed. "That's encouraging."

"She also asked me if I knew this friend of hers who had died. Like it really mattered to her. Not someone my age, someone her age, she said."

"How old was she?" Mark asked.

"Oh, wow, old. Not little old lady old, but way old enough to be my mother or your mother."

"Who was this friend?"

"Said his name was Alexander. Said all these nice things about him. So I remember thinking, Alexander the Great. And it stuck in my mind."

Mark was silent. "My Dad's name was Alexander," he finally said.

"Was? Is he, dead?" Julia whispered.

"Yeah, freak accident a couple of years ago. I really miss him."

*Mark looks so sad.* "Weird coincidence. I'm sorry," she said.

"Listen," he said. "That's in the past. I can't change it. But I would really like it if I could take you to some places in Boston that you haven't seen yet. Would you go with me?"

She smiled and nodded.

"And I'll do my best to find a French restaurant for us, so you can show off reading the menu."

"*Très bien!*" She laughed.

\*

Winter gradually, grudgingly gave way to spring that year as Julia and Mark continued to see one another. They met at least once a week and texted each other multiple times a day, every day, often with photos attached. Their friendship grew strong during the three months they had been dating.

Elena Gonzalez passed by Mark's house one Thursday morning on the way to work at Starbucks. She would walk by again, on the way home, and perhaps linger on the street, or walk back and forth a couple of times, hoping to run into him. So far she had not. Maybe he lived in the dorm or something. Elena had learned Helen's routine: Monday, Wednesday and Friday she went to the gym. Must be. She came home all flushed wearing sweats. Tuesdays she usually went grocery shopping. On Thursdays she went to the beauty parlor, came home with her hair all nice. Helen was very boring. But Mark was so wonderful! She recalled the last time they spoke, when they had met after his father had drowned. She could still feel the wonderful hug he had given her. He loved her. She knew it. But when she would text him to ask how he was, did he want to get together, he always dodged her. Why? Not knowing ate at her. She sighed. She had to get to work. They had her on the cash register; if she performed well they said she could train to be a barista. Who the fuck cares? She hated her job. The most annoying part was how all the rest of them loved it there, tying on their stupid aprons, raving about how good the coffee smelled, the light roast, the dark roast, how they were helping the world by paying people in Ethiopia fairly for their stupid coffee beans. Fuck that! Who cares about some losers in the Middle East?

*

"What do you say to a quick coffee, before we go see my Mom?" Mark asked.

"I will never turn down coffee," Julia answered.

"There's a Starbucks on the way," Mark said.

They entered, and it was quite crowded, with nearly all the seats taken. "I see a free table, all the way back," Mark said.

"I'll go grab it. Can you get me a cappuccino?" Julia said, and slipped toward the back of the room. Mark watched her go, admiring her slender but muscular legs.

Mark approached the counter to order. Elena stood before him, in Starbucks regalia.

"Elena! You're working here now?" Mark said.

"And you, are you babysitting?" Elena asked, letting a little sarcasm leak into her tone.

"What? No, she's our age, just petite. She goes to Harvard. Really smart."

"Yeah. What do you want?" Elena asked tersely.

Mark placed the order, and when it was ready, came to the table with their coffee.

"This is so good. Thanks," Julia said, sipping the cappuccino.

"So, ready to meet my Mom?"

"Yeah, I guess. Let's go." She stood and stretched, shifting her weight to her left leg and twisting her fingers together behind her back. She reminded Mark of those ballerina statues you see in museums. Everything about her was so nice, he reflected. He wondered what she would think if she knew how he'd gotten his start in life. Maybe she'd be horrified. Some people from the South were so conservative. He would hate to lose her. But maybe she wouldn't care. Maybe she'd judge him based on the present, not on the past.

Mark waved to Elena as they left, but she looked away. He shrugged. She wasn't happy, but he didn't know what else he could do. Better avoid this Starbucks in the future.

Helen was admiring her French manicure- a little more expensive but worth it. Chi-chi was just wonderful with a nail file. She may have put on some weight over the years, but her hands were still beautiful. Then the doorbell rang. That would be Mark. She headed for the door.

"Hello there. This is Julia?" Helen eyed the diminutive girl before her. Cute little thing.

"Yes, ma'am," Julia answered.

"Come in, take off your jackets, have a seat."

"Wow, what a nice house!" Julia said. Not huge and fancy like the McDade's house, but very attractive and comfortable.

"Thank you," Helen said, pleased. She had started doing the house cleaning herself to save money and because she had read that it burned calories. Could be as good as a gym work-out, the article had said. "I have a few little snacks; let me get those," Helen said, disappearing into the kitchen.

"Can I look at your pictures?" Julia asked. There were framed photographs all over the living room.

"Sure," Mark said.

"What a great picture!" Julia reached for a photo of Mark as a young boy, sitting on a man's shoulders, desperately trying to hold onto a full-size basketball. "You were so cute!" Her voice grew soft. "Is that your Dad?"

"Yeah." He sounded wistful.

Helen returned to the living room carrying a tray with nachos, salsa and guacamole. "It's all natural, from Whole Foods. Mark loves Mexican."

"I know. We went to a Mexican place on our first date."

Helen joined them as they looked at the photos. She adjusted the angle of several photographs, careful to keep her movements controlled and graceful. She let her right hand linger on the shelf, next to a school picture of Mark in fourth grade.

Julia reached past Helen for a photo of Mark as a child on a beach. "Where is this?" she asked.

Helen noted with dismay that next to Julia's dainty little white hands her own looked plump, the skin blotchy and crisscrossed by fine wrinkles. Helen withdrew her hand quickly.

"That's on Cape Cod. We used to go every summer when I was little," Mark answered.

"Yes, that's right. Then when Mark got older we started going to Hawaii. There was a resort a travel agent found for us that was really lovely." She clasped her freshly manicured hands together, trying to minimize the amount of skin visible.

"Wow! Two more places I've never been!" Julia said.

"Cape Cod is easy- you can just drive. We can go there," Mark said.

"You're the best, thanks," Julia said.

*This girl seems to really like Mark. I hope he will be happy; he deserves it,* Helen thought.

"Mom, remember how Dad was always chasing us around with sunscreen when we went to the beach?" Mark asked. He turned to Julia. "My Dad was a fanatic about protecting skin from the sun. Once, in Hawaii he went up to this redhead, a total stranger, and gave her some sunscreen. Told her she was getting sunburned and should protect her skin."

"I am having incredible déjà vu," Julia said. "I was in Turkey on a trip with a group from school, and same thing, some guy came up to me and gave me sunscreen. Nice man. Weird coincidence, huh?"

"Yeah. Weird," Mark said.

Julia directed her attention to a formal wedding photo of Helen and Alex. "That's your Dad? Where'd that dark hair of yours come from?"

Helen inhaled quickly and stood silent, waiting for Mark to respond.

"Um, uh, good question, I guess. I never really thought about it," Mark sputtered.

"Mark's grandmother had dark hair. I think it skipped a generation," Helen said.

*Oh my god,* Julia thought to herself. *I bet Helen bleaches her hair. How embarrassing!* "I just asked because I don't look much like anyone in my family. I'm tiny and everyone else is pretty big. My parents make this joke about a mix-up at the hospital." *This silence is so thick you could cut it with a knife,* Julia thought. *What is it?*

"Well!" Helen said brightly after a long pause. "Look at the time. I should get dinner started." She whisked out of the room.

Elena approached the Eastgard home. It was dark, and she didn't think anyone inside would be able to see her, so she left the sidewalk and peered into a window. She could see through to the living room. Helen was there as usual, then walked out of the room. She took a few steps, to get a different angle. There was Mark! He was smiling. He looked happy. That was nice. Then, he turned and – there was the little bitch from Starbucks. He pulled her to him and kissed her. This was awful. She was too short for him and she was practically flat-chested. Really disgusting! How could he? How could he possibly prefer that stupid little tramp to her? She started to cry. She wiped her eyes impatiently and turned to leave. As she walked, she stepped on a small rock. She stopped, picked it up and flung the rock at the window, resulting in a loud crack. She had hit the glass where it met the window frame, and the glass remained intact. She retreated immediately into the neighbor's yard. But she saw with satisfaction that Mark and the little bitch jumped apart. Mark ran over to the window and looked for the cause of the sound. His face in the window was so handsome. Then *she* joined him at the window. Fury washed through Elena. She'd love to wring the little whore's scrawny neck. She picked up another rock and threw it, harder, right at the little bitch's face. The window shattered. Mark and Julia jumped away. Elena wanted to stay, to see what Mark and the fucking whore would do now, but she'd better get going. She didn't want to get caught.

# CHAPTER 68

"It's so beautiful today! Thank god it's finally almost warm," Julia said. She and Mark emerged onto Boylston Street from the Copley Station of the Green line train, holding hands.

"It's only April. This is a fluke, so let's enjoy the hell out of it while we can," Mark said.

"Global warming?" Julia slipped off her sweater. The lacy top she wore underneath left her arms bare; the warmth of the sun on them was intoxicating. That man she'd met at Troy would not approve, but too bad.

"After the winter we've had, I won't complain," Mark replied.

"Can we go sit down somewhere and just enjoy the sun?"

"Sure. There's Copley Square. We'll find someplace to sit."

"Wow, it's gorgeous!" Julia said. The plaza had broad flower beds ablaze with red tulips.

"This is where the Marathon ends. Right here."

"Ah. So is this where the bombing was? It happened here?"

"Yeah. The first bomb went off across the street. The second bomb went off in front of Marathon Sports, just down the street."

"That was before I started college here," she said, and then stood quietly, remembering all she had heard about that terrible attack.

"It won't happen again. There's a lot more security now," Mark said.

"What are all the buildings around? They're beautiful!"

"Okay, straight ahead of us is the Copley Plaza Hotel. Stately old place. When we both turn 21, or when we both have fake IDs, we can go into their Oak Bar and have a cocktail."

Julia took in its solemn facade, its bow-front center flanked by columns. "I like it!"

"Then to the left is Trinity Church."

"How pretty! Unusual style, isn't it?"

"Yes. It's built in what they call Richardsonian Romanesque."

"It's absolutely swarming with saints! Life-sized saints, doll-sized saints. Look, even an animal head. And another. And gargoyles!"

"Yeah, the facade is kind of crowded. But look how Trinity Church is reflected in the walls of the Hancock building, that shiny skyscraper right next to it. They planned it to be like that when they put up the Hancock building."

"Brilliant idea! How do you know all this?"

"My Dad. He knew everything. And was glad to tell you all about it."

"I wish I had known him."

Mark nodded. "Me too. He would have liked you."

"Mark, look at the fountain." Julia walked over and smiled at a vigilant young mother at its edge and her toddler. The toddler was barefoot, standing on the step just below the surface of the water. "Do you think we can, dip our feet for a minute?" Without waiting for an answer, she pulled up her skirt, sat at the edge of the fountain, whipped off her sneakers and dunked her feet.

Mark sat next to her, wrapping his arm around her shoulders.

"This is so decadent; I love it!" Julia said, gently splashing the cool water with her feet. Then she looked up and across Dartmouth Street. "That's your library!" She thought of her own small town's library; it suffered greatly by comparison.

"Well, it's the main library. We have a lot of smaller libraries."

"It's very impressive!" Another monumental building, orderly and beautiful, executed in pale gray stone, featuring tall arched windows.

"The inside is very interesting also. There's some beautiful artwork. You can take tours to see the interior."

"Which you did with your Dad?"

"Exactly." Mark laughed. "But anyway, for example, there's a big room for meetings or functions, whatever, with a story about Sir Galahad and his quest for the Holy Grail painted on the walls. And there are two big lions carved in marble inside, and you can rub their tails for luck. Other stuff too. There's a cafe, and a courtyard with a fountain with this cute little statue. Not your average library."

"I want to go rub the lion's tail," Julia said dreamily.

"Whenever you finish soaking your feet." He ran his fingers through her silky hair.

The skin of her temples tingled under his fingertips. Julia sighed. "Okay. Feet are out." She rested them on the stone rim of the fountain to dry. They rose and continued their walk down Boylston Street.

"Now we're in Kenmore Square," Mark said. "My territory! Across the street, that's the BU Bookstore where I work a couple afternoons a week. And just down that way is Fenway Park, home of our beloved Red Sox."

"Oh, yeah, I see it."

"Are you okay to walk more? Feet tired or anything?"

"No, I'm good. Bring it on," Julia said.

"Okay then, let's walk back in the direction we came from, but down Commonwealth Avenue rather than Boylston. There are some beautiful old homes along Comm Ave, and there's a mall along its whole length with statues strategically placed in chronological order having to do with the history of our area."

"Okay. Can there be a coffee break along the way?"

"Absolutely. We'll take a one-block detour to Newbury Street and get coffee. Come on." They got their coffee and continued hand in hand down Commonwealth Avenue until they came to its end at Arlington Street.

Julia put her sweater on. "It's gotten cool," she said.

"Sun's gone down." He checked the weather on his phone. "But it's still nice. Shouldn't get too much colder today. Want to walk through the Public Garden?" Mark gestured across Arlington Street.

"Sure." By this time dusk had replaced the sparkling daylight. Street lights softly illuminated the Public Garden; their tall black posts disappeared in the darkness, while the lights on top seemed to float in the air just out of reach. Dimly lit figures strolled silently on winding paths. Someone on the opposite bank of the Garden's swan boat pond played the flute; a haunting melody drifted across the water.

"What a magical place this is! It's like, like when the elves were leaving Middle Earth," said Julia.

"You like the Lord of the Rings too?"

"Oh yeah, I read those books at least three times."

"I saw all the movies when I was a kid." *The man I thought was my father took me to all of them.*

She spoke softly, reluctant to disturb the enchanting scene. "Thank you for showing me all these wonderful things today. You're an awesome tour guide. You know, all my life I've been trying to get away from where I was, trying to find where I belong. But here, this is all so beautiful. Maybe this is it."

"Of course, you belong here, right here," Mark said, hugging her. They drifted along the paths that crisscrossed the park, the gathering darkness imparting a sensation of privacy to their quiet walk. "Are you getting hungry?" he finally asked.

"Mmm, yeah. You want to get dinner?"

"I was thinking I could cook dinner for you. If you want."

"In your dorm?"

"No. We can go to my house. There's a Green line train stop close to it."

"Won't we be in your Mom's way?"

"No. My Mom is away. She and my Aunt Kelly went on a spa weekend in the Berkshires to celebrate their birthday. They're twins."

"Well, sure, that's a good idea. What are you going to cook?"

"I only know how to make spaghetti. Okay?"

Julia laughed. "Sure." She and Mark had done no more than kiss. What wonderful kisses those were! She wondered if there would be more tonight.

\*

Mark went directly to the kitchen and began to assemble the ingredients he would need to prepare dinner.

"Can I do anything to help?" Julia asked.

"No, I've got this. Do you want to turn on the news, see what's going on?"

"Sure." Julia turned on the TV and stopped when she got to Channel 7. The local news program was underway. As the anchor asked the weatherman for the forecast, Julia drifted around the living room, studying the family's photographs. Some of the older photos showed a Helen who had been absolutely stunning. Julia sighed. She looked like the kind who would have been a cheerleader all four years of high school, and probably Homecoming queen in her senior year. She had really put on weight over the years, Julia noted, remembering how she looked now and glancing at other photos from later years. Mark's Dad was quite attractive too, but in contrast to Helen, he had stayed lean. No surprise that Mark was so gorgeous.

"Pasta's ready, come sit down," Mark said, carrying a big pot of spaghetti with sauce mixed in.

"Wow, I was so caught up looking at those photos of your family I didn't even realize you'd set the table. This looks completely legit!"

"Hey, I was raised right. Let me give you some spaghetti."

Julia wrapped spaghetti around her fork and tasted it. "This is really good. Could I cook you dinner sometime? I can cook Cajun."

"I'd love that!"

"And I'll do the dishes."

"We can do them together."

"Deal."

After dinner, they cleared the table and washed dishes together. As they finished, Mark asked "Are you tired? I can drive you home if you want. Mom went in Aunt Kelly's car."

"I'm not really tired. Are you?"

"No, not at all. I think the red sauce gave me a second wind. Tell me something. How come, that first day we met, I practically had to beg you to have coffee with me?" Mark asked her.

"I don't know. I mean," Julia's voice trailed off.

"What? Tell me."

"Well. Okay. I came from a small town in Louisiana, where guys mostly ignored me or made fun of me. Too nerdy. Too little. I just didn't fit in. Then I got here, to the big city. I didn't expect much, but then once at a party, this good-looking guy came up to me and I actually thought he liked me. Turned out he was a smooth talker, with, well, no interest in me beyond that one night." Julia paused, and then fixed her eyes on Mark. "Do you think less of me?"

"No, of course not," Mark said.

"I felt so bad about it for a long time and told myself I needed to know people better before I trusted them. Especially good-looking guys. Then along you come, and suddenly want to have coffee with me. I was thinking, this can't be for real, and I would only get hurt all over again." She looked at him and smiled. "But I'm very glad with how it's working out."

"Julia?" Mark put his fingers on her cheeks and bent his head close to hers. "I need to tell you something. About myself. And if you want to ditch me, I will understand."

"You look so serious. What is it? You can tell me," she said.

"Let's go sit down. I have a story to tell you, and it's kind of a long story," Mark said. They sat on the couch, and he took her hands in his. "I haven't told anyone else about this. My mother finally told me, a couple of years ago, after the whole thing blew up in her face, but made me promise to keep it all a secret. But I feel I have to tell you, because it might change how you feel about me. It's not fair for me to keep seeing you, without you knowing who, or what, I am."

And then he related the story that began more than 30 years ago, the enmity between Alexander Eastgard and Hector Gonzalez, the death of Alex's friend Patrick Close, and Hector's role in it, his mother's affair with Hector, his own attraction to a girl who he learned was his half-sister, his mother's confession, overheard by Alex, that Hector, and not Alex was his father, and finally the drowning death, presumably suicide, of his father, or at least of the man he had always thought was his father.

"He was such a wonderful man, always so good to me. But then that night when he found out I wasn't his, the look he gave me, the look of so much sadness. Sadness and, and horror. That was the last time I saw him. Next thing we heard was that he had drowned. I don't think it was my fault, exactly, but my existence led to his death. And that's hard to live with."

"Oh, Mark, I had no idea. I'm so sorry."

"And I really, really almost had sex with my half-sister, and that knocked me down, totally put me off dating. I hadn't gone out with anyone since all that happened, until I met you."

Julia shook her head. Poor Mark! "So, why me?"

"When I saw you, I just knew you were different from everyone else, with so much depth." And he knew that a big part of it was that Julia was so very different from Elena, Elena with whom he had almost made a terrible mistake.

"Thank you." She looked down.

"Julia, look at me. I have to say this. You have to hear it. I'm a bastard, the old-fashioned kind where my parents weren't married, almost guilty of incest, indirectly responsible for the death of a very good man. If you want to run, I'll understand."

"None of this is your fault, and none of it changes who you are."

"Thank you," Mark murmured softly.

"I'm glad you told me," Julia whispered. "Thank you for trusting me. I will keep your secret."

"Thank you, my sweet Julia," he said. He embraced her. "Do you realize that we've been talking all night? It's almost light. Look!" He drew her out onto the patio behind the house, arms around her to keep her warm.

Julia and Mark watched in silence as dawn crept, mist and spun-silver, from the night-black earth and slowly warmed to gold, and all the world changed from black-and-white to color.

Mark put his hands on her face, his fingers in her hair and kissed her. *When I kiss you I can taste all of you, what you've done, where you've been, what you dream about,* Mark told himself. *I can taste your restlessness, your ambition. You're very complicated for such a small person. One day I'll tell you all of that.* In the tremor of her deltoid under his hand he knew her fear. "I can't get past your eyes."

*Did he really say that?* She returned his kiss, passionately.

"I've wanted us to be together like this for so long, but I couldn't, before I told you what you were getting into."

"I understand," she whispered. She trembled as he pulled off her shirt and unhooked her bra, and finally she knelt before him, wearing only her jewelry.

"These things also," Mark said softly. "I want there to be nothing to keep us apart."

Julia took off her earrings. Mark took her left arm and removed her bracelet, and then each of her rings, one by one. She had never felt so vulnerable, but she looked hopefully into his eyes.

He pulled her gently toward him and made love to her with all his heart. Later with her head nestled in the hollow of his shoulder, Mark fell asleep. She relaxed in his arms, warm and secure, and wept silently for the miracle of being wanted.

They slowly woke up around midday. "How are you?" Mark asked her.

"Good," she said, her voice muffled by the covers over her head. "You make me feel safe."

Mark looked at her, cuddled up against him. Perhaps if he were good to her, could make her happy, it would somehow make up for the wrong done to his Dad.

# CHAPTER 69

"Abuelita, you know that boy I told you I liked? You said he was so cute. A *papacito*, you said. He just ignores me. He's going around with this pale skinny little girl who goes to Harvard," Elena said, her face in a pout.

"Elena, are you sure?"

"Yes, I saw them holding hands walking down the street." Also they kissed and giggled after, but that was too painful to repeat.

"Thin? Pale skin?"

"Yes, practically built like a boy."

Anita lowered her voice to a hoarse whisper. "Could he be, could he be, a *mariposa*?"

"No, I don't think so," Elena replied, recalling his reaction to her breasts. "Maybe he likes that she goes to Harvard."

"No, boys do not care about that sort of thing. Truly, I believe they prefer a woman who is not too smart."

"I have a picture." Actually Elena had multiple pictures, but no need to let her grandmother know that. She pulled out her iPhone and selected an image.

Anita sniffed. "Not a real woman. *Una muñeca de porcelana*. A porcelain doll. He will get tired of her. If he is very lucky you will still be interested in him when he does."

*

Elena hovered outside Mark's house. She had learned that he worked at the Boston University Bookstore in Kenmore Square on Tuesdays, Thursdays and Saturdays, and got off at 6pm. Nothing much happened on Tuesdays, but Thursdays were now different. As before, Helen would drive off and return late in the afternoon with her hair done. But now, in the afternoon on Thursdays that girl would arrive via the Green line, often toting groceries. Mark would arrive last, also on the T. On days when she brought groceries, she would go to the kitchen and start cooking before Mark got home. Once Mark got there, they would sit down together like a big happy family and have whatever the little bitch cooked. When the little whore didn't bring groceries, Helen would usually bring home stuff from Whole Foods, and they would eat that. One time someone ordered pizza and they all sat on the couch and watched something on TV while they ate. Mark didn't go home on Saturdays; he usually went straight from work to Harvard to meet his whore. She knew because she'd followed him discreetly onto the T when he got off work, and then watched him get off at Harvard Square.

*

"Julia, this is absolutely wonderful!" Helen said.

"Yeah, fantastic as always!" Mark added.

"It's my Mom's recipe. I can't take credit," Julia answered.

"But this must be so difficult to make. So many flavors, so rich!" Helen said. She ate, taking just a nibble at a time. She recalled that she used to take much smaller bites back when she was thin. She was trying to revert to that habit.

"This is jambalaya. It's not hard at all. You just throw everything together."

Helen looked at Mark and Julia, "Seriously, I want to thank you, both of you for having dinner with me every week. It's so nice to have the company, as well as the delicious food."

"Well, thank you for having us. And thank you for letting me use your kitchen. It's such a struggle if I want to cook something at school," Julia said.

"And it works out perfectly. Julia doesn't have afternoon classes on Thursdays, so she has time to shop and cook. I get off my job and jump on the T and get here right in time to eat. Talk about having it made!" Mark kept his tone light, but he knew that spending time with his Mom was the right thing to do. Mom didn't have anyone to lean on, except him.

*

Elena entered the BU Bookstore in Kenmore Square and looked around for Mark. Before heading out, she had dressed with care, choosing a flattering blouse that beautifully displayed her enviable décolletage. She had put on make-up, not too much, and sprayed her wrists and cleavage with J'Adore perfume. Now she looked past the check-out counter, and around the room. Toward the front of the store, all kinds of BU clothing was on display. Elena walked slowly among tables and racks with T shirts, hoodies, sweat pants and hats, checking out the people around her. No Mark. She passed into the rear part of the store, where most of the books rested and continued her search. There he was! Organizing books in a section designated 'Romance.' *Let that be a sign!* She walked over to him and tried to sound casual. "Mark! Hi, I didn't know you worked here."

"Elena! Hey, how's it going?"

*He's smiling but he sounds nervous,* she thought. She frowned as he turned back to his shelving. "Going good. Good. What's new with you?"

"Aw, you know. More of the same. Study, study, study. Then work here some days. Generates a little spending money."

*Liar!* "Yeah, I know what you mean. I see you're busy..."

"Yeah. It's always something."

*Why won't he look me in the eye? Probably embarrassed about not answering my texts.* "Want to get some coffee?"

"I really should finish," Mark started to say, but then saw her face fall. She was his sister. He couldn't treat her badly. He glanced at his watch. "It's about time for my break. Coffee would be good. There's a café in here, just past the front door."

"I saw it. That'd be fine," Elena answered. *Progress,* she thought.

They walked together toward the front of the store, ordered their coffee and then sat down across from one another at a small table in the bookstore's little café.

"You still working at Starbucks?" Mark asked.

"Yeah. Not too exciting, but like you said, it's spending money."

"That's good. Do you think about what you'll do going forward? Think you'll go to college eventually?"

*He cares about me, about my future!* "I'm just not sure yet. What would your advice be?"

"I think you should seriously consider going to college."

"I'm just not, you know, academic."

"You could go to community college. That shouldn't be too stressful. Then when you finish there you could think about getting a bachelor's. You'd get a better job for sure."

"Maybe. I could think about it. Do you know any community colleges?"

"No, not really. But you could easily google it. There have to be some. There's so much opportunity in this area. You just have to reach for it."

"You would help me?"

"Sure, I would." *You're my sister. I want you to be happy.*

"Mark..." Elena wasn't sure if she should bring up the topic of the little bitch or be happy that Mark might be willing to get together to talk about schools with her. Should she be patient, maintain contact, and be there when he got tired of the little whore?

"Well, I should get back to work. They'll get annoyed if I take too long a break." Mark swirled the last of the coffee in his cup and downed it.

She couldn't wait. She had tried being patient. "Ah, Mark, that girl you were with in Starbucks. Is she, like, your girlfriend?"

Mark leaned back in his chair. He answered with care. "Yes. She's really sweet."

Sweet sounded noncommittal. Sweet was not hot. *She* was hot. There was hope. Maybe he just didn't realize how she felt. Boys could be complete idiots sometimes. She'd have to spell it out. She gave him her most sultry look and inhaled deeply, making her breasts bulge up toward him. "Mark, what happened to us?"

Mark sighed. "Elena, you're so wonderful and so beautiful but I'm with her now. The time just wasn't right for us." He looked into her eyes: they were so green. His own eyes were light blue-green. His mother had blue eyes. Their absentee father must have green eyes. Elena started to cry.

"No, don't cry. Please, Elena, please." Mark put his hand on her shoulder. He noted with chagrin that the manager was looking his way.

"I thought you loved me!"

"I'll always love you." And he did, in a way that she didn't know. He wanted to tell her, wanted so much to come clean, but knew that the revelation would not be kept quiet, and his Mom would end up disgraced.

"Well then, why? What happened?"

"I'm with her right now. She needs me." *And I need her…*His phone pinged. He glanced at it.

"Is that her? Are you meeting her?"

"Having dinner with Mom," Mark said.

She knew that was misleading, but she said nothing.

The manager was glaring at Mark. In a moment he'd be on his way over. "I'm so sorry, but I should go. Boss is giving me a dirty look."

She dried her eyes on her napkin. "I understand." He had said he loved her. His feelings had not diminished. He probably was just too honorable to break up with the little bitch, for some stupid reason. Boys could think stupid things. How had he slipped away from her and ended up with that little whore?

*

Elena waited patiently that night until her grandmother had gone to bed. Then she crept quietly to the pantry and extracted the gun from its hiding place. She stepped into the bathroom and stood in front of the mirror. She held the gun against one side of her face and slowly drew it across to the other side, kissing it lightly as it passed her lips. Then she held the gun against her breasts, wishing for Mark's hands in place of the gun. It had been her secret for so long, it was almost a part of her. Her secret friend. She held the gun, pointing up, against her cheek and examined her face in the mirror. *I am beautiful. I am hot. And I will get what I want.*

*

Julia and Mark ascended the beige staircase of porous travertine that led to the second floor of the Boston Museum of Fine Arts.

"Don't these stairs look moth-eaten?" Julia remarked.

"More like Swiss cheese, I think," answered Mark.

"I'm not really getting a cheese vibe from these stairs; maybe you're getting hungry. Come on, I want to show you something," Julia said.

"Can't wait!" They entered a spacious room

"I love this painting; it's my favorite one at the MFA." Julia gestured to the huge canvas that dominated one wall: Automedon with the Horses of Achilles.

"What about it do you love?" Mark asked.

"The energy, the power, the strength, the intensity," Julia answered. "And also, you look like Automedon." If Automedon would just turn so she could see his face straight on, see his eyes, she would know that Mark had gone back in time and served as the model.

"Thanks, but I'm not *that* buff."

"Pretty close though, Marcus."

"Marcus! Where'd that come from?"

"I don't know, you just seem like more of a Marcus than a Mark. Today at least."

"Exactly how many Marcuses do you know?"

"Only you- you're one of a kind."

They turned again to the painting.

"Two of Achilles' three horses were immortal, children of Zephyros, the west wind. There's a haunting passage in the *Iliad* where one of them, given the power of speech, reminds Achilles that his time on earth is running short," Julia whispered. "There was a legend that said that if Achilles stayed away from Troy, he would have a long life. If he went to Troy he would achieve everlasting glory, but he would die there. At one point Achilles was so mad at Agamemnon that he planned to sail for home, which would have saved him. But when Hector killed his best friend, Patroklos, Achilles stayed at Troy to kill Hector, and his own fate was sealed."

"How do you know all this?"

"We have this amazing teacher. I take one of his classes every semester. In his class, it's as though he transports us back through time, to the age of heroes. He makes it all seem so real." Julia stopped and turned to him. "Thanks for coming; you're really a good sport."

"My pleasure! This is fun," he answered.

She turned to him and looked at him with her deep blue eyes and spoke, "In front of me I see, More magic than the two moons of Capri."

"What does that mean? Two moons of Capri?"

"Nothing much. But you know what? I think you're magical," Julia said. "Oh, that was dorky. You must think I'm the biggest dork."

"No, I don't. And if you were a dork, you'd be a little dork."

"See! I knew you'd think I was a dork," moaned Julia.

"No, I think you're sweet. You're romantic. You're like someone from some other time," he said, and put his arm around her shoulders. "Have you had enough of Automedon? Because I'm starting to get jealous. Do you want to show me your second favorite painting?"

"I love you, Mark," Julia said.

"I love you too," he said.

Julia started to cry.

"What's wrong, sweetheart?" Mark asked.

"No one ever said that to me before."

"Never?"

"No, not ever. No."

"I'm glad then that I'm here to tell you. Because you deserve it." They joined hands and proceeded to the next room.

*

The following Thursday Julia made shrimp Creole for Helen and Mark, to rave reviews. Mark and Julia moved to the TV room while Helen stepped into the kitchen to get the dessert. Julia found her eyes drawn once more to the photos around the room. As she studied them, she felt the spirit of the man who had raised Mark. She wished she had known this man who Mark loved so much.

"Mark, if you can't, or you don't want to talk about it, please just tell me. I know you said that your Dad drowned, but what exactly happened?" She spoke softly, hoping that Helen would not hear.

"I'll tell you. I don't mind. He went out sailing one day after work and a terrible storm started up, and he capsized. We used to sail together a lot, and we always stayed in the river. But somehow the sailboat that day got into Boston Harbor. They found the boat washed up on one of the harbor islands, but they never found my Dad." Mark paused. "He's out there somewhere. I keep hoping one day he's found. It doesn't make a difference really, but I'd feel better if he could be laid to rest. It would be good for my Mom as well."

"They never found him?" She repeated. The fortune teller's words rang in her ears, speaking of her friend named Alexander: *They never found his body.*

Mark shook his head.

Julia paused. "Remember how I mentioned I'd been to Salem, and had my fortune told?"

"Yeah, I do."

"And the fortune-teller asked if I knew anyone named Alexander? And how she seemed to think he was just wonderful?"

"I remember."

"I've been wondering whether she did actually mean your Dad. I know it's a long shot, but her name was Giulietta. With a G. Did he ever mention someone with that name?"

"No. For sure he didn't know any fortune-tellers."

"He never went to Salem?"

"If he'd gone to Salem, he would have taken me and Mom. We've never been there."

Julia pondered this. "Could it be she knew him from the hospital where he worked, and he didn't know she told fortunes? Or that he knew her before she was a fortune-teller?"

Just then Helen returned to the room with a plate of mint Milano cookies.

"Mom, did you or Dad ever know anyone named Giulietta?"

"Giulietta with a G," Julia added.

Helen stared at them.

"Julia had her fortune told in Salem and she thinks the fortune-teller might be someone Dad knew. Her name was Giulietta."

Helen paused, wondering about the implications of this conversation. She set the cookies down on the coffee table. "Giulietta. I haven't thought about her in years! There was a Giulietta in our high school class. She went by Giuli." Helen sat in the chair next to the couch.

"That's her! Has to be," Julia said. "She said such nice things about someone named Alexander. I thought it might be a coincidence, but I think she must have meant Mark's Dad."

"She went to senior prom with Dad," Helen said.

"Wait, you didn't go to prom with Dad?" Mark asked.

"No. He did ask me but someone else had already asked. So he ended up going with Giuli."

"Who'd you go with?" Mark asked.

Helen looked down, remembering. "Oh, ah, this other guy." Her tone suggested he should drop that topic. "But I'll tell you something. Giuli, well, I could tell she was crazy about Dad. Crazy about him. She just radiated it. That prom may have been the high point of her life for all I know." Helen remembered Giuli's chubby physique, her frizzy red hair; Helen had felt sorry for her. Whatever became of Giuli, she was probably happier now than Helen herself was.

Julia stood and studied the photographs more closely. What did she know about this man, Alexander Eastgard? He was an intellectual. He was attractive. There he was with Helen and Mark on the beach, he in a broad-brimmed hat, she with sunglasses, Mark squinting into the sun. Mark had said he was neurotic about using sunscreen. Looked like the same kind of hat that guy in Turkey had given her, the guy Betsy said looked like Indiana Jones. Maybe there's a secret club of people who are weird about sun exposure and they all have the same kind of hat. Julia stood, holding her half-eaten Milano, and studied the photo more closely. There was something vaguely familiar about him. Then the breath caught in her throat. No, it couldn't be. Her brain was playing tricks on her, merging a completely unrelated memory into the present. She had to calm down. She had to stop imagining crazy things. She had to sit down with Mark and Helen and act normal.

*

As soon as she got back to her house, Julia pulled a chair over to her closet and climbed onto it so she could see onto the top shelf. She grasped Indiana's hat and pulled it toward her. She began to tremble. She had not been this nervous since receiving her acceptance letter from Harvard. She put one hand onto the back of the chair and carefully climbed down. Her heart was pounding as she willed her hands to move the hat away from her chest, to turn it upside down so she could see inside. There was the label inside that read, 'If found, please call,' with space for the owner's phone number. A phone number had been neatly entered, probably with an indelible marker. She didn't recognize it, but it started with 617, like most phone numbers in Boston, not New York. That didn't prove anything, she told herself. She glanced at her phone. Kind of late, but she couldn't wait until morning. Her fingers shook, but she entered the number, and then waited. It rang once, twice, three times, and then a woman answered.

"Hello? Hello?" It was Helen! No mistake about it, Julia thought.

"Sorry, wrong number," she said in a husky voice, hoping it would not be recognized, and hung up quickly.

Julia's mind was racing with the enormity of her discovery. She clasped her phone to her chest. What was his name? All she could remember was that it wasn't Alexander. Her mind was too unsettled to recall that detail from almost a year ago. She pulled up her contact list and skimmed it. She couldn't find it the first time through and forced herself to slow down and review the list more carefully. There it was: Patrick. No last name. Of course not. Then she groaned. What an idiot she was! She could have just searched for New York and she would have found him right away.

What should she do now? Tell Mark? Call Patrick, or rather Alexander? What if his number had changed? She'd have no way to find him. But if she did reach him, what should she say? Oh god! It was almost midnight by this time. She should get some sleep and think about it.

Just before she went to sleep her phone pinged. Mark! She smiled as she picked up the phone to read his text: 'Mom n my aunt r going to spa taking grandma weekend after next. Mothers day. House to ourselves' Then a winking smiley face. She replied with a smiley face and a heart. Helen would be away that weekend. Perhaps she could fit that into a plan.

# CHAPTER 70

The man who called himself Patrick Close turned up the collar of his light coat to keep out the wind. It had been almost two years since he moved to New York City. Spring had arrived, but nights were still cold, and he waited for his second full summer here with anticipation, eager for the return of the warmth. As he ambled down the sidewalk, he reflected on his life, his new life, his solitary existence. He had a number of casual acquaintances, but his inherent decency prohibited him from forming close friendships. He realized that he was still an attractive man. Many were the women who smiled at him, or chose the empty stool next to his, when he stopped by a bar for a drink, hoping to catch his eye. But he could not initiate a relationship which would be a lie. Had he done the right thing, running from his old life? He continued to walk, and the wind continued to wail. He truly, deeply missed Mark. Strange sort of existence, he reflected, being someone else's ghost.

Could things have been different? Could he have changed all this? Perhaps. The most important decisions of his life had been made impulsively, he had come to realize. His decision to leave History and go to medical school, because of his Dad's illness. Not a bad decision really. He had done well in an honorable profession. He had helped many people over the years. But it had never been his love. He had been fascinated with the world around him, with exploration, with the battles and the wars and the conquests that had molded the world into its present state. Perhaps he should have stuck to History. Studying medicine hadn't allowed him to help his father, after all. Or his mother.

He had loved the wrong woman. His marriage was cursed. He had been so elated that Helen accepted him; he had never asked whether she was truly happy, truly satisfied. Clearly, she had not been. He knew she had been enamored of Hector Gonzalez in high school. He never spoke of him with her. Never asked if she was over him. No. Instead, unwittingly, he had brought them together, in New York City. She said she had been lonely. So she contacted the one other person in New York that she knew. Alex had no love for her; that was gone. But he had come to understand how it could have happened. People can do crazy things when they're lonely. And when his marriage and his son turned out to be completely different from what he had always thought, what had he done? He had fled. And why not? Everyone who loved him was dead. He never wanted to see Helen again. There was the dread of the legal proceedings, the paperwork, the division of assets, the accusations, the emotions; those things that had led Buck to take his own life. But he had not thought through the consequences of his chosen course. What freedom he now had! But the isolation was terrible. Would it have been better if he had stayed? He wished he knew what Mark thought. Was it possible that Mark still loved him? Did Mark hate him? The shock of learning the truth about Mark's parentage had faded. If there was one burning regret he had, it was his loss of Mark.

What if he had not struck Hector that one day decades ago, and not made an enemy of him? What if he had just walked past Hector and helped Patrick to his feet? Would everything have been different? Hector would not have hated the two of them so much. Patrick might still be alive. Alex would not have those terrible nightmares, trapped helpless behind a fence while Patrick died before his eyes, again and again, still haunting him after so many years. Perhaps Hector and Helen would not have had an affair; Hector's hatred of Alex likely played a role in that as well.

*

The man called Patrick Close rose from the bed in his tiny studio apartment, brewed coffee, showered, shaved and dressed in his uniform suit. With the arrival of May, the weather was finally mild and sunny. He enjoyed the walk to Union Square, to catch the 6 train going uptown. He emerged at 86th Street and turned south to walk the short distance to the Metropolitan Museum of Art, where he worked as a guard. As usual he began his day by saluting Cardinal Richelieu, who responded with his customary sneer.

"I'm elsewhere today, *mon Cardinal. 'A bientôt*," he whispered, and then headed to his station in the Arms and Armor section of the museum. The museum had an impressive collection of suits of armor for the knights of Europe and for their horses, armor for warriors from the Middle East and even India, and weapons of all sorts-short knives, broadswords, axes, exquisite jeweled ceremonial daggers. Patrick eyed the swords jealously. He would love to have a chance to swing some of those, check their balance, test their edge. Ah, to have been a knight in shining armor! Perhaps one of Arthur's own... Then he heard footsteps- visitors to the museum. He quickly returned to his station near the door, from which his mandate was to protect the museum's collection, maintain order, scold people using cell phones, call for help in the case of a medical emergency, give directions and answer questions about the items in this room. Of all the different areas he stood guard over, this was the only one truly popular with young boys. Mark would have liked this; too bad they never came here.

He was surprised to feel his own phone vibrating in this pocket. Unlikely to be anyone interesting. Whoever it was, he couldn't answer; cell phone use on the job was not allowed.

He returned from work that day, turned on the news, extracted a heavy glass mug from the freezer and poured a Sam Adams into it. He sat and listened to the sports while enjoying the frosty beer. As he changed clothes, he removed the phone from his pocket, and only then remembered his missed call. There was a voicemail: a girl's voice, hard to understand in the scratchy recording. He listened again. Julia, she said she was. Julia! That young girl from Harvard. He'd met her in Turkey. At Troy. She wanted him to call her back. He stared at the phone for a long time. What could she want? What harm could there be in calling her?

"Julia? This is Patrick calling back, yes, Patrick from Troy. You're coming to New York next Saturday? Sure, I can meet you. 11, 11:30, you think. Where should we meet?" Patrick pondered this. What would be easy? "Meet me on the steps of the Metropolitan Museum of Art. Take the Lexington Avenue train to 86th Street, get off and go south a couple of blocks. Everyone knows where it is. Just ask if you have any trouble." He'd make sure he had next Saturday off. It would be fun to see little Julia. She would be here for a few days, he would give her his take on the best sights in New York, and she would be on her way.

# PART 6

End Game
Saturday, May 7, 2016

# CAMBRIDGE, MASSACHUSETTS

4:30 am. Julia's iPhone emitted a cheerful trill. Julia groaned, then suddenly remembered why her alarm was set to this god-awful hour. She jumped out of bed, took a quick shower and headed out into the pre-dawn darkness for the Harvard red line train station. She arrived at 5:21, just in time to catch the first train of the day at 5:23. She boarded an empty car and rode to South Station, exited the station and ran down the street to the bus terminal. She arrived at 5:45, grabbed coffee and a sesame bagel from Dunkin Donuts, and hopped onto the Megabus to New York City.

Julia climbed the steps to the upper level of the double-decker bus. She stuck the bagel into her shoulder bag; she would eat it later, when she got hungry. She sipped her coffee slowly as the scenery whipped by, and shortly after the bus crossed into Rhode Island, enough caffeine had kicked in to permit Julia to comprehend the enormity of her plan. *There's no turning back now*, she told herself. *I have to do this. For Mark.* She had rehearsed in her mind the series of steps she had to take upon her arrival in New York City, which subways to take from the bus station towards her destination, which way to turn upon exiting the subway, who she had to find, and what she would say when she found him. It sounded logical and straightforward, but when she thought about actually carrying out her plan, her stomach curled up in a tight knot and she wondered if what she was doing was crazy.

# SALEM, MASSACHUSETTS

Giulietta Stewart awoke with an overwhelming sense of foreboding. She listened unmoving but all she could hear was the sweet chirping of little birds, invigorated by the sunshine and mild weather. She turned her head cautiously toward the window, but from her bed could see nothing unusual, just a few branches bursting with pale green leaves celebrating the arrival of spring. *Primavera*, mother would say. A bright red cardinal alighted on the branch closest to her window.

*He's looking at me, and he's red as blood,* Giulietta thought with horror. She sat up abruptly, tossing her bedspread aside. The flurry of bedclothes startled the bird and he disappeared. She cautiously eased herself out of bed, clinging to the edge of the headboard for support. But as soon as her feet touched the floor, her head began to pound and lights flashed fluorescent in back of her eyes. The pain in her head grew. It was like a sword slicing through the left side of her skull, or like a building that had collapsed, with every brick, every rafter, every chunk of concrete that fell landing on her head. She sank to her knees and her head dropped into her hands. Something terrible would happen today.

# BROOKLINE, MASSACHUSETTS

Helen Eastgard closed her suitcase and slid it off her bed and onto the floor, wheels down. She was looking forward to the Mother's Day weekend with her Mom and Kelly. If there was any good thing that had come from the whole disaster with Alex, it was an improved relationship with Kelly. Kelly actually seemed to like her, went out of her way to look out for her. Helen considered her life as it stood now. In some ways, it had come full circle. Alex was gone. Hector was gone. Mark was a wonderful boy, but he was mostly gone now too. She still had her mother, her father and Kelly. They were all older, but it felt like she had re-entered the small, safe world she had known before they moved to Brookline so many years ago.

Elena Gonzalez strolled casually down Mark's street on her way to work at Starbucks. She paused as she approached Mark's house. There was a flurry of activity: a car she didn't recognize was in the driveway with the trunk open. Helen was in the act of emerging from the house pulling a wheeled suitcase while two other women, one around Helen's age, and one older, stood outside the door chatting. Maybe the older woman was Helen's mother. Maybe the other was Helen's sister. Tomorrow was Mother's Day. Maybe they're all going to celebrate somewhere together. The younger of the two women reached into the trunk and rearranged the suitcases already there to make room for Helen's. *They'll be gone for at least one night, if not two,* Elena calculated. *If Helen is gone, Mark will bring his whore here, and fuck her here. Won't that be nice, having the house to themselves.*

Elena adjusted her headphones and continued down the street at a leisurely pace. Her phone rang. Crap! It was the manager of that shithole. Undoubtedly to remind her that she was late for work. That job sucked. She declined the call and put her phone back into her jeans pocket. She took one last look over her shoulder. They were all in the car now, pulling out of the driveway, heading away from her.

Elena sauntered into Starbucks, a scowl on her face.

Fanny, the manager, strode forward. "Elena, can I have a word with you?"

"Yeah." Elena kept her tone non-committal. If Fanny gave her any shit, she would get it right back. But Elena had been working here for so long, maybe there was a law she had to get a raise or something, so she'd wait to see what Fanny would say.

Fanny gestured for Elena to enter the tiny room that served as storeroom and makeshift office and shut the door once they were both inside. "Elena, I won't mince words. You are hardly ever on time, but today, you're 45 minutes late. This is unacceptable."

Elena watched with interest as Fanny's face and throat got red and blotchy; that always happened when she chewed out Elena. "It's Saturday morning, for god's sake! What's wrong with taking it a little slow?"

"Saturday morning is an exceptionally busy time at this Starbucks. We need our people to be here and performing at their peak. What if we all showed up late?"

"I guess people would figure out they need to slow down on Saturdays, and not act like spoiled brats if they don't get their damn coffee exactly when and exactly how they want it," Elena said. *Fanny needs a good fuck; she's wound way too tight.*

"Our clients are not spoiled brats. What a thing to say! Our conversation today serves as a final warning: one more late arrival, one more significant error, and we will have to let you go. Understood?"

"Yeah," Elena muttered. She headed for the cash register. The image of the car with Helen in it driving away from Mark's house wouldn't leave her. What would happen there tonight? *I wonder if the fucking whore will come early and cook something like she does on Thursdays.*

"Hi, I'll have the light roast coffee of the day with just a little room for cream," some person in front of the counter said to Elena.

"What size?" Elena responded.

"Small. I mean tall. You know."

"Yeah, I know."

"Oh wait, is it too late to add a flavor shot?"

Elena grimaced. "No, no problem."

"Vanilla shot, then. Thanks."

"You can collect your drink at the end of the counter," Elena said, jerking her head to the right. The customer ambled obediently to the end of the counter.

She hoped it would slow down so she could think about what she should do later. *Is today the right day?*

One after another they came, requesting cappuccino, lattes, herb tea, chai, pastries, bagels. Elena handled it all with reasonable competence. Then two girls came in, clad in sports bras and leggings, hair pulled back in messy ponytails. Elena glanced at them. One of them looked vaguely like Mark's little whore. Elena entered their orders with angry keystrokes. "Pick up down there," she muttered at them. They went off giggling. A couple of minutes went by, then the one that looked like the whore came back, stepping in front of the first person in line.

"Excuse me. Excuse me?" the girl said. She set a hot drink in front of Elena. "I did not order this."

"Yes, you did. That's a cappuccino," Elena countered. *I hate you. Go away!*

"I wanted a frappuccino. I just worked out. I don't want a hot drink!"

"Next time order a frappuccino. Who's next?"

"Excuse me, but I did order a frappuccino. Can you correct your error, so I can have the right drink?"

*Fuck you, bitch!* Elena glared at her, then turned around and headed for the storeroom. She ripped off her apron, grabbed her jacket and approached Fanny. "I'm going home. I'm ill."

"You don't look ill. There are three people waiting. Please put on your apron and take care of them."

Having to put up with that goddamn basic bitch who looked like the little whore was making her sick. The whore had to go. "I'm ill. I'm on my period. I can't stand. That's why I was late. It was painful to walk."

"Ah-ha. You can pull up a stool and sit on that while you work," Fanny said.

"I have to go lie down."

"Is there a problem? Some of us need to be somewhere," a man in line called out.

"Excuse me. I still don't have the right drink!" work-out girl said, her voice now shrill.

"Get back to work," Fanny said, keeping her voice low.

"Excuse me? I just want a frappuccino. Why is that so hard?"

Elena rounded on work-out girl. "Fuck you!" Then she turned to Fanny. "Fuck you!"

The color drained from Fanny's face. "Elena, I am sorry to say that you are terminated."

"Fuck that. I quit." She flounced out of the Starbucks, enjoying the look of horror on work-out girl's face.

# NEW YORK, NEW YORK

Anxious though she was, Julia gasped when she got her first good look at the skyline of New York City: an impossibly dense forest of skyscrapers! In just a few minutes, she would be there, in the midst of those towers, navigating the subway, hopefully without getting lost.

*

The man who called himself Patrick saw her first, a petite girl with shoulder length dark hair, bundled up in an oversized Harvard sweatshirt, seated on the museum's steps, hugging her legs to her chest. He folded his New York Times, crossed the staircase and sat down next to her.

"It's the lady with the wine-dark eyes, in New York!"

She looked up at him and smiled. She had gotten this far. Now came the hardest part. She studied his face.

"How are you?" she asked.

"I'm good. And you? Harvard treating you right?"

"Oh, yes. Almost finished my sophomore year."

"So now you're here in New York. You came all by yourself?"

"Yes."

"First time in New York? It can be overwhelming! You must be brave."

*I'm brave alright. It's my wisdom that's in question.* "Not really. I just had to come."

"But by yourself! You don't have a friend, a boyfriend who would come with you?"

"I do have a boyfriend. He's working. Couldn't come."

"A boyfriend. What's he like?"

Her throat constricted, and her heart raced at a crazy pace; it was hard to talk. She spoke slowly, deliberately, trying to calm down. "He's so nice. And smart and cute. He is very sweet."

"And loyal and honest?"

"He is." She paused. Should she continue? Should she forge ahead and change this man's life? She had come this far. Too late to turn back. "But he's sad." That sounds stupid, childish, she told herself. "I mean, there's a sadness about him that colors the rest of his life."

"Why? What's wrong?"

"He's had a tragedy in his life and he can't get past it."

"What is this tragedy?"

"His father died."

"I'm sorry for him. My father died when I was in, well, when I was a little older than you. It can be difficult. It was recent?"

"Not so recent. A couple of years. Almost two years."

"Two years and he still can't get over it? He must have been very close to his father."

"Yes, they were very close. Do you have children?"

The man called Patrick looked away. "No. No, I never had children."

"Seriously?" It came out harsher than she had intended.

He looked at her, startled. "Well, I..., ah, what do you want to see? I brought a subway map for you, in case you didn't have one."

She'd better get this out before she completely lost her nerve. "My boyfriend, his father drowned sailing. They used to do that together. But they never found his body."

The man called Patrick stared at her.

"His name is Mark. Mark Eastgard. You're Alexander Eastgard, aren't you?"

He shifted in his seat on the steps, without speaking, offering no denial, no affirmation.

She grabbed his arm. "Don't run. I'm a runner too. I can keep up with you."

The feel of her fingers, tight on his skin, shocked him. When was the last time anyone had touched him, touched him with emotion? It had been a long time since he'd had physical contact with anyone, other than the occasional impersonal handshake. And then, what she'd said!

Julia had made her accusation. She had said what she came to say, and now emotion rolled through her and she began to cry. "You have no idea the effect this has had on Mark. He thinks you killed yourself, because of him, because he exists."

"How did you-?"

"It's just a crazy coincidence. I met Mark, and he talked about you all the time, how great you were and how much he missed you, and then after we were dating a long time, he told me about how, how you weren't his father, not his biological father. He told me the whole story. Otherwise, he's kept it secret all this time. Helen didn't want him to tell anyone. And anyway, it was so hard for him to talk about."

"Helen." There was a bitterness in his voice.

"Okay, so she's not the brightest bulb in the box but she's not an evil person. As best I can tell, after this prize-winning screw-up with that other guy, she buckled down and did the best she could for you and Mark. She's not so principled, not so high-minded, and she was scared. So she never owned up. Never told anyone. She thought you were a happy family and that's what ultimately counted. Years passed, and she thought she'd got away with it. And then finally she only told Mark because of another bizarre coincidence, when he'd started dating his half-sister, and she wanted to keep them apart."

"But why did you put me together with your boyfriend's father?"

"Pictures in the living room in your old home in Brookline. You haven't changed much. There was a phone number written in that hat you gave me. I called it and Helen answered."

The man called Patrick sighed. A long time passed before he spoke. Betrayed by his cherished hat! "Mark misses me? I was afraid he would hate me. I've missed him so much."

*He's finally admitted who he is!* "Come back with me," she said softly. "Please come back with me and see Mark. Please."

"Why didn't you and Mark come together?"

"Well, I wasn't completely sure I was right about this until I talked to you. And what if I'd brought Mark, and you saw him and wouldn't come talk to him, or you said something mean to him. I would have made it worse. He doesn't know anything about this."

"I wouldn't do that. I never wanted to hurt Mark. I'd love to see him. Bring him here."

"Just come with me now. It's not even noon. You can see him and be back in New York tonight if we leave now. We can be in Brookline before Mark gets home from work."

"I can't go there. I still can't look at Helen."

482

"No, she's away."

"Away? Where?"

"She and her Mom and Aunt Kelly went for a Mother's Day spa weekend in the Berkshires."

"A spa weekend! Where'd she get the money for that? Does she have a job?"

"She sold your Mom's house. Mark said they got a lot for it. They're living off that."

"Sounds like I've missed a lot."

"Come with me! Just for an hour or two. Then you can come back here. No one has to know but Mark." She stood, waiting for him to stand.

He sat immobile, head in hands.

"You can't just sit here. You owe it to Mark. You owe him big time. What you did, leaving like you did, it's as bad as what Helen did. Worse, even. Poor Mark is just caught in the middle. You have to make this right."

He looked away, across 5th Avenue, at the elegant buildings of the Upper East Side.

"You can't run from this. Are you a coward?" She asked. His body jerked; that stung.

After a long while, he turned to her and nodded. "I'll go with you. I'll see Mark, and I'll come back here tonight. After that, if he wants, he can come here. He'd like New York."

*

Alex and Julia sat together on the Megabus. Julia sat tense in her seat, hands clasped together so tightly that her fingers hurt. *Let's go!* She thought, willing the bus into motion. She glanced at Alex. He sat on the aisle, quiet, lost in his thoughts. He could still bolt, she knew. *Close the door and let's move!*

Finally, the bus's engine rumbled into action, and slowly pulled away from the curb and onto its route north. Only after Manhattan Island was no longer visible, did Julia dare speak.

"Do you mind if I ask, what have you been doing for the past couple of years?"

"You mean, for work?"

She nodded.

"Well, right now, I'm a museum guard. I enjoy it. It's low stress. Great being surrounded by works of art."

"The museum where we met?"

"Yes."

"You weren't afraid someone would recognize you? So many people visit there."

"Yeah, but who looks at the guards? Once I did see someone, a couple I knew from before. Passed right in front of me. They never even looked at me. That's one thing about New York. People mind their own business. Everyone's in a hurry, coming and going. They don't notice the people around them while they're in transit."

"You said right now you're a museum guard. Were you doing something else before?"

He smiled. "Yes. I've worked on container ships. I've always loved the sea. I've been around the world a couple of times."

"Is that right? What's it like?"

"Conditions are extremely spartan. A lot of down time. I got to read so much. But the places we go! I've been through the Panama Canal, the Straits of Hormuz, the Suez Canal. I've been to so many ports in Europe and Asia and North Africa. Amazing sights!" The stars he'd seen, a thousand miles from land! Pulling into faraway harbors, where the colors are different, the smells are different, no Westerners in sight, like Marco Polo or some adventurer from the heyday of the British Empire.

"When you were in Turkey, had you been on one of those ships?"

"That's right. I wanted to see Istanbul, so I picked a ship stopping there. Then I picked up another ship in Istanbul and sailed home."

"What's home? Where do you live?"

"I have a good deal. I rent a tiny studio in a building in Little Italy. There's a restaurant on the ground floor. An old Italian guy owns the building. He lets me stay for pretty low rent and when I'm gone, my stuff gets locked up and he puts it on Airbnb. I help with maintenance when I'm in town. It works."

Julia nodded. She looked out the window. She recognized the scenery: they were already in Rhode Island. "Hold on." Her voice dropped to a whisper. "If you did all that, you must have had a passport. How did you get a passport?"

He looked around cautiously. No one else was nearby. "I had all the necessary documents. I just applied."

"Applied as who?"

He smiled a wry smile. Why was he telling her all this? In a way, she had earned it. "The name I gave you."

"Could you, would you be willing to tell me how you did it?"

He sighed. "I suppose. Why not?" he said with a low laugh. He paused for a long while before speaking. "I had a friend. My best friend. Patrick."

"I heard about him. You took his name!"

"People were always saying we looked like brothers. We sort of did. Similar coloring, similar builds. But then he was killed." Alex's voice caught in his throat. The terrible scene flashed before his eyes, yet again. It would never stop, never. *I sent him out! I could have stopped it. But I didn't move fast enough and then it was too late.*

"I heard about that too. I'm so sorry," Julia whispered.

"When I found out what Helen had done, I moved out. Moved into my Mom's house. When Patrick died, his mother gave me his wallet. It had photos of our friends, and she thought I'd want them. But his license was there, and it had his social security number. I requested a copy of his birth certificate, and with that, and the old license, I got a new license. Got it mailed to my Mom's house. ID to start a new life."

"Nobody ever realized you had, sorry, a dead person's ID?"

"No. He- died so long ago. Decades ago. And he was born in a different state- New Hampshire. The record-keeping wasn't like it is now."

"But you must have needed some money to leave Mass and get an apartment."

He nodded. "I kept quite a bit of cash in a safe at home. I went to our house when I thought Helen and Mark would both be out and took the money. I also had an awesome coin collection. Well, still have. I took that too. As a last resort, I could have sold some coins. Some of them are quite valuable. I took my few things with me and went to New York and found that apartment. Then I came back, and..." He paused.

"And you jumped off a sailboat into a terrible storm. You weren't afraid of drowning?"

"I wasn't afraid of dying. But I didn't seek it either. I had put an old wetsuit on under my clothes and had a life preserver from the boat. I brought a change of clothes with me, wrapped in plastic, in an old backpack of Mark's. The storm was bad. No one was out, and no one was looking when I swam to shore. I changed clothes, made it to the bus station and went to New York. It wasn't hard."

"Why New York? You could have gone anywhere."

"I knew New York. I went to med school there. I always liked it."

"It wasn't because Hector was there?"

"At first it was. I tracked him down and confronted him."

"Did you, did you, do anything to him?"

"I wanted to. The night that I found this all out, I was not in my right mind. I was so angry. I can't explain to you how angry I was. Insane with anger. I would have killed him. But when I found him, he was so pathetic. He'd become a drug addict. He barely remembered Helen. He knew nothing about Mark. Kept begging me for cigarettes. So I walked away from him. But then I looked around, and there I was in New York. And I think that planted the seed of the idea to move there. Leave everything behind and go."

"Look, we're in Boston already. I was thinking, let's get a taxi from South Station and go to your old house. Mark will be getting off work soon. I'll text him that I'm there. I think I'll let him find out about you when he gets there. Is that okay?"

Alex gave a silent nod.

# BROOKLINE, MASSACHUSETTS

Elena Gonzalez left Starbucks, went home, changed into non-descript clothing, tied her distinctive hair into a tight knot, slipped an item from the pantry and then another from a drawer in the kitchen into her shoulder bag and then made her way toward Mark's house. She glanced up and down his street. No one. She approached Mark's house. Mark was working today, she knew. Still, to be sure the house was really empty, she rang the doorbell. No response. She glanced to her left and to her right. No one. She knelt, lifted the fake rock by the door, extracted the key, unlocked the door and quickly replaced the key. She stepped inside and closed the door. She took a deep breath. She had entered a house without permission- that was a crime. She had crossed a line. She could walk out the door right now and no one would ever know she was here. She could still walk out. And go back home, and get some other crappy job and go there, day in, day out, for the rest of her life. No! She was going through with it. And she would be there at Mark's side to help him and they would get back to where they were before his father died. She would do it. All she had to do was wait patiently, do what she had to do, and leave.

Mark always got off work at 6:00, and then got home by 7:00. The slut usually showed up a couple of hours earlier and did her stupid cooking. Elena had some time. She walked quietly to the back of the house, opened the window next to the back door, pulled a short kitchen knife from her purse and cut a ragged L-shaped tear in the screen, creating a defect large enough for an arm to stick through, close enough to the door to reach though to unlock the door from the inside. She folded the edges of the tear inward so it would look like the cuts were made from the outside. She decided to leave the door in the unlocked position, in case she forgot to do it later. That was easy. Now she just had to wait.

She retreated toward the center of the house and cautiously sat down on a step near the bottom of the staircase. She took off her shoes so she would be able to move more quietly, and set them on the step behind her. When she had last been here with Mark, he had kissed her so passionately, right on these stairs. He'd been hard for her. She had felt it. Why did he hold back from her now? Why was he going around with that scrawny little bitch from Harvard? Did he feel sorry for her? If so, good. Time to put her out of her misery.

*

Julia and Alex approached the front door. She bent down and took the key from the bottom of the fake rock.

"That's still there?" Alex asked with a short laugh.

"Yep." Julia looked up at him. His face was gray and drawn. "Are you okay?"

"I don't think I can go inside."

"Are you, are you just going to stand out here?"

"We can go sit on the patio in back. I can wait for Mark there."

Together they walked along the side of the house to the patio and sat down in the Adirondack chairs. The chairs looked weather beaten. He re-stained them every spring. Before he left. No one was doing that now.

"Alex, thank you for coming," Julia said.

"Thank you for making me come. It's the right thing to do."

They sat in silence until Julia's phone pinged. "Mark's on his way, almost here. I'll tell him to come to the back when he gets home." She sent the text, then set her phone in her lap.

A few minutes later Mark walked into the driveway and around the side of the house to the back patio. When he saw Julia he smiled, but his greeting died in his throat, as Alex stood and met his eyes.

"Dad! You're alive! What- where have you," Mark stammered.

"I'm so sorry, Mark. I was so wrong. I never wanted to hurt you. I missed you so much," Alex said.

"Did Julia find you?" Mark asked.

"She did. She's a smart girl. Very determined." Alex said.

"Dad, what happened? Where have you been? What have you been doing?" Mark asked.

"I'm going to go inside and let you two talk," Julia said. As she departed, she looked back and saw them seating themselves and talking intently. She returned to the front door, unlocked it and went inside. She walked over to the couch in front of the TV and turned on the news. She opened her laptop and booted it up.

From the shadowed stairwell, Elena saw the little bitch enter, heard her drop onto the couch. Carefully, slowly she peered around the edge of the wall. The back of the couch was toward her. She couldn't see Julia, but she knew that she must be sitting on the couch. Elena reached into her bag for her special friend, the one she'd kept secret for so long. She had to get this over with. But she wasn't sure she could do it if she had to walk around the couch and look the little whore in the face. She could do it if the bitch would stand up and have her back to her. Then she'd have time to take careful aim and do it.

Julia sat on the couch, skimming through her homework assignment. She sensed movement from the patio. She stood, facing the back of the house, and walked to the back door. It had gotten dark while Alex and Mark were talking, and she couldn't see distinctly, but it looked like they were both smiling. Julia reached for the knob of the back door to go out and join them, and then noticed the cut screen. Had someone tried to break in?

Elena tiptoed from her hiding place on the stairs, and saw Julia standing at the back door. *Let her keep her back to me and I can do it*, she told herself. *She sees the cut screen. Who the fuck cares? Soon she won't know anything. I'm close enough. I can do it.* Elena lifted the pistol to shoulder height and aimed at Julia.

Alex stood and approached the back door; a look of horror crossed his face. Although Elena had not noticed him, she stood in the brightly lit room, and he could see her well. In an instant Alex took in her face, her thick black hair, her green eyes, and knew her for Hector's child. She held a gun, trained on Julia! The light on the gun seemed a flash of sunlight on bronze. A terrible NO roared in his brain and the fence that had kept him from Patrick, the fence from his nightmares, appeared before him, indifferent, unyielding, and then the fence merged with the door, the back door, and it was solid and implacable and would keep him out.

Julia, even in the dim light discerning a change in Alex's face, turned around and saw Elena, six feet away, hatred in her eyes, shaking hands on a gun pointing at her. Julia froze. Alex put his hand on the knob and miraculously it turned. The fence dissolved. He was free to act. He opened the door just as Elena shut her eyes and started to squeeze the trigger. Alex grabbed Julia and spun her around, blocking her from Elena. The bullet hit Alex square in the back. The impact knocked him over, and Julia with him. He tried to rise, but the bullet had entered his heart, and he could not move.

Mark bounded in behind Alex. "Elena! What did you do?" he wailed.

"Oh my god!" Elena moaned. She dropped the gun and ran from the house.

"Are you hit? Are you hurt?" Alex asked Julia. It was already difficult to speak.

"No. No," Julia said, running her hands along her body to check. "I'm calling 911. Don't move."

Alex saw that she was unharmed. At last, finally, this was well done.

Mark crouched down next to Alex.

*This time I'm leaving for good*, Alex thought. *Julia said I owed Mark. I hope this is enough.*

Aloud he said, "I love you, Mark. I love you more than I've ever loved anyone. I'm so sorry for running. I'm so sorry. Please forgive me."

"I already forgave you! But don't talk. Rest. The ambulance is coming."

He shook his head slightly. "Too late for me. Take care of this little one. She acts tough, but she needs you."

That made Mark smile. "I knew that."

Mark's and Julia's anxious faces blurred above him. "Listen to me. This was my choice, no regrets," Alex whispered. "Bury me next to Patrick." A faraway roar of victory surged in his ears and slowly faded away, and darkness covered his eyes.

"Hang on, Dad. Please hang on," Mark begged.

But Alexander Eastgard was gone.

"Mark, he gave his life for me. He barely knew me, and he gave up his life for me," Julia said, tears running down her face.

Mark took her hand and they sat together in silence.

Finally, Mark spoke. "He was always my hero. What he did for you, for us, that's what it means to be a hero."